PRAISE FOR THE BRIDGE KINGDOM SERIES

"Heart-pounding romance and intense action wrapped in a spell-binding world. I was hooked from the first page."

—Elise Kova, *USA Today* bestselling author
of *A Deal with the Elf King,* on *The Bridge Kingdom*

"Exquisite, phenomenal, and sexy, *The Bridge Kingdom* is the epitome of fantasy romance perfection. I adored Jensen's world and characters. Aren and Lara were magnificent individually and together, a couple you'll root for from beginning to end."

—Olivia Wildenstein, *USA Today* bestselling author
of *House of Beating Wings*

"An epic, action-packed tale of love, revenge, and betrayal."

—Jennifer Estep, *New York Times* bestselling author
of *Kill the Queen,* on *The Traitor Queen*

"The next installment in the Bridge Kingdom series is not to be missed. Do not walk to pick up this book. Run."

—Jennifer L. Armentrout, #1 *New York Times* bestselling author
of *From Blood and Ash,* on *The Inadequate Heir*

BY DANIELLE L. JENSEN

THE MALEDICTION TRILOGY

Stolen Songbird
Hidden Huntress
Warrior Witch
The Broken Ones (Prequel)

THE DARK SHORES SERIES

Dark Shores
Dark Skies
Gilded Serpent
Tarnished Empire (Prequel)

THE BRIDGE KINGDOM SERIES

The Bridge Kingdom
The Traitor Queen
The Inadequate Heir
The Endless War

SAGA OF THE UNFATED

A Fate Inked in Blood

THE
INADEQUATE
HEIR

THE
INADEQUATE
HEIR

DANIELLE L. JENSEN

NEW YORK

Published in the United States by Del Rey, an imprint of Random House, a division of Penguin Random House LLC, New York.

DEL REY and the CIRCLE colophon are registered trademarks of Penguin Random House LLC.

Originally published as an audio original by Audible in 2021 and subsequently self-published in print and digital formats by Danielle L. Jensen in 2022. "The Calm Before the Storm" was originally self-published in digital form by the author in 2022.

LIBRARY OF CONGRESS CATALOGING-IN-PUBLICATION DATA
Names: Jensen, Danielle L., author.
Title: The inadequate heir / Danielle L. Jensen.
Description: New York: Del Rey, 2024. | Series: The Bridge Kingdom series; 3
Identifiers: LCCN 2024043324 (print) | LCCN 2024043325 (ebook) |
ISBN 9780593975244 (trade paperback; acid-free paper) | ISBN 9781737924807 (ebook)
Subjects: LCGFT: Fantasy fiction. | Romance fiction. | Novels.
Classification: LCC PR9199.4.J455 I53 2024 (print) |
LCC PR9199.4.J455 (ebook) | DDC 813/.6—dc23/eng/20240916
LC record available at https://lccn.loc.gov/2024043324
LC ebook record available at https://lccn.loc.gov/2024043325

Printed in the United States of America on acid-free paper

randomhousebooks.com

1 2 3 4 5 6 7 8 9

Title page art by Vibrands Studio © Adobe Stock Photos

Book design by Sara Bereta

Map: Damien Mammoliti

For the bookworms with big dreams

THE
INADEQUATE
HEIR

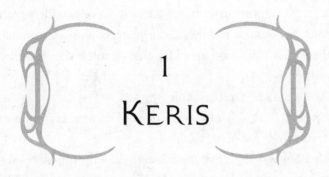

1
KERIS

KERIS VELIANT, LATEST HEIR TO THE THRONE OF MARIDRINA, FOLlowed his father down the gangplank and onto the pier of Southwatch Island. They hadn't spoken a word to each other during the short crossing, his father remaining on deck while Keris closeted himself in the captain's quarters. Though in truth, even if they'd stood side by side the entire voyage, the result would've been the same: the taciturn silence of two men well aware that each wished the other dead.

A masked Ithicanian, his shoulders stooped with age, approached, bowing low. "Welcome back to Southwatch, Your Majesty." Then he inclined his head toward Keris. "Welcome, Your Highness. I understand this is to be your first venture through our bridge?"

Keris opened his mouth to answer, but his father interrupted, "Are they here?"

"His Grace sends his regrets, I'm afraid. His presence was required elsewhere."

A flicker of disappointment passed through Keris at the Ithicanian king's absence. Aren Kertell was a man much discussed, though the rumors surrounding him were at odds with his recent actions. Actions that had the Maridrinian people singing his name in the streets, claiming him a king that all rulers should aspire to emulate.

And Keris's father hated him for it.

Yet King Silas Veliant showed none of that ire, his tone steady as he asked, "What of my daughter?"

Lara. She was Keris's younger sister—his only full-blooded sibling in the sea of half sisters and brothers produced by his father's harem. He hadn't spoken to her in over sixteen years—not since she'd been taken away to be raised in secret. Keris had believed her dead until the day she'd passed through Vencia on her way to be married to the king of Ithicana as part of the Fifteen-Year Treaty. A bride of peace, they'd said.

Keris didn't believe *that* for a heartbeat.

The Ithicanian said, "It is the queen's preference to remain at His Majesty's side, though she sends her regards."

"I'm sure."

On the surface, his father's voice was cool, but for the sake of his own self-preservation, Keris had long ago made a practice of reading the tiny tics and tells that gave away his father's true sentiments. As such, he heard the hint of amusement in the king's voice, the tone causing Keris's skin to prickle. What amused his father tended to elicit a rather different reaction from everyone else.

The Ithicanian's eyes narrowed slightly, and wary of anything that might jeopardize his escape to Harendell, Keris said, "I'm sorry to have missed my sister, but pleased to hear of her loyalty to your king. Give them both my best wishes."

His father huffed out a soft chuckle, giving Keris a condescending pat on the cheek. "My son is sentimental. Gets it from his mother."

That would be the mother you murdered, you cold-blooded reptile? Keris wanted to say, but today was not the day to test his father's patience. Not when he was so close to finally escaping him. "We all have our faults, Your Grace."

His father's azure eyes, which were twin to Keris's own, regarded him, unblinking. "Some more than others." Then he clapped his hands sharply. "I came only to see your sister and her husband. Given they are absent, I don't care to belabor my presence. Let's get this over with."

Sentiment was *not* one of King Silas Veliant's faults.

The pier turned into a flurry of activity, two dozen young Maridrinian men in tight coats made with vibrant fabrics disembarking, the stiff breeze tugging at their slicked-back hair, much to their obvious consternation. The smell of wine came with them, which accounted for their overloud voices as they shouted at the sailors to take care with their belongings or suffer the lash. Between his teeth, Keris asked, "Who are they?"

His father crossed his arms, a slight smile growing on his face. "Your entourage."

"I'm going to university, not to court, Your Grace. This is an unnecessary expense."

"You are heir to the throne of Maridrina," his father answered, "which means you must arrive in Harendell with a suitable entourage." Under his breath, he added, "You're embarrassment enough—no need to add to the shame."

Don't argue. Keep your damned mouth shut, Keris silently ordered himself. But the temper he usually kept in check was rising. "This will cost a fortune. Better for us to go by ship. It's the calm season—there's no reason not to." On a ship, it wouldn't matter if these men behaved like idiots, whereas the Ithicanians had rules of conduct for their bridge and no patience for those who broke them, which these buffoons would inevitably do within the day.

Perhaps that was what his father was counting on.

"Don't be a fool, Keris. The seas are swarming with Valcottan vessels, and the last thing I need is for my heir to be killed."

"Given my eight predecessors are in their graves, I'd think you'd be used to that by now."

The words sneaked out, and Keris immediately braced for the blow, long used to his tongue earning him beatings. Yet instead his father gripped him by the shoulders, pulling him close so that his mouth was inches from Keris's ear. To anyone looking on, it would appear nothing more than an intimate exchange between father and son, but Keris's arms were already numb with pain from where his father's thumbs pressed against nerves.

"Your older brother was twice the man you are," his father hissed. "I'd exchange your life for Rask's in a heartbeat, if such a thing were possible."

And not just Rask. Despite Keris having brothers who were arguably worth less than the detritus of humanity, his father held every one of them in greater esteem. It was only Keris whom he hated, only Keris whom he mocked without mercy.

"I wish Rask were still alive as much as you do." Not because he'd liked his brother, but because with Rask performing all the duties the heir was supposed to do—soldiering, politicizing, and warmongering—Keris had been able to avoid them. But Rask had gotten himself killed in a skirmish with the Valcottans, and Keris's greatest fear since his brother's death was that he'd be able to avoid soldiering, politicizing, and warmongering no longer. Which was why his father not backtracking out of his agreement to allow him to go to Harendell had seemed like nothing short of an act of God.

Which, given he was a disbeliever of the first order, made Keris extremely suspicious.

"You are pathetic and weak, and your tongue is not worthy of speaking your brother's name." His father's grip tightened. "But you are still my son. Which means I must find ways to capitalize upon your attributes, limited though they may be."

And there was the catch.

Of course his father wanted something from him. He wouldn't allow Keris to go without making him pay a price. "What will it be, Father? Spying on the Harendellians, I assume?"

He chuckled, and the sound made Keris's skin crawl. Then his father released his shoulders. "No, Keris. I've spies aplenty. But rest assured that I will find a way to use you to my benefit." And without another word, he strode up the gangplank and disappeared onto the ship.

Not spying, but *something*. And whatever it was, Keris knew he wouldn't like it.

The old Ithicanian still stood a few paces away, waiting patiently. "If you'd follow me, Your Highness, we will get under way. We have restrictions on what is allowed through the bridge, which means all persons and baggage are subject to search. And"—his eyes flicked to the stacks of chests and to Keris's entourage—"that might take more time than anticipated."

HOURS WAS WHAT IT TOOK, the Ithicanians removing them to a stone warehouse where *everything* was thoroughly searched before being loaded into narrow wagons. And though Keris had watched his father's ship sail away, he couldn't escape the sense that *something* would happen that would see him not in Harendell but back in Maridrina, once again immersed in a war he wanted no part of. A war he was opposed to on every possible level.

"They ready?"

A female voice caught his attention, and Keris lifted his face from the book he was reading to find an Ithicanian woman striding into the warehouse, several other armed Ithicanians on her heels. She was tall and lean, her dark-brown hair shaved on the sides of her head and the rest pulled back into a long tail at the back. She wore the drab grayish-green tunic and trousers that the Ithicanians favored, her thick leather boots rising to her knees and a multitude of weapons belted at her waist. Her arms were bare except for the vambraces buckled around them, her skin tanned but for the few pale scars lining it that suggested she was no stranger to combat. Like the rest of her countrymen, she wore a leather mask, making it difficult to guess her age with any certainty, but Keris doubted she was more than twenty.

The old Ithicanian nodded. "Their luggage is in order. An overabundance of drink, but they assure me it is for the journey, not to sell." His jaw tightened. "Their . . . *conduct* gives verity to the claim."

"Lovely. There is nothing I like better than escorting drunk Maridrinian pricks."

Keris laughed.

Her head jerked sideways, gaze lighting upon Keris where he leaned against the wall, far away from his companions.

After coughing to clear his throat, the old Ithicanian said, "This is Crown Prince Keris Veliant. The queen's elder brother."

The woman inclined her head. "My apologies, Your Highness. I regret you overhearing my comment."

But she did *not* regret saying it. Keris liked her already. "Given I'm quite sober, I assume you're delighted to escort *me*."

Her hazel eyes flickered with amusement. "Sober . . . but you *are* a Maridrinian."

"And a prick, as luck would have it." He smirked at her. "I hope your king pays you well."

"Not well enough." She gestured toward his entourage. "If you'll join your companions, Highness, you'll be searched for weapons, and then we'll be on our way."

Keris made no comments as one of the soldiers accompanying her searched him from head to toe for weapons, pulling off his boots and inspecting their soles, the man's efficiency suggesting he'd done this a hundred times and knew his business well. Keris's entourage, on the other hand, snickered and laughed through the whole affair, making comments that had Keris grinding his teeth. He was on the verge of shouting at them to shut their damned mouths when one of them said to the Ithicanian woman, who was kneeling while searching him, "You look well practiced in this position, girl."

Every Ithicanian in the room went still, their anger palpable even to the fools in his entourage, whose faces quickly drained of humor.

Shit.

The Ithicanian woman's jaw had visibly tightened, but she said nothing as she finished her search. Then she stood abruptly, her shoulder catching the idiot between the legs hard enough that he screamed. Toppling over, he lay on his side, cursing and moaning while he clutched his groin.

The woman turned to the old Ithicanian, snapping, "There a Maridrinian ship in port, Rin?"

"Two."

"Good. Pick one and tell them they're taking His Highness and his men back to Vencia. Passage through the bridge is denied."

Keris's stomach dropped, panic rushing through his veins. He'd known this would happen. That his father would find some way to go back on his word.

"Raina." The old man's voice was disapproving. "Prince Keris is Queen Lara's brother."

Her eyes flicked to Keris, looking him up and down. "We'll take him, then. But not the rest."

It was tempting. Oh so terribly tempting to take the woman up on her offer and go through the bridge alone, but Keris knew his father would make him pay for such a decision. He always did.

"I'm sorry for his disrespect." Walking over to the woman—Raina—Keris stopped a courteous distance from her. "He's a fool, but he doesn't deserve to die."

"I didn't hit him *that* hard." Her voice was withering. "He'll live."

"Not if you send him back." Keris lifted one shoulder. "My father tolerates embarrassment poorly. The unfortunate sot will be dead within an hour of making port unless he finds the courage to jump overboard on the journey back."

"Perhaps he should have considered the consequences before he spoke."

"I doubt he's capable of that much foresight." Keris glanced at the men, who were silent for once, and he could see in their eyes that they knew the threat was real. Not only to the idiot on the ground but to all of them. "They won't step out of line again; you have my word."

She exhaled a long breath, rocking on her heels. "Don't make me regret this."

"We will be on our best behavior."

Even with her mask, he saw her eyes roll. But she gestured to the wagons. "Get in."

His entourage scurried toward the traveling wagons, polished affairs with well-upholstered seating that were pulled by pairs of mules. Comfortable enough, but far too close in quarters for Keris's liking. "Do you mind if I walk?"

Raina shrugged. "Be my guest."

The caravan creaked into motion, nine more heavily armed Ithicanians flanking the wagons as they trundled out of the warehouse and into the light rain. Raina led the way, and Keris followed at her heels, his eyes going up the slope to the cavernous mouth of the bridge. Mist emanated from the gray stone as the rain struck it, and as they approached, a heavy steel portcullis rose, the rattling of chains rivaling the distant rumble of thunder.

Raina cast her face skyward, the rain splattering against her mask. "Be glad you chose not to go by ship, Your Highness."

Keris eyed the dark opening, the steel bars of the bottom of the portcullis looking remarkably like teeth. "Why is that?"

"Because there's a storm coming." Then, taking a glowing lantern from one of the waiting guards, she led Keris inside the bridge.

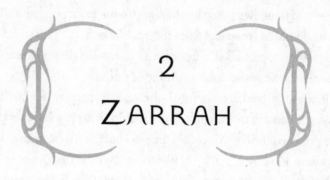

2
ZARRAH

Lieutenant Zarrah Anaphora, niece to the Empress of Valcotta, cast her eyes skyward, watching the clouds swirl north, the deck beneath her feet rising and falling with growing violence. "The calm season is coming to an end, would you not agree, cousin? Time for us to return home?"

"Soon. But not yet." Her cousin Bermin's voice was deep as the thunder rolling in the distance, and she cast a sideways glance to where he stood at the rail. Head and shoulders taller than her, and more than twice her weight, Prince Bermin Anaphora was everything that could be asked for in a warrior. Unparalleled in strength and bravery and martial skill.

Unfortunately, he was also something of an idiot.

Which was why, when their fleet returned to Nerastis, Zarrah would be taking command of Valcotta's armies.

The letter she'd received from the empress containing the orders was hidden in an inner pocket of her uniform, and it took a great deal of self-control not to take out the heavy piece of stationery, the power it granted her making her blood boil with anticipation. Making her want to reach for the knife belted at her side, the opportunity to enact the revenge she'd sought for nearly a decade so close she could almost taste it. Especially with Vencia only a half day's sail away.

A shout filtered down from the lookout above, and a heartbeat later, the captain of the ship was at her cousin's elbow. "General, there is a fleet on the horizon."

"How many?"

"Fifteen, at least, sir."

"Hmm." Her cousin pulled a spyglass from his belt, Zarrah doing the same.

Since the Ithicanians had sided with the Maridrinians and broken the Valcottan blockade on Southwatch, her cousin's fleet had been patrolling the Ithicanian coast, gleefully sinking any Maridrinian ship that came in range even while it protected the Valcottan merchant vessels risking the violent seas to bypass Ithicana's bridge. They'd had a few glorious skirmishes with the Maridrinian Navy, but their murderous prick of a king, Silas Veliant, seemed content to use his forces to protect his own merchant vessels running the gap to Southwatch.

Except judging from the flags flying on the ships racing in Zarrah's direction, that was about to change.

Her pulse throbbed, her weapons begging to be drawn, to be drenched in Maridrinian blood. Vaguely, she heard her cousin give the orders to sound the alarm and ready for battle, her ears ringing a heartbeat later as the bells jangled, the dozen ships that formed Bermin's fleet echoing them.

Soldiers poured onto the deck from below, men and women armed to the teeth and ready to fight, and Zarrah pulled loose her staff, lifting it into the air. "Perhaps fortune will smile on us today and there will be a Veliant princeling aboard," she shouted. "And when we are through, we'll sail back to Nerastis with the vermin dangling from the mainmast by his entrails!"

The soldiers roared, lifting their own weapons to the sky, all eyes fixed on the approaching fleet.

Laughing, Zarrah lifted her spyglass. But her heart skipped, anticipation washed away by concern even as those in the crow's nest shouted warnings.

Not fifteen ships, as had originally been counted, but many more. Twenty. Thirty.

And though they must have caught sight of the Valcottan fleet by now, they weren't moving into position to attack. "Cousin . . ."

Bermin didn't answer, so she twisted to grab him, her hand looking like a child's against his massive forearm. "Look! They're bypassing us."

All around her, soldiers paused in their preparations and moved to the rail, eyes on the fleet that was upward of fifty ships, all sailing wide of the Valcottan fleet and heading north.

"Where are they going?" someone muttered.

But Zarrah knew. The empress had said this moment was inevitable—it was only a matter of when and how. Yet knowing didn't lessen the shock. "They're attacking Ithicana."

Bermin made a sound of agreement, then rested his elbows on the rail, a slight smile curving his round cheeks.

"We must engage." Zarrah's heart thundered in her chest. "Disrupt the attack!"

Bermin ignored her. "Stand down."

The alarm bells went silent, no one on deck speaking a word.

She rounded on him. "They're stabbing Ithicana in the back! We need to engage and send warning to Southwatch."

"No." Her cousin's word rolled across the deck like thunder.

"We have to!" The words came out breathy as panic rose in Zarrah's chest. Silas Veliant wouldn't commit this many ships to an attack unless he was certain of victory. And if Ithicana fell, it would mean the bridge and all its wealth in Maridrinian hands. In her *enemy's* hands.

"You bed down with snakes, you must expect to be bitten," her cousin answered. "The empress saw this and warned the Ithicanian king, but he seemed more content to listen to the snake in his bed."

The soldiers around them laughed. Zarrah did not. "Our ship is faster. We can beat them to Southwatch and warn them. If Ithicana knows the Maridrinians are coming, they'll at least have a chance of repelling them."

"And risk having them fire their shipbreakers at us? I think not. And as it is, the empress was specific that if this were to come to pass, we were not to interfere." Her cousin motioned to the captain. "Set sail for Nerastis. It might be the Rat King has left himself exposed, and we must capitalize upon the opportunity."

As alluring as that opportunity was, Zarrah *knew* what would happen if they allowed this. Had seen the results of Maridrinian raids before, burned homes and slaughtered civilians and orphaned children, and the sickening helplessness she felt every time she came too late to stop it churned in her guts. The same helplessness she'd felt ten years ago when Silas Veliant had murdered her mother and left Zarrah for dead.

"We must act!" Cold coils of panic filled her guts. "If they take Ithicana, it will be a massacre. Not just soldiers, but families. Children! We must intervene."

The soldiers within earshot shifted uneasily at her words, their eyes moving to the fleet, every last one of them familiar with the outcome of a Maridrinian attack. But her cousin only shrugged. "It is not our concern. Ithicana spit upon our friendship, and now they will pay the price."

Except it wasn't Ithicana's people who deserved to pay.

The letter in her pocket giving her the authority to take command burned like fire, but her aunt had been specific: *Say nothing until you are returned to Nerastis.*

Zarrah's mind warred with the order, with her desire to do something, anything, to stop what was about to happen to Ithicana. "Cousin, please. King Aren may have spit on our friendship, but it will be his people—innocents who had nothing to do with that decision—who will pay the ultimate price. For them, we should do this."

Bermin only shook his head. "Let this be motivation for Ithicana to choose a better king." Then he roared, "Now, set sail!"

Ignore your orders and take command, her conscience screamed. *Stop this!*

But instead, Zarrah only watched in silence as the Maridrinian fleet passed, heading north toward Ithicana's destruction.

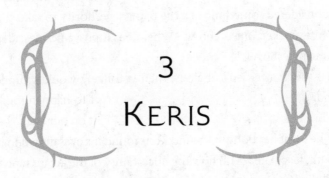

3
KERIS

INSIDE THE BRIDGE, THE AIR WAS THICK AND DAMP, THE SMELL filling his nose that of mildew and manure, along with something Keris couldn't quite name. Like petrichor, but different. Unique.

"It's the material the bridge is made from," Raina said, answering his unasked question. "It creates a distinct odor. Outsiders always wrinkle their noses when they step inside."

Outsiders. Like there was Ithicana and then there was everyone else. "It's quite . . . intense." It was the kindest word he could part with.

"Count yourself lucky, Your Highness. When the Harendellians run cattle, it smells like shit for weeks, which is about how long it takes to clean up the mess."

"Surely a warrior such as yourself isn't relegated to such a task?" Given the mystery surrounding the Bridge Kingdom and its people, Keris had no reason to be sure about anything they did, but he found that compliments loosened tongues.

Raina's mouth, which was the only part of her face that was

visible, curved into a smile. "I did a year of it when I was sixteen. It's considered something of a rite of passage."

Keris cocked one eyebrow. "What does it prove besides adeptness with a shovel?"

"If the answer isn't obvious, then you likely wouldn't understand."

"Try me."

She bit at her bottom lip, and Keris found his eyes drawn to her mouth, fascinated with how the uncertainty of the act juxtaposed with the ferocity of the rest of her. "It demonstrates you are willing to do what it takes to prove your loyalty and earn the trust and respect of the king and the commanders."

"If so much could be gained from shoveling animal feces, then stable boys would be revered. And yet I've not found that to be the case," he replied, testing the waters to see if pricking her pride would cause her to reveal anything interesting.

But Raina was not easily baited. She glanced at the caravan traveling behind them. "Ithicana is a nation built on secrets, and one must earn the right to know them."

Secrets that the world was desperate to know, none more so than Keris's father. King Silas Veliant had what could only be described as an obsession with Ithicana's bridge. With its secrets. Its profits.

With possessing it himself.

And while Maridrina and Ithicana were ostensibly allies, Keris wasn't of the opinion that his father would let that get in his way if the opportunity arose to snatch the coveted bridge from Ithicana's hands. Loyalty and trustworthiness were *not* attributes Keris would ascribe to his father any more than he would sentimentality. Though if the rumors he'd heard were true, Keris's sister, Lara, was different.

Or pretending to be.

"Has my sister earned the right to those secrets?" Keris bit the inside of his cheeks the moment the question came out. *Stay out of it!* he silently screamed at himself. *The less you know, the better.*

"Depends on who you ask."

It was a shame his good sense never ceased to be silenced by his curiosity. "I'm asking you. Forgive my questions; it's only that I know little of my younger sister. We were raised apart."

"I've heard." Raina switched the lantern she carried to the other hand. "Why is that?"

"To protect her from the Valcottans," Keris answered, though he knew that to be a lie. There was nowhere more well guarded than his father's harem in Vencia. Lara had been taken away for another reason. Another purpose.

And it was only a matter of time before that purpose revealed itself.

"She's very beautiful." Raina cast a sideways glance at him. "She looks like you, Your Highness, if you don't object to me saying so. You have the same eyes."

Veliant blue. In all likelihood, Keris inheriting his father's eye color was the *only* reason he hadn't been labeled a bastard and cast aside. Whether that was a blessing or a curse, Keris wasn't entirely certain. "That doesn't tell me what she's like."

"She makes His Grace very happy."

Keris smirked. "You're only saying that because I'm Maridrinian, which means that I *must* think the sum of a woman is whether she makes men happy."

The corners of her mouth turned up. "Am I wrong?"

"Oh, yes. I'm far more selfish than you're giving me credit for— I only care if they make *me* happy."

She laughed, a high, tinkling sound like wind chimes on a summer day, the echoes of it filling the dark expanse of the bridge, making Keris smile.

Then his father's voice echoed through his thoughts: *Rest assured that I will find a way to use you to my benefit*, and his smile fell away.

"Are you well, Your Highness?"

"Quite," Keris said, and then belied his own words by walking a little faster.

KERIS LEANED AGAINST THE INSIDE of the bridge, watching the flickering flame of a lantern. He was exhausted from a day's worth of walking, but unlike his snoring entourage, he couldn't fall asleep on the bedroll the Ithicanians had provided.

Sleep never came easily to him, especially when he wasn't alone or protected by solid walls and a locked door. He'd been stabbed in the back—literally—too many times for *that*. Such was the nature of being a Maridrinian prince, the sheer number of brothers ensuring constant jockeying for position, which often meant eliminating the competition. Keris had survived this long because his brothers hadn't perceived him as a threat, choosing instead to murder the best warriors and most ambitious politicians among them. It had all worked very well until the last of his elder brothers had been killed, leaving Keris as heir, whether he wanted to be or not. And the heir was always the greatest target of all.

The slight scuff of boots caught his attention, and he looked up to see Raina step into the pool of lantern light from where she'd been standing guard farther up the bridge tunnel. She stopped next to a sleeping Ithicanian, shaking him awake. The man rose without hesitation, buckling his weapons on as he walked to take the place she'd vacated. The other Ithicanians keeping watch did the same—a finely oiled machine that ensured nothing happened in the bridge that Ithicana did not see.

Raina's eyes landed on him. "You should rest, Your Highness.

We've many more days of walking, and if you can't keep the pace, I'll have to ask you to ride with your friends."

Keris wrinkled his nose, casting a sideways glance at the unconscious group of men. "They aren't my friends." He didn't have friends.

Unbuckling her sword belt, Raina sat on the ground with her legs crossed, weapon resting on her knees. "Who are they, then?"

"They are what my father deems *suitable company.*"

"If the ability to imbibe an immense amount of wine is what it takes to be deemed *suitable,* they are excellent choices indeed."

His entourage had drunk and gambled through the entire day, their laughter raucous and grating, although they'd kept to Ithicana's rules. "I can't blame them. This is a terrible way to travel. Walking in the damp and the dark, eating cold food, sleeping on the ground. Never mind the cost in gold."

Raina's teeth gleamed white in the lantern light as she smiled. "Pay us or pay the tempests, Highness. Every traveler has a choice."

"Are the storms really so bad?" They were violent and unpredictable enough along the northern coast of Maridrina, but there were dozens of harbors with storm walls and breakwaters to protect ships from the worst of the onslaught.

She made a soft noise of confirmation. "It is said the bottom of the Tempest Seas gleams with the gold spilled by a hundred thousand sunken ships, and that the treasure is guarded by the countless souls sucked beneath the waves, their greedy fingers always reaching up for more."

"Then I'll count my good fortune to have solid stone beneath my feet." He knocked a fist against the bridge floor. "Even if it makes my back ache."

The Ithicanian who was standing guard nearest to them coughed, and Keris noted how Raina's shoulders jerked, her head turning toward the man. Not startled but guilty, fraternization between the Ithicanians and those they were escorting being strongly discouraged.

"It's late." She moved to the pallet the other Ithicanian had vacated, pulling the blanket over her shoulders. "You should rest."

Keris didn't answer, only picked up the book next to him, angling it toward the light. He was close, so painfully close to escape. When he was on Harendellian soil, he'd be away from his father's influence.

And only then would he sleep easily.

KERIS ONLY CAUGHT FITS AND snatches of sleep through the night, yet again he chose not to ride in the travel wagons but to walk, each step he put between himself and his father like a weight lifted off his chest, each passing hour filling him with more confidence that this wasn't an elaborate ruse to put him in his place. Another way to bring him low.

To temper his boredom, he examined the interior of the bridge and those who traveled it. The strange stone the structure was made from was smooth and uniform, the only marks the numbers stamped into the floor that appeared to mark distance. Keris counted the paces between them, the consistent number of steps suggesting that they measured distance traveled within the bridge, which snaked and wove between the islands and piers it rested on, rather than the actual linear distance traveled north, making it impossible to determine precisely where in Ithicana they were.

Despite it being the calm season, there was more traffic than he anticipated, the bray of donkeys and the thud of boots rivaling the groaning draft of wind that filled the endless tunnel. Dozens of wagons, some in long convoys, passed by, and while most were loaded with goods being transported from Northwatch to Southwatch by the Ithicanians, there were some with travelers from other nations, predominantly Harendellians. Regardless, the wagons were always escorted by heavily armed Ithicanians, the eyes behind their masks watchful, their hands quick to their weapons at any sudden movements. Only once was his party passed from behind: a group of twelve Ithicanians who eyed Keris's entourage with interest before jogging ahead, not one of them uttering a single word.

Likely as a result of her comrade's scrutiny, Raina avoided Keris for most of the day, but late that night, after she'd returned from watch and curled up on her bedroll, he heard her murmur, "Is it true you're going to Harendell to study at university?"

Aware that the Ithicanian standing only a dozen paces away could hear the conversation, Keris said, "Yes. It's long been a dream of mine, though my father only recently agreed to it. We're both happier to see less of each other, and if I am in Harendell, he need not see me at all."

"Why?"

"Why do I wish to go to university or why do my father and I not see eye to eye?" Not waiting for a response, he said, "The answer to both is the same: I prefer books to swords."

Her tone was wistful as she said, "You aren't alone in that."

"In having an odious father or in having a fondness for large libraries?"

"Both." She curled an arm under her head, eyes glinting from behind her mask. "My father was a watch commander until recently, so there was never any other option than me picking up a sword."

"I'm not certain there is any other option for me, in the long run. At some point, I'll have to come back and take up the fight against Valcotta."

That endless, pointless war.

Raina traced a finger along the ground, and he noticed that she was closer to him than the prior night. Close enough to touch, though he did not. And would not.

Her hand stopped moving, and for a moment, he thought she'd fallen asleep. Then she said, "When you are king, you will have the power to end the war, if you want."

Keris laughed softly, knowing it sounded bitter. "War is easy. It's peace that is the challenge. An Ithicanian should know that better than anyone."

"We have peace right now."

Keris's skin prickled and crawled, and he turned his head to see one of the men in his entourage watching him from his bedroll, the man's eyelids easing shut under Keris's scrutiny. "Peace is like a dance," he said softly. "It only works if both partners are listening to the same music."

And Maridrina only knew the drums of war.

THREE DAYS. THEY'D BEEN WALKING in this endless dark tunnel for three days, and the claustrophobia of it was setting in.

As was exhaustion.

Sleep, you idiot, Keris silently ordered himself, shifting on his pallet. But it wasn't the discomfort that was keeping him awake; it was that he couldn't shut down his mind. Couldn't silence the endless thoughts and fears and anxieties that circled his brain. And each time his body forced him to drift off, he'd jerk awake, heart racing in his chest.

Finally, he gave up, rolling into a seated position, blanket tangled around his ankles, the only light coming from a pair of lanterns turned down low. His entourage slept in a row along the side of the bridge, several of them snoring and all of them stinking of wine, the ground littered with empty bottles. Farther down the bridge, the travel wagons were stopped against the wall so as to leave room for any southbound traffic they encountered—a necessity, given that his entourage had begged to stop early that night, pleading exhaustion. Keris thought the Ithicanians had agreed only to silence the whining.

Glancing in the other direction, Keris peered at the still form of an Ithicanian sleeping against the wall, swiftly determining it wasn't Raina. Which meant she was on watch farther up the tunnel.

Keris rose, starting in that direction.

"Stay in camp, Your Highness," the Ithicanian standing nearby ordered.

Turning so that he was walking backward, Keris held his arms out. "Where exactly do you think I'm going to go?"

When the man didn't answer, Keris rounded the bend into the darkness, jumping slightly as Raina's hand closed over his arm. "Where are you going?"

"To find you."

She huffed out an amused breath. "Why?"

"Because you're the only person in this cursed bridge whose presence I find tolerable."

"Tolerable, is it, Your Highness? Such a compliment! My cheeks are burning."

"Impossible to tell, given that mask you wear. If a blush is to be the reward for my kind words, I've been robbed."

"Perhaps you should lodge a complaint. We take theft *very* seriously in Ithicana."

Leaning against the wall next to her, Keris inhaled the faint scent of soap that clung to her despite the fact bathing wasn't a possibility on the bridge, the water they transported with them reserved for drinking. So strange to be surrounded by oceans and a kingdom where it rained almost continuously, and yet inside the bridge, water was precious. "Why do you wear them?"

He had his own opinions on why the Ithicanians wore masks when dealing with outsiders, but he was curious what she'd say.

"I'm as beholden to the laws as any other, that's why."

Keris remained silent, waiting. Waiting. And when she cleared her throat, he smiled at the darkness.

"I suppose it's because it makes us more intimidating in battle. Adds to the reputation that we're not quite human." Her fingers brushed against his, little more than a glancing touch that might have been accidental but wasn't.

"You seem very human to me."

Raina made a noncommittal noise. Then in a rush of words, she said, "I think it's just another way to keep us separate—another wall between Ithicana and the *outside*."

Keris was inclined to agree. "Would you take it off, if you could?"

"It's forbidden. Just as is leaving. Just as is being anything other than a weapon whose purpose is to defend the bridge. Just as is this conversation."

Her voice was edged with bitterness, but Keris wasn't very good at leaving well enough alone. "That wasn't my question."

Silence. "Yes," she finally whispered. "If it were my choice, I'd do all of those things."

Pushing away from the wall, Keris faced her, lifting one hand to curve it around her cheek. And when she didn't pull away, he slipped his thumb under the leather of her mask, easing it upward.

Her breath caught. "I can't."

"Can't?" he asked. "Or won't?"

Raina didn't answer, but her fingers caught hold of his other hand and interlaced with his fingers. She pulled him closer so that her breasts pressed against him; their eyes locked in the faint light.

"I've a ship meeting me at Northwatch." Keris leaned closer, a loose tendril of her hair brushing his cheek as he said into her ear, "You could come with me."

It was madness to make such an offer, tempting the ire of both his father and the Ithicanian king. But Keris knew what it was like to be a prisoner to circumstance. What it felt like to want to escape.

"They'd hunt me down and execute me as a traitor."

All for leaving. "Is Ithicana a kingdom or a prison?"

"Both."

One of the men in his entourage let out a loud snore that echoed down the bridge, but Keris ignored it, focusing on the shadows of her face. On the way Raina gripped his hand. On the ache of desire building in him.

Then Raina reached up, and together, they drew off the mask, revealing her face. It was hard to see clearly in the gloom, but he traced his fingers over her rounded cheekbones, over the arch of one eyebrow, then bent to kiss her bow-shaped lips.

A ragged breath escaped her, then her arms were around his neck, dragging him closer, their hips pressing together as her tongue slipped into his mouth. He caught his balance against the wall of the bridge, the rock damp beneath his hand as he lifted her, groaning as her long legs wrapped around his waist.

He moved from her lips to her throat, and her breath was hot against his forehead. "Take me with you," she whispered. "I want to go with you."

"I will." To do so would infuriate two kings, but neither would do anything for fear of aggravating the other, so what did it matter?

He felt her tangle her fingers in his hair. The juncture of her thighs pressed hard against him as he tugged at the laces holding the neck of her tunic together, pulling the fabric down to expose her pert breasts. He kissed them reverently, then drew one peaked nipple into his mouth, satisfaction filling him as she whimpered, her hands drifting down his body to tug at his belt.

Then the sound of hooves reached them, and Raina tore her

lips from his, sliding down his body to land with a thud on her feet even as her hand went to the weapon at her waist. In the distance, a pool of light appeared, revealing a donkey pulling a wagon under the escort of four masked Ithicanians.

Lifting her fingers to her mouth, Raina gave a series of whistles, then straightened her clothes.

"Your mask," he muttered, and she jumped, swiftly retrieving the leather from where it had fallen.

But it was too late.

They'd seen.

The Ithicanian leading the donkey opened her mouth as they approached. "Aster's going to beat you bloody if he finds out you were messing around with a Maridrinian, Raina. Especially if he hears you were doing it while on duty. Get your ass back around the corner and I might consider keeping my mouth shut about what I just saw."

Not waiting for a response, the woman hauled on the donkey's lead, slowly walking around the bend, none of the other Ithicanians saying a word as they followed.

"Who's Aster?" Keris asked.

"My father."

"All the more reason for you to get on that ship."

Raina didn't answer, only tugged on his arm, leading him after the wagon. Ahead, all of his entourage had sat up in their bedrolls. As Keris watched, several stood, pulling on their boots, appearing entirely more sober than they should be, given the wine bottles scattered about them. And all of them were looking anywhere but at the approaching wagon.

Keris's skin prickled. "What's in that wagon?"

"Goods from Harendell. Steel, likely."

Weapons.

Realization slapped Keris in the face, and he shoved Raina back the way they'd come. "Run!"

As he said the word, his countrymen leapt at the wagon, dragging the cloth off to reveal glittering steel. In a heartbeat, they'd snatched up weapons and turned on the Ithicanian guards, who were pulling their own blades free.

And instead of running, Raina only drew her own sword, racing in the direction of the battle. Most of the Ithicanians were already down, and his countrymen turned on her, lifting their weapons.

"Raina!" Keris broke into a sprint, racing after her.

She crossed blades with one man, kicking him in the knee and then gutting him, but as she turned to engage another, a shadow flitted up behind her. As the individual stepped out from behind the wagon, Keris recognized him as the man who'd disrespected her at Southwatch, his face bright with glee.

"Look out!" Keris screamed, snatching up a fallen weapon.

But it was too late.

Grinning, the man lunged and shoved his sword into Raina's back, the tip appearing through her chest. She gasped as he jerked it back out, and Keris threw himself forward, catching her as she fell. "What are you doing? They are our allies!"

But they weren't; Keris knew that. Or rather, he knew that his father was no ally to Ithicana.

He lowered Raina to the ground and pressed his hands against the gaping wound in her chest. Blood bubbled up between his fingers, her mouth opening and closing wordlessly as she fought to breathe. As she fought to live.

Beyond, several of his father's soldiers were feeling along the floor of the bridge; then a stone hatch popped open on silent hinges, the fresh scent of the sea filling the air. "Right where she said it would be," one of them muttered. "Get down and get out, and we should be right in front of Midwatch."

She.

Lara.

Then the man who'd stabbed Raina stepped into Keris's line of sight. "I'm afraid your trip to Harendell is to be cut short, Your Highness. Will you be a good little prince and sit here nicely while we take Ithicana, or do we need to resort to ropes?"

Keris lunged, but the soldier was ready, and in a heartbeat, three of them had him pinned, another wrapping ropes around his ankles, then around his wrists. They proceeded to arm them-selves with more of the weapons from the wagon before dropping down the hatch.

Then there was nothing but the thunder of his heart and Raina's ragged, wet breath. He met her gaze. "I didn't know."

A tear ran down her cheek.

"This is the last thing I want." His eyes burned. "I'm sick of war. Tired of the endless fighting. It's the reason I was going to Harendell—not because of the books, but because I can't stomach any more killing. I wanted a different life."

Wasted words.

Wasted sentiment.

Because the eyes staring back at him were as still as glass.

4

ZARRAH

ZARRAH DREW HER BLADE OVER THE MARIDRINIAN'S THROAT, then let him drop, his last gasping gurgles filling the air as she strode to where her soldiers were laying out bodies. "How many?"

Yrina, her closest friend and second-in-command, rose from where she knelt next to a farmer's body. "Ten, we think. We'll need to let the flames die down before we can check the ashes."

So many. Zarrah's stomach hollowed even as her eyes passed over the dead, all farmers. All Valcottan. All people she was sworn to protect. "Children?" It was hard to ask, but she made herself do it, swallowing a swell of sickness as she waited for a response.

Yrina shook her head. "Those who could fight managed to hold back the raiders while the children and infirm hid in the woods. A small mercy."

Small indeed. Many of those children were now orphans of violence, much like Zarrah was herself. Like her, they'd seen the Maridrinians slaughter their parents and destroy their homes. A moment that would forever change the course of their futures, and she wondered how many would pick up weapons so as to never see themselves hurt like this again. How many of them would join the fight against their nation's nemesis. How many of them would, like her, dedicate their lives to achieving victory in the Endless War.

"It could've been worse," Yrina said. "Every member of every family could've been lost, but they weren't. We got here in time to help, and they've you to thank for it."

Not in time to help everyone, Zarrah thought, staring at the dead farmer, his stomach sliced open by a Maridrinian sword.

She'd taken command of the Nerastis garrison the moment they'd sailed back into the harbor, caring little when her cousin Bermin shouted and raged about being stripped of the role of general. The first thing she'd done was triple the number of scouts watching the border for raiders and double the number of patrol camps stationed up and down the countryside. Already it had paid dividends, her soldiers having intercepted several raiding parties before they had a chance to work their devilry. But the Maridrinian rats had generations of practice at this form of warfare, and they were adapting to her tactics, as the day had proved.

"The horns are a mistake!" a deep voice boomed from behind her. "We'd have killed twice their number if we'd used stealth."

Zarrah turned from the bodies to find Bermin riding up behind her, his massive mount splattered with blood and her cousin equally covered in gore. "It looks as though you caught more than a few fleeing rats."

"Some." He spit on the ground, then dismounted. "Their horses are fast, so many more will escape back across the border. An opportunity they wouldn't have had if you hadn't warned them we were coming."

It was one of the many strategies they disagreed on. Bermin preferred to approach the raids with stealth so as to kill as many

Maridrinians as possible, whereas she preferred to put the run on them with signal horns, thus saving as many Valcottan lives as she could. But the bigger difference between how she and Bermin worked was that Zarrah never limited her strategies to just one element.

No sooner had that thought rolled through her head did Yrina say, "Smoke," and the group all turned to look at the crimson puffs in the distance. Zarrah smiled in satisfaction before turning back to Bermin. "Just because *you* didn't kill them doesn't mean they got away. I had archers waiting to pick them off."

Her cousin huffed, crossing his thick arms. "You dedicate too many of our forces to defense, Zarrah. It's been weeks since we crossed the border. Makes us look weak. Makes Valcotta look weak."

The Maridrinians had lost more soldiers in recent weeks to Zarrah's strategies than they had in the last year of Bermin's, so Zarrah doubted *weakness* was the word the rats were spitting as they licked their wounds.

"Gather the bastards' heads," she ordered, taking the reins of her horse from one of her soldiers. "Burn the bodies." She turned to Yrina, about to give the order for soldiers to remain to dig graves for the dead farmers, but motion caught her attention. Shading her eyes from the brightness of the sun, Zarrah peered at the brush. Someone was hiding. "I thought you found all the children?"

"We did," Yrina answered, but Zarrah was already walking toward the brush, her hands up to indicate she meant no harm. The child would be terrified, and though Zarrah was one of his or her countrymen, she was still a soldier. "It's okay," she said softly. "You can come out now. It's safe."

"Zarrah!" Yrina called. "Hold back."

Zarrah ignored her friend because she knew the fear this child was feeling. Knew the horror. And she remembered how she'd prayed to be delivered from it. "Let me help you."

A form exploded from the brush. Not a child but a man.

A Maridrinian soldier.

"Die, you Valcottan bitch!" he screamed, then sliced at her with his sword.

Instinct took over.

Zarrah ducked under the blade, rolling across the ground and then back onto her feet in a flash. Pulling loose her weapon, she held up a hand to stop Yrina and the others from attacking. "You should have run when you had the chance."

"Better to die with your blood on my hands," he hissed, eyes gleaming with hate.

But his hate was a paltry thing compared to hers.

She knocked the blade from his grip, then swung again, taking his legs out from under him.

The Maridrinian sprawled on the ground, but Zarrah kicked him in the ribs, flipping him over. "Pick up your weapon."

He retrieved his sword, rising unsteadily. Then he attacked.

Zarrah's staff was a blur of motion, blocking his swipe and then flying under his guard to slam against his arm, bone breaking. The Maridrinian screamed and dropped his weapon.

"Care to try again, or do you want to run?"

"So that your archers can shoot me in the back?" he demanded. "I heard you, Valcottan. There is no escape."

"Maybe you'll get lucky." She pressed forward, the Maridrinian stumbling out of reach. "Rats are good at scuttling through small, dark spaces."

"You're supposed to let us retreat," he snarled. "Those are the rules. Those have always been the rules!"

Her anger turned to blistering rage, her vision red, because this murderer didn't deserve escape. Didn't deserve any mercy beyond what he'd shown her people, which was *none*. "The rules have changed." Then she swung her staff with all her strength.

It struck his skull with a resounding crack. He dropped like a stone, but she struck him again because she wasn't through. Would never be through delivering vengeance upon the Maridrinians who'd orphaned the children of her people.

Until she had revenge on the Maridrinian king who'd orphaned her.

HOURS LATER, ZARRAH TROTTED HER horse into the stable yard of her garrison, the sound of the purple banners flapping from the minarets loud in her ears. A lifetime ago, when Nerastis had been a thriving city and under Valcottan control, the palace had been the winter residence of emperors and empresses, but now it was populated only by soldiers.

Cracked stone and boarded-up windows from prior attacks by Maridrina had gone unrepaired, the pale walls bore scorch marks and soot stains, and one of the towers stood in ruins. The interior was little better, the walls naked but for the pale shadows of where priceless artwork had once hung and the furniture either cheap or aged. Rooms that a hundred years ago had held parties and spectacles filled with the upper echelons of Valcottan society were now filled with rows of bunks and soldiers' belongings, the massive chandelier that had once turned the dining room into a rainbow of color apparently at the bottom of the River Anriot, courtesy of a long-dead Maridrinian princeling.

The only consolation was that the Maridrinian palace on the north side of the river was in equal disrepair, neither side controlling the city, therefore neither side seeing much point in funding repairs.

"Take the heads down to the river and send them across," she ordered. "Aim for their palace."

"Disregard that order," a familiar voice said, and Zarrah looked up to find Petra Anaphora, Empress of Valcotta, standing in the palace entrance.

Dropping her horse's reins, Zarrah pressed her hand to her heart, lowering her head in deference. "Your Imperial Majesty. My apologies, I'd not been made aware of your arrival."

"That's because I wished it to be a surprise, General." The empress descended the steps, jeweled sandals making soft thuds on the stone, her silk garments fluttering on the breeze. Petra Anaphora retained the beauty she'd once been famed for, though now there were creases around her eyes, and her halo of hair was more silver than black. Courtesy of a militant dedication to training, her body was all lean, hard muscle, the stomach revealed by her short blouse as flat as Zarrah's own.

She approached, her hands curving around Zarrah's head as she kissed both her cheeks. "Beloved niece, we have been too long apart."

A flood of warmth filled Zarrah's veins, her aunt's presence always a comfort. "To what do we owe the honor?"

"Necessity, I'm afraid." Her aunt slid her arm through Zarrah's, tugging her toward the entrance. "A change of strategy." Her eyes flicked to the soldiers holding the bag of heads, Bermin standing next to them, hand pressed to his heart and expression unreadable. "Burn them."

Zarrah blinked. "But that's not—"

"What we do?" Her aunt gave a tight nod. "Trust me. No one wishes more than I to fling those murderous rats back across the Anriot to their fellows as a warning of what fate awaits those who attack Valcotta, but circumstance demands it."

"What has changed?"

"The opportunity I predicted has finally been presented to us. But let us retreat to more comfortable quarters to discuss what must be done to capitalize upon it."

They made their way to the royal apartments, ensconcing themselves on soft cushions while the servants her aunt traveled with presented them with wine and delicacies of a far higher caliber than was typically found within these walls.

Never one to waste her time on small talk, her aunt said, "Silas has bitten off more than he can chew with the bridge. As I anticipated, the Ithicanians are still fighting him at every turn, and will continue to do so. War is in their blood, even more than it is in ours. They won't concede defeat."

The events at Southwatch still caused a swell of sickness in Zarrah's stomach, for she knew better than most what atrocities the Maridrinians were capable of. Already reports were filtering in of Ithicanian corpses dangling from their bridge, and she always forced herself to read the details. For while she'd not caused it, she'd also done nothing to prevent it. Yet she schooled herself to remain silent and listen to her aunt's explanation of her motivations, because if Maridrina holding the bridge would see them made vulnerable to Valcottan blades, it was worth it.

It had to be.

"Silas is losing soldiers by the dozens," her aunt continued. "Soon he'll need more men in Ithicana or risk losing his hard-gained prize, and there is only one place he can source them."

"Their garrison in Nerastis."

Her aunt smiled. "Correct. And we will encourage this decision on his part by not giving him any reason to keep them here."

Understanding flickered through Zarrah's mind. "We wait until he's depleted the ranks here and then move against those who remain, taking Nerastis back under control."

"Even so." Her aunt took a long mouthful of wine, her eyes

gleaming. "He cannot hope to hold both prizes, which means he will have to choose. And holding the bridge has been his obsession for most of his life."

"Ithicana's loss is our gain."

Such was the cost of war; Zarrah knew that as well as anyone. Knew that sacrifices had to be made to achieve victory and that she should be looking forward with anticipation to how Valcotta could use the opportunity to strike a blow. Yet every time she blinked, Zarrah found her mind's eye filled with children's corpses hanging from the bridge.

Silence stretched between them, then her aunt said, "You don't agree with our passivity in the Ithicanian conflict."

A statement, not a question, so Zarrah didn't bother denying it. "We may not have been allies, but neither is Ithicana our enemy. Whereas Maridrina is. To allow the rats to triumph over those who have been our friends for the sake of our own gain sits poorly with me, regardless that it provides us an advantage."

"As it does with me, but Aren Kertell left us little recourse." Motioning for a servant to refill their cups, her aunt ate a chocolate, her eyes distant as she considered her next words. "I know you desire to save everyone, my darling, but it's not always possible. Sometimes one must choose, and when one is in power, the sacrifices are a hundredfold harder. If we'd intervened to warn Southwatch, Maridrina would have blamed us for the failed invasion and turned their might south upon us. And instead of Ithicanian corpses soaking blood into the earth, it would have been Valcottans."

There was logic to her aunt's words, but they did not ease the sourness in Zarrah's gut. "That doesn't mean we need to make it easy for them. If we attacked, it might allow Ithicana a chance to regroup."

"And their gain would be our loss." Her aunt's voice was flat.

"This is the first opportunity we've had in decades to retake what is rightfully ours without catastrophic losses, and you'd throw it away?"

"I . . ." Zarrah swallowed, emotions warring between her loyalty to her aunt and her sense of what was right. "Silas shows no sign of reducing his numbers in Nerastis. The latest princeling arrived with three hundred new men, and they've been aggressive in their raiding. Don't we risk them seeing our passivity as a weakness they should exploit?"

Another wave of the hand. "Silas has to put in a good showing for the heir. Once this one dies, which, if what the rumors say is true, is inevitable, Silas will take back those men. And then we will strike."

"But how many civilians do we risk losing in the meantime?" Frustration slipped into Zarrah's voice despite her best efforts. "How many Valcottans will die because the Maridrinians believe we won't retaliate in response to their murders?"

"Courtesy of your fine defense strategies, hopefully not many. But as it is, I dislike your tone, General. Remember whom you speak to."

Zarrah lowered her eyes, staring at the large, silken cushion on which her aunt sat. "Apologies, Empress. I find my emotions running high with a Veliant in Nerastis."

And not just any Veliant, but Crown Prince Keris. The latest of Silas's sons to command in Nerastis, the king's bloodthirsty progeny as vicious in their raiding as their monster of a father. Yrina had reported yesterday that the spies had finally caught sight of the Rat King's heir. Pretty enough to be a girl and, of course, with eyes of Veliant blue.

"You are not alone in your desire to see all the Veliants dead," the empress said. "His presence boils the blood of every Valcottan in Nerastis. But we must nurture our rage. Must temper it into a weapon that we will use against the Maridrinians when the time to attack is right. And your rage, dear one"—she reached across the space between them to cup Zarrah's cheek—"will be the sharpest blade of them all. I have no doubt in my heart that it will be *you* who removes the princeling's head."

"It would be an honor."

"You're already proving to be a fine general. And, eventually, an even finer empress."

Empress. Though for years rumors had swirled that Empress Petra favored her niece over her own son as heir to the Empire, this was the first time she'd voiced her intent to Zarrah's face. "You honor me, Auntie. Truly."

"You are as a daughter to me, dear one." The empress leaned forward to kiss Zarrah's forehead. "As alike to me in mind and spirit as if you'd been born of my body, and it will be you who carries on my vision for Valcotta when I am gone." A smirk lit her aunt's dark-brown eyes. "Although if God is good, he will grant me many more years to guide you to your full potential."

Zarrah forced herself to smile, though the thought of losing the woman who'd raised her since she was fourteen made her stomach clench, old panic rising in her chest. "I pray for this also, Auntie. Would wish for your immortality, if such a thing were possible."

The empress laughed, then pulled Zarrah into her arms, holding her close. Squeezing her eyes shut, Zarrah listened to her aunt's heart the way she had as a child, her unease receding.

"I know your pain better than anyone, my love," her aunt murmured. "Your grief is my own. And together, I promise we will have revenge on Silas Veliant."

A promise that had kept Zarrah going in the dark days after her mother's murder. She'd been fourteen and had gone with her mother, the empress's younger sister, to visit the estate of a friend, not an hour's ride south of Nerastis. Just before dawn, Maridrinian raiders had struck, slaughtering the guards and estate workers alike. And then they'd turned on the villa.

Like it was yesterday, Zarrah could remember her mother begging she be spared. That she'd do anything if only they'd allow her daughter to *live*. And Zarrah's dreams were haunted by the laughter of King Silas Veliant himself as he agreed. As he hacked off her mother's beautiful head, his men fixing her body to a cross in the middle of the gardens while Zarrah screamed.

But he'd kept his word.

They'd tied Zarrah to the base of the cross with her mother's head in her lap. For *two days*, she'd wept and screamed and struggled against her bonds as blood and worse dripped onto her, as the hot sun turned her mother's body to rot.

And then the empress had come.

Galloping into the villa with her war party, she'd been the one to cut Zarrah loose. To clean the filth from her body and hold her close night after night as the terrors took hold. Who, after witnessing weeks of weeping, had put a staff in Zarrah's hand and said, "Tears will not bring your mother back. Put all your sorrow and all your rage and all your passion into becoming a weapon, and fight to prevent this fate from ever befalling another Valcottan child. I promise you, we will make Silas Veliant *bleed* for what he has done."

Zarrah had never put the staff down, her desire to protect those who couldn't protect themselves fueling her day after day. Had struggled and trained under the best arms men in the Empire, become a warrior few would pit themselves against. Ruthless and dangerous, hundreds of Maridrinian raiders dying at her hands. And yet for all of that, more nights than not, she still woke with the echoing sensation of blood dripping on her face, and of Silas Veliant, azure eyes as cold as a reptile's, laughing while she screamed.

A knock sounded at the door, and a moment later, her aunt's bodyguard, Welran, entered. "Empress." He bowed low. "Your entourage is ready to depart."

"Our time together is always too brief, dear one." The empress stood, the gold bangles on her arms jingling as she straightened her voluminous lamé trousers. "But if I abandon Pyrinat for too long, the nobility will cease their quarrels with one another and turn to conspiring against me until they receive a reminder of who rules. Which is why I have several villas to visit on my journey back—best they remember I know where their families live."

"You are beloved by the people, Auntie." Zarrah rose to her feet. "They'd not dare move against you."

"The nobility are *not* the people." Her aunt tapped Zarrah's nose. "And love means little in politics."

Together, they strode through the corridors of the palace, a large honor guard waiting for them in the courtyard. Zarrah's cousin, Bermin, stood waiting with them.

"Mother." He pressed his hand to his heart. "I came to bid you farewell and safe travels."

"Our parting will be brief if I hear you aren't abiding by your cousin's orders, Bermin," the empress snapped. "She is my chosen, and when you dishonor her, you dishonor me. Am I clear?"

Zarrah winced internally, but Bermin only inclined his head. "As you say, Mother, so shall it be."

"Good." The empress paused next to her waiting horse. "Much goes into victory, dear one, but timing might well be the most critical piece of all. You will keep our forces to this side of the Anriot, no matter what provocation." Then she leaned closer, breath hot against Zarrah's ear. "And when the princeling gets himself killed and his men return north to fight Ithicana, we will strike."

Zarrah pressed her hand to her chest. "Yes, Empress. Safe travels."

Her aunt mounted in one swift motion, and without another word, led her escort out into the city.

Only to be passed by a rider galloping in.

A scout.

"Raiders," the man gasped, slipping off his lathered mount. "They hit a village."

The Maridrinians *never* raided twice in one day. Zarrah's stomach plummeted. "How did they get past our scouts?"

"We think they traveled south along the edge of the desert and then cut inland, returning by the same path. They were gone by the time our patrols arrived. Forty-three dead, all farmers and their families."

Forty-three. "Children?"

The scout gave a grim nod, and Zarrah had to clench her teeth to keep from vomiting.

"Cowardly vermin," Bermin snarled. "We must retaliate immediately. Attack their garrison and make them pay in blood."

"No." Zarrah swallowed the taste of bile. "The empress was clear in her orders. We will not cross the Anriot for any reason." She looked to Yrina. "Increase patrols."

"Yes, Gen—"

"To do nothing makes us look weak," Bermin interrupted. "It dishonors the dead."

Frustration and guilt bit at her guts, but Zarrah only flattened her palms against her thighs, looking up at him with a measured expression. "And yet that is what the empress has ordered me to do."

"Forty-three dead, Zarrah! Many of them children! The Maridrinians are rats that deserve nothing more than extermination!"

The ferocity and passion in his voice were the reason soldiers loved to follow him into battle, but Bermin saw no further than the length of his sword. "We will avenge them when the time is right, but that time is not now, cousin."

He eyed her coldly, looming over her with his enormous bulk, his voice patronizing as he said, "Good little Zarrah. Perfect little Zarrah. Always listening to Auntie's orders even when it means sacrificing her own honor."

Zarrah exhaled a slow breath. Since he'd been removed from command, Bermin's efforts to goad her into making mistakes had increased. But unlike him, she possessed a modicum of self-control. "Increase the eastern patrols. We might not be able to avenge the dead, but at least we can protect the living. If you catch them, show them no mercy." She added, "Now, if you'll excuse me, the hour is late, and I've work yet to do."

She heard Yrina give the orders, and then the sound of footfalls as her friend ran to catch up. They walked through the corridors together, and only when they were in Zarrah's suite, the doors shut, did Yrina say, "I'd sooner believe you're related to a lump of rock than that idiot. Did Her Imperial Majesty drop him on his head when he was an infant? Perhaps more than once?"

Rubbing her temples, Zarrah said, "His bravery is unparalleled, and his soldiers would follow him into fire. That is no small thing."

Yrina lifted up one hand. "Bravery." Then she lifted the other. "Stupidity. They can follow him where they like—I wouldn't follow him across a room."

Not answering, Zarrah went to the expansive windows to look out at the growing night. The Valcottan palace was perched on a hill on the southern edge of Nerastis, giving her an unimpeded view of the massive city. At night, it was beautiful: a sea of colored lights and flickering flames, the River Anriot flowing through its center like a serpent. Yet the shadows concealed that most of the buildings were rubble, the streets reeked of waste, and the marshy edges of the Anriot were home to countless rotting corpses that had yet to be consumed by the river's inhabitants.

"What reason did the empress give for her orders?" Yrina asked. "It's unlike her not to desire retaliation."

Zarrah explained the empress's intent, but Yrina's frown only deepened. "It's a good strategy, but it's going to cost us. If the Maridrinians don't fear retaliation, their appetite for raiding is only going to increase, and we can't stop them all. We could lose hundreds of civilians waiting for Silas to withdraw his men to reinforce his armies in Ithicana."

"The empress is wise." Zarrah wasn't sure if her words were for Yrina or herself. "And she knows how to fight Maridrina—she's been doing so all her life."

"But do you agree with this plan?"

"Of course I agree with it." The words slipped from her tongue without hesitation because her aunt had *never* led her astray. And yet . . . Zarrah couldn't push aside the sourness that came with knowing an entire nation had been sacrificed as a part of her aunt's ambitions to strike a heavy blow against Maridrina. For all it was strategically brilliant, it felt . . . *lacking* in honor. "We just have to do more to protect our borders while the plan comes to fruition."

Yrina opened her mouth as though to say something, hesitated, then said, "That's a problem for tomorrow. Care to take a trip into the city for the night? I know a few establishments where the drink is tolerable, and they employ men pretty enough to make you forget your cares for an evening. I could arrange an escort?"

The last thing Zarrah wanted was to be in a noisy drinking establishment with people pressing in on all sides. As it was, she felt like she could barely breathe, her stomach twisting with nausea. What she needed was air.

"Another night. I'm tired."

"It's always another night, Zar. We've been at each other's sides for half our lives, and yet I can count on one hand the number of times you've set aside duty for a night of entertainment. Valcotta isn't going to lose the Endless War because you took a few hours to relax."

For a heartbeat, she considered it. Except Zarrah remembered the handful of times—how stepping away from her sworn path, even for a moment, felt like she was betraying her purpose. "Have a drink for me. I need to come up with some strategies to tighten our borders."

Yrina shrugged, then pressed a hand to her heart. "I'll leave you, then. Perhaps tomorrow will bring orders to fight. Until then, I drink. Good night, General."

"Good night," Zarrah murmured, waiting until the door clicked shut before moving onto the balcony. A salty breeze blew in from the sea, and leaning her elbows on the balustrade, she stared across the city at the illuminated domes of the Maridrinian palace, which was sure to be full of Maridrinian nobility. And the crown prince who had given the order for the raid, vermin, just like the rest of his bloodline.

Drip.

A warm droplet splattered against her forehead. Zarrah gasped, stumbling back and swiping her hand across her skin, certain she'd see blood.

It was only water.

Swallowing hard, she forced herself to look up, irrationally certain she'd see her mother's rotting corpse hanging above her. But it was only droplets of beaded water that had collected on the overhang from the earlier rains. Yet panic still crawled in her belly, dragging her back to the moment when she'd been tied up and helpless. And God help her, but she hated it. Hated the Rat King.

Hated that whole goddamned family.

When the princeling gets himself killed . . . we will strike. Her aunt's voice echoed through her head, and a thought followed on its heels.

She could kill him.

As long as she made it look like either an accident or like he'd been assassinated by one of his grasping younger brothers, no one would be the wiser. With Prince Keris dead, the men who had been sent with him would likely be recalled north immediately, which would mean the raids would ease. And then it would be nothing to wait until her aunt was ready for her to attack.

The life of one murderous Veliant prick to spare the lives of potentially hundreds of Valcottan innocents.

Retreating inside, Zarrah dug through the piles of papers on her desk until she found a description. *Possessed of little military acumen. Notorious whoremonger with a fondness for wine and flamboyant attire. Shoulder-length blond hair. Medium height and light build. Eyes of Veliant blue.*

Memories of eyes that color filled her head, along with Silas Veliant's laugh. Zarrah shivered, then scowled at herself for the reaction.

She was no longer a child to be intimidated, especially not by a princeling.

Pulling off the dark-purple coat of her uniform, which was marked with Valcotta's crest and signifiers of her rank, she then tossed it inside. The wind brushed her bare arms and raised gooseflesh on her skin. Strapping her staff to her back, Zarrah flipped a leg over the balustrade so that she was sitting on the edge.

The empress had ordered her to keep the Valcottan forces to this side of the Anriot. But she'd said nothing about Zarrah herself remaining so contained.

Taking a deep breath, she jumped.

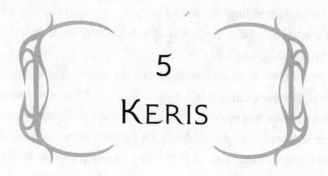

5
KERIS

KERIS ROLLED ONTO HIS BACK, HEART THUNDERING AND SWEAT beading on his brow, his breathing as ragged as that of the woman next to him on the silk sheets.

"Feel free to leave. There's coin in the pocket of my trousers, wherever they are."

The courtesan raised herself up on one elbow, pushing her golden-brown hair back over her shoulder. "Most men like to talk afterward, Your Highness."

"Most men are idiots." He moved onto his stomach. "But I'm sure you've noticed that."

She made a humming noise that indicated neither agreement nor disagreement. "But not you, Your Highness. They say you're very clever."

Keris snorted, the sound muffled by the pillow. "I'm sure *they* say a good many things about me, but nothing quite so flattering as that."

She shifted on top of him, her thighs pressing against his sides, her fingers digging skillfully into the knotted muscles of his back.

But having had knives stuck into those very muscles, Keris tensed at the contact, rolling so that he was in a position to defend himself, if need be.

"You should go," he said. "I'm not interested in conversation."

The courtesan straightened from where she'd been kissing his throat, her eyes narrowing. "Why? You think because I'm paid company that I'm not clever enough to do more than lie on my back?"

"On the contrary. From what I've ascertained from our few hours together, you're clearly clever enough to know that saying anything interesting around me is dangerous. Your mistress caters to patrons on both sides of Nerastis, and girls who get caught talking too much tend to find themselves floating facedown in the Anriot."

"As if I'd take the coin of Valcottan scum."

He smirked, amused by what was likely false patriotism. "Just the coin of Maridrinian scum."

She was quiet, seeming to contemplate his words, green eyes regarding him thoughtfully. "Why do you take up with paid girls at all, Your Highness? You could have an entire harem of beautiful young wives whose loyalty was ensured. You're going to be king of Maridrina one day."

Catching a lock of her hair, Keris twisted it around his finger. "Did you know, lovely, that I had eight older brothers? And that for a moment in time, each of them *was going to be the King of Maridrina one day*. Tell me, do you know what happened to my brothers?"

Her jaw tightened. "They died, Your Highness."

"Precisely. So what do you think the odds are that, of all of Silas Veliant's sons, I'll be the one to survive long enough to take the crown? What do *they* say about that?"

Silence. Then, "They say that you'll be in a grave before the year is out."

"And they are very likely correct."

The courtesan smiled, revealing straight, white teeth and a spark of bravery that he found distinctly appealing. "You didn't answer my question, Your Highness."

Lifting her up by the waist, Keris rolled, setting her gently on her feet next to the bed. After handing her the gown that she'd discarded on the floor earlier, he then located his trousers, the garment clinking as he lifted it. Keris pulled a handful of coins out of his pocket and gave them to her. "Given the odds of me surviving are low, it seems unkind to take a wife, never mind a whole harem of them. Paid girls don't weep when their customers meet untimely ends."

Her head cocked. "How interesting that you believe your wives would."

Despite himself, Keris laughed. "Careful, girl. I might decide to keep you for another few hours if you're not more sparing with your wit."

She walked toward the door, retrieving one silk slipper and then another. Fingers resting on the handle, she turned to him, offering a slow smile full of promises. "My name's Aileena, if you liked me enough to see me again, Your Highness."

He did like her. But the second the thought crossed his mind, the room seemed to shadow and Raina's dead eyes filled his vision, reminding him that the things he liked got broken. The people he liked got killed.

Never again.

"If I cared what your name was," he said, "I would've asked."

Aileena stared at him for a heartbeat, her eyes wide with hurt; then she was gone, the door slamming shut behind her.

Lying on his back, Keris pressed his forearm against his eyes, taking deep, measured breaths, trying to gain control of the miserable twisting guilt that filled his core. Guilt that had haunted him ever since that cursed night in Ithicana's bridge.

Why hadn't he seen it coming?

The door opened and shut, and a familiar voice said, "Well, Keris, just when I think you can't stoop any lower, you prove me wrong. Just what did you say that was bad enough to make a whore cry?"

Not lifting his arm from his face, Keris said, "I told her I wasn't interested in knowing her name."

"You're a prick, you know that? Why would you say such a thing?"

"Because I liked her."

Keris could all but feel his younger brother roll his eyes, then Otis said, "This is why no one likes you, Keris. You're an awful person."

"*You* like me."

"No, I do not. I am merely inured to your acid tongue. Now, for the love of God, put some clothes on. I don't need to see so much of you so soon after eating dinner."

Groaning, Keris pulled on his trousers and then walked barefoot across the room to where Otis stood surveying the shithole that was Nerastis, the city clearly visible through the gaping hole in the tower's domed upper floor. Younger than Keris by a matter of months, Otis was tall and broad, his brown hair slicked back in the current style, his beard trim and neat. Rubbing his own cleanshaven chin, Keris asked, "Father send you?"

"Yes. He's heard that you are refusing to attend meetings of the war council to discuss strategy. That all you're doing is alternating between burying your face in books and burying your face in the breasts of Nerastis women."

Picking up a glass of wine that he'd abandoned at some point,

Keris drank deeply. "Accurate." Or at least, partially so. Ever since the attack on the bridge, he'd been unable to focus on his studies, ever reminded that the pursuit of them had seen Raina killed. A kingdom conquered.

Why didn't I suspect his plan?

Otis rounded on him, his blue eyes filled with frustration. "Why are you behaving this way? This is your chance, Keris! Father's giving you the opportunity to prove yourself worthy of the crown, and you're throwing it away!"

"I'm not interested in proving myself to him." Especially given that proving himself to his father meant becoming a killer like every other goddamned member of his family, women included. It was almost a shock that Veliant children weren't born with their hands stained red.

"You're going to get your own throat slit." Otis's face reddened in the way it always did when he was upset, his hand reflexively touching the pocket where Keris knew he kept love letters from his late wife. Her ship had been sunk by the Valcottans several months ago, and the letters were deeply precious to him. "You're his son. He doesn't want you dead, but Maridrina must come first . . ."

Keris shrugged, draining the glass and setting it aside.

"This isn't still about you getting caught unaware with the Ithicana invasion, is it? God, Keris, let it go. It's history."

Keris stared into the darkness of the night, seeing the light fade from Raina's eyes. Seeing Ithicanian blood pooling on the gray stone of the bridge. "History, is it? It seems like only yesterday that Father used me to start a war."

Otis snorted. "Don't flatter yourself. The force you were with was but a small piece in a very large plan."

"*Lara's* plan." And if only he'd allowed Raina to send his escorts back to Vencia, it might have failed. His cowardice, his selfishness, had been Ithicana's doom as much as his conniving sister.

"Apparently." Otis rolled his shoulders with obvious discomfort, not alone in his unease that their father had kept their sister in a compound in the Red Desert, allowing Serin to turn her into a fundamentalist warrior bent on Ithicana's destruction. The revelation that she'd been responsible had come from the Ithicanians themselves, those who'd been captured spitting at Lara's name, referring to her only as the *traitor queen*.

"Has Serin found her yet?"

Otis shook his head. "She's either dead or disappeared into the wind."

Given what she'd accomplished, Keris hoped it was the former. And that it had not been swift. "And the Ithicanian king?"

"Stubborn bastard is still fighting. There are orders to take him alive, if possible."

"To what end?"

Leaning against the raw edge of the dome's broken wall, Otis gave him a long look. "Never mind Ithicana, Keris. Never mind the bridge. Never mind Lara. *You* need to focus that mind of yours on the Valcottans and taking the southern half of Nerastis back under Maridrinian control. The ranking officers are meeting downstairs in an hour to discuss strategy. Join them."

To take the rest of Nerastis would mean hundreds, if not thousands, of lives lost. And for what? To hold a larger piece of the rubble that was this city? Keris refused to be part of such an undertaking. "I wouldn't have the slightest idea of where to begin. You go instead—everyone will be happier for it."

"Likely. But I'm not in command. I'm not the heir."

Keris slapped his younger brother on the shoulder. "Soon enough, Otis. Soon enough."

Otis's face darkened, and in a flash of movement, he slammed Keris against the wall hard enough to rattle his teeth. "Don't ever say that. No matter how much you irritate me, you're still my brother, and I do not want you dead."

They stared each other down for several long moments, Otis's fingers digging into his shoulder hard enough to leave bruises, but then his younger brother turned away. "The Valcottans have a *woman* in command now. Zarrah Anaphora. She's barely more than a girl."

Lara is barely more than a girl, and she brought down the impenetrable Bridge Kingdom, Keris considered saying, but instead muttered, "So I hear."

"You could beat her and take the southern half of Nerastis. I know you could, if you put your mind to it. Do it, and your life will be safe."

Except losing wasn't what made Keris's blood run cold; it was that he *knew* he could win. He'd stood in on war council meetings and felt his head fill with strategies for victory, his mind all too capable of distancing itself from the realities of war, if he allowed it. And if he did it once, he had no confidence that he wouldn't do it again and again until his hands were as drenched in blood as his father's. "No. You go. Tell them I'm with a woman. Or too drunk. Pick your excuse."

"*Are* you drunk?" Otis demanded.

"No. Although that's easily remedied."

His brother's jaw clenched and unclenched, but then he exhaled. "Fine. But in exchange, you have to agree to train with me again. At the very least don't make yourself an easy target for an assassin."

"The perception that I am an easy target has kept me alive for most of my life, Otis. I'm not inclined to jeopardize it. I will take this, though." Reaching across the space between them, Keris plucked loose the dagger shoved in his brother's belt and examined it. The edge was dark with the poison his brother favored. One that was slow to work but always fatal without the antidote. "You know how I love knives."

Otis cast his eyes at the painted ceiling. "Do you have any idea how dreadful that sounds?"

"Says the man who poisons his knives."

"Only when I fight Valcottans. The bastards deserve no less."

Keris knew better than to comment, for when it came to Valcotta, Otis's hate was practically religious in its fervor. As it was for so many Maridrinians, and the Valcottans were no different.

Otis headed toward the door. "Good night, brother. Enjoy your wine and the sleep that follows."

Keris waited until the sound of his brother's boots echoed down the stairs, then he bolted the door. Retrieving a black shirt and hooded leather coat, he found his discarded boots and pulled them on before tucking a variety of knives into various hiding places.

Stepping to the edge of the broken floor, scaffolding running up the tower beneath him, Keris breathed in the scent of the air, a mix of sea salt and the filth of the city, his eyes taking in the glow of a thousand lights. Nerastis came alive at night.

And so did he.

Stepping out onto the scaffolding, Keris jumped.

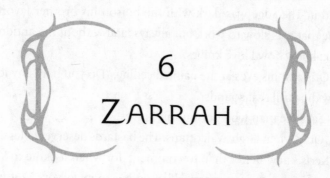

6

ZARRAH

HER HEAD DOWN, ZARRAH WOVE HER WAY THROUGH THE rubble-strewn streets of Nerastis. Near a third of the buildings were collapsed, and the rest were near enough to it that venturing into any of the establishments meant risking being buried alive.

Not that it stopped anyone.

Groups of her soldiers staggered drunkenly around the rubble, laughing as they ventured into the tap houses and brothels and opium dens, those who worked within them watching on with eyes filled with equal parts cunning and despair. Rats skittered forth from dark alleys, disturbed by the moans of pleasure from those too cheap to pay for a room or the despondent weeping of those who'd succumbed to vice or circumstance. Both would net bodies for her patrols to dump into the river to feed the alligators come morning.

Orphans ran wild, picking pockets and begging on corners before returning to the hovels they called homes, their beds little more than flea-infested rags. One raced toward Zarrah, a boy not more than eight, but the focus in his gaze spoke to his intent. Not interested in arresting children tonight, Zarrah tossed him a copper before he had the chance to slip a hand into her pockets, but the boy only glared at the metal and then spit at her feet.

Gritting her teeth, she carried on. Because this was Nerastis: lawless and dangerous and miserable, and though both Valcotta and Maridrina fought endlessly to possess it, neither did anything to improve it. Perhaps that would change once Valcotta held the whole of the city, but her gut told her that her aunt's eyes would only travel farther north into Maridrina and that Nerastis would continue to languish.

The closer she got to the Anriot, the more mixed the company became, Maridrinians venturing to this side of the river despite the risks, much as her people did to the northern side of the water. Soldiers who fought each other during the day sat around rough tables, cards in hand, whores from both nations perched on their knees. The games often turned into brawls, which resulted in more corpses to feed to the Anriot's alligators, and Zarrah gave the gatherings a wide berth, making her way down to where the street fell apart into rubble, the swampy ground consuming the cobbles.

Countless bridges had been built over the wide river, but all were destroyed, leaving behind only the remains. Rotting pieces of timber, slimy rocks, and twisted steel sat just beneath the surface of the water, providing the daring multiple ways across if they were willing to risk the snapping teeth lurking in the depths.

Zarrah followed the narrow path, which was flanked by twisted trees on both sides, her boots sinking into the spongy ground, the scent of rot rising to assault her nose. Ahead, a guttering torch was stuck deep into the earth, marking where one was to cross, its twin flickering on the Maridrinian side.

Dropping into a crouch, she scanned the opposite bank for signs of Maridrinian patrols, then the river for signs of motion, but there was only the ripple of water over the collapsed bridge, the air full of droning insects that bit at her skin.

This is madness.

Zarrah shoved away the thought. Madness was allowing the princeling to live when every day he did so, more of her people died as a result.

Tightening her grip on her staff, Zarrah used it for balance as she slowly picked her way across the river, both her bravery and her balance precarious on the slick stones. The cold water seemed to know whenever her boot slid in the murk or her toe caught on a piece of lumber, grasping at her legs and trying to send her toppling so as to feed its inhabitants. But each time, she managed to keep her balance, making it past the deepest point in the middle. She was almost there.

Splash.

Zarrah's heart leapt at the faint sound, which was followed by three more in quick succession.

She'd been spotted.

Pulse racing, she quickened her pace, but her boots kept sliding into gaps in the stones, causing her to stumble. And out of the corner of her eye, she saw faint ripples in the water from the approaching reptiles, eyes glittering in the torchlight.

Idiot, Zarrah silently cursed herself. *This is what you get for leaping forward without a proper plan.*

Then her foot caught.

Panic flooded her as she tried to pull herself free, but her boot was wedged in debris. She jerked on it hard, using her staff as leverage, only to fall on her ass with a splash, her ankle twisting painfully, the water up to her armpits.

And from all around, there were splashes as more creatures took notice.

Her breath came in fast little gasps as she twisted her foot this way and that, trying to free it. She'd seen what the alligators did, how they worked together to tear apart prey, ripping larger animals into pieces that they'd gulp down whole. She wouldn't have a chance.

Her fingers fumbled at the laces of her knee-high boot, her hands shaking. "Come on," she said between her teeth. "Come on!"

Then it was loose. Grinding her teeth against the pain, she dragged her foot free of the boot. Zarrah scrambled forward right as one of the reptiles lunged.

A gasp of terror tore from her lips, and she fell sideways, water closing over her head.

Swim!

Zarrah kicked hard, aiming toward the bank, her staff still clutched in one hand. Something banged into her leg, and she sobbed, choking on the foul water. Then her knees hit the bottom, and she was crawling up the bank.

But some sixth sense warned her.

Rolling onto her back, Zarrah lifted her staff right as a mouthful of teeth lunged toward her. The weapon went down the alligator's throat and its jaw snapped shut, head whipping from side to side, tearing it from her grip.

Her heels digging into the mud, she scrambled backward, then flipped onto her feet. Zarrah ran up the bank, not pausing until she reached the tree line and the shattered cobbles of the street emerged from the earth. There she paused, hands resting on her knees as she gasped in mouthfuls of air, her heart pummeling the inside of her ribs.

Her night was *not* going as planned.

Because she didn't have a plan, only a goal. To be impetuous was to invite disaster, and she'd proven that tonight. And now she was stuck in enemy territory, soaking wet, down her best weapon, and with only one fucking boot.

But going back the way she'd come wasn't an option. The collapsed bridge was crawling with alligators lured in by the commotion, which meant either trying one of the other collapsed bridges upstream or waiting for a drunk Maridrinian to attempt to make his way back across, only to find himself met by a few dozen mouthfuls of teeth, thus providing a distraction.

Zarrah debated her options, but as she did, her gaze was drawn to the Maridrinian palace looming in the distance, torchlight flickering off its domes, the highest of which was still under repair, the damage courtesy of a Valcottan catapult.

Good little Zarrah, her cousin's voice rippled across her thoughts. *Obedient little Zarrah.* Then his mockery turned into Silas Veliant's laughter, those cursed azure eyes filling her vision.

With his laughter chasing her, she started toward the home of her enemy, in search of honor.

And vengeance.

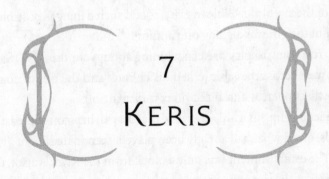

7

KERIS

KERIS EYED THE CUP THE CHILD HANDED HIM, WHICH DID NOT look like it had seen a wash in some time, then shrugged and took a long swallow of the ale.

And nearly spit the contents on the table in front of him.

Eyes watering, he turned to the child. "What is this? Piss?"

"Yes, sir." The girl inclined her head, a grin rising to her face, which appeared the product of a union between a Maridrinian and a Valcottan. "But I assure you, it is our finest piss. My mother sends me out at dawn to sit beside the palace sewers to collect the royal offerings, which we serve to only our best of customers. Liquid gold, it is, sir."

Keris laughed, amused not only at the thought of being served his own urine but at the thought of being up at dawn to deliver it. Those early hours were the only ones where he slept. Pulling a silver coin out of his pocket, he held it up. "Find me something drinkable, and this is yours."

The girl's eyes gleamed with hunger. "I'll find you something fine enough for Crown Prince Keris himself."

Keris nearly choked, covering his reaction with another mouthful of the awful ale. "A clean glass, too, if such a thing is possible."

But the girl was already off running.

"You going to play or keep whining about your drink?" One of the men across the table jerked his chin toward the pile of coins: mostly coppers with a bit of silver mixed in.

Picking up his cards, Keris glanced at them, considered the odds, given what had already been played, then folded.

The establishment was only a block from the River Anriot, the stench of the swampy waters nearly enough to drown out that of spilled drink, vomit, and worse that permeated the air. The building had only three walls, the front having been caved in during the last bombardment from Valcottan catapults, and the tables were all broken doors balanced on barrels, the chairs a mismatched assortment salvaged from around the city. A typical venue this close to the river, which tended to cater to common soldiers, the officers and nobility preferring the more expensive locales around the palace.

Keris liked it because there was almost no chance of him being recognized.

The girl came back, carefully balancing a glass of wine, which she handed to him.

"Well? Try it!"

He dutifully took a sip. The wine was not nearly as bad as anticipated, and he flipped the silver coin in the girl's direction, wishing she'd spend it on something worthwhile, like shoes, but knowing it was more likely to go into her mother's pocket.

The lanterns hanging from the ceiling swung back and forth on the breeze, casting dancing shadows as he played, lost to the rhythm of counting cards and amassing coins that he didn't need. He enjoyed gambling, but what really lured him out was the opportunity to listen to what people had to say. When they saw Keris

Veliant, people filtered their words for fear of offending him, but when they saw an anonymous Maridrinian, men and women spoke their mind. Curiosity had always been his greatest vice, and he plucked and pried tidbits of information from the men around the table, storing them away for later consideration.

Yet as engrossed as he was, habit had him look up as a figure passed the building. A woman, judging from her shape, her chin-length hair concealing her face. A *Valcottan* woman, given the voluminous trousers. And to top it all off, a soldier, as she wore a high-laced military boot.

Boot. Singular. For her other foot was naked as a babe's, which, in combination with her soaked clothing, suggested that her crossing of the Anriot had not gone . . . *swimmingly.*

In the distance, Keris picked up on the sound of horse hooves, no doubt a Maridrinian patrol. And without breaking stride, the Valcottan woman cut into one of the abandoned buildings across the street.

Curiosity piqued, Keris folded his cards and scooped his winnings of copper and silver into a purse, which he tied tightly to muffle the jingle of metal. "Good night," he said to the other players. "And good fortune."

If any of them answered, Keris didn't hear, his attention all for the building the woman had entered. Walking on silent feet, he ducked inside, stepping carefully over debris, wrinkling his nose at the stench of rat droppings and mildew. Moonlight filtered through holes in the floor of the second level, and peering upward, he noted that the ceiling had collapsed during one of the bombardments. One of the walls was canted inward at an alarming angle, and to his right, the floor had fallen into the cellar. The whole damn structure was probably a good windstorm away from collapsing entirely, but hearing the squelch of a wet boot, Keris pressed on.

The soft leather of his own boots made no sound as he climbed the stairs, stepping over the body of a dead bird, one hand extracting a knife in case he ran into trouble. His heart beat at a steady clip, and he paused at the top of the stairs, eyes searching the shadows, but what remained of the room was empty.

Where had she gone?

The floor groaned under his weight as he crossed to one of the walls. Bending his knees, Keris leapt up, catching hold of the edge and praying it would hold as he heaved himself on top, the shadows from the neighboring building cloaking his motions. He crouched in place, scanning the rooftops of Nerastis until he picked up a flicker of motion.

You should report her to a patrol, a voice whispered in his head. *A sober Valcottan soldier on this side of the banks only means trouble.*

But if he reported her, she'd be captured, and the best she could hope for was to be killed quickly. It wouldn't matter if she'd done anything wrong or not: She was the enemy.

You could let her go.

Except that would mean if she got Maridrinian blood on her hands, it would be on his as well.

Which left only one option. To deal with her himself.

Keris ran down the length of the wall and leapt onto the next building, following her path through the city toward his palace.

8

ZARRAH

SWEAT MIXED WITH THE DRYING WATER OF THE ANRIOT AS ZARrah meandered across the rooftops of Nerastis, the sound of music, laughter, and drunken soldiers covering any sound she made as she leapt from building to building, heading toward the palace.

The princelings always had their rooms at the top of the main tower. Given her spies reported that, unlike his predecessors, Keris Veliant rarely left his rooms, she assumed that was where she'd find him. Climbing the stairs of that tower would be impossible, but the repair scaffolding that ran up the side was another matter. Like her own palace, most of the windows were broken, so gaining access would be easy. Then she'd find his room, smother him in his sleep, and escape, with no one the wiser.

Her bare foot was scraped and bruised, but Zarrah ignored the pain, pausing on the roof of one of the garrison barracks and surveying the wall that encircled the palace. The Maridrinians loved walls. But *her* people loved tearing them down, and she could see the sloppy repairs that had been made to the damage from the last

major battle—broken and uneven blocks of stone mortared together, platforms of wood placed across them for the patrols that
circled the ramparts. And beneath one such platform, there was a
gap. A gap *just* large enough for a slender woman to squeeze
through.

A scraping sound caught her attention.

Dropping low in the shadows, Zarrah scanned the rooftops
around her, but there was no sign of motion. *Just a cat*, she told
herself, easing over the edge. *Or a bird.*

Climbing down the side of the building, she pressed her back
against it, eyeing the thirty feet of open space between her position and the base of the palace wall. It was not well lit, and there
was still debris from the last battle large enough to provide some
cover.

Watching the progress of the soldiers patrolling the wall, Zarrah waited until a pair had passed and then crawled to the first pile
of debris, where she lay flat in its shadow. Another patrol passed,
and she repeated the exercise until she was able to roll against the
base of the wall.

Her pulse was a dull roar, but her fear had fallen away, replaced
by the intense focus she felt going into battle. Glancing up, she
listened for the thud of passing boots, then climbed the rough
wall, moving as fast as she dared until she reached the gap beneath
the platform. Wriggling under it, she paused to catch her breath,
taking the moment to peer down into the courtyard surrounding
the building.

There were at least a dozen wagons, soldiers working to unload
knives, swords, and other weapons, the metal glittering in the
moonlight. All the Harendellian steel the Rat King had spent a
year transporting through the bridge, which, if the rumors were
to be believed, was integral to the invasion of Ithicana. And now
he intended to repurpose it against Valcotta.

Waiting for another pair of soldiers to pass over her, Zarrah jumped, landing in a pile of hay. She rolled down the side, then took several quick steps to hide behind two barrels. There were endless shadows this late at night, and she moved between them until she reached the base of the palace, where the decorative stonework created two parallel walls about two feet deep. Resting her shoulders against one, she braced her feet against the other and slowly worked her way higher and higher, trusting that the soldiers on the walls were more focused outward than inward.

Reaching the top of the main structure, she crawled to one of the towers, which had scaffolding running up the side that she swiftly scaled, her eyes on an open window, curtain flapping in the breeze. Cautiously, she looked over the sill and into the darkness inside.

A lamp burned on the table next to the bed, but the blankets were untouched, the room empty of life. She rolled inside and crouched behind heavy velvet drapery, sucking in a few deep breaths to calm her racing heart before she stepped out into the room.

In the years she'd served in Nerastis, they'd sacked this palace a total of three times, but in none of those battles had Zarrah actually gone inside this infamous structure.

It was not what she expected.

While the palace itself was grand and imposing, the room she stood in was sparsely furnished, the furniture either worn or inexpensive, the stone floors and walls barren of any adornment. Only the bedding spoke to the importance of the room's inhabitant, and Zarrah ran her finger over the fine silk before picking up the lamp, her eyes lighting on a discarded Maridrinian uniform draped across the back of a chair.

Picking it up, she noted the silver braiding and the turquoise and silver pins indicating the owner was a high-ranking officer, but it was the weight of something in the pocket that captured her attention. Extracting a packet of letters, she smiled at the sight of the royal seal on the front of one. Official correspondence, which meant there might be something in them of use. She shoved the papers into her pocket for later perusal, then sloshed the lamp to judge the level of oil, considering her options. She needed a distraction once she killed the prince to ensure she got out of this alive.

Then a low voice said, "I don't think you've really thought this through."

Zarrah jumped, nearly dropping the lamp as she whirled toward the open window.

On the sill perched a figure, his hood shadowing his face but the knife in his hand clearly visible. As she watched, he stepped down to the floor, moving with such utter silence that Zarrah knew he could've slit her throat before she'd even felt the press of the blade.

Her hands turned cold, and she pulled free her own knife, backing away as he prowled toward her.

"You're planning to start a fire, correct?" His accent was Maridrinian, his tone soft, with an edge of amusement. "Though to call *this* a plan is an insult to the word."

Zarrah's hackles rose, but she was not one to let her temper get the better of her. "And yet you climbed all the way up here to stop me."

"You *wound* me, Valcotta. I'm not here to stop you but rather to offer my advice on how to turn this fool's errand into a *roaring* success." He chuckled softly. "One: You will require somewhat more than half a lamp full of oil. Two: You will require somewhat more than a bed's worth of fuel. Three: If a body count is your aim, you really ought to start the fire at the *bottom* of the tower, not near the top. And four: If you wish to emerge from this venture unscathed, you will hand over those letters."

Her aim was a body count of *one*, but she was not opposed to making it more. A slow smile rose to Zarrah's face, and she patted her pocket before leaping onto the bed, the silk cold beneath her one bare foot. "Why? Are they yours?"

"They're certainly not *yours*. Hand them over and I'll let you go. You've proven yourself to be only a marginal threat, so I feel able to do so with a clear conscience."

Whatever the contents of these letters were, they were important. And the fact he hadn't raised the alarm suggested that whatever they contained, it wasn't something he wanted anyone else reading, which meant they were for officers' eyes only.

Zarrah weighed and measured her options. She could kill him and then go after the prince, but if there was a scuffle, someone would hear and shout an alarm, rendering escape nearly impossible. Or she could take the lesser prize of the letters and make a run for it now, saving the prince for another day. "Toss the knife under the bed and I'll consider it."

"I think not."

With her index finger, Zarrah twisted the knob on the lamp, the flame rising until it licked the edges of the glass. Extracting the packet of letters, she brushed them through the flame, laughing when he tensed. Not only were they important, but they were something he didn't want destroyed. Orders, was her best guess. "Knife."

An aggrieved noise exited his lips, and with a flick of his wrist, he tossed the knife under the bed. "Letters."

Stepping off the bed, Zarrah circled him, making sure to keep the papers close enough to the flame that he wouldn't risk taking them by force.

"Not very trusting, are you, Valcotta?" His tone was light, but there was no mistaking the tension radiating from him. He was taller than she was, and while not bulky, he was bigger than her. And Maridrinians were notoriously good grapplers.

"Nor you, Maridrina." She backed toward the window. There'd be only one chance at this, and she needed a running start.

"Letters." The velvet softness of his tone had been replaced with a steely edge. "You are testing my patience."

Zarrah's heart throbbed, her hands clammy and her stomach tight. "Your word you'll let me go?"

"You have it."

Her arm shaking, Zarrah held out the package of letters. Her muscles tensed as he came close, reaching out one gloved hand, his shadowed eyes so intent on the prize that he didn't see her other arm swing wide, launching the lamp past him.

"A Maridrinian's word doesn't mean shit," Zarrah hissed, then she threw herself at the window, the scaffolding already ablaze. Her foot hit the windowsill, and with her eyes fixed on the target beyond, she leapt into the air.

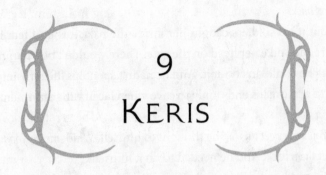

9
KERIS

KERIS GAPED IN ASTONISHMENT AS THE WOMAN JUMPED OUT OF the tower window and over the flames, Otis's letters still clutched in her hand.

"Shit!" Racing to the window, he looked through the smoke to see her land hard on the dome of the neighboring tower, where she slid, hands and feet scrabbling for purchase.

She was going to fall.

Keris gripped the sill, heedless of the flames and helpless to do anything as she slid faster and faster, the letters now between her teeth, her hands fumbling with the harness around her chest. Just as she reached the lip, the straps came loose and she flung a loop out, the leather catching on a cornice.

Keris's breath came out in a loud whoosh, his heart pounding as she dangled in midair. Then she swung her legs back and forth before sailing onto the balcony. She quickly disappeared into the room beyond, emerging moments later with a sheet, which she tore into lengths and then knotted together.

Call the alarm! logic screamed inside his head. *You need to get those letters back!*

But if his soldiers caught her inside the palace, they'd tear her apart and spike her head on the gate. There wouldn't be a damned thing he could do about it. And he hadn't spent his life refusing to kill to achieve his ends, only to cave when faced with a moment of adversity.

You let her get this far, he thought to himself. *Which means you need to get them back.* And he needed to do it himself.

Cursing under his breath, Keris backed up across the room and then sprinted toward the open window.

10
ZARRAH

ZARRAH WAS HALFWAY DOWN HER MAKESHIFT ROPE WHEN SHE
heard a loud *thump* and the sound of something heavy sliding
down the metal dome. She looked up in time to see the Maridrinian slip over the edge, deftly catching hold of her harness and
swinging onto the balcony.

What the hell is in these letters?

Ignoring the burn in her palms, Zarrah slid down the sheet-
rope. Her bare foot screamed in pain as she landed on the roof of
the palace, bits of shattered rock cutting into her flesh as she raced
to where she'd climbed up. Shouts of alarm rose from the soldiers
below, the fire having been spotted. A quick upward glance revealed the scaffolding was nearly engulfed, which would provide
an ideal distraction.

Although, not from everyone.

Crouching low, Zarrah wedged herself between the two decorative walls. But before she dropped below the roofline, she
looked back. The Maridrinian was already down the sheet-rope
and was sprinting toward her. Shit. She needed to get out into the

city, into that mess of broken buildings and its million places to hide.

When she reached the ground, Zarrah paused to watch the soldiers drawing buckets of water from the well, everything chaos and confusion.

Horses and wagons rushed out the gates to avoid the falling pieces of burning wood. She rolled under a passing wagon, clinging to the underside and cringing as bits of manure fell through the slats.

The wagon passed through the gates and into the maze of city streets, but Zarrah held on, wanting to get as far away as she could before she risked revealing herself. Then the wagon hit a large hole in the cobbles, jouncing her loose. She landed hard on her back, the skin on her elbows shredding as she skidded to a stop. Zarrah ignored the pain and rolled sideways into the shadows of an opium den, shrieks of laughter, both male and female, filtering from the rooms above even as shouts of "Fire! Fire!" spread through the city.

Keep going. He's not going to give up that easily. You need to get across the river.

Zarrah limped down an alley until she found an easy place to climb. On the roof, she had a clear view of the palace, the scaffolding an inferno. An impressive sight, but she knew it had done nothing more than inconvenience their efforts to repair the palace. She could only pray that the letters yielded something worth the lost opportunity to spill Veliant blood.

She leapt onto a neighboring rooftop, retreating by the same route she'd taken on her way to the palace, hoping that the alligators had dispersed or found easier quarry. Because she needed to get back across that river. As soon as dawn lit the sky in the east, the unspoken peace between Maridrina and Valcotta would shatter, and being caught on the north side of the river would not go well for her.

Soldiers and civilians alike had given up their carousing to watch the fire, droves of them heading in the direction of the palace to gawk. As she leapt from the roof of a tavern onto yet another brothel, a loud roar filled her ears, and Zarrah glanced back in time to see the scaffolding collapse, a cloud of sparks and smoke filling the air.

Then the skin on her neck prickled and she whirled, finding herself face-to-face with the Maridrinian.

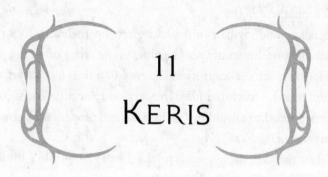

11
KERIS

THE GLOW OF THE FIRE ILLUMINATED THE VALCOTTAN WOMAN'S face, which, if he was being honest, was far more beautiful than he'd first appreciated. Her brown skin was glossy from heat and exertion, and strands of her short, dark hair clung to her rounded cheekbones. If not for the knife that had appeared in her hand, he might have imagined the bow-shaped lips of hers engaged in a number of intriguing activities.

"That"—he gestured to the glow of flames—"is going to be a significant inconvenience for me."

Her voice dripped with sarcasm as she said, "So sorry," then stepped sideways, searching for a way around him. But Keris moved with her, growling, "Give me the damned letters, Valcotta. They're no good to you."

She opened her mouth as though to respond, but instead stepped backward off the side of the building. He swore as he heard her hit the ground, her feet pounding away before he'd even reached the edge.

But he knew which way she'd go.

Twisting, he raced across the roof to jump to the next, rolling as he hit and then on his feet in a flash, tracing a path across the city. He leapt and climbed, never hesitating because to give up momentum would see him plunge to his death.

His knees ached and his fingers were cramping from climbing by the time he reached the tap house where he'd sat earlier and dropped into the alleyway. The tables were nearly devoid of patrons now, all the Valcottans wisely having taken their leave when they'd seen the flames.

All except for one.

His eyes picked up motion in the shadows of a building, her slender form barely visible as she crept down the street, gaze focused on the path leading to the Anriot. But before either of them could make a move, the clatter of hooves on cobbles filled the air, and a patrol galloped into view. "Block the river crossings!" one of the men shouted. "Then we'll begin a search of the city to find the culprit. His Highness wants the individual on the executioner's block by dawn!"

Damn Otis and his efficiency.

Keris watched the woman stare at the patrol, weighing her chances of getting around them and across the river without taking an arrow in the back.

They weren't good.

She was going to get herself killed, and all over Otis's stupid letters. *Don't do it*, he willed her. *Think of something else.*

She ignored his silent plea, body tense with the stillness of someone about to leap into action. Which left him with little choice.

Shoving his hood back, he shouted, "Goddammit, woman," then staggered drunkenly into the open. "Where are you hiding? I wasn't done with you yet!"

He could feel the soldiers' eyes pass over him, marking his nationality but not his identity before they continued with what they were doing, and Keris broke into a stumbling run toward the woman, catching her by the arm. "Took my coin without earning it!" he shouted, then hauled her in the direction of one of the brothels, keeping himself between her and the soldiers to hide her from clear view.

Kicking open the door, he barely spared a glance for the room full of soldiers and naked flesh before he pressed her against a wall, pinning her wrists above her head and twisting his hips so that she wouldn't try to knee him in the balls. "Letters. Now."

She squirmed, trying and failing to slip his grip, but his brother had trained him well. Then she stilled, dark eyes fixing on his for a heartbeat before she screamed, "Thief!"

The shrill panic in her voice caught the attention of everyone in the brothel, and the sturdy madam presiding over it turned and fixed her eyes on them. Though she must have known Zarrah was not one of her girls, there was apparently some unwritten code that demanded solidarity among whores, for she roared, "Not in my house!" then pulled a cudgel out from under a table. Keris yelped, ducking as the heavy wood swung past his face.

The Valcottan woman scuttled into the room, sobbing, "He doesn't think he needs to pay!"

"Thief!" the madam shrieked at him, swinging her cudgel and forcing Keris to step backward or lose his teeth. "Get out!"

Across the room, the Valcottan woman grinned, then she ran toward the stairs. Cursing, Keris dodged the madam, leaping over whores and patrons alike as he gave chase. A door slammed as he reached the second level, and a heartbeat later, he heard shouts of shock, then anger. Kicking in the door revealed the Valcottan woman on the windowsill about to jump, and he clambered over the trio of naked forms on the bed, reaching for her.

Too late.

He jumped without looking, catching the rooftop and jerking himself upright with a violent pull, and then he was running. Chasing her across the rooftops and through buildings and down alleys as they wove their way upstream, bypassing all the collapsed bridges now barricaded by soldiers, torchlight flickering off their armor.

If she had a plan or a destination in mind, he couldn't guess it, his focus all for keeping her in sight while maintaining his footing as stone crumbled and roofs threatened to collapse, the darkness hiding countless pitfalls that could send either of them to their death.

And then they were out of the city, the woman racing along the edges of the swamp toward the distant bluff. At the top, there was a large lake formed by a dam. She'd have to circle it, and on the open ground he could risk the speed he'd need to catch her.

The roar from the dam's spillway grew in intensity, the air tasting of water as they ascended the bluff. But as she reached the top, instead of heading around the lake, she cut right. Keris's stomach dropped as she raced along the dam to where the crumbled stone fell away, nothing but blackness and water in front of her.

"Valcotta!" he screamed. "Don't do it!"

12
ZARRAH

CRAMPS TORE APART HER SIDES, HER THROAT BURNING WITH each rapid breath, but there was no time to pause. No time to rest when she could hear the Maridrinian in fast pursuit, never allowing her to get far enough ahead to hide.

Without the ambient light of the city, it was a struggle to see in the dark, and Zarrah tripped and stumbled over deadfall and debris, reliant on the roar of the waterfall to guide her in the right direction as she scrambled up the slope.

As she burst from the trees, she saw the moon gleaming off the small lake formed by the ancient dam. She limped along the top of the dam itself, the rocks crumbling with age and slick with moisture from the waterfall's spray. At the center of the dam was the gap that formed the spillway. She knew it was eight feet across, but now, standing at the edge and watching the dark waters roar through it to plunge thirty feet onto broken rocks, it seemed infinitely wider.

And the safety of the far side infinitely farther away.

"Valcotta, don't do it!"

Zarrah turned her head. The Maridrinian had reached the top of the dam, but he'd stopped a dozen paces back, his hands raised, no weapon in sight.

"While you've led me on quite the merry little chase, having to climb down to retrieve your broken body is not how I wish to end it," he continued. "Give me the letters and we can both walk away from this alive."

Terror was thick in her veins, and it was tempting, oh so damnably tempting, to hand the letters over. Except Zarrah knew to do so would see her dead. A Maridrinian's word meant nothing— especially when given to a Valcottan. That she had his precious letters was the *only* reason he hadn't killed her yet.

Taking a deep breath, Zarrah steeled herself against fear and pain, took a few running steps, and then jumped.

Wind whistled past her ears, the water roaring beneath her. She hit the far side of the dam, the impact driving the air from her lungs. Her nails scrabbled against the slick rock, her legs dangling, toes unable to find purchase because the water had eroded the sides of the spillway.

"Shit!" Panic rose as she tried to climb, but her arms shuddered from the strain of supporting her weight, too spent and exhausted to pull her higher.

She was going to fall.

Her fingers slipped, her nails ripping, and a shriek tore from her lips as the rock crumbled.

Then a gloved hand closed around her wrist.

Gasping in a breath, Zarrah looked up to see the Maridrinian above her, balanced and steady as though he knelt in a palace corridor, not on a crumbling dam with death on all sides. Though he must have jumped over her, she hadn't seen him. Hadn't heard him.

"The letters, Valcotta." His voice was strained. "Give them to me."

"Only to have you drop me?" She put as much heat into the words as she could, which was difficult with the cold river waters kissing the toes of her bare foot, beckoning her into its flow. "Pull me up first."

"Only to have you run again? I think not."

They stared at each other. Though Zarrah couldn't see the color of his eyes in the shadows, they burned into her. Neither of them was willing to concede, but with the way his arm was starting to shake from strain, the decision was soon to be made for them.

Do not give in, Zarrah screamed at herself. *He is Maridrinian, and even if it means your death, you must never concede! Your honor demands it!*

"Your word," he said through his teeth. "Your word that if I pull you up, you'll give them back."

Her terror strangled her, but Zarrah managed to say, "You have my word. I'll return them if you pull me up."

"All of them."

"For fuck's sake, yes!" she gasped. "All of them! On my honor!"

The Maridrinian heaved, pulling her upward so that she was sprawled on her stomach, both of them crawling away from the edge. Body shaking, Zarrah climbed to her feet, but before she could get her bearings, the Maridrinian was behind her, knife at her throat and his free arm pinning hers to her sides. "Walk."

Limping, she started around the curved dam, not stopping until she'd reached the bank. Back on Valcottan soil, such as it was. There they paused, her back pressed against his chest, both of them gasping for breath. And though the sharp edge of his knife stung the skin over her jugular, it was the warmth of his breath against her cheek that she felt as she turned her head. Away from the stench of the city, she could smell him now: the clean scent of soap along with the spice of a subtle cologne, beneath which she picked up the faintest odor of smoke and sweat.

"The letters, lovely." His voice tickled her ear, and he loosened his grip so she could move an arm.

The last thing she wanted to do was to give up her prize after all of this, but with his knife against her throat, she hadn't much choice. And as it was, she'd given her word.

Reaching into her pocket, Zarrah extracted the package and held it up.

"In one of my pockets, if you will. My hands are rather occupied at present."

Scowling, she shoved her hand between them, feeling the hard muscles of his stomach as she jammed the letters down the front of his trousers. He jumped as her fingers brushed his cock, and she used the distraction to twist away from the knife.

He only chuckled, tucking a lock of damp hair behind his ear before sliding the knife into a hidden sheath. "Good night, Valcotta," he murmured, then inclined his head. "I'll show myself out."

And without another word, he whirled, racing down the length of the dam and leaping the gap, easily reaching the other side. Not so much as breaking stride, he disappeared into the darkness.

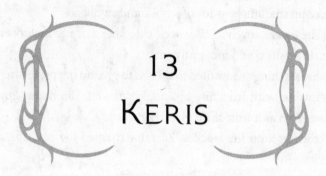

13
KERIS

WITH NIGHT DRAWING TO A CLOSE, NERASTIS WAS FINALLY QUI-
eting down for a few hours of respite, for which Keris was profoundly grateful as he trudged through the streets.

Everything hurt.

Countless scrapes and bruises, but it was his shoulder that had
him gritting his teeth. He'd barely made it across the spillway in
time to catch her, but the angle had been bad, and muscles had
torn. Climbing anything higher than his own bed would be next
to impossible, and already he could feel the walls of circumstance
closing in on him. Without his ability to scale walls and secret his
way in and out of the palace, he'd be stuck with an escort if he so
much as wanted to peek his head outside the walls.

As it was, his favored route was currently ash, the Valcottan
having decimated the construction scaffolding he typically used.
He could only pray that none of the burning embers had found
their way onto anything important in his rooms. Many of his
books were irreplaceable, but then again, so were the letters in the
inner pocket of his coat.

Striding through the open gates with enough authority that no one contested his presence, Keris unfastened the tie holding his hair back as he entered the palace, sweaty locks falling around his face. Servants and soldiers were running every which way, and above the din, he heard his brother bellow, "I don't want a stone in this city left unturned until we find my brother! There isn't a chance they got him across the Anriot, which means they have him hidden somewhere in Nerastis."

Shit.

"We must entertain the real possibility that Prince Keris is dead, Highness," another voice answered, Keris recognizing it as that of a captain named Philo.

"If they'd only cared about killing him, they'd have slit his cursed throat!" Otis shouted. "He's alive, but we need to find him before they decide to cut their losses."

"Good morning, gentlemen." Keris stepped into their conversation.

His brother's eyes widened, then narrowed with growing anger. "Where have you been?"

"With a lovely pair of ladies at the Pink Rose," he answered, naming the most expensive courtesan house in Nerastis—and one infamous for its discretion. "What happened to my palace?"

"Without an escort?" Otis's ears turned red. "Have you lost your bloody mind, Keris? This isn't Vencia. You can't just go gallivanting around by yourself."

"I just told you I wasn't by myself."

"Keris—"

His exhaustion had eaten away his patience for being treated like a wayward child, so he interrupted Otis. "Was there a fire?"

"Yes, the Valcottans managed to torch the repair scaffolding. No significant damage but—"

He'd had enough of this conversation. Injecting panic into his voice, he shouted, "My books!" Keris broke into a sprint, taking the steps two at a time as he circled to the top level, finding the door to his rooms kicked open, likely courtesy of Otis, and the space filled with servant women sweeping ash off the floor. His gaze went immediately to the chest where he kept his most precious possessions, but it appeared unscathed. "Thank God for small mercies."

Otis appeared behind him, breathing hard. His brother caught him by the arm and dragged him into the bathing chamber, slamming the door shut behind them. "I thought they'd taken you," he said in a low voice. "That they'd scaled the scaffolding and stolen you out of this fool's choice of a bedroom right from under our very noses. But the Valcottans had nothing to do with it, did they? You climbed down of your own volition so that you could go fraternize with the masses as someone other than yourself. Was the fire just a way to cause a distraction so you could get out the gates, then?"

"I—"

"You could've gotten someone killed, you know. Several of our men have burns from falling debris, never mind that it's going to take at least a week to rebuild the scaffolding."

Guilt bit at Keris's stomach, for despite not having been the one who'd set the fire, he was responsible for allowing the Valcottan woman close enough to do so.

"I'm tired of this, Keris. I've only been back in Nerastis for a day, and I'm already tired of your childish methods of showing your displeasure over your circumstances." Otis scrubbed his hand through his hair. "I know how much you hate fighting. How much you abhor killing. How much you are against our invasion of Ithicana and our war with Valcotta, but what I don't understand is why you can't accept that this is the hand you've been dealt. War is in the blood of our people, and you're heir to the throne, so you need to either become the man this kingdom needs or accept that your life will be a short one."

Keris crossed his arms. "I have accepted my lot, Otis. It is you who continues to struggle."

Silence stretched between them, so tense that he wondered if it would come to blows, as quarrels between Veliant brothers often did. Except usually, it was Otis delivering blows on his behalf.

But Otis only stepped back. "There are days I hate you, Keris. And today is one of them. But since I know you're not going to do a damn thing but go back to being the useless bastard you always are, I'll go clean up your mess. And then I'll organize a raid across the Anriot, because it is a far better thing that our men believe a Valcottan got past our defenses than that their crown prince was stupid enough to set his own palace on fire."

And without giving Keris time to muster a retort, his brother flung open the door and left the room.

Leaning against the wall, Keris balled his hands into fists, forcing himself to take deep, measured breaths, wondering if it wouldn't be better to just concede. To go down to the war room and plan raids across the border. To ride out with the men and coat his blade with enemy blood for the glory of Maridrina. To be the heir his father wanted.

To do what it took to ensure his own survival.

Go after him, a voice inside his head whispered. *Apologize. Promise to change.* But his body didn't move, and as seconds turned to minutes, his heart ceased its pounding, and the angry sweat that had risen to his skin slowly cooled.

Stepping out of the open door, he nodded at the servants as he exited the room, heading down two flights of stairs to the floor containing Otis's room. The corridor was empty, so there were no eyes to see him pick the lock on the door and swiftly shut it behind him. His brother had clearly not had an opportunity to come back, his uniform jacket still slung over the chair as it had been when Keris left.

Smoothing the sheets, Keris then extracted the package of letters from his pocket, examining them to ensure there was no obvious damage. He'd seen them in Otis's hands enough times to know them well, and in his mind's eye, he could see his brother's thumb running over the edges of the twelve precious letters that were all he had left of his wife. His eyes skipped over an official missive from his father, which was likely what had inspired Valcotta to steal the package in the first place. Yet as Keris ran his own thumb over the edges of the love letters, counting, his stomach dropped when he reached only eleven. He swiftly recounted, but the number was the same.

One of them was missing.

"Shit!" he snarled. "She kept one!"

Then the memory of the Valcottan woman's voice filled his ears. *All of them! On my honor!*

And there was nothing more important to a Valcottan than her word. Which meant one thing for certain: Keris hadn't seen the last of the beautiful thief.

14
ZARRAH

Just after dawn, Zarrah limped inside the gates of the Valcottan palace, several of her soldiers racing to her side.

"It's nothing," she said. "A bar fight that I found myself in the middle of." Then she made her way up to her rooms and collapsed on her bed in exhaustion.

A second later, the door opened.

"I'm feeling hurt, Zar," Yrina said. "It appears as though you went out for a bit of fun without me."

"It wasn't fun." Zarrah kept her eyes closed, feeling the press of the Maridrinian's chest against her back. The heat of his breath against her cheek. "A good reminder of why I don't go drinking with soldiers."

Her friend made a noise that was simultaneously pity and amusement, then Zarrah felt the bed sink and heard Yrina's soft intake of breath. "God, woman. Did you run through a field of broken glass?"

"Is it that bad?"

"It's not good. Where is your other boot?"

Probably in a gator's belly was the answer, but Zarrah said, "Lost it in the fight."

Yrina whistled between her teeth. "You really were out for some fun."

The bed shifted. Water splashed. Zarrah clenched her teeth as Yrina immersed her battered foot in a basin, washing it clean before she began picking debris out of Zarrah's flesh with a pair of tweezers. The smell of alcohol filled the air, and Zarrah had only a second to bury her face in her pillow to muffle her scream as Yrina doused her foot, cleaning the rest of the Nerastis filth from the wounds.

"You going to tell me what you were doing on the other side of the Anriot when the empress specifically ordered otherwise?"

"I wasn't."

"Don't lie. You reek like river water." She paused, then asked, "Did it have something to do with the fire at the Maridrinian palace?"

Yrina was sworn to her and had always kept her confidence. But more than that, Zarrah hated lying to her friend. "Fine. Yes." Zarrah kept her face buried in her pillow to hide the heat burning across her cheeks. Never mind that her actions were in deliberate violation of the empress's orders, what she'd done had been nothing short of a total disaster. She felt a fool and had nothing to show for it but a shredded foot and a stomach full of shame.

Yrina was uncharacteristically quiet as she wrapped a bandage around Zarrah's foot. Then she murmured, "Don't let Bermin goad you, Zar. Remember, it is in his best interest to see you make mistakes. The empress is fickle, and that which she giveth, she can easily taketh away. For you to remain as general of this garrison, you must be perfection in her eyes."

And to the empress, perfection meant obedience.

"I'll leave you to get some rest," Yrina said. "And I'll start a rumor that you lost your boot beating the woman who looked too longingly at your lover."

Zarrah groaned into the pillow. "Don't you dare."

"Perhaps you're right," Yrina said thoughtfully. "That's not something you'd do. You'd beat your *lover* with the boot for inviting temptation, right?"

"I don't have a lover."

"That's half your problem. You'd enjoy life a great deal more with a man dedicated to your pleasure." Yrina swatted Zarrah across the ass, finally luring her out from under the pillow if only to scowl at her friend's departing back.

The *last* thing she needed was the distraction of a lover. Over the years, she'd taken a handful of men into her bed for a night or two, but she'd always been careful to keep it to that, knowing that hers would be a carefully selected political union, not a love match. A consort from a powerful Valcottan family, the union bringing strength to the Crown. And in recent months—years, if she were being honest—she'd not brought any men to her bed at all, for they weren't a distraction she could afford.

Exhausted as she was, the sun was already glowing through the stained-glass windows of her room, sending spirals of color across the white silk of her sheets. Past time for her to have been up and completing her exercises, which meant sleep wasn't an option.

What she needed was a cold shower to slap some alertness into her.

Limping to the adjoining chamber, Zarrah unfastened the buckles of her leather corselet and discarded it on the floor, followed by the silk camisole that was still glued to her skin from sweat.

Her fingers ached as she unfastened her belt, but as she tugged down her trousers, she heard the distinct sound of crinkling paper.

Frowning, Zarrah reached into the deep pocket and withdrew

a folded letter, her heartbeat accelerating as she slowly unfolded it. Perhaps her efforts had netted her something worthwhile after all.

Unfolding the letter, she read. *Dearest O, every minute we are apart feels like an eternity* . . .

What in the name of God had she stolen?

Starting over, Zarrah read the letter once, then again, searching the overly poetic piece of nonsense written by a woman named Tasha for any sign of a code, but there was none. Nothing that was even the slightest bit useful.

She'd risked life and limb to steal that bastard's *love letters.*

But that wasn't what set her heart to racing, her stomach threatening to empty its contents onto the glass-tiled floor. No, the worst of it was she'd promised to give the letters back. All of them.

And a Valcottan always kept her word.

HER DAY DID NOT IMPROVE.

The Maridrinians raided not an hour after she returned—likely in retaliation for what they perceived as an assault on their palace. They attacked one of her patrols, the battle short yet fevered, resulting in heavy casualties on both sides, and each time she spoke words over one of the fallen, her guilt pooled higher in her guts until Zarrah was certain she might drown in it.

Dead because of her actions. Actions that had netted her *nothing* but shame for undertaking such an ill-considered escapade in the first place.

And now, with full dark having fallen over Nerastis, she had to go back across the Anriot to return a stupid love letter.

The roar of falling water intensified as she approached the dam, the moon her only source of light as she stepped onto the top of it, heading slowly toward the gap in the middle, where she stopped at the edge.

Water surged through the spillway, the flow black and ominous, and fear prickled up her spine. Without the adrenaline of the chase, it seemed madness to try to leap the gap, but she had little choice. Honor demanded she return the letter, no matter that it was nothing more than flowery drivel, and there was no other way to get across that didn't risk her being caught, as the bridges were being watched.

"You can do this," she muttered, readjusting the new staff strapped to her back. "Jump over. Return the letter. Jump back." And then she could shove this particular embarrassment to the bottom of her mind, never to be thought of again.

Or so she hoped.

Taking a deep breath, Zarrah retreated down the top of the dam, taking careful strides so that she'd hit the edge just right when she sprinted back. Turning to face the gap, she voiced a silent prayer, then broke into a run.

Wind tore at her hair as she rounded the dam, her pulse rivaling the waterfall in intensity.

You can do this.

Her boots pounded against the stone, drawing her closer and closer. She gathered herself, readying to leap.

Then she skidded to a stop, nearly toppling over the edge as her nerves betrayed her.

"You're a bloody coward!" She twisted on her heel, intending to try again, when a laugh caught her attention.

Her eyes jerked across the spillway, landing on a dark figure standing on the edge, moonlight turning his blond hair to silver.

"Don't give yourself such a hard time, Valcotta." His tone was amused. "Not everyone has the nerve for such a leap."

She scowled at him, but there wasn't much she could say.

Rocking on his heels, he called, "I believe you have something of mine. Was the reading of it everything you hoped it would be when you stole it?"

Her cheeks burned. "I didn't mean to take it." Though she couldn't see his face clearly in the darkness, Zarrah knew he'd lifted an eyebrow, so she hastily added, "I meant to return them all. The one stuck in my pocket. It's here." Digging it out, she held the folded paper up to the moonlight.

"I believe you." He tilted his head. "But you didn't answer my question."

God, but he was a bastard.

Except while she was fumbling for a reply, he gestured at her to back up, and before she could shout at him that she was perfectly capable of jumping across herself, he'd retreated a few paces and was sprinting toward the gap.

Zarrah's heart caught in her throat as he jumped, a dark shadow flying over the deadly water to land beside her on nearly silent feet. A silence broken by a sharp intake of breath, and he pressed a hand to his shoulder before reaching out the same hand to her. "Letter."

Zarrah silently handed it over, his gloved fingers warm where they brushed hers.

"Thank you." He backed up several paces, obviously intending to jump across, their exchange over.

Without thinking—which she was starting to believe was an escalating issue for her—Zarrah said, "I risked a great deal under the mistaken belief that I'd found myself a prize worthy of my life, yet you risked your life knowing that scrap of paper contains nothing but bad poetry, O."

He huffed out a laugh. "I am most certainly *not* O."

"Then why—"

"O is a . . . *friend*, of sorts. Those letters are from the wife he lost a year ago to a shipwreck, and they are deeply precious to him."

"I . . ." Her stomach twisted with a mix of shame and admiration. Shame at herself for having pilfered such precious items and admiration that this man had risked life and limb to retrieve them for the sake of another. "My apologies. I would never have taken them if I'd known it would cause such hurt."

"A strange line to draw, given that you took them on the hope they'd give you information that would see him—and his countrymen—dead."

"I have principles. Whether you understand them matters little." She needed to be done with this conversation before her pride took any more abrasion, but curiosity held her feet in place even as it gave voice to a question that had haunted her. "Why didn't you sound the alarm? Why chase me down yourself?"

He was silent, and the moon chose that moment to move out from behind a cloud, clearly illuminating his face, which was every bit as striking as she'd remembered. All high cheekbones and straight lines, though his lips were absent the smirk she'd begun to associate with him. The wind blew softly over them, and her nose caught the subtle scent of spice, the smell of which filled her with the absurd desire to move closer. To breathe deeper.

"If I'd sounded the alarm, they'd have captured you, and a swift execution would've been the most mercy you could've expected."

Zarrah had known this crossing the Anriot. Known that if she were caught, she'd have been brutalized before her head was removed and catapulted across the river for her countrymen to find. "Why should you care for the life of your enemy?"

"Because I've seen enough death to last me a lifetime, and if I have my way, I'll never be the cause of it." His eyes, rendered colorless in the darkness, regarded her steadily. "And just because Valcotta is Maridrina's enemy doesn't make you mine."

That was *exactly* what it meant, but instead of arguing, she said, "You do not sound in favor of the Endless War."

He turned to look out over the glowing city, but Zarrah kept her eyes on him, watching as the wind teased a strand of his hair free from the knot at the back of his head. He was in his mid-twenties, was her guess, and while his clothes were nondescript, his cleanliness suggested he enjoyed a certain amount of privilege. Likely one of the endless noblemen who filled the Maridrinian Army, there being no other purpose for them.

He gestured at the city. "Explain to me how this place is worth fighting over?"

There were reasons. The land surrounding Nerastis was tremendously fertile, the port large enough to support significant merchant traffic, and the weather calmer than it was anywhere on the continent.

As though sensing her thoughts, he said, "How many men and women do you suppose have died in the war over this city?"

"Who can say?" Though she knew the answer: tens of thousands. It was surprising the earth itself wasn't stained red, so many had fallen in this place.

"Even if it were only one, it would be too many," he said. "Because this is a war fueled not by the desire to improve the lives of the people but by the greed and pride of kings and empresses, and no one should have to give their life for that."

She snorted in disgust. "Perhaps by Silas Veliant's greed, but the empress fights for honor and vengeance."

"I'm sure that's what she would have her soldiers believe is her motivation. It is likely the reason they tell themselves they fight, because it is much more palatable to face death in the name of honor than because it was the job you were hired to do. It's certainly what Maridrinian soldiers tell themselves; that I can tell you for a fact."

Zarrah opened her mouth to argue that was ironic, given his people were honorless dogs, but then shut it again, as it was no argument against his point.

"Do you know who started the Endless War, Valcotta? Who

threw the first punch?" He didn't give her a chance to answer. "*No one does,* though of surety both sides blame the other. The only thing that can be said with certainty is that an emperor and a king long dead both wanted this land and had too much pride in their hearts to split it down the middle. And though thousands have died to claim it, Nerastis sits in ruins and much of the land around it is fallow. Anyone who thinks it is honorable to continue such a fight is a goddamned fool."

Zarrah jerked, hand going to her weapon as fury rose in her heart. "If you had any concept of what your people have done to mine, the number of orphans they've left in their wakes, you'd—"

"I do understand, because *your* people have done the same to mine. And you must take a hard look at yourself if you think a child of Maridrina is worth less only because they don't bend the knee to the same crown." He gave a sharp shake of his head. "Back and forth and back and forth, and all it yields is corpses, their children growing up with hate in their hearts to take up weapons and continue the cycle anew."

His words were too close, too personal, though he couldn't possibly know the truth. "What would you have us do? What other solution is there but to fight?"

Silence.

"I don't know," he finally said. "It's easy to want change, but far more difficult to find ways to achieve it. And impossible to achieve it when those in power want the status quo, which is why I dream no further than finding a way to extract myself from these circumstances."

She dropped her hand from her weapon, feeling oddly disappointed with his answer, though she wasn't certain why. "What good are idealistic words when you do not act upon them? You criticize the actions of others but then lift up your hands in defeat when asked for solutions to the problem. I might be a fool, but at least I'm a fool who tries to make a difference. Whereas you are . . . *useless.*"

The Maridrinian visibly flinched, though he recovered swiftly. "Better useless than dead."

"I disagree. If you truly believe in something, you should be willing to suffer for it. To die for it, if need be. Which tells me that you either don't believe your own words or that you are a coward."

He stared at her in silence, then said, "Valcotta, I believe you are far cleverer than I first gave you credit for." The moon cast shadows across his too-handsome face. "And perhaps more of an idealist than you realize."

An idealist? She blinked, then took a step forward to catch his arm. "Who are you?"

The smirk returned and, reaching down, he took her hand and lifted it, his lips just barely grazing her knuckles, the sensation making her stomach flip. "There is something to be said for anonymity, Valcotta. Especially when one's mind is not aligned with the will of one's country. And most especially when one is considering action." He let go of her hand, her skin immediately begrudging the absence of his touch. "Good night."

And without another word, he leapt over the spillway and disappeared into darkness.

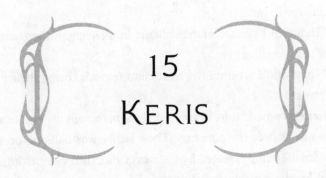

15
KERIS

"IT WAS ON THE FLOOR OF MY ROOM." KERIS HANDED THE LETTER to Otis. "So you can cease and desist in your threats to the maid-servants."

Otis muttered, "I haven't been threatening them." His denial was at odds with the current state of the staff, which, since his brother had realized the letter was missing, could only be described as frazzled. "But how did it get in your room?"

"The answer will have to remain one of life's great mysteries." Settling himself on a chair, Keris sorted through a stack of his books on the neighboring table, the desire to read settling upon him in a way it hadn't in a long time. But instead he asked, "What word of Ithicana?"

He could feel his brother's scrutiny, but Otis eventually said, "They are still fighting, despite the storms and our forces turning their own defenses against them. We've reopened trade along the bridge."

"With the same trade terms as the Ithicanians used?"

Otis shook his head. "As compensation for the continued use

of her navy, we are allowing the Amaridian queen to use it without charge or tax."

"That will have the Harendellians in a frenzy. Father tempts fate."

"They won't act until the next calm season. Losing their fleet isn't worth it."

Keris frowned at the book he'd chosen, though his consternation wasn't over the contents. Their father was banking on the Ithicanians being defeated by the next calm, thus eliminating his need for the Amaridian Navy and the cost associated with it. If Ithicana kept fighting, Maridrina would not only have war on all sides, it would be bankrupt, which would mean increasing taxes on their already-beleaguered people. "Taking the bridge was folly."

Otis made an aggrieved sound. "Never mind Ithicana. You promised to train with me, and don't think I'm not convinced you didn't steal my letter to cause enough of a stir to get yourself out of it."

The Valcottan woman's face appeared in his mind's eye, his memory replaying how her jaw had tightened at the thought of having taken an item of sentiment and the hurt its loss would've caused. "Think what you'd like."

Otis gave him a shove. "Find your sword and meet me in the stables. I need a gallop, and you need some sunlight—you're the color of a corpse."

"You've forgiven me, then?"

"Not even close. But you are my responsibility whether I wish it or not, so I have no choice but to endure your company. Now, quit procrastinating and find your bloody sword."

THEY WAITED UNTIL THEY WERE out of the city, then broke into a fast gallop up the road, mud from recent rains splattering their boots as they raced north. Overhead, the sky was the purest shade of blue, without so much as a cloud in sight, the sun heating the back of Keris's coat as he leaned over his mount's neck. Away from the swampy Anriot and filth of Nerastis and the fallow grounds, the air smelled of ocean brine and verdant fields, and his eyes moved over the men and women working them.

There was a great deal of wealth to be made here, but it came at a cost that was impossible to miss: Burned remains of homes and barns dotted the landscape, blackened frames reaching up to the sky like fingers. Here and there, the ground had been razed, and as the wind shifted, the stench of rotting flesh filled his nose. Possibly slaughtered livestock, but equally likely it was the casualties of a Valcottan raid. In the distance, he caught sight of a Maridrinian patrol, sun glittering off the steel of their weapons. Dozens of such groups patrolled the border, but there was too much ground for them to protect every inch of it, and the Valcottans were opportunistic in their attacks.

Otis cut inland down a narrow track, and Keris guided his mount after him, urging the horse to more speed. He liked to ride. Liked to ride fast, which was rarely an option with an escort. But while *he'd* never be allowed out of the city without an escort, Otis suffered no such limitations. Not with his reputation as a warrior and the respect that went along with it.

Reaching a wider spot in the path, Keris dug in his heels, surging past his brother and laughing when Otis lifted his hand in a vulgar gesture. Neck and neck, they raced their horses east until they reached a copse of trees, only then slowing to a walk.

"This will do," Otis declared, swinging off his mount, Keris reluctantly following suit. With the horses tethered to some trees, his brother pulled out his sword.

Keris eyed the weapon. "Must we?"

"Yes. There's a difference between people believing you're skillless and actually being so, and that difference is survival."

"I prefer knives."

"Pretend it's a very big knife."

Sighing, Keris extracted his own sword, hating the weight of it in his hand. Knives had purposes beyond violence, but the blade glittering in the sun was good for nothing but killing. Holding the sword felt like tempting fate.

If you truly believe in something, you should be willing to suffer for it. To die for it, if need be. Which tells me that you either don't believe your own words or that you are a coward. The memory of her words simultaneously angered and inspired him. All his adult life, he'd been espousing the virtues of peace and been called a coward for believing in such ideals.

But never once had he been called a coward for not acting on them.

Otis moved to attack, and Keris halfheartedly parried, going through the motions that he'd been forced to learn as a child. The clang of steel against steel set his nerves on edge, sending flickers of memories through his mind. Memories of his father screaming at him that Veliant men were warriors and to be otherwise was womanly and soft. How he'd shrieked at Keris that he was a weakling for refusing to learn, not seeming to understand that learning would've been the easier path.

How many beatings would it have spared him? How much mockery and vitriol would have gone unvoiced if he'd become as accomplished with the weapon as Otis and his other brothers?

Except juxtaposed with those memories was the one of his father strangling his mother to death and the oath that he'd sworn on her lifeless body that he'd die before becoming anything like the man who'd sired him.

Otis snapped, "Quit defending and attack!"

Grinding his teeth, Keris lunged into a feeble offensive, his brother countering it with enough force that his weapon was knocked from his hand.

"Pick it up!"

The words filled Keris's ears, except it wasn't his brother's voice he heard but his father's, and red filled his vision. With a snarl of anger, he dived under Otis's upraised blade, tackling his brother to the ground with violent force. They grappled, rolling across the ground, their fists flying, but he managed to get his arm around Otis's throat. Squeezing, he waited until his brother frantically tapped on his arm, then held on a moment longer for good measure before shoving him down to the dirt. "I don't like swords."

"Fine." Red-faced, Otis dragged in several breaths, then shook his head. "How someone as lean as you can be so god-awful strong is a mystery to me."

"Books are heavy."

Otis huffed out a laugh, then his eyes narrowed. "Are you hurt?"

Keris was rubbing the shoulder he'd injured catching Valcotta the night of the fire. Grappling had done it no favors. "It's nothing." And knowing that given the chance, Otis would fret over him worse than one of their aunties, he unfastened the hamper attached to his brother's horse, then peered inside. "Did you pack me a picnic lunch? How sweet. If not for our shared blood, I might be starting to question your intentions toward me."

Casting his eyes skyward, Otis muttered what sounded like a prayer for patience, but before he could say more, distant screams filled the air. And as the wind blew over their faces, so did the smell of smoke.

16
ZARRAH

Despite the exhaustion plaguing her, Zarrah had slept only fitfully, her mind unwilling to let go of her conversation with the Maridrinian. Not only the words, but that she'd had a conversation with him at all.

While many Valcottans tolerated Maridrinians, in commercial and occasionally social contexts, Zarrah engaged with them only on the battlefield. She had long believed herself honorable in her refusal to have anything to do with Maridrinians that didn't involve steel and staff and *their* blood. And yet last night, she'd talked to one of them about *peace* between their nations. Had called him a coward for not pursuing it.

And he, peculiarly, had called her an *idealist* for believing so.

A less accurate word for her character she didn't know. Her life was dedicated to the Endless War and to exacting vengeance against the Veliant family, and she'd crossed the border more times than she could count, leaving Valcottan justice in her wake.

Except what if it hadn't been justice at all?

The idea infuriated her, but as hard as she tried to shove it aside, it kept returning to her mind. Kept scratching at her conscience with the suggestion that in trying to avenge what had been done to her as a child, she'd instead made herself the villain in the stories of countless Maridrinian children. That in trying to defeat Silas Veliant, she'd become him.

She forced herself to focus on the report she held, which was from a spy in Harendell who'd discovered the whereabouts of the Ithicanian queen. Yet despite the information being unexpected and strange, she had to read it three times before retaining any of it.

"Why do you fight?" The question leapt from her lips, and Yrina looked up from the reports they'd been reviewing together to regard her.

"For any number of reasons, as well you know. Last night I got in a fight because one of Bermin's fools spilled my drink."

Zarrah had noticed her friend's minor injuries when she'd come in earlier and accurately assumed an alehouse brawl. "Someone with a nose as large as yours shouldn't pick fistfights. Is it broken?"

Yrina rubbed at it. "Nah. It's made of steel. And he looks worse, I'll have you know."

"I've no doubt." While Zarrah had been raised in the privilege and comfort of Valcotta's capital, Yrina was from the northeast edge of the nation, part of one of the nomadic and highly militant desert tribes. She'd been born swinging her fists, been wielding a blade before she could walk, and had killed a dozen men before she'd reached womanhood. The empress had personally selected Yrina to be Zarrah's close guard after her mother had been killed, and she'd swiftly been won over by the other girl's humor. "But that's not what I meant. Why do you fight the Maridrinians?"

"For the honor and glory of Valcotta."

Yrina said the words without hesitation, but the swiftness in the saying caused Zarrah to frown. "Of course. But . . . are there other reasons?"

Yrina set down the report she was holding. "For you, sister. Where you go, I will follow, and your path leads to Maridrinian blood and vengeance."

Unease fluttered in Zarrah's stomach. "And if I did not exist in your life? Would you fight?"

Yrina's round face scrunched into a grimace, brown skin creasing around her hazel eyes. "I'll not hear talk like this, Zar."

"Not my death. I mean if we had never met."

Her friend leaned back in her chair. "This is a strange line of questioning. Is it a test?"

It was, but not for Yrina. "Humor me."

Yrina shrugged. "Might be that I would. The pay is good and the accommodation posh in comparison to other posts." She swiftly added, "And of course, there is honor in spilling Maridrinian blood."

A swell of nausea rose in Zarrah's stomach. "Is it your opinion that the majority of the garrison shares these sentiments?"

"Why?" Yrina scowled. "There isn't to be a cut in pay, is there? Because honor doesn't fill the belly or pay for an attractive man to tell me I'm pretty. I think the empress forgets that, if she cares at all."

God spare her, had the Maridrinian been right?

"No," she answered weakly. "No pay cut. Only idle curiosity."

But Yrina had been at her side for a decade and was not so easily fooled. Leaning over the desk, she took Zarrah's hands. "Not everyone has been hurt by the Maridrinians the way you have, Zar. But that doesn't mean that we are not loyal to you. Your hurt is our hurt, and we will die to give you the vengeance you deserve. Trust in that."

Words intended to give comfort, though they did the exact opposite. All the violence she'd perpetrated in her life, all the death she'd enacted, had been easy to live with, knowing it was honorable and just. But what if it wasn't? What if everything she'd done—or in the case of Ithicana, not done—had been, as the Maridrinian had suggested, in the name of ambition?

No! The word of denial ricocheted through her skull because vengeance was not ambition. The Maridrinian didn't understand how much the empress had suffered at Silas Veliant's hands, her beloved younger sister slaughtered and left to rot.

Except it wasn't the Maridrinian people who'd killed Zarrah's mother.

She bit at her thumbnail, remembering how she'd pleaded with Bermin to warn Ithicana because the nation's innocents didn't deserve to pay for the choices of their king. Yet wasn't that exactly what she'd spent the past decade doing? Making Maridrinian innocents pay for the crimes of Silas Veliant? A good, clean fight between armies of soldiers was one thing, but that wasn't how the Endless War was fought. It was fought with ugly raids intended to strike against those who could least defend themselves, and in that, she was just as guilty as any Maridrinian princeling.

A knock on the door pulled her from her thoughts. "Come."

A sweaty-faced scout entered, pressing a hand to her heart, and Zarrah recognized her as one of Yrina's. "What's happened? A raid?"

The scout shook her head. "It's His Highness."

Zarrah's heart skipped, because Bermin had gone out on patrol earlier. "Has he been hurt?"

"No, General," the woman answered. "He's crossed the Anriot."

"Oh, shit," Yrina muttered. "He was going on last night at the alehouse about how not retaliating against the Maridrinians was dishonorable. But I thought he was just drunk."

He's gone raiding.

Leaping to her feet, Zarrah broke into a sprint, heading toward the stables.

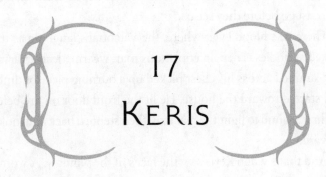

17
KERIS

"RAIDERS." OTIS WAS ALREADY SHOVING HIS SWORD BACK IN ITS sheath and moving toward the horses. "We need to go. We need to get you back to the safety of Nerastis."

Keris to safety, while his people were slaughtered by raiders. The screams grew louder, shrill and terrified and desperate. "No."

Snatching his sword up from the ground, Keris flung himself into the saddle and dug in his heels, galloping toward the attack. Tree branches scraped and caught at his clothes, but he ignored the stinging pain just as he did Otis's shouts for him to stop.

He burst out of the copse, reining in his horse to take in the scene before him.

It was a farmhouse and barn, the latter already engulfed by flames. Animals ran this way and that, as did field workers, the Valcottans shooting them in their backs as they tried to flee. The few who tried to fight were cut down, blood spraying and bodies falling, the air suddenly absent of screams.

"Keris, there's nothing we can do," Otis hissed as he caught up.

"It's too late! We'll warn a patrol on our way back to the city, but we must go before they see us."

There was blood everywhere, the Valcottans laughing as they kicked at bodies. Then an enormous man wearing leather armor that strained across his chest picked up a burning piece of timber and started toward the house. He lit the front door on fire before circling around to light the rear exit, then stepped back and looked upward.

And that's when Keris saw the faces in the window. A woman and two children, eyes wide with terror. Without thinking, he dug his heels into his mount's side and galloped toward the home.

Through the smoke, the Valcottans caught sight of him and shouted their alarm, and Keris vaguely heard Otis blowing on a signal horn to alert patrols in the area. But there wasn't time to wait for them. The house, made entirely of timber, would be an inferno long before the patrols could reach them.

An arrow flew past his face, catching at his hair, but Keris only bent low over the horse's neck. The Valcottans were moving to intercept, but his animal had been bred for speed, and only the big man stood in his way.

Eyes stinging from the smoke, Keris watched as the Valcottan man hefted a staff longer than he was tall, knees bending as he readied to swing it at the horse's legs.

The animal tensed beneath him but didn't falter, galloping straight toward the soldier.

Steady, Keris willed it. *Steady.*

The Valcottan swung, the staff a blur.

But as the horse shied away from the weapon, Keris dove off the side, shoulder taking the man just below the chin. They hit the ground together, the Valcottan choking and clutching at his throat. Keris ignored him and raced to the door, only to stumble back from the heat.

There was no way inside. But over the crackle of flames, he could hear the screams from the family trapped within.

Think.

The other soldiers converged on Otis, the sound of blades crashing against blades loud as he fought them back. But he was only one man against a dozen, and if he were killed . . . Keris twisted, hand going to the sword at his waist, but Otis shouted at him, "Get them out!"

Keris's instincts took over, pulling him down the length of the house. There were no windows on the ground floor, but there was a rain barrel resting against the wall. Keris leapt onto it and jumped as high as he could, catching the edge of the window frame on the second level, his injured shoulder screaming. Boots scrambling against the side of the building, he heaved himself up, then kicked in the glass, shards tearing at his clothes as he slipped into the smoke-filled home.

A fit of coughing immediately took control of him. Keris ripped off his coat, holding it over his mouth and nose as he felt around in the darkness for a door, finding it open to the hall beyond.

Tears flooded down his face, vision entirely obscured, but he followed the screams for help and found the stairs. Ascending them swiftly, he opened the door to the attic, then slammed it shut behind him before turning to face the terrified family. "Help is coming," he gasped, praying it was true, because he had no idea how he was going to get them out of this mess. Heroics were not one of his competencies.

The boy, who looked no more than six or seven, said, "One of them followed you in!"

The words barely had a chance to register before the door burst open, a coughing Valcottan rushing through, weapon raised.

Keris jerked free his own sword and the blades met with a

crash, all the apathy he'd displayed with Otis vanquished by the adrenaline racing through his veins.

The other man was bigger, but Keris had always been fast, his speed making up for his lack of skill as they fought in the small space, the family screaming and diving out of the way even as smoke billowed through the open door.

He coughed with every other breath, his eyes streaming tears, but he stayed between the Valcottan and the family, knowing the man would kill them if given the chance. Blocking a downstroke that made his injured shoulder shudder, he kicked the door shut and shouted at the mother, "Get the window open!"

"It's stuck!" she sobbed. "It won't open!"

"Break it!"

The woman didn't move, but the boy picked up a wooden box and threw it, the glass shattering and fresh air rushing in.

But it would buy them only minutes.

The Valcottan scrubbed at his eyes with his free hand as he fought, face wet with tears, and Keris saw an opening in his guard. Then another.

Attack! He swore he heard Otis's voice in his head. *Kill him!*

"No!" he snarled back, refusing to consider it.

The patrols would be here soon. The Valcottans would retreat. All he had to do was hold off until then.

But smoke rose between the floorboards, the growing heat having nothing to do with exertion.

They were running out of time.

The Valcottan attacked again in earnest, Keris's injured arm starting to give, but he managed to parry blow after blow, staying on the defense. And when the Valcottan stumbled and Keris saw an opening, he swung his fist.

His knuckles stung as they collided with the man's temple, sending him falling back. But the Valcottan didn't drop his weapon.

"They're retreating!" the boy shouted from his position by the window. "They're running away."

And Maridrinian horns were blowing.

"If you run, you might escape," he said to the man through coughs. "Go."

The man spat, the glob steaming as it hit the overheated floor. "This is vengeance, you Maridrinian rat. An eye for an eye for the innocent lives you took."

Otis's raid. The one Keris and Valcotta had instigated.

Then the Valcottan lunged, blade directed at the boy. Keris didn't remember moving but found himself between the two. Everything seemed to happen very slowly and all at once as the tip of his blade punched through the man's leather armor, sliding between his ribs.

The Valcottan stared at Keris, eyes wide with shock, then slowly he dropped to the ground.

Dead. He's dead.

I killed him.

It felt like he was watching the scene from a distance. As though watching someone else entirely, hearing someone else cough, feeling someone else's pain. Then the sound of someone shouting his name snapped him back into the moment.

"Keris!"

Otis's voice echoed over the roar of flames and cracking timber.

"Keris, you need to get out! It's going to collapse!"

"Shit!" Retrieving his coat from the ground, Keris used it to smash the rest of the glass out of the frame, the heat seeping through his boots painful. Leaning out, he saw Otis below him, face smeared with blood but alive.

Lifting the boy, Keris told him, "Be brave," then tossed him away from the flames licking the sides of the building. Otis caught him easily. Beyond, the patrol burst into sight on galloping horses, but Keris paid them no mind, his attention on the girl.

"I'm too scared," she wept as he balanced her on the sill. "It's too far down."

"It's not that far. And if you do it, you'll be able to tell all your friends you were rescued by Prince Otis Veliant."

The girl turned to gape at him, then her face grew determined, and she jumped.

"Go," he said to the mother, nearly shouting in frustration as she hesitated on the windowsill, asking, "Who are you?"

"No one of consequence. Now jump."

The woman leapt. Otis was too entangled with the daughter to catch her, but the woman landed well enough, rolling over the dirt.

Climbing onto the sill, Keris winced as the heat hit him in the face, flames reaching up to singe his boots. It was an easy jump for him—or would be, if they'd get out of his way.

"Move!" Coughing, he bent his knees. Then timber cracked and the building fell out from under him.

18
ZARRAH

HER HORSE LABORED BENEATH HER AS SHE GALLOPED THROUGH the Maridrinian countryside, Yrina and her group of soldiers in hot pursuit. They were in enemy territory, which meant an attack could come from all sides, but Zarrah found herself not caring. All that mattered was stopping the raid. She told herself it was to protect her cousin from the empress's wrath, but in her heart, she knew it was something deeper.

She didn't want to be a villain.

Bermin's party had left clear tracks in the damp earth, but they had more than an hour's head start. More than enough for him to enact slaughter upon whatever farm he selected, though he'd be smart enough to attempt to avoid Maridrinian patrols. For all his talk of honor, he wouldn't be looking to lose his life in exchange for avenging a farmer's death.

The faint smell of smoke tickled her nostrils, and Zarrah slowed her horse as she searched the horizon.

There.

A black column reached up to the sky, growing taller by the

second. Far too large to be burning debris and the wrong color for a grassfire. This was undoubtedly her cousin's work.

Twisting in her saddle, she said, "We're going to force Bermin to retreat, on the orders of the empress. You will not engage or harm the Maridrinians unless your own life stands in the balance, understood? I want scouts in the surrounding terrain— Maridrinian patrols will come to investigate the smoke, and I want to be gone before they arrive. Now, move!"

Cracking her reins against her horse's haunches, she raced in the direction of the smoke, Yrina and the rest on her heels.

She burst from a copse of trees, her horse galloping through wheat nearly up to her knees as she headed in the direction of a burning barn, flames flickering up the side of the neighboring farmhouse. Her eyes danced over the familiar faces of her cousin's soldiers, not seeing Bermin among them. Then the low bellow of a Maridrinian horn filled the air.

"Shit!" Yrina shouted from behind. "It's one of their patrols! Has to be!"

Which meant this might not be a matter of forcing her cousin to retreat but rescuing his ass from this poorly laid plan.

Bermin's soldiers abruptly sprinted toward the far side of the farmhouse, the air filling with their shouts of alarm.

Pulling free her staff, Zarrah circled her horse around the burning home, her gaze recoiling from the dozen corpses of men and women littering the yard—farmers whom Bermin and his soldiers had massacred, their eyes staring sightlessly at the sky. How many of them had children hiding in the woods or in cellars, stifling their sobs while they looked on?

How many children were among the dead?

This wasn't war; it was cold-blooded murder. Fury raged through her, and part of Zarrah wanted to turn her horse around and leave Bermin and his men to be slaughtered by the incoming patrol.

But the thought fell away as she rounded the building and found Bermin's men fighting not a Maridrinian patrol but a single man, his sword blade flashing in the sunlight. He felled one of Bermin's soldiers, then another, but he was deeply outnumbered. Which meant it was only a matter of time until they cut him down.

"Zar!" Yrina shouted, and she followed her lieutenant's pointing finger to where Bermin writhed on the ground, clutching at his throat.

"Get him out of here," she ordered, then flung herself off her horse and into the fray.

"Fall back!" she shouted at the soldiers, their eyes widening as they recognized her. "That's a fucking order, you fools! Fall back!"

Four of them listened. Three did not.

Cursing, she tripped one of them with her staff, sending him toppling out of the way, then jabbed another in the ribs before she was forced to block a blow from the Maridrinian. And then another. He was big for one of them, tall and broad of shoulders, with dark hair and eyes, his skin tanned brown from the sun.

"We're done here," Zarrah snarled. "Back down and we'll leave you alive."

His eyes flashed, and he wiped away the blood threatening to drip into one of them. "You're still alive," he snarled. "Which means *I* am not done."

He moved to attack but hesitated, his gaze skipping to the burning farmhouse.

Zarrah took advantage of his distraction, cracking him across the ribs and sending him staggering. "Stay down!"

Rounding on her cousin's soldiers, she growled, "You forget who is in command. Retreat, or I'll kill you myself for this insubordination."

But they didn't answer, their attention behind her.

Zarrah ducked, sensing the attack. The Maridrinian's blade

sliced just above her head. Twisting on her heels, she straightened and swung her fist, catching the man in the face hard enough that he fell on his ass.

Then Yrina was there, flanked by four of their soldiers, her eyes flashing with enough fury that Zarrah knew she'd seen what Bermin's soldiers had done. Or *not* done. Yrina lifted her blade. "I'm going to cut—"

"Later," Zarrah snapped. "Listen!"

More horns in the distance, a patrol only minutes away.

"Our comrade is inside," one of Bermin's men said. "Went into the house after the other Maridrinian."

The house that was an inferno. "Then he's dead. Either way, we can't remain." Because from the sounds of those horns, it wasn't just one patrol galloping in their direction.

Her soldiers pulled Bermin's men onto their horses' backs, Zarrah catching her mount and following. They broke into a gallop across the fields, but she risked a backward glance, catching sight of motion in the upper-floor window. Children being dropped to the safety of the ground, a woman following suit. Then a man balanced on the frame, barely visible through the smoke, where he hesitated.

Which was a mistake.

The building collapsed in a roar of flames, the man disappearing into the smoke.

An unexpected flicker of grief flashed in Zarrah's chest, and she pressed her hand to her heart in a show of respect for the man's sacrifice before turning her attention to the road ahead.

And the changes she intended to enact once she reached the end of it.

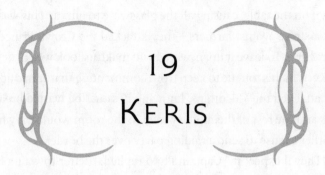

19
KERIS

KERIS LEAPT, THE HEAT WASHING OVER HIM SO INTENSE IT HURT, his lungs burning from smoke and embers as he hit the ground and rolled. And kept rolling until fresh air filled his lungs, his shoulder screaming in pain.

"Keris!" Hands gripped his arms, shaking him, and he looked up to see his brother's face. "Keris, are you all right?"

"Wonderful," he croaked. "Never been better."

Pushing up onto his hands and knees, he saw the mother with her arms wrapped around her two children, faces stained with soot. All around them were the bodies of their family and fellow workers, the yard and field splattered with blood and parts. Then his eyes skipped to the burning pile of lumber that was all that remained of the farmhouse, a body sitting near the top of it. A body that still had his sword shoved through its chest.

You killed him.

Twisting away, Keris vomited into the dirt.

———

"WE NEED TO RETALIATE IMMEDIATELY!" Otis slammed his fist down on the table, causing all the glassware to jump. "This wasn't just a strike against farmers—they attacked the Crown Prince of Maridrina. To leave it unanswered will make us look weak."

Keris bit his tongue to keep from commenting that *he* had actually attacked the Valcottans, knowing it would be wasted breath. Otis and the rest of the military men in the room would only find another excuse to send a raiding party over the border.

"They'll expect it," Captain Philo replied. "Better to wait a few days, then coordinate a strike. Perhaps by sea this time? There are a few villages close to the coast that would make prime targets."

Civilians. Keris's jaw tightened, knowing the raid would look the same as the scene he'd left behind at the farm. Bodies of people who'd never held a weapon in their lives. Bodies of people who only wanted to work the land and care for their families. Bodies to stack upon the thousands who'd already died in this sickening back-and-forth between nations that accomplished nothing.

What would it take to end it?

"Given they were likely retaliating against our recent raids, perhaps we'd be better served to strengthen our border patrols than to incite them further."

Every man in the room went silent, all eyes fixing on Keris. His first inclination was to dismiss his own words, to back away from the situation as he'd always done. But the Valcottan woman's criticism was fresh in his head, so instead he found himself saying, "Our capital goes hungry for want of crops, and yet we put all our effort into killing Valcottan farmers rather than protecting our own and allowing them to farm the highest-yielding land in Maridrina."

"We protect them by demonstrating to Valcotta that there are consequences to attacking," Otis answered. "It's how it's done."

"How it's done," Keris repeated. "Yet year after year, hundreds of farmers and their families die beneath Valcottan blades, which suggests the strategy is not particularly effective. Perhaps it's time to try something different."

"With respect, Your Highness," one of the men said, "it might be better to leave military strategy to those with training and experience, especially given you've made it clear to us that you have no interest in involving yourself."

Retorts rose and fell, but none reached Keris's tongue, because he wasn't entirely sure what he wished to accomplish other than to put an end to raiding, which wasn't within his power. The men took his silence as agreement and returned to their debates over when and how to raid, drawing maps in front of them.

They wouldn't hear anything he said because they *wanted* to raid. Wanted to leave death and destruction in their wake. For all they claimed to be acting in the interests of those they were supposed to protect, it wasn't the truth. They were killers.

Keris stared into his glass, some trick of the light making the wine look like blood. His stomach twisted, bile burning in his throat.

You're a killer, too.

On the ride back to Nerastis, Otis had filled his ears with platitudes. That Keris had had no choice but to kill the man. That if he hadn't, he'd have been the one who wound up dead. And when none of that worked, that the Valcottan would've slaughtered the woman and her children. "You saved their lives," Otis had repeated over and over. "You're a hero."

He was no one's hero.

"It had to have been Zarrah Anaphora," Otis said, drawing Keris's attention back to the conversation. "There's no one else in Nerastis with the authority to override Prince Bermin's commands."

Keris glanced at his brother. "There was a woman there?"

"She arrived at the head of another force while you were in the farmhouse," Otis answered. "Likely as reinforcement, but the little chit turned coward at the sound of the patrol horns and called the retreat. Ran off with her tail between her legs."

"Was she the only woman?" Unease rose in his chest. "Or were there others?"

"There were several women in her company." His face was filled with disgust. "All of them dressed like men."

"Repugnant practice," one of the generals muttered, another pounding his fist against the table, declaring, "It's unnatural."

Keris was tempted to point out that Maridrina's most recent victory against Ithicana was the result of a woman's strategy but instead rose to his feet. "If you'll excuse me, I find this conversation tremendously tedious."

As he strode from the room, he heard Otis giving the other men final instructions for the raid, but then the sound of boots followed him, and a second later, his brother slung an arm around his shoulders. "I know it doesn't feel this way, Keris, but what happened today was a good thing. You rode into battle and took down Bermin Anaphora, for fuck's sake. The empress's son and one of the most formidable fighters in Nerastis—*you*! If you'd change your mind and allow me to share that information, the men in that room would revise their opinion of you."

Keris struggled not to cast his eyes skyward, uninterested in being in the good graces of those idiots. "No."

"At least in the report we send Father—"

"I'd prefer you refrained from mentioning my involvement." Their father would be pleased, yes, but not out of pride. It would be because he'd see it as a victory against Keris in their endless battle of ideology.

Otis was silent, then muttered, "He'll find out regardless. Nerastis is full of the Magpie's spies, and if I exclude that you were with me, he'll know it was because you asked me to, which will be worse."

Keris's jaw clenched, knowing his brother was right and hating it. "Fine. Say I was there, but nothing else."

"Let's not dwell on that which cannot be changed." Otis pulled him closer, then gave him a shove forward, making Keris stagger. "Let's go find some entertainment in the city. A pretty girl to soothe your battered morals. I'll arrange an escort."

Keris opened his mouth to argue that he was in no mood for entertainment, but then shut it again. Escaping the palace right now would be impossible, but escaping a brothel . . . Keris forced a smile onto his face. "Lead the way."

BOTH OF THEM KEPT THEIR hoods up, though the dozen guards Otis had handpicked for their escort likely gave away their identities. Even so, Keris was happy enough to keep his face relatively unknown to the people of Nerastis, anonymity key to his ability to blend in among them.

They entered the brothel, the main level having been cleared of other guests so that the royals could have their pick of the girls. Spotting Aileena, Keris nodded at her. To her credit, the only surprise she showed was a slight raising of her eyebrows before she dropped into a deep curtsy and led him toward the stairs.

The air was heavy with scented oil and perfume, all to hide the smell of sweat and sex that permeated the popular establishment. The dim light provided by lamps fixed to the walls every dozen feet gleamed through glass of Valcottan make.

"I must say, this is an unexpected privilege," Aileena murmured. "I had believed I displeased you during our last encounter."

"The only one who did anything displeasing was me." Keris shook his head when she opened the door to a room facing the street. "A quieter room, if you would."

Shrugging one graceful shoulder, Aileena opened the door on the opposite side, revealing a room dominated by a large bed made up in lavender silk, the drapes a deeper shade of purple shot with silver thread. He smirked. "I thought you didn't entertain Valcottans."

She shrugged. "Business is business."

"And a cock is a cock." He went to the window and pulled aside the drapes to peer at the alley.

She gave a soft chuckle. "I wouldn't say that, Your Highness."

He turned around to find that she'd removed her dress, now wearing undergarments made of golden chains and glittering jewels. Gilt and glass, but becoming nonetheless. Yet despite having tasted the pleasures Aileena had to offer, *his* cock did not so much as twitch at the sight, his mind's eye filling with the memory of dark eyes, silken brown skin, and a body honed by a life spent working on her feet, not her back. But more than that, it was Valcotta's words that filled his head, her fearless voicing of things that most were too terrified to even think. "Speaking of business, lovely, I've something of a proposition for you . . ."

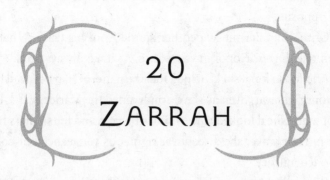

20
ZARRAH

"HAVE YOU LOST YOUR GODDAMNED MIND? THE EMPRESS LEFT specific orders *not* to raid."

Bermin crossed his arms, scowling. His throat was swollen and bruised from the battle. "Orders I don't agree with. She seems content for Valcotta to look weak while Maridrina's strength only grows."

Zarrah ground her teeth. "It's treason, cousin. The only thing saving you from execution is your title."

Bermin rasped, "I'd rather die a thousand times than sacrifice my honor."

"Honor, is it?" She spat the words in his face, fury rising in her chest. "What exactly did you prove today other than that we are as murderous as they are?"

Her cousin stared at her in confusion, which only fueled her anger.

"It wasn't soldiers you attacked today; it was unarmed farmers and their families. Perhaps you might explain to me how slaughtering children proves your prowess as a warrior, for I say it does the opposite."

Grimacing, Bermin wiped her spittle from his face. "What is wrong with you? Honor in vengeance. As it has always been."

And for so long, she'd helped fuel the pattern. Had believed her actions righteous even as she'd condemned the Maridrinians. Except when she'd looked at the bodies Bermin and his soldiers had left in their wake, she'd seen not righteous vengeance but cold-blooded murder.

"You will abide, Your Highness. Or I will send you back to Pyrinat. It is your choice. Now, get out."

She twisted away, not watching him leave in favor of staring out the window at the city, shadows stretching long as the sun set. Her gaze moved east to the bluffs, the dam little more than a shadow in the distance. It drew her like a compulsion, beckoning her, because there was no one here who would understand. No one she could tell that a Maridrinian had put the spark of an idea in her head, and that against her will, it now blazed like a bonfire.

No one she could tell, except perhaps for the Maridrinian himself.

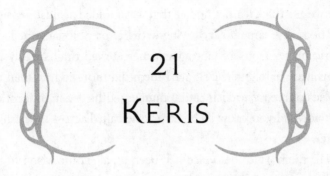

21
KERIS

After a few minutes of haggling over a rate, Keris had kissed the courtesan on the cheek and handed her triple what they'd agreed upon before slipping out the window into the Nerastis night.

He had no reason to believe Valcotta would be there. And yet his heart pounded rapidly as he exited the city limits and headed up to the old dam, the roar of the waterfall growing with each step he drew closer.

Why are you here? a voice whispered from deep inside his head. *What is it about this woman that causes you to risk life and limb to speak to her?*

"She listens," he replied to the voice. Except it was more than that. Valcotta didn't just listen: she *heard*.

Stepping onto the top of the dam, he moved around the curved stone, coming to a stop at the edge of the spillway, his eyes drinking in the sight on the other side.

Moonlight gleamed off her dark hair, the short locks brushing her polished cheeks as the breeze blew against them. As always, she wore a thick leather bodice that was molded against her slender body, the same breeze toying with her hair blowing the loose fabric of her trousers taut against her curved thighs. Only her arms were bare, but the sight of them did more to him than the naked courtesan he'd left eating candies on the bed in the brothel.

"How did you know I'd be here?" she called across the rushing water.

His memory of her voice had been a pale comparison to the reality of it. A voice he could listen to for the rest of the night. And for many nights to come.

"I didn't. Only hoped that fortune would favor me with your presence."

She tilted her head. "You're the first Maridrinian to ever call my presence a favor of fate."

He smirked. "With a face like yours, I cry false. I'm sure you leave half-cocked Maridrinian corpses everywhere you go, Valcotta."

She burst into laughter, easing the tension that had been seething through him since the raid. Calming his heart even as it made his pulse race.

"That is the worst compliment I've ever received in my life."

Keris gave a deep bow, then motioned for her to step back. Clenching his teeth because he knew this would hurt, he sprinted to the edge and jumped. His boots made no sound as he landed, but the impact sent pain lancing through his shoulder, causing him to stumble and catch his balance against her shoulders.

Her skin was feverishly warm even through his gloves, and as Keris inhaled, the scent of lavender and leather and steel filled his nose. A warrior, yes, but also very much a woman, and they stood only inches apart, his hands gripping her shoulders and one of her hands pressed against his chest, holding him steady.

"You're hurt." She lowered her hand from his chest. "You shouldn't have jumped."

She was probably right, but the reward of being close to her felt very much worth the risk. "It's nothing. An old injury come back for a visit."

"There is little worse than uninvited guests."

God help him, but he wanted to drown in her voice. "I hope you speak metaphorically of my shoulder and not literally of my presence on Valcottan soil, for if it is the latter, my feelings will be tremendously hurt. I might weep."

She smiled. "Why are you here?"

"Why are *you* here?" When she shook her head, he sighed. "I was reminded today exactly why I didn't want to come to Nerastis. Why I don't wish to be in Maridrina at all, for that matter."

"Then how fortunate you now stand on Valcottan soil."

It *was* fortunate, though it had nothing to do with the soil. "I know a good many who'd debate that statement, but I'll let you have it."

"How magnanimous of you." She tilted her head, quietly waiting for him to say more, and yet the truth of what had driven him to the dam stuck in his throat, not something he'd admit even to Otis. Especially not Otis, who hated the Valcottans so thoroughly for what they'd taken from him that he'd see Keris's beliefs as a form of betrayal.

She's different. The thought rippled through his head, though he had no reason to believe it. He barely knew this woman, this *soldier.* And yet he found himself saying, "You've witnessed the aftermath of raids against your people?"

She nodded. "Many times."

"I have not. *Had* not, that is."

"Until Bermin's raid on that farm today." She exhaled a long breath. "Was it as you expected?"

"Yes. And no." Keris turned to the glittering city, the mist rising to dampen his hair and clothes. "The silence is different than other silences. It's not the lack of words, but lack of motion. The still hearts and unmoving chests. The empty eyes." Visions of the farmers at work juxtaposed with them lying in pieces across the farmyard and fields, and he blinked, trying to force them away. "One moment going about their lives, the next, their lives cut short. And for what?"

"Vengeance." The word came swiftly from her lips, then she hesitated and added, "Retaliation for the loss of our people in the recent raid is the reason Bermin gave."

A raid that the two of them had unwittingly caused.

"Yes, an eye for an eye. Yet those your people and mine would seek vengeance against care nothing for the lives taken." He remembered how Otis had barely seemed to see the carnage around them. How the patrols who had come had been wild with anger over the sight and absent any grief for the loss.

Reaching down, he picked up a rock and threw it hard, swearing as pain lanced through his cursed shoulder. "Those in power don't care in the way they should."

"I care." Her voice caught. "It breaks my heart every time I see it. I feel sick with guilt for not having prevented it. And . . ." Valcotta hesitated, then blurted out, "Have you ever had an idea lodge in your thoughts like a spark, and rather than your efforts extinguishing it, they only cause it to burst into flame? And for those flames to illuminate the world in such a way that you half wondered if you'd been blind before?"

"Yes." Because her words had lit a spark in his own mind, though he hadn't decided what, if anything, he intended to do about it.

Turning away from him, she sat, legs hanging over the edge of the dam. Keris lowered himself to the damp stone next to her, immediately feeling the waterfall's mist dampen his trousers.

"My mother was murdered in front of me by Maridrinian raiders when I was fourteen. She didn't even know how to hold a weapon, but she fought to save my life. They tied me to the cross holding her body and left me there to die."

Keris's stomach clenched. It was a cruelty his father had made popular in his younger years before he'd inherited the throne, and many of the soldiers in Nerastis continued to use it in honor of him. "I'm sorry."

She didn't respond, only sat in silence for a long time before finally saying, "I dedicated my life to becoming strong enough to fight back against men like the one who killed her. To protecting those who could not protect themselves. To defending Valcotta from those who'd harm her. And to the pursuit of vengeance. But along the way, I lost myself. Forgot myself. And all that remained was the need for vengeance." She looked up at him. "That was the truth the spark revealed to me."

"And now you seek to find yourself again?"

She nodded. "Except that when I do, I fear there will be no place for her in Nerastis. Or anywhere in Valcotta."

That had always been the way he'd felt. As though his true self were so at odds with the man his father—and all of Maridrina—wanted him to be that it would be impossible for him to survive unless he escaped. That was why he'd been so desperate to flee to Harendell. Except his cowardice had consequences, his selfishness used as the linchpin in Lara's and his father's plans to invade Ithicana. And while he'd not caused the Endless War between Maridrina and Valcotta, in refusing to use his own power to try to mitigate the harm it caused his people, was he not complicit?

If you truly believe in something, you should be willing to suffer for it. To die for it . . .

"There will be a retaliation for the raid today," Keris said softly. "One of some significance."

She tensed, then shifted closer to him as though they were co-conspirators in danger of being overheard. "When? Where?"

"Telling you that would make me a traitor to my nation."

Valcotta was quiet, then she said, "A traitor to your king. And to the princelings and their sycophants in that domed palace. But not a traitor to your people—not a traitor to the innocents who have no say in this war and yet give their lives in payment for the actions of those who do."

Keris felt what she was saying in his core, and yet if he did this, his soldiers would die where otherwise they would not.

As if hearing his thoughts, she said, "The soldiers in your barracks chose this life. Are paid handsomely for it. And what's more, Silas Veliant and his ingrate sons care a great deal more for the loss of a soldier's life than they do a farmer's. Lose enough of them, and they might cease with the raids for the sake of keeping their hold on Ithicana. And . . ." She hesitated. "I think for my empress, if she lost the need to retaliate, it would be the same."

Keris wondered what Valcotta would think if she knew he was one of those ingrate sons. Not just a princeling living in the domed palace, but *the* princeling.

"We can't stop this war," she said. "But perhaps we could change the nature of it."

The spark she'd lit in his mind was a spark no longer but a flame, and it illuminated a far different future for himself than he ever imagined. "Can I trust you, Valcotta?"

She leaned toward him, her cheek brushing against his jaw, the sensation sending a rush of desire through him. Her breath was hot against his ear as she whispered, "I think we both know that the question is whether I should trust you."

He huffed out a breath, not entirely certain whether it was his head, his heart, or his cock that was making this decision. Only that he was making it. "Have you enough authority to influence strategy?"

She lifted one eyebrow. "Do you have enough importance to know anything worth influencing strategy over?"

He laughed softly. "I do."

But it was there his words stalled. She was an officer in the Valcottan Army. A sworn enemy of his people. And this was treason of the highest order. But if he did nothing . . . "In four days, when the moon has waned enough to attack by sea under the cover of darkness, they will come. And we've spies in your garrison, so ensure you keep this information close until the final hour."

Silence stretched between them, the tension so thick he could hardly breathe, then she whispered, "Who are you?"

There was a part of him that wanted to answer. A part of him that believed the path they were walking down demanded there be no lies between them. Except his identity, his *name*, was a curse, for it tied him to his father. And the revelation of it might well burn this moment to the ground. "One step at a time, Valcotta. I've already bared my throat enough tonight."

Instead of answering, she reached up, hand closing over his throat. "If you are lying to me, I'll slit your jugular. You know that, yes?"

Keris's heart hammered in his chest, fueled by fear and desire and anticipation, but more than that, by the sensation of being more *alive* than he'd ever been. He could hear the rapidness of her breathing, feel the heat of it against his face, and God help him but he wanted her. Except he knew it would be on her terms or not at all, and he wasn't willing to jeopardize this fragile trust between them, on which so much depended, by allowing his cock to make stupid decisions. "On my honor, those are the plans as they stand tonight. I heard them with my own ears."

Her hand didn't move from his throat, only tightened, her nails digging into his skin. He stared down at her, watching her lips part, watching as who she was warred with who she wanted to be. And though logic told him that he should be glad when the latter won and she lowered her hand to her side, he had to fight the urge to provoke its return.

Pulling away before his body could betray him, Keris rose to his feet. But before he jumped back across the spillway, he turned. "When will I see you again, Valcotta?"

She smiled, her teeth bright in the moonlight. "When I find out if your word is good, Maridrina." And then she disappeared into the night.

22
ZARRAH

FOUR DAYS AFTER MEETING WITH THE MARIDRINIAN, ZARRAH crouched behind some rocks and brush overlooking one of the handful of inlets south of Nerastis's port. On her left, Yrina watched the dark seas intently for any sign of motion, and on her right, Bermin glowered.

"Mistake to pull our eastern patrols." His voice was a raspy whisper and would be for some time, courtesy of the blow he'd taken during the raid. That his throat hadn't been crushed beyond repair was likely only because her cousin had a neck like a tree trunk. "If they hit one of the villages, we could have dozens of casualties in a single night with us none the wiser. This is folly."

It was an enormous risk; Zarrah knew that. But some risks were worth the reward, and though logic said otherwise, she trusted the Maridrinian's intent. It was impossible not to when she'd seen the naked grief on his face for those Bermin and his soldiers had slaughtered. Grief that she knew in her heart wasn't feigned. He wanted to see an end to the raids and was willing to risk his own life by committing treason to do it.

Except for this to work, she ultimately needed to be willing to do the same. Willing to put her soldiers, many of whom were friends, at risk by betraying their raiding plans. Yet if the raids could be stymied, how many innocent lives would be saved?

"Time will tell," she finally answered Bermin, unwilling to argue when what happened tonight would either prove the Maridrinian's word was good or that she was a naïve fool.

The moon above was little more than a sliver of light, but stars filled the clear night sky with brilliant silver sparks beyond counting. The only sound other than the breathing of her comrades was the roar of the waves rolling onto shore, and caught in the lulling rhythm, her mind drifted, her head filling with visions of the Maridrinian's face.

God, but he was something to behold. The sort of beautiful that should be the domain of a woman, except there wasn't anything feminine about him. Not the solid grip of his hands on her shoulders as he'd caught his balance against her. Not the rock-hard muscle of his chest beneath her palm. And most certainly not the masculine scent of spice and exertion that had filled her nose or the rasp of stubble that had brushed her hand when she'd caught hold of his throat.

Too close. They'd been too close. And yet her body—apparently as traitorous as her mind—had ached to move closer.

The sound of an oar slamming in a lock ripped her back into the moment, and Zarrah focused her gaze on the distant waves.

Yrina lifted a hand and pointed. "There."

That it would be this inlet, of the six others she currently had under watch, was something of a stroke of luck. But there was no denying the faint sounds of at least two longboats coming into shore, and a heartbeat later, her ears picked up the scrape of wood over sand.

Not two longboats, but three, all of them loaded with Maridrinian soldiers. Equal numbers to her own, but Zarrah's force had the advantage of surprise. Lifting the bow she held in one hand, she nocked an arrow, seeing all the archers in her force do the same.

"Hold." She toed the line between the enemy force being far enough up the sand to be hit and still leaving them an opportunity to escape. She owed the Maridrinian that much. "Hold."

The enemy force reached the midpoint of the beach, close enough to strike with good shots but only a quick sprint back to the boats if they chose to escape. "Shoot!" She loosed an arrow.

A second later, the air filled with the hiss of arrows. And she wasn't the only one who heard it.

"Ambush!" a vaguely familiar voice shouted, and Zarrah aimed at the shadowy form.

Her arrow flew through the air, grazing the soldier's arm. He jerked, but instead of calling for a retreat, he shouted, "Charge!"

Fool! Zarrah dropped her bow and lifted her staff, screaming, "For Valcotta!"

The two forces collided, clashes of steel and screams of pain drowning out the surf; it was difficult to discern friend from foe in the darkness. Zarrah fought back-to-back with Yrina, her staff whistling through the air, cracking bones even as she blocked swipes from Maridrinian swords, her arms shuddering from the impacts.

She didn't fight to kill, leaving groaning men in her wake even as she silently pleaded, *Fall back. Retreat.*

But Maridrina was a kingdom built on bravery and pride, and they kept coming. Kept fighting even as her reinforcements arrived.

Zarrah's skin prickled and she whirled, barely managing to evade the blood-drenched blade that nearly took off her head.

"We meet again, *Zarrah.*"

She instantly recognized the man she'd fought during Bermin's raid. The one who'd done his damnedest to cut off her head despite knowing she'd been trying to retreat. "That's General Anaphora, you Maridrinian rat."

"I'll accord no titles to the likes of you."

Though she could barely see him in the dark, she felt his disdain. His hate. Felt her own rising despite knowing she had no more ground to stand on than he did. They were both killers. Both murderers. "Retreat while you have the chance!"

"Not while you still stand!"

She swung at his head with no intent to hit him, but he rolled, coming up on his feet swift as a cat, sword slicing at her hamstrings. Zarrah jumped, the blade sliding under her boots. But instead of landing on flat ground, her foot slid along a slick tree root, sending her staggering.

Pain seared across her arm, and she gasped, throwing herself sideways and out of range of another blow from his sword. She scrambled to regain her footing, staying on the defense as he drove her backward down the hill.

In her periphery, she could see the Maridrinians falling back to the boats, recognizing this was a fight they couldn't win, but the stubborn bastard refused to run.

Then one of them shouted, "Highness, we must retreat!"

Highness. This was not a common soldier, not a man here only because he'd been ordered to fight. This was one of the Rat King's sons. A Veliant prince.

Hate, blistering hot and merciless, boiled up from her heart, driving aside logic and reason, caring nothing for the consequences that would come from killing him. With a wild scream, Zarrah threw herself at him, attacking in earnest where before she'd held back.

Her staff struck him on the arm, sending his weapon flying and him backing down the beach as he fumbled for a knife.

"I'm going to kill you, Veliant," she snarled. "I'm going to cut out your black heart and feed it to the dogs!"

"Zarrah! Hold your ground!"

She heard Yrina's shout of warning, saw the Maridrinians racing up the beach in an attempt to rescue their prince. Knew she'd be overrun but found herself not caring.

Another swing of her staff, and he was on his ass, scrambling backward. Pulling her knife, she bared her teeth, moving in for the kill.

Then strong hands caught her around the middle, hauling her back.

"We've won, little Zarrah," Bermin's voice rasped in her ear. "Allow the rats to scuttle back to their side of the Anriot, where they can lick their wounds in shame."

"Let me go!" she screamed, but her cousin's grip was implacable. "He's a Veliant!"

Her soldiers muttered angrily, demanding pursuit, but Bermin only said, "Do not allow your emotions to rule your good sense, little Zarrah. The princeling's pride will give you another chance; you need only bide your time. And if it is not this one, it will be another who you bring low."

She would not stop at just one. For when it came to the Veliant family, her need for vengeance was no spark.

It was an inferno.

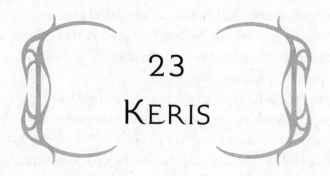

23
KERIS

KERIS PACED BACK AND FORTH ACROSS HIS ROOMS, HIS SKIN clammy and his stomach twisted into knots.

Of course Otis had insisted on going. Of course Otis insisted on being the one to deliver Maridrina's revenge.

It could be no other way.

Nothing Keris had said in an attempt to dissuade him from joining the raiding party had made a difference, and short of commanding his brother to remain, which would've raised questions he couldn't answer, there'd been nothing he could do to keep Otis from sailing into an ambush.

"Shit." Visions of his brother's corpse being laid at his feet filled his eyes. "Shit! Shit! Shit!"

Otis was more than his half brother—he was Keris's best friend. His only friend, if he was being truthful. For their entire lives, Otis had protected him. Against their brothers, against their father, against the world. That they didn't have a damned interest in common and fought more days than not didn't matter. They were blood, and if Otis were harmed . . .

A knock sounded at the door. Not bothering to answer, Keris jerked it open, the servant on the other side leaping back in alarm. "Well?"

"You wished to be informed when the raiding party returned, my lord." He blinked at Keris. "They've returned."

"Is my brother with them?"

"I don't know, my lord. Only that there are many injured."

No.

Pushing past the man, Keris ran down the circular stairs, checking his pace only when he reached the bottom. The main level of the palace was a flurry of activity, servants carrying basins of water and bandages toward the rooms that served as the infirmary.

A scream of pain echoed down the corridor, groans and sobs growing louder as he approached. His heart throbbed, his breathing more labored than it should've been from the stairs as he entered the room, taking in the sight of soldiers sprawled on cots, physicians and their assistants working to stem the blood that seemed to coat most of the room.

Keris's eyes jumped from face to face, but none of them was his brother.

None of them was Otis.

A wave of dizziness washed over him, then a loud voice in the distance said, "I'm going to kill that Anaphora girl, mark my words! The next time, she's not walking away unscathed!"

A wave of relief forced Keris to catch his balance against the wall as the world swam. Giving his head a shake, he rounded a corner, finding his brother in the adjoining chamber with several other soldiers, a physician engaged with stitching up a nasty gash along Otis's left bicep.

Crossing his arms, Keris leaned against the doorframe. "Things not go well?"

Otis's gaze flicked to him, then he swore and moved his glower to the physician. "I've known tailors to show more care with fabric than you currently show my flesh."

"Perhaps if you refrained from gesticulating until he's finished . . . ?" Keris gave his brother a smirk, then laughed when Otis flipped him his middle finger. He could handle his brother's annoyance because he was *alive*.

"They were waiting for us, Keris. Had an ambush ready the moment we stepped away from the boats."

"How could they have known where you were landing?" Keris asked, because not asking would be strange.

"I'm not sure they did." Otis clenched his teeth as the physician ran the needle through again. "It appears they anticipated a raid by sea and moved the majority of their forces to defend the coast. Though they would've had to leave the east exposed to do it." He shook his head, brow furrowed. "A bold move. If we'd gone by land instead of sea, we could have struck a significant blow against them."

She'd trusted him. The realization settled into Keris's core, sending a spill of emotion through him that he didn't entirely understand. Such a simple act, and yet it had saved how many innocent lives? "What will be our next move?"

"Attack again." His brother pulled his bloodied shirt over his now-bandaged arm. "And soon."

He'd known it wouldn't just take one stymied raid to stop the cycle, but Keris still struggled not to grind his teeth at his brother's response. The stubborn refusal to see any path forward but war. "When?"

Otis rubbed at his temples, then frowned, focusing on him. "Since when do you care?"

Shit. "Given you nearly got yourself killed, it's a matter of personal interest. You're the only person in Nerastis that I don't have to pay to tolerate my presence, and I'd feel your absence keenly."

The frown didn't smooth from his brother's brow. "You should attend the next raid. You need not be in the thick of it, but it would be good for morale to have you there after this mess."

Keris laughed. "Now, there's a jest."

His brother sighed. "The men believe that you look down upon them, Keris. That you see them as lesser than you for a myriad of reasons. And I understand how they feel, for you treat me in much the same way."

Keris's hands turned cold, his stomach hollowing because he could hear the hurt in his brother's voice. It made him feel ill; there were only a small handful of individuals dear to Keris, and Otis was one of them. "I hold you in high esteem, and you damn well know it."

"No, you don't."

Bewilderment flooded him, because for all they'd butted heads over a million topics during the course of their lives, never had he given his brother cause to believe he didn't hold him in the greatest of regard.

Before he could answer, Otis said, "You have pit yourself against Father, no matter how much it costs you, and the only people you hold in esteem are those who also stand in defiance against him. Which means you esteem no one, for the rest of us aren't so willing to risk our lives for ideologies that only work on paper."

This was utter bullshit. He admired his brother, respected his talents even if they weren't the sort he aspired to himself. "That's—"

"The truth, Keris. And most days I admire your stubbornness, but today . . ." Otis gave a sharp shake of his head. "It doesn't matter. Just go back to your books, brother. Forget I asked anything of you."

Except he *had* asked.

All their lives, Otis had been the only one of his brothers to accept Keris's refusal to fight. To accept his abhorrence of violence and war, even if he didn't agree with it. Had defended him against everyone who'd tried to force him to change and protected his back from those who'd tried to kill him for refusing to do so.

What had changed?

Keris knew the answer without asking. He was acceptable to Otis as a brother, but not as an heir. Not as a king. And now that he was heir and in line to become king, Otis, like everyone else, would try to force him to be just like their father.

Keris swallowed the rising ache of grief that threatened to strangle him. He couldn't stand the thought of losing his brother, but neither was he willing to concede everything he stood for. And with Otis's hatred of Valcotta, there was no chance that he'd be able to convince his brother to pursue peace.

But maybe . . . maybe he could convince him of the merits of avoiding war. For his brother was no fool. If the cost of raiding became too high, the loss of soldiers' lives too great, he'd desist. And while a stalemate wasn't the same thing as peace, the results might well be the same. "I'll think about it. The raid."

Otis's eyes widened in disbelief. "*You'll* fight?"

I'll fight, Keris silently replied. *Just not the battle you think.* "I was thinking a more observational role, but if I must." He crossed his arms. "Just . . . just keep me informed of the plans. You know I hate having things sprung upon me."

"I'll involve you with every decision." Genuine pleasure filled Otis's dark eyes, more proof that his brother wanted him to be someone other than who he was. But Keris shoved down the hurt. "You'll have to excuse me now, for I can feel dawn starting to warm the sky, which means it's time for me to go to bed."

"Thank you for this concession, Keris. You won't regret it—not once you've earned the loyalty of the men."

Keris walked away without answering. When it came to standing in defiance of his father, he'd never once conceded.

And never would.

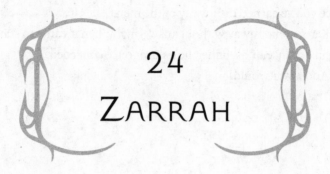

24
ZARRAH

CHEERS MET ZARRAH AND HER SOLDIERS AS THEY RODE BACK into Nerastis, word that they'd repelled the Maridrinian raid having flown ahead of them. Civilians and soldiers alike lined the streets, hands held to their hearts in respect for those who'd fought, those who'd died, and those who'd come home victorious.

Zarrah could feel the shift in sentiment in her soldiers. Far too often, they arrived on the heels of a raid, too late to do anything but step over the bodies of dead civilians as they pursued the Maridrinians back across the border. But this had been a good, clean fight, and instead of heading straight to the war room to make plans for retaliation, nearly everyone wandered off in search of leisure or sleep, only Bermin following her as she went to her office, a healer waiting to stitch up the deep cut on her arm.

"They sing your praises." He closed the door behind him. "Victory is sweet, but you and I both know this was luck. If the Maridrinians had come by land, it would have been a very different story."

"What is it you want, cousin?" What *she* needed was sleep, yet what she *wanted* was the sun to be setting, not rising, so that she could meet the Maridrinian at the dam. Already her pulse thrummed, anticipation distracting her as the healer unraveled the sticky bandages and set to cleaning the wound, which stung but wasn't deep enough to be of particular concern.

The chair across from her creaked as Bermin settled his bulk into it, the dark bruises on his throat vivid in the sunlight shining through the window behind her. Blood from the battle splattered his clothing, and between the two of them, the room was beginning to reek.

"How did you know?" he finally asked, leaning back, his arms crossed behind his head. "You wouldn't have left us so exposed if you weren't certain."

Zarrah shrugged, the healer muttering in annoyance as she fumbled one of the stitches. "After your actions, a significant retaliation was inevitable. With little moon, it's easier to transport a larger force at speed via the sea. I had our spies in the Maridrinian palace watch the stables and inform me if horses left."

"They take horses out all the time on patrol."

"Senior Maridrinian officers don't condescend to ride patrol, cousin. But they do love the glory of a raid—it was their horses that I had watched."

Bermin's brow furrowed, and he rubbed thoughtfully at the few days of stubble darkening his chin. "How did you know it would be last night?"

"I didn't." She lifted one hand. "My intent was to keep watch over the shores until the moon lit the sky, then once again split our patrols between east and west. Was only luck that they came the first night we stood watch."

"Luck." He dropped his hand from his chin. "Didn't feel like luck, little Zarrah."

God, but she *hated* when he called her that. "If you have a point to make, make it. Otherwise, if you'll excuse me, I've reports requiring my attention."

"So diligent." He smiled. "When do we attack again?"

Because this hadn't been *his* victory, it had been hers.

"We don't." Zarrah nodded at the healer, who'd finished working on her arm and was now leaving the room. "As you said yourself, pride will send them back across the Anriot, and I intend to meet them head-on. No more of us arriving minutes too late to save the lives of those we are supposed to protect, Bermin. Until the empress orders otherwise, we will defend our borders. Nothing more."

His nostrils flared, wheels turning in his dark eyes. Then he shrugged. "I live by your will, General."

Liar, she thought, but only smiled, watching as he left the room.

THE MARIDRINIAN WAS WAITING WHEN she arrived at the dam, both of them carrying muted lanterns in deference to the utter blackness of the moonless night.

"You were true to your word, Maridrina," she called across the gap, her pulse racing faster than the climb warranted.

"Such little faith." He set his lantern on the edge of the spillway. "Mark the edge for me, would you? I've no interest in shouting across a waterfall."

She set her lantern down on the edge, backing up to give him space but remaining close enough to catch his arm if he slipped. Fear bit into her chest as he retreated out of the faint glow of the lantern, his boots scraping against rock as he sprinted forward and leapt, little more than a shadow until he landed like a cat next to her lantern. And though he was steady, Zarrah caught him by the arm, pulling him away from the edge. "Don't you fear falling?"

He glanced back at the spillway, then shrugged. "Seems counterproductive. Besides, I won't be half so lucky as to die from a fall—it's just not in the cards."

She opened her mouth to ask what he *did* fear, then found herself not wanting to talk about such grim things. "They came exactly as you said they would. It was good information. Thank you."

"Should we be expecting retaliation?"

She shook her head, following suit as he sat on the edge of the dam, legs dangling. "It was a clean fight—and one which we won. It has contented spirits in the barracks, at least for a time." Inhaling, she wrinkled her nose. "Why do you smell like you just came from a brothel?"

He smirked. "Because I did."

A flicker of jealousy burned in her stomach, but before she could tell herself that she had no right to the emotion, he added, "I have an arrangement with one of the girls in order to give myself cover for my nocturnal wanderings, as I've no desire to be followed. Especially of late."

"And you think you can trust her?"

"I don't trust anyone. But she's a clever girl who knows it's in her best interest not to betray me, never mind that I pay her more for her silence than I would for her services." His elbow brushed the bare skin of her arm as he turned to look at her, sending prickles of sensation through her body. "Does no one notice your absence?"

"There's a rumor that I have a lover in the city." She shrugged one shoulder. "I don't discourage it."

"Do you?"

The question came out quickly, and Zarrah smiled at the darkness. "Jealous, Maridrina?"

He huffed out a breath. "I'm merely concerned for the longevity of your relationship with the poor sot, given you spend more nights than not here with me. He must seem very boring in comparison."

"You've a high opinion of yourself."

"I find false modesty tedious."

A laugh pulled from her lips, and when Zarrah turned her head, she found him watching her, his face serious. "Is something wrong?"

"No." His voice was soft. "Everything is far from wrong." Then he coughed and looked away. "Except in the case of your rumored lover. How long will he hover by the door, awaiting your attention, before resigning himself to the comfort of his right hand? I'm starting to feel guilty, which is typically only a sensation I burden myself with when I've received something in return."

Holding a hand to her mouth, Zarrah tried and failed to stifle another laugh. "Just what are you begging me for, Maridrina?"

"Release."

As her eyes widened, he laughed, teeth white in the darkness. "From the burden of guilt, Valcotta. Curb your filthy thoughts and tell me that I'm not keeping you from anyone so that I might sleep easy."

This was dangerous ground, and if she were smart, she'd stop things now before they went any further. Because already she felt like she was standing at the end of a precipice, knees bent and ready to leap. Yet she found herself saying, "Sleep easy, then. My nights are yours and yours alone."

He leaned closer, and her heart leapt with anticipation even as her skin flushed. But he only murmured into her ear, "And they say Valcottans are merciless."

A slight shudder ran through her, an ache building in her core. "Don't get used to it."

He chuckled, then rose in a smooth motion before reaching

down to pull her up, his gloved hand strong and warm against her naked palm. "My fellows are currently licking both wounds and pride, but the latter will drive them to move against Valcotta. Their plans are not fixed, but when they are, I need to be able to get word to you."

"Can you meet me again tomorrow night? At midnight?"

"Midnight." Lifting her hand, he brushed his lips against her knuckles, and then he turned away.

She didn't want him to go.

Didn't want this conversation to end.

"Maridrina?"

He looked over his shoulder. "Yes?"

This is insane, logic screamed at her. *Utterly and entirely foolish.*

But her heart said otherwise. "I don't suppose you'd like to get something to eat?"

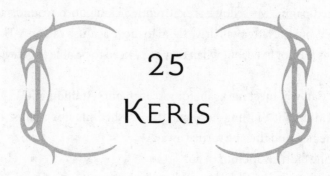

25
KERIS

YOU HAVE LOST YOUR BLOODY MIND, KERIS THOUGHT TO HIMSELF as he followed Valcotta down from the dam and into the enemy side of Nerastis. *If you get caught, a quick death is the best you can hope for.*

And a fool's hope, at that.

"Best to keep your hood up," she murmured. "There will be Maridrinians aplenty on our side at this time of night, but you're likely to draw some attention."

He smirked. "A hazard of being so attractive, I suppose."

Valcotta huffed out a breath of amusement, then pulled up her hood. "I was thinking of that blond hair of yours, but you're correct: Your ego burns bright as the sun."

Staggering sideways, Keris clutched at his chest but dutifully drew his hood forward to conceal his hair and shadow his face, tucking his gloves in a pocket because Valcottans didn't wear them. Which meant they both blended in as they wove through the broken streets lined with drinking establishments and opium dens and brothels, the majority of people keeping to the shadows of hoods and scarves as they pursued vice and sin.

And maybe he did fit in, for what was fraternizing with the enemy if not a sin? What was his addiction to her conversation if not a vice that was as likely to get him killed as anything the people in these parts consumed?

Yet he found himself unable to stop moving closer to her, inhaling her clean scent and allowing his eyes to drift over the hard curve of her bottom as she climbed over a stretch of rubble. She turned and offered him a hand, and his pulse roared at the sensation of her skin against his, palm callused from combat, though the top was as smooth as silk. The last thing he wanted was to let go, but not even he was bold enough to walk hand in hand with a Valcottan soldier on this side of the Anriot. "Where are we going?"

"I know a place."

She turned down a dark alley, stepping over refuse, rats skittering ahead of them. It was dark and smelled terrible, the walls to either side teetering precariously. "You haven't brought me here to do me in, have you, Valcotta?"

"We'll see how the night goes." She turned to face him, the torchlight from the street illuminating her face, so painfully lovely his breath caught in his throat.

Imagine what she'd say if she knew who you were? The thought soured his stomach, and he looked away.

Valcotta's head tilted. "What's wrong?"

Nothing. And everything. "I don't like rats."

"Then you must really dislike your king."

More than you know, he thought, allowing her to take his hand and tug him forward.

"We're nearly there."

There was a tiny common room that smelled of cooking, tobacco, and the dark ale the Valcottans favored. The roof had collapsed at some point in the past, and boards were stretched across to replace it, from which dangled strings of colored lanterns. Like on the Maridrinian side, the furniture was scavenged and thus mismatched. There were six groups of patrons, but unlike most establishments, none were gambling and all were eating.

Valcotta pulled him down into a chair at one of the empty tables, a stout old woman appearing a moment later to set a stub of candle in front of them. "You're wanting to eat, then? Pay first."

Valcotta smiled, and Keris found the world fading to a blur as he examined her face in the candlelight, the soft glow illuminating her smooth skin and rounded cheeks, her bottom lip enticingly plump. And her eyes. Wide and dark and rimmed with thick lashes. He stared at them while she ordered and generously paid the old woman.

Then Valcotta focused on him, gaze expectant, and Keris found himself grasping for something to say. Theirs were always conversations of a forbidden nature, not things they could discuss surrounded by people. Yet idle chatter felt no more fitting, like the only conversation there could be between them were topics dear to the heart. "You're beautiful."

As soon as the words were out, Keris cursed himself, because he was normally better at this. Better at knowing exactly what to say to make women smile and laugh and eventually fall into bed with him. Except with her, he found himself wanting more.

She doesn't even know your name.

"We haven't even had a drink yet," she said with a laugh. "I wonder what you might say when the ale begins to flow."

His cheeks burned. "Bad poetry, I expect. Later I might sing, and the shame I'll feel come dawn will mean I can never see you again, so perhaps I should drink water."

"If you drink the water served here, you will suffer more than shame; that I promise."

The proprietor returned with ale, setting the glasses of dark liquid between them. Keris took a mouthful, the cool, bitter drink welcome on his tongue. He waited for the woman to depart, then asked, "Do you like it? Soldiering?"

She drained half her glass. "Yes. I like the order and routine of it, and I like defending my country." Her head tilted sideways. "What exactly is your role here? And don't say soldiering, because I'll know that's a lie."

This was dangerous territory. For while he was far from the only useless nobleman loitering about the palace, if he said too much, she might suspect his identity. "I'm a spy."

She blinked, and he laughed. "I'm jesting. The best spies are those with unmemorable faces, which we've already established is not the case for me. The truth is, I'm an administrator—I keep the palace books in order. I was selected because I have perfect spelling, grammar, and penmanship."

Her eyes narrowed. "That's a lie."

"Only part of it. My penmanship is as flawless as my face."

"Fine." She rested her chin on one hand, eyes narrowed. "What do you like to do when you *aren't* doing the thing you won't confess to?"

Treason, Keris thought even as he said, "I like to ride."

One of her eyebrows rose. "Ride . . . ?"

"Horses, Valcotta. Get your mind out of the gutter. Fast horses." He paused as the proprietor set a platter of food between them, all of it unfamiliar. "I like climbing and gambling and reading."

"Reading?" She leaned forward. "That . . . I didn't expect that." Then she frowned. "Or maybe I did. What do you read about?"

Her reaction eased the tension that had formed in his shoulders, because he was used to the admission eliciting sneers and derision. Which he'd long since stopped caring about, but from her . . . "I like to read about what other people think."

"Think about what?" She picked up a piece of what appeared to be a fried bread of sorts, then took a delicate bite.

"Anything. Everything." He examined the food, feeling disarmed by her question, though he didn't know why. "If one only knows one's own mind on things, does one really know anything at all?"

"I'd never thought of it that way." Her brow furrowed. "When I was a girl, I read a great deal. But it's been an age since I've picked up a book."

"Why did you stop?"

"My mother died." She gave a sharp shake of her head. "I . . . When she died, I dedicated myself to becoming someone who couldn't be hurt like she'd been hurt. And I suppose part of that was setting aside anything that didn't help me achieve that goal." She hesitated. "My aunt encouraged my dedication, facilitated it, so all my time was spent learning to fight. And perhaps that was to my detriment."

Keris didn't comment, sensing that she was lost to her thoughts on the matter, and instead sampled some of the food. They ate in silence for a long time, and only once the old woman had taken away the trays and refilled their glasses did he say, "All the books didn't disappear from the world because your young self decided to abandon them. They are still waiting for you."

"I wouldn't know where to start." She sipped at her ale. "Or where to find the time."

"What about right now?" Unfastening his coat, he reached inside and pulled a small volume from the inner pocket.

"You have one *with you*?"

"Always." He dragged his chair around so that he was seated

right next to her, deeply aware of how her leg brushed against his, feeling the heat of her through his trousers. "This is a book about stars."

She frowned. "What about them?"

"What they mean. Or groups of them mean, I suppose is more accurate. It's a translated text from one of the nations north of Harendell, where they believe the stars tell the stories of their ancestors." Pulling the candle in front of them, he held the book behind it so that the tiny script and sketched diagrams were illuminated. Flipping through the pages, he paused when the sight of a constellation in the shape of a whale caused her to lean forward with interest. Smiling, he read the story to her.

And as he read, Valcotta leaned into him, her knee brushing his and her shoulder resting against his chest, the scent of her hair ensuring that none of the words he read registered in his mind.

None of this would be happening if she knew who you were.

The thought caused him to stumble on a word, and he snapped the book shut. "If I read any more in this bad light, I'll blind myself."

She looked up at him, her eyes searching his and making him profoundly grateful for how the darkness turned everything to shades of gray. "You read well."

"Practice. I've a number of female relatives who enjoy stories." As soon as the words slipped his lips, Keris cursed himself for the carelessness that came with too much drink, but she only asked, "You've many?"

More than I can name. "Enough that Nerastis seems peaceful by comparison."

Valcotta laughed, her eyes shining with delight, and then she froze, her gaze going to the entrance.

And that's when he heard it.

The solid thump of a large group walking with purpose, and

then a female voice shouting, "We're conducting a roundup, loves! Show us your faces, and if your faces be Maridrinian, you better start running now!"

Fuck.

"Goddammit!" Valcotta dumped a handful of coins on the table, then grabbed his hand and dragged Keris across the space. "Is there another way out?" she demanded of the proprietor.

"Through the kitchen." The woman smirked. "Better run fast."

They stumbled through the tiny kitchen, Keris nearly overturning a barrel in his haste. Then they were in a narrow alley, refuse squishing beneath their feet as they sprinted to the end. Instead of racing into the street, Valcotta slid to a stop, Keris nearly knocking her over. God help him, he was too drunk for this.

"Shit," she hissed. "There's a patrol out there."

And staying where they were wasn't an option, because from behind them, he heard the old woman announce, "A rat went scampering that way."

"Climb!" He caught Valcotta by the waist, lifting her up to a narrow window, which she scrambled inside before reaching down.

"There he is!"

Keris shoved the book he still held inside his coat and jumped, catching her hand and praying she was strong enough to hold his weight.

He was a fool to have doubted her, because Valcotta heaved, drawing him high enough that he could reach the sill. Keris hauled himself in as the patrol raced down the alley toward them.

"He's in the building! Go! Go!"

He landed on top of Valcotta, but she rolled him off, whispering, "We need to get to the roof. They'll surround the building and then come inside."

Heart racing, Keris climbed to his feet and took her hand, leading her cautiously through the darkness until he found a set of partially collapsed stairs. Balancing on the banister, he jumped to catch hold of the upper level, clenching his teeth as the floor groaned beneath his weight. Valcotta followed, and they eased across the floor to where the roof had collapsed, the sounds of the patrol entering the building echoing from below.

The entire structure seemed to shift and move as Keris climbed out onto what remained of the roof, keeping to the shadows so as not to be seen by those below. "Which way?" he asked softly as Valcotta joined him, her eyes panning the rooftops.

"We'll have to be fast," she murmured. "Keep up and don't fall." Then she jumped.

"They're on the roof!" Keris heard the shout as he leapt after Valcotta. He rolled across the neighboring roof, on his feet in a flash and running. Adrenaline drove away the effects of the ale, but he was still hard-pressed to keep up. Valcotta raced across the rooftops, pausing only occasionally to listen for pursuit before sprinting onward.

By the time she pulled him down in the shadows next to a broken chimney, Keris was panting for breath.

"We wait here," she said softly. "They'll have given up by now in favor of easier catches, so we need only wait until they've rounded up the quota and you can get out of the city."

It had to be close to the third hour of the morning, which meant only a few more hours until dawn. If he didn't get back across the Anriot before then, he'd be stuck. And once his escort came knocking at Aileena's door and realized Keris was not in with the courtesan, there'd be a panic.

Yet as Valcotta leaned back against the rubble next to him, her hip pressing against his, Keris couldn't find it in himself to regret coming with her.

"I take it this roundup wasn't planned?" he asked.

"No." Her tone was sour. "Smacks of Bermin's doing."

The familiar way she spoke of the Valcottan prince piqued his interest. "You don't care for His Royal Highness?"

"He's an idiot fueled by pride rather than intelligence," she scoffed.

"Most princes are."

Her body shook with a silent chuckle, but then a cold south wind blew over them, and she shivered. Pulling off his coat, he handed it to her. "Here."

"That hardly seems fair."

"It's fine. The cold doesn't bother me." Which wasn't the slightest bit true. He was Maridrinian and despised being chilled. But she didn't need to know that.

Valcotta took the garment, toying with the sleeve for a moment before slipping it on.

Then she shifted so that they were pressed together. His heart leapt, and after a moment's hesitation, he put his arm around her shoulders, drawing her against him. The flickers of desire that had been tempered by the pursuit of patrols flared back to life, but he kept his hands to places that would cause no offense.

It was a clear night, the stars an ocean of sparkles, and taking her hand, he used her finger to trace a constellation. "Do you see it?"

"The whale." There was wonder in her voice. "So strange to think we can see the same shapes in the sky as those living half a world away, and in the seeing know the stories of people we've never met."

"Some of them." He traced the outline of a bear. "Some you can only see in certain parts of the world. Or at certain times of the year."

"Why?"

"I don't know." Their fingers interlocked, and his eyes moved from the stars to their hands, taking in the image of it. Committing it to memory lest it never happen again. "Perhaps there is some higher power that knows which stars we need to see when we look up, which stories we need to hear. That knows which constellations will lure us to travel the world so that we might see them with our own eyes, adding them to the map of sparks in our minds."

"A map of where we've been," she murmured.

"And where we might go." He lowered his arm, keeping hold of her hand as he turned to look at her.

Kiss her.

God help him, but he wanted to. But he wouldn't do it unless she asked, and she had not. Very likely would not.

"Where would you go?" she asked. "If you could?"

Always, the answer had been somewhere, anywhere, other than where he was. To escape.

But that had changed. "If I had the choice to be anywhere in the world, I would choose right here."

She exhaled a soft breath, half laughter and half surprise, then curled tighter against his side as the wind gusted over them. "Show me another shape in the sky."

Keris scoured his memory for every constellation he knew, which was many, for he'd always been the sort to look up and see things others didn't. He spoke until his voice grew hoarse and her breathing deepened, her arm growing limp as her head drifted down against his chest, sleep taking her.

For a long time, he remained still, holding her against him and listening to the city grow quiet as the soldiers retreated back to the garrison. Soon there was only the sound of the wind and the warmth of her breath against his throat.

You need to go, he told himself. *You need to get back before you are missed.*

But he didn't want to leave her. Didn't want to let go of this woman who should be his enemy and yet had somehow become the one person he could trust with everything.

Except his name.

Chest aching, Keris eased his arm out from under her, gently lowering her head so that it was cushioned by the hood of his coat. Then, with the faint glow in the east beginning to light the sky, he traced a word in the soot of the broken chimney before abandoning the building to race the dawn back to his side of the Anriot.

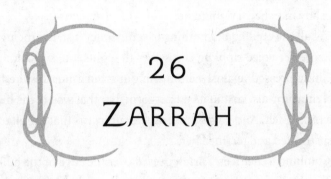

26
ZARRAH

She woke to the light of dawn glowing in her eyes, a slow smile rising to her lips as she turned her head.

Only to find herself alone on the rooftop.

Zarrah's stomach hollowed, but then her eyes latched onto a word written in large letters in the soot stains on the chimney.

Midnight.

Warmth filling her, she pulled the collar of the Maridrinian's coat up, inhaling the spicy scent of his cologne. Heat flooded through her veins, chasing away the headache caused by too much ale and replacing it with an aching need that could only be satisfied in one way.

By one person.

"You've lost your mind," she muttered to herself. "And clearly forgotten the purpose of all this."

Forgotten the reason she was seeing him, which was to facilitate an end to raids across the border. To stop the senseless slaughter of civilians.

Not to fall in bed with a Maridrinian who was more handsome than any man had a right to be.

Yet all the chiding did nothing to temper her lust, the memory of his velvet voice rippling across her thoughts, the sensation of his body pressed against hers making her burn hot despite the cool morning air. Lust in its purest form, but that wasn't the limit of what she felt. And it was those other sentiments that simultaneously thrilled and terrified her.

Climbing to her feet, Zarrah peered over the edge of the building. Seeing it was clear of traffic in the alley below, she climbed down and headed toward the palace. Though she didn't want to give up the warmth of his coat, wearing it would raise questions, so she tucked the expensive leather under one arm.

But she took the book out of his pocket first.

As she walked through the streets, Zarrah flipped through the pages, her eyes drifting over the writing, the stories making her smile.

It was a forgotten joy, reading for pleasure.

One of many things she'd given up in her desire to be strong, in her desire for vengeance, in her desire to please her aunt.

When was the last time she'd done something for no reason other than it made her happy?

Seeing an approaching patrol, Zarrah tucked the book back into the pocket, nodding at her soldiers as they stopped to salute. More salutes as she strode through the empty gates, and Zarrah forced her thoughts to what needed to be accomplished. To the endless reports she needed to read and drills she needed to oversee.

"Where in the name of God have you been?" Hands closed over her shoulders, pulling Zarrah sideways into a corridor.

Yrina.

Her friend shook a finger in her face. "All damned night I've been searching for you, Zar. All. Night. Had to organize a bloody roundup to hide what I was doing, but you were nowhere to be found."

Zarrah opened her mouth to lie about where she'd been, but Yrina's eyes latched onto the Maridrinian's coat. "What's this?" She jerked it out of Zarrah's grip, holding it up. "This is a *man's* coat." Her fingers moved over the leather. "An *expensive* man's coat. Does it belong to your lover?"

"Give it back, Yrina." She reached for the coat, but her friend danced backward. "I borrowed it from a civilian friend and didn't have the chance to return it."

Yrina lifted the leather to her nose and inhaled. "Bergamot. Ginger. And red cedar, if my nose does not mistake it." She inhaled again, then rolled her eyes back, groaning. "My God, Zar. If you aren't sleeping with whoever owns this coat, there is something deeply wrong with you." Then she frowned. "Except this isn't . . . this isn't a Valcottan cut. It's—"

"Harendellian," Zarrah snapped, trying to curb the rising panic in her stomach. "And it takes more than expensive cologne to get my trousers off, Yrina. Now, perhaps you might explain *why* you organized a roundup of Maridrinians for the sake of tracking me down?"

All humor vanished from her friend's face. "Because *she's* here."

She. The empress. "When? And why? She was supposed to return to Pyrinat."

Yrina exhaled a long breath. "She does not keep me in her counsel, Zar. All I know is that she was not pleased to discover you absent, especially given no one knew *where* you were. And I'm not sure there is a lie in the world that's going to get you out of this one."

Shit. Zarrah closed her eyes, knowing that she'd gotten herself into this mess and had no one to blame but herself. "Put those in my room for me, please. Somewhere the servants won't find them."

"Those?" Yrina lifted one eyebrow, then fished the book out of the coat's pocket, reading the cover. Her other eyebrow rose to join its mate. "Stars," she murmured. "Color me intrigued." Then she wandered down the corridor, flipping through the pages of the Maridrinian's book.

Straightening her clothing and praying the smells of her prior night's activities didn't cling too strongly, Zarrah headed to the training yard to face her aunt.

Empress Petra of Valcotta stood at the center of the nearly empty yard, only her bodyguard, Welran, and a servant holding a pitcher of water in attendance. She wore training leathers, her eyes closed as she moved through the same exercises she'd completed every morning for as long as Zarrah had been alive.

Zarrah stopped at the edge of the sand, standing at attention while her aunt finished, trying to keep her racing heart in check. Not once had she disappointed her aunt, not like this. And though her aunt didn't know the half of what Zarrah had done, what she did know still smacked of defiance.

Which was something the empress had no tolerance for.

Without speaking, her aunt went to a rack of weapons and selected two staffs, one of which she tossed to the ground at Zarrah's feet before accepting a glass of water from the servant. Eyes on Zarrah, she drank deeply before setting the glass back on the tray.

Her mouth dry as the sand they stood upon, Zarrah retrieved the staff and moved to the center of the space, taking her position.

The empress attacked.

A blinding whirl of wood, which Zarrah barely managed to block, her arms shuddering from the impact. Then another and another, her aunt putting her on the defense and giving her no respite.

She never did.

At her best, Zarrah was barely a match for the older woman, who made up for the strength age had sapped with a lifetime of experience. But today, Zarrah was far from her best. She was exhausted from nights of little sleep, her body stiff from lying on a rooftop, and her mind sluggish from ale.

Crack.

The blow caught her across the ribs, ripping a gasp from her lips and sending her staggering. Zarrah rolled as her aunt swung at her again, trying to give herself the space to regain ground, but her aunt relentlessly pursued.

Crack.

Pain spidered down her hip and she staggered, struggling for balance, but her head was spinning with thirst. Her aunt hooked her leg, sending Zarrah toppling onto her back and knocking the wind from her lungs.

Before she could suck in a breath, her aunt's staff whirled, driving straight toward Zarrah's face. She lifted her own weapon to block the blow, but it tangled in her ankle, and she braced for the pain.

The staff stopped a fraction of an inch from her cheekbone.

"Shameful!" Her aunt threw the staff to the sand, then spat on it for good measure. "Not since you first picked up a weapon have you fought so poorly."

"Apologies, Your Imperial Majesty." Zarrah climbed to her feet, head lowered, stomach filled with self-loathing for having embarrassed herself so horribly. "I—"

"Oh, I know exactly what you've been up to, girl." Her aunt inhaled, then wrinkled her nose. "Rumpled, stinking of liquor and sweat and *man*, your eyes dull from lack of sleep." She rounded on Welran and the servant. "Leave us."

They departed without question, leaving Zarrah and her aunt alone in the silent yard. For a long moment, the empress said nothing, and Zarrah's mortification grew with every heartbeat. Her aunt had raised her, had given her everything she wanted and guided her on her chosen path. To her aunt, Zarrah's behavior must appear as though she were spitting in the face of all those gifts.

"I arrived to word of a great victory against the Maridrinians who dared to step onto our soil, victory delivered by my chosen heir," the empress slowly said. "An heir I expected to greet me with plans for how we might capitalize on this win. Except instead you were out drinking and rutting in the slums of the city like some common soldier. If I wanted an heir like that"—her voice rose— "I'd have named my own cursed son!"

Zarrah flinched, looking away. "One night's misstep. And one that will not happen again."

"Don't you lie to me!" Her aunt's palm cracked against her cheek, the pain making Zarrah's eyes water. "Don't you lie, girl. This was not the first night, nor even the second. Do you think you aren't watched?"

Zarrah's blood ran cold, though instinct told her that if the empress knew everything, she'd be on her way to be executed for treason.

Her aunt pressed her fingers to her temples, drawing in a deep breath. Then she fixed Zarrah with a steady gaze that seemed to see into her soul. "I know it is hard, dear one. Always having to hold yourself above the rest, never a moment's respite. I know what it's like to want to lose yourself in a lover's touch, or to drink and laugh until dawn with comrades. But those are pursuits denied women such as you and me. Women who rule, or who are destined to rule, must never let their guard down. Never lose their focus."

Zarrah gave a tight nod, knowing that her aunt lived by her words. That she held herself to the same standard of conduct.

"I don't want to lose you, my love." Her aunt stepped closer and cupped her cheek. "If I'm hard on you, know that is why. But if my path is no longer the one you wish to follow . . ."

"It is!" Alarm filled Zarrah's chest, fear that because of one mistake, her aunt would send her away. "It's all I want."

Liar, a voice whispered in her head, but she shoved it away.

Her aunt's eyes glinted liquid bright, and she scrubbed at them. "It's rare that you remind me of your mother, for she was ever impetuous. Ever seeking life's pleasures, no matter the risks that came with them. But you remind me of her today, and that terrifies me."

A tear rolled down her aunt's cheek, and Zarrah stared at it in horror, having never seen the empress weep before. To be the cause of such grief made her ill.

"It was your mother's recklessness that got her killed. I told her not to travel so close to the border. Told her it wasn't safe, but she was desperate to visit her lover, and he was to meet her there for an assignation."

Zarrah gaped, having never heard this before. "I don't remember a lover . . ."

"She hid her lovers from you out of respect for your father, may his soul rest in everlasting peace." Her aunt smoothed the fabric of her trousers. "Like yesterday, I remember the news reaching us in Nerastis that the villa had been raided by the Maridrinians. How my heart plummeted and fear took over as we rode as fast as we could." Her voice caught. "And when the wind blew over us, carrying that smell, I knew we were too late."

Zarrah's own eyes burned with tears, the words dragging up emotions that she fought so hard to keep buried.

"They'd lined the road with the bodies of every soul who lived at the villa." Her aunt's eyes were distant as she spoke. "I remember searching them for your face, praying that you'd escaped, that you were safe. And when I found you tied beneath your mother's body, covered in gore and flies, I thought I'd lost you." She sucked in a ragged breath. "And then you looked up at me."

Tears poured down Zarrah's cheeks, because that moment was burned into her soul. Her aunt, her empress, her savior.

"Silas Veliant stole my sister from me," her aunt said. "But he unwittingly gave me an heir who will carry on my legacy. Who will ensure that he and all his brood will pay for their crimes. Who will never put down her weapon in our Endless War." Her eyes bored into Zarrah's. "You *will* give me my vengeance, won't you, Zarrah? You *will* be my weapon against him, and all those that come after him?"

Zarrah swallowed hard but nodded. "Yes, Your Imperial Majesty. On my honor, vengeance will be yours."

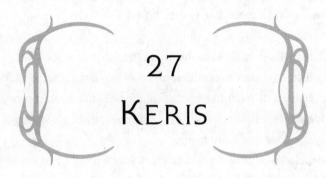

27
KERIS

THREE NIGHTS IN A ROW, MIDNIGHT HAD COME AND GONE WITH-
out Valcotta making an appearance.

The first night she hadn't shown, he'd been terrified something
had happened to her. That by leaving her alone on the roof as he
had, he'd unwittingly condemned her to a dark fate. Or that she'd
been identified as having been with him during the roundup and
was being punished. He'd debated going to the Valcottan side of
Nerastis to search for her before abandoning the notion. In the
city itself, it would be a needle in a haystack, and he was not fool
enough to go lurking about the garrison in the hopes of finding
her.

Those initial fears had diminished when he'd rooted through
reports from their spies the following day, none of which mentioned the death or punishment of a senior Valcottan officer. What
they *did* mention was that Empress Petra herself was back in
Nerastis. Her presence provided a probable explanation for Valcotta's absence on the second night, for some duties could not be

set aside. Yet by the third night, with the empress once again departed south, Keris began to question if Valcotta's absence was by choice.

If, for whatever reason, she no longer wanted to see him.

Which of course meant that his head was consumed with endless theories of what her reason might be. That she'd discovered his identity. Or he'd offended her in some manner. Or she'd gotten what she'd wanted from him.

Or what he'd revealed to her about himself wasn't to her liking.

"What did you think?" he muttered as he walked through Nerastis, having left Aileena eating candy and counting her coins in her room. "She's a soldier, and now she knows you're a scholar who carries books around in his pocket."

It would have been one thing if it had been about a serious topic, but of course it had been one about stars and silly folktales. Something to be read to children. He kicked a loose cobble, watching it spin off into the shadows, cursing himself for allowing her to see a part of himself that he normally kept hidden. For letting down the wall of sarcasm and indifference that years of mockery and contempt had forced him to build so high.

"This is the last night. If she isn't there, I'll know."

In truth, it was the last night he could risk it. Aileena had warned him that the hours he was supposedly spending in her company were raising eyebrows, her mistress going so far as to suggest he intended her for a formal mistress. And to be seen as holding that much of his favor would put the courtesan at risk.

Raina's sightless eyes flickered across his vision, and Keris squeezed his own shut for a heartbeat, sucking in deep breaths to control the twist of guilt in his stomach. It was better if Valcotta didn't come. Better if she stayed away from him.

And yet as he finally made it to the dam, he couldn't curb the swell of anticipation. The hope that he'd find her standing on the far side of the spillway.

Wasted hope, because as he rounded the curve of the dam, it was to find the edges of the spillway had crumbled on the Valcottan side, widening the gap to an impossible jump. Beyond, there was nothing but shadows.

28
ZARRAH

You must strive for perfection. Her aunt's parting words echoed in her ears. *To be above reproach so that no one will question your fitness to rule.*

For nearly four days, Zarrah had done just that. Up at dawn to complete her exercises, then to spar with Yrina, redeeming herself on the training ground, at least, before her aunt departed the city. She ran the garrison through endless drills, showing her soldiers no mercy, just as she showed herself no mercy as she sat at her desk for hours, combing through reports, eating while she worked, stopping only when the palace clocks struck the midnight hour.

For at that point, it would be too late.

Too late to venture out to the dam to see if he waited on the far side of the spillway. Too late to risk the temptation of his presence. Too late to question whether the path she walked was the one she wished her feet to remain upon.

Which was good, because in the darkest hours, it felt like her willpower crumbled. Felt like all the fantasies that daylight and duty had kept at bay gathered so as to overwhelm her the moment she was alone in her rooms. They drove her to pull his coat from where it was hidden deep in her wardrobe, the scent of him still clinging to the butter-soft leather. Compelled her to burn her lamp for hours past when she should be asleep, reading and rereading the book of stars and stories, the memory of his voice echoing through her head.

And now it was the fourth night since she'd slept in his arms on a Nerastis rooftop, the clock showing that it was nearly the midnight hour, and she knew if she went back to her rooms, it would be more of the same. "Enough, Zar," she snarled at herself. "You are acting like a lovesick girl, not a soldier. And certainly not like a general or heir to the throne."

She needed to put an end to this, once and for all.

Zarrah rose to her feet and stormed through the corridors, wrenching open the doors to her quarters. In three strides, she was across the room with her wardrobe open, coat and book in hand.

"Burn them." She stared at the objects in her hand. "Be done with this. Move on."

But the thought turned her hands to ice and hollowed out her core. "Why?" she demanded softly. "They are just *things*. And not even particularly valuable things."

Which was true, but the thoughts and emotions they inspired *were* valuable. *Too valuable* for her to cast aside or destroy.

Give them back, then.

Zarrah chewed on the insides of her cheeks. There was little chance he'd be at the dam, for not only had nights passed since they'd planned to meet, but it would also be past midnight when she arrived. She could leave the coat and the book weighted down with a few rocks, and he'd either eventually come to find them or . . . not. Either way, there was a finality to leaving them.

Decision made, Zarrah turned her thoughts to how she might see it done. There was no chance the empress hadn't left orders that she—and her windows and doors—be watched, which meant she was going to need help getting out.

Tucking book and coat under her arm, Zarrah left her rooms, making her way down the hall to Yrina's much more modest quarters, where she knocked at the door. Cursing and swearing emanated through the wood, but then the door opened to reveal her sleep-rumpled friend. At the sight of her, Yrina straightened, eyes sharpening. "What's wrong? Has something happened?"

"No, nothing." Easing into the room, Zarrah went to the window and looked out. "I need a favor."

"Can I do whatever it is in the morning?" Yrina's eyes went to the leather coat rolled under her arm. "Ah."

"I need to return these things. And to end . . . *it*."

"It?" Yrina lifted her eyebrows. "You mean your *friendship* with the man that smells like leather and spice and reads books about stars?"

Zarrah's cheeks burned hot. "Correct."

Silence stretched between them, then Yrina said, "Are you sure?"

"Yes. I know it's risky with my aunt's spies watching my every move, but I need to do it. So I need you to cover for me."

"I meant," Yrina said slowly, "are you sure you want to end it?"

"Of course I am." The words tore from her lips before Zarrah had a chance to think about whether they were true. "Why wouldn't I be?"

She wasn't sure if the question was for Yrina or herself.

She'd dedicated her life to achieving victory in the Endless War. To avenging her mother's murder at any cost. To carrying on her aunt's legacy by making Valcotta strong. Seeing the Maridrinian ran counter to all of that.

Didn't it?

"I don't know . . ." Yrina said. "Maybe because these past weeks are the first time I've seen you this happy."

Happy. It was as though a missing piece fell into place, finally providing an explanation for what it was she was giving up. Not a coat or a book, but a feeling that had been absent in her life. Zarrah wanted to scream with frustration, because this wasn't what should make her feel happy. It should be achieving goals and winning victories, not staring up at a starry sky and dreaming of a world with no more war, no more bloodshed. "You're reading more into this than you should."

"I don't think I am." Dark-brown eyes fixed Zarrah with a steady gaze. "I think you're ending it because the empress is making you, not because you wish it."

"She didn't ask me to end anything." What she'd asked was for Zarrah to not lose sight of the thing most important to her: avenging her mother's death. Because her aunt knew that if she didn't achieve that goal, it would weigh upon her soul.

Yrina cast her eyes skyward. "Perhaps not in so many words, but there isn't a person in the palace who doesn't know how her temper flared over you deigning to give yourself *one night* of liberty after our victory. She controls every aspect of your being, Zar, and has since your mother died."

Frustration boiled in her stomach that her friend was so badly missing the mark. Why didn't Yrina understand that the empress teaching Zarrah to control herself wasn't the same as controlling her? "She's trying to ensure I have the skills necessary to rule Valcotta!"

"No, she's trying to ensure that even after she's in the grave, she'll still rule, for she will have created an heir exactly like her!"

Zarrah's temper burned hot, because Yrina, of all people, knew that she had no tolerance for harsh words against the empress.

Her aunt was her savior, the one who'd given her life and purpose after everything had been stolen from her. Who'd named Zarrah heir instead of her own son. Visions of her aunt weeping when she'd believed that Zarrah was losing her path filled her mind's eye, carrying with them guilt and grief from knowing she hadn't just disappointed her empress but herself. "You're out of line."

"Am I?" Yrina paced back and forth across the room. "I've watched how she's groomed you, Zar. How she's made certain that you have nothing in your life beyond the goals and priorities that she's set for you, so that she can threaten you with taking them away and leaving you with *nothing*. How she makes you feel as though you have *no one* but her, that no one cares for you like she does. And I hate that awful look of adoration that climbs on your face whenever she walks into the room, because it's clear to me and everyone else that she's manipulating you!"

"My aunt loves me!" Zarrah snarled.

Yrina snorted. "Love, you say? She's got an interesting way of showing it, given that the moment she got wind that there might be someone else in your life, she arrived to put an end to it."

"To focus me!"

"To control you! That bitch is incapable of love."

Fury raged through Zarrah's veins. "Mind your tongue, Yrina, or find yourself deprived of it."

Yrina didn't so much as blink. "Those are *her* words. *Her* threats. Always spoken when anyone dares to offer an opinion contrary to her own."

That wasn't true. Her aunt had advisors whose counsel she heeded, and she always allowed Zarrah to speak her mind.

But does she ever listen?

"I don't know who this man is, Zarrah," Yrina said softly. "And I don't know if it's something he's done or said or if he's just that good a lover, but he's changed you." She hesitated. "No, not *changed.* He's just caused you to remember who you really are. So don't think it a coincidence the empress showed up when she did."

Was that true? Zarrah immediately rejected the thought as lunacy. The empress was not so controlling as to toss aside travel plans solely to police her niece's idle hours; she'd merely taken the opportunity to refocus her while she was here on other matters.

Except . . . what had those other matters been?

What had been the reason her aunt had returned to Nerastis?

It occurred to Zarrah for the first time that none had been given, and she'd been so caught up in regaining her aunt's favor that she'd not noticed the visit was rather purposeless. "Thank you for your insight." Her voice was colder than she'd intended, but it was better than betraying her unease. "Now, will you cover for me, or do I need to take my chances alone?"

"Of course I will." Yrina's shoulders slumped, and she ran one hand through her curly hair. "Go. End it, if that's what *you* want."

Except it wasn't so simple as that, which Yrina would have understood if she'd known the truth of who this man was.

You don't even know who he is, the voice in her head whispered. *You don't even know his name.* "I won't be long."

Yrina caught her wrist. "I love you, Zar. I only want you to be happy; please remember that."

"I love you, too." And though there was more she should have said, some acknowledgment that there was perhaps some truth to her friend's words, Zarrah said nothing, only slipped out the window into the night.

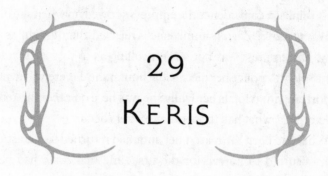

29
KERIS

You should go.

A refrain that had repeated in his head for what had to be over an hour, yet Keris remained sitting on the damp rock of the dam, his eyes fixed on the shadows of the opposite side, now out of reach. And it wasn't only Valcotta who was out of reach, but the dream she'd ignited in him that he could be something more than what he was. Someone better. Leaving felt like he'd be giving up not only on her but on himself.

She's not coming. And you are what you are.

Keris rose to his feet, turning from the spillway. But as he did, the shadows stirred. Freezing in place, he held his breath, waiting. And she appeared.

"I brought your things," she called over the roar of the water. "I should've brought them sooner. I'm sorry."

He eyed her for a moment, then called back, "You're not here because of a coat and book, Valcotta."

Looking anywhere but at him, she was silent. Then she lifted her beautiful face, shadowed eyes latching onto his. "Seeing you, speaking to you . . . it's forbidden. You are Maridrinian, which means you are supposed to be my enemy."

Something had happened. Something had changed. "*Supposed to be.*" He tilted his head. "Except I'm not."

"You are!" Not even the waterfall was loud enough to drown out the frustration in her voice. "If we met on the battlefield, I'd kill you without thought."

"Handily, I'm sure. I'm not a particularly gifted fighter." Sarcasm pushed its way into his voice despite his best intentions because her words stung. "If you don't want to be here, then why are you?"

"To tell you it's over. To say goodbye. To give you back your goddamned things so I don't have to look at them!"

"Well, you've said it, then. And the gap between us has grown too large to jump, so feel free to toss said things over the edge if they cause you such consternation. I care not."

"Fine." She tossed his coat into the falls, and Keris cursed under his breath because he'd *liked* that coat. But when she held up the book, clearly intending to throw it next, he found himself stepping forward. Not because of the book itself, for it was neither rare nor expensive, but because of what it represented. A moment that he didn't want thrown into a spillway to be lost and forgotten.

Valcotta hesitated, withdrawing her outstretched hand to press the book against her chest, the simple action making his own chest ache.

"What is it that needs to end, Valcotta?" he called across the water. "What part terrifies you so much? Because I don't think it's me."

Her shadowy form shivered. "You don't understand. I need to *be* a certain way. I need to *think* a certain way. Because if I don't, not only do I risk losing everything I've worked for, but I risk losing myself."

"Or maybe you'll find yourself." His hands balled into fists, and he wasn't sure if he was talking to Valcotta or to himself. "You told me once that if you truly believe in something, you should be willing to suffer for it. To die for it. Well, I think that if you truly believe in something, you should *live* for it."

Valcotta stiffened, staring at him, then she twisted on her heel and strode down the dam.

He'd pushed too hard, and in doing so, had pushed her away. Keris shoved his hands through his hair, desperately searching for the right thing to say to get her to come back. "Valcotta, wait!"

She slid to a stop and turned to face him, and his heart leapt. Then she shouted, "Back up."

Back up? Realization slapped him in the face. "Valcotta, no! Valcotta, it's too far!" But she was already sprinting toward the gap. A gap a full foot wider than it had been the last time she'd failed to make the leap. "Stop!"

She jumped.

30
ZARRAH

BOOK STILL CLUTCHED IN HER HAND, ZARRAH SPRINTED TOWARD the gap. It drew closer with every step, the blackness seeming an impossible distance to leap, the deadly water rushing through it fighting the volume of her thundering heart for supremacy.

"Stop!"

Gathering herself, Zarrah took one final stride, and without hesitation, she jumped. She flew across the gap, stumbling slightly as she hit the far side. And then his arms were around her, pulling her away from the edge.

"Have you lost your mind?"

His breath was warm against her face, and she tilted her head up to meet his gaze even as she inhaled the scent of spice filling her nose. "An unreasonable accusation, given how often you jump across, Maridrina."

"That's different." He still hadn't let her go, his grip on her arms tight, their bodies only inches apart. Except those inches felt like miles when what she wanted was the press of him against her. To experience in the flesh what she'd only felt within the confines of her dreams.

"Why is it different?"

He exhaled softly. "Because watching you jump was the most terrifying moment of my life." And before she could answer, his lips descended on hers.

What her imagination had conjured was a pale shade to the sensation of his mouth on hers, the kiss fierce with terror and desire, the intensity making her knees tremble. Still holding the book, she wrapped her arms around his neck, eliminating those cursed inches between them, her fingers pulling loose the tie holding back his hair, the locks that spilled around his face like silk against her skin.

His hands moved from her shoulders, sliding down to the small of her back even as their lips parted, his tongue delving into her mouth and chasing over hers with soft strokes that Zarrah swore she felt down to her core. Shivers burst over her skin, a tight, curling sensation filled her belly, and an aching pulse rose in intensity between her thighs. Then he pulled away, resting his forehead against hers. "Not here, Valcotta," he murmured. "If I'm going to have you, it will be somewhere I can do it properly and without interruption."

It was madness to consider going into the city with him. She was a general and the future empress of Valcotta, and he was a Maridrinian whose name she didn't even know. But none of that felt as important as the need to have his lips back against hers and his body between her legs. "Where should we go?"

WITH HER HAND IN HIS, the Maridrinian led her through Nerastis, the people filling the streets paying them no attention, their minds all on their own pleasures. They stopped in front of a building less derelict than most and he took her inside, the main floor dimly lit by a handful of lamps.

"Room," he said to the greasy man sitting behind a counter eating equally greasy pastries.

"An hour?"

The Maridrinian snorted, then said, "The rest of the night," and Zarrah's stomach flipped, a fresh rush of desire making her skin burn hot.

The greasy man rolled his eyes. "Lass like that and you'll be down in half an hour, but it's your silver coin."

The Maridrinian didn't answer, only sent a piece of silver flipping through the air, then caught the key the man tossed to him in return.

Zarrah's heart pounded in anticipation as he led her up the stairs and then down the hall, fumbling with the lock and nearly dropping the key before he got the door open, the slip making her smile.

The room was large, the walls and floors bare, but the bed beneath the window looked clean enough to justify the ridiculous price, the thin curtains above it blowing on the breeze. A single table held a lamp, and as she watched, the Maridrinian turned the flame up high, allowing her to see him more fully than she ever had before.

He was paler than most of his countrymen, who tended to darken in the sun, his shoulder-length hair a dark blond that reminded her of fields of wheat. His eyes were light, although their exact hue was lost in the shadows that danced across his face. And that face . . . He was beautiful in a way that defied reason, that made her want to stop and stare. That made her want to touch him again, if only to prove he was real. "You really ought to spend more time in the sun."

A slow smile rose to his face. "But all the best things happen at night."

The velvet tone of his voice tightened something deep in her core, suggesting that tonight, at least, he was right.

They circled each other, Zarrah setting the book on the table before unfastening the harness that held her staff to her back and dropping it to the ground, her knives following suit.

With her past lovers, all had been conducted in the dark, for she'd never felt comfortable being exposed. But with him, she felt different. She'd already exposed her soul to him, and Zarrah *wanted* him to see the rest of her.

So she moved to the buckles of her leather corselet, then slowly down her chest before casting aside the garment. Beneath, she wore only a thin bodice of purple silk, and with a quick jerk, she pulled it over her head, then allowed it to flutter to the ground. Her nipples immediately peaked, and her thighs turned liquid as his hungry gaze moved to them.

But when he took a step in her direction, she clicked her tongue and shook her head, not wanting to rush the moment. "Not yet."

"You're very domineering, Valcotta." His hands went to the buttons of his coat. "And I think quite used to giving commands."

"And to being obeyed."

He gave a soft growl of frustration but stopped unbuttoning his coat, his eyes never moving from her as she unlaced one boot and then the other. She unfastened her belt, her trousers slipping down to reveal she wore nothing underneath.

She heard his breath catch, felt the tension rise as though he were barely contained. As if she might blink and find him across the room, his hands on her naked body and his tongue in her mouth. The thought of it had her slipping her hand between her thighs, fingertips finding her body wet and wanting. Zarrah used one fingertip to circle the sensitive flesh that was the center of her pleasure, leaning her shoulders against the wall, her eyes never leaving his.

"Valcotta," he murmured, "if this is the torment you envisioned for me, you could have done it from the far side of the dam."

She smirked. "But then I wouldn't have known whether it was fear or self-control holding you in place, and if I am to be satisfied, I demand the latter."

His chuckle was dark and full of promises. "With me between your thighs, Valcotta, you are ensured satisfaction."

This wild and wanton side of herself was unfamiliar, and yet . . . *not*. Like it had always been there but had never found cause to be unleashed. Now it was free, and it felt like this was who she'd been all along. "Prove it."

Her eyes closed for what felt like only a heartbeat, but when she opened them, he was in front of her. His lips brushed her earlobe, causing a tremor to run through her as he said, "Gladly."

The ever-present question of *who are you?* flickered through her mind, only to be vanquished as he lifted her. Her back slid up the wall until she could feel the heat of his breath against the apex of her thighs, the sensation tearing a gasp from her lips.

She was entirely exposed, supported only by the strength of his arms, her sex inches from his face. He was in control, and she should have hated that, but instead it made her burn hotter. Made her spread her thighs wider so the folds of her sex parted and he could see all of her, her core pulsing with need.

"Some things I won't be robbed of." He kissed the inside of one of her knees, and then the other, making her shiver. "And being the one to make you come is foremost on that list."

He lowered his face, and a moan tore from Zarrah's lips as his mouth took the place of her fingers, sucking and teasing her sensitive flesh. Her thighs tensed, but he only pressed them wider, holding her up as though she weighed nothing at all. She gasped, wild, aching lust making her body thrum and her skin burn like wild-fire.

Then he pulled away to look up at her. "Are you sure you want to do this, Valcotta?"

"Yes," she gasped, for there was nothing she wanted more. No one she wanted more. "I need . . ." *You* was the word she wanted to say, but she couldn't give that much up to him. "I need it."

He laughed softly, then lowered his mouth and slipped his tongue inside of her. Tasted her thoroughly before running his tongue up her sex to the knot of nerves that pulsed with need, closing his mouth over it. Zarrah sobbed as he sucked and stroked the part of her that seemed to hold every sensation in her body, her back arching against the wall as his fingers dug into her thighs.

The tension built and built until pleasure washed over her like the breaking of a dam. Zarrah screamed as her body shuddered, as he sucked her flesh hard, dragging waves of pleasure from her. She tangled her fingers in his hair to hold him there, her body bucking in his grip.

Only when her shudders eased did he lower her down, kissing her lips, her jaw, her throat, a soft groan exiting his lips as she wrapped her legs around his body.

"I want more," she breathed into his ear, rocking her hips against him, inhaling his scent. "I want everything."

Everything that she'd denied herself for so long. Everything that hadn't been possible until she'd met him.

"Then everything you shall have." He carried her over to the bed and laid her on her back, the sheets rough against her skin.

Zarrah's heart skipped as he straightened, his eyes locked on hers as he pulled off first his coat and then a shirt of expensive linen, revealing a torso that might well have been carved from ala-baster, every muscle taut and defined. His boots made soft thuds as he kicked them free, his belt clinking as he unfastened it, and anticipation caused her breath to quicken.

But though his desire was visibly apparent, there he paused, his eyes drifting over her nakedness. "A body to match the voice."

Was that a good thing? She wasn't sure. "How so?"

"Beautiful." Her breath caught as he bent to kiss her navel, then looked up at her. "Something I would gladly lose myself in every night of my life, if such a thing were possible."

Emotion flooded Zarrah's chest, making it hard to breathe, because while she'd been many things to many people, no one had ever spoken this way to her. No one had ever expressed such feelings for her. Until this moment, she hadn't felt the absence of the sentiment, but now she half wondered how she'd live without it. How she'd live without *him*.

Though she knew she'd have to.

What was happening between them was forbidden. There was no possible future in it. Yet instead of tempering the heat burning through her body, it only made her want him more.

His lips kissed lines of fire up her torso, then his mouth closed over the tip of one of her breasts, making her back arch. She tangled her fingers in his hair, her other hand running over the hard muscles of his shoulders, which flexed beneath her palm as he shifted to her other breast. She whimpered, the sensation of his tongue stroking her nipple spiraling down between her thighs, the need to be filled by him so intense it almost hurt.

Catching her heels around his hips, she pulled him closer, snarling in frustration as she felt the fabric of his trousers instead of bare flesh, but he silenced her with a kiss even as his hips pressed down, his hardness rubbing against her, teasing her with what was to come. What she *needed* to come.

Twisting her body, she rolled him onto his back, abandoning

his lips to taste the lobe of his ear, her heart speeding as his fingers interlocked with hers, knuckles digging into the mattress as he allowed her to hold him down.

She heard the rapidness of his breath, felt the thunder of his heart against her breasts as she moved, her tongue flicking over the pulse at his throat before moving down, exploring the hard planes of his chest and the tensed muscles of his abdomen.

Her hands drifted to the top of his trousers. He lifted his hips beneath her, allowing her to pull them down, revealing the hard length of his cock. While he kicked away the garment, it was her turn to look up, knowing hers was the smile of a devil as she met his gaze. Then Zarrah lowered her face, taking as much of him in as she could.

He groaned as she moved, her tongue circling him until he gasped, "You're going to break me, Valcotta, and my pride can't take passing that front desk with less than an hour gone by."

Zarrah didn't stop.

Instead, she lost herself to the rhythm, to the pleasure of feeling his body shudder beneath her touch, his breath coming in rasping gasps. And only when she sensed he was at her mercy did she shift her weight upward, knees to either side of his body, not hesitating as she drove her hips down, his cock plunging into her.

Whether it was him or her who cried out, Zarrah couldn't have said, only that the world spun sideways as she rocked against him, his grip on her ass driving her downward with more force with each stroke.

He let go of her to push himself up, capturing her mouth with his, her breasts crushed against his chest, the ferocity and passion unlike anything she'd ever experienced.

Tension built again in her core, rising and rising, and then his hand shifted between their bodies, his thumb finding that knot of pleasure between her legs, stroking her with the same rhythm.

Zarrah screamed, her head falling back as he drove her need for release to the point of agony.

Then her body shattered, pleasure lancing through her and bright spots of light filling her eyes. Over and over, her core convulsed so that she could barely draw a breath. She felt his body shudder as he climaxed, the pulse of him filling her, the moment seeming to last an eternity and yet be over in a heartbeat, the Maridrinian collapsing back against the bed and taking her with him.

Her softened body molded against him, her cheek pressed against his chest as they lay in the light of the flickering lamp, too spent to do anything but breathe.

Only when her heart finally slowed did Zarrah lift her face to regard him. "You could probably get half your coin back, if you wanted."

He lifted a hand to stroke her cheek, then coiled one lock of her hair around his finger. "What I want," he said, "has nothing to do with silver," and he rolled her onto her back. Smiling, Zarrah closed her eyes, allowing him to draw her back down into the depths of pleasure.

As if both of them recognized this would be their only night together, they slept little. Wrapped in his arms, Zarrah drifted off only a handful of times, but always the need for *more* would wake one of them, and they'd begin anew.

Though she'd had her share of lovers, it had never felt like this. Like she'd been made for the man whose lips consumed her, and he for her. Never had she felt such an insatiable desire that cared not for sleep or obligation or the rising threat of dawn, only for having his body against hers, in hers, his tongue, his fingers, his cock pulling her over the edge so many times she lost count.

No matter that it might be to her own ruin.

A sliver of sunlight spilled from beneath the thin fabric of the drapes, casting a line of gold across the Maridrinian's back. Resting on her elbow, she traced her finger over a scar illuminated by the light. A knife wound was her guess. It looked like the blade had missed the gap between his ribs, slicing through muscle instead of into his lungs. "Who stabbed you in the back?"

He exhaled a slow breath, his eyes still closed, cheek still pressed against the mattress. "One of my brothers."

There was no emotion in his voice. No indignation or outrage or hurt that a family member had tried to kill him. Which she supposed wasn't surprising. He was clearly of noble birth, which meant whoever his father was, he likely had a harem full of wives and more children than he could count. More sons than could reasonably be given any inheritance, which meant siblings ridding themselves of one another in order to have a chance at wealth and title upon their father's death. "Your people don't understand the meaning of family."

"The men don't," he murmured. "But the women understand it well enough to make up for our idiocy."

She snorted, because the women of his country were forbidden to fight. "Maridrinian women are weak."

He gave a slight shake of his head. "They are stronger than you could possibly imagine." Then one eye opened, regarding her from the shadows. "Do you have siblings?"

A dangerous question, given that too many details would make her identity an easy guess, as there were few senior female officers in the Valcottan garrison, and she had the highest ranking. "Isn't ours a union resting on anonymity, Maridrina?"

He lifted one shoulder and then closed his eyes, sighing as she continued to trail her fingers over the muscles of his back.

She found herself wanting to tell him. Wanting to reveal the truth of herself, despite the danger, because it seemed strange that she should feel so much for a man who knew so little about her. And she about him. "No siblings, but many cousins." She leaned onto her right arm, wincing as a jolt of pain shot through it, the wound she'd taken in battle aching beneath its bandage. "My father died when I was a baby, and you know what happened to my mother. I was raised by one of my aunts."

"I'm sorry." He reached up to take hold of her hand, pressing her knuckles to his lips. "I lost my own mother young. Would that it had been my father, and my life might have turned out far differently."

"You are at odds with him?"

His body shook with silent laughter. "That would be an understatement. My father is an unrepentant prick the world would be better off without. Though if you asked him, he'd no doubt say the same about me."

Curiosity flooded her with the need to keep asking questions, but the strength of the sun was growing. And if she didn't get back to the Anriot before dawn shifted to day, she'd be stuck on the Maridrinian side until nightfall. There was no way Yrina could hide her absence for that long. "I need to go."

His brow furrowed, and he rolled onto his back, tugging her on top of him. Desire burned across her skin as she felt him harden beneath her. "Once more," he said under his breath. "We'll be quick."

"It's not once been quick," she reminded him, but he only lifted her hips, lowering her onto his cock, her aching body shuddering as he filled her. A beam of dawn light peeked through the curtains, and she reached up to pull them wide, wanting to see him at least once without the cloak of shadows.

He turned his face away from the light, squeezing his eyes shut against the brilliance. "Stay all day." His hips moved against hers. "And all night."

"I'll be missed." Sorrow filled her chest because all she wanted to do was to say yes. To stay here with him and ask him all the questions that burned in her heart.

He sighed, turning his far-too-beautiful face into the sunlight. "As will I."

And then he opened his eyes.

The glow of the dawn revealed what neither moonlight nor lamplight ever had: irises of such a deep azure blue that it was like staring into the depths of a shifting sea. A color so rich and vibrant that it was almost inhuman. The sight of it sent a shock through Zarrah's body as sure as if she'd been doused with icy water. For the Maridrinian's eyes were the identical color to those of the man who'd looked at her and laughed while he'd slaughtered her mother.

Words of a report long forgotten filled her mind: *Shoulder-length blond hair. Medium height and light build. Eyes of Veliant blue.*

Zarrah's throat closed, but she still managed to get out, "You're Keris Veliant."

His jaw tightened. Reaching up, he jerked the curtain closed so that they were again concealed by shadow. "I was under the impression we weren't doing names, Valcotta."

Oh God, what had she done? "Just tell me the truth."

"What difference does it make?"

All the difference. All the difference in the world. "Tell me!"

He was silent, and her heart skittered in her chest, part of her hoping against hope that she was wrong. That he was someone else entirely. But then he met her gaze. "Yes. I'm Keris Veliant."

Zarrah recoiled, almost falling off the bed as she scrambled away from him, her skin icy cold and her vision pulsing in and out of focus. What had she done? What had she done?

He followed her off the bed. "What does it matter what my name is?"

"It matters." Zarrah could barely get the words out, the world shifting as though she stood on a rocking ship, none of her clothes seeming to be where she'd left them.

"Why?" he demanded. "I'm the same man as I was before. The same man you spent the better part of the night *fucking,* I might add."

She flinched, covering up the motion by dragging on her trousers, trying not to think about the stickiness of her skin. Trying not to think of how she'd spent the night not in the arms of just a Maridrinian but in the arms of the future king of Maridrina. How the son of her greatest enemy had tasted every inch of her. Had spilled himself into her. Oh God, what if she got with child?

Bile surged up her throat, and Zarrah just barely managed to get to the side table to grab the basin sitting on top of it before she heaved her guts into it. Her eyes stinging, she turned to look at him. "I would never have done this if I'd known who you were. You are more my enemy than anyone in Nerastis."

Not some hapless nobleman forced into service against his will but the crown prince in command of Maridrina's forces. Her opponent in every possible way. Not just a stupid decision but a treasonous one. Her aunt would have her executed if this were ever discovered, and as it was, her honor would never forgive this.

"I am not my father." His hands balled into fists at his sides. "You more than anyone know that."

"I didn't go to your palace to burn it, Veliant," she whispered. "I came to put a knife in your heart. And if I'd done so, my actions would've seen the empress heap me with accolades for striking a blow against the Rat King, whereas now I should fall on my own sword for the shame of what I've done."

"Then kill me now." He was across the room in a flash, scooping up a fallen dagger as he went, forcing it into her hand. Gripping her fingers tight over the hilt and then pressing it to his throat.

"Do it," he repeated, azure eyes liquid bright. "But know that my father will lift a cup of wine in your honor for ridding him of me."

Do it, a voice whispered inside her. *Redeem what honor you have left.*

His breath was warm against her face, the lips that had kissed hers so reverently all night thinned with tension as he stared into her eyes, daring her to do it.

Zarrah's hand quivered. It wasn't that she'd spent a night in the arms of the Crown Prince of Maridrina that had shaken her to the core; it was all the nights that had come before. All the things that he'd said. That she'd said.

That in the saying, Zarrah had fallen for him in a way she'd never fallen before.

She straightened her fingers, the blade slipping through them to drop to the floor. "I'm going. And let this be as though it never happened."

As if such a thing were possible.

Slipping around him, she gathered the rest of her things and headed to the door. Only to find him standing there ahead of her, trousers on and hand holding the planks of wood shut.

"You can't go out there now, Valcotta. The sun is up and the midnight truce is over. If you're caught, it won't go well."

"I won't get caught." Even in the daylight, the rooftops would be safe. No one ever looked up.

"Valcotta . . ."

"Do not stand in my way, Veliant," she hissed. "You have no right."

His fingers flexed against the door as though he were considering arguing, but it was he who looked away first. "Be careful."

"It isn't your problem."

Not allowing him the opportunity to say more, Zarrah yanked open the door and then slammed it shut behind her, striding swiftly down the corridor to the stairs. The greasy man remained at the front desk, and he gave her a lascivious smile as she passed, mumbling, "I've always preferred Valcottan girls."

He deserved a broken nose, but she couldn't risk putting him in his place. Not with the sun fully in the sky and her very much in enemy territory.

Stepping outside, she blinked against the bright sunlight, nausea twisting in her belly and her head starting to throb. The streets of Nerastis were quiet, but in the distance, she could hear the sounds of hoofbeats: Maridrinian soldiers already on patrol.

Hurrying down the length of the building, Zarrah moved into an alley and climbed onto a stack of crates to gain access to the rooftops, then moved swiftly across them in the direction of the Anriot.

The smells of cooking mixed with the scents of chamber pots being emptied into the streets, but she paid them little mind, relying instead on her ears to guide her away from threats, all her thought on picking out the voices of soldiers and the hoofbeats of horses from the shrieks of babies. Of women shouting at men to rouse themselves. Of men returning their own forms of abuse on the women. She felt dizzy and unwell, her balance off and her body weak.

You fell for Silas Veliant's son.

The thought distracted her as she leapt between rooftops, and her foot slipped. Biting off a scream, Zarrah flailed her arms as she fell, then landed hard on a pile of crates. The wood shattered, pain lancing through her, but she scrambled to her feet, knowing she needed to move quickly.

As she started to climb, a voice from the front of the alley caught her attention, and she turned to find a man flanked by soldiers, his face familiar. "Well, now," he said, eyes full of recognition. "Look who we have here."

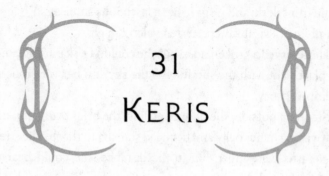

31
KERIS

His ears filled with a roaring sound as she abandoned the room, leaving him alone with nothing but the remembrance of her reaction in his head. The horror in her eyes when she'd realized his identity, how her disgust had caused her to spill her guts, everything that had passed between them washed away by his name. By the fucking blue eyes he'd inherited from his father and the legacy that came with them.

"I hate you!" He slammed his fist against the wall, his knuckles splitting and agony racing up his wrist. But the pain was nothing compared to his hatred for his father. A hundred miles away, and still, he took *everything* Keris ever cared about.

Ever loved.

Doubling over, he sucked in breath after breath, his stomach twisting with hurt that she'd left and fear that she was out in his half of the city alone, everything about her making her a target. But there had been no stopping her.

Valcotta was not a woman to be contained, but he still had to fight the urge to go after her. Had to fight the urge to tail her across the city to ensure she got across the Anriot safely.

What if she doesn't make the jump?

Bile rose in his stomach, and Keris clenched his teeth, his breath coming in ragged gasps. *She can do it,* he silently told himself. *She's capable—she proved that much last night.*

And as it was, his own absence had inevitably been noticed. He'd told Aileena that if he were ever discovered gone from her rooms she should say that he'd left to go back to the palace, which meant if he didn't arrive there soon, Otis would start a search. Which would only complicate matters for Valcotta.

Swiftly donning his clothing, Keris headed downstairs.

"You're late," the pig at the desk said. "That'll be an extra copper."

It was tempting to tell the bastard to fuck himself, but instead Keris flung a handful of coins at his face, limiting himself to the satisfaction of watching a silver coin bounce hard off the man's greasy forehead as he exited the building.

The rising sun was already hot, not a cloud in the sky to mute its blinding rays, and he pulled up his hood as much to shield his eyes as his identity as he strode through the streets toward his broken palace.

I would never have done this if I'd known who you were. You are more my enemy than anyone in Nerastis.

He felt sick, in need of sleep and an entire pitcher of water, his throat dry as dust, his eyes burning. But it was grief that choked him, drowning his anger and leaving him hollow.

There would be no more nights meeting her at the dam. No more conversation with what seemed the only person in this cursed city he could actually talk to. And never again would he have the chance to touch her perfect skin, to kiss those lips, to bury himself between her thighs, the wild pleasure of the prior night unlike anything he'd ever experienced.

What did you expect? he asked himself. *Your name is poison, and everything you touch turns to rot.*

Ahead, the gates to the palace loomed, and though all was quiet, there was a tension in the air that didn't exist during the midnight truce. The people who were already out and going about their business had a caution to them, knowing full well that with the sun in the sky, either side might be priming for an attack.

Stopping in front of the gate, Keris pulled back his hood, the eyes of the guards on duty widening in recognition and shock. "Your Highness," one of them said as they opened the gate. "We've been searching for you all morning. Prince Otis is scouring the riverfront."

Shit. "Too much wine," he answered. "I fell asleep on my way back."

One of his father's generals approached, his thick arms crossed over his monstrous chest. The huge man cleared his throat, and Keris girded himself for whatever chiding would come from wandering the city without an escort, but instead the man said, "We received word that the Ithicanian king has been captured and is being brought to Vencia."

Captured. Keris cared little for Aren Kertell himself, what he'd learned about the man from Raina not endearing the Ithicanian king to him in any way, but his stomach clenched at what it meant for Ithicana. Whether he was worthy or not, Aren's people followed him, and without his leadership, their resistance to the Maridrinian invaders might crumple. Which was logically what he should want, except the thought of his father triumphing—of him becoming the Master of the Bridge, in truth—made Keris want to vomit. "I see."

"With the capture, your father foresees an end to the conflict in Ithicana, which means we'll have the resources to escalate our own situation. To take back the southern half of Nerastis from the

Valcottans. It is your father's will that you commit yourself to achieving this particular end."

Commit himself to war.

Keris's head began to throb, and he rubbed at one temple. "Let's wait until our hold on Ithicana is certain before biting off more than we can chew with the Valcottans. Now, if you'll excuse me—"

A loud commotion from outside caught his attention, shouts and cries of triumph splitting the air. Keris turned to see Otis striding in his direction, a wide grin on his brother's face. Which was rather unexpected, given that Otis had been out hunting for him. "Of all the days for you to be up at this hour, Keris, this was the one to do it. We've caught ourselves *quite* the prize."

His gaze skipped past his brother to the pair of his soldiers dragging a figure between them dressed in Valcottan garments. The individual had a sack over her head, but that didn't stop him from recognizing the slender brown arms that were bound at the wrist. Arms that had been wrapped around him not an hour ago.

Keris's stomach dropped, his skin turning to ice as she was forced to her knees in front of him, her wrists bleeding from the tight ropes and arms marked with livid red blotches that would turn to wicked bruises, the wound on her arm no longer bandaged but torn open and bleeding.

"Caught her in an alley on her way to the Anriot," Otis said. "She put up quite the fight, but we were able to subdue her."

"Who is she?" The words slipped out, a question Keris had asked himself a thousand times but now one he wished he'd never have an answer to.

"The most powerful woman in Nerastis." Otis yanked the sack off to reveal the face Keris saw in his dreams. The face of the woman he'd fallen for in a way he hadn't believed possible.

Otis caught Valcotta by the hair, jerking her head back. "Allow me to introduce General Zarrah Anaphora."

32
ZARRAH

SHE STARED UP AT HIM, THOUGH IT WAS HARD TO SEE WITH ONE of her eyes swollen shut and her brain fuzzy from the blows she'd taken. But she heard the Maridrinian clear enough as he said, "Who harmed her?"

The princeling who'd captured her frowned. "What difference does it make? She fought back. This is Zarrah Anaphora, Keris. She's the Empress of Valcotta's niece. The heir apparent. Do you know what a blow to the Valcottans her capture will be?"

"Not as big a blow as us catapulting her back across the Anriot, piece by piece," one of the soldiers said, and the rest of them laughed, their eyes full of murder. Zarrah struggled not to flinch, because she knew they'd do it. Had *seen* them do it.

"No," the Maridrinian—Crown Prince Keris, she reminded herself—said after a long pause, his brow furrowing, "that won't be what we are doing."

"Now isn't the time to get squeamish, Keris," Otis hissed. "This bitch killed Rask."

Keris gave a weary sigh. "It's not the manner in which you wish to execute her that concerns me, Otis, but rather that you intend to kill her at all."

Otis. O. It had been his letters that she'd stolen and that Keris had chased her across the city to get back. Which meant it was Prince Otis, one of the most brutal murderers of her people since Silas himself had commanded the garrison, whom the Maridrinian held in such high regard.

"As you said," Keris continued, "this woman is a prize second only to the empress herself. And yet you'd spend all her worth on a few minutes of satisfaction?" He tsked. "A short-sighted decision, and I think not one Father would thank me for allowing you to make."

What did he intend? What did he plan to do with her?

The men surrounding them clearly were wondering the same thing, all of them staring at their prince. "What do you want to do with her, then?" Otis demanded.

Keris shrugged. "She's collateral we can use in negotiations with the Valcottans. With her, we might see an end to the blockades on Southwatch, but the empress won't negotiate for the return of a corpse."

Gods, no. Zarrah blanched at the thought of being used in such a manner, and the other princeling appeared equally horrified as he blurted out, "But—"

Keris leveled a finger at his brother. "I am in command here, Otis, which means she is *my* prize. If I personally deliver her to Father in Vencia and she proves as valuable as I believe, it will be me he thanks."

The princeling's jaw tightened. "He's only going to kill her. This is a waste of time."

"Perhaps, but that's his decision to make, not yours. And to that end, from this moment forward, I want her treated with the *utmost* care and consideration. The last thing I need is one of you heavy-handed pricks accidentally killing her and ruining my chance to win my father's favor."

It had all been lies. If he wanted Silas Veliant's favor, every single thing he'd said to her had been a lie. Blood boiling, she lunged at him. "You fucking Maridrinian bastard!"

The men caught her shoulders, slamming her into the ground with enough force that her eyes glazed.

"Enough!" Keris ordered. "Stand down!"

But instead of listening, one of the men kicked her several times in the ribs, each blow drawing a gasp of pain from her lips. It only ended when Keris snarled, "Did I or did I not just give an order that she was not to be harmed?"

"But Your Highness—"

"Did I or did I not give you an order?"

The man swallowed hard. "You did, my lord."

"I don't give you lot many orders." His tone was frigid. "But when I do, I expect to be obeyed. And there are consequences to doing otherwise. Otis, have him whipped."

The princeling's jaw tightened, but he nodded. "How many lashes?"

"How should I know?" Keris straightened his coat. "Keep count, and when he stops breathing, bring me the number."

Zarrah stared at him in horror, unable to reconcile the man she'd fallen for with this creature. With this *monster*.

"Keris—"

"I want this win," he interrupted. "See it done. And then put the woman somewhere safe and keep her under close guard. If anything happens to her, the man responsible will consider this one's fate"—he jerked his chin at the pale-faced soldier—"merciful. Now, if you'll excuse me, I'm in need of both bath and breakfast."

And then Keris turned on his heel and walked away.

Everything was blurry and distant, though whether it was because the blow to her head had concussed her or she was in shock, Zarrah couldn't have said as she watched Keris disappear down the corridor.

"You heard him," Otis snarled. "Put her in one of the cells, and for the love of God, don't let anything happen to her. Veliant blood runs through Keris's veins, and not one of you should ever forget what that means."

The blood of her mother's murderer ran through his veins, and she'd just seen proof of it. She'd slept with a monster. Given herself to a monster.

Otis turned to the soldier who'd been sentenced to die. "Do you submit yourself to your fate willingly?"

The soldier was blanched of color, clearly terrified, but he nodded before turning his gaze on her. "My only regret is not aiming for your face, you Valcottan bitch."

"I'd say next time"—she forced a smirk onto her face—"but it doesn't look like that's in the cards."

Fury flashed in the man's gaze, but Otis hauled him backward, voice cool as he said, "I'd temper your optimism, General. Just because His Highness believes your life holds value does not mean His Majesty will agree. And when our father hands you over to Serin to see what secrets that pretty little head of yours holds, you'll be cursing Keris's name for not handing you over to me."

Serin. The Magpie. Zarrah's blood chilled. The Maridrinian spymaster was infamous for his skill at torture, and many of her countrymen had died from his ministrations after telling him everything he wished to know. As trained as she was, Zarrah doubted she'd fare any better. "I already curse your brother's name."

The expression on Otis's face as he led the condemned man away suggested she wasn't alone.

Two soldiers caught her under the arms, hauling her upward,

but the motion was more than her rattled brain could take, and she vomited on the ground, barely hearing their muttered curses of disgust. The corridor swirled around her, a blur of color, and Zarrah struggled to remain conscious as they dragged her forward.

I curse you. She silently sent the words to where she imagined Keris bathed and dined in all the luxury befitting his station. But the true words, the ones in her heart, were, *How could you?*

Because he's an honorless Maridrinian and a monster, just like his father, a cruel voice answered. *And you're a fool for having ever trusted him.*

It was the last thought Zarrah had before she slipped from consciousness.

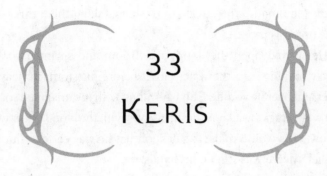

33
KERIS

WALKING AWAY FROM HER WAS THE HARDEST THING HE'D EVER done in his life.

But he had no choice.

Not when getting her out of this alive depended on him playing his part to perfection, which meant behaving exactly as everyone expected him to.

As much as he could.

Never in his life had he ordered someone whipped, much less ordered an execution. Yet he'd seen the desire for revenge in the eyes of his soldiers and known that if he didn't make the consequences of harming Zarrah clear, one would kill her and then proclaim it an accident.

The necessity of it did nothing to ease the roiling in his stomach, which, despite being empty, was threatening to heave itself up his throat as he ascended the stairs two at a time, whistling cheerfully. "Draw me a bath," he said to one of the servants he passed. "And get me some breakfast. With water, not wine. I need a clear head."

"Right away, my lord." The woman curtsied, but Keris was already spiraling up the last flight of stairs, taking them three at a time now, his mouth sour.

He shoved open the door to his room and sprinted across, barely making it to the water closet before his stomach heaved. Over and over he vomited, his ears filling with the imagined sound of a whip cracking against flesh, his eyes with the blood that would follow. Otis would make it quick, of that he was certain, but the soldier's death was still on his hands.

In more ways than anyone knew.

Ribs aching, Keris pushed himself up and returned to his bedchamber, where he drained a glass of water and tried not to think about Valcotta—about Zarrah—broken and bleeding in the prison cells below. Yet for all his efforts, visions of her in increasingly worsening circumstances rolled through his thoughts, and a cold sweat rose to his skin.

There was no other path he could have taken, no other choice that he could've made. At least, not one that wouldn't have seen them both dead.

Not even he had the power to give the order to release her—especially not given who she was. Even before her rise to command, she'd been an infamous warrior on the battlefield, responsible for countless Maridrinian deaths, including—if the rumors were true—the death of his elder brother Rask. And while Keris might raise a glass to her for that particular death, Rask had been revered by the soldiers in Nerastis.

He could spout orders until he was blue in the face. Order dozens of men whipped for defiance—they'd still refuse, because their loyalty to him was a paltry thing compared to their desire for revenge.

There was only one person with the power to spare her. Only one person the soldiers respected and feared enough to set aside their need to execute Valcotta.

The King of Maridrina.

The thought of relying on his father made his stomach twist, but in the seconds he'd had to think of a plan, he'd seen no other solution. The soldiers would allow her to live because they feared his father. And because they believed what he'd do to Valcotta would be far worse than anything they'd come up with.

They were probably right.

Servants entered the room, bobbing curtsies at him as they carried buckets of steaming water to warm the bathing pool, the air soon filling with scented oil as sconces were lit.

You need to go to her, his conscience screamed. *You need to make certain she's safe.*

Instead, Keris pulled off his clothes, then headed into the bathing chamber, barely seeing the large pool circled by candles or the rose petals scattered across the surface of the water. If he showed *any* sign of empathy for Valcotta, he risked losing what authority he had.

Slipping into the tepid depths, he leaned back against the curved stone basin, then shut his eyes and reached blindly for a glass of water and drained it.

This plan had only bought him time; the idea that his father would use her as a bargaining chip in negotiations with the empress was a fool's hope, it being far more likely that he'd execute her as entertainment for the masses. Which meant Keris had to get her free *before* they reached Vencia.

Think, he ordered himself. *Come up with a solution!*

Yet every time he blinked, Keris heard the sound of her skull bouncing off the tile. Saw her eyes glazing. She could be dying in a cell. Could already be dead while he was up in his tower soaking in the bath.

If she is, there is nothing you can do to help her, he told himself even as a tremor ran through him. *Believe that she is alive, and turn your head to keeping her that way.*

The first step was getting her out of Nerastis. Otis would push to transport her by ship to Vencia, which would not only make an escape more difficult but also cut the time he'd have to orchestrate it by more than half. It had to be by land, which would necessitate a heavy escort.

Think.

Even on the road, finding an opportunity for escape would be nearly impossible. He'd need assistance, either in the form of someone breaking into camp to free her by force or providing a sufficient distraction that he could set her free himself. But he had exactly zero allies in this. Being an enemy soldier was bad enough, but Valcotta was also the future empress. Was the woman who'd fought against these men time and again, killing their friends, their loved ones, their commanders. Help wouldn't come from Maridrinians.

Then who?

Mercenaries? They certainly could be bought, but likely not in so short a time period that they'd be of any use. He needed help that was already here, already available.

The Valcottans?

He sat up straight in the bath, water sloshing everywhere. The Valcottans would be desperate to get her back. If they knew she was alive and traveling by road, they'd inevitably try to rescue her.

A plan formed in his mind, and he picked up a bar of soap and set to scrubbing the sweat from his body, refusing to consider how it had gotten there. Except memories forced their way through. The devilish smile on her lips as she'd tormented him. The taste of her on his tongue as he explored her every curve. The vision of her above him, back arched and head thrown back as she climaxed.

He'd slept with Zarrah Anaphora. Heir to the Empire his own kingdom had warred against for generations.

Would he have done it if he had known the truth of who she was?

Would she?

Even as the question arose in his thoughts, he shoved it away, remembering the horror in her eyes when she'd realized who he was.

Zarrah Anaphora *hated* him, and nothing he did would change that.

The truth caused hot pain to lance through him, his hands to ball into fists, and a scream of anger and frustration and grief to rise up his throat. But Keris clenched his teeth to silence it. No matter how she felt about him, he cared for her. *Deeply.* And he'd cut his own throat before he'd allow any more harm to befall her. Would do whatever it took to protect her, no matter the cost.

But for there to be any chance of his plan working, he needed General Zarrah Anaphora to trust him.

And that might be the most impossible task of all.

34
ZARRAH

ZARRAH WOKE WITH A START, THE SCENT OF SMELLING SALTS heavy in her nose and a stranger bent over her.

She recoiled from his reaching hand. "Don't touch me!"

"I am a physician to the royal family." His tone was cool. "Stay still while I examine you, or I shall have these men hold you down. His Highness has made it quite clear that he wishes for you to survive long enough to be judged by the king, and I've no desire to tempt his wrath."

His Highness. Keris. The fog in Zarrah's brain cleared, and memories came crashing through, echoes of the Maridrinian espousing the virtues of peace juxtaposed with those of the prince ordering a man whipped to death for disobedience, her mind refusing to see them as one and the same.

Except they were.

Had it all been an elaborate ruse to capture her? Had he known who she was this entire time? Had everything he'd said been a lie?

The last was somehow the worst of all. God help her, but she'd felt alive in those moments when she'd believed she might make a difference. In those moments when she'd believed that, together, they might change the nature of this war.

In those foolish moments when she thought that it might be possible to end the fighting altogether. When her hate for her enemies had paled beneath the glow of passion she'd felt at the Maridrinian's words. At his touch. At what he'd inspired within her.

Not the Maridrinian, a hateful voice whispered at her. *Prince Keris Veliant, the son of your mother's murderer!*

Pain and nausea filled her, and Zarrah submitted to the physician's examination even as she clawed aside her emotions in favor of thought for her path forward. For escape. Because it would be better to die trying to escape than to allow them to execute her. Better for her to die with honor than to allow them to use her against her people.

"How do you feel?" the man asked, frowning at the wound on her arm where the stitches had broken open. It ached nearly as badly as her skull, the skin around it blanched where it wasn't streaked with blood.

"Dizzy," she mumbled. "My head throbs."

He hesitated, then said, "A bad concussion." He picked up a needle and began restitching her arm, then covered it with a pungent poultice and a thick bandage. When he'd finished, he said to the guards, "She needs to be kept awake, and if that isn't possible, woken every hour. I'd say fetch me if she won't rouse, but if that happens, nothing I can do will save her. Fresh water only, no wine. And get her cleaned up. She smells of sweat and soldier."

He departed, and a few moments later, a servant—little more than a child—appeared with a washbasin and what looked like a dress, her eyes wide with trepidation. "I'm to help you wash, miss."

"I don't need help," Zarrah answered, unwilling to admit weakness. But the soldiers ignored her words and pushed the girl inside, locking the door. With their arms crossed, they stood watching with faint smiles on their faces until the girl said, "Please turn your backs. His Highness gave orders she was to be treated with courtesy."

"She's dangerous, girl. There is no chance of us turning our backs to her."

The girl's face tightened, and she reached for the blanket at the foot of the bed, then held it up to form a screen.

A small act of kindness, though it was no doubt motivated by fear. Either way, it was the most privacy she could expect, and Zarrah grudgingly pulled off her clothes, using the cloth to clean her body, which ached from head to toe with bruises.

When she was as clean as could be managed without a bath, Zarrah eyed her own garments, which were splattered with blood and vomit, then pulled the Maridrinian dress over her head, the thin wool rough against her skin, which was used to silk and leather. The cut left her arms and a large portion of her back bare, and she shivered as a draft struck her. The act of washing had rendered her exhausted, and she slumped down on the cot, her heart racing, the world swimming in and out of focus.

Where is he? she found herself wondering. *Is he sitting in his tower, gloating over my capture? Or does he truly care so little that he is, as he alluded, asleep in his bed, with not a thought for me at all?*

The girl departed with her soiled garments, then returned with a tin cup of water and a crust of bread. The water Zarrah guzzled gratefully, but her stomach revolted at the thought of food, and she left the bread sitting on her cot.

Yrina would be out searching for her by now. Would have raised the alarm, and Zarrah wondered what her friend had told the garrison. Whether she'd given the whole truth, hoping it would aid in the hunt, or if she protected Zarrah's secret still. Once word of her capture on this side of the Anriot reached Yrina's ears, her friend would suspect the truth—that Zarrah had been with a Maridrinian. That Zarrah had lied to her.

Shame burned over her skin, briefly chasing away the chill, then footfalls echoed down the corridor, the draft carrying a familiar spicy scent and the voice that had once inspired her dreams. "Please tell me she's still alive, preferably in one piece."

"Yes, Your Highness," one of the guards answered. A heartbeat later, Keris appeared in front of her cell, freshly bathed and dressed immaculately in a deep-blue coat that matched his eyes, trousers pressed, and his boots so polished they reflected the lamplight.

Rising on wobbly knees, Zarrah gripped the bars and faced him. She wanted to scream, *How could you?* Wanted to hammer her fists against the bars with all the rage in her chest, all the hurt in her heart, if for no other reason than to get a reaction from him. Yet she clung to her composure. "Come to preen?"

Keris shrugged, then brushed a fleck of lint off one shoulder. "Tempting, but better to wait until you're safely delivered to Vencia. Accidents happen, after all, and I wouldn't care to embarrass myself by celebrating too soon." He gave her a weighted look that her battered brain couldn't process, then waved a hand at one of the guards. "Go. I wish to speak to General Anaphora, and she's more likely to speak freely without you staring daggers at her."

"I must advise against you being alone with her, Your Highness. She's more dangerous than she looks."

"Then how fortunate she's locked in a cage." Keris turned to glare at the man. "Go."

Given she could barely stand, Zarrah didn't feel very dangerous at all. And yet she readied herself to reach through the bars. If she could take him hostage, escape might be possible. And if not that, she'd satisfy herself with taking his life before his countrymen took hers.

Heart in her throat, she watched as the soldier's jaw worked back and forth, a rush of anticipation filling her when he saluted sharply and strode down the hall. Only when the sound of his footfalls had faded did Keris turn back to her, the blithe indifference gone from his face, his expression heavy with concern. "How badly are you hurt?"

"What do you care?" It took concerted effort not to spit the words in his face, but she needed to lure him closer, not drive him back.

"Given I just ordered a man whipped to death in order to protect your life, I'd say a great deal."

He gripped the metal just above her hands. Well within reach, if she was quick. And yet Zarrah stood frozen in place as he added, "I'm going to get you out of this, but I need your help."

All the flippancy was gone, his gaze intense. The prince was vanquished, and the Maridrinian stood before her once more. Yet logic screamed at her not to trust him. That this was only a ruse. That she should attack. But Zarrah only stared at him, tasting the blood now dripping from her nose, his face blurring in and out of focus.

"Dammit." White fabric appeared in his hand to press against her nose. His fingers were warm where they brushed her skin. "I know your head is rattled, Valcotta, but you need to focus. I've only got a minute before Otis comes barreling down here in my defense."

Valcotta. Zarrah's legs shook, only her grip on the bars holding her upright. And behind the Maridrinian, the light pulsed.

"I can't keep you here," he said. "Nerastis is too lawless, too wild. It's only a matter of time until someone murders you in your cell."

"Then let me go." Her tongue felt thick, and it took all her concentration to form the words.

"If I thought they'd listen, I'd give the order," he said. "But there isn't a chance of them allowing you to go free, and Otis has half the garrison guarding you for fear of an escape or rescue attempt. To get you free, we must leave Nerastis."

His voice sounded far away, as though they stood atop the dam with the spillway between them once more.

"I'm going to argue that your value as a political prisoner demands the Crown decide your fate, which means bringing you to Vencia. Along the way, I need your people to attack our party to liberate you."

Her mind sharpened for a heartbeat, seeing the trick. Seeing his endgame. "Kiss my ass." Her heart was racing so swiftly, she swore it would wrench from her chest. "You think I'm such a fool as to lead my people into an ambush?"

His jaw tightened, likely from anger that her battered brain saw through his plan. "I intend no such thing. Which I realize requires you trusting me, but—"

Rage flared in Zarrah's chest, though it wasn't for him. It was for herself. "I did trust you. So it's no wonder you think me the fool."

Silence.

She watched his throat move as he swallowed, his eyes narrowing with frustration or anger, she wasn't sure which. Then he closed them.

Grab him, a voice screamed inside her head. *Capture him! Kill him! Do something!*

"You've no reason to believe me, Valcotta, but I had nothing to do with your capture beyond being the reason you were here in the first place."

"Liar!" She gave her head a sharp shake, but it only caused pain to lance through her skull and nausea to swirl in her stomach.

"I warned you not to go. I told you to wait until nightfall. But you were too busy being horrified over my family name to see reason."

"Your father murdered my mother," she snarled. "Laughed as he cut off her head and had his men stake up her corpse. Laughed as he put her head in my lap and left me for dead!" And instead of striking a blow against him by killing his son, she'd fallen into bed with him.

He recoiled. "*My* father killed your mother? I—"

"You're the same as him. All the Veliants are." She coughed on the blood dripping down the back of her throat. "You're monsters, just like him."

He flinched, then shook his head. "I'm nothing like him."

"Says the man who just ordered someone whipped to death."

"To protect you!"

"Do you really expect me to believe that?" She spat blood on the floor in front of him. "The spies said you were a womanizer and a drunk, but they also said you were very clever. Don't think for a moment I'll fall for more of your trickery. I see who you are now."

His grip on the bars tightened, his knuckles blanching, and her eyes went to them, remembering what it had felt like to be touched by those hands. It had felt so real. Had felt so right. How could she have felt that way about someone so heartless? So cruel? "You'll have to content yourself with my death," she whispered, her eyes burning. "For I won't allow you to use me against my people."

Then her knees buckled and Zarrah collapsed, feeling his hands catch her around the waist as he said, "Goddamn your honor!"

Honor was all she had left, tarnished though it was.

He lowered her to the ground, then Zarrah felt his hand curve around her cheek, lifting her face to look at him. "I'm not allowing you to die just because you had the misfortune of crossing paths with me, Valcotta." His throat moved as he swallowed. "Zarrah."

Her chest tightened, and she pulled away from him, slumping against the stone floor, her body cold. "Kill me. Or leave me. Or if you must stay, know your words fall upon ears now wise to your deception."

Silence stretched between them, broken by a loud bang and the shout of "Keris!"

He glanced down the hall, then leaned forward. "If you give up now, you'll never have vengeance. My father wins."

Zarrah squeezed her eyes shut, seeing Silas Veliant's face. Hearing him laugh and laugh and laugh as her mother's blood rained down upon her.

"Fight to live," Keris said, "and you will *live to fight*."

Live to fight.

Otis appeared, his face splattered with blood that she could only guess was from the man he'd whipped to death. "Have you lost your mind, Keris? Do you have any idea how dangerous she is?"

His voice was light as he said, "So everyone keeps telling me." Keris rose. "But thus far I've been rather disappointed. All she's done is faint. What did the physician say?"

"That she's concussed and will either die tonight or live to meet her end in Vencia."

"Let's pray for the latter," Keris answered. "Now, if you'll excuse me, I'm somewhat short of sleep and in need of a nap. Make arrangements to transport her north by road—the Valcottans are thick upon the seas, and they'll be after us as soon as they learn we have their general."

"It will be done," his brother answered, but he remained where he was as Keris strode off, humming a tune.

The princeling watched his brother go, then turned back to her, the blood splattering his face at odds with the words written to him in those love letters. As was the hate in his eyes. "You and yours are a scourge upon this earth," he hissed. "You took those I loved most and slaughtered them. Don't think there won't be a reckoning."

Pulling herself upright, Zarrah stared him down as best she could with the world slowly turning to black around her. "Perhaps so. But it seems it won't be coming from you."

"Don't be so sure," he said, then darkness once again pulled her under.

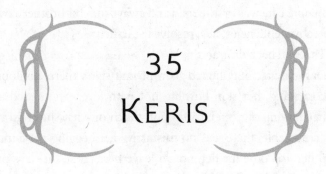

35
KERIS

THE CARRIAGE BOUNCED UP THE ROAD, KERIS'S TEETH RATTLING with each rut and rock a wheel hit, his ass already bruised despite the thick cushion on the seat.

But none of it registered.

Not with Valcotta sprawled on the bench across from him, her wrists and ankles bound, and her eyes glazed from the head injury she'd taken. She drifted in and out of consciousness, the *out* a mercy, because when she was awake, he could see the pain in her eyes, her jaw clenching and unclenching.

And there was nothing he could do to make it better, even his words of comfort silenced by the soldier who sat next to him on the bench.

Otis had insisted. "I'm not allowing you to ride alone with her. She's dangerous, Keris. All of this could be an act to get you alone and kill you."

"I'm not helpless, you know."

"I didn't say you were! But she's a trained soldier, and I've seen firsthand how well she fights. And you're . . . well, you're *you*."

"How flattering." But Keris didn't bother with further argument. Once he was on the road and away from his brother's overprotective tendencies, he'd resolve the issue.

That had been days ago.

Days of watching Zarrah grow progressively worse, no longer able to stand, her skin burning hot with fever. She tossed and turned, crying out often. Although much of what she cried was indecipherable, there was no mistaking her begging her aunt to help her, to come for her, not to leave her. Yet as the days progressed, her delusions turned to someone named Yrina, whom she begged over and over for forgiveness. The servant girl he'd brought with them did her best to get her to drink, but he didn't need to be a physician to know that she was dying.

And she was doing it surrounded by her enemies, because the Valcottans had made no move to rescue her. The farther north he took her, the less likely it was that they would.

"Won't be long now, Your Highness," the guard sitting next to him said. "Valcottan bitch has got one foot in the grave. Might as well turn back to Nerastis so that she still looks herself when we throw her corpse across the Anriot."

White-hot fury burned through Keris's veins, the desire to pummel the man making his hands ball into fists and his vision turn red. But that would accomplish *nothing*, least of all sparing Zarrah this fate.

Pulling open the window of the coach, he banged on the side. "Stop. Stop right here."

"Is there a problem, Your Highness?" asked one of the soldiers riding close to the precious cargo. "Has the prisoner—"

"The prisoner is the same. But I'm tired and in need of a nap." He gave a pointed look at the man sitting next to him. "Find a horse or ride with the coachman. I care not."

"But—"

Keris flattened his gaze, and the man blanched, swiftly acceding to his request without further argument.

It was a power that came from fear. The power his father wielded so well, everyone around him too terrified of what he might do to *ever* argue. A power that Keris had never wanted to have, and yet in one act he'd gained it. His stomach twisted, but instead of yielding to the sensation, he pulled the curtains shut and then knelt next to her.

"Valcotta?" He pushed her sweat-soaked hair off her face. "Can you hear me?"

She stirred, then her eyes cracked to reveal dilated pupils that stared at him without focus. "Where . . ."

"A few days south of Vencia. And there has been no sign of your people."

Her lip quivered. "Good."

"I dislike fatalism, Valcotta," he said, because if he didn't speak, he'd crack. Would break down and scream, because he'd done everything right. Had ensured that dozens had seen her alive. Ensured there was no secrecy surrounding his intent to take her to Vencia. The Valcottans knew what had happened and where she was, yet had done *nothing* to retrieve her.

Which meant they'd abandoned Valcotta to her fate.

"Your comrades are cowards. Every last one of them."

She smiled, but it didn't reach her eyes. "Angry your little plan didn't work, Princeling?"

Though the sentiment was not unexpected, her words still stung, with the knowledge that nothing he could say, nothing he could do, would ever be a match for the distrust his name provoked in her. Not just distrust . . . *hate*. Hate placed in her by his father and then compounded by his brothers and by his cursed sister, ensuring that the world believed that all who possessed the Veliant name were monsters.

He wanted to scream. Wanted to pound his fists against the floor of the carriage, wanted to put a knife in his own heart, because everyone he cared about met this end. His affection was murder, his name poison, and he couldn't escape it. "Is there anything I can do that will make you believe that I want you both alive and free? Anything that will make you believe I don't conspire against you or your people?"

Valcotta opened her mouth, then closed it again, staring at him in silence for so long he thought she refused to give him any answer at all. Then she whispered, "Give me your knife."

His heart skipped, hope rising in his chest only for it to be dashed as she said, "Let me go out there and die fighting. Die on my feet. And then make sure my people know it, so they'll not suffer my shame. You do that, and I'll die knowing you are a different man than your father."

"No." The word jerked from his lips, because gaining her trust only for her to lose her life was nothing he'd ever agree to. He refused to consider it. Refused to sit back and watch his soldiers slaughter her. "You get better and I'll give you a knife to fight your way out."

"I'm not going to get better." A tear trickled down her cheek. "And if you wish to prove to me that all that passed between us was *real*, you'll allow me to die with honor, not wasting away like this."

Every part of him wanted to argue. Wanted to tell her that this was a mistake, that she'd recover, that he'd get her free.

Except that was a lie.

She was dying, and would denying her the chance to die on her feet be a mercy to her? Or to him?

Keris slowly pulled a knife from his boot, then pressed it into her palm even as indecision warred in his chest.

Valcotta stared at the knife for a long moment, then lifted her face to meet his gaze, her pupils so dilated that no color remained. "Thank you."

"It was real." His chest tightened painfully, making it hard to breathe. "I swear it, Valcotta. Everything I said. Everything I did. Everything I felt."

"I believe you. But that doesn't change who you are."

Nothing would.

Sliding an arm underneath her, he lifted Valcotta upright so that she was sitting, then unfastened the knots binding her wrists and dropped the ropes to the floor.

"Tell them I untied myself while you were sleeping," she said. "And attacked you."

"You'll be dead, so what does it matter what I say?" He couldn't keep the bitterness from his voice, the darkness rising in his heart whispering that the world might be better if he joined her in the grave.

"It matters to me." Clenching her teeth, she dragged herself to her feet, moving behind him, but he was painfully aware that if she hadn't been holding on to his shoulders, she'd have fallen.

"Call the alarm. Tell them to stop the carriage."

They'd kill her. It would be over in moments.

And he couldn't do it. Couldn't stand back and let her die. Couldn't lose her like that.

"Do it!"

He'd get them to stop the carriage. And then *he'd* fight to get her away. He'd die trying to give her a chance, even if it was the chance to die free. "Guards!" he shouted. "Stop the carriage!"

The carriage lurched, nearly sending them both sprawling. He caught her, accidentally pulling the bandage loose from her arm, revealing the injury beneath. Rather than having healed into a pink line, the skin around the lesion was the gray of a long-dead corpse, and horror filled him as understanding dawned.

The carriage ground to a halt, and he jerked the knife out of her grip, shoving it in his belt just before the guards opened the door to find Valcotta in his arms. "Get me somewhere with a healer," he snarled at them. "She's been poisoned."

And he knew exactly by whom.

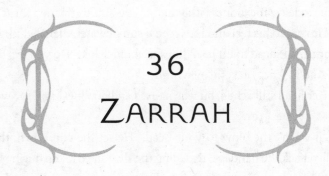

36

ZARRAH

THE WORLD WAS A BLUR AS SHE FADED IN AND OUT OF CON-
sciousness, first too hot and then too cold. Darkness fell, and Zarrah was vaguely aware of Keris lifting her. Carrying her out of the
carriage and into a building, his voice loud as he berated the soldiers. Told them he didn't want them anywhere near her because
they'd damaged his prisoner enough.

Then louder still, him shouting, "You will treat her or, for the
love of God, I'll have you hanged in the square for murder!"

"But she's Valcottan!"

"And I am the Crown Prince of Maridrina." Through the waves
of pain she heard the faint edge of panic in his voice, and it twisted
at her heart. "You will do what I say!"

And then nothing.

ZARRAH WOKE TO THE SOUND of a rooster crowing, the breeze
blowing over her smelling like horse shit and hay. Blinking, she
tried to sit up. Only to find herself tied to the bed on which she lay.

"I'm sorry." His voice was hoarse. "It was the only way they'd agree to leave me alone with you."

He rose to his feet and retrieved a cup of water, then slid a hand beneath her head to lift it so that she could drink. "Do you feel better?"

Her head still ached, but the nausea and dizziness and fog were mostly gone. "Yes."

"It wasn't the blow to your head." He set the cup down, then pulled back the bandage, revealing the slice she'd taken during her capture. It looked as though it had been cut open again and all the dead flesh removed before it was restitched. It was going to leave a significant scar. "There was poison on the blade of the weapon that gave you this. Nightbloom."

Poisons were not her forte, but even she had heard of nightbloom. It hailed from Amarid and was very expensive. Slow to act and always fatal, unless properly treated.

"Who cut you?" he asked. "Whose weapon gave you that injury?"

"I think you know."

"Otis." His jaw tightened. "He knew you were dying and said nothing."

It was possible that the other prince wasn't aware that he'd cut her that night in battle on the beach. It had been dark, and everything had happened so quickly. But her gut told her otherwise.

Keris let out a slow breath, then sat back on the chair, elbows resting on his knees. The sleeves of his shirt were pushed up to reveal his forearms, muscles flexing as he regarded her. In the faint light, she couldn't make out the color of his eyes, and with his hair pulled back as it was, he again appeared the anonymous Maridrinian she'd made love to. But then her gaze jumped to where his coat was draped over another chair, the brilliant blue fabric barely visible beneath all the gold embroidery, and he once again was the Veliant prince. "What is your intent?"

"Same as it has always been," he answered. "To help you to escape. And while you were recovering, I think I discovered a way out of this mess."

Zarrah's stomach flipped, but she kept her expression neutral. "Why would you take such a risk?"

"I—" He broke off, giving his head a sharp shake. "I care about you, Valcotta. More than you seem to realize." His face twisted with grief. "Because of my name, because of who my father is, everyone I care about ends up dead. I refuse to allow you to join their ranks. My dreams are haunted enough as it is."

He'd said it was real. The moments in the carriage before she'd passed out were blurred with fever and pain, but she remembered that. And with that memory came all the others. Of him pressing a knife into her hand, of him allowing her to hold it to his throat. Logic told her that it was madness to believe a Veliant prince would work against his father, would betray his nation, and yet instinct told her that was exactly what Keris was doing.

"Who did he kill?" she found herself asking, knowing it was her heart and not her head that wanted the answer.

His jaw tightened, then he sighed. "The Fifteen-Year Treaty between Maridrina, Harendell, and Ithicana was signed when I was just a boy. Not long after, my father's soldiers took all of his daughters of a certain age from the harem, giving no explanation for where they were being taken. Or for what purpose. All the women accepted it, except for my mother. She tried to go after my sister to get her back, but she was caught. My father strangled her to death in front of me and the rest of the harem to make a point to us of what happened to those who crossed him. Had his men hold me down when I tried to help her. And then he left her body in the middle of the harem garden for weeks so we'd all have to watch her rot." His voice caught. "I still wake up in terror with that smell in my nose."

Zarrah's breath caught, horror filling her chest because she knew that smell. Knew what it was like to watch a mother's flesh blacken and foul. To watch the flies swarm and the buzzards circle overhead.

"Fifteen years later, my sister Lara reemerged from the Red Desert and was sent to Ithicana. And given what she did to that kingdom, I think it fair to say that my father killed the sweet little girl I knew and brought to life a creature made in his image. A monster. A queen who leaves the corpses of her enemies in her wake."

Zarrah shivered, something about the story sending unease through her chest.

"I know you have no reason to trust me, Valcotta. But at least take some comfort that I hate my father every bit as much as you do."

She shouldn't believe him. Shouldn't trust him. And yet in this, every one of her instincts told her that he was telling her the truth.

Rising to his feet, Keris shocked her by unfastening her bindings. As she sat, he handed her a knife. "Beneath the window is a barn," he said. "Climb across it and you should be able to jump over the pigpen to the neighboring building, then drop down into the alley. After that, escape is whichever way you choose."

He was letting her go. And not just letting her go but giving her a route for escape.

"Hit me on the back of the head hard enough to knock me out," he said. "That way, if worse comes to worst and you're recaptured, I'll still be alive to try to help you."

This was her moment. Her chance to get away and return to her people in Nerastis. Yet Zarrah found herself hesitating, wondering if escape was truly the path to reclaiming the honor she'd lost.

Silas Veliant was her enemy. The man who'd murdered her mother. The one she desired vengeance against.

"Dawn is nearly here, Valcotta," he said quietly. "It needs to be now, or the opportunity will be lost. As soon as the sun rises, we travel to my father's palace in Vencia, and once you're inside, there will be no escape."

Not just inside the city, but inside the Rat King's impenetrable palace—a goal long denied her people. As Keris's prisoner, she'd have the chance to get closer to Silas than she'd ever dreamed possible.

Perhaps close enough to kill.

Rising to her feet, Zarrah shifted the knife in her grip so that the pommel was down, seeing Keris tense as he readied himself for the blow.

The enemy of my enemy is my friend.

Could she trust Keris with her plan? Did he hate his father enough to see it through? She wavered, uncertainty churning through her thoughts, but then he looked up at her.

And that *cursed* blue hardened her resolve.

Zarrah swayed on her feet, allowing the weapon to slip from her hand to land with a clatter. "I . . ." She let her knees buckle, rolling her eyes back as she dropped.

Swearing, Keris caught her, and Zarrah kept her eyes closed and her body limp as he settled her back on the bed.

"Your Highness?" a concerned voice called through the door. "Are you well?"

"Fine," he snapped, and she could feel his frustration. His panic. "I dropped something."

The doorknob jiggled, and Zarrah forced herself to breathe deeply as Keris cursed under his breath, fumbling to retie the ropes binding her to the bed.

"Your Highness?" the voice called, then again, with growing alarm: "Your Highness, please open the door."

"Calm yourself!"

Her ears filled with the sound of the latch being unfastened, the door opening, then boots scuffing against the wooden floors.

"Apologies, my lord," the man said. "But word you are traveling to the city with a prisoner has preceded us to Vencia, and an honor guard was dispatched to ensure your safety. They arrived in the night and are waiting to escort you the rest of the journey."

"It's not even dawn, and the prisoner is still unconscious. Tell them to wait."

The guard cleared his throat. "There is concern that the Valcottans might yet attempt rescue, my lord. Better that we not tarry. I'll arrange for a stretcher to carry the prisoner to the carriage."

Silence.

Zarrah held her breath, waiting to see if Keris would argue. Whether he'd find a reason to delay their departure so as to give her another chance to escape. And whether in doing so, he'd stymie her own growing plans.

"His Majesty sent word with them that you were to come with all due haste," the man finally added, and it was all Zarrah could do not to smile as Keris answered, "Then I suppose we must do so. Arrange the stretcher."

She kept her eyes closed as they carried her out to the carriage and settled her on the bench, her nose filling with Keris's spicy scent as he joined her inside. Then a whip cracked and the carriage moved forward, the horses soon urged into a fast canter, pulling them north.

Toward Vencia.

Toward the palace of her enemy.

And once she was inside, Zarrah intended to cut out Silas Veliant's heart.

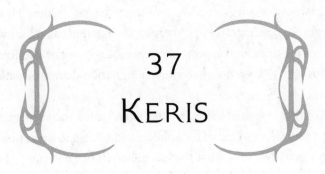

37
KERIS

How had things gotten so terribly out of his control?

Keris bit at his thumbnail, staring out the window but not seeing the homes and businesses lining Vencia's streets as they bounced over the cobbles, moving ever closer to his father's palace.

Valcotta sat slumped against the side of the carriage, her eyes closed, her cheeks still hollowed from the toll the poison had taken on her.

It had been unreasonable to expect her to be physically capable of escape after how sick she'd been, and yet it had still been a shock when she'd fainted in his arms. There was something about her that had always seemed indomitable—she who, on her deathbed, had still been willing to pick up a weapon and fight. And if not for the fact she'd slept nearly the rest of the journey, he'd have questioned whether her faint had been an act.

Sweat ran in rivulets down his spine, the steady throb of his pulse loud as they rolled through the gates of the palace, the carriage rocking as it came to a halt, causing Zarrah to sit upright.

"We're here." He searched her face for a hint of her thoughts, but she gave only a grim nod, then squared her shoulders. He had to fight the desire to take up a weapon and attempt to get her away. Except the time for weapons had passed, and now he had to rely on his wits to keep her alive long enough to find another path to escape.

Someone opened the door, and Keris exited the carriage, his heart thundering. One of the soldiers reached up to catch hold of Zarrah's bound wrists, but she jerked herself free and stepped out of the carriage, chin high. Even in her rough woolen dress, her hair unwashed and tangled, she looked like an empress, not a prisoner.

I will get you out of this, he silently promised her. *No matter the cost.*

Turning to one of the servants who was offering towels to wipe the grime of travel from his hands, Keris asked, "Is he here?" There was no need to be specific. In this palace, only one man mattered.

"Yes, Your Highness." She accepted back the soiled towel. "In his office. I'll send word to him that you have arrived with the . . ." Her gaze flicked to Valcotta, expression darkening.

"Prisoner?" he supplied before the servant could come up with anything disparaging. "No need. I'll go to him directly."

But before Keris could move, a scream split the air, loud and piercing and full of fear.

A scream that had come from the inner sanctum of the palace. Where all of his aunts and youngest siblings resided.

Uneasy, Keris motioned for the soldiers to bring Valcotta and strode across the stable yard to the gates of the inner walls. As he drew nearer, his eyes landed on two hooded figures on their knees, wrists bound. "Who are they?"

The soldiers guarding them exchanged looks, then one reluctantly replied, "Ithicanian prisoners, Your Highness. Serin is . . ." The man trailed off, and Keris's mouth soured. God, but he despised that creature.

"Does my father know the Magpie is playing with his toys in the garden?" He immediately waved a hand at the man, silencing any need for response. "Never mind. Of course he knows."

The soldiers swiftly searched him for weapons, then swung open the gate. Keris moved into the sanctum, the scents of flowers and misting fountains filling his nose even as his eyes filled with the sight of Serin ripping the fingernails off a hooded woman's hands, an unfamiliar man chained to a bench before them.

What madness was this?

"How do we get into Eranahl?" Serin's words reached Keris's ears. "No? Let's see how she holds up to losing her fingers."

"Pull out the damned gate!" the chained man screamed, and Keris fought the urge to intervene.

This was happening on his father's orders, which meant he was powerless to stop it. To try would have consequences he couldn't risk with Valcotta's life at stake.

"How do we manage that?" Serin picked up another tool, and the chained man fell to his knees.

"*Please.*" The desperation in the man's voice made Keris's stomach twist. Especially since he knew this was the least of the horrors Serin was capable of conjuring. He was a sadist of the first order.

"A strategy, Aren," the Magpie crooned. "Give us a strategy, and this will all be over."

Aren. The Ithicanian king.

Realization struck Keris, but before he could react, the woman being tortured twisted free from the guards holding her. She threw herself at the Ithicanian king, then reached up with her bound hands and pulled the sack from her head.

At the sight of her face, the Ithicanian king's eyes widened in surprise before quickly turning to horror. Not whom he'd expected, apparently, but most assuredly someone he knew.

"Idiots," Serin hissed at the guards. "Get her back!"

The men stalked closer, their eyes wary despite the king being chained and outnumbered. And Keris knew the hesitation would cost them as resolve flashed over the Ithicanian's face—an unwillingness to allow the young woman to suffer any further. Serin saw it, too, and he shrieked, "Stop him!"

But it was too late.

With a quick twist of his muscled arms, the Ithicanian king broke the woman's neck, the crack audible. As was Zarrah's soft intake of breath from where she stood at his elbow.

An act of mercy. That was what it had been. But from the look in the king's eyes, it would still weigh upon his soul.

"Hang her up," Serin ordered, and Keris pressed his hands to his thighs to keep them from clenching, forcing himself to watch as the men dragged the dead girl over to the wall, leaving streaks of crimson in their wake. One of the soldiers above dropped a rope, which they fastened around her neck, the trio hauling her up until she dangled out of reach from one of the cornices, the blood dripping from her foot splattering against the green of the lawn. A wave of dizziness ran through Keris, old and painful memories rising to the forefront of his thoughts at the sight.

Then Serin said, "Bring out the other two prisoners."

Enough. He'd watch no more of this.

Crossing his arms, Keris snapped, "Good God, Serin! Don't you have holes and dark places where you conduct this sort of business? What's next? Beheadings at the dinner table?"

Displeasure rose on the spymaster's face at the sight of him, but that didn't stop Keris from picking his way closer, avoiding the splatters of blood on the path.

"Your Highness." Serin gave a slight bow. "You are supposed to be in Nerastis."

As though the bastard hadn't known Keris was coming. And

whom he had with him. "Yes, well, we captured ourselves quite a prize. It seemed prudent that I ensure she arrive in one piece. Broken things make for less valuable leverage."

Serin's gaze went past Keris, his bushy gray eyebrows rising in recognition, his shock masterfully feigned. "General Zarrah Anaphora, the empress's niece. You've outdone yourself, Highness. You'll be in your father's favor."

"I doubt that."

Serin's eyes gleamed in unspoken agreement. "Now that you've delivered her, I assume you'll be returning to Nerastis immediately."

Ignoring the statement, Keris pushed his hair behind one ear, focusing on King Aren, who remained kneeling on the ground. He was both tall and broad, the heavy muscles of his arms visible even through his clothes. As formidable as was rumored, and rather obnoxiously good-looking. "Is this the Ithicanian king, then? I must say, he's less terrifying than I anticipated. I'm rather disappointed to see that he does not, in fact, have horns."

"The *former* king. Ithicana no longer exists."

Keris glanced at the corpse hanging from the wall, this performance suggesting a rather different truth from the one the Magpie offered. Suggesting that both Ithicana and its king remained very much a problem. But involving himself in this was not something Keris could afford to do. "My mistake. Do carry on."

Stepping past the Ithicanian, Keris started in the direction of the tower, but the sound of Valcotta's voice stopped him. Turning, he found her on her knees before the king.

"I am sorry, Your Grace." Her eyes glittered with unshed tears. "For all that you have lost. And for the part I played in that coming to pass. I pray one day to have the opportunity to atone."

What was she talking about?

Before Valcotta could say more, one of the soldiers dragged her upright, snarling, "The only thing you should be praying for is that His Majesty chooses not to spike your head on Vencia's gate, you Valcottan wretch!"

Valcotta spat in the man's face, but as he lifted his hand to strike her, Keris snapped, "Have you forgotten the fate of the last man who struck my prize?"

It disgusted him to refer to her in such a manner, but fear was the only way he could protect her right now.

Blanching, the soldier muttered to Zarrah, "Move along." But beyond them, Keris didn't miss the way Serin's brow furrowed with interest at the reaction. And garnering Serin's interest was the last thing he needed.

Play your part. Be who he expects you to be. With the thought in his head, Keris continued toward the tower but called back over his shoulder, "Make sure you clean up your mess, Magpie." And then he stepped inside, readying himself to face his true opponent.

38

ZARRAH

ZARRAH'S PULSE THRUMMED AS SHE WAS PULLED AWAY FROM THE Ithicanian king, her stomach a twist of emotions, the first and foremost guilt.

She knew what had happened in Ithicana after the invasion. Had heard stories of the slaughter enacted by Maridrinian hands. But there was a difference between hearing stories of suffering and seeing it with her own eyes.

You are complicit, her guilt whispered as she followed Keris up the seemingly endless stairs to the top of the tower. *That girl's torture at the Magpie's hands? Her death? The look in the king's eyes? All burdens you must share.*

Her mind drifted, remembering the moment she'd watched the Maridrinian Navy sail past her fleet to attack Ithicana, struggling to understand the choice she'd made. Found herself certain, if presented with a similar circumstance, that she'd walk a far different path. And her eyes went to Keris, convinced that for better or worse, it was knowing him that had changed her.

She would atone for the mistakes of her past. Not just for the sake of her honor but for the sake of herself. And she'd do it by killing Silas Veliant.

Reaching the top of the stairs, Keris paused, waiting while one of the guards stepped inside the chamber, the other glowering at her with undisguised hatred. As had every Maridrinian who'd laid eyes upon her since her arrival.

The guard stepped back outside. "He'll see you now, Your Highness."

"Perfect. Would've been a shame to have walked up all those stairs for nothing." The guards searched them for weapons, then Keris stepped past them and into the room, the man holding her arms shoving Zarrah after him.

The top of the tower was enclosed primarily with glass. While she was certain the view was impressive, her eyes went immediately to the man sitting behind a heavy desk, elbows resting on the arms of his chair, azure eyes twin to Keris's. Eyes that had given her nightmares for more than a decade.

King Silas Veliant of Maridrina.

Rage, blistering hot and fierce, scorched through her, and despite her wrists being bound, it was all Zarrah could do not to lunge at him. To claw his eyes out and rip his heart from his chest. But she'd get only one chance, and she needed to make it count.

"Keris." Silas's voice was deep and dripped with authority. "I didn't give you permission to leave Nerastis." Then his gaze moved to Zarrah. "Or to bring a *Valcottan* into my home. Explain yourself."

Keris shifted, rolling his shoulders, and Zarrah sensed his fear. "Apologies for the slight, Your Grace, but keeping her in Nerastis while I waited for a message to reach you, and for you to reply in kind, risked the Valcottans attacking in an effort to retrieve her."

"One of the many reasons we don't bother with prisoners." The king steepled his fingers. "I believe the current practice is to dismember them and catapult the pieces back over the Anriot, though I confess it's been some time since I visited the city."

"Yes, well, I deemed that shortsighted."

"Shortsighted?" The king's eyes narrowed.

"As I believe you've been made aware, this is General Zarrah Anaphora. The empress's niece, captured on our side of the Anriot."

"*General* Zarrah Anaphora." The king laughed, as though her holding the military title was the epitome of ridiculousness. She clenched her teeth because the alternative was to bare them, and it was better that he believed her cowed. Better that he believed her a helpless woman right up to the moment she slit his throat.

Silas rose to his feet and circled the desk. Then he waved a hand at the guards who'd followed them in, dismissing them. Only when the door shut behind them did he add, "Caught by you, Keris?"

"Hardly. That would require me lowering myself to patrol, which you know I have no tolerance for. Otis caught her trying to cross back over the Anriot."

"Makes one wonder what she was doing on our side in the first place. Do you know?"

Keris shook his head, and Zarrah couldn't help but imagine how his father would react if he knew the truth. "She refuses to say."

"Perhaps we might let Serin speak to her."

It was impossible to hide the flash of fear that lanced through her, and Silas smiled. Reaching out, he caught her by the chin, lifting her face to regard her thoughtfully. Zarrah cringed at his foul breath, the feel of his touch making her nauseous. Yet it was well worth it, because he was now within reach. And if he exposed his back to her, she might get the chance to snap his neck.

"I'd rather avoid Serin's involvement," Keris said. "If what's going on in the gardens is any indication, all we'd have when he was through with her is information of dubious value and another corpse to add to the décor."

"The walls, I'm afraid, are reserved for Ithicanians and Aren's viewing pleasure. I wouldn't want him to think I hang just anyone up to rot in my garden."

Keris flinched, swiftly adding, "Why not just kill him?" to cover the reaction.

The king dropped his fingers from Zarrah's chin and shook his head. "That's not your concern. Obviously you have a reason for bringing this girl here. Speak your mind."

Zarrah forced herself to breathe, lest she betray her own trepidation over what Keris intended to say.

"The Valcottans have several of our people prisoner in Pyrinat. We *could* offer her in exchange for their release, but I propose something more . . . *ambitious.*"

Zarrah tensed, her guts in ropes.

"Oh?" The king's brow furrowed in interest even as her stomach sank like lead at the prospect of being ransomed. At the thought of being used to extort concessions from her aunt.

The trust built when Keris had offered her the opportunity to escape wavered, replaced once again with the fear that he'd been playing her this whole time. That his agenda had always been to further himself, and she a fool to believe otherwise.

Keris's plans don't matter, she silently reminded herself. All that mattered was her finding a way to kill the creature standing before her.

Keris cleared his throat. "Even with Ithicana on the brink of falling—"

"It has fallen," Silas interrupted sharply. "All that remains is to clean up the rubble."

"Allow me to rephrase. Even with our hold on the bridge secure, it benefits us little with Valcotta stymieing trade. One might argue that at this point, all it is doing is *costing* us."

It was costing Valcotta, too. Dozens of merchant ships were already lost to the Tempest Seas' violent and unpredictable weather, but her aunt had declared she'd stop trade entirely before paying Silas Veliant a copper to use the bridge.

"What I propose," Keris continued, "is that we offer General Anaphora up in exchange for a trade agreement between Maridrina and Valcotta, which would see gold in our pockets and their heir back"—he glanced in her direction—"breathing and in one piece."

Zarrah barely heard his words, her pulse roaring as Silas started to turn, exposing his back to her. This was her chance. She'd get her bound wrists around his neck, and it would be over.

You can do this. You can end this.

Then Silas paused and met her gaze, a smile rising to his lips. He *knew.* Knew she wasn't cowed, knew what she intended, and his eyes gleamed as he backed away from her, taking a seat at his desk. "Breathing and in one piece, so she can again cause us trouble."

She wouldn't get the jump on him. Not now, not like this. Which meant she needed to find a better opportunity, and that meant staying alive long enough to do so.

Which meant she needed to play along with Keris's plan.

Keris slipped into the chair across from his father. "I didn't say it was a perfect solution. But killing her would incense the Valcottans enough to move against us, which would not be ideal, given that much of our forces remain engaged with quelling the Ithicanians."

"Why am I not surprised that you'd offer up a strategy that avoids war?"

"Not 'avoids war,' Father. Just avoids us losing one."

Silas was silent for a long time, wheels of thought turning in his eyes, then he lifted one shoulder. "There might be merit to this plan of yours, Keris. I'll keep the girl here while I consider if what we might gain in exchanging her is worth more than the goodwill executing her would earn me with our people. But don't bother unpacking your bags—I'll forgive your decision to deliver her to Vencia, but you *will* return to Nerastis with all haste."

If the order surprised him, Keris didn't show it. "I thought you might allow me the opportunity to negotiate the agreement, Your Grace." He hesitated. "We both know that I've no head for military matters, but such is not the case when it comes to economics. Allow me the opportunity to prove my worth." His jaw flexed. "Please."

Using the word had cost him. She could see it, and judging from the thoughtful expression on his father's face, he'd seen it, too.

"This is unlike you, Keris," the king said after a long moment. "And that makes me mistrustful of your intentions, which are nearly always contrary to my own."

Keris exhaled a soft breath, then nodded. "In that, this is no different. I wish to live, and to achieve that end, I must earn your favor in whatever way I can."

The silence stretched, Zarrah's heart racing as she watched the king consider Keris's request. If he sent his son away, Zarrah knew she was a dead woman. Without Keris to argue otherwise, Silas would choose the path that protected his pride, and she'd likely never get the opportunity to try to kill him. But if Keris bought her time . . .

"You may remain for as long as I perceive your efforts yield some worth," Silas finally answered. "But fail in this . . ."

"I won't fail you, Father."

Instead of answering, the king turned on Zarrah, running his tongue over his bottom lip. "And you, *General*. I will grant you my hospitality for now, but if you make any effort to escape, rest assured that I won't hesitate to remove your head." He smiled. "Much like I did your mother's."

Logic burned away, reason turning to ash. The world around Zarrah turned bright, blood roaring in her ears as a scream rose in her chest. As her hands balled into fists, every inch of her wanted to attack. Wanted to rip out his eyes and his tongue and then carve him apart piece by piece. But she was bound wrist and ankle, the guards outside only a dozen paces away.

You will get only one chance.

So she took a deep breath, digging for calm as Silas laughed at her. The same laugh that filled her nightmares.

The laugh that had brought her here.

He rose to his feet. "I cherish that particular kill. Now, if you'll excuse me, I have another prisoner requiring my attention."

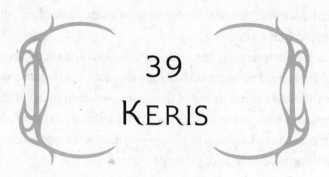

39
KERIS

I CHERISH THAT PARTICULAR KILL.

Anger simmered in Keris's guts as he pulled Valcotta from the room, knowing that if she were subjected to any more of his father's barbs, she'd try to kill him, consequences be damned.

Either that, or Keris would try to kill the sadistic prick himself.

Avoiding Valcotta's gaze, he growled "Bring her" at the guards waiting outside the door, then started down the stairs. He exited on the second level in order to take one of the enclosed walkways that connected the tower to the other buildings of the inner sanctum. As he crossed, his eyes flicked to the three corpses now hanging from the wall, crows already circling above.

Aren Kertell remained chained to a bench, his face blank and unreadable as he stared at the corpses, Serin nowhere in sight. Which meant the Magpie was probably on his way to meet with Keris's father to discuss whatever he'd learned from the prisoner king. It wouldn't be long until the bodies started to stink, until the flies began to swarm and the birds to pick at their flesh, and dizziness swept over him as memory juxtaposed with reality.

Shaking his head to clear it, Keris stepped into the harem's quarters, which, despite the hallway being empty, were loud with female chatter, shouting children, and a few crying babies. "Go back to the main palace," he said to the soldiers, taking Valcotta's arm himself. "This place is not for your eyes."

And not waiting to see if they complied, he pulled Valcotta along with him, allowing the door to slam shut.

She looked with curiosity at the closed doors lining the curved hallway, her tone cool as she asked, "What is this place?"

"The harem." His voice was sharper than he intended, his apprehension over the conversation he was about to have with his aunt nearly as bad as he'd felt over the one with his father. "Men aren't allowed in here."

She arched one eyebrow at him and Keris sighed. "Obviously I'm exempt. I meant men who are not of my family."

Her eyes brightened. "So there are no guards?"

Giving her a long look of warning, he said, "There are," the verity of the statement revealed as they reached the apex of the curved hallway, where two such guards stood outside a closed door. "But they've had certain parts removed, if you get my meaning."

Zarrah let out a shocked breath, but she said nothing as he gave a firm knock on the heavy wood. After a moment, it swung open, revealing an exceptionally beautiful woman with ivory skin and hair so blond it was nearly white.

Lestara was the daughter of a king of one of the smaller nations north of Harendell, having been offered as a bride in exchange for one of Keris's half sisters. She was several years younger than Keris was himself, but because she had the habit of looking at him like he was something she might one day consume, he said, "Good morning, *Auntie*."

Lestara's eyes widened at the sight of him, and she dropped into a low curtsy. "Your Highness! We hadn't been made aware you were in Vencia." Then she caught sight of Zarrah, and the pleasure on her face was eaten away by anger. Despite having lived in Maridrina less than a year, the harem's prejudices had already worn off on her. "Why is there a *Valcottan* in our house?"

She said *Valcottan* like Keris might say *worm*, and for no reason other than to goad her, he said, "I finally decided to get married."

Lestara's amber eyes bulged, but the joke was ruined as a voice belonging to an older woman said, "He's teasing you, girl. Not even Keris has the balls to marry a Valcottan. Mostly because he knows I'd chop them off myself if he ever did so."

"What an awful thing to say, Auntie Coralyn." He tugged Valcotta into the room. "You know how attached I am to them."

The matriarch of the royal harem snorted and took a long sip of steaming tea, eyeing him up and down. After his own mother was murdered, Coralyn had personally seen to Keris's upbringing, and even after he'd grown too old to live within these walls—his father uninterested in competition, least of all from his sons—he'd remained close with her by letter and frequent visits. She'd intervened often between him and his father in his youth, and though it had not come to pass, had fought tirelessly on his behalf for him to attend university in Harendell. Not because she had any time for philosophy but because she'd recognized that remaining in Maridrina would be the death of him.

"You'd better have a good explanation for this, boy. And it better *not* have anything to do with her pretty face."

"Otis captured her, not me, so if you're going to cast stones, direct them at him. I merely recognized her worth and decided to capitalize upon it."

"Oh?" Coralyn crossed her arms. "Care to elaborate, or are you more interested in standing there looking smug?"

"This is Zarrah Anaphora. She's . . ." Keris trailed off as every woman in the room rose, their faces darkening. On the surface, the harem seemed soft and civilized, but he knew better. Knew what they were capable of, if pressed.

"You can't kill her." He stepped between Zarrah and the other women. "I'm going to ransom her back to the empress in exchange for a trade deal with Valcotta. I'm afraid that requires her alive, so control yourselves."

One of Coralyn's eyebrows rose. "Sometimes you are too busy being clever to think about whether what you're doing is smart, boy. Do you have any notion how many of the harem's sons have been lost to the Valcottans? This woman personally murdered your brother."

Keris made a face. "You yourself said Rask was an idiot and a sadist, Auntie. Don't go pretending to be morose over his loss."

Coralyn opened her mouth, but the retort in her eyes never reached her lips as Zarrah said, "I didn't murder him. I met him blade to blade on the field of battle, and while fate favored my life over his, he died with his weapon in his hand, cursing my name."

Silence fell over the room, and Keris clenched his teeth as he waited for wrath to fall upon her. And him.

But Coralyn only lifted one shoulder in a shrug. "Better a weapon than his manhood, I suppose. We've had a few lost in the brothels over the years, and it's truly embarrassing for all involved."

Zarrah laughed softly, and the tone of it made Keris's skin prickle with memory. The last time he'd heard her laugh was when she'd been naked in his arms. Was before she knew his name. He shoved aside the sensation. "Rask notwithstanding, I'm well aware of the enmity between her family and ours. But our coffers grow thin, and if you wish to remain in the style to which you're accustomed, we need Valcottan revenue from the bridge."

"I dislike this, Keris. You've brought a fox into the henhouse."

"You don't need to like it. You need only find her a room and ensure she is kept in comfort fitting her title. And while she might be a fox, don't pretend you and yours are helpless hens, because I know better."

His aunt made a noncommittal noise, then took a mouthful of tea. "Fine. But this will be on my terms, Keris. My rules. Is that understood?"

"I wouldn't dare presume otherwise."

The look she gave him said that she didn't believe that for a heartbeat. Taking hold of Zarrah's arm, he inclined his head to the women and started toward the door. "Which room do you want me to put her in?"

"The one at the end of the hall has bars on the window. And a secure door. It will do." Then Coralyn eyed Zarrah. "I'll arrange for more appropriate attire."

"Excellent." He edged toward the door, but Coralyn's hand latched onto his arm with surprising strength.

"You aren't going anywhere until we discuss the matter of compensation, Keris." Gesturing to a servant, she rattled off instructions as pertained to Zarrah's attire, then opened the door and barked at the two guards outside, "Take the prisoner to the room at the end and stay with her until I arrive to inspect the security."

Neither guard argued—they knew better than to cross Coralyn—one taking Zarrah's arm and leading her out, the servant trailing after them.

"Sit," Coralyn said. "Have tea with us."

Equal parts annoyed and curious about what the harem wanted from him, Keris obliged, sipping from the steaming cup that Lestara handed to him and waiting while the women settled themselves. His father had somewhere around fifty wives, but only twelve were currently present, playing court to their unofficial queen. Never mind that of all his wives, Keris's father despised

Coralyn the most. *Meddlesome, sour-tongued old hag,* he always called her, but not even Silas Veliant was stupid enough to attempt undermining the harem's order.

"You might have noticed that we are hosting another prisoner," his aunt finally said. "King Aren Kertell of Ithicana."

"King no longer, I'm told."

One of her eyebrows rose, and he added, "I witnessed a portion of Serin's performance with him in the gardens. There's nothing I can do about it, if that's what you're suggesting. My father is more likely to listen to the harem's complaints than mine."

"I'm aware." She sipped her tea. "Silas has forbidden any of us to speak to Aren, but you are under no such restrictions. There is information we hope he can provide us."

He eyed her for a long moment. "About Lara, you mean?"

"Yes. And the rest of your sisters."

Keris had been nine when his father had taken Lara and his half sisters away without any explanation. All the five- and six-year-old daughters stolen from the harem, their fates kept secret until last year when his father had arrived back in Vencia after a trip to the desert, and in his company, one of the missing girls.

Lara.

She'd immediately boarded a ship and sailed off to Ithicana, the bride destined to fulfill Maridrina's half of the Fifteen-Year Treaty between Ithicana, Maridrina, and Harendell. Upon his return from the nuptials at Southwatch Island, his father had explained that she and her other sisters had been kept in a secret compound in the Red Desert in order to protect them from Valcottan assassins. The others, he'd said, would continue to reside there until he'd found appropriate matches for them.

Lies, on every level, though the truth hadn't been revealed until his father invaded Ithicana using a plan of Lara's invention, his sister apparently having been trained by Serin himself as a spy. And a deadly one at that. "Lara's either dead or a ghost on the wind. And my other sisters are still in their secret compound in—"

"If that's where they are, then why is Serin hunting them?" Coralyn interrupted. "And why is he hunting Lara?"

Keris's jaw tightened. *Loose ends.* His father hated leaving anyone alive who might cause him trouble in the future. But why did his father have cause to doubt the young women he'd turned into fundamentalists who blindly followed his orders no matter the cost? "Don't you think if Aren knew where Lara was that he'd gladly give her over?"

"He probably would, if he wasn't in love with her."

Keris huffed out a laugh. "Maybe he was once, but Lara stabbed him in the back. Betrayed him and Ithicana, costing him his throne, his liberty, and the lives of countless of his people." As he blinked, Keris again saw the light fading from Raina's eyes. Lara had killed her as surely as if she'd wielded the blade herself. "He'd have to be a damned fool to still care for her."

"I'm not unaware, Keris. Yet during that despicable scene in my gardens, Serin tricked Aren into believing the girl he was torturing was Lara. And he pleaded she be spared."

More than pleaded.

The vision of Aren on his knees, shouting, *Pull out the damn gate!* filled Keris's head, and he frowned. "If it is so, then he's not going to give up Lara's whereabouts to you, me, or anyone else. He has no reason to trust us."

"Then find a way to give him one so that we might find out what he knows of the harem's lost daughters," Coralyn said. "That is the price of our hospitality for your Valcottan."

If his father or Serin caught him meddling with the Ithicanian king, it wouldn't go well for him, and as it was, Keris needed to focus on negotiating with the empress. Needed to focus on getting

Valcotta free. But he knew the harem was dangerous if crossed, and if he didn't pay their price, it wouldn't be long until a *freak* accident took Valcotta's life. "Fine. But accomplishing this will be difficult. Maybe even impossible."

Coralyn reached across the table and patted his cheek. "You've always been cleverer than the Magpie, Keris. I have every faith you'll deliver."

"I'm glad you do." He rose to his feet. "Take care of my Valcottan." And without waiting for a response, he exited the room.

He had a negotiation to begin.

40
ZARRAH

ALL THE LUXURY IN THE WORLD WOULDN'T MAKE UP FOR THE fact the room had bars on the window and a bolt on the door.

It was a prison.

And it wasn't lost on Zarrah that it wasn't a prison intended for individuals such as herself but rather for wives of the King of Maridrina. Likely girls who were reticent about being wed to an aging monster who'd treat them like broodmares. The very thought of it made her sick, and she added them to the list of people who'd see vengeance when Silas fell to her blade.

A cold voice from behind her interrupted Zarrah's thoughts. "Allow me to make myself very clear, Zarrah: this is my house. You will dress in the clothes I provide. Conduct yourself in a manner I find fitting. Speak only to those who speak to you first. And you will never lay so much as a finger on a single member of this household."

Turning, Zarrah found the wife called Coralyn standing behind her, flanked by two guards. Perhaps in her mid-sixties, the woman was stately in her gown of amber brocade, her hair perfectly coiffed, and the jewels on her fingers, wrists, ears, and throat worth enough to purchase one of the more costly homes in Vencia.

"If you cross me on any of these things, I'll have you killed, and I don't care what Silas or Keris has to say about it. Am I understood?"

A hundred retorts rose in Zarrah's thoughts, the foremost being *I could kill you before those two fools moved, you old Maridrinian hag*, but instead she gave the slightest of nods. If pandering to a harem wife was what it would take, then pander she would.

"Not only are you Valcottan and a member of the Valcottan royal family, but you are a soldier responsible for the death of at least one of our sons by your own hand. And indirectly the cause of the death of many more. You may anticipate courtesy from the women of my household, but do not expect kindness. Am I understood?"

"I understand and will abide." Right up to the point she put a knife in Silas Veliant's heart.

"Good." Coralyn snapped her fingers, and servants moved into the room carrying a bath, several others on their heels. "Measure her for gowns. She's a princess of sorts, so she is to be dressed accordingly. I've a reputation to uphold, and I won't have her returning to Valcotta to spread rumors that the Veliant house is cheap."

Then she approached, caught hold of Zarrah's wrists, and untied the ropes.

"Lady Coralyn," one of the guards said, his eyes widening with distress. "Are you certain this is advisable? She's a killer."

"So am I." Coralyn looked up to meet Zarrah's gaze. "And I can see in your eyes that you've a brain between your ears. You won't cross me, will you, dear?"

"I wouldn't dream of it, Lady Coralyn."

The old woman patted her cheek. "Good girl. You can dine in here alone once you are bathed. I'm certain, after the journey from

Nerastis, that you're desperate for privacy and silence. God knows, Keris does like the sound of his own voice." Yet as she turned, she told the guard, "Keep the door locked and under guard at all times."

Zarrah allowed the seamstresses to measure her without comment, trying not to stare longingly at the bath as the servants filled it with steaming water and set a tray of salts and soaps and scrubs to one side of it. As soon as the seamstresses departed with their notes, she stripped off her filthy garments and stepped into the steaming water, wincing as she looked down. The poison had leached her strength, eating away at both muscle and curve, and she looked as weak as she felt. It disgusted her, so she sank under the water, all sound turning muffled.

God, how long had it been since she'd had a proper bath? Not since before she'd met Keris on the dam that fateful night. Not since he'd had her in every possible way, and she him. Beneath the water and with her eyes closed, memories of that night drifted over her. Of how he'd devoured her with a look. How he'd made her feel more powerful and alive than she had in years, if ever. How it had felt to be joined with him, not just in flesh but in thought.

That was the Maridrinian. Not Keris Veliant.

She wasn't certain if it was because of the act he played that she couldn't reconcile the two or that she subconsciously didn't want to. Didn't want the man she'd fallen for to be the same man as the one she reviled in every possible way. And it drove her to madness that in one moment, her gut told her he was on her side and in the next that all his words were a manipulation intended to achieve his own ends.

It doesn't matter, she told herself. *If he realizes your intent, he'll try to stop you.* Because as much as Keris seemed to hate Silas, the man was still his father.

And yet . . . Zarrah's hair drifted in the water, brushing against her cheeks, her eyes still closed as she remembered how he'd spoken of Silas. *My father is an unrepentant prick the world would be better off without.* His words whispered through her thoughts, tempting her. Making her *want* to trust him.

The need to breathe grew too intense to be denied, and Zarrah sat upright in the bath, gasping in a mouthful of air and ignoring the alarmed looks of the pair of servant women. Resting her chin on her knees, she squeezed her eyes shut. *The words were the bluster of a man pretending to be something he is not,* she thought. *If he meant them, he'd have taken action long ago.*

"Something to drink, my lady?" one of the servants asked, holding out a glass of wine. Zarrah accepted it, suddenly feeling more exhausted than she had since she'd been on her deathbed.

The man you fell for isn't real, but Keris Veliant is, she told herself. *He was a fabrication. An act. A pretense. Which means you didn't fall for him at all.*

Or so she would keep telling herself.

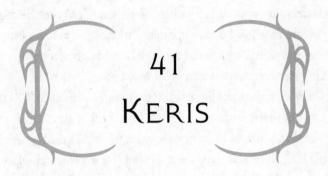

41
KERIS

VALCOTTA WAS BEING EXCEPTIONALLY AGREEABLE.

And that made Keris exceptionally nervous.

For all she'd made no move against his father, there'd been no mistaking the murder in her eyes when she'd come face-to-face with her mother's killer. She wanted him dead; there was no doubt. And in that, their thoughts were aligned.

It was the method that had him concerned. He'd bought her time, but that mattered little if she got herself killed in the pursuit of honor and vengeance.

Sitting up straight, Keris winced as his spine cracked from hours of leaning over pen and paper. He was in the heir's quarters in the tower, though this was the first time he'd been here since Rask died. His things had been brought from his residence in the city, but there were still traces of his elder brother, most notably the furniture. It was all sized as though for a giant, the bed large enough for ten, the heavy wood covered with gold leaf and the bedding vivid indigo with gold stripes.

He hated every piece of it.

But more than that, he hated being parted from Valcotta. For days upon days, he'd been at her side, and her absence, especially in this place, had his nerves on edge. Not only because she was surrounded by enemies but because he knew her mind, at least, would not be sitting idle. Which meant it was only a matter of time until she took action.

Closing his eyes, Keris allowed his thoughts to drift, visions of Valcotta filling them. He'd seen hardened warriors reduced to tears in his father's presence. Yet despite the bastard threatening her life and digging into the wound of her mother's murder, Valcotta had stood defiant, never losing control. Every bit the empress she was destined to become, and the vision of her stirred heat in him that, for long days, had been tempered by circumstance.

"Idiot," he muttered. "You're the last man she wants anywhere near her."

And even if it were otherwise, he'd not pursue pleasureful ends. Not because the risk of being caught was high, for that had never stopped him before, but because he refused to take anything from her while she was held prisoner.

Yet that did nothing to stop memories of their night together from filling his mind's eye. Memories of her slowly stripping naked, of the way she'd looked at him while she'd touched herself, of the way her ragged breaths made his cock stiffen. God help him, but no woman had ever driven him wild like she had, all thought pushed from his head and replaced with the need to touch her, to taste her, to pleasure her until she screamed his name.

Except she didn't know your name, you jackass. And if she had, she'd never have allowed you near her.

The thought was akin to having a bucket of ice water dumped

on his crotch, and Keris opened his eyes to stare at the ceiling, feeling a growing hollowness in his chest. It wasn't the absence of her body that was carving his insides out; it was the absence of her voice in his ears. That was what he craved, what he *needed*, more than he cared to admit.

A knock sounded at the door, and when he rose to unbolt it, Keris bit back an annoyed sigh at the sight of the Magpie standing in the stairwell. "What do you need, Serin? I've been on the road, and I am weary."

"Only a moment of your time, Your Highness."

It was tempting to slam the door in the spymaster's face, but Keris was curious as to what the man might want. Stepping back, he gestured into the room. "Wine?"

"Water, if you have it. I've work left to do tonight that requires a clear head."

Work that probably involved torturing the King of Ithicana, but Aren Kertell was not Keris's primary concern. "As you like." He poured the spymaster his water and wine for himself, then settled back at his desk. Serin perched on the seat across from him.

"I understand from your father that you're of a mind to use the Valcottan girl to negotiate with the empress. I must say, you show more foresight than your predecessors."

"I *am* more intelligent than all of them combined. Thank you for noticing."

Serin made a face. "Indeed, although a penchant for self-aggrandizement is an attribute you all share."

Keris shrugged. "No one is perfect, Serin. Now, what is it that you want?"

"I think there is merit to moving your negotiations south to Nerastis." The Magpie took a sip of his water. "The proximity will allow speed of negotiation, and while you are there, you can return to your studies of war."

"What an interesting dichotomy: to be both negotiating and fighting with the same people at the same time."

"Such is politics." Serin gave him a tight smile. "And it would please your father greatly."

"My father? Or you?" Keris put his boots up on his desk, eyeing the old man. There were bloodstains on his robes. "Because I think him content to have me here as long as I serve him well."

"With respect, Highness, when did you start caring about pleasing your father? All your life you've made sport of doing the exact opposite."

"Since it became a matter of life or death." Sipping at his wine, which was very good after the swill that was served in Nerastis, Keris added, "I'm never going to impress him with my martial skills, so I must impress him with my cleverness."

"Maridrinian kings are famous for their prowess on the battlefield, not their cleverness."

Laughing, Keris lifted his glass in a toast. "I believe you just called my father stupid. Bravo! You're braver than I gave you credit for."

"You twist my words, Highness."

"No, Serin. I hear *exactly* what you are saying." Setting his glass on the table, Keris rose. "I've no intention of returning to Nerastis until I've achieved what I came here to do, which is to impress my father enough that he doesn't have you dispatch someone to stick a knife in my back."

"He'd order no such thing. Truly, Highness, your imagination runs wild."

"Does it?" Keris leaned across the table, close enough to see the pieces of dried skin that clung to the man's gray stubble. "Then why are you hunting my sister?"

"Because Lara is a traitor."

Keris barked out a surprised laugh. "Don't use the games intended for Aren Kertell on me, old man. I know you raised her to betray the Ithicanians and that you hunt her only because you dislike loose ends."

"Not a traitor to Ithicana, Highness. A traitor to Maridrina."

"How so? She delivered my father the bridge, for God's sake. She did the impossible."

"There is a certain amount of mystery and confusion surrounding your sister's actions, Keris, but there is one thing we know for certain: Her heart and loyalty belong to Aren Kertell."

Keris was immediately reminded of what Coralyn had said. That the King of Ithicana was still in love with his wife. "Stabbing a man in the back is a peculiar method of showing affection, but I suppose it's no surprise. She was raised by *you*, after all."

Serin gave him a sour smile. "Indeed. Which is why I know that she will go to the ends of the earth to protect those she loves, even if it means betraying kingdom and crown. She is fierce and brave and tremendously dangerous when provoked, which makes her a liability we can no longer afford. Whereas you, Highness, are a timid, cowardly little shit who is a threat to no one but yourself. Your father will not see you assassinated because it's not worth his time. And because some whore you've angered will likely do the job for us soon enough."

The Magpie rose and went to the door. "Get yourself back to Nerastis, Keris. Go back to your wine and women, and leave the ruling to those of us who know how to wield power."

Fuck off was the thought that rose in his head, but Keris only exhaled and glared at the man's departing back. Forcing his eyes back to his letter, he reread his proposal to the empress, his words blurring in and out of focus. A fine balance between asking enough that his father wouldn't suspect but not so much as to put off the empress. Whether he'd succeeded, only time would tell.

Swearing softly, Keris signed and sealed the letter, shoving it

into one of the enameled tubes his father used for official correspondence.

As he strode down the stairs, he silently prayed, *Let this work. Let
the empress buy her free of us.* Yet even as the thought rolled through
his head, another came on its heels. One that whispered that, regardless of the outcome, it would be his father who was the victor.

42
ZARRAH

DRIP. DRIP. DRIP.

Zarrah jerked awake, her skin drenched and her heart beating chaotically in her chest. She peered into the dark, certain she'd see her mother's corpse dangling above her. Certain that the dampness on her skin was blood and that when she looked down again, her mother's head would be in her lap.

But her hands were empty.

All around was darkness, the smells unfamiliar, the bedding beneath her fingers cotton rather than silk. Then female laughter filtered through the walls, and she *remembered*.

She was in Vencia. In Silas Veliant's palace. In the harem's quarters.

Tap.

She jumped at the noise, searching the darkness, only to hear it again.

Tap.

It came from the direction of the window, the sound what must have triggered her dream. She rose and donned a silk wrap over the nightdress she wore, then walked cautiously to the window. It was small, perhaps three feet across and four feet high, and beyond the frosted glass were steel bars that were bolted to the stone of the window frame.

Tap.

Kneeling on the cushioned window seat, she unfastened the latch on the glass and swung it inward.

Only to have a pebble strike her in the forehead. Swearing under her breath, Zarrah pressed her head to the bars and looked down into the shadows.

"Valcotta?"

Keris's whispered voice filtered up from bushes at the base of the building three stories below. Picking up the pebble that had struck her, Zarrah stuck her arm through the bars, then aimed at the slight movement she saw.

And was rewarded with a muttered curse as her aim struck true.

"I need to talk to you."

The gardens, with their pathways and topiaries and illuminated fountains, were empty, but there'd be guards on patrol and servants moving about, so a conversation shouted up three stories seemed ill-advised. "Go away."

The shadows moved, but instead of departing into the gardens, Keris started scaling the wall, the only handholds the places where the mortar had eroded between blocks of stone. But that appeared to be enough, for he swiftly climbed the side of the building, the shadows hiding him from sight.

Reaching her windowsill, he caught hold of the bars and pulled himself up so that he was perched on the narrow ledge, the scent of spice filling her nose and sending her pulse racing. Annoyed with herself, Zarrah snapped, "What do you want?"

"To see if you are all right."

She couldn't see his face in the darkness, only the outline of his shape against the ambient light of the garden. Broad shoulders and trim waist, his coat strained tight over the muscles in his arms. "Define *all right*."

He waited in silence, and she closed her eyes, listening to his breathing, which was rapid from the climb.

"The harem has been courteous," she said. "And I've been given everything I need. Your food is terrible, though. Someone needs to inform the cook that with salt, less is more."

Keris laughed softly. "He cooks to my father's taste, and everyone else's preferences are inconsequential."

"Does your father have any redeemable characteristics?" Not that there was anything that could redeem him in her eyes.

"None. Though that's probably just as well, given that you're planning to kill him." And before she could answer one way or another, he added, "Don't bother denying it, Valcotta. Even if you hadn't been radiating murder when you saw him, you do have something of a reputation."

"He deserves to die."

"You'll get no argument from me on that, but it's not such an easy thing to accomplish. He never goes anywhere without his bodyguards, who are *loyal*, and even if you did manage to get him alone, he's an accomplished fighter. And he'd be armed, whereas you'll be lucky to get your hands on anything more dangerous than a butter knife."

"Then give me a weapon."

"I don't have one to give you—I'm the crown prince, and even I'm not allowed weapons within the inner sanctum. Believe me, Valcotta, when you are as universally reviled as my father, you either become very paranoid or you find yourself dead."

"What about poison?" It disgusted her to use such a method, but if that were the only option . . .

"Everything and everyone who comes in those gates is searched. He has the best tasters in the kingdom, dogs that are trained to sniff for poisons, and he has the habit of changing dining plans at the last minute. He's also recently become very obsessed about his cutlery being tampered with, which is why he brings his own to every meal."

She glared at him, though he wouldn't be able to see her expression in the dark. "For someone who says he'd like to see his father dead, you aren't particularly helpful." And despite what he'd endured at his father's hands, she still didn't trust that Keris wasn't trying to protect his father.

"If killing him were easy, he'd *be* dead." Keris shifted his weight so that he was sitting on the ledge, one arm hooked through the bars, sleeve pushed up. And she found her eyes drawn to that pale expanse of skin. "While I've no doubt you're capable of finding a way, Valcotta, I've no confidence that you'd survive long enough to enjoy your vengeance. And *your* life matters infinitely more to me than *his* death."

Her heart flipped, and Zarrah silently cursed herself for a fool to be so moved by pretty words, especially given she'd seen how easily he lied. Biting the insides of her cheeks, Zarrah considered her response for several long moments before deciding on silence.

Keris exhaled a frustrated breath. "I've sent a letter to the empress with proposed terms for your release."

Zarrah listened as he explained the proposal, knowing that there was little chance of her aunt agreeing to such steep demands and that she would likely counter. Yet admitting so would be folly. Her longevity depended on her having value, and because killing Silas would be no easy task, she needed to keep the Maridrinians convinced she was worth more alive than dead. Especially Keris.

"The Harendellian ambassador is facilitating the negotiations, given that your people have a habit of sending our messengers back without their entrails, but it will still take weeks for us to receive a response."

Weeks.

That was how long she had before her aunt inevitably countered, which she suspected would see Silas past the limit of his patience, and her subsequently executed. A few weeks to kill a man who expected death to come from every angle, most especially from her.

Keris was watching her with an uneasy expression, likely motivated by her silence, so she said, "You grew up in this place. There has to be some way to get out."

"If there is, I never found it." He was silent for a moment. "It was designed as a prison. For close to two hundred years, it's served as the home of the king's harem, and not every woman brought here comes of their own volition. Their fathers and brothers and uncles force them into marriages to secure alliances with the Crown or for financial gain or for political favors. Or because the king saw their face"—his voice turned bitter—"and decided he had to possess them. Which means for two hundred years, women have been trying to escape this place. Every possible avenue has been discovered and removed, and with the Ithicanian in residence, it's even worse. Because now they aren't just containing unhappy noblewomen; they are containing a renowned warrior who probably knows a dozen ways to kill a man without a weapon."

She knew a dozen ways to kill a man without a weapon, but Zarrah said nothing.

"And despite all of that, I'd invite you to try. Except my father has made it clear that if you are caught pushing your boundaries, he *will* kill you."

The fear of death was rarely enough to dissuade her.

"I know it's against your nature to sit idle, Valcotta. But *please* allow me the opportunity to try to get you free of this place via negotiation *before* you consign yourself to death."

She needed time to regain her strength, so it was easy enough to shrug. "Who wouldn't like to be pampered like a harem wife for a handful of weeks?"

"You." He leaned against the bars. "And be wary of the wives. I put you in this building rather than elsewhere in the palace because nothing happens in here without Coralyn's say, and because she refuses to allow Serin in her house. But the harem is just as dangerous as you, albeit in a different fashion. Their lives are *hard*, but they protect them fiercely even as they hunt for ways to increase their power. If you cross them, they'll be just as quick to see you dead as my father or Serin."

She'd been raised to hold Maridrinian women in contempt, but already she'd seen that the notions put into her head were far from accurate. "Fine."

Keris was silent for a long moment, then said, "I'm sorry for this, Valcotta. I should never have let it go as far as it did between us, should have walked away that night on the dam and never looked back, because everyone who gets close to me ends up hurt. It was a mistake."

He regrets you. A sharp pain radiated through Zarrah's chest, and though she silently berated herself for being an idiot, it refused to fade. "I made my own decisions, not you. I'll not have you take responsibility for that which I chose freely."

"A choice you wouldn't have made if I hadn't deceived you about my identity."

"What deceit?" Her anger flared, though she wasn't sure if it was at him or at herself. "Neither of us confessed who we were, Keris. We agreed to it."

He hesitated, then said, "Maybe so. But a hundred times over, I thought of what it would mean to tell you the truth. And every time, I knew that if I told you my name, the best I could hope for was a knife in the heart. So like a coward, I kept it to myself. And in doing so, caused you worse hurt than all the blows my soldiers rained down upon you." He moved his arm, reaching for her, then hesitated and withdrew it to the far side of the bars. "I hate having caused you so much suffering."

Emotion flooded her chest, making it hard to breathe, much less speak. "The same could have happened to you when you ventured to my side of the Anriot. We both took risks. Both engaged in the same deception. And if blame is to be cast for the current situation, it should be cast at my feet for losing my head when presented with the truth and getting myself caught."

"Anyone in your position would have reacted the same."

"You didn't." No, when presented with her identity, he'd instantly come up with a plan to save her life.

Keris tilted his head, seeming to consider her words. "It's not the same. I was raised to believe Valcotta my enemy and to despise your people, but such political animosity is a product of the head, not the heart. Whereas your hatred is born of a personal loss, and therefore rooted in the heart. Matters of the heart do not bow to logic or reason. Anyone who does not understand that has either never lived or is devoid of a heart themselves." He was silent, then added, "On that note, I should go."

Without waiting for her response, he started to descend.

Zarrah reached through the bars, wanting to pull him back, the word *wait* rising to her lips.

But he was already lost to the darkness.

ZARRAH WOKE AT DAWN LITTLE more rested than she'd been the prior night. Her dreams were plagued, and she'd lost count of the number of times she jerked awake, soaked with sweat and Silas's laugh ringing in her ears.

But exhausted or not, her days to accomplish her ends were numbered, so lazing about in bed was not an option.

You need to get strong again, she told herself. *Strong enough to fight. Strong enough to kill.*

Strong enough to win.

So she drew upon the exercises Yrina had taught her when she'd been chosen as Zarrah's close guard, the other girl as fit as a person could be, whereas at fourteen, Zarrah had been as soft as a harem wife. Exercises to make her heart and lungs capable of enduring lengthy battles, muscles tough enough to cut through flesh and bone, and reflexes sharp enough to compensate for her smaller size. *You will never be the strongest,* her friend's voice echoed through her thoughts. *So be the fastest. The smartest. The fiercest!*

God, but she missed Yrina. Missed having someone she could trust, not only to guard her back but to confess her worries to without fear of judgment or betrayal.

The last words you had with her were in anger, a voice whispered. *You threatened to cut out her tongue for confessing her own worries.*

Her skin turned cold, her stomach hollowing with shame for having behaved so.

You brought your own fate down upon you, her conscience whispered viciously right as the door to her room opened, Coralyn stepping inside. The woman looked her up and down, Zarrah all red-faced and sweaty, then shook her head. "You'll make a very fit corpse." Then she snapped her fingers, and two servants came in with a platter of food. Fruits and cheese and cured meats, along with tiny pots with contents Zarrah couldn't identify, the scents strange.

"Your new clothes will be brought in shortly. Though you'll

need to be bathed before they can be tried on. Then you'll be escorted for a walk in the garden."

"May I run in the garden instead?" Given no one was likely to run alongside her, it might give her more opportunities to see things that would otherwise be hidden from her. Like a way to get close to Silas Veliant.

"Absolutely not. What you do in here while you are alone is your own business, but you will act the part of a lady when eyes are upon you."

Taking orders from a Maridrinian matriarch in a fuchsia brocade gown and jeweled slippers ground her nerves, but Zarrah remembered Keris's warning. These women were dangerous, and this one perhaps most of all.

Zarrah forced herself to smile. "As you wish, Lady Coralyn."

After the woman departed, she sat at the table and ate, forcing as much food into her stomach as she could fit. *You must get healthy,* she chanted to herself. *You need to be strong.*

Afterward, the servants again brought in the large tub, filling it with tepid water and scrubbing the sweat from her body. More servants arrived with an armload of Maridrinian dresses, all made of thin silks and cut to entice. And while she normally had no time for such things, as she looked into the mirror, Zarrah found herself not averse to what she saw.

Bronze silk hung from narrow straps, the fabric clinging to her body as though it had been made for her. Which she supposed it had. The neckline was cut down to below her navel, revealing the inner curves of her breasts and the hard lines of her abdomen, the back so low that wearing any undergarments was impossible. On her feet were sandals of bronze leather decorated with bits of gold. Her wrists were encased in glittering cuffs, and her ears were laden with black diamonds that brushed her shoulders.

Her hair was held back from her face with golden clips, and one of the servants applied cosmetics, lining her eyes with kohl, highlighting her cheeks with gold dust, and painting her lips a dusky rose. If seduction had been her goal, she'd have felt well dressed, but if she had to run or fight, she'd have been better off naked.

Clever old bat, Zarrah silently grumbled, allowing the guards to escort her along the corridor and then down the stairs, the doors opening to reveal the garden.

All of the harem seemed to be out, the women rolling balls across the lawn or playing games at the tables. But the laughter and conversation and commotion faded to a drone as Zarrah was slapped in the face with the stink of corpse.

Bodies still dangled from the inner walls, flies buzzing around them and crows picking at their faces. Though Zarrah had seen more corpses than she could ever count, the similarities to what happened to her mother had her massive breakfast threatening to rise up her throat.

Then male laughter caught her attention, and Zarrah turned to see Keris dodging between topiaries and fountains. He was dressed only in shirtsleeves and had a young girl balanced on his shoulders while a horde of children racing at his heels screamed, "Catch them!"

He jumped on the edge of a fountain, racing around it only to leap off the other side, the girl on his shoulders shrieking with delight even as Coralyn shouted, "Show caution with your sister, Keris!"

Ignoring her, he circled the garden, staying well away from the corpses as he led the children on a merry chase, displaying the agility and strength that, logically, Zarrah knew he possessed. And yet it still surprised her. For a moment, it was as though the prince had exited the scene and the Maridrinian had taken his place, causing her chest to tighten and an unwanted longing to fill her core. *You can't want one and hate the other,* she snarled at herself. *That's madness.*

Yet the admonition did nothing to temper the flare of anticipation filling her as he wove in her direction, distraction rendering him oblivious to her presence. He was almost upon her, looking over his shoulder and shouting at his younger siblings that they'd never catch him, when the children caught sight of her.

"Valcottan!" several of the elder ones screamed, and Keris slid to a stop, nearly colliding with her. He caught his balance, his eyes widening as he took in her ensemble. "Valc . . . Lady Zarrah. I . . ." He trailed off, seemingly at a loss for words.

His reaction was a dangerous one, and yet it made her heart skip with something other than fear. Especially as his gaze ran down her body, her nipples tightening as he lingered on her breasts before returning to her face. If any other man had looked at her in such a way, she'd have blackened both his eyes for his troubles, but violence was the last thing on her mind. Forcing her tone to a coolness that belied the flood of heat between her thighs, she said, "Your Highness."

The corner of his mouth turned up. "I see the harem has been playing dress-up."

Zarrah should've been offended. Should've snapped back that she wasn't a doll to be played with. Instead, she said, "They seem to think your preference is that I dress in Maridrinian styles."

"I didn't realize that it mattered what I thought of your attire."

It didn't. It shouldn't. Her tongue ran across her lips, his eyes moving to her mouth as she did. "Are you suggesting that you'd prefer me dressed in something different?"

Why had she asked that? What he thought of her clothing didn't matter, and she certainly had no intention of scampering off for a costume change. Yet she found herself holding her breath as Keris looked her over once more.

"*Dressed* is rarely my preference, my lady, but"—he inclined his head—"I appreciate you taking my desires into consideration."

Zarrah's skin prickled with goose bumps as tension mounted between them, entirely inappropriate, given they weren't alone, the children, including the girl sitting on Keris's shoulders, watching with interest.

"Good," Coralyn said. "You two have found each other."

Zarrah jumped at the sound of Coralyn's voice, turning to find the old woman approaching down the path.

"Keris, rather than running about like a fool with your siblings, perhaps you might direct your excess of energy into exercising your prisoner."

Keris lifted one eyebrow, showing no sign of discomfort despite the fact his aunt might well have heard him flirting with said prisoner. "She's not a horse. Surely she can exercise herself."

"And get into all manner of trouble while she does it? *You* will walk with her and ensure she keeps to the paths. Take your little sister with you—she weeps when you put her down." Coralyn snapped her fingers at Zarrah's guards, who stood a respectful distance away. "Remain within arm's reach."

With an aggrieved sigh, Keris started down the path, adjusting his younger sister so that she sat more squarely on his shoulders. Her legs, Zarrah saw, were underdeveloped enough that she doubted the girl capable of walking far unassisted, much less racing around the gardens with the other children.

"What is your name?" she asked the child, who was a pretty little thing, her hair so blond as to be nearly white, her eyes a soft brown.

"Sara." The tiny princess regarded her with interest. "Is it true that you are a warrior?"

"It is, yes."

"I'm not allowed to learn to fight," the girl said. "Only the boys are. It's not fair."

It wasn't fair the way Maridrinian women were limited, but

Zarrah said, "Not all battles are won with fists and swords. Some are won with words and a clever head."

A faint smile rose on Keris's lips, but he said nothing.

"That sounds dull." The girl drummed her heels against her brother's chest as though he were a horse. "Walk faster, Keris."

"Then I'll be too winded to give our guest a proper tour of our home. What will Auntie Coralyn say?"

"Horses don't talk," the girl declared. "I will give the tour."

With the guards on their heels, they walked through the gardens and buildings, Sara keeping up a steady stream of explanation about the purpose of every building and every room, pointing out guards on the walls and even going so far as to tell Zarrah that Silas's rooms were near the top of the tower. It was a positive wealth of detail that Keris could never have provided without raising serious questions but which the guards seemed to ignore as the prattling of a child.

And it all served to confirm what Keris had already told her: Finding a way to the king would be no easy task.

Maybe an impossible one.

Only when Sara finally ran out of things to tell her did Keris ask, "Do you feel sufficiently exerted, Lady Zarrah? The midday sun does not agree with me."

She risked a sideways glance at him, seeing that his skin, which was far more used to the moon than the sun, was beginning to pinken. A teasing remark rose to her lips, but Zarrah bit down on it. One did not *banter* with one's captor. "Yes."

"Good." They circled around to where the wives were gathered. Keris lifted his sister off his shoulders and set her next to a wife, the woman a handful of years older than Zarrah and extremely beautiful. "We'll go riding soon, Sara," he said. "I promise."

"I hope your horse is faster than you are." The girl stretched up to kiss his cheek. "Good day to you, brother. You may leave now."

The women all laughed at the dismissal, the one who must be her mother saying, "You are so kind to her, Keris."

He made a face. "Kindness has nothing to do with it. She's been raised by the harem, which means she tells me what she wants, and I have no choice but to obey. And on that note, I will now flee before any more demands are made on my time."

Twisting on his heel, he walked away.

Zarrah watched him go, ever curious as to what was real and what was an act when it came to him. Whether he knew himself.

Sensing eyes were upon her, she turned her head to find Sara's mother watching her, gaze curious. Which was a welcome change from the hate most of the women directed at her. "Your daughter is quite clever," Zarrah said. "You must be very proud."

"I am. Sadly, her father sees only her flaws." The woman glanced down at the girl, who was embroiled with a wooden puzzle. "She is to be sent away to the church."

Not the worst life, but a hard one. And not one, Zarrah thought, suited to the girl's temperament, which meant she would suffer. Judging from the way her mother's jaw quivered, she was in agreement. Part of Zarrah recoiled from confessing anything to these people, yet she found herself saying, "My mother was taken from me, so Sara has my sympathy. It is a harsh thing for a girl to grow up absent her mother."

"There is nothing I can do."

Likely true, but Zarrah despised the passivity. The resignation and acceptance of defeat before the battle had even been fought. "My mother begged for me to be spared right until the moment your husband cut off her head."

The woman flinched, then looked away. "I'm sure she was a great warrior and prepared for such sacrifice."

Staring at the bodies hanging from the wall, Zarrah closed her eyes, trying to remember her mother's face while she'd been living but seeing her only in death. "She'd never lifted a weapon in her life. But all good mothers will die for the sake of their children." Then she inclined her head. "If you'd excuse me, my lady. I've spent too many days confined, and I would walk some more."

She started to move away, but the mother caught her wrist. "Zarrah." Their eyes met, and the mother swallowed. "I spent a year in the room where you currently reside. During that time, I came to appreciate the tapestry that hangs behind the bed. It has the most exquisite . . . *depth*."

Zarrah felt her curiosity flicker to life, because if this wife had once considered herself a prisoner . . . "I will give it close attention. Enjoy your afternoon."

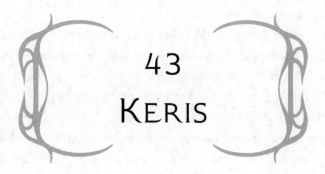

43
KERIS

WHAT IN THE NAME OF GOD HAD POSSESSED CORALYN TO DRESS Valcotta like that?

Waiting for the guards to open the gates to allow him to pass, Keris scrubbed his hands back through his hair, trying and failing to push away the image of Valcotta in that scrap of bronze silk under which she was clearly wearing nothing at all. He'd been hard within an instant, and if not for Coralyn insisting that Sara accompany them, he'd have spent the entire walk searching for a way to get her alone.

Stepping through the gates, he accepted his knives from the guards, then tucked them into various hiding places on his person. He needed to get out of these walls, but with Vencia boiling hot over an increase in taxes, he had no intention of walking its streets unarmed.

"Your Valcottan looks like her mother."

Keris straightened with a jerk, eyes snapping to where his father was handing over the reins of a horse to one of the stable hands. "I suppose you would know, Your Grace. I understand you personally cut off her head."

His father chuckled. "A kill handed to me on a silver platter. And unlike Petra, Aryana was no warrior, though she did fight. When that didn't work, she begged."

For her daughter's life, Keris thought, but said nothing.

"I'm sure Aryana would be horrified to learn what a violent, murderous woman her daughter has become," his father continued. "She and Petra spent their lives at odds, and I can't help but wonder if Petra raised Zarrah as she did to spite her sister. For how better to do so than to turn the daughter of the woman who fought so tirelessly for peace into a leader in the Endless War?"

Valcotta had never mentioned that her mother had been a proponent of peace. It made him wonder if she had even known. "Is there something I'm supposed to be gleaning from this, or are you merely regaling me with a favored war story?"

"I only wish to impart information about your adversary." His father slung an arm around Keris's shoulder, and it took effort not to pull away. This was how his father behaved with Otis and his other brothers, but never with him. Neither of them had desired the familiarity.

What are you up to? he silently asked as his father pulled him with unrelenting strength in the direction of the training yard.

"Petra is a hard woman. If you believe her swayed by sentiment, you are sorely mistaken."

"You speak as though you know her."

His father smiled. "In a manner of speaking, I do. But in this case, my words come from the lips of a more concrete source."

Keris's blood chilled, every muscle in his body tensing as his father opened a door and headed down a set of narrow steps into the outer palace's sublevels. It was dark and damp and smelled of mold.

And blood.

Vaguely, Keris had known that there were cells down here. That Serin's workshop was down here. But he'd never had cause, nor desire, to explore the spymaster's domain. Why had his father brought him?

"We've a new prisoner," his father murmured as though sensing his thoughts. "One I believe in which you'll take a personal interest."

Keris's pulse roared, the walls pressing in as his father nodded at a guard outside a cell door. "Open it."

The hinges creaked, the cell swinging open to reveal nothing but blackness. Taking up a lamp, his father stepped inside, leaving Keris no choice but to follow. And as the pool of light moved farther into the space, he had to stifle a sharp inhalation as a Valcottan woman was illuminated.

She was passed out, the chains around her wrists and ankles bolted to the floor, her clothing soiled and torn. And the torture that had been inflicted on her body . . . Twisting away, Keris vomited against the wall, a wave of dizziness washing over him.

"Weak stomach," his father said with disgust, and Keris forced himself to straighten. To wipe his mouth on his sleeve.

"Who is she?"

"Yrina Kitan, a captain in the Nerastis garrison. And if what Serin tells me is true, a personal friend of Zarrah Anaphora."

Yrina. Memory flooded him, of Zarrah whispering the name over and over when she'd been poisoned, begging for the unknown person's forgiveness. Keris's skin turned cold, his eyes moving over the broken woman. Her injuries were not something she could survive. But he had to try.

"What do you hope to gain from this, Your Grace? We're in the midst of negotiating with the empress, and you allow Serin to ply his craft on a Valcottan soldier? This is not just cruelty; it is *folly.*"

His father snorted. "The empress has little ground to stand on, given one of her soldiers broke into my palace and killed four of my men."

The woman stirred, her remaining eye opening to fix upon Keris and his father. "I see you brought one of your princelings, Your Grace," she said around a mouthful of broken teeth. "Teaching him your ways?"

"I'd once believed that a lost cause," his father answered. "But his capture of your princess has given me new hope."

Keris stiffened, a fresh wave of sickness rising in his stomach, because this was the first time he'd ever heard a word of praise from his father. And it was because of *this*.

"As it is, Yrina," his father continued, "I don't think there is anything more of use that you can tell us."

His eyes flicked to Keris. "The empress, it seems, was only a day's ride from Nerastis when you captured her niece. And it was Petra's orders that there would be no pursuit. No rescue. Which suggests she either fears the repercussions of invading Maridrina to retrieve her niece or that she doesn't care enough about her niece to bother doing so. And the Petra *I* know fears *nothing*."

Yrina stiffened, telling Keris that she agreed with his father's sentiments toward the empress.

"Or perhaps she anticipated that we'd be willing to negotiate. What you've done to this woman does us no favors."

"Perhaps," his father answered. "Either way, you've a point, Keris. It wouldn't be ideal if this were discovered, so I think it best that we . . . *bury* the problem."

Keris flinched as his father reached over and extracted the knife tucked into his belt. "This is your venture. Your gambit to prove to me that you're worthy of being my heir. That you're worthy of the Maridrinian crown. And part of being king is a willingness to do the dirty work."

He forced the knife into Keris's hand, squeezing his fingers shut around the hilt. "See it done."

There was no chance this woman would survive. Even if Keris refused to kill her, his father would do it. Or one of the guards. Or Serin. Or they'd leave her to succumb to her injuries. To do it himself would be a mercy, because at least he would make it quick. So he stepped toward her.

Keris kept his eyes on Yrina, who, though her face was shattered, stared at him in defiance. "Do your worst, little princeling." Her voice was slurred. "If you have the nerve for it."

He didn't have the nerve for it. The proof of that was in the vomit splattered against the wall. In the sweat rolling in beads down his back. In the rapid hammer of his heart.

"Do it." His father leaned against the wall. "Prove your worth."

The words echoed in his head: *Prove your worth, prove your worth, prove your worth.* "Fine. But I neither need nor want an audience."

One eyebrow rose, and his father said, "If this is an attempt to weasel your way out of this, put aside those foolish hopes. I will check that she's dead. And lest you play the same tricks as your sister, I'll ensure she *remains* dead."

Keris had no notion of what his father was referring to, but neither did he care. "Out."

"Don't disappoint me."

The door settled shut with a resounding thud, and Keris swallowed the sourness in his mouth. His palms were clammy, and he flexed his fingers around the pommel of the knife as he dropped to his knees in front of the chained woman, turning the flame down low on the lamp because he knew eyes would be watching through tiny holes in the walls.

And listening.

Yrina watched him warily, and as he stepped forward, she

lunged against her chains. Only to fall back against the floor, gasping in pain.

But still dangerous.

Moving quickly, he dropped to his knees, catching her from behind and pulling her back against him. She struggled, cursing and swearing, but went silent as he said softly in her ear, "You and I want the same thing, Yrina."

"And what is that?" She strained against him, looking for a weakness.

"Zarrah's freedom."

"This is a trick."

"No." He kept his grip tight, knowing that she'd try to kill him if he gave her a chance. "I know your name, for it was on her lips when she was in the grips of poison-induced delusions. You mean something to her. And she means something to you, else you'd not have come against the empress's orders."

Silence. Which in and of itself was neither confirmation nor denial, but she'd also ceased struggling. Was listening to him. So he pushed forward. "In the days before her capture in Nerastis, Zarrah was disappearing at night. She was seeing me."

"Lies." As the words hissed from Yrina's lips, she twisted out of his grip and wrenched the knife from his hand. In a flash, she was behind him, blade at his throat.

Shit.

He didn't move, wondering whether it would be better to let her kill him or to scream for help. Then her body stiffened and she whispered, "Bergamot. Ginger. Red cedar. Oh my *God.*"

He had no idea what she was talking about, but he was afraid to move, lest she slit his throat.

"The man she was seeing gave her a book," she said. "What were the contents?"

Keris squeezed his eyes shut, pain filling his chest, for if Valcotta had shared that with this woman, she was more than a comrade. She was a friend. "Stories about stars."

"It is you." She let go of him, slumping to the ground. "Oh God, Zarrah. What a mess you've got yourself into." Then she lifted her face. "Do you care for her?"

"Yes." He hesitated. "Very much so."

She gave a slow nod, and then words poured from her lips. "It's not Zarrah who should be asking for forgiveness, it's me. The empress ordered her not to see you any longer, but I encouraged it. And when Zarrah didn't return, I told the empress that I believed she'd crossed the Anriot to see her lover. I hoped she'd allow us to move across in force to search, but I was wrong. She ordered us to stand down, and when word came that you were taking Zarrah to Vencia, she told us that Zarrah had earned her fate."

Keris clenched his teeth, panic rising in his chest. "If she refuses to negotiate, my father will kill Zarrah."

"Then you must find another way to get her out." She pressed his knife into his hand. "And you must silence the truths that both of us have revealed."

Yrina's death would crush Valcotta. The knowledge her friend had died trying to save her would be a weight upon her soul, dragging her down. And it was because of him.

Because he'd turned back that night at the dam.

Because he'd pursued her.

Seduced her.

Lied to her.

Failed her.

"I can't," he whispered. "I can't do that to her."

"Leaving me alive will do far worse to her," Yrina answered, lifting his hand so that the knife pressed against her jugular. "I can't take any more of Serin's torture. I'll break and bring you both down with me."

Think of a way to get her out, his conscience whispered. *Save this woman!*

"I—"

Yrina jerked sideways, the tip of his knife sliding into her flesh like a hot blade through butter. Blood splashed over his hands, sprayed him in the face, and Yrina slumped in his arms.

"Tell Zarrah that I love her," she whispered, and then she went still.

A tremor ran through him, and Keris sucked in breath after breath, but it didn't feel as though any air reached his lungs. He lowered Yrina to the cell floor and clambered to his feet, falling against the door. "Open it!"

He waited for the sound of the bolt opening, for motion, for voices, but there was nothing. His father was going to leave him in here. Leave him in here to stare at the corpse of yet another woman he'd gotten killed. Panic raced through his veins, and he hammered his fists against the wood, screaming, "Open the fucking door!"

It opened.

His father stood in the opening, blocking Keris's route to escape. Panting for breath, he tried to get past, but his father didn't move. "She's dead. Let me out."

"Very dead, from the look of it." His father's shoulders began to shake, and he laughed. Not a chuckle, but a great belly laugh of delight, tears running down his face. "God strike me down, I didn't think you had it in you, Keris. But it appears I underestimated your desire to survive."

Keris's hand tightened around the dagger he still clutched, his fingers sticky with blood, and all he could think of was how good it would feel to plunge it into his father's chest. Not once but over and over until that *laugh* was silenced. Until those awful eyes glazed to lifelessness.

A shiver ran through him, because as much as he denied that violence was in his blood, it was still there. Still a part of him. And if he unleashed it, he'd be more than capable of slaughtering his father where he stood.

But then what?

He'd be executed for patricide, and Otis would become king. Though he loved his brother dearly, Keris knew that Otis would execute Valcotta without hesitation and that things would carry on as they always had, never changing.

Find another way.

Keris forced his fingers open, the knife falling to the stone at his feet with a clatter. "Was there something else you required of me, Your Grace?"

He swore he saw a flash of disappointment in his father's eyes. "No, Keris. You can go back to *negotiating* with the empress."

44
ZARRAH

THE BALANCE OF HER DAY WAS A MADDENING COMBINATION OF stilted conversation or being outright ignored by the harem, and Zarrah used her time to watch and listen. Yet as the day progressed into evening, she found herself thinking more about what Sara's mother had said, wondering what secrets hid in the tapestry in her room, her mind conjuring thoughts of weapons woven into the threads or instructions for some secret route of escape.

By the time she'd forced another over-salted dinner down her throat, Zarrah was vibrating with anticipation, pleading exhaustion until Coralyn allowed her guards to escort her back to her room.

The second Zarrah pulled off the cursed heels that were murdering her feet, she ran silently to the tapestry, which hung floor-to-ceiling behind the headboard. Old and faded, it depicted two women weaving, the work mediocre and the subject dull. Frowning, Zarrah glanced at the door, then knelt next to the bed. The area where the fabric was tacked to the wall showed wear, as though it had been refastened many times. Yet it was dusty enough that she doubted it had been removed for cleaning in years.

Zarrah unfastened the corner and pulled it away from the wall as much as the bed would allow, peering into the dark space. But she could see nothing in the dim light, so she shoved her hand behind the tapestry, the stone wall cold against her overheated skin. She was nearly at the limit her arm could reach when her fingers brushed a deep groove. Her heart racing, she traced along the groove, realizing that someone had carved away the mortar around one of the large stone blocks in the wall.

And left behind their tool.

Withdrawing her hand, Zarrah stared at the small nail, the tip dull from endless chiseling. She eased the bed away from the wall and crawled behind it, lifting the tapestry to stare at the block, seeing a dozen names carved into the surface. A dozen women who, over the years, had all worked to create an escape from this place.

And they'd very nearly made it. Beneath the block and around the sides, the mortar was gone, and sunlight shone through. There was only the mortar along the top still holding the block in place.

Zarrah scratched her name on the block. Set the nail back in its groove. Fixed the tapestry into place. Tonight, she'd pick up work where the other women had left off, and when she succeeded where they had failed, she'd have the first step in her plan.

Going to the window, she looked up at the tower where Silas slept.

And she smiled.

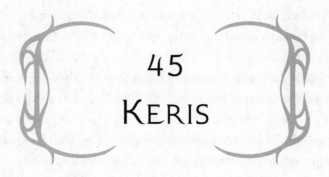

45

KERIS

HE WAS DRUNK.

Which, contrary to the rumors about him, was something Keris never allowed himself to become. It lowered his guard, loosened his lips, and risked sleep so deep that he'd never hear the assassin coming. But tonight, that was the oblivion he sought. To escape the endlessly replaying sensation of his knife siding into Yrina's throat, hot blood spraying him in the face, and her words in his ears.

Find another way.

Except there *was* no other way. The sanctum was locked down, even trusted servants forbidden from exiting the inner gates, and the inner walls were thick with guards whose attention never wavered. Not with the Ithicanians ceaseless in their attempts to reach their king. And not with Yrina having killed four of their own in an effort to reach Valcotta.

Coralyn had come to see him at some point during the afternoon. She'd eyed the empty wine bottles with disapproval before moving books aside to sit on a chair. "I saw the blood. Who did your father kill?"

"He didn't kill anyone." Keris drained his cup and promptly uncorked another bottle. "I did."

The silence that stretched made him sick, the anticipation of what his aunt would say making him want to shout at her to get on with it. To say what she needed to say.

"What did you think would happen, Keris? The moment you arrived in Vencia with Zarrah Anaphora in tow, you stepped into the arena. Now you have a choice: You can fight for the crown, or you can lie down and die."

"I never wanted to be king," he answered, staring blindly into the distance. "Ran from it all my life, because I knew I was ill-suited for the role."

"I'm aware." Coralyn sat on the sofa next to him. "And I've long done my best to support you in your flight from duty, even if I didn't agree with it. If you'd kept your head down, you might have outlived your father and inherited, then abdicated to one of your brothers. But in showing a willingness to play the game, you've removed that option. Your father's eyes are on you, but worse, the *Magpie's* eyes are on you. Which means you must either bend to their power or take it from them."

"I'd gladly carve out both their hearts, if I could manage it."

Coralyn snorted. "I didn't raise you to be a drunken fool, boy. You cannot murder your father, nor can you be seen as complicit in his death. The former would see you executed, and the latter would have the people label you a coward. You must find another way."

"What other way?" he shouted, those cursed words triggering him. "There is no other way!"

She rose to her feet. "I see you are too deep in your cups and self-pity to see reason, so I'll leave you. But when you've climbed out of this useless pit of morosity, we will speak again. Good evening, Keris."

That conversation had been hours ago. Curfew had passed, the windows of the harem's house all dark. Lured out of his rooms by the quiet and the need to be away from the bottle, Keris sat on the bench where the Ithicanian king was so often chained, rain pouring from the sky. Unlike Aren, he ignored the corpses, his eyes instead fixed on Valcotta's window.

He needed to confess.

Except she'd hate him for it. His father had murdered her mother, and now he'd murdered her closest friend. And if he didn't find another way to get her out of this mess, Valcotta would lose her life as well.

Find another way.

But all he could think of was apologizing to her. Of explaining that there had been no choice, or at least, no better choice. Of begging for her forgiveness.

Keris rose to his feet and walked toward the base of the harem's building, ignoring the sheets of rain slapping him across the face as he reached down to grab a handful of pebbles.

But his nerve failed him.

Swearing softly, he sat against the wall of the building, staring upward. "She deserves the truth," he muttered as thunder rolled, the rain like icy pellets striking his skin. "Don't be a coward."

Find another way.

His eyes went to the corpses of the Ithicanians swaying in the wind, his stomach contents rising as he wondered what had been done with Yrina's body. It was more of the same—people who'd been willing to die to rescue the person they cared for. But unlike Valcotta, Ithicana showed no sign of giving up hope. They kept coming despite knowing they'd most likely die.

What would happen if they had help on the inside?

The thought struck him like a punch to the stomach, and Keris straightened.

The Ithicanians were working blind, none of them familiar with the interior of the palace or where Aren was being kept, which meant they were destined to fail. But what if they were given the information they needed? What if *he* helped them orchestrate an escape for Aren?

And what if Aren took Valcotta with him?

A thrill of excitement raced through his veins, even as the countless obstacles to such a plan shouted that it was impossible.

He had no way to get in contact with the Ithicanians, especially given that Serin would have him followed every time he left the palace. And even if he somehow managed it, the Ithicanians had no reason to listen to him. Would probably slit his throat and toss him into the sea for his trouble.

Unless their king ordered them not to.

Wheels turned in his head, pushing aside the haze of wine as Keris considered how to make such a thing happen. And then it struck him.

The enemy of my enemy is my friend.

Keris scrambled to his feet and climbed out of the foliage, then strode down a path, once again steady. Ignoring the protests of the guards at the harem's quarters, he went inside, taking the stairs two at a time. The guard at the top said, "Highness, with respect, it is after curfew—"

Keris pushed past him. "How the hours fly." His boots squelching, he strode down the corridor, then opened the door to Coralyn's rooms and navigated the dark entryway to reach her bedchamber.

A lamp burned low on a table, revealing his aunt sound asleep among piles of silken cushions. "Auntie?"

She jerked upright, blinking at him. "Keris?" Then her face hardened. "Have you lost your bloody mind, boy? You cannot be in the harem after curfew—your father will think you are carrying on with one of the women and have your head."

"I'm too drunk to fuck, but thankfully not so drunk I can't think. I've had an idea."

"Foulmouthed child!" She swung her legs out of the bed, reaching for a dressing gown. "What is it that you want?"

"This isn't about what I want." He dropped onto a chaise. "It's about what *you* want."

Her eyes narrowed. "Oh?"

"You want to know what Aren knows about my sister and her whereabouts."

"*Sisters.*"

"Yes, yes." He waved a hand at her to sit. "But he's no reason to give us anything, much less information about the wife he foolishly still loves."

"Keris . . ."

He ignored the warning in her tone. "So you will have to offer him something in exchange."

"What are you suggesting?"

"An end to his people getting themselves killed trying to rescue him." Her mouth opened to respond, but Keris kept going. "If you offer to facilitate communication with the Ithicanians ordering them to stand down, I think he'll give you the information the harem wants."

That was only the first step. He'd need to gain Aren's trust before the man would ever agree to an organized rescue attempt. And Keris needed time to convince Coralyn that the harem should risk their own lives to help a foreign king.

His aunt's brow furrowed, then she shook her head. "If I suggest as much, he'll believe me a pawn in one of Serin's tricks to try to catch the Ithicanians who are undoubtedly in Vencia. He's no fool."

"Debatable," Keris answered. "But in any case, that's why you aren't going to offer him anything—you're going to wait for him to ask for it, which he will."

"Why? He has no reason to trust us and many reasons not to."

"Because you're going to give him certainty with the knowledge you have a common enemy."

She stared at him for a long moment. "The Magpie." At his nod, she cocked her head. "And what, pray tell, is in this for you?"

Possibly nothing. Possibly an alliance that would see Valcotta freed of this place. "I'm merely fulfilling my half of our agreement. This was what you wanted in exchange for keeping Zarrah Anaphora under your wing while I negotiated with the empress."

"Bullshit, boy. You weren't sitting out in the rain fretting about your deal with *me*. What are you up to?"

Rising to his feet, Keris held his arms wide. "Playing the game, Auntie." And without another word, he left the room.

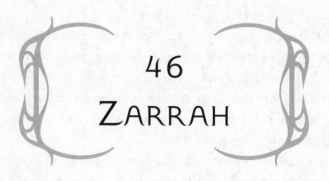

46
ZARRAH

ZARRAH TRIED NOT TO SCOWL AS THE SERVANTS GATHERED THE cutlery used for the garden lunch, one of the guards carefully counting each piece before following the servant to the kitchens, where everything was washed and locked up for the next meal. It was the same for glassware and every other mundane object the harem might require that could potentially be used as a weapon: kept under lock and key and strictly accounted for. And though she'd been here for days, she hadn't been able to steal so much as a spoon without them noticing.

It's no matter, she reminded herself. *A length of fabric torn from a sheet is a weapon. The clasp on a brooch is a weapon. A pillow is a weapon. I am a weapon.*

Seated next to her, Sara shifted restlessly, eyeing a plate of desserts at the center of the table, of which she'd already had three. Zarrah asked, "Would you walk with me?"

The little princess looked to Coralyn, who gave a slight nod, and then said, "Gladly, Zarrah. But only if you tell me more stories of battles."

Smiling, Zarrah rose and helped the child to her feet. What the girl needed was a cane, but that was another thing Silas apparently considered a weapon. It made Zarrah sick how little regard he showed his own children, but Sara seemed unconcerned, gripping Zarrah's arm to steady herself as they moved slowly down the path.

"Let us walk around the tower and then back." Zarrah knew the limits of the child's endurance well, for Sara had been her constant—and only—companion. The harem still kept their distance, and Keris . . . Keris, she hadn't seen since their walk in the garden on her first morning in Vencia.

She wasn't the only one who'd noticed his absence.

"Boy keeps the hours of a two-copper courtesan," she'd heard Coralyn complaining earlier to Lestara, a rare beauty who, despite not being Maridrinian by birth, seemed to hold the greatest grievance against Zarrah. "Out all night and then sleeps all day. It's insufferable."

Lestara had only shrugged. "Can you blame him? There's little to entertain him within these walls. Once he inherits, I think you'll find we can scarcely get rid of him. Not that I'd *want* to get rid of him."

"Mind your words, girl," Coralyn had snapped. "If Silas hears talk like that, you'll suffer. As will Keris, despite him showing no more interest in you than he does Elouise."

The wife Elouise was the eldest in the harem, wrinkled, deaf, and smelling of prune juice. Zarrah had struggled not to laugh at the look the comparison brought to Lestara's face, although she could hardly blame the woman. Silas was old, smelly, and sadistic, whereas Keris was young, handsome, and charming. The woman probably prayed nightly that her husband died in his sleep and wept every morning to discover he had not.

But regardless of Lestara's dreams for her future, she was right in one thing: Keris had been notably absent. And not knowing the reason why was driving her to madness.

"Tell me a battle story, Zarrah," Sara said, interrupting her thoughts. "One from long ago when you were young."

"As opposed to recent battles, where I am old and feeble?" Smiling, Zarrah dug into her memories, bringing forth a tale the princess would find worthy. The words flowed from her lips even as her eyes went to the tower, and to the guards standing at the entrance of the base, both armed and deadly. More patrolled the bridges linking the tower to the buildings, leaving every entrance under guard. And the men never abandoned their posts.

She circled the base of the tower, pausing when she heard the child's breathing begin to labor. "Rest here."

They sat together on a bench, the tower blocking them from the harem's sight, though Zarrah's pair of guards stood nearby, expressions bored.

"I will be leaving the palace soon," Sara said, toying with the fabric of her dress. "My father is sending me away." Twin tears rolled down the girl's face. "I don't want to leave."

Your life will be better away from this place, away from your father, Zarrah wanted to say, but instead asked, "Have you ever been outside of Vencia? It is a very beautiful country."

Sara looked up at her with red eyes. "I've never been outside of the palace."

Sickness filled Zarrah, for Silas didn't just treat his wives like prisoners; he treated his children that way as well. Born and raised in captivity, and now liberty was in Sara's grasp, but it felt like punishment. "To be a warrior, one must be willing to venture beyond the walls and face one's fears. And though no one has given you a weapon, you are still a warrior, Sara."

Sara frowned, but then nodded, wiping away her tears.

"Shall we carry on?" Zarrah asked. "Your mother will wonder where you have gone off to."

"Sara!"

Zarrah straightened at the distant call, not a female voice, but male.

"It's my brother!" The little princess tugged on Zarrah's arm so that she'd walk faster. "Let's find him!"

Zarrah's heart skittered in her chest at the sound of boots against the pathway, her skin prickling with anticipation. She saw him before he saw her, and not for the first time, Zarrah felt her chest tighten into breathlessness at the sight of him. Sun reflected off his honey-blond locks, which were pulled behind his head as he'd always worn it during the nights in Nerastis. It revealed the square lines of his jaw and the high planes of his cheekbones, utterly beautiful and yet so profoundly masculine that her toes curled. Her body didn't care that he was her enemy or that he was the son of the man who'd murdered her mother. It didn't even care that she didn't wholly trust him—it only cared for the unchecked lust coursing through her veins. She wasn't sure if it was better or worse that she knew *exactly* what it felt like to have his tongue in her mouth, his hands on her breasts, and his cock buried deep inside of her.

What she did know was that her body wanted all those things again.

Keris lifted his face and their eyes met, and what looked almost like panic filled his expression. "Lady Zarrah." He inclined his head, eyes fixing on the ground before her.

"Your Highness."

His throat moved as he swallowed, looking everywhere but at her. "Do you wish to go riding, Sara?"

The girl went still. "Truly? Auntie Coralyn will allow it?"

"I don't intend to ask. Here, I've smuggled out all the things you'll need."

He stepped to his sister's side and fastened a black cloak over her dress, and as he did, the spicy scent of his cologne filled the air. His sleeve brushed Zarrah's bare arm as he straightened, sending a shiver running over her skin. She knew she should move, but the chance it might happen again kept her rooted in place. "Is there word from the empress?"

Keris stiffened, and a flutter of unease filled Zarrah's chest. Had something happened? Had her aunt given the Maridrinians reason to believe she wouldn't negotiate? But he only said, "The Harendellians won't even have reached Nerastis yet, much less—"

"What have you been doing these past days?" Sara interrupted. "Auntie Coralyn says that you are a two-copper courtesan, as you sleep all day."

Instead of laughing, Keris frowned, still avoiding Zarrah's gaze. "I haven't been sleeping. I've been occupied." He dropped to his knees and pulled off her delicate slippers.

"With what?"

Zarrah could have kissed the girl, for that was precisely what she wished to ask but couldn't. Not with the guards within earshot.

"Unpacking my books." He pulled tiny boots onto her feet, jaw tight as he fastened the laces.

"But it's been days since I've seen you." The princess crossed her arms. "And we've servants for such things so that you might spend your time with me."

"I've more important things to do than to keep you company!" he snapped.

Zarrah started in surprise, the harsh response unexpected and out of character.

The child stared at him with wide eyes full of hurt, and guilt immediately flooded Keris's blue gaze. "That was a wretched thing for me to say, and I'm sorry for it." He rose to his feet and picked her up, kissing her cheek. "If it were my choice, I'd climb down from the tower and spend all my hours with you. But there would be consequences to doing so, so prudence demands I spend my time elsewhere."

With visible effort, he lifted his head to meet Zarrah's gaze. "When we receive your aunt's response, you will be the first to know. Good day to you, my lady." With Sara in his arms, he turned on his heel and walked away.

Something had changed. His tension. His temper. His inability to look her in the eye . . .

There was something he didn't want to tell her, and *that* was why he was avoiding her.

Zarrah started to stride after them, not entirely certain what she intended to do, only that she could not be complacent, but her feet caught in Sara's slippers, sending her stumbling. Catching herself against the wall of the tower, she held on to a gap between the stones while she righted her sandal on her foot.

Then she froze, Keris's words repeating in her ears. *I'd climb down from the tower . . .*

She looked up, eyes picking out the innumerable hand- and toeholds where time and weather had eroded the masonry. An idea formed in her head, difficult enough to verge on impossible, which meant it was nothing any of them would expect.

Keris might not be willing to climb down.

But that didn't mean Zarrah couldn't climb up.

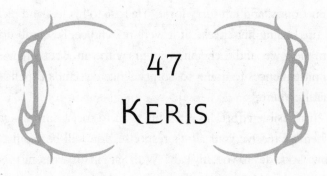

47

KERIS

"YOU'VE HAD NO RESPONSE FROM PETRA, I TAKE IT?"

The question was inevitable. It had been weeks since Keris sent his letter south to Valcotta, but thus far, the only response was silence. And given what Yrina had told him, silence was the best he could hope for.

Keris shifted his weight in the chair, ever unnerved by his father's eyes, which were currently fixed on him. "No. But the winds have been southerly, so the Harendellians might well be delayed in returning with the empress's response." An excuse that would satisfy for only another handful of days, but Keris made it anyway.

"You've put all your eggs in one basket," his father said. "And I fear you're destined to find them all broken."

He had. But the basket was not the Empress of Valcotta but rather the King of Ithicana. He only said, "It's rumored the Valcottans lost another three merchant vessels to the Tempest Seas, so the empress may be feeling pressure to ease her restrictions on using your bridge. It's not only goods lost but lives. Her own people will insist she lift the embargo. Perhaps Serin has heard whispers of that already."

The Magpie made a face. "Of course, but she's also doing an admirable job of fueling the fires of hate toward Maridrina using her niece's imprisonment. They are willing to suffer for the sake of harming our revenues with the continued embargo."

His father gave a soft snort. "More likely they know how their empress handles dissent, especially dissent against the Endless War. Those who speak against it soon speak no more."

Again, Keris was struck by the incongruity between the empress's reputation and how his father spoke of her. He rose to his feet and went to the window to look out over the city. "There's another fire. Looks to be in the wharf market."

Cursing, his father rose and joined him, his face darkening. "Malcontents. Nothing suits them. They demanded food and I got it for them. For my troubles, they burn my city. I should let them starve for their spite."

Serin coughed, and Keris had to fight to curb a smile as the spymaster said, "That is not the source of their discontent, Your Grace. It's that they believe you've executed Aren Kertell, and they are demanding proof he is still alive."

They believed *that* because Keris had been out gambling and drinking every night, subtly sowing rumors that Aren was being tortured for information. His goal was to incite the Ithicanians enough to keep up their rescue attempts. The unintended side effect was that he'd also incited his own people. All of Maridrina was in a frenzy over their king's perceived behavior toward the man who'd saved them from starvation, and thanks to an expensive bottle of wine, a pretty courtesan, and a memorable night for the Harendellian ambassador's manservant, the ambassador himself was now demanding proof that the Ithicanian king's heart still beat.

"Tell them he's very much alive."

In the reflection of the glass, Keris watched Serin's jaw tighten. Probably because he'd love to see Aren Kertell killed in the most gruesome of manners. The spymaster's lust for blood was part of what kept Keris up all night. If Serin accidentally killed Aren, Keris's plan to free Valcotta would be ruined, and it was not lost on him that it was only his father's insistence that Aren remain alive that kept him so.

"I have my people giving assurances that Aren is alive and well, Your Grace," Serin answered. "Unfortunately, the people seem . . . disinclined to believe our assurances."

They didn't believe them because Keris had *also* started a rumor that Aren's death had been an accident that the King of Maridrina was desperate to keep silent. "You could always tour Aren about Vencia and give them proof."

"Don't be a damned fool," his father snapped. "I'll not pander to those who dare to call me a liar, never mind that this is Ithicana's doing. They're starting rumors to incite the masses. Have the malcontents thrown in prison and we shall see the end to it."

Keris shrugged. "Was only a suggestion."

"With respect, Your Grace," Serin said. "Perhaps we might pursue a different approach. One that would silence the malcontents without giving them the sense they hold any power. If we were to invite the Harendellian ambassador, who is a neutral party, to see that Aren Kertell is well, he might then provide comfort to the people."

"The bastard has been demanding a meeting for weeks," his father snarled. "I'll no more pander to Harendell than to the people. Already they squawk over terms on the bridge. We cannot show any sign of weakness."

"Then arrange it under the guise of something else," Keris suggested, gently guiding his father's thoughts. "And don't include only the Harendellian; include all others in the city of note, most especially the ambassador from Amarid, because that will truly grind the Harendellian's nerves."

"You propose a social engagement?"

"You know how the Harendellians love pomp. And entertainment."

His father rubbed his chin. "True. This has merit."

"I mislike this idea, Your Grace," Serin said, his voice grinding at Keris's nerves. "Within the sanctum, we have total control. The moment we bring Aren outside of it, we risk—"

"Then we host it within the sanctum. Tonight, so no one has the time to conspire." His father smiled. "Have Coralyn arrange it. The old hag understands pomp, if nothing else. And it will give the harem something to do other than complain. See it done, Serin."

"As you wish, Your Grace." Serin bowed, the spymaster's irritation palpable as he shuffled from the room, though whether it was over the king ignoring his counsel or whether he sensed a plot not his own was afoot, Keris wasn't certain. There was little to be done other than to press forward.

Keris had done his part to ensure all the key players would be at the same table, and now it was up to Coralyn to make the most of it. "I'm sure whatever she arranges will be a roaring success. Now, if you'll excuse me, I've—"

"You will attend as well, Keris. I grow weary of your aunts' complaints about your whoremongering in the city. And bring the Valcottan—might as well strike two birds with one stone and ensure Petra knows we aren't negotiating with a corpse."

Keris couldn't help but stiffen. Since Yrina's death, he'd done his best to avoid Valcotta, their one encounter proof that he couldn't control himself around her. Telling her the truth would be a disaster, but he was unable to look her in the eye with deception in his heart. And instead of each day growing easier, it had felt like every passing hour he swallowed another mouthful of poison. That the deception was for the sake of her freedom, for the sake of her *life*, was no balm, because he knew she wouldn't see it that way. All she'd see was a murderer.

Swallowing the sourness in his mouth, Keris said, "I'd rather not. I have some new books that need to be shelved."

"It wasn't a request," his father answered. "Be there, or I'll burn every last volume to teach you a lesson."

A sacrifice Keris would've gladly made, but given the same threat had been used successfully against him dozens of times before, he needed to allow it to work now or raise suspicions. Grinding his teeth, Keris left the room, ignoring the guards as he went down flight after flight of stairs to the door to his chambers. He unlocked it and went inside, then twisted the bolt behind him.

Everything depended on Aren Kertell. Without an alliance with the Ithicanians, there would be no rescue, which meant Keris had to do whatever it took to make this meeting between Coralyn and Aren come to pass. Even if it meant sitting next to Valcotta through dinner and lying through his teeth that everything was as it should be.

He crossed to the window, ripped aside the drapes, and swung open the pane, then immediately regretted it as a wave of stink slapped him in the face. Clenching his teeth, Keris searched the paths for her, but the harem was notably absent.

The reason for which became apparent as his eyes lighted upon Aren.

The King of Ithicana was chained to his bench, staring at his rotting countrymen dangling from the wall. How he personally felt about the man, Keris wasn't entirely sure. Once, before he'd met him, he'd been disgusted by how Aren ruled his kingdom, keeping his people locked inside like prisoners. Then he'd been disgusted by the man's stupidity for trusting Lara, for loving the woman who was more Silas Veliant's progeny than any other. But now . . .

Now he felt equal parts pity and admiration for the king. For Keris knew the pain of this particular torture, and it had been visited upon Aren eighteenfold. Yet despite his obvious grief, the Ithicanian remained defiant. Time and again, he tried to escape, using guile and strength and skill. But though he had successfully killed two guards and injured several more, a prisoner Aren remained.

"I'll get you out," Keris muttered. "Just don't get yourself killed before I do it."

There were too many risks to the man's life.

Serin taking things too far.

A guard accidentally killing him.

Yet as he watched Aren straighten, expression grim, Keris realized there was a third threat to the King of Ithicana's life that he hadn't considered: the man himself.

A look of determination filled Aren's face, every muscle in the man's body tense as though in preparation for action. "Don't you fucking dare." Panic rose in Keris's chest because he needed the king *alive*. "Don't you dare take your piece off my board!"

He had to do something. Had to find a way to give Aren a reason to keep his heart beating until Coralyn could speak to him at dinner.

Everything depended on it.

Except Serin or his lackeys would be watching, which meant Keris had to do it in a way that wouldn't burn his plans to the ground by revealing his allegiances.

Think! he screamed at himself. *A clue! Something, anything, that will give him a reason to hold on a few more hours.*

But there was *nothing*.

Then a gust of wind whistled past. The corpses swayed and danced, scattering the carrion birds that had been pecking at them.

Birds.

Rushing to his shelves, he tore into them, searching for a particular volume.

There.

He flung it open, flipping through the pages until he found the familiar illustration of a magpie, his eyes dancing over the words *opportunistic, they will feed on the chicks of songbirds.*

Keris slammed the volume shut and tucked it under his arm, then left the room, struggling not to take the stairs two at a time. A pair of guards opened the doors at the base, and he strolled out into the gardens, schooling his face to blankness.

Please don't let me be too late.

His heart pounded as he wove through the paths, then stuttered as his eyes latched onto the still-living Ithicanian king.

Aren's whole body was tense, his eyes full of the resigned determination of a man ready to end his life because he saw no other path forward. He leaned, readying to dash his own skull against the hard stone of the table, and it was all Keris could do not to throw himself at the man to restrain him.

But Serin was always watching, and he dared not give himself away.

Aren closed his eyes and took a breath, and Keris clenched his teeth to keep from screaming, *Don't do it!*

Step. Step. Step. He put weight into his stride, hoping the noise would cause the man to look up, but Aren only gripped the table with his manacled hands, knuckles turning white, the resolve in his expression so great that Keris wondered if stopping him were even possible.

But he had to try, so he said loudly, "The wives are starting to complain about the smell. Can't say that I blame them."

The King of Ithicana twitched hard enough that his chains rattled against the table, his bloodshot eyes fixing on Keris, recognition filling them.

"It's a terrible practice." Keris squinted at the bodies lining the walls, their putrefying flesh crawling with insects, drawing old, painful memories to the forefront. "Never mind the smell; it invites flies and other vermin. Spreads disease." Feeling his stomach twist, he looked back to Aren. "Though I expect it's far worse for you, given that you know them, Your Grace. Especially given they died trying to break you free."

Aren's hazel eyes darkened, and it seemed he hadn't noticed Keris's use of his title despite it being forbidden. "You are . . . ?"

"Keris."

"Ah." Aren's tone was flat. "The *inadequate* heir."

Given you've proven yourself to be a particularly inadequate king, that seems a tad self-righteous, Keris wanted to say, but he hadn't come here to needle the man. He'd come to facilitate an alliance and achieve an end, which meant every word needed to be chosen with care. Setting the book on the table, he said, "Eight older brothers who fit the mold, all dead, and now my father is stuck trying to weasel his way out of naming me heir without breaking one of his own laws. I'd wish him luck in the endeavor if not for the fact that his and Serin's weaseling is likely to see me in a grave next to my siblings."

The king leaned back in his chair, the chains on his manacles rattling, reminding Keris that the man was dangerous, even when restrained. "No desire to rule?"

"It's a thankless burden," Keris replied, knowing it was no answer.

"True. But when you have the crown, you can change the décor." Aren gestured at the corpses lining the garden walls.

Keris laughed despite himself, wondering if under other circumstances he'd have liked this man. *Probably not.* "To rule is a burden, but perhaps especially so for a king who enters his reign desirous of change, for he will spend his life wading against the current. But you understand that, don't you, Your Grace?" The guards who were listening in on the conversation would believe he spoke solely of Aren's reign, but he prayed the Ithicanian was more intelligent than that.

"You're the philosopher," Aren said. "Or was that, too, part of the deception?"

A flicker of confusion ran through him, and then Keris understood. Aren was referring to the part Keris had played in the invasion of Ithicana.

It had been Aren who'd given Keris and his entourage permission to travel the bridge, and it was unlikely that the Ithicanian king was aware that Keris's participation in the invasion had been unwitting. Aren believed him complicit, which meant he'd not see Keris as a potential ally. But perhaps the truth would sway him. "I think Serin took particular glee in using my dreams in such a perverse fashion. It is one of the only instances in which he has successfully pulled the wool over my eyes, the shock of being trussed up and stuffed in a corner while my *escort* invaded Ithicana not one I'll soon forget. Even still, I might have forgiven the duplicity if my father had allowed me to carry on to Harendell in pursuit of my studies, but as you can see"—he stretched his arms wide—"here I am."

"My condolences."

Not enough. He needed to do more to sway the man's opinion of him. "Imagine a world where people spent as much time philosophizing as they did learning to swing weapons."

"I can't," Aren answered bitterly. "The only thing I know well is war, which doesn't say much given that I'm on the losing side of this one."

"Losing, perhaps . . ." Keris knew that he was treading on dangerous ground, given this conversation would be reported back to Serin. And to his father. "But not yet lost. Not while Eranahl stands, and not while you still live. Why else would my father insist on these theatrics?"

"Bait for his errant daughter, I'm told."

"Your wife."

The only answer he got was a glower, and Keris found himself questioning his aunt's belief that Aren still cared for Lara. Except Coralyn was a master at reading people—and manipulating them—and he'd never known her to miss her mark. Which meant he needed to dig deeper.

"Lara." Keris rubbed his chin, forcing his face into a mask of idle curiosity. "She's my sister, you know."

"If you meant that to be a great revelation, I'm afraid I have to disappoint you."

Keris chuckled even as motion in the distance had him scanning the garden for spies. But it was only a bird splashing in a fountain. "Not my half sister. We have the same mother, too."

Aren straightened, interest rising in his gaze. And something else. "What of it?"

Keris ran his tongue across his lips, reluctant to speak on this, though he knew it was necessary to establish that they had a common enemy. Keeping his voice low enough that the guards would pick up only bits and pieces, he said, "I was nine when my father's soldiers took my sister—young enough to still be living in the harem, but old enough to remember the moment well. To remember how my mother fought them. To remember how she attempted to sneak out of the palace to go after my sister, knowing in her heart that my father intended her for some fell purpose. To remember how, when she was caught and dragged back, my father strangled her himself in front of us all. As punishment. And warning."

The only other person he'd told this story to was Valcotta, but now that it was unearthed, it appeared it desired to be shared.

"What game are you playing, Keris?"

It's good to see you're clever enough to realize that one is being played, Keris thought, then rested his hand on his chin so that his fingers partially obscured his mouth before saying, "A long one, and you are but a singular piece on the board, albeit one of some significance." He gave the Ithicanian king a measured stare. "I sense that you're considering removing yourself from the game. I ask that you might reconsider."

Disgust flared in Aren's eyes, and he looked away. "As long as I'm alive, they'll keep trying to save me. And keep dying in the attempt. I can't allow that."

And the time they had for this conversation was over. Appearing from behind a topiary like some sort of village peeper, Serin approached. While he was still out of earshot, Keris said, "Keep playing the game, Aren. Your life isn't as worthless as you think."

Then Serin was upon them, his obnoxious voice filling the air. "A questionable choice of company, Your Highness."

Keris shrugged, knowing that the blasé attitude ground on the spymaster's nerves. "I've always been a victim of my own curiosity, Serin. You know that."

"*Curiosity.*"

"Indeed. Aren is a man of myth. Former king of the misty isles of Ithicana, legendary fighter, and husband to one of my mysterious warrior sisters. How could I resist plying him for details of his escapades? Sadly, he hasn't been particularly forthcoming."

There was an edge of frustration in Serin's voice as he said, "You were supposed to have returned to Nerastis. You need to study with your father's generals."

Words of wishful thinking. It was unusual for the spymaster to make such a slip, which made Keris uneasy, but he played along. "My father's generals are boring."

"Boring or not, it's a necessary part of your training."

"*Mag, mag, mag!*" Keris mimicked a magpie's call, laughing inside as the man's eyes lighted with fury. He hated the moniker, and especially hated the woman who'd given it to him. "No wonder the harem wives christened you so, Serin. Your voice truly does grate on the nerves." He rose to his feet. "Was a pleasure meeting you, Aren. But you'll have to excuse me, the smell is making me quite nauseous."

Turning, he sauntered across the courtyard as though he hadn't a care in the world despite his heart being in his throat. Despite his nerves being stretched so tight he thought he'd vomit. Inside the cool confines of the tower, he lost control of his pace, the need to ensure Aren had taken the bait making him leap up the stairs three at a time, rounding the corners at dizzying speed.

He unlocked the door to his rooms, then strode to the window to look down. And hissed between his teeth as another corpse was dragged across the garden, Aren watching in silence as the guards hung it on the wall.

Please, he prayed. *A few more hours. A few more hours, and we can make this stop.*

Then Aren squared his shoulders, and Keris knew his efforts had been in vain. That he was about to watch a man die, and with him, all of Keris's plans. Frustration flooded him, but also guilt that he'd not done more. And grief that yet another life would fall beneath his father's bootheel.

Yet instead of dashing his skull against the stone of the table, Aren reached out and opened the book, flipping through the pages before pausing. Reading.

Keris didn't have a chance to see how the King of Ithicana reacted as a familiar voice said, "Give me one reason not to kill you where you stand."

48
ZARRAH

"THIS IS A KINDNESS," SHE SAID TO CORALYN, ACCEPTING THE folded garments. "Thank you."

"You've ruined three gowns in as many days with your *exercises*," the harem wife sniffed. "Perhaps these will show more longevity. Although allow me to make myself abundantly clear: You will not wear these scandalous items outside your room, or I will have them burned. Understood?"

"Yes, Lady Coralyn." Zarrah waited for the woman to remove herself, then unfolded the garments. Voluminous trousers and a snug bodice made of black silk, cut in Valcottan style. She sighed as she slipped them on. Not only for the familiarity after weeks of wearing Maridrinian garments but because she had been growing concerned that she was going to have to assassinate Silas Veliant whilst wearing only her undergarments, for her plan wouldn't accommodate billowing skirts.

She went to the window and stared up at the tower where her enemy lurked, blissfully unaware that this was the last day he'd draw breath. For tonight would be a moonless night, and under the cover of darkness she would make her move.

Her hours of effort removing the mortar that secured the stone block had finally been rewarded, and all it would take now was pushing the block out and she'd have her method of escape, her own body serving as the weapon she'd use to take Silas's life, for she'd not managed to acquire another.

But it would be enough. It *had* to be enough.

Unbidden, her eyes moved from Silas's glass-enclosed office at the top to a window at the midpoint.

Keris's room.

She'd seen him only a handful of times since their encounter on the day he'd taken his sister riding, and always from a distance. Though she'd had weeks to get used to his choice to avoid her, the sting hadn't lessened. If anything, it had only grown worse.

Because she didn't know the reason.

Was he losing the negotiation with the empress? Had he realized that escape was impossible? Or had Keris just become bored with her, which was certainly fitting with his reputation?

Why did it matter to her at all?

She was here to kill his father, which meant all of Keris's efforts ran counter to her own, as did any form of relationship between them. It was *better* he was avoiding her. It was good that they had nothing to do with each other. Because it would make what she was about to do all the simpler.

Then the curtains moved, and logic disappeared as Keris stepped to the window, looking out.

God spare her, but he was easily the most beautiful man she'd ever set eyes on, and that he had a mind to match seemed unfair. Knowing that the glare on the glass of her own window would hide her, Zarrah stared at him in a way she couldn't when subject to prying eyes. His honey-blond hair was loose, the breeze catching at it, and a yearning to brush the silky locks back from his face hit her like a battering ram.

Squeezing her eyes shut, Zarrah took several measured breaths. *You must focus,* she reminded herself. *Tonight, you will achieve the vengeance you dedicated your life to.*

Not with war. Not with raids. But by killing the man who'd murdered her mother with his own hands.

The moment she opened her eyes, her gaze shot back to the window. But Keris was gone. Biting at her lip, she rested her hands on the sill, only to have a flash of blond hair catch her attention. Keris was in the garden.

"Stay put, Zarrah," she said to herself. "Leave well enough alone."

Except she realized that while the gulf between them might be for the best, knowing that it was so was not enough. She needed a reason for Keris's choice. Needed the truth, even if the truth hurt. And today would be her last opportunity to hear the truth from his lips.

Ripping off her new garments, Zarrah pulled on a gown and then hammered on the door until one of the guards opened it. "I wish to go to the gardens," she said. "Now, please."

Not waiting for a response, she squeezed past them, her bare feet silent on the carpet as she walked as quickly as she could, for breaking into a run would raise alarm. And she couldn't risk them stopping her, as this might well be the last chance she ever had to speak to Keris.

To know the truth. To—though she couldn't voice the words— say goodbye.

She shoved open the doors at the bottom of the stairs, wove through the garden paths, then slid to a stop.

Keris sat across from Aren, who was glaring at him like he'd like nothing better than to wring his neck. They were speaking, but she was too far away to hear what they were saying. Keeping behind a hedgerow, she watched them through the leaves, ignoring the mutters of her guards.

What are they talking about?

A smell filled her nose, sour and stale, and Zarrah's skin crawled. Slowly, she looked over her shoulder, her palms turning to ice as she found the Magpie standing behind her.

"Bold of Keris to get so close to Aren, given that the man knows of his involvement in the invasion," he said. "Idiot is going to get himself killed."

Involvement? Zarrah stilled herself, refusing to show any reaction. This was no idle conversation. Serin had a purpose. Yet she couldn't help but say, "I hadn't realized Ithicana's invasion was a family affair."

"Oh, yes." Serin smiled at the corpses. "The Ithicanians never suspected the ruse because His Highness's desire to study in Harendell was long known to their spies."

She stood in silence as the spymaster detailed what had come to pass inside the bridge. How Keris had led a group of elite warriors, then, using duplicity and clever timing, had slaughtered his Ithicanian guards.

"Keris's force cracked open Midwatch Island itself," Serin continued. "Well worthy of accolades, if not for the fact he was but a small piece in Lara's grand scheme, so hardly anyone is aware Keris was even involved."

Zarrah certainly hadn't known he was there. Every bit of intelligence Valcottan spies had given her spoke only of *Lara*.

"I believe he hoped it would win his father's favor, but His Grace was unimpressed. As he has been likewise unimpressed with Keris's attempts to use you to negotiate. The king favors sons with steel in their spines, fighting men who won't hesitate to take the kill."

This was a lie. Zarrah didn't believe for a heartbeat that Keris had led a critical piece of the invasion. For one, he would want nothing to do with it, and two, Silas would never trust him with something of that magnitude. "Is there a point to all this prattle? I care little of the grasping of a Maridrinian princeling."

"My pardon, of course. I was merely trying to illuminate His Highness's motivations for killing Yrina Kitan."

Yrina? Zarrah swayed on her feet, breath driven from her chest. Yrina wasn't here; she was in Nerastis. She couldn't be dead. "Pardon?"

Serin pursed his lips. "I see Keris has not informed you of the casualty. The coward likely fears your reaction."

The world around her seemed to pulse, a sour taste filling her mouth. "I . . . How?"

"The captain was captured attempting to infiltrate His Majesty's inner sanctum, presumably to reach you. She killed four trusted soldiers, necessitating her execution, which Keris volunteered to carry out. Silas was most impressed with his conduct— I've not heard the end of it."

It couldn't be true.

Yrina couldn't be dead.

Keris couldn't be the one who'd killed her.

Zarrah gasped in breath after breath of air, but it didn't feel like any of it reached her lungs. "When?"

"The day after you arrived, I believe."

The day he'd started avoiding her at every turn. And she, like a fool, had thought it was because he'd grown tired of her.

Unless Serin was lying.

Unless this was a scheme.

"You seem to doubt my words," Serin said. "By all means, ask the prince for the truth. You've placed your life in his hands, so his word, at least, should be something you can trust. Now, if you'll excuse me, I have a gift I must present to Aren." He motioned at her guards. "You two may be required momentarily. Come with me."

Serin strode out from behind the topiary toward Aren and Keris, but Zarrah barely registered the exchange between the men, seeing only red. Hearing nothing beyond the silent scream of grief ricocheting around in her head, because Yrina was dead.

Her comrade, her confidante, her *friend* was dead.

Dead, because Zarrah had chosen to allow Keris to bring her into this palace. Dead, because she wanted a chance at vengeance instead of escaping. Dead, because Zarrah had been so blinded in her pursuit of Silas Veliant's death that she'd failed to realize her sworn bodyguard and closest friend would defy every order and come after her.

The pain of it swelled like a rising tide, threatening to overwhelm her, to drown her, and then her eyes fixed on Keris, who was on his feet. Who was walking toward the doors of the tower.

He'd killed her. Had murdered Yrina to impress his father and then avoided Zarrah like a coward rather than owning up to his actions.

Zarrah's focus narrowed, her eyes moving to her guards, who'd followed Serin, their necessity made apparent when more of Serin's men dragged another Ithicanian corpse into the gardens, Aren having attacked them many times before. But then Serin lifted a hand and motioned to the two men guarding the doors to the tower. They abandoned their posts, moving cautiously into position, their focus entirely on the Ithicanian king.

Zarrah didn't hesitate.

Once she'd slipped inside the building, she took the stairs two at a time, counting the levels until she reached the one that held Keris's room. She swung open the door, then silently closed it behind her, eyes fixed on Keris's back, where he stood looking out the window. "Give me one reason not to kill you where you stand."

Keris whirled around, gaping in shock. "Valcotta? What are you doing in here? Why . . ."

"Did you do it?" she demanded, watching the color drain from his face. "Did you kill Yrina?"

The silence that followed made her want to vomit, because part of her had hoped . . . had *prayed* that Serin was lying.

"I'm sorry. Let me explain what—"

She wasn't interested in explanations.

In a heartbeat, Zarrah was across the room, the silk of her skirt ripping as she lifted her leg and twisted, his protests a drone in her ears. Her foot connected with his head, and he fell sideways, stunned. "Valcotta, just listen to me!"

"I'm going to kill you, you lying Veliant prick!" She threw herself at him, fists striking hard and fast, hearing his grunt of pain as she connected. "How could you?"

"I'm sorry!" He blocked her next blow. "I didn't have a choice!"

"There's always a choice," she snarled, striking him below the ribs, drawing a gasp from him. "You chose to invade Ithicana. You chose to kill Yrina. You're the same as everyone in your bloodthirsty family, but at least the rest of them don't pretend to be anything different!"

"Ithicana was no choice!" He twisted, sending them both rolling into a stack of books. "And neither was Yrina!"

"You're a liar! You did it to impress your father! You did it because you want to be king!" She got behind him, arm around his throat. "And I'm going to kill you for it. Then your father. And then the rest of your twisted family."

And she squeezed.

Keris clawed at her arms, trying to pull them loose, but Zarrah gritted her teeth and held on, her skill against his strength.

Tears rolled down her cheeks because she'd been so certain he was different. So certain that he truly wanted peace.

So certain that she could trust him.

But it had all been lies.

Fury gave her strength, and Zarrah pulled tighter as his fingers dug into her skin. There was no explanation. There was nothing he could say that would make this right.

Then he went limp. Not dead yet, but if she held on a few moments longer . . .

If you kill him, you'll never know the truth of what happened to Yrina. The thought sent a rush of panic through her, and Zarrah let go of Keris's throat, rolling him off her. For a heartbeat, she stared at him, certain that she'd gone too far, but then he sucked in a ragged gasp of breath, eyes fluttering open, his gaze unfocused. He started to sit, but she straddled him, pinning his wrists to the thick carpet beneath him.

"Tell me what happened. All of it," she said. "Leave nothing out."

Keris sucked in breath after breath, but then he met her gaze. "I didn't know they'd captured Yrina until my father brought me down to her cell," he said. "There was no way to get her out; there were too many guards. And even if it had been possible, Serin had . . . *hurt* her in ways that weren't survivable."

Tortured her. Zarrah's chest constricted, her mind supplying endless visions of what Yrina must have endured.

"My father gave me the choice: to kill her or to allow her to die a slow, painful death. I . . . Mercy was the only thing I could give."

Mercy. Her tongue felt thick, her throat tight. "Serin said you did it to earn your father's favor."

Keris gave her a sideways glance. "You believed him?" He gave a sharp shake of his head. "Serin used Yrina's death to manipulate your emotions. To drive you toward a purpose. To . . ."

"Kill you." Zarrah bit the insides of her cheeks, realizing now that the guards abandoning their station had been no misstep. The

Magpie had known *exactly* where she'd go. Which meant he knew she was in here, and now she'd have to face either the consequences of having attacked Keris or questions she couldn't answer for why she hadn't killed him when given the chance. "I allowed grief to blind me, and I believed the worst."

"Sometimes the worst is true."

Silence stretched between them, then he said, "I should've told you about Yrina, but I didn't want to hurt you. Didn't want you to hate me." He sucked in a ragged breath. "It was the act of a coward."

How would she have reacted if he'd told her? Would she have been reasonable? Would she have listened to his explanation? Or would she have lashed out in grief? Zarrah wasn't certain, but she did know that she'd rather have heard of Yrina's death from Keris than from Serin. "You should have told me." She swallowed hard. "Please don't keep things from me. Even if they hurt, I need to know." She looked down at him, meeting his gaze. "I can't trust someone who deceives me, no matter the motivations. Yrina's death was not your decision, but you chose to keep it from me. Chose to avoid me rather than to face the consequences of the truth."

Keris exhaled a long breath. "I'm sorry. For deceiving you, but also for my part in her death."

"You offered her mercy." And she knew better than most that to be merciful often necessitated bravery, but God help her, this hurt. It was her decisions that had brought Yrina here, which made her more the cause of her friend's death than anyone.

"I told her the truth. About you and me."

A flicker of panic bit at her guts, fear that in learning the truth, Yrina had spent her last moments feeling betrayed. That she'd died believing Zarrah was a traitor. "Why?"

"So she'd know you weren't alone. So she'd have the peace of knowing that someone was trying to get you free."

"Then you should have told her you were negotiating with the empress. She knows my aunt would never abandon me to die."

His jaw tightened. "The empress personally gave the order that no one was to go after you. Yrina defied the order."

A jolt ran through Zarrah, her breaths coming quickly yet not seeming to deliver air. "So she died a traitor to the Crown and knowing that I lied to her."

Silence.

"She didn't care about any of that, Valcotta. She willingly chose death to protect you, and her last words were to request I tell you that she loves you."

A knife to the heart would have hurt less, and Zarrah doubled over, forehead pressed against his chest as she fought to breathe. "Was it quick? Please tell me you made it quick."

"It was quick."

There was something about his tone that told her what his words did not. "She did it herself, didn't she? You weren't the one who killed her."

He didn't answer, and she looked up to see that his eyes were closed, fingers pressed to his temples and face pale. "Keris?"

"I hesitated." The words caught as he added, "I wanted a chance to think of a solution, a way out, but . . ."

Of course he had. Of course he'd refuse to concede to death being the solution. "Sometimes, there is no way out."

His eyes snapped open. "I will get *you* out, Valcotta. One way or another."

Except she hadn't come to this place to escape. She'd come for blood and vengeance. But for all her admonitions about honesty and trust, she couldn't tell him that. So Zarrah only gave him a tight nod, easing her grip on his wrists.

But she didn't climb off him, remaining where she was, straddling his hips. Rising meant leaving, and she didn't want to be alone in her grief. In her guilt.

Keris shifted beneath her, fingers interlocking with hers, and the tenuous control she had over her emotions shivered. Her chest was so tight, and she feared if she opened her clenched jaw, a sob would tear loose. Yet she managed to say, "I should go. I need to go. Serin knows I'm here."

Instead of answering, Keris sat upright, and Zarrah instinctively shifted her weight so that her legs were wrapped around him, resting her forehead on his shoulder. She exhaled, shuddering, and tears forced themselves free. *Don't cry*, she told herself. *You're strong.*

Not strong enough.

A sob ripped from her lips with such ferocity she thought it would tear her apart. Might have torn her apart, except Keris wrapped his arms around her, holding her close. Holding her together as sob after painful sob clawed its way out of her body. Only when they eased did he loosen his grip, one hand moving up and down her naked back.

The sensation sent a stab of heat into her core, igniting a throb between her legs, and she clung to the sensation rather than attempting to vanquish it. Focused on how the silk skirt of her dress was pushed up to her waist and that she wore nothing beneath, her naked sex pressed against him. On how the low-cut neckline had pulled sideways to expose one of her breasts. On how the growing hardness beneath her betrayed that he'd noticed these things as well.

She ground her hips against him, her desire ratcheting higher as he groaned softly, his fingers trailing over her naked thighs. Then he said, "You need to get out of the tower before Serin comes looking. He can't catch us like this."

Because it would be the death of both of them. Yet such logic meant little when she wanted to drown her grief in his touch. Wanted to drive away the pain in her heart with lust. Wanted to fall asleep wrapped in his arms so that he might ward away the nightmares that were sure to come.

Except she wasn't selfish enough to disrespect Yrina's sacrifice by getting herself killed before accomplishing what she'd come to Vencia to do, so Zarrah rose and straightened her dress. "Serin believes I came in here to kill you. We need a reason why I didn't. An excuse for me being here."

"Think of one on the way down." Keris caught her hand, then led her to the door and hauled it open. "We can't linger."

The sound of footfalls echoed in the stairwell.

"Shit!" Panic filled Keris's gaze.

An idea struck her.

She hauled Keris up the stairs, whispering as they climbed. "Tell the guards upstairs that I have information for the king and I wish to negotiate. Then follow my lead."

"What information?"

"Trust me."

Keris gave a tight nod, then caught hold of her elbow, leading her up. They reached the first pair of bodyguards, one of them saying, "You aren't supposed to be alone with her, Highness."

"I'm not." Keris looked over his shoulder, then frowned as though surprised to see Zarrah's escort missing before shrugging. "I'm sure they'll be along shortly. This can't wait."

"Highness . . ."

Keris ignored the man, pulling Zarrah up the stairs to the top level, where yet another set of guards waited. "She wishes to negotiate with His Grace. Says she has information he'll consider valuable."

The guard knocked, then stepped inside, reappearing a moment later to nod at Keris. "He'll see her."

The guards fastened her wrists with manacles, and taking a breath to steel herself, Zarrah went inside, the chains jingling with each step.

Silas sat with his boots up on his desk, arms folded behind his back, and a glass of amber liquid sitting in front of him. "You've been busy, Keris. It's been less than an hour since you left my presence, and already you've managed to have an unsanctioned conversation with Aren Kertell, as well as found the time to facilitate a confession of some sort from Lady Zarrah here."

"Serin's tactics have broken the man's will, and he's on the cusp of taking his own life, which will cause us significant consternation," Keris answered. "The Magpie allows his passions for torture to take precedence over your goals, Your Grace. You might remind him who rules, because I believe he may have forgotten."

Something flickered in Silas's eyes . . . annoyance? Or something more? "You may have a point. Now, what is it that Lady Zarrah wishes to discuss?"

Lifting her chin, Zarrah allowed her grief to swell, the prick of tears in her eyes unfeigned as she said, "Your spymaster informed me that an individual of some importance to me was apprehended and killed." She shot a look of venom at Keris, who shifted uneasily. "Killed by *his* blade."

Silas's jaw tightened. "What of it? The woman murdered four of my soldiers. If you are seeking an apology, you are wasting your breath."

"That's not what I want." A tear spilled down her cheek. "Yrina was my bodyguard. And friend. I'd see her remains treated with respect and returned to the Red Desert. And in exchange, I'll offer you information about your daughter."

"Which one?"

"Lara." It was old information. Probably useless as far as locating the traitor queen. But from the way Silas slid his boots from his desk and straightened in his chair, Zarrah knew she'd chosen well.

"I've no notion of what Serin did with the remains, but if such a thing is possible, I will see it done," he said. "That is, assuming your information is good."

"Our spies told us that she was seen in several coastal villages in Harendell," she said. "In taverns every night."

Silas grimaced. "Yes, yes. We received the same information. It is of no worth, as she disappeared before assassins could track her down."

"Did your spies also inform you that she was drinking to excess every night?"

"I fail to see how tales of her *celebrations* are of any worth."

Probably because he was a man. And his spies were men. Whereas the Valcottan who'd reported this information had been very much a woman. "Not celebrating, Your Grace. She drank alone, refusing to have anything to do with other patrons, drinking to such excess that she was often sick in the gutter, at which point she'd drag herself back to a boardinghouse, always alone." An easy mark, which the traitor queen of Ithicana had to have known. "She favored harbor taverns, particularly those with active trade between Harendell and Southwatch market."

Silas stared at her, still not comprehending.

"She behaved like a woman with deep regrets. A woman with nothing left to lose. A woman desperate for information about those she left behind. And if, as you say, she's now gone from those taverns, it is because she learned the news of her husband's capture."

"She's coming for him," Keris said softly, a hint of disbelief in his voice, and Zarrah gave a slight nod. "A spy's worth is not always in what they see and hear, but in how they interpret it."

A smile of delight rose to Silas's face. "Indeed. And it is news well received. I shall discover the fate of the remains of your countrywoman."

"Thank you." The words stuck in her throat, but Zarrah forced them out. She'd take them back when she took his life.

A knock sounded at the door, the guard stepping inside. "Serin is here, Your Grace."

The spymaster entered. Though he must have been surprised to see her standing there with Keris, still very much alive, none of it registered on his face. "Aren has agreed to attend a dinner with the ambassadors tonight."

"Excellent." Silas sipped at his drink. "I'm going to need you to dig up the corpse of that Valcottan woman. Pay a merchant to dump the body in the Red Desert."

"Why would we do such a thing?"

"As payment for information the Valcottans had about Lara that *you* didn't."

There was a threat in Silas's tone, but instead of blanching, Serin's gaze darkened with anger. "What information would that be?"

"Information on Lara's behavior and state of mind," Silas answered, then repeated what Zarrah had told him.

"It would be good information if not for the fact it presumably predates Lady Zarrah's capture in Nerastis, suggesting that it is *old* information and likely of little use."

She couldn't help but tense, because if Silas agreed, he might deny Yrina dignity in death.

"You're an idiot if that's what you think," Keris said. "And even if it proves useless, the fact remains that it is information your spies failed to accurately report, Serin. You must be losing your touch."

"My son makes a valid point."

Zarrah didn't so much as blink, but watching the spymaster

squirm, knowing full well that his scheming had been turned back on him, sent a rush of vicious pleasure through her.

"I will endeavor to tighten my web," Serin finally said. "But as for the matter of the body, I'm afraid that will be impossible."

Zarrah felt her stomach drop and her hands turn to ice even as Silas demanded, "Why?"

"Because it was burned," Serin answered. "And the ashes were tossed in the sewers with the rest of the shit."

The world spun in and out of focus. *In the sewers* . . .

"My regrets, Lady Zarrah," Silas said. "I'll be sure to make the proper arrangements if any more of your people attempt rescue, although I'd not hold my breath."

She couldn't get enough air into her lungs. "You monster!" She flung herself at Serin. "I'm going to rip out your goddamned heart."

Then she was flying backward, her shoulders aching from the force the guard had used to jerk her chains. She ignored the pain and lunged again, but the guard was strong. He kicked her in the back of the legs, knocking her to the ground, his boot between her shoulder blades.

Zarrah felt hot breath against her cheek, and she twisted her head to see Silas bent close. "You are expected at dinner with the ambassadors tonight. Be on your best behavior." Then he rose. "Lock her in her room."

The guards dragged her backward, kicking and screaming, but as the door slammed shut between them, she met the King of Maridrina's gaze and made a silent vow.

Tonight, Silas Veliant would breathe his last.

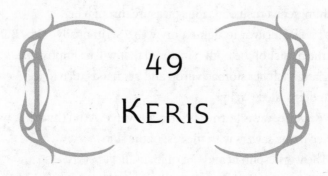

49
KERIS

SERIN WAS TRYING TO KILL HIM.

Which meant his father was losing patience with Keris's ploys, and that meant time was running out. Though whether that would see his father dead or Valcotta dead, he wasn't sure.

There had been no missing the promise of murder in her eyes—a fate his father had earned, but if she managed to follow through, the consequences would be catastrophic. If his father's guards didn't slaughter her, which was unlikely, her life would still be forfeit. The people would demand her death, and even with the crown on his head, he'd be in no position to deny them. It would necessitate him trying to escape *with* her, which would border on an impossible task.

Not that he wouldn't try.

And the Endless War would be catapulted into a fevered pitch, his father a martyr fueling Maridrina's wrath and the empress, from what he was learning, more than happy to return in kind. Especially if Valcotta ended up on the executioner's block.

His mind spiraled down and down, imagining worse and worse

scenarios, until he felt sick with anxiety. He needed to talk to Valcotta, needed to explain to her that Aren might be the key to her escape, but getting her alone was nearly impossible. A few more hours was all he needed, for the harem had a plan to allow Coralyn a moment to speak to Aren over dinner and gain the man's support.

Which had to work.

Keris pressed his fingertips to his temples, his head aching and every muscle in his body tense, hating that he was dependent on the Ithicanian king. On that man whose error in falling for Lara's duplicity was the cause of *all* of this. "He's desperate," he told himself, stomping down on the guilt that rose in his chest. "You've seen the proof of that." Desperate enough to take his own life to keep any more of his people from dying trying to rescue him, but the desire to live was still there, else he wouldn't have taken the bait Keris had left him with that book. Aren was looking for options, and if the harem could connect him to his people, options he would have.

Unless Zarrah tried to stab his father with a dinner fork.

"Fuck," he muttered, resuming his pacing, visions of her screaming in rage as she was dragged from his father's office rolling through his mind's eye. What were the chances she'd gained control over her grief in the intervening hours? What were the chances she was seeing clearly? What were the chances that the burning need for vengeance hadn't consumed her entirely?

None.

The clock at the base of the tower tolled the seventh hour, the loud *bong* causing him to jump. A message. He needed to somehow give her a message that she'd see prior to dinner. He picked up a piece of paper, then discarded it as too risky. Swearing, he snatched up a book on economics and flipped through the pages until he found a section on the bridge. In pencil, he scribbled, *Take no action until after the meeting.* Then he tucked the volume under his arm and left the room.

The sky was yet clear, but in the distance, the gathering clouds suggested an incoming storm, the breeze carrying the faint scent of rain. Servants moved through the gardens, lighting the lamps along the path, glowing lanterns already floating in circles in the fountains. And along the base of the wall, torches burned every few feet, leaving no shadows for *anyone* to hide in, the guards standing high above, ever vigilant.

Please let this work, he silently prayed as a guard opened the door to the harem's building and he climbed the steps to the second level where the dining room was located. Only to stop in his tracks.

Valcotta descended from the upper floor, one hand holding the skirts of her blue silk gown, the other resting on the banister. All signs of the rage she'd exhibited earlier were gone, her face serene as she walked past him. The silk was thin enough that he could see the outline of her legs, the back cut to just above the curve of her ass. He jerked his gaze from her swaying hips only for his eyes to fix on the long column of her neck, golden clips holding her black curls at the base of her head. Unbidden, his mind drew forth the taste of her lips on his, the feel of her skin beneath his hands, her laugh in his ears. What he wouldn't give to go back to that perfect moment in Nerastis before everything had gone to shit.

Before she'd known his name.

Blood running hot, he strode into the room and sat on the chair next to the one a servant was pushing under Valcotta, then promptly opened to the page he'd written on, pretending to read, though nothing registered. There was no chance she'd miss his message—she was too observant for that. Valcotta said nothing, but the scent of her filled his nose with every inhale, causing his cock to stiffen.

He wanted to talk to her. Wanted to touch her. But there was no chance they weren't being watched, so he continued to scowl at his book.

Three noblemen who were long supporters of his father's reign entered the room, but Keris barely noticed, every muscle in his body tensed as he anticipated whether she'd say something. Whether she'd do something.

But Valcotta remained silent, not so much as moving until guards trooped into the room, Aren Kertell in tow. The guards chained his manacles to the legs of the table, then took away the glassware within reach, a servant returning with a small tin cup, which was filled with wine.

As the men stepped away, Valcotta rose, and from the corner of his eye, Keris watched her press her hand to her heart in respect, not sitting until Aren gave the slightest of nods. Which meant all eyes were on her when the real player in this game entered the room.

Coralyn took a seat at Aren's right and immediately struck up a conversation, their voices low enough that he couldn't hear from his end of the table.

More men filtered in, taking their assigned seats. Next to Valcotta sat the ambassador from Harendell, who was blond, with an enormous nose. Across from her sat a red-haired man with freckles who looked Amaridian. A supposition that was supported by the glowers the two men gave each other. Amarid and Harendell were *not* on good terms, though they tended more to embargoes and assassinations than all-out war.

"General Anaphora," the Harendellian said. "It was with regret that we heard of your capture in Nerastis, but I'm pleased to see that Silas is keeping you in a manner befitting your name and station. One can never tell with the Maridrinians. Violent bastards, to a man, though I suppose you know that well."

Keris gave a soft snort of annoyance. "I *am* sitting right here, you know."

The man squinted at Keris, clearly poor of eyesight. "Forgive me, which one are you again? Silas has so many sons, I find myself struggling to keep track."

"He's Crown Prince Keris, you idiot," the Amaridian said from across the table. "Heir to the throne and the one negotiating with the Valcottans."

"Oh, of course. Forgive me, Your Highness. No disrespect intended. Last I heard, Prince Rask was heir."

"He's dead." Keris pointedly moved his attention back to his book, staring blindly at the pages.

"Perhaps you might fill my ears with news of my homeland," Valcotta said to the Harendellian. "How fares my aunt, the empress?"

"My countrymen have not yet returned with word of her response to the Maridrinians, if that is your inquiry. But rumors are that she closed herself in her room and wept for a day and a night when she heard you were taken."

A rumor quite at odds with what Yrina had told him. Was the Harendellian lying to appease Valcotta, or had the empress created the rumors herself to keep her reputation intact? Once, Keris would have thought the former, but now he suspected it was the latter.

He heard a soft chime, and Keris closed his book and rose, watching as his father entered the room. As always, he was flanked by bodyguards and his current favorite wives, including Lestara. She went to a seat at the far end of the table, her eyes meeting Keris's briefly.

The harem was ready.

"Do we need to find you a lighter set of chains, Aren?" his father said, and Keris looked to the far end of the table and saw that the

Ithicanian king remained sitting. "Perhaps we could have one of the jewelers fashion you something less burdensome?"

The heavy links joining Aren's manacles clunked and rattled ominously against the wood of the table as he reached for his tiny tin cup of wine and drained it. Then he shrugged. "A lighter chain would make a fine garrote, but there is something more . . . *satisfying* about choking a man to death. I'd ask you if you agreed, Silas, but everyone here knows you prefer to stab men in the back."

Keris silently cursed. If Aren got himself killed after all the work Keris had done to get him here, he was going to piss on the idiot's grave.

Silas frowned. "You see, kind sirs? All the Ithicanians know is insults and violence. How much better now that we no longer have to deal with their ilk when conducting trade through the bridge."

The Amaridian ambassador thumped his hand against the table in agreement, but the ambassador from Harendell only frowned and rubbed at the gray stubble on his chin. And next to him, Valcotta squared her shoulders, the silk of her dress whispering with the movement. "I'm afraid Valcotta does not concur with your sentiment, Your Grace. And until Maridrina withdraws from Ithicana and you release its king, Valcottan merchants will continue to bypass the bridge in favor of shipping routes."

This was what he'd been afraid of. Valcotta knew nothing of Keris's plans for tonight. Had no idea that gaining an alliance with the Ithicanian king might see her freed. And she was *angry*. He could feel the hate simmering off her despite her mild expression. Fresh grief from Yrina's death meant her heart was making her decisions, not her head.

His father gave her a withering glare. "Then your aunt best get used to losing ships to the Tempest Seas. And you would do well to remember your place and curb your tongue, girl. Your presence is only a courtesy. You should be thanking me for sparing your life, not testing my patience with your prattle. Your head would look rather nice spiked on Vencia's gates."

Keris's hand tightened reflexively on the stem of his wineglass as Valcotta shifted next to him. Was she trying to pick a fight with his father? Was she trying to gain herself a chance to get close to him? For a fighter like Valcotta, everything was a weapon. A fork. A shard of broken plate. The snapped-off stem of a wineglass. And this was the first time she'd been in his father's presence without chains binding her wrists. Keris tensed, readying himself to intervene if she tried to make a move, because it could *not* be Valcotta who killed his father.

From his end of the table, Aren said, "As one intimately acquainted with this issue, Silas, allow me to let you in on a little secret: An empty bridge earns no gold."

The Amaridian ambassador cast a sideways glance at Silas. Judging from the way his father's jaw flexed, he hadn't missed the look. Keris's skin crawled as he felt his father's anger rising. Silas hated not being in control of a situation, but what he hated most of all was mockery. It would be well within his character to lash out with violence, if for no reason other than to remind everyone whom they needed to fear. And Valcotta was the person he was most likely to strike.

Unless Keris drew his attention elsewhere.

He opened his mouth, readying a quip that would bring his father's wrath down on him instead, but before he could say anything, music began to play, emanating softly from where the musician was seated behind the curtains. Keris hadn't even been aware the individual was there.

Lestara rose to her feet and began to dance, a slow and seductive set of movements. Every male gaze in the room went to her *except* his father's, who was assuring the rather distracted Amaridian that he should not believe rumors, for the bridge was indeed turning a profit. The music volume increased, and his father scowled, forced to repeat his words as the Amaridian stared at him in confusion, conversation drowned out.

Exactly as the harem had planned it to be. Out of the corner of his eye, Keris watched Coralyn converse with Aren, doing a far better job at making whatever they were discussing seem like idle dinner chatter.

"Has Amarid's partnership with Maridrina been a profitable one?" Valcotta asked the ambassador. "I can't help but think the losses you must be taking in ships and crew far outweigh what profit you've gained via preferential treatment on the bridge."

The Amaridian opened his mouth, but Keris's father snarled, "Silence your tongue, woman. You weren't invited to this dinner to discuss politics."

Valcotta rested her chin on one hand and gave the Harendellian a conspiratorial smile. "I believe he wished to prove to you that I am still alive."

"What was that, dear?" The man frowned at her. "I'm afraid I'm a touch hard of hearing."

"I'm still alive!" Zarrah shouted, provoking a glare from his father.

"Oh, yes." The Harendellian nodded vigorously. "There was a great deal of concern about King Aren's well-being."

His father's face purpled at the use of Aren's title, his eye flicking to the conversation between the man in question and Coralyn, then back to the conversation in front of him, then to the Amaridian, who was staring with undisguised lust at Lestara's breasts as she swayed around the table, the other noblemen little better.

"Somewhat less vigor," his father shouted at the musician. "I can barely hear myself think!"

What he wanted to demand was for Coralyn to cease her conversation with Aren, but that would grant Aren power in the eyes of all in the room, which his father's pride couldn't tolerate. Keris opened his book, struggling not to smirk as sweat beaded on his father's brow.

"Your wife is tremendously talented, Your Grace," the Amaridian said. "I must say, Maridrinian women are famed the world over for their beauty and grace. Especially in the bedroom."

His father clearly didn't hear the man's words, for he showed no reaction. And Keris had seen him kill men for lesser insults.

"The woman is clearly from Cardiff, you daft fool," the Harendellian declared. "I can tell from the pallor. And her eyes. We've a saying in Harendell: Beware the amber eyes of Cardiff, for if you look too long, they steal your soul."

"Superstitions," the Amaridian snapped. "Though I'd expect no less from you."

The men devolved into bickering, as Keris had anticipated they would, the volume growing louder and the musician playing louder to compensate. And at the far end of the table, Coralyn smiled and laughed, though the gravity of their conversation was betrayed by the seriousness of Aren's expression.

Take the bait, Keris silently pleaded as he stared blindly at the pages of his book, flipping them from time to time. *Give us what we need.*

"Enough!" his father shouted at Lestara. "Sit down!"

Lestara returned to her seat, the entire table silent as Silas rose to his feet, glaring at the ambassadors, though Keris knew his ire was for Coralyn. "I invited you here as a show of respect for your kings and nations, and you betray my hospitality by bickering and disrespecting my wife." He rested his hands on the table. "Get the fuck out of my house."

The Harendellian slowly rose to his feet. "With respect, Your Grace, I—"

"Out!"

The noblemen and ambassadors all silently rose and bowed before departing under the escort of guards. When they were gone, Aren said, "If I'd known your dinner parties were such lively affairs, I'd have accepted the invitation sooner." Then he rose, his chains rattling. "I'll take my leave for the evening."

Keris's father gave a tight nod at the guards, who unshackled the Ithicanian king and took him from the room. "This one, too." He jerked his chin at Valcotta, and she shrugged and rose, departing on Aren's heels, the female musician following after her.

"We will eat in peace," his father declared, then sat back down, the servants soon appearing with the main course.

Peace was *not* the word that Keris would have used for the rest of dinner, but it was silent until the last of the dishes had been removed and his father leaned back in his chair, a glass of cognac balanced on his knee as he regarded them. "It was well done," he finally said, his eyes on Coralyn. "What did you learn from him?"

Shock radiated through Keris as Coralyn sipped at the tea one of the servants had brought her. "Likewise, Your Grace, you played your part to perfection. Aren was entirely convinced that I was speaking to him against your will."

Keris opened his mouth to comment, then closed it again, realizing that he was not the master of the scene he'd believed he'd orchestrated.

"He does not know where Lara is or where she might have gone," Coralyn said. "Nor her sisters, though he told me one of them is dead." She set her cup down and gave his father a long stare.

"Marylyn gained access to Midwatch prior to the main attack, her goal to secure Lara, kill her if necessary," he answered, then drained his cup. "Aren, she was supposed to kill."

Marylyn. The name was familiar, but in truth, Keris only had a vague memory of many of his half sisters who were taken into the Red Desert at the same time as Lara. His mother had always kept both him and Lara close to her, unwilling to share the burden of motherhood the way the rest of the harem did, which meant that he and Lara had bordered on inseparable before she'd been taken. He wondered if she even remembered him, or if time and distance had erased him from her memory as Marylyn had been erased from his.

"They are your *daughters,* Silas." Coralyn's voice was cold. "You should not have pitted them against one another. They are family."

All of Keris's half brothers were family, and yet they were encouraged to murder one another to ensure the strongest inherited.

"Cast your blame at Lara's feet," his father snapped. "Her loyalty was supposed to be to this family. To Maridrina. And yet when faced with a handsome young husband, she forgot who she was. Where she came from. Family is everything, and she betrayed us."

"But the others did not, yet still you allow your Magpie to hunt them. Not to bring them back to their family in Vencia, but to put them in the ground."

A look of disgust flashed over his father's face, and he waved a dismissive hand at her. "You think you want them, but you don't, Coralyn. They are violent, murderous creatures."

"Because you allowed Serin to raise them that way!"

Coralyn *never* shouted. Keris shifted uneasily in his chair, realizing that he'd underestimated her desire to learn his sisters' fates. And to get them back.

"To achieve an end!" His father exploded to his feet, pacing back and forth across the room. "And it worked! Once Ithicana has fallen entirely, Maridrina will be poised to become the most powerful nation on two continents. Poised to create alliances that will allow us to drive Valcotta back so that we might reclaim the land we need to sustain our people."

He slid to a stop, leveling a finger at her. "You know better than anyone that my father left a weak legacy. A nation dependent on others for survival—and we suffered for it. But I accomplished the impossible, which means my son will inherit a nation that is not to be trifled with. You wanted these results, Coralyn, so don't you dare lose your spine because you mislike the manner in which I achieved them."

His son. Not Keris, but whichever one of his half brothers managed to inherit. Nothing new, nothing unexpected, but for reasons Keris couldn't articulate, it hurt more than Serin and his father conspiring to kill him.

"There is nothing more important than family, Silas."

His father silently regarded Coralyn for a long moment, then asked, "Then why do you care so much for the fate of the daughter who betrayed us? Lara is the *key*, Cora. With her, we can break Aren and get the information we need to win this."

Cora? Keris blinked, having never heard his father speak with such familiarity to his aunt. Always, he spoke of her with disdain. Resentment. Frustration. But there was a rhythm and comfort to this argument that suggested his father kept his aunt far deeper in his counsel than Keris had realized.

Silence.

"He said he doesn't believe that Lara will take your bait." The words came out in a rush of annoyance. "But he was clearly lying. I saw the fear the idea inspired in his eyes, and if he fears her trying to rescue him, it's because he believes it's possible."

"Do you?"

Keris held his breath, waiting for his aunt's response, for it would validate the information Valcotta had given his father about Lara.

"Yes. I think she'll come for him and that you'll be forced to face the monster you created, Silas."

His father smiled. "You are rarely wrong about such things. Did you learn anything else of use from him?"

"Indeed. Your father married a woman named Amelie Yamure. You might not recall her, for she was only in the harem for a short time before she went missing, presumed dead. I learned tonight that she was an Ithicanian spy sent to infiltrate the inner sanctum. I also learned she is Aren's grandmother."

Keris didn't bother hiding his surprise at *that* revelation. His grandfather had been wed to an Ithicanian spy?

"Why would Aren tell you this?" his father asked, posing the very question Keris was thinking.

"He has strong opinions on our customs, and when I suggested he had no basis for his views, he offered her experiences up as an example. It's been an age since she was here, but we can only assume that she's the source of Ithicana's information on the inner sanctum's defenses. Consider her perspective and you might better defend against their continued intrusions."

Frustration boiled in Keris's veins, because his aunt was achieving the exact opposite of the ends he'd hoped for. And there was nothing he could do about it.

His father rubbed his chin. "You've learned more from him in a few minutes of idle chatter than Serin has from weeks of torture."

Coralyn snorted softly. "The man is trained to resist Serin's techniques, but I do not think a lifetime isolated within Ithicana prepared him for political machinations." Then she rose to her feet. "I did what you asked. Now you'll hold up your end of the bargain. Give your word that you'll allow the other girls to live out their lives in peace. That you'll call off Serin and threaten him with consequences if any of them are harmed."

"Done." His father rose to his feet and left the room, leaving Keris alone with his aunts. Lestara rose and retrieved a drum the musician had left behind, beating a rhythm and singing in the language of her homeland loud enough that any listeners would be unable to hear the conversation within the room.

Keris leaned back in his chair. "Well played, Auntie. What does Aren think he's getting in exchange for this information?"

"What he believes he'll receive matters little, given that I have what I want."

"So . . . you lied to him?" Keris didn't know why that surprised him, but it did. Coralyn was most certainly not above deception, but this felt . . . *off.*

She lifted one brocaded shoulder. "For the ruler of a nation that depends on trade, he's a poor negotiator. One should always hold back full payment until the goods are delivered."

Sickness filled Keris's stomach, along with frustration with himself for not anticipating that she'd have her own agenda. "Did he give you a method to reach his people?"

"Yes."

"How?"

Her head cocked. "Why do you wish to know, Keris? I was under the impression you were ambivalent about Aren's fate."

"I am. But I grow weary of my family being surrounded by corpses. Give me the contact and I'll put an end to this." It was risky, because Serin's men *always* followed him outside the palace, but what choice did he have? He needed the Ithicanians to help him free Valcotta.

"It's not worth the risk of your father catching you meddling, Keris. Serin is watching you, looking for any possible mistake. And if you believe I'll risk you for the sake of my gardens smelling more appealing, you don't know me in the slightest."

His panic was rising, because he was losing control. Had lost control. "I need to do something."

"Why? Why is this so important that you'd risk *everything*? Not only yourself, but your sisters, for if your father realizes I was the one who told you the information, which he will, he'll renege on his promise to stop hunting your sisters. We can endure the corpses, but we *cannot* endure more of our children dying."

Because I cannot endure her dying! was the thought that screamed to be voiced, but he couldn't. The harem hated Valcottans. They hated Zarrah. "Because it's too much like what was done to my mother."

Coralyn's expression softened. "I know it is, dear one. But it won't last much longer. Once Aren realizes I haven't helped him, he'll put an end to this himself."

"You're crueler than I'd believed, Auntie." And he hated it. Hated that the one he loved like a mother was capable of this.

"Family is everything." Coralyn motioned for the other women to follow her toward the door, though she paused to pat his cheek. "And there is little I won't do to protect the harem's children. Goodnight, Keris. Perhaps tomorrow will bring an end to all our woes."

50
ZARRAH

THE HAREM HAD BEEN UP TO SOMETHING TONIGHT AT DINNER—
even without the note Keris had written in his book, that would
have been obvious. But Zarrah didn't dwell on what the conversation between Coralyn and Aren might have achieved as she allowed the servants to prepare her for bed because after tonight,
none of it would matter at all.

The clock in the tower struck the first toll of the ninth hour, an-
nouncing the harem's curfew had begun. It was time. Zarrah swallowed down the twist of emotion in her stomach, but her grief
refused to be vanquished. As did her regret.

What she wouldn't give for the chance to say goodbye. To apologize for the grief her actions would cause. To tell him—

Tap.

Zarrah jumped, whirling around to face the window.

Tap.

Her pulse roared with equal parts anxiety and anticipation, and
she extinguished the lamp and went to open the window. Faint

mist rolled over her, and in the distance, lightning crackled across the sky.

Zarrah pressed her forehead against the bars and looked down into the darkness, her heart rivaling the thunder that rolled across the city.

And then he was there.

Keris swung himself up so that he was seated sideways on the ledge, one arm through the bars to hold him on the narrow perch. Then he said softly, "I've got news." Zarrah's heart skipped with the sudden certainty that her aunt had agreed with Keris's terms. That she was to be freed, and her opportunity for vengeance was lost. But then Keris said, "Aren Kertell provided Coralyn with a way to contact his people in exchange for her giving them his orders to stand down in their rescue attempts."

It wasn't at all what she'd expected him to say, and for a moment, she was at a loss for words.

"She won't act on it. She made a side deal with my father and revealed much of what Aren told her in exchange for him agreeing to make Serin cease his hunt of my half sisters."

"Backstabbing old bitch."

Keris shrugged. "She held back critical details from my father, the most significant of which was that Aren gave her a way to contact his people in Vencia. She has refused to share that knowledge, but that's of no matter. I'll get it from Aren himself, meet with his people, and give them the information they need to make a successful rescue attempt."

Zarrah blinked, then realized his intent. "Your plan is for them to rescue me as well."

"Yes."

"Keris . . ." She exhaled. "This is a mad plan. What the Ithicanians are most likely to do is either *kill* you on first sight or kidnap you in an attempt to ransom you for Aren."

He laughed. "They'd have better luck kidnapping and ransoming my father's horse."

"Which is why you shouldn't risk it. It won't work!"

"It might. The Ithicanians are *desperate*. They'll agree."

"It won't." Her heart was thundering in her chest. "Don't pursue it."

Keris was silent for a long moment, then he said, "If I didn't know better, Valcotta, I might think that you didn't *want* to escape."

Zarrah's hands turned to ice, because if Keris suspected her intentions, he'd try to stop her. Would pursue this mad plan to save her no matter the price. A price that didn't have to be paid.

Yet she didn't want to lie to him.

"My freedom isn't worth your life, which is very likely the cost of all this."

"On that, we'll have to agree to disagree, Valcotta. If falling on my own sword would miraculously get you free of this mess, I'd do it. But given it would prove ineffectual, I'll take what risks I must to secure the help of those who *can* accomplish this task."

His voice was angry, bitter, but given this might be their final moment alone together, she refused to deceive him with false hopes. Thunder rolled in the distance, the storm moving closer, and she knew that if she didn't get under way soon, rain and wind would render the climb impossible. But instead of sending him away, she whispered, "Why do you still call me that?"

Silence.

"Because knowing your name didn't change who you were to me. Didn't change how I felt about you. And . . ." Zarrah heard him swallow. "And perhaps because I refuse to let go of the moment when all things felt possible, including being with you." He hesitated. "I can stop calling you that, if it's what you want."

It was the last thing she wanted.

His hand slipped through the bars to cup her face. "I'd fallen for you before I knew your name. You are everything I can never be. You are powerful and strong and brave. You make me believe I can be better. You give me hope. You *are* my hope."

"Keris . . ."

He moved his thumb, pressing it to her lips. "No matter what the future brings, know that you hold my heart."

Zarrah's own heart went wild in her chest, because God help her, it felt an eternity since he'd touched her like this.

She'd once believed there was no going back to the way she'd felt about him when he'd been the anonymous Maridrinian reading her stories about stars. Believed that moment impossible to reclaim. And in that, she'd been correct. Knowing the truth about him, seeing the *true* him, had created a storm of emotion in her heart that was a hundred times more intense. Of all the stars mapped in her mind, his burned the brightest.

"I should go," he said. "I put you at risk by being here."

Zarrah reached through the bars, catching hold of his shirt, her hands tightening into fists because she didn't want to let him go. Didn't want to lose him, either through her actions or his. Because though she was too terrified to name the emotion setting her heart on fire, she felt it nonetheless. "Don't go."

Every breath she inhaled carried the scent of spice, and it triggered a flood of desire, flashes of memory rolling through her mind. Of his lips trailing over her body, fingers tracing lines of fire over her skin, of his tongue teasing her aching sex. Of his cock thrusting into her until she screamed, echoes of that pleasure sending a shudder through her.

There'd never be another chance to have him touch her, because regardless of whether she succeeded in killing Silas tonight or not, she was unlikely to survive long to revel in it.

This was it.

This was the end.

"I want you." She caught hold of his hand, interlocking his fingers with hers, sliding his palm over her breast and hearing his intake of breath. "I *need* you."

"Valcotta . . ." His voice was ragged, and because she sensed protest on his lips, she reached through the bars. Slid her hand down the front of his trousers, taking hold of his already-stiffening length, his skin hot against her palm. "I want this."

She stroked her hand up and down, remembering how he liked it, which was *not* gentle. Her eyes drifted shut and she listened to his breathing accelerate as he hardened beneath her touch.

He groaned, letting go of the bars with one hand to catch hold of her wrist, his fingertips tracing over the veins and making her body ache with need. But then his grip tightened, and he drew her hand out of his trousers, pushing her arm back through the bars. "I won't take pleasure from you while you are a prisoner. You might have morals beyond measure, Valcotta, but I suffer such a dearth of them that I fear in sacrificing this one, I'll have no morals left at all."

"That is such a lie." Her core throbbed, her thighs slick with desire. "And you seem to forget that in denying yourself, you deny me as well."

He didn't answer. Frustration filled Zarrah, because he was going to deny them this moment, not realizing it was the last chance they'd ever have.

"You make a valid point." He reached through the bars to catch hold of her waist, his hand hot through the thin silk. "You are an excellent negotiator."

"It helps when one knows what one wants." She pressed her face to the bars, sighing as his hand moved over the curve of her ass, her eyes drifting shut. "Kiss me."

She felt his breath, heard the raggedness of it, and then his lips were on hers, tongue in her mouth, kissing her with the desperation of one too long denied. She slipped her arms through the bars, dragging her nails over his shoulders and digging them into the hard muscles, relishing his groan.

"God help me, Valcotta, you undo me like none other."

"Because you are mine." She didn't care that logic said such a dream was impossible. "And no one else's."

He caught hold of the straps of her nightgown, the silk spilling around her body to pool over the curve of her hips. She whimpered as his thumb brushed over the tip of one breast, allowing him to pull her against the thin bars, his mouth lavishing one nipple, then the other, the scrape of his teeth on her sensitive skin driving her to madness.

Lightning splintered the sky, wind brushing against her naked torso, her skin cold except where his mouth turned it to fire. He gripped the bars with one hand, but the other was under the skirt of her nightdress, fingers trailing up her inner thigh. Higher and higher, and then they brushed over her silk undergarments, the growl that exited his lips telling her that he'd found them soaked with lust. "I want to see you."

She spread her legs, knees moving to brace against the sides of the window frame, her hands gripping the bars as she leaned back, feeling his eyes drink in her body with every flash of lightning.

He stroked a finger over the sodden silk, the fabric rubbing against the apex of her thighs and sending shudders through her, tension growing in her core.

"Please." She needed more. Needed all of him. "This is torment."

"Which you deserve." His finger slowly circled the center of her pleasure. "You have caused me a great deal of frustration."

"Not on purpose." She was shaking, wild with need. "Whereas your torment seems quite purposeful."

He laughed softly, and then his finger slipped behind the fabric, the feel of his skin against hers nearly shattering her. She sobbed his name as he stroked her, finger moving down to tease her entrance before sliding inside of her.

Her body bucked, and she gripped the bars, thrusting herself against him and nearly sobbing as he slipped a second finger inside her. "Is this more what you had in mind?"

"Yes. God, yes." She rode his fingers like a wild thing, moans tearing from her throat as his thumb rubbed against the knot of nerves, her tension mounting even as the storm moved closer. Then she felt his fingers curve inside her, stroking as she thrust down, and her body shattered. Wave after wave of pleasure washed over her, forcing her to clap a hand over her mouth to muffle the screams of his name, the climax leaving her spent.

But not sated.

She was coming to realize that she never would be. That she could never have enough of him. That a lifetime wouldn't be enough and that even in the Great Beyond, she'd need his touch.

His arms moved around her, pulling her against the cold steel of the bars. Holding her until her breathing steadied, one hand gently stroking her spine.

"We're going to win this, Valcotta," he finally said. "You and I are going to beat them. It can be no other way."

I will win, she thought, her eyes burning. *But we will lose.*

She whispered, "You should go. It's going to rain."

He kissed her once, long and lingering and so full of passion that she felt her resolve falter. But before she caved entirely, he pulled away and slipped into the night.

Grief threatened to overwhelm her, fueled by guilt that she was deceiving him. That he'd have to deal with the fallout of her actions. Yet it had to be this way, so Zarrah built up walls around every emotion, allowing only her anger to walk free.

As she cast her eyes upward to the tower, like clockwork, a glow flickered to life in Silas Veliant's chambers.

It was time.

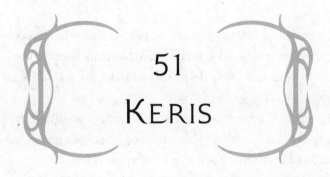

51
KERIS

YOU SHOULD NOT HAVE DONE THAT, HE BERATED HIMSELF AS HE slipped through the gardens. Never mind if you got caught—it's immoral to touch her while she's a prisoner.

Yet denying her anything that she wanted, especially pleasure, bordered on impossible for him. He'd do anything to make her smile. To make her laugh. To take her away from this awful circumstance, if only for a moment.

Hands closed on Keris's shoulders, and a voice whispered, "Have you lost your *fucking mind*?"

He twisted, nearly punching whoever it was in the face before recognizing his brother. "Otis? What are you doing here?"

"Hardly the most pressing question." Otis scanned the dark gardens, his face barely visible in the shadows. "What were you thinking? If you were caught, Father would gut you like a fish."

Keris felt the blood drain from his face. "Caught doing what, precisely?"

"Don't play coy. Not with me." His brother leaned closer. "I followed you out into the gardens to talk to you, but you disappeared.

Only I *know* you, so I had a mind to look up. Or *listen* up, as the case might be."

Horror filled Keris's stomach, his palms turning to ice, because if his brother had heard what he and Valcotta had been doing . . .

"Only you would have the bloody audacity to cuckold Father in his own house. Who was it?"

Cuckold . . . The word sent a rush of relief running through him, because his brother thought it had been one of the harem wives. He crossed his arms. "It's hardly your business."

"Tell me, or I'll ask Coralyn whose window that is."

Fuck. "Fine. It was Lestara." The most believable of any of the women, as well as the most palatable, given she hadn't given birth to one of his half siblings. "I hope you'll do me the favor of keeping your mouth shut."

Otis snorted. "For her sake, I'll keep silent. But if you've got any sense in you, you'll end it. There are countless women in Vencia who'd be happy to warm your bed without the risk of Father chopping off your most offending member."

Thank God for small mercies, Keris thought, relief nearly causing his shoulders to sag. *And large ones.* "For once, you speak wisdom." He slung his arm around his brother's shoulders. "Care to venture out for the night? Find some women and wine and a game of cards?"

"Would that I could, but Father wishes a report on the state of Nerastis."

"And what is the state of that shithole?"

Otis exhaled a long breath, allowing himself to be led in the direction of the tower. "Quiet as a grave. The Valcottans are sticking to their side of the Anriot, and when we raid, they defend but don't pursue. They're up to something, mark my words."

"Or they recognize that antagonizing those who have their princess is an excellent way to get her killed."

Otis's voice was tight as he said, "I heard about your plans to negotiate your way into Father's good graces."

Otis's anger wasn't unexpected. His brother wasn't interested in negotiating with Valcottans, only slaughtering them. "The situation with Ithicana is dire, Otis. Father has bankrupted himself, including running up an enormous debt with Amarid, in order to secure a bridge that is making almost no money. We need Valcotta to resume trade at Southwatch, and this negotiation could achieve that."

Otis snorted. "It won't work, you know. Valcotta is *wealthy*— just for spite, the empress will sacrifice a hundred ships to the Tempest Seas rather than pay us a cent."

Keris *did* know, but admitting so was counterproductive. "The empress is beholden to her people. I don't think they'll be willing to sacrifice so much for the sake of pride."

Silence.

"It's never the simple path forward for you, is it?" Otis said bitterly. "I say cut off the Valcottan bitch's head and stake it on the gates."

The threat sent anger twisting through him, but Keris forced himself to laugh as the guards opened the doors for them. "The empress would retaliate, and with Father embroiled with holding Ithicana, he wouldn't be able to send reinforcements. I'd lose Nerastis, which I'm fairly certain would see *my* head spiked on a gate." Casting a sideways glance at his brother, he added, "You allow your hatred for Valcottans to cloud your judgment, Otis."

He instantly regretted the comment as Otis scowled. "Easy for you to say, given you don't seem to hate them at all."

This was dangerous ground. The Valcottans had killed Otis's wife when they sank the ship she sailed upon, so for his brother, this was no political grudge. It was every bit as personal as Valcotta's, and Otis hadn't half her empathy for those who were harmed in his path for vengeance. "I know this is a bitter tonic for you, brother, but I can't afford to allow my senses to be muddled with emotion right now."

They climbed the stairs, Otis silent and Keris's thoughts twisting over how close he'd come to being caught. His brother would hold his tongue—the consequences of doing otherwise were far too high, for both Keris and Lestara. But it meant that he needed to keep his distance from Valcotta at least until his brother departed, which would hopefully be soon. Otis knew his habits too well, knew *him* too well, which meant he wouldn't be fooled for long.

Reaching the door to his room, Keris paused. "Do you want me to come with you to meet with him?"

Otis leaned against the stone of the stairwell. "No, it's better you don't. I've not your mastery of composure, and I hate listening to his mockery of you, which I know is inevitable."

Guilt soured Keris's guts, because his brother was so cursedly loyal. Even when Keris didn't deserve it. "When you're through, seek me out. We'll go find some entertainment in the city."

"I'd settle with wine and a well-padded sofa. My ass has been too long in the saddle."

Keris laughed. "I'll send someone to raid the cellar and then leave my door unlocked. Good luck." He watched as his brother climbed the stairs two at a time, knowing it wasn't Otis's luck that he needed to worry about.

52
ZARRAH

ZARRAH WAITED UNTIL IT WAS NEARLY THE TENTH HOUR, THEN eased her bed away from the wall, revealing the block she'd pushed partially outward. It would be loud when it fell, so she needed to time this just right.

She tucked the nail into her bodice, then braced her heels against the block of stone and waited.

Her heart beat like a drum in her chest, her palms clammy, sweat beading on her brow. From fear, yes, but also from anticipation. Tonight, she'd regain the honor she'd lost in capture. Tonight, she'd have vengeance. For her mother. For Yrina. For herself.

Bong.

The first of ten tolls of the clock, and she shoved her heels against the stone, hands braced against the floor. It made a grinding noise as it shifted, then stuck.

"Come on!" She shoved harder as the clock tolled a second, third, and fourth time. But it wouldn't move. The cursed thing was wedged tight.

Bong!

"Stupid piece of shit!" She tried with her hands, slamming them against the block, but it wouldn't move.

Bong!

She switched back to using her feet, sweat drenching her skin as she pushed and shoved, the seventh and eighth and ninth tolls rolling through the inner sanctum.

"You can do this!" She slammed her feet one last time.

The block shifted, sliding forward and falling, her feet slipping through the opening in the wall. Heart in her throat, Zarrah clenched her teeth, waiting for the crunch of it hitting the brush below.

Bong!

By fate or luck or intervention of a higher power, the block landed right as the tenth toll sounded, the rolling echo drowning out most of the noise. Still, she held her breath, waiting to see if anyone came to investigate.

But no one did.

There is no going back now.

Checking to ensure she had everything she needed, Zarrah tossed her velvet cloak down. Then she rolled onto her belly and stuck her legs through the opening, shimmying backward, swearing as her ass wedged in the opening. Pushing with her palms, she ground her teeth and forcefully pushed her body through, angling her shoulders and allowing her weight to pull her down until she was hanging from the opening by her hands.

She climbed lower, fingers and toes finding all the tiny cracks and grooves Keris used, then eased herself into the bushes. She retrieved the cloak, put it on, and ensured the hood was pulled forward. Then she strode onto the pathway, moving with total confidence toward the tower.

Anyone who saw her would believe her a wife summoned to

attend the king, but her heart was still in her throat as she passed one guard, then another, both nodding respectfully at her. Instead of going to the entrance, as Zarrah rounded between topiaries, she cut left, keeping to the shadows and making her way to the base of the tower.

She pulled off her cloak and wrapped it in a bundle that she tied to her waist. Taking a deep breath, Zarrah started climbing.

Time and weather had eroded the mortar between blocks of stone, and in places pieces of rock had cracked off, giving her end-less choices of handholds, but by the time she'd climbed thirty feet, her arms trembled with exhaustion.

And she was not yet halfway to Silas's window.

Keep climbing! she screamed at herself, for, excluding the risk of falling, her greatest worry was that the guards manning the inner walls would see her shadow on the tower. If that happened, not only was her chance at killing Silas lost but she'd also get an arrow in her back for her troubles.

This high up, the stink of the corpses on the inner walls was fainter, the smell of the coming rain filling her nose. Yet it was no mercy, because it was carried by a fierce breeze that buffeted her body, threatening to pull her from her perch.

Keep climbing.

Glancing up, she determined herself more than halfway, and so she risked a backward glance. Soldiers moved along the top of the inner wall, their eyes on the well-lit base. More stood in the turrets on the corners, eyes equally watchful. But they were all looking down, their concern for someone trying to escape, not for some-one trying to climb into the belly of the beast.

The stone she gripped with her right hand abruptly gave way.

A gasp of terror tore from Zarrah's lips as she dropped, the fin-gers of her left hand screaming as she dangled from them, her toe-holds lost.

She scrabbled for another handhold, her breath desperate gasps until she managed to shove her fingers into a gap, her toes finding holds.

But below, she heard voices. Sensed motion. Men approached the base of the tower, obviously drawn by the sound of the piece of rock striking the bushes.

Climb, she screamed at herself. *Hurry!*

Ignoring the shuddering pain in her fingers, Zarrah worked her way higher, reaching a window, on the top of which she perched for a moment's rest.

Keris's window.

Guilt filled her stomach, because he was the one who'd pay for her actions tonight. He'd be the one who'd have to order her executed for murdering his father and who'd have to manage the empress's subsequent retaliation. But there was no other way: Silas Veliant needed to die.

Keep going.

Stretching tall, Zarrah found another fingerhold, moving higher and higher until she was beneath the king's open window. Catching hold of the edge, she pulled herself up, listening.

But there was only silence.

She eased inward and cautiously slipped behind the billowing curtain, pressing her back against the wall. Then she inched sideways and peeked around the heavy fabric.

The room was dimly lit, the lamps turned down low, but it was enough to see that it was full of heavy furniture and dark fabric, the artwork gracing the walls depicting scenes of battle, many of them decidedly gory.

Her ears picked up a rhythmic thumping from behind the closed door of the adjoining room, along with male grunts, which grew louder with each passing second. A woman's sounds of pleasure, probably feigned, merged with the grunting, and Zarrah cringed at exactly what was going on in the bedchamber.

It's of no matter, she told herself. *It isn't as though the wife is likely to linger.*

Then the door to the stairwell opened, and the Magpie appeared. He hesitated, listening to the activities going on in the bedroom, then sighed and took a seat on one of the sofas, pouring himself a glass of wine.

Zarrah wasn't certain if she wanted to scream in frustration or crow in delight. Because while Serin's presence made this a greater challenge, it also meant she might kill two birds with one stone.

Breathing slowly, Zarrah flexed her fingers and toes before extracting the nail and slipping it between her knuckles.

The bedroom door slammed outward, Silas calling over his shoulder, "Stay on your back, woman. If this doesn't take, I'll be returning you to your homeland and revoking our trade agreement. I didn't bargain for a barren wife." Then his eyes fixed on Serin. "Well? Did it work?"

The spymaster sighed. "I think it too soon to say, Your Majesty. We need to allow time for the ambassadors to spread the word to the people that Aren is not only alive but well. By tomorrow, I'll know more."

"I know you disliked this plan. But I can't help but think that it has more to do with who proposed it than the plan itself."

The Magpie inclined his head. "I seek only the success of your ventures, Majesty. But . . . I'd be wary of any *ideas* that come from the prince's lips: Keris is meddling, and his eyes are on the crown."

"And it's about goddamned time."

Zarrah blinked in surprise, watching as Silas strode across the room and threw himself down on the sofa opposite his spymaster before leveling a finger at the man. "I've told you, Serin. I've always told you: My son will be neither pushed nor led. Not through any amount of force. He has to decide to do something himself, needs to make the idea his own, at which point, he's intractable. And now that he's decided he wants to live, wants to be heir, he will become everything I dreamed of and more."

"With respect, Your Grace, I don't agree. Maridrinian kings are warriors and generals, which Keris is decidedly not. He's bookish. He can't even wield a sword."

Silas laughed. "You mistake *can't* for *won't,* Serin. Keris drew a line in the sand to spite me over the death of his mother, but he's too logical to spite a corpse. Once I'm in the grave, he'll embrace his bloodline and become the man he is meant to be."

"By then, it might be too late." Serin filled a cup of wine and handed it to his master. "The people make mockery of him, but more than that, the soldiers have no respect for him, and he will need them to rule this kingdom. Your Grace is yet in the prime of life: Think how much further in their graces he'll slip in another five years? Another ten? Whereas someone like Prince Otis *already* commands their respect. He's a man they'd gladly follow."

Silas waved a hand. "Otis is a fine boy, but he lacks vision. Lacks the intelligence to raise Maridrina up high."

"Keris will burn your legacy to the ground." Anger flared in the Magpie's eyes, and he slammed his glass down on the table. "He will take all that you've fought to achieve and set it aside for the sake of his *principles.* Surely you see that in the way he attempts to negotiate with Valcotta rather than warring with them."

Silence hung in the room, and Zarrah held her breath. Every moment she tarried risked her absence from her bedroom being discovered. Risked alarms being raised. But she felt compelled to hear the end of this disagreement before she took the choice out of both of their hands.

"Which is why I must allow him the opportunity to see that his principles only function on the page, not in reality," Silas answered. "Petra will refuse his attempts to negotiate. We know this. Keris will be forced to recognize reality, and necessity will drive him to embrace the Veliant way of ruling. But he needs to come to that realization himself."

Ice filled Zarrah's belly. What reason did Silas have to be so certain that her aunt would refuse to negotiate? The closeness of their relationship was well known, which meant he had to be aware of what she meant to the empress.

"I dislike this," Serin said. "I cannot set aside the knowledge that he is of identical blood to Lara, who betrayed you in favor of her husband. They are both of the womb of *that woman* who shamed you so, Majesty."

Silas's face darkened, and he leaned across the table. "Lara is *your* mistake, Serin. You may have made her a weapon, but you failed to instill in her a true sense of loyalty, which allowed her to be swayed in a way that Keris never will be. For all his failings, for all his faults, Keris is loyal to his family and to Maridrina. And if you so much as—"

A sharp knock at the door caused him to break off, and Zarrah's heart sped with the certainty her escape had been discovered. That she'd lost her chance.

"Come."

The door swung open, but instead of a guard stepping inside to bring warning, a young man entered.

Keris's brother Otis.

He bowed low. "You summoned me, Your Grace?"

The king cast a sour glare in Serin's direction, suggesting that it had been the spymaster who'd done the summoning, but then he rose and embraced Otis. "It warms my heart to see you, my son. How fares Nerastis?"

"Quiet, Your Grace, but—"

The bedroom door opened, and Lestara stepped out. "I would take my leave, Your Majesty," she said, bobbing a curtsy.

"I told you to stay where I left you, woman," Silas snapped, rising to his feet. "Get back in that room!"

Except it wasn't Silas's reaction to Lestara that drew Zarrah's eye, but Otis's.

The color drained from his face, and he stared at Lestara as though she were a ghost. Serin noticed the reaction, too, his brow furrowing as his eyes skipped between Lestara and the prince.

Silas pushed Lestara back into the bedroom, following her in even as he berated her carelessness. But instead of listening to his father's tirade, Otis strode to the window.

Adrenaline pumping through her veins, Zarrah pressed herself against the wall, holding the corner of the curtain with her fingers to keep the wind from revealing her as Otis looked out.

"Serin," he said, "who sleeps in that room there? The one in the shadows."

Zarrah held her breath as Serin approached, joining the prince at the window. "Which one, Highness?"

"There. You can't see it in the darkness, but there is a window."

The Magpie was silent, and her mind raced, wondering which window the prince was pointing at. Wondering why the sight of Lestara had provoked this line of questioning.

"That room is where Zarrah Anaphora is kept, Highness, as it is the one with the bars. It is quite secure, if that is your concern. For all her faults, Coralyn shows every caution when it comes to the harem's safety."

"So it's not Lestara's room?" Otis's voice was stilted. Breathy, and Zarrah's mind raced as she tried to puzzle out what he was thinking.

Serin huffed out an amused breath. "Certainly not, Highness.

Lestara is favored and has rooms next to Coralyn's. There." He hesitated, then said, "Why do you ask?"

Silence.

"The Valcottans killed my Tasha." Otis's voice was barely audible. "Sank the ship she was on. There were no survivors."

Zarrah's chest tightened, because it was probably the truth. Her aunt's fleet sank Maridrinian vessels constantly. Zarrah had personally ordered the sinking of several, though they'd all been naval vessels.

"A tragedy that should never have occurred, Your Highness. She was with child, no? Traveling on a naval vessel to visit you in Nerastis?"

Serin's voice dripped with sympathy, but Zarrah's instincts jangled with the certainty that if she could see his face, it would be wearing a smile.

"Yes." Otis's voice was strangled. "She'd intended to surprise me. If I'd known, I'd never have allowed her to take the risk."

Serin made a soothing noise that made Zarrah's skin crawl, for no one could take comfort from such a monster.

"Yet instead of strangling Zarrah Anaphora like she deserves, my father sees her treated like a princess. Offers to return her, unscathed, in exchange for *trade terms* that will never hold."

"It's Keris's plan, but your father seems inclined to indulge him." Serin sighed. "I can't fathom how terrible that must feel, Your Highness. The Anaphora woman deserves to have her head on a stake, yet for the sake of trade negotiations, she sleeps peacefully in your family home."

Otis's breath was ragged, the scent of sweat rising from him thick. Zarrah's own heart beat a frantic rhythm. Because while she was not certain why the sight of Lestara had triggered him, she *could* see the direction Serin was pushing Otis. To take matters into his own hands and kill her.

Serin cleared his throat. "I . . . I hesitate to bring this fell information to light, but I do believe there is something you should know."

"What information?"

Beads of sweat rolled down Zarrah's back as she waited for Serin to reveal the information that would've sealed her fate if she'd not already intended to die tonight. Because she *knew* what the spymaster was about to say.

"We've no way to confirm the truth of it, but the rumor is that Zarrah ordered Tasha's ship sunk. And logic tells us that it could only have been her or Bermin, which means it was an Anaphora who saw your wife dead."

A ragged sob tore from Otis's lips, and Zarrah's eyes burned with guilt. Serin's words were no lie. There was every likelihood it had been her who'd given the order, which meant she was responsible for an innocent woman's death. An unborn child's death. Echoes of the love letter she'd stolen rippled through her mind, the fierce declarations of love from a woman who had deserved a better fate.

"She deserves to die."

The snarled words tore Zarrah back to the moment, because there was no chance that Otis wouldn't leave this tower with murder in his heart. He'd likely get his wish for her death, although not in the manner he hoped for.

"Zarrah does deserve death, Your Highness. But your father has given specific orders that she is not to be harmed until Keris has the opportunity to see his plans through."

"Not this time. He's not getting his way in this." Otis whirled away from the window, crossing the floor with rapid strides to exit the room, and Serin chuckled softly before he twitched the curtains shut.

Zarrah forced herself to breathe, peering around the edge of the curtain to see that Serin had resumed his position on the sofa. There was no chance of her getting past him to the bedroom without him raising an alarm, and if she didn't catch Silas unprepared, she'd be unlikely to overcome him before the guards arrived.

Shit.

Sounds of Silas shouting at Lestara filling her ears, Zarrah leaned sideways and looked out the window. Her eyes skipped between the base of the tower and the covered walkway that connected the tower to the harem's building.

Would Otis go now?

Would he burst into the harem's quarters, and into her room, no matter the consequences?

She knew he would. Had heard it in Otis's voice that he was past logic. Past reason. There was only anger and the desire for vengeance.

The moment she was discovered missing from her room, the alarm bells would ring, and the guards would be in here.

Quit yelling at Lestara and get back in this room, she willed Silas even as she kept her eyes on the paths to the harem's quarters. She'd give herself until she saw Otis make his move, then she'd have no choice but to make her own.

But Otis never appeared.

Had he taken a different, secret route? Had he gone to secure some form of weapon by perhaps bribing a like-minded guard?

Or had she been wrong about his intent?

"Don't move a muscle!" Silas's voice shot her attention back to the room. "Where is Otis?"

Now or never. Zarrah squared her shoulders.

"His Highness took his leave," Serin answered. "He was out of sorts over Keris's actions in regards to the Anaphora woman. Which is understandable, given the losses he's suffered at the hands of the Valcottans."

Silas snorted. "Is he still weeping over his wife? It's been a god-damned year."

Zarrah barely heard his words, realization dawning on her as her mind leapt from the moment Otis had blanched at the sight of Lestara's face to when he'd snarled, *He's not getting his way in this.*

Otis wasn't going to kill her. He was going to confront his brother. And God help her, Maridrinian princes killed one another all the time for reasons lesser than this.

"I'm famished," Silas said. "And you promised me an update on the rebels contesting Petra's rule."

"They've pressed north out of their strongholds in the deep south, though their primary weapon is one Petra uses so adeptly herself."

"Propaganda. Or murder?"

"The former. My spies tell me that Petra is struggling to silence the woman's father as effectively as she did her mother. If they move against her, it would be a good opportunity to retake Neras-tis."

The words were little more than noise in Zarrah's ears, panic raging through her veins because if Otis picked a fight with Keris, she *knew* who'd lose the encounter.

The men moved to the next room, where a table sat with trays of food, Silas sitting in one of the chairs and the Magpie standing next to him, both with their backs to her.

She'd smelled the sweat pouring off Otis. Had heard the rage and betrayal in his voice. Zarrah knew that if she didn't warn Keris, didn't help him, she'd regret it.

Except if she left now, she'd lose her chance to kill Silas. A chance that she might never have again.

Choose.

Indecision warred within her. Once she'd have chosen vengeance without hesitation, but . . . she couldn't lose Keris as she had Yrina.

Revenge was not worth his life.

Zarrah eased onto the windowsill and lowered herself over the edge. Only to hesitate, because she'd never climb down in time.

Then an idea occurred to her.

Easing back inside, she pulled on the velvet cloak tied to her waist, drawing the deep cowled hood forward so that it obscured her face. Then she moved on silent feet to the door, praying that Silas and Serin would think it only a servant if they noticed a noise at all.

The guards outside glanced at her, one of them frowning, but neither spoke to her nor impeded her progress, believing her Lestara as she glided down the stairs. She held her breath, waiting for one of them to notice her bare feet were brown, not ivory, but the guards didn't stir.

Rounding the bend, she broke into a faster pace, her feet making soft pats as she descended, coming to a stop outside Keris's door. She pressed her ear to the thick wood.

In time to hear a loud crash and a cry of pain.

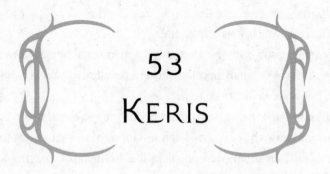

53
KERIS

KERIS WAS PUSHING A BOOK CAREFULLY BACK INTO ITS SPOT ON his shelves when he heard a faint click.

"That was quick," he said, turning around. "What did he—"

He had a second to register the fury on Otis's face, then the blow caught him in the stomach and drove the wind out of him.

Gasping, Keris staggered backward and fell, his brother on him in an instant.

"How could you?" Otis grabbed him by the shoulders, slamming him against the floor.

"I don't—"

"Don't deny it!" his brother snarled. "I know it wasn't Lestara, because Lestara was upstairs being serviced by our father. That was Zarrah Anaphora's room. That was Zarrah Anaphora you were fucking."

Panic flooded his veins. "I wasn't—"

"Don't lie to me, Keris!" Otis slammed him against the ground hard enough that Keris's teeth rattled. "It makes perfect sense. How you kept disappearing in Nerastis, trying to disguise it by buying the tongue of that courtesan. I let it go because I thought you had a girl in the city, but it was her, wasn't it?"

"You've lost your mind!"

"Have I?" Otis shouted the words, spittle striking Keris in the face. "What other reason explains how you behaved when she was captured? You ordered a good man whipped for doing his duty. Whipped to death, despite you never having ordered *anyone* punished our entire lives. It was because he hurt your *lover*! Because you wanted to protect your *Valcottan whore*! Admit it!"

Keris's mind raced, hunting for a way to deny it, a way to get himself out of this situation. But there was *none*. All it would take was Otis telling their father what he'd seen, what he'd heard, whose room it was. The harem wouldn't lie to protect him, not once they knew the truth. Deception would not see him clear of this, which left him only one path.

"It's true. It was Zarrah."

Otis went still, staring down at him as though the shock of the truth was enough to temper his anger. "How did you cross paths with her? How was that even possible?"

Keris swallowed hard, mind hunting for a way out of this mess even as the truth flowed from his lips. "I caught her in the Nerastis palace. She stole your letters from Tasha, believing them military correspondence. I chased her down to get them back, and . . . we talked. Neither of us knew who the other was."

"But you knew she was Valcottan."

"I didn't care. I still don't." He exhaled a long breath. "I refuse to hate a nation of people because of the choices made by rulers and generals."

"But she's one of those generals!" Otis shouted, his anger rising as his shock faded. "It was on her orders that Tasha's ship was sunk! She murdered my wife! She murdered my unborn child!"

It was a military ship, Keris wanted to protest. *She had no reason to believe civilians were aboard.* Except he knew they were empty words, because Tasha *had been* aboard. Words and intentions wouldn't bring the dead back to life.

"So that's what all this is about, then?" Otis demanded. "This sham of a negotiation? To free your lover?"

It was more complicated than that. Had grown in scope with every passing day, but Valcotta was, and always would be, at the heart of it. Saving her mattered more than anything else. "Zarrah isn't like the empress. She doesn't want war for the sake of pride and vengeance—she wants to see an end to the needless slaughter of innocent people. If she inherits the crown, there is a chance we could end this war."

Otis stared at him, tears dripping down his cheeks to splatter Keris in the face. "I don't want the war to end. Not until we've killed every last one of them and hung them from stakes to rot. Not until we've made them pay for every fucking thing they've taken from us. Not until that bitch pays for what she took from *me.*"

Keris's stomach hollowed, for he could see in his brother's eyes that his grief was too painful, his anger too intense, for Otis to see beyond either emotion. For him to want anything but vengeance.

"I'm going to give you the choice, Keris. Either you go down those stairs and kill that woman with your own hands, or I'm going to execute you as the traitor you are before killing her myself."

He could agree to it. Say he'd kill her in the hopes of finding a way out of this on the way to Valcotta's rooms.

Except he knew there was no way out.

All delaying would accomplish was one of them killing the other in front of his aunts and younger siblings in the harem's house. And they'd witnessed enough horror. "Then you're going to have to kill me now."

Otis's face twisted with grief. "So be it."

He reached for Keris's throat, but Keris was already moving. He twisted out from under his brother, then rolled to his feet, barely getting an arm up to block the fist swinging toward him.

Otis attacked again, raining blows down upon him until Keris's arms screamed in pain.

But he kept defending. Kept buying himself time to come up with a solution that wouldn't see Otis or Valcotta dead, because he couldn't live with losing either of them.

Then one of his brother's fists got past his guard and took the choice from him.

Stunned, Keris dropped, stars spinning in his eyes, his vision clearing as Otis wrapped his hands around Keris's throat.

Panic surged. He clawed at Otis's hands, desperation causing him to strike his brother in the face, but Otis didn't seem to feel the pain.

His chest spasmed with the need for air, the need for just one breath, the need to live . . .

And then Otis's hands were torn from his throat, his bulk disappearing in a blur of motion.

Keris gasped in a breath, then another and another, his vision clearing to see his brother fighting what looked like a harem wife wearing one of their distinct black cloaks. Then the hood fell back, revealing her face.

It was *Valcotta* fighting his brother, meeting Otis blow for blow with grim resolve, driving him back with skill and speed.

"Serin was manipulating you, Otis. I heard it all. He wants Keris dead, but your father won't oblige, so he is setting you up to do the dirty work."

How could she have heard? What was she doing in the tower? Keris dragged himself to his feet, a wave of dizziness striking him as Otis threw himself at Valcotta, fists a blur.

"Serin didn't make you sink my wife's ship!" he screamed, snatching up a stool and snapping off the leg. "Serin didn't make my brother fall into your bed! You've taken everything from me, you Valcottan bitch, and my greatest regret is not putting my sword through your heart when I had the chance!"

He swung at her with vicious force, and Valcotta's eyes widened. She stepped back, her foot catching on a stack of books. She stumbled as Otis swung again, aiming for her head.

"No!" Keris lunged, slamming into his brother with greater force than he intended, sending Otis staggering sideways.

Glass shattered.

Keris lifted his head, seeing his brother fall backward, arms pinwheeling as he tried to catch hold of the window frame.

"Otis!" He reached, his fingers brushing the leather of Otis's boots as his brother plunged from sight.

Thud.

Cold shock rippled through Keris as he stood.

No. It wasn't possible. Otis hadn't fallen.

He took one step. Then another. Gripped the window frame and looked down. His stomach twisted, the contents rising.

Otis *had* fallen.

On the pale paving stones below, his brother's body was sprawled, blood spreading around him in a great dark pool.

No.

"Keris."

This wasn't supposed to happen.

"Keris?"

He slowly turned to find Valcotta behind him, her eyes wide.

"It wasn't your fault," she said. "It was an accident. Serin drove him to this moment. The Magpie wants you dead, and he goaded Otis into this. It's his doing."

If only that were the case.

The fog of shock disappeared, reality rushing over him. Guards would have seen Otis fall. It was only a matter of time until they came up to Keris's room to investigate.

Grabbing Valcotta's arm, he pulled her hood forward to conceal her face and then dragged her to the door. "Hurry." They raced down and down the stairs. "React like one of the harem wives would, and then get back to their quarters. If you're caught here, both of us will be dead, and all of this will be for nothing."

He burst through the door to find the four guards bent over Otis's still form, bubbles of blood rising from his lips. *God, he was still alive.*

Behind him, Zarrah let out a bloodcurdling scream that echoed through the gardens, then clutched at his arm, sobbing.

"Go!" He gave her a shove. "Fetch Coralyn. Tell her to summon the physician."

She gave a jerky nod, then hurried down the path as fast as she could without breaking into a run, none of the guards paying her attention, their eyes on him.

"He fell from your window, Your Highness," one said. "What happened?"

"An accident." His throat was tight, the words strangled. "He . . ."

Otis moved, turning his head, his mouth forming Keris's name, though only a gurgle came out.

On leaden feet, Keris approached, dropping to his knees to grip his brother's hand, seeing that it wouldn't matter how fast the physician came, for these injuries weren't survivable. He lowered his head, keeping his voice soft enough that only Otis would hear, his heart aching. "I'm so sorry. This was the last thing I wanted. You're my brother, and I love you."

Otis tightened his grip, the force of it grinding the bones of

Keris's hand, the look in his brother's eyes one that would haunt him forever. Not pain. Not fear.

But betrayal.

"I'm sorry," he repeated, because no other words would come. "I'm so sorry."

But Otis's chest was still, the spark fading from his eyes and leaving behind nothing but a corpse.

A female scream split the night air, and Keris turned to see Lestara with her hand over her mouth, his father standing at her arm, expression unreadable. Beyond, Serin lurked in the shadows.

Keris's body quivered, every part of him demanding that he go after the spymaster. That he strangle the life out of the monster for what he'd done.

Except in this, he couldn't blame Serin. Only himself.

"God in heaven, what has happened?" Coralyn dropped to her knees next to him, his father's physician arriving a heartbeat later, though the man almost instantly withdrew to be replaced by more women, who pushed Keris back, tears running down their faces. The gardens filled with a chorus of their wailing, servants looking on in horror.

Keris took one step back. Then another, before colliding with something solid. He twisted to find his father behind him.

His father crossed his arms, looking Keris up and down before saying, "You did what you had to do."

"It was an accident." His tongue was thick in his mouth. "I didn't mean for him to fall."

The corner of his father's mouth twisted up. "I saw the state of your room when I came down. It was you or him, I'm sure, although I think it a shock to all that it's you who is still breathing. I'm impressed."

Keris's stomach heaved, forcing him to clench his teeth and swallow vomit, the alternative to spew on his father's boots.

"Get used to it, Keris," his father said. "When you are heir, you are the target of all. You can expect no loyalty from your brothers, and all but the cowards will come for you at one point or another. If you live to inherit, they'll come for your sons." His smile grew. "It is the way of it, and it is also the reason you have no uncles still living. Do you understand me?"

How many had his father murdered, first to get the crown and then to keep it? How much blood was on his hands? The questions circled Keris's head, but he only gave a tight nod. "I understand."

"Good." His father pushed past him, shouting, "Quit your wailing, women! The fool picked the fight and lost it, which means he deserves his fate." Then to the servants, he ordered, "Clean up this mess and make the arrangements."

Keris stood in silence, watching as the weeping women dispersed. As the guards lifted his brother's body and took it away. As the servants mopped up the blood.

Then his skin abruptly prickled with a sixth sense that he was being watched, and Keris turned to find Serin standing in the shadows. "My condolences," the spymaster said. "I know you and your brother were once close."

Keris's hands fisted, the need to rain violence down upon the man causing him to see red. Except while his father might forgive Otis's death as part of the life of an heir, the murder of his most trusted advisor was an entirely different matter. "I didn't mean for Otis to lose his life. Whereas I think *your* intentions for the encounter were far different, Magpie."

"Your death would please me, it's true." Serin rubbed his chin. "But it would be foolish to make an attempt on your life while you are in your father's good graces, and I am *no fool*, Highness. Far better to wait for your inevitable fall from favor that will come when these negotiations fail. And they'd fail far sooner if Zarrah Anaphora were to meet her tragic end. When Otis inquired which room was hers in the harem, then departed in such a rage, I thought he'd make my hopes reality by slaughtering the woman."

Keris's heart skittered, dread filling his stomach.

"Yet it wasn't her room he went to, but yours. It wasn't her life he attempted to take, but yours." Serin smiled, revealing his discolored teeth. "One can't help but wonder why."

"He wanted *me* to kill her." Keris met the man's stare, letting him see the truth staring out. "Said it was a matter of loyalty."

"Why did you refuse? Surely your brother is worth more to you than some Valcottan woman."

Keris needed to be away from this conversation, from this line of questioning, because his nerves were too rattled to spar with this man. But walking away would be just as damning as saying the wrong thing. "As you said, Magpie, my longevity is dependent on remaining in my father's graces, and to accede to Otis's demands would turn those good graces to ash. I did what I had to."

"Chose your plans, and your own life, over your loyalty to your dearest brother? Over his *life*? That seems a deviation in character, Your Highness. A darker side of you that I find quite shocking."

"It is rich indeed for you to cast judgment on anyone's principles, Magpie, for you are devoid of them."

"No judgment, Highness. My shock comes only from learning that you are more like your sister than I'd ever imagined."

Like Lara, who'd destroyed a nation and the man she ostensibly loved for the sake of her plans. "I am nothing like Lara. If I wish to stab a man, it will be in the chest, not the back."

Serin smiled again, smoothing his robes. "And thus my point stands. Good night, Your Highness. I hope you find pursuits that bring you peace." Without another word, the spymaster walked away.

54
ZARRAH

HEART IN HER THROAT, ZARRAH HURRIED THROUGH THE GARden paths, then ducked into the shadows beneath her window, crouching low in the brush. She held her breath, waiting for any indication that the guards had realized she was not Lestara.

You left him.

Sickening guilt filled her core, making her want to double over as Keris's face filled her mind's eye. Shock. Horror. Grief. He'd *loved* his brother, and now Otis was dead. Not because he deserved such a fate but because his grief over his wife had been manipulated by that monster of a spymaster.

Though Serin was not alone at fault. Otis's wife was a casualty of the Endless War. But rather than comfort him, those around Otis had used his grief to fuel his hatred, for it was as keen a weapon as any sword. They didn't want him to heal, didn't want him to move past his grief and anger, because then he'd no longer be a pawn they could use to achieve their ends. He'd believed himself righteous—the master of his own destiny—never once seeing that he was a pawn in a war between rulers.

They'd been manipulated in the same way, she and Otis, their grief weaponized to fight a war where the only people who died were those who didn't deserve to.

As she'd stared at his body, broken and bloody on the ground, the scream that had torn from her lips had not been feigned, the horror slicing through her soul visceral and cutting and cruel, for it wielded the truth.

A female shriek pierced the night, coming from the direction of the tower, jolting Zarrah into action.

She shoved the stone block into the deepest part of the brush, as there was no way for her to replace it, then swiftly scaled the wall. Again, her hips got stuck climbing through the opening, but with a dozen silent curses, she toppled into her room.

Which was exactly how she'd left it, no sign that her absence had been noted.

Though her body was exhausted and aching from the blows Otis had landed, Zarrah swiftly put the room back in order.

Only then did she go to the window.

Topiaries blocked her view of the base of the tower, but light spilled outward from the scene. She didn't need to see it to imagine it, only prayed for Otis's sake that his end had come swiftly. Prayed that Keris wasn't holding himself to blame.

The former was far more likely than the latter.

Her adrenaline faded, leaving her weary and hollow, but Zarrah didn't move from her place at the window. Through the walls, she heard the wailing of women, felt the pain and grief of a son lost falling over the palace like a pall. But eventually the light around the tower faded, servants and guards retreating until all was still. Silent.

A knock sounded.

Zarrah jerked, turning as the bolts on the door unlatched. Coralyn stepped through with a lamp in hand, shutting the door behind her. Her eyes were red and swollen, but her voice was steady as she said, "I believed you the trump up my sleeve, Zarrah, and I'm rarely wrong about these things."

An icy chill spread across Zarrah's skin. For it was not just empresses and kings who used rage and grief as a weapon.

It was also harem wives.

"Why didn't you do it?" Coralyn set the lamp down on a table, crossing her arms. "You made it to his room. I *watched you* climb through his window. I gave you the opportunity to see him dead, and yet Silas breathes while another of our sons does not."

If Coralyn believed she'd killed Otis, Zarrah suspected she'd already be dead. "I had nothing to do with him falling."

"I never said that you did."

Zarrah met the woman's cold stare, her mind racing. Coralyn learning she'd been with Keris would be nearly as catastrophic as *Silas* learning the truth, which meant she needed to tread carefully. Especially given that her story needed to align with what Lestara had likely revealed. "I made it to his room when he was still with Lestara and erred in hesitating to kill him while he was in bed with her. Serin arrived, then Otis soon after, and there was no good opportunity."

"Lestara was attempting to provide you a distraction, you fool."

Zarrah forced her face to darken with feigned anger. "We might have gotten further if you'd been more forthright about your intentions."

"I needed proof I could trust you with my intentions, first. Now I have it, and here we are. What happened next?"

Zarrah debated what course to take and settled on replying, "What difference does it make?"

"Given Otis is dead by Keris's hand, what happened in the tower tonight makes every difference."

What had Keris told Coralyn? What reason did he give for the accident? Not knowing meant that Zarrah was walking forward blind, and if she blundered in what she told Coralyn, she might inadvertently step over a cliff edge. "Otis spoke with Serin and then left. After that, I very nearly had the opportunity to kill Silas when he sat down to eat, but then—" A gesture out the window finished the explanation with appropriate vagueness. "You're a clever one, Coralyn. I didn't think you'd stoop to using a Valcottan to assassinate your husband."

The old woman didn't so much as blink. "What did you overhear? Specifically, what did they say to Otis?"

Rising to her feet, Zarrah took a sip from the water glass next to her bed. "Why would I tell you anything? What's in it for me?"

"You need me to hide the evidence of your escape." Coralyn cocked her head, giving Zarrah a considering stare. "And because you need me to facilitate another opportunity to take your vengeance."

There was no denying it. For one, if the old woman decided Zarrah wasn't a tool she could use, she would probably find a way to kill her. And two, working with Coralyn was likely the only way she'd get another chance to kill Silas. "Silas went to chastise Lestara, leaving Otis and Serin alone." She repeated the conversation word for word, finishing with, "I thought he'd left to come here to kill me."

"But he went to Keris's room instead?"

Zarrah shrugged. "Of that, you know more than I do. I used the commotion caused by his death to get back here undetected."

There were holes in her story. Inconsistencies that Coralyn undoubtedly noticed, but as long as she didn't arrive at the truth, that was all that mattered.

Silence.

Coralyn finally said, "If I give you another opportunity, will you take it?"

She didn't trust Coralyn as far as she could throw her, but they did have the same goal: Silas's death. With the woman's help, it was possible she might achieve her goal *and* get out alive, but that meant showing Coralyn that she wasn't going to tolerate being used. Giving Coralyn a considering look, Zarrah drained her water. "Maybe I negotiate my freedom instead by offering Silas information about which of his wives is trying to have him murdered."

Coralyn snorted. "If my death is worth so much to you, then by all means. But it won't earn you your freedom."

A fact of which Zarrah was well aware, but if Coralyn believed Zarrah would do her dirty work without something in exchange, she had another thing coming for her. "I'll kill Silas, Coralyn. But only if you find a way for me to escape afterward."

"That's not possible."

Maybe it wasn't. Keris hadn't found a route for escape. Neither had Aren. But Zarrah's instincts told her that Coralyn had the cunning to achieve what the men had not. "Put your mind to it, my lady. Until then, I'll continue to enjoy your hospitality."

The old woman's eyes darkened with fury, her hands clenching. It was the first time Zarrah had ever seen Coralyn's control fracture, and she wasn't certain whether to feel triumphant or worried. Probably the latter.

"I *will* think on it, Zarrah. But in the meantime, you will remain confined to this room at all times."

Not ideal, but better than dead, which might well be the alternative.

Coralyn retrieved her lamp, then held out her hand. "Give me the nail."

Zarrah didn't want to give it up. Tiny as it was, it was still the only weapon she had. But if she wanted Coralyn to believe her a willing ally, she needed to provide some proof. So Zarrah handed it over.

Coralyn gave her a cool smile. "Let's hope I find reason to give it back to you in the future. But until then, I hope you continue to enjoy my *hospitality*."

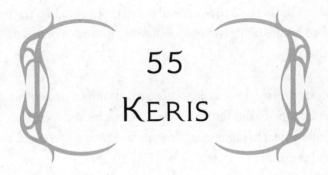

55
KERIS

HE NEEDED TO GET OUT OF THE PALACE. AWAY FROM THE ENDLESS stink of corpse, the judgmental eyes of the wives and servants, away from the goddamned *silence*. Because in the silence, he heard the same noise over and over.

Thud.

The sickening, wet thump of his brother hitting the ground replayed through his head, his eyes filling with the sight of crimson pooling around Otis's body. Of the look of betrayal in his eyes.

Thud.

Keris flinched, glancing to his right, where men tossed heavy sacks onto a cart, rainwater splattering with each impact. His stomach roiled, and he looked back to the slick cobbles ahead of him, swallowing the sourness. What he needed was somewhere loud. Somewhere busy. Somewhere his face wasn't known. Somewhere he could *be* someone other than who he was.

You're a goddamned coward.

He should've stayed in the palace. Valcotta was in a precarious position, for if it were discovered she'd gotten out of her room, his father might kill her for the infraction. But he just couldn't stay. Couldn't be there. Couldn't spend the night cleaning up the mess created by the fight, endlessly replaying his final words with his brother.

Thud.

Keris pressed his hands to his ears, trying to drown out the sound. Rain soaked through his cloak, but he still looked to the sky, allowing it to hammer against his face. Wishing it could wash away his mistakes.

A scuff of a boot against stone caught his attention, but Keris didn't turn. It was one of Serin's minions, tasked, as always, to follow him through the city. He knew their faces—knew how to lose them—but as he glanced down a dark alleyway that would allow him access to the rooftops of Vencia, a wave of vertigo nearly caused him to stumble.

Thud.

He didn't want to climb. Climbing meant being up high. Being up high meant risking falling, and with the way he was feeling, it would almost be inevitable.

And maybe he deserved it.

Instead, Keris pushed open the door to a loud alehouse with a sign above it reading *The One-Eyed Parrot*. A wave of heat rushed over him, carrying with it the scent of spilled booze, sweat, and cooking, his ears filling with the raucous shouts of drunks and music played by a drummer with middling talent.

Spying a table with a group of men playing cards, he approached. "Room for another?"

Eyes flicked up, and Keris waited for them to recognize him. But Vencia knew Prince Keris as one always dressed in flamboyant attire, his hair perfectly coiffed, and with an escort on his heels. Not a sodden man in shirtsleeves and a plain cloak, hair pulled back in a messy knot. "You got silver?" one of them, a thick man with a receding hairline that he made up for with a dense beard, asked. "We don't play for coppers."

Keris debated pointing out that the pot in the center was more copper than not, but instead said, "Yes."

"Then sit. We'll deal you in next round."

Keris settled in the chair, motioning to the barmaid to bring him a glass of wine. From the corner of his eye, he saw Serin's man take a seat at the bar, watching him in the tarnished mirror that sat behind the row of bottles. When the girl brought Keris his wine, he lifted it and smirked at the man, who only cast his eyes upward and took a drink from his own glass.

The bearded man won the hand and scooped the pile toward him. The skinny one sitting across from him shuffled and swiftly dealt. Keris glanced at his hand, then met the bet the bearded man placed, which was a single copper. "Don't think your luck will hold another round?"

The bearded man spat on the floor. "Got nothing to do with my luck. Fault lies with the king and his taxes. If I don't come home with the coin I left with, my wife will chop off my parts and sell them to feed our children."

A complaint about his father that Keris had heard many times before, and he gave a sympathetic nod as he watched the other players for tells. Not because he cared about winning but because he needed to keep his mind busy.

Thud.

He covered his flinch by drinking deeply from his glass, forcing himself to focus on the game and not the feel of his brother's boot slipping through his grasp.

"Bastard will see us all starved and in the streets before conceding he's bit off more than he can chew with that cursed bridge he stole from Ithicana."

The other men nodded their agreement, the skinny one adding

his own glob of spit to the floor as he muttered, "Backstabbing Veliant thief."

Keris had fueled this anger in the people with his rumors about Aren, and old habits died hard. "To the victor go the spoils, in cards and in war."

He'd kept his voice light, but that seemed not to matter, for the faces of all three darkened, the bearded man saying, "This was no war. A war is fought face-to-face with weapons in hand, not by sending a princess with a pretty face and nice tits to stab a man in the back. Not only was there no honor in it, our *beloved* king has nothing to show for it but snake-infested islands and empty pockets."

"And a royal prisoner," Keris added. "You wouldn't want to forget that."

"He brings shame upon Maridrina," the skinny man said. "The Ithicanian king treated us as true allies, and this was how he was repaid."

Keris made a noncommittal noise, swapping out a card, then lifting a hand to the barmaid. "A round on me, love."

She brought him a glass of wine and the men more ale, which went quickly down throats, the men's grievances against the crown—and his father—voiced with increasing volume and intensity. And not just at his table, but at all of them, men and women alike crying foul against the taxes, the Endless War, the hunger, the invasion of Ithicana, and the imprisonment of Aren Kertell, all of them blaming one person.

His father.

For as long as Keris had been alive, there had been no love lost between his father and the people. But he was feared, which allowed him to maintain total control. In recent years, the people's ambivalence had moved to dislike, and then, after the invasion of

Ithicana, into outright hate. But still . . . fear had kept them in check. Yet listening to the players and the other patrons, feeling the roiling rise of fury in the room, Keris realized the balance had tipped so far that fear no longer had the power to silence them.

One man could not stand against a king and hope to win. But a nation . . .

Keris listened and played and bought round after round until the noise in the room was near deafening with shouts for the liberation of Ithicana and its king. Then he asked his now very drunk companions, "What do you see as a solution to Maridrina's woes?"

"I say"—the bearded man drained his cup—"that Silas Veliant is not fit to reign. I say," he shouted above the noise, "that Maridrina should pull him from the throne! I say death to the king!"

"Hear, hear!" Keris said, then rose and went to the bar. Sitting next to Serin's spy, he said, "I hope you're taking notes of all this so you might accurately repeat it back to your master."

The man twitched. "You incent them toward treason, Your Highness."

"I merely listen to the voices of the people." Leaning back against the bar, he rested his elbows on the damp surface, watching as his gambling companion's cry for his father's death spread through the room. "Their thoughts and actions are their own."

"And will be punished accordingly," the man snapped. "They all deserve to be arrested. To have their heads removed and spiked on the gate as traitors to the Crown."

"Ah, yes. Because that will undoubtedly regain the goodwill of the people."

The spy made a face. "Crawl back into your books of idealism, Your Highness. The people need not love their king; they need only fear the consequences of crossing him. Consequences, I might add, from which you are not exempt."

Keris sipped at his wine, knowing he'd had too much but not caring, because the people had more power than he did. The power to see change accomplished.

They only needed someone to guide them in the right direction.

All his life, Keris had run from the crown, not wanting any part of it. Yet now he found that the desire to take that crown from his father burned like wildfire through his veins. Not only because it would give him the power to liberate Valcotta. Not only because he'd be able to free Aren Kertell and withdraw from Ithicana.

But because he wanted to *rule*.

So Keris lifted his glass and joined the voices of his people as they screamed for Ithicana's liberty. For Maridrina's liberty. "Death to the king!"

The spy's face drained of color. "Your father will hear of this."

"I certainly hope so." Keris leaned closer to the man. "He needs to answer for crossing his people. And for crossing *me*."

Vaguely, he realized that his voice sounded like his father's. Cold and threatening and cruel. But with the heat of wine and anger and grief firing through him, Keris didn't care. The spy blanched, seeming to finally understand that what sat next to him was no sheep but a wolf.

The spy tried to rise. "Your Highness—"

Keris shoved him back onto his stool, then raised his voice, loud enough to be heard over the noise. "This is one of the Magpie's spies!"

The men and women near him went silent, their eyes fixing on the spy, whose face went pale.

If you truly believe in something, you should be willing to suffer for it. To die for it.

To kill for it.

"I bet he's here spying on us and plans to scuttle back to his master!" Keris shouted. "And you *all* know how Silas Veliant punishes dissent."

Tension rose, the room growing silent as word spread.

"That true? You one of the Magpie's creatures?" his bearded gambling companion finally demanded.

If the spy had held his ground and denied it, he might have lived. But the man's nerve failed him, and he bolted to the exit.

Everyone in the bar surged, several moving to block the door.

"Spying on us, are you?" the bearded man said, driving the spy backward into the bar. "And just what are you planning to tell your master?"

"Nothing," he sniveled. "I won't tell him anything. You have my word!"

Keris smiled, for that was about the worst thing the spy could've said to these people.

"Your word?" the bearded man demanded. "Your word is worth less than the rag I wipe my ass with." The crowd laughed, their starved eyes merciless. For the Magpie's reputation was no secret to them. "You serve a sadist. You find him people to cut up for his own entertainment. Might be time for you to have a taste of what that feels like."

"You can't hurt me! There will be consequences!" He twisted around, and his eyes met Keris's. "Highness, please! Keris!"

Keris tensed at the use of his name, waiting for the mob to turn their ire on him, but the bearded man only laughed. "I thought your pretty face looked familiar. Should have known it was you, given you're the only man in the goddamned city with the balls to defy him."

Shock radiated through him. That ... that wasn't what the people thought of him. They thought he was a weakling and a coward. The worst excuse for a prince to bear the Veliant name. Time and again, Keris had been told as much. Yet there were others in the crowd nodding, watching him not with disgust but with . . . with respect.

And he refused to disappoint them.

"Defiance is no longer enough." Keris met their gazes. "Maridrina needs to be led by someone like-minded to its people. By someone who respects the people, not someone who sets Serin upon them for speaking their thoughts."

The crowd shouted their agreement, calling again for the death of his father. For the death of Serin. For the death of the spy standing before them.

The crotch of the man's trousers turned damp, a puddle of fear pooling around his boots. "I don't serve Serin! I serve whoever wears the crown! I could serve you!"

"You'll never serve me," Keris answered, then gave a nod.

Like unleashed hounds, the mob descended with fists and feet. So many of them that Keris swiftly lost sight of the spy, though he heard his screams. Heard his pleas.

Heard his silence.

Keris waited long enough to ensure the spy was well and truly dead; then, with the shouts of his people ringing in his ears, he stepped out into the night.

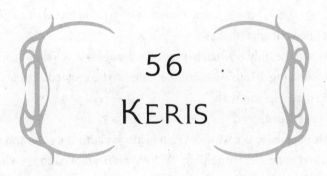

56
KERIS

"KERIS, WAKE UP!"

He jerked upright with a start, nearly falling off the side of his bed.

"Keris!"

It was Coralyn. Even muffled by stone and heavy wood, he recognized his aunt's imperious tone. Rubbing at his eyes, Keris pulled on the pair of trousers he'd left discarded on the floor and then padded barefoot across the room, fastening his belt as he went. He unbolted the door and swung it open. "Good morning—"

"It's early afternoon, you lazy creature. You keep the hours of a prostitute."

Since Otis's death, his nights had been spent in the city, stirring up dissent against his father, his days trying to find a way to get Aren alone, though he'd had no luck with the latter. And when he did sleep, it was only to be jerked awake by the sickening thud of his brother's body hitting the ground. He was exhausted beyond reason, but Keris didn't want her knowing why. "There's a reason I keep their hours; it makes it easier to—"

She leveled a finger at him, silencing the rest of his quip. "Don't even go there, young man. Knowing of your habits is enough. I don't need the details."

Given the only woman to grace his thoughts was Valcotta, Coralyn knowing details was most definitely to be avoided. "What is it that I can help you with?"

"I need an escort."

He glanced at the window, rain pelting against the glass and the howling wind clearly audible. "Why? You're allowed to go where you will. And you know how I dislike getting wet." A lie, the truth being that he didn't want to be subjected to her interrogation about what had happened with Otis. While he might have convinced Serin of his ruthlessness, Coralyn wouldn't be so easily fooled.

She snorted. "As though I care about your preferences. Get dressed. Clearly you need time away from these rooms so that the servants might have a chance to clean up." She wrinkled her nose. "Be quick about it."

KNOWING HIS AUNT DESPISED WAITING on anyone, Keris forwent a shave and settled on a swift wash, realizing she might have had a point about the servants when he examined the limited contents of his wardrobe. Donning something more subdued than he was known for wearing, he stepped out of his chambers and made his way down the steps, finding his aunt waiting on the second level.

"Sara is leaving today," she said. "Your father can't be bothered to take her, and her mother hasn't the fortitude for it, so it will have to be you and me."

Sighing, he nodded and offered her his arm, a pair of servants holding canopies over their heads against the rain as they stepped out of the tower doors. His eyes immediately went to the spot where Otis had landed, a wave of dizziness passing over him as he walked over it.

Thud.

He took a steadying breath, but each blink of his eyes revealed his brother's body, blood pooling around it, Otis's eyes full of betrayal.

Don't think about it, he told himself. *It's done. You can't fix it. Focus on what you can fix.*

That thought had his gaze moving to the harem's building, to Valcotta's windows. Coralyn was keeping her confined, the reason given that she believed her at risk from Serin. It made him ill that she was effectively being kept in a cell, but there was nothing he could do but push forward with his plans. Since he had failed in learning how to reach the Ithicanians to secure their support, he'd turned to making plans to overthrow his father by way of force. His lieutenants, led by his bearded gambling companion, whose name was Dax, were gathering loyal men and women. As soon as there were enough of them to overwhelm the palace guard, Keris would have them move against his father.

And put the crown on *his* head.

His stomach flipped with a strange mix of anticipation and terror at the freedom he'd have with all that power. Power not just to free Valcotta, but to change Maridrina for the better. To make peace with enemies and form alliances that would make his country strong.

But those were thoughts for another time. Right now, his family needed to be first in mind, most especially his little sister.

Sara stood in front of the gates, her mother on her knees before her, sobbing and clutching at his sister's hands. Her tears intensified as he and Coralyn drew close.

"Please. Please don't take her away!"

"You are making this harder than it needs to be," Coralyn said.

"This is a wondrous opportunity for Sara, and yet you behave as though it were a punishment."

Sara's mother only cried harder, clinging to her daughter, who looked on the verge of tears herself. "I can't lose her. Please, Keris, speak to the king. Convince him that this is a mistake!"

"He won't be moved on the matter," he answered, and in truth, that felt a mercy. His sweet sister would leave this place of misery and death, and even if it were not the life she dreamed of, it would be better than this one. "I'm sorry."

Her eyes turned bitter. "Are you sorry, Keris? Do you even care that you're taking yet another of our children away from us?"

He flinched, pain ricocheting through his chest, because he had no defense.

"Sara, it is time," Coralyn announced, and more of the wives moved to catch hold of her mother's arms, drawing her back. "Say goodbye."

Sara's chin quivered, but she squared her shoulders. "Goodbye, Mother. Goodbye, Aunties."

Keris offered her his arm, her fingers clenching harder than they usually did as they slowly made their way through the gate toward the waiting carriage. He helped her inside while the servants loaded the few belongings she'd been allowed to take with her. Coralyn followed them in, handing Sara a long, wrapped parcel. "For you, dear one. I've been wanting to give this to you for some time."

Wiping at her eyes, Sara unwrapped the parcel, extracting a polished cane sized for a child, her eyes widening. "Is this . . ."

"To help you walk, my love, because you will need to rely on your own strength going forward."

Keris's eyes burned, and he looked out the window as the carriage exited the palace.

It was always this way with Coralyn, her knowing what those of her family wanted. What they needed. When he'd been a boy, it was she who'd procured the books he'd so desired, using her own allowance to purchase them because his father had believed them a waste of coin. Even after he'd left to be fostered until he was of age, books he'd coveted would arrive for him in unmarked packages, her ability to know what he needed uncanny. And he found himself wondering what he'd ever given her in return.

They rode in silence, the carriage exiting the city through the south gate, forced to move slowly on the muddy roads until they reached the large estate where the church's young acolytes were trained. The Veliant family had long been notorious for having little time for matters of faith, but his father was not fool enough to cut the funds used to support it, especially since it gave him an avenue for disposing of his inadequate children without question.

A pair of older women dressed in robes awaited them at the entrance, both curtsying low to Keris with murmurs of "Your Highness" flowing from their lips.

"His Majesty is giving into your care his daughter, Princess Sara Veliant, with the expectation that she be treated according to her rank," he said, feeling Sara press closer to his side. Feeling her fear and apprehension, because it was his own.

"With respect, my lord," one of the women answered, "in this place, there is no rank except for that which one earns in service."

Which meant his sister would be dressed in rough garments and forced to sleep on a narrow cot in a cold room with no one to comfort her, then made to labor to earn her meals. Hard for any child, but for Sara, it would be harder. "Perhaps that is so, but outside these walls, rank *does* matter. And there will come a time when it will be *me*, not my father, whom you will come to when this place has needs that faith alone cannot provide. I will be more amenable to gifting resources to those who have shown kindness to my most favored of sisters."

Behind him, Coralyn made an aggrieved noise, but the woman only inclined her head. "The princess will be shown every love and kindness, my lord. You have my word."

"Wonderful. I look forward to your updates on her progress, and you may expect me to visit from time to time."

"It is our preference..." The woman trailed off as Keris met her with a cool stare. "We would be honored, of course."

Drawing Sara away to a bench against one wall, he sat next to his sister. "If you have troubles, you will send word to me or to Coralyn. Bribe the servants to carry your messages, if you have to. But you shouldn't fear—they will treat you fairly." Promising anything more felt too much like a lie.

His tiny sister stared at him, her large eyes welling up with tears. "I don't want to stay here. I want to stay with you. Why can't you move back to your house in the city? Then I could live with you."

His heart broke into a hundred pieces, because under different circumstances, he'd have done just that. But it wasn't just the palace she was safer away from. It was him. "That's not how it's done, Sara. You know this."

She bowed her head and began to weep, and he pulled her against him, smoothing her hair. "It's not for forever, sister. I'll get you back."

She lifted her head to look at him, surprise driving away her grief.

"I'll need some time to do it," he said. "But as soon as I'm able, I'll take you away from this place."

"Do you promise?"

"I promise." Pulling a handkerchief from his pocket, he dried her face. "Except when I do, I'll be needing your assistance for a good many things, so you must remain strong until then, understood?"

She squared her shoulders and nodded, and then her eyes drifted over his shoulder. "You should go. Auntie Coralyn is giving you a *look*."

"Thank you for the warning." He kissed her forehead. "Keep this conversation between us." He rose, fixing the waiting women with a long stare that promised there would be hell to pay if he was crossed, before offering his aunt his arm.

"I see you've stooped to threatening nuns," she said as they stepped outside. "I can't help but wonder if there's much lower you can go, boy."

"One can always go lower."

She sniffed. "In the effort to save yourself, please don't forget yourself." Stopping in her tracks, she said, "I fancy taking some air."

"It's pissing rain."

She cast him a baleful glare for his language. "Find a canopy to hold over my head."

Cursing under his breath, Keris retrieved one from the carriage, his consternation not for the rain but for the conversation that was to come, for he was certain that it would pertain to Otis. Already his chest was tight, his mouth dry at the thought of not just having to relive the moment but of having to spin lies to hide the truth of what had happened.

Together, they walked around the rear of the building, Keris angling the shade to keep the rain from dampening her, though it meant he was soaked through by the time they reached a gazebo. Climbing the steps, he set aside the shade and took a seat on one of the benches. "As much as I appreciate the opportunity to say goodbye to my sister, Auntie, perhaps you might explain your true reason for dragging me out of Vencia."

"There's always someone listening in Vencia." She sat next to him, frowning as the wind tugged a lock of her hair loose from its coif. "And we both know Serin takes a particular interest in you, Keris. You are not the sort of man he wishes to serve, and he aims to see you removed from succession. We've already seen the proof of that."

He stiffened, and she gave him a sideways glance. "We both know it was Serin who drove Otis to attack you. His plot failed, but that only means he'll try again and again until he succeeds. We need him dead, but your father relies too much upon him to give him up. Which means for you to survive, we need your father dead or removed from power. I imagine you've come to the same conclusion, and it is your efforts to achieve his removal that have been occupying your midnight hours, not whoremongering."

Keris crossed his arms, unwilling to reveal anything, given that his last alliance with his aunt had netted him nothing.

"I know it's you riling the masses against your father, boy. You're pushing them to overthrow him, possibly to even kill him, but what is less clear is why you believe they'll put you, another Veliant, on the throne in his place. What's more likely to occur is that they'll slaughter this entire family, and Maridrina will descend into anarchy. You're wielding a cudgel when what you need is a knife."

There was far more finesse to his plans than *that,* but Keris only said, "What do you propose?"

"That you use your sister as your knife. An option made much more feasible given that Lara is in Vencia. And she isn't alone."

Shock rippled through him with enough force that his jaw dropped. "Lara? How—"

"Aren gave me a contact in the city, his hope that I'd give the individual a message to desist in their attempts to rescue him. I went to meet this contact but found more than Ithicanians. Lara is with them, as are your missing half sisters, warriors all."

Keris abruptly found himself pacing, though he had no recollection of rising, a mix of emotions churning in his gut, the foremost of which was anger. Lara was a liar and a traitor and a killer. She'd started a goddamned war. Was responsible for the deaths of thousands of people. If not for her . . . "Why is she here?"

"Because of Aren. She and his people are united in the desire to see Ithicana's king freed."

How Lara had gotten the Ithicanians to stomach her presence, Keris couldn't begin to imagine. "She's a creature of Serin's making, and we can't trust her."

"He left his mark on her, to be sure, but she's not his creature. And certainly not your father's."

"I'll have nothing to do with her," Keris snarled. "What she deserves is a knife in the heart, and while the Ithicanians might not have the balls to do it, don't think I'll show any such hesitation if she crosses my path."

Though he refused to look at her, Keris could sense his aunt's scrutiny as she asked, "What happened to you that night in the bridge?"

Turning his back on her, he closed his eyes, the vision of Raina gasping for breath, blood bubbling from her chest, filling his mind. "I told you. They trussed me up like a pig when I protested their actions and I was left in a cart until the battle was finished."

"Yes, I recall your bitter complaints." She hesitated. "But knowing you as I do, it wasn't what was done to *you* that you blame your sister for but what was done to someone else."

"They murdered my escort. They were good people."

"That was your father's doing, not Lara's."

"Bullshit!" He rounded on her. "She enabled him by being his tool."

"You think she had a choice?"

He stared his aunt down. "Yes. The same one I had. The same one I still have."

Neither of them spoke, the only sound the rain pattering against the roof of the gazebo and the wind racing across the land, the echoes of the typhoon over Ithicana.

"You two could be twins, you are so alike in face," Coralyn finally said. "And both equally unforgiving, though your sister is significantly less self-righteous about it. She erred, Keris. She knows it and is trying to right wrongs. In that, I say she is your better, for while you have not erred, you do nothing but point fingers at the wrongs around you."

"I'll hear no more of this." Turning on his heel, Keris made for the entrance to the gazebo, but his aunt's voice stopped him in his tracks.

"For the sake of your mother, you will sit. And you will listen."

Grinding his teeth, he turned.

"Lara intends to free her husband, and the harem has decided to assist her and the Ithicanians in this venture."

Less Lara's involvement, this was *exactly* the alliance he'd hoped for, but now he found himself not wanting any part of it. "Why? And why, for that matter, did you go to see Aren's contact? You indicated to me that by winning my father's promise to leave my sisters alone, you were content. What changed?"

She was quiet, eyes searching his for a long moment before she said, "The circumstances surrounding Otis's death caused me to reconsider. When I learned Lara was with them, I realized she could be of use to us. If we give her the opportunity, she's more than capable of killing your father. And more than willing."

"You're suggesting we use Lara to assassinate my father?" He frowned, pushing aside his anger in an effort to think clearly. "That's why you are agreeing to work with them? Not to rescue

Aren Kertell but because you believe she will use the opportunity to take revenge? And then . . . and then the expectation is that I'd use my newly gained crown to free him if he's not escaped already?"

"Correct." Coralyn stopped in front of him, her perfume thick in his nose. "Aren is a good man, and I believe the world will be better for his freedom. But I'll sacrifice his life in a heartbeat if it sees Silas dead, Serin along with him, and you on the throne."

Ignoring the last part of her statement, he said, "There has to be an easier way to murder him. One that holds less risk for the harem." And one that didn't involve his sister.

"You think I haven't tried? For years, I've been trying to sneak poisons into the inner sanctum. Only twice have I succeeded, and both times, your father's poison testers fell while he lived. I can't even get a weapon larger than a butter knife through those gates."

"But you think you can get Lara and her companions *in*?"

Coralyn nodded. "I'll take a select group of the wives shopping. But it will be Lara and her sisters who return with me. I'll choose women who look alike, and the younger women always keep their faces concealed outside the palace. Then I'll hide them in the harem until it's time."

"That's a piece-of-shit plan, Coralyn. What if the guards checking them for weapons notice they aren't the same women?"

She glared at him. "For someone with an enormous vocabulary, you do tend to dig from the bottom of the barrel. But as to your question, you'll just have to trust that I know what I'm doing."

It occurred to him that if Coralyn had desired Valcotta free, she probably could have arranged it. But the harem's hatred for the enemy nation ran too deep for that to ever be a possibility. Keris bit at his thumb, slowly warming to the plan, which did show much more artistry than his intended coup. "You're certain Lara will kill him? Because if she just takes Aren and runs, it will be you and the rest of the harem who pay the price. My father might be an idiot, but Serin isn't. He'll know you arranged it."

"Lara gave her word. She hates your father every bit as much as you do—I believe she'll die before leaving with your father still alive."

And Lara was a trained assassin. "You have a plan for getting her in. But what about out? It isn't as though I'll have instantaneous control, which means my father's soldiers will kill her, Aren, and whoever is with them. As it is, I'll look culpable if I just allow Lara to walk away. And she's not going to agree to any of this without an escape route."

"Lara believes Aren will have insight once presented with expanded resources."

Keris shook his head, seeing the flaw in the plan. "Aren will never agree to this. One, Lara is involved. Two, it puts his people at risk, which is something he's desperate to avoid."

"Think of a way to convince him."

The only way to convince Aren would be to make the reward worth the risk, which meant the reward had to be greater than his own freedom. "What if I promise I'll withdraw our army from Ithicana if he and his people manage the assassination during the escape?"

"Do you believe he'd trust you?" Coralyn asked. "Easy enough for you to deny making any such promise when you take the crown, leaving him with only his freedom for his efforts, which you've suggested isn't enough incentive."

"True." Keris bit at his thumbnail again, barely feeling the pain or tasting the blood as he considered the problem. Not only did he need a worthwhile incentive but he also needed to give Aren a reason to trust that the promise would be delivered upon.

Which meant the incentive needed to come from someone whose word was gold.

And Keris knew just the woman.

Catching his aunt by the elbow, he flipped the shade over her head to block the rain and then tugged her out of the gazebo. "I think it's time I had another conversation with Aren Kertell."

57
ZARRAH

CORALYN WAS NOT ONE FOR IDLE THREATS.

True to her word, the woman had kept Zarrah locked in her room since the night of her failed assassination attempt, the only people she saw being the servants who brought her food and bathwater. The stone block had been mortared back into place in the wall, though how the harem had managed it without being seen, Zarrah didn't know.

It was maddening, being imprisoned this way.

With nothing to read and nothing to do, Zarrah spent hours exercising, pushing her body to the limit, with Yrina's imagined voice driving her on until she collapsed into bed at night, exhausted. But that was better than the waiting.

Waiting for Keris to come to an agreement with her aunt.

Waiting for Serin to try to kill her again.

Waiting for Coralyn to present another opportunity to rid the harem of Silas.

She wanted to scream. Wanted to fight her way out. Wanted to be able to rely on her strengths instead of being forced to face her weaknesses, of which patience was her worst. Where she dominated was the battlefield, with soldiers and weapons and strategies, not in political machinations.

You played your hand, Yrina's voice whispered in her ear. *Now you must see how the other players respond.*

"I can't wait any longer," she answered, knowing that she spoke to a ghost. That she spoke to herself. "I need out of this room. Need to fight."

Then you're going to lose.

A knock sounded on the door.

Zarrah twitched, rising shakily to her feet as one of the guards stepped inside. He looked her over, his mouth curling in disgust. "Make yourself presentable. The king orders you to attend him."

"I'm a prisoner, not one of his wives," she answered, ignoring the flutter of nerves in her chest. "How I look matters little. Take me to him now."

The man opened his mouth to argue, then huffed out a breath and gestured for her to exit the room.

Ignoring how her trousers and blouse clung to her sweaty body, Zarrah moved into the corridor, her bare feet making no sound as she was led to the doors to the covered walkway, where two of the king's bodyguards waited.

As did an unexpected noise.

Glancing to the walls, Zarrah frowned at the roar emanating from beyond them. It sounded to her like an angry mob. And not one that numbered in the dozens but rather one that numbered in the hundreds. Possibly thousands. "What's going on?"

"Not your concern," the guard snapped. "Hands behind you."

Zarrah allowed him to fasten manacles to her wrists, then a set to her ankles. Normally they didn't bother restraining her until she was about to step into Silas's chambers, and she wondered if the mob was what had provoked the extra caution. What were the people so angry about?

Chains clinking, she walked across the walkway to the tower, her eyes drifting over the gardens below, immediately fixing on Keris.

Her heart skipped, for it had been days since she'd seen his face. Days since she'd heard his voice, and she willed him to look up, needing that connection, but he was deep in conversation with Lestara, several of his younger sisters skipping around them.

"Spends so much time with women, he practically is one," the bodyguard holding her wrists said to his fellow. "Useless weakling. I can't believe he's lasted this long."

It amazed her that these men, trained soldiers, didn't see the truth. When she watched Keris move, she immediately saw the raw strength in the press of muscle against his embroidered coat. The balance and grace in every step that came from a lifetime on rooftops. The swift instincts of one who might choose not to fight but was more than capable of doing so. But it was his intelligence that made him a force to be reckoned with.

And she expected the day these men realized the danger that walked among them, it would be too late.

The guard opened the door to the tower, cool air washing over Zarrah as she started up the endless stairs. They reached the top, and the guards outside the doors to Silas's offices searched her for weapons before allowing her inside.

"Good morning, Zarrah." Silas sat with his boots up on the desk, a glass filled with amber liquid balanced on one knee. Serin stood next to the window behind him, face unreadable. "I have news."

Her heart skipped, then raced.

"The Harendellians sailed into port this morning," he said. "With your aunt's response to my son's proposal."

Sweat broke out on her already-clammy palms. Her aunt hadn't abandoned her. "Oh?"

"I'll allow you to read it yourself." He tossed a folded piece of familiar stationery to her side of his desk, the purple wax of the empress's royal seal snapped in half.

The chains on her wrists rattling, she picked it up and unfolded it, her eyes skimming over the two sentences of text. The familiar signature.

I'll allow my niece to die a thousand deaths before negotiating with a Veliant. Do with her what you will, but be prepared for the consequences.

Petra

Zarrah's stomach hollowed even as a shaking breath exited her lips. She'd known her aunt wouldn't concede to Keris's terms, but she'd thought the empress would draw out the negotiation. Would look for another way to secure Zarrah's freedom. Would buy time for Zarrah to free herself. Not . . . not this.

She read the lines a second time. And a third. Searching for something, anything, that indicated the empress hadn't abandoned her. That she'd fight for her. That she still loved her.

But there was nothing.

Her aunt would allow Silas to kill her before conceding an inch. Would allow him to murder her because her death would put fuel to the fire of the Endless War. As her aunt had used her as a tool in life, she'd now use her as a tool in death.

Zarrah couldn't help but wonder if that meant her aunt had never cared about her at all.

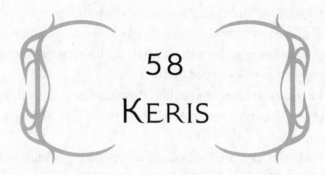

58
KERIS

SINCE THERE WAS NO WAY TO ARRANGE FOR A PRIVATE CONVERsation with Aren, circumstances necessitated doing it in full view of Serin, his father, and all the many watching eyes within the inner sanctum.

Fortunately, Keris was no longer working alone.

"Loud enough that no one can overhear," he murmured to Lestara. "And have the girls block the view of us so that reading lips will be a challenge."

"How do you know he'll come?" she asked.

"Because for one, he's waiting for news that Coralyn met with his people. Two, he's watching us from his window." Leaving her to organize his little sisters, who were all dressed in a rainbow of dazzling silks, Keris stared at the book in front of him, none of the words sinking in.

Be patient, he told himself. *Aren believes he needs you more than you need him.*

If only that were the case.

Long minutes passed, then the sound of footsteps filled his

ears, chains clinking as Aren settled onto the bench across from him. Not wishing to appear eager, Keris refrained from looking up from his book until Aren's guards stepped back. "Good morning, Your Grace. Come to enjoy the brief respite from the storm?"

"Rain doesn't bother me."

"No, I suppose it wouldn't." Keris set his book on a spot on the table that had dried in the sun, then fixed his gaze on the lingering guards. "Is there something you need?"

Both men shifted uncomfortably, probably wondering if they'd be rewarded for allowing Keris to get himself killed. "He's dangerous, Your Highness," one said. "It's best we remain close in case he needs to be restrained. He's very quick."

Keris bent to look under the table at Aren's legs. "He's chained to a stone bench. Just how feeble do you believe I am that I can't outpace a man chained to a bench?"

"His Majesty—"

"Is not here. You two are close enough to be part of the conversation, and from this brief exchange, I can already tell that I've no interest in further discourse with either of you. Plus, you are in the way of my little sisters' practice. Move."

The guards glared at him but complied, though one said, "Scream if he causes you trouble, Highness. It's what the wives have been told to do."

Keris forced his face into a mask of boredom despite the irritation rising in his chest. *Don't worry about what they think,* he told himself. *You can replace them all once you are king.* "Noted."

He turned his attention back to Aren, who was scrutinizing Keris's forearms with a furrowed brow. Tugging down his sleeves, Keris kept his tone bland as he asked, "Now, how might I be of assistance, Your Grace? More reading material, perhaps?"

"As enlightening as your bird book was, I'll pass."

"As you like." Keris tucked his hair behind one ear, which was his signal for Lestara to begin. A moment later, his sisters began to twirl around him and Aren, clapping their hands loudly in time to the music, the scarves they carried obscuring their conversation from view.

"You risk a knife in the back with the way you treat your father's men," Aren said, his gaze moving from the girls back to Keris.

"That risk is there regardless of what I say or do." Keris rested his elbows on the table. "Like my father, they took my lack of interest in soldiering as a personal insult, and short of turning myself into something I am not, there is no path to redemption with either. My bed is made."

Aren rubbed his chin, seeming to consider the words. Seeming to understand that everything, by necessity, would have hidden meaning. "There are ways to popularity other than swinging a sword."

"Like feeding a starving nation?" Keris held a hand to his ear. "Listen. Do you hear them?"

Aren frowned, turning his head outward to listen, the sound of the protests Keris's men had incited a dull roar in the distance.

"A rumor is swirling that you are being tortured for information about how my father might defeat Eranahl," Keris said. "Such dreadful ideas the masses come up with while cooped up during storms. Idle hands may do the devil's work, but idle minds . . ."

Achieved Keris's ends.

"I'm surprised they care."

"Are you?" Keris wrinkled his nose, the humbleness of Aren's words ringing false. "My aunt believes you to be cleverer than you look, but I'm beginning to question her judgment."

"Did you just call me *stupid?*"

Given my sister played you like a fiddle, I can only assume she loves you for your looks, Keris thought, though he said, "If the shoe fits . . ."

Aren didn't rise to the barb, wheels turning behind his hazel eyes, albeit somewhat more slowly than Keris would have liked. Especially given they were short on time. "Allow me to help you along. Would you say that understanding the nature of the Ithicanian people was key to you ruling them successfully?"

"I didn't rule them successfully."

That, you did not. "Don't be morose."

Aren glowered at him, but whether the man liked him or not mattered little. He needed Aren brought back to life and to the forefront of the game, and if it took anger to do it, then so be it. His effort was rewarded as Aren snapped, "Obviously it was key."

"Extrapolate. I'll know from the expression on your face when you come to an understanding."

Aren closed his eyes, taking a deep breath as he thought.

Think faster! Keris silently shouted at him. *We don't have much time.* Then Aren huffed out a quiet breath of understanding. "Finally!" Keris clapped his hands as though in mockery, though in reality, it was a signal to Lestara. "I thought I might have to wait all morning."

"The Maridrinian people don't want the bridge."

"That they do not. They've gained nothing from it, but it has cost them a great deal."

It was like watching fireworks over the harbor, realization after realization flashing over Aren's face. Unable to keep from taking shots at the other man, Keris said, "I imagine this is how parents feel when their child learns to speak. It's tremendously satisfying to see this display of intelligence from you, Your Grace."

"Be quiet," Aren replied, still deep in thought as he mulled over the revelations, and Keris waited for him to understand why his father was so desperate for Eranahl to fall. Then Aren asked, "When will the money run out?"

Keris smiled at a pair of his little sisters as they twirled past him, both girls grinning at him, well aware he was up to something, if not what. "The coffers, I'm afraid to say, are completely dry." Spent paying Amarid for the use of their navy. Spent on Harendellian steel weapons. Spent on paying the wages of thousands of Maridrinian soldiers. And paying the death payments to the families of those who'd fallen.

"You seem remarkably pleased to be heir to a nearly bankrupt kingdom."

"Better *that* than a grave."

Aren made a noncommittal noise, so Keris added, "If Eranahl surrenders, my father won't need the Amaridian Navy any longer. And given he's unlikely to be merciful to those surrendering, Ithicana will no longer be a threat to Maridrina's control of the bridge. My father's position will be the most powerful it has ever been. So you see, Your Grace, a great deal is dependent on the continued survival of your little island fortress."

"First and foremost, your ability to take the Maridrinian crown from your father by way of a coup."

Keris didn't blink. "First and foremost, my *life*. The coup and crown are merely a means to an end." A truth and a lie in one, for if Lara delivered, no coup would be required. But he couldn't reveal her involvement to Aren.

"You're risking a great deal telling me any of this," Aren said. "And I fail to see to what end. My involvement changes nothing. If anything, my death will serve to turn your people further against your father. But I also know we wouldn't be having this conversation if there wasn't something you wanted from me."

This is the moment. And yet despite all the work he'd put toward getting here, Keris found himself unable to voice his request, because it would put Valcotta at risk. Serin might again put Aren to torture, and the king might well give her up in an effort to end his pain.

But it appeared Aren did have a brain between his ears, because he said, softly enough that only Keris could hear, "Zarrah."

How had he guessed? Unease rolled through Keris's chest, but he had to press forward. Had to bait him with the truth so that he'd believe the lie. Keris gave the slightest nod of affirmation, knowing it wasn't just Serin's people watching but Lestara, who'd report everything back to the harem.

"You want me to arrange for her escape."

Keris nodded again, watching as Aren mulled over the confirmation of what he suspected the Ithicanian had guessed long ago. *How did he know?* he wondered. *What gave it away?*

Had anyone else seen what Aren had seen?

"Why do you believe I'd risk my own people to save her when I'm not even willing to risk them to save my own skin?"

He'd taken the bait of the truth, and now Keris needed to hook him with a lie.

"Because," Keris said, "if you do it, she's promised Eranahl will be supplied with enough food to outlast my father's siege."

"I can't see the empress agreeing to that."

"Zarrah's a powerful woman, and the deal is with her, not the empress. Take it or leave it."

She'd be furious at him for making the promise without consulting her, despite the fact that speaking with her had been impossible. But Keris didn't care. Would stoop low and sacrifice every drop of his own honor if that was what it took to get her out of this place.

"Allying with your kingdom's greatest enemy to win the crown." Aren gave a low whistle. "If your people discover that bit of information, it will cost you."

Aren wanted this to work. Keris could see it in his eyes, the glitter of hope where he'd believed there was none. Guilt rose in Keris's chest at the deception, but he quashed it. If Lara succeeded in

assassinating their father, Aren wouldn't need Valcotta's help—
he'd have the King of Maridrina's. "Agreed. Which is why it's much
better for both of us if it's perceived that you and yours were responsible for liberating her."

"You've access to my people now. You don't need me for this."

Keris grimaced, deeply wishing that were the case. "Serin
doesn't trust me, so I'm under near-constant surveillance when I
leave the palace, which means I can't contact your people directly.
I need the harem to facilitate communication. But here's the rub:
They despise Valcottans, so there isn't a chance of them agreeing
to this plan of mine." He probably *could* contact them himself, but
he didn't trust that they wouldn't reveal his request to free Valcotta
to Coralyn.

"And your solution to this rub?"

"The harem won't help me free Zarrah. But they will help free
you." Keris smiled. "Which is why you're going to use them to help
orchestrate your own escape, and when you run, you're going to
take Zarrah with you."

Aren stared at him for a long moment, weighing the risks with
the potential reward. "All right. What do you need from me?"

Keris nearly slumped from the relief that flooded through him.
This was going to work. He was going to *make* it work.

"We can get your people in, likely six of them," he answered.
"What they need is for *you* to figure out a way to escape once they
remove your chains."

Inclining his head, Aren said, "I'll see what I can come up with.
But I think this conversation is over."

Seconds later, boots thudded against the ground, and Keris
turned to find one of his father's personal guards standing behind
him. "His Majesty wants to speak with you, Your Highness," he
said. "Now."

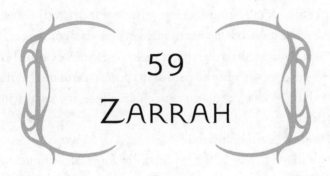

59
ZARRAH

STOMACH HOLLOW AND A DULL ROAR OF NOISE DEAFENING HER ears, Zarrah set the letter back on her enemy's desk.

I'll allow my niece to die a thousand deaths before negotiating with a Veliant. Do with her what you will, but be prepared for the consequences.

It couldn't be real. Couldn't have been written by the same woman who'd come to Zarrah's rescue. Who'd untied her and cleaned away the rot and gore. Who'd raised her like her own child. Who'd made her strong.

Who'd promised her vengeance.

"Not the response you'd hoped for, I'm sure," Silas said, stealing back her attention. "Especially given she was like a mother to you after her sister's death. This must be a tremendous blow."

It wasn't real. Couldn't be. Had to be a forgery. A trick of Serin's hand because he wanted Keris's plans to crumble so that he could see him dead.

As if hearing her thoughts, the Magpie said, "If you doubt its authenticity, I'd be glad to arrange a meeting between you and the Harendellians."

Her jaw trembled, and Zarrah clenched her teeth. But that didn't stop her eyes from burning or her stomach from hollowing as the realization that *this was no trick* sank into her core.

"You thought she'd do what it took to get you back. Truly believed she'd sacrifice her pride to save you." Silas rubbed his stubbled chin. "Which means you are either a fool or caught within her thrall."

Her thrall. Zarrah shivered.

"It's like watching a blind woman see for the first time," Silas said. "What was clear to all around her now revealed in shocking clarity."

Her skin was cold, and for the first time in her life, Zarrah felt as though she stood entirely alone, no one at her back. No one left who cared whether she lived or died, and she had no one to blame but herself.

Silas shifted, his boots thudding against the floor. "Petra leaves me with little choice but to execute you as an enemy of Maridrina."

His words should have provoked fear, but all Zarrah felt was numbness.

A knock sounded at the door, and a guard stepped inside. "His Highness is here, Your Grace."

"Good."

Keris entered, his eyes skipping among the three of them. "You summoned me, Your Grace?"

"Petra has declined to negotiate."

Keris's jaw tightened, but no shock filled his eyes. And Zarrah realized in that moment that he'd anticipated this outcome. That he'd seen the facts and known her aunt wouldn't sacrifice her pride to save Zarrah. Part of her wanted to scream at him, *Why didn't you tell me?*

Except she knew the answer: She wouldn't have believed him.

Just as she hadn't believed Yrina. When it came to her aunt, she'd been, as Silas had said, blind.

Silas said to him, "I told you it wouldn't work, but you needed to see proof with your own eyes that not everything can be resolved with pretty words and negotiation. Sometimes, you have to take what you want by *force*. And sometimes you need to remind your enemies of the consequences of crossing you."

Keris's face drained of color. "We can't execute her. We'd be—"

"Playing into Petra's hands." Silas huffed out an amused breath. "Favor for Petra's pursuit of the Endless War has been in sharp decline over recent years, especially with the rebels in the south contesting her right to the crown at all, for there are many who believe it was not she who was the chosen heir but rather her younger sister." He jerked his chin at Zarrah. "Her mother."

Zarrah blinked, his words entirely unexpected. Especially since she'd never once heard anyone contest her aunt's right to the throne. But before she could give more thought to the comment, Silas continued.

"Petra is using Zarrah's imprisonment as a way to fuel the enmity between our nations, and executing her niece would only add fuel to the fire she's so laboriously built." He smiled. "I'm not in the habit of giving her what she wants, so I'm inclined to keep Zarrah alive for the time being."

Alive.

The word should have filled her with relief, but Zarrah felt nothing. Nothing but a gaping void in her chest left by the stolen certainty of her aunt's love. Her mother had been taken from her. Then Yrina. All she had left was—

"Zarrah will remain my guest in Vencia," Silas said. "But you, Keris, you need to set yourself on a path to becoming a man worthy of the crown. Get your affairs in order and pack your things, then get yourself back to Nerastis."

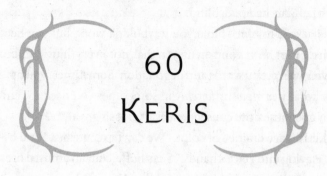

60
KERIS

"YOU NEED TO LEAVE," CORALYN SAID, HER EYES FIXED ON HER fellow wives, who were practicing a dance they never intended to perform. "Then there is no chance of you being seen as culpable. As it is, your father grows weary with your excuses for remaining."

She wasn't wrong.

It had been days since his father had ordered him to depart Vencia, but Keris had been dragging his feet, coming up with reason after reason why he wasn't ready to get on a ship to sail to Nerastis, and his father's temper was burning hot even as Serin's delight grew.

But Keris couldn't leave. *Wouldn't* leave.

Not with this whole rescue scheme hanging in the balance as they waited for Aren Kertell to solve the impossible problem of how to escape an inescapable palace. Not while Valcotta remained a prisoner locked in a gilded cage.

Valcotta. Unbidden, the memory of her face filled his mind, her eyes numb from the revelation that her aunt saw more value in her dead than alive. He couldn't imagine how that felt, for while his own father bore no love for him, neither had he ever pretended to. Silas never portrayed himself as anything other than the heartless asshole that he was, whereas Petra had spent the last decade deceiving Valcotta into the certainty that she was loved, only to betray her at her most vulnerable.

Now all the hope rested on Aren Kertell's shoulders.

Like a caged tiger, Aren tested the limits of his enclosure, never hitting the same place twice. But thus far, all his efforts had yielded was beatings from the guards.

"He's not coming up with anything that I haven't already thought through and dismissed," Keris muttered under his breath. "We've put all our eggs in the basket of a dimwit."

"He's not a dimwit," Coralyn chided, giving him a scowl. "You merely decided to dislike him at some point and refuse to see his attributes. Besides, Lara says he'll deliver, and your sister is most definitely *not* a dimwit."

"Just murderous and backstabbing."

"She is neither of those things." There was anger in his aunt's voice. "I've heard the truth of what occurred in Ithicana from her own lips."

"Truth from the mouth of a trained liar."

"She's got no reason to lie to me."

He snorted. "I'm sure that's what Aren said while he was thrusting away between her legs."

"Keris, shut your goddamned mouth, or I swear, I'll get every woman in the harem in here to hold you down while I wash it clean with soap."

Coralyn didn't make idle threats, so Keris crossed his arms and kept his teeth clamped shut.

"Will you hear her story, or is your intent to remain willfully deaf to anything that contests your misguided opinions?"

A dozen retorts rose to his lips, but his day would not be improved with the taste of soap, so he said, "Fine."

The story that flowed from her was not at all what he expected. And his sister not quite the monster he'd believed.

"They'll never forgive her," he said once Coralyn was finished. "It doesn't matter that it was a mistake, or that Lara didn't intend for it to happen. Thousands of Ithicanians are dead because of her actions, and no amount of atonement will bring them back to life."

"She knows that, and she doesn't seek forgiveness." Coralyn took a mouthful of tea. "But perhaps you might give her yours."

He closed his eyes, remembering his father's men attacking their Ithicanian escort. Remembering how the light faded from Raina's eyes. Remembering when he'd realized that his desire to escape war had been the linchpin in starting one. Remembering how, in that moment, he'd *hated* Lara as much as he did their father.

All that had come to pass might not have been Lara's intent, but that didn't mean it wasn't her fault. And Keris had never been of a forgiving nature. "She's a means to a mutually beneficial end, after which we need never see each other ever again."

"You are so cursedly stubborn," Coralyn snapped. "There is nothing more important than family. Everything you do, every move you make, should be with a mind to protecting your family."

His irritation rose. "I'm planning my own father's assassination and giving the harem what it wants. Isn't that enough for you, Coralyn?"

"If I believed it was *for us,* it would be enough. But I've heard what the people are screaming outside our walls, and it is *your* words coming from their lips. I fear that with the crown on your head, your pursuit of ideals that have no place in our world will be the death of everyone I hold dear."

Unease chased aside Keris's irritation, and he rounded on her. "Just what is it that you think I plan to do?"

"I don't know." His aunt touched her fingers to her temples, closing her eyes. "Promise me, Keris. Promise me that you'll not make decisions that put this family in danger. Promise that you'll put your family first."

"I . . ." It should've been an easy promise, because the last thing he wanted was anything to happen to his aunts or siblings, but the words caught in his mouth. And he was spared having to say anything more when motion outside caught his eye.

Aren threw one of his guards off the side of the covered walkway, the man pulling the Ithicanian king with him. They fell, the guard taking the brunt of the fall in a way that suggested he'd never rise again.

Aren was on his feet, weaving his way through the garden and racing past screaming women, moving as quickly as the chain strung between his ankles would allow.

Alarm bells rang, the guards falling into action, but Aren kept moving, dodging around potted plants and statuary.

"He's heading for the sewer grate," Coralyn said with interest. "Do you suppose—"

Before she could finish, one of the guards struck Aren in the back of the head, knocking him to the ground. More guards dogpiled the king, pinning him down, and Keris watched with grim fascination as his father approached, several of the wives on his heels.

"I could have told him the sewer wouldn't work," Keris muttered, watching his father taunt the Ithicanian king, a smile on his face at however Aren had responded.

"He'll come up with something," Coralyn said. "Have more faith."

A hard thing to do while watching Aren writhe and fight

against the guards like a feral beast, his father giving one final smirk before walking away.

The guards slowly untangled themselves to reveal Aren's form. But instead of glaring at them, Aren was staring at the tower rising above him. Aren's eyes remained on it as the guards dragged him to his feet, but as he walked, his gaze went to the window where Keris and Coralyn stood watching. And he gave the slightest of nods.

Elation flooded Keris, driving away all the anger and uneasiness of Coralyn's accusations, because Aren had figured out a way to escape.

"You'll just have to trust my intentions," he said to his aunt. "Trust that if I'm given the chance to rule, I'll do what I think is right."

His aunt smiled, then wrapped her arms around him, holding him tight in a way she hadn't since he was a boy. "I know you will, dear one. Just as I'll do everything in my power to ensure you succeed."

61
ZARRAH

"Your arms have healed."

Zarrah touched one forearm, the swelling from the blows she'd taken from Otis gone, the bruising faded to yellow that was easily covered by cosmetics. She was lucky he hadn't struck her face, for that would have been a difficult injury to explain, given the story she'd provided Coralyn. "Does that mean I will regain my liberty?"

Long days of being trapped inside her room, seeing no one but Coralyn's trusted servants, had driven her to the point of madness, and she was desperate to step outside. To breathe fresh air again.

"Yes," Coralyn answered, taking a seat and crossing her ankles beneath the chair. "If you play your cards right, these hours will be the last you ever spend within the comfort of my hospitality."

Zarrah's heart skipped, then raced, and it was a struggle not to hold her breath as she waited for the woman to say more.

"Tonight," Coralyn said, "the Ithicanians, with the harem's assistance, will attack during a dinner Silas is hosting for the ambassadors. Their intent is to rescue their king, and I've arranged for them to take you with them. After you kill Silas."

Zarrah blinked in shock, for the last thing she'd expected was a plan of this scope. "Why would they agree to help me? Ithicana and Valcotta are at odds."

"Because I made the harem's assistance conditional upon it. They've given their word."

Zarrah narrowed her eyes, distrust flooding her core. "Why? Why not have the Ithicanians kill him during Aren's rescue, given they certainly have cause? Why involve me at all?"

The old woman lifted one shoulder. "My reasons are manyfold. But the foremost is that you're the only one I trust to kill Silas no matter the personal cost to you. He murdered your mother. Cut off her head and left you tied beneath her body while it rotted. You won't leave him alive."

Zarrah's instincts told her that Coralyn's words were the truth even as they screamed there was far more at play. "Why? Aren and his people desire vengeance against Silas just as much as I do."

A furrow formed in Coralyn's brow, though it swiftly smoothed away. "I fear they'll place rescuing Aren ahead of that vengeance, and I can't risk that. I need certainty, Zarrah. I need to *know* that Silas will breathe his last tonight. If he survives a day longer, my favorite nephew might not."

"You mean Keris." Zarrah's hands turned cold, because she could see the real fear in Coralyn's eyes, and it infected her own heart, though she was careful to keep it from her face.

Coralyn inclined her head. "I assure you, if the situation was not dire, I'd not take these risks. Nor would I lower myself to an alliance with a Valcottan. But the Magpie wants Keris dead, and he's very skilled at getting what he wants."

She wasn't lying.

Zarrah knew better than anyone that Serin had set a target between Keris's shoulders, but she'd also heard Silas forbid any harm to come to his son. "I was under the impression Silas had ordered him to depart to Nerastis, which would put him out of Serin's reach for a time, no? Why are you so desperate, Coralyn?"

"Because he won't leave!" The words exploded from the old woman's lips, and in a flash, she was on her feet. "Cursed, stubborn boy has drawn a line in the sand and refuses to go."

Keris was still here.

She hadn't seen him once since his father had ordered his departure. Although her heart had told her that he wouldn't leave without some form of goodbye, each day that had passed, her uncertainty of whether he remained had grown. Knowing that he hadn't abandoned her filled her with warmth even as concern that he was putting his life at risk to remain ratcheted up her anxiety. "Is Keris involved in your plot with Aren? Is he aware you conspire to kill his father?"

Coralyn waved a hand at her dismissively. "Of course not. He'd never agree to use you as his assassin."

A prickle of suspicion ran across Zarrah's skin because she *knew* Keris had facilitated Coralyn's meeting with Aren at dinner. "Why not? Silas's death serves his ends."

Something flickered in the old woman's gaze, something that looked a great deal like anger, but it was gone in an instant. "You're Valcottan, Zarrah. Using you would violate his rather rigid morals, so it's better not to involve him at all."

Because Keris had been raised to hate Valcottans. Just as she'd been raised to hate Maridrinians.

Zarrah couldn't help but wonder what Coralyn would think if she knew the truth about her and Keris. She'd raised him, which meant it had been *she* who'd attempted to instill that hate in him. That he'd chosen to walk a different path made him a better man in Zarrah's eyes, but Coralyn would see it as a betrayal. The thought filled her with sadness, but her suspicions eased. Not because she trusted the woman but because she knew that Keris would never agree to using Zarrah to assassinate his father, though his reasons were far different from what his aunt realized.

"I know you don't care for Keris," Coralyn said. "To you, he's just the Veliant who captured you and brought you to this prison. But to me, he's the son I never had. There's nothing I wouldn't do to protect him."

To Zarrah's shock, tears spilled down the woman's cheeks. "His younger half brothers have been filtering into Vencia, and I know it's Serin who has lured them here. The Magpie was able to turn Otis—Keris's most loyal brother—against him, so it's only a matter of time until one of the others tries to kill him. And Silas only encourages it. Pits them against one another like dogs, certain that the most vicious is his worthy heir. I . . ." Coralyn trailed off, then scrubbed at her face. "So yes, Zarrah. I'm desperate. But so are you. We could both come out ahead if we set aside our animosities and work together."

A sour taste of anxiety filled Zarrah's mouth as she watched Coralyn pace the room, the underarms of the woman's gown darkening with sweat, her fear very real.

Keris was in danger.

Coralyn was presenting her with the chance not just to kill Silas but to protect Keris. For if Silas was dead, Keris would be king. He could put an end to Serin with an executioner's ax. And that was just the beginning of what he might achieve, especially if the Ithicanians managed to get her out alive. Zarrah could return to Valcotta as the woman who'd killed Silas Veliant with her own hands. An honorable kill. Her aunt would have no choice but to grant her favor, keeping her as heir. And when the day came that she inherited the throne, she fully intended to be the woman who ended Valcotta's role in the Endless War.

Squaring her shoulders, Zarrah met Coralyn's gaze. "Tell me Ithicana's plan."

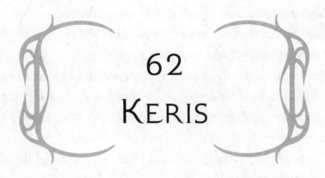

62
KERIS

HE'D WATCHED LARA AND HIS OTHER HALF SISTERS WALK through the gates of the inner sanctum, and if he hadn't known it was them, he'd have been as fooled as the guards who'd searched them.

Dressed in the gowns and scarves of the wives who'd left with Coralyn earlier that day, they'd laughed and chatted with one another as they strolled into the gardens, greeting the women and children they passed by name as they made their way into the harem's house, where they'd remain until the moment they attacked.

No one suspected, not his father, not Serin, not any of the guards, because the harem never risked their own. But tonight, they risked everything to kill his father.

There were a thousand ways this could go wrong, for everything depended on Keris successfully manipulating the players in this vast scheme of moving parts. Depended on him tricking enemies into working with enemies, each of them with a different vision of what the events of tonight would achieve, none aware of the others' goals.

Lara believing she'd get her husband back.

Aren believing he'd gain an ally in saving Ithicana.

The harem believing his father would breathe his last.

The mob believing they'd crown a new king.

They weren't wrong in holding such beliefs, but what none of them realized was that Keris stood at the heart of this scheme and that every move they made was to achieve *his* goal: freeing Valcotta.

It was no small amount of irony that she remained the wild card in this mad plan. Valcotta had no idea what would descend at dinner tonight, no idea the critical role she played, which meant she was walking into the line of fire completely blind. And he had no way to warn her.

Reaching her was impossible.

He knew because he'd tried. Over and over, but between Coralyn and his father's *precautions,* he'd been stymied at every turn.

"You will not attend dinner tonight," Coralyn had ordered him. "If you're there, the survivors will question why you didn't fight. If you do fight, you might get yourself killed. You've done your part. Now let Lara do hers by killing your father. By midnight tonight, you'll be the King of Maridrina."

Which would mean exactly nothing to him if Valcotta didn't get through this dinner unscathed.

She could be killed by his father's guards.

She could be killed by Lara or his sisters.

But what terrified him most was that she'd be seated, unshackled, in a room with his father. The man who'd killed her mother. Who'd ordered the death of Yrina. The man she'd already tried to kill once.

And there was *nothing* to stop her from trying again.

The plan was for him to stay out of it, to let Coralyn ensure all the pieces were in play, to trust that those pieces would do their part. But . . .

"Fuck the plan," he muttered, then pulled on a coat and headed down the stairs.

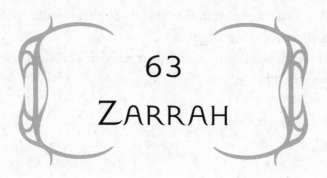

63
ZARRAH

EVERY TIME SHE'D GONE INTO BATTLE, ZARRAH HAD WORN leather and steel and been armed to the teeth. But tonight, in what might be the most important battle of her life, she wore a silk gown and had only a dull nail for a weapon.

It felt like enough.

Her heart beat like a war drum as she made her way to the dining room, guards hurrying to keep up with her long strides. *Wait for the attack before you make your move against Silas,* Coralyn had cautioned. *Do it before all is in place, and you'll ruin any chance of escape.*

When will they attack? Zarrah had asked.

You'll know when the moment is right was the only detail she'd been given, then Coralyn had pressed the precious nail into Zarrah's hand before saying, *Don't fail this time,* and leaving Zarrah in the care of the servants.

She wouldn't fail. She couldn't fail, because this wasn't just vengeance. It was about saving Keris's life.

And saving her own.

"I told you to get yourself to Nerastis!" Silas's voice slapped her in the face as the doors swung open, the king turning to glare at her before rounding back on Keris, who stood before him with his arms crossed. It seemed a lifetime since she'd seen him, and her stomach flipped as she looked him over, struggling to feign disinterest.

"I haven't finished packing."

"You've got an army of servants! Use them!"

Keris shrugged. "Some things are too valuable for me to allow others to pack. Far better for me to do it myself." His eyes flicked to Zarrah, meeting her gaze steadily before moving back to his father. "I'll finish after dinner tonight."

It was a message.

"Forget dinner," Silas barked. "Get back to your rooms, pack up your useless drivel, and get on a ship south. Am I understood?"

"A deal for passage has already been struck with the captain." Keris glanced at Zarrah again, and there was a hint of desperation in his blue eyes that didn't match his bored tone. "Bastard negotiated hard—his family will be eating well for the next few months. Apologies for committing you to the expense without permission."

"Least of my fucking concerns!"

Keris wasn't talking to his father—the words were for her. He was trying to tell her something that couldn't be said in front of his father, and the fact that he was risking it at all meant it was urgent. Before Zarrah could puzzle her way through his coded language, Silas rounded on her. "I will have silence from you tonight, woman. You're attending this dinner as proof your heart still beats, lest your aunt claim otherwise."

He's nervous. Nothing in Silas's expression betrayed the emotion, but Zarrah felt it. Smelled it in the stink of the sweat dampening his collar. And she wondered if some primal part of him sensed that countless individuals who desired him dead would soon descend on him. If he sensed that this night would be his last.

"At least the mob outside our gates doesn't care about her," Keris interjected. "They only care about Aren Kertell. Perhaps you ought to follow his lead, Lady Zarrah. People will do all sorts of things for you if you promise to deliver them from hunger."

Another message, but she had no idea what it meant.

Silas snorted in disgust. "That mob outside is your sister's doing, Keris. Her and Ithicana's desperate attempt to get Aren out in the open. But I've never pandered to the masses, and I won't now. If she wants him, she'll have to come and get him."

"My only regret is not being here to see it," Keris said. "Now, if you'll excuse me, I've packing to get to."

Inclining his head to his father, Keris strode from the room, not giving Zarrah so much as a passing glance.

Leaving her alone with Silas and her guards.

No shackles bound her wrists or ankles, and Zarrah's muscles quivered with the desire to move. To slip the nail hidden in her belt between her fingers, then swing hard, driving the steel into his skull.

As if sensing her thoughts, Silas's eyes fixed on her, his hand drifting to the sword at his waist. The last thing she needed was to be shackled to the table because Silas finally recognized her for the threat she was.

"You seem nervous, Your Grace," she purred. "Please don't tell me that the *great Silas Veliant* is afraid of an unarmed woman."

The guards heard her and stepped forward, but Silas lifted a hand, and they stopped in their tracks. Then he moved.

Zarrah saw it coming. Could have blocked the blow or dodged, but instead she allowed his fist to slam into her cheek.

The blow sent her staggering and she nearly fell, pain ricocheting through her face and her eyes watering. Then he had her by the hair, slamming her down on the table. Glasses shattered, the vase of flowers at the center toppling sideways and spilling its contents across the tablecloth.

"You believe you are untouchable"—his breath was hot against the back of her neck—"but you're not. It serves my purposes to keep you alive, but that doesn't mean I won't hurt you. Doesn't mean I won't make your life a living hell." He twisted his hand in her hair, her neck screaming as he forced her to look up at him. "Once Eranahl falls, I will turn my eyes south to Valcotta. And when I march, I have every intention of carrying your corpse as my banner."

He jerked her like a rag doll, forcing her down in her chair. "Get a servant in here to clean her up," he snarled at the guards. "Before the ambassadors arrive."

Her face ached, and her skull burned where he'd torn out her hair, but Zarrah still struggled not to smile as he strode from the room, her wrists and ankles remaining unshackled. *Your pride will be your downfall,* she silently whispered, then sat still while a servant woman repaired her smeared cosmetics, several others hastily setting the table to rights.

They'd barely finished when more guards arrived with Maridrinian noblemen, and on their heels arrived the ambassadors from Harendell and Amarid, as well as several others she didn't recognize.

"We were sorry to bring such disappointing news," the Harendellian ambassador said to her as he took his place. "We'd hoped the empress would see the merit of negotiation, but it seems the bad blood between your nations outweighs her affections."

His words sent a lance of pain through her chest, but Zarrah only inclined her head. "She must make decisions that are for the good of Valcotta, not the good of her heart. Though I appreciate your efforts."

"It is always the hope that one can avert war through one's efforts," he answered. "But I think there is no averting this one."

"Maridrina and Valcotta have been at war for generations," she said, eyes skipping down the table to where Coralyn was seating herself.

"Raids and skirmishes and blockades are not war, girl," the ambassador said. "You aren't old enough to have seen what happens when two nations matched in hatred truly collide. The skies will turn black from the ash of the dead."

Unease flitted through Zarrah's chest, but before she could answer him, Aren Kertell entered the room, all eyes going to him.

He took his usual seat at the end of the table, nodding and offering courtesies to Coralyn while his chains were secured. Zarrah couldn't make out what the old woman said to him in response, but her face turned serious, and she pressed her hand against his. Zarrah's heart skipped, then sped, because it was the first proof that this escape plot was real, not a trick on the harem's part to get Zarrah to do their dirty work.

Her gaze moved around the table, searching the faces of the unfamiliar men. She'd presumed them ambassadors or noblemen, but was it possible they were Ithicanians in disguise? Except even if they were armed, there weren't enough of them to overwhelm the guards standing around the perimeter.

Silas stormed into the room, not surrounded by his wives, as was his custom, but very much alone. He barked, "Where are they? If you begin shirking your duties, your days of extravagance at the Sapphire Market will come to an end."

Coralyn inclined her head. "The harem's girls will be along shortly, *husband*. They've prepared a performance for you. Given the effort they've put into making it memorable, you might consider giving them your full attention when they arrive."

Zarrah kept her face smooth even as she slipped the nail from her belt, placing it between the knuckles of her closed left fist. This was it. This was the moment, and she readied herself to strike when the Ithicanians exploded through the door. She'd only have a heartbeat before Silas got his weapon out, and she needed to make it count.

A glowering Silas flung himself into his chair, immediately downing a glass of wine, oblivious to the fact death sat at arm's reach.

"Your Grace," the Amaridian ambassador said, "have you had a chance to respond to my queen's letter?"

"The letter demanding payment?" Silas snarled. "Perhaps you might explain to me why I should pay her anything, given that Amarid has failed to uphold its end of the bargain?"

The man's ears turned red. "How so? You've had full access to our naval fleet for *months*."

Zarrah only vaguely heard their argument, her ears trained on the closed doors, listening for the sound of running feet or fighting. For anything that would give her the ounce of warning she needed to leap to her feet and swing her spiked fist at Silas's skull.

But there was nothing.

Servants stepped in, bearing the salad course, and Zarrah ate methodically, the food tasting like sawdust. Where were they? Where were the Ithicanians?

Perhaps they'd been caught.

Perhaps they'd never been coming at all.

Salad stuck in her throat, and she choked, needing to take several gulps of wine to ease her coughing.

"You all right, dear?" the Harendellian asked. "Do let me know if you need—"

The main door flung open, and Zarrah lurched upward. Only to freeze at the familiar sight of the harem's musicians.

Two men pounding vigorously on drums, followed by another two shaking cymbals. Zarrah eased back into her seat as they circled the table, taking up positions on opposite sides of the room. They kept up the furious beat, then with a resounding thunder went silent.

The guards' eyes were on the open door, and Zarrah glanced down the table of men to see if this was the distraction, if this was the moment when Ithicana would strike, but all the men were watching the doorway with interest.

So she turned her head to see what they were gaping at.

Six harem wives had appeared. They were dressed in gossamer silks that concealed little of their bodies but most of their faces. The bells fastened to their wrists and ankles tinkled a soft music, but it was the drums of her own heart that filled Zarrah's ears because she saw what the men did not. Her eyes flicked over the dancers' bodies, seeing the hard muscles of their arms. Seeing the faint marks of scars on their skin, visible through the cosmetics that attempted to hide them. Seeing the vibrant azure of their eyes, the color sending adrenaline roaring through her veins.

None of the women were harem wives. But neither were they Ithicanian.

Zarrah held her breath, waiting for the men to see what she saw. For *Silas* to notice that none of these dancers were his wives.

No one said a word.

Because they saw only what Coralyn intended them to see. Curved breasts barely concealed by thin bodices, the rose hue of the women's peaked nipples visible through the fabric, as was the apex of their thighs each time they passed before a lamp. The men gaped at the display of female flesh, the one man who should be able to identify them too busy glaring at Coralyn to see the truth.

It wasn't wives circling the room; it was Silas Veliant's daughters.

A lithe woman began to dance, the tiny shakes of her wrists making the bells decorating them jingle softly. She swayed through an elaborate set of steps, hips moving from side to side seductively. Her blond hair was streaked with lighter strands from hours in the sun but otherwise was an identical color to Keris's. The others joined her, replicating her motions in perfect unison, the musicians creating a rhythm, but Zarrah kept her attention on the blonde.

She circled the table, bare feet rapidly striking the floor in a complicated series of steps that filled the air with music. She spun, long locks swinging out behind her before falling to brush against her naked lower back. There was a predatory grace to her, and every muscle in Zarrah's body tensed with certainty that this woman was *dangerous*.

They all were.

Yet the men at the table were oblivious to the knowledge they were being circled not by women but by hunters. By tigresses costumed to look like housecats.

It was only a matter of time until they pounced, and Zarrah needed to be ready when they did.

The blond woman rounded behind Silas, and Zarrah watched her lift her face, gaze upon the opposite end of the table. Out of the corner of her eye, Zarrah watched Aren's face blanch of all color.

It was all the confirmation that Zarrah needed: The woman was Lara Veliant, the traitor queen of Ithicana, Aren's wife and Keris's younger sister.

The thought of him sent a jolt of memory through her. *If Lara wants him, she'll have to come and get him.*

What had Keris responded? Zarrah dug into her memory, but the words were already bubbling up to meet her.

My only regret is not being here to see it.

Keris knew Lara was coming tonight. Knew about Coralyn's plans, despite the woman saying otherwise. Yet he'd been warning Zarrah of what was to come, which suggested he was unaware Coralyn had involved her, otherwise why take the risk? Zarrah stared blindly at the dancers, digging through her memory of the conversation.

A deal for passage has already been struck with the captain. Bastard negotiated hard—his family will be eating well for the next few months. Apologies for committing you to the expense without permission.

The captain . . . it had to be Aren whom Keris had negotiated with, the passage her escape, except she'd already known that. Coralyn had told the Ithicanians her assistance was predicated on them taking Zarrah with them.

Perhaps you ought to follow his lead . . . People will do all sorts of things for you if you promise to deliver them from hunger. Zarrah silently swore, realizing that Coralyn had lied. The Ithicanians weren't taking her with them in exchange for the harem's assistance; they were taking her because Keris had committed *her* to supplying Eranahl.

And she was supposed to follow Aren's lead.

Except the King of Ithicana was gaping at his dancing wife, clearly shocked by her presence.

He wasn't the master of this plan, only a piece on the board of . . . of whose scheme? Who had masterminded this plan? Keris or Coralyn? Zarrah wasn't certain, but it was very clear that the two were not entirely aligned.

The drums took on a frenzied pace, finishing the piece with a rattling crash of cymbals as each of the women struck a final pose, though Zarrah's pulse remained frenetic as she waited for them to make their move.

Because when they did, she'd make hers.

"Well done!" Coralyn cried out, clapping her hands. "Beauti-fully performed, my lovely girls. Weren't they stupendous, Silas?"

Silas gave her a sour smile. "Wonderful, if somewhat over-loud." Then he waved a dismissive hand, and the young women backed into the shadows of the walls, heads lowered.

All, that is, but one.

Lara took three quick steps and jumped, landing on the center of the table like a cat, glassware rattling.

"What are you doing, woman?" Silas demanded. "Get down and get out before I have you whipped."

"Now, now, Father." Lara walked down the table, kicking over glasses of wine with every step, and Zarrah shivered, hearing Keris in her voice. "Is that any way to greet your most *favored* of children?"

Silas's eyes widened as she pulled away the veil concealing her face and allowed it to flutter down onto a plate. Zarrah's chest tightened, because there was no mistaking her as anything but Keris's flesh and blood.

"You little fool." Silas rose to his feet and pulled his sword. "Just what did you think to accomplish by coming here tonight?"

Hard as it was, Zarrah tore her attention from Lara to glance to the shadows where the other women were cowering behind the guards, sobbing in feigned fear and begging the men to protect them.

Lara wasn't the threat. She was the distraction.

The other dancers moved, hands flitting out to palm knives from the belts and boots of the soldiers whose eyes and weapons were trained on the Ithicanian queen.

"You lied to me. Manipulated me. Used me—not for the benefit of our people, but for your own benefit. To satisfy your own greed." Lara's voice filled her ears, and Zarrah felt the other wom-an's fury. *Knew* that fury, because it burned in her own heart.

Zarrah tore her gaze from Lara and her sisters and found Coralyn wasn't watching them. She was staring at Zarrah with such hatred that it was hard not to recoil. Not the political hate between people of enemy nations—this hatred was personal.

Zarrah's skin turned to ice, dread filling her stomach, some sixth sense telling her why Coralyn despised her so much.

She knew.

Coralyn knew there was something between Zarrah and Keris, and she hated Zarrah for it. Hated her for pulling her precious *son* away from the path she intended for him.

The path to the throne.

Though Coralyn had been clear about her intentions, Zarrah only now truly understood them. Coralyn hadn't brought Zarrah here just to ensure Silas died. She'd brought her here to kill any chance of Keris pursuing peace with Valcotta. To kill any chance of Keris pursuing Zarrah by ensuring she murdered Silas in front of the ambassadors, who were impartial witnesses.

Kill him, Coralyn mouthed. *Have your vengeance.*

There was a time Zarrah would have leapt at that chance. Would have seen no greater honor than putting this vile man who'd caused so much harm, had caused *her* so much harm, in his grave. But now . . . now she saw how the consequences of her actions would unfold. How word would spread that the King of Maridrina had been slaughtered in his own house by a Valcottan, and Silas would cease to be a monster to his people.

He'd be a martyr.

As Silas's heir, Keris would have no choice but to march his armies south in pursuit of blood and vengeance, for to pursue peace in the face of his father's murder would be nothing short of suicide. And the empress would meet him head-to-head, generations of hatred culminating in a war of such violence that the ground would be soaked with blood. Thousands dead. Thousands more orphaned.

And for what?

So Zarrah could have a moment of righteous delight in achieving vengeance for her mother's murder? So that she could go back to Valcotta and be honored by the empress who'd abandoned her? Was what she'd gain worth the horror she'd be unleashing on so many others?

It was not. Seeing it so clearly now, Zarrah questioned how she'd ever thought it could be.

There was nothing to be gained from her killing Silas tonight, not even the knowledge it would protect Keris. Because if she killed his father, it would mean condemning him to a fate he'd see as worse than death.

Zarrah refused to do that to him.

So she met Coralyn's gaze and mouthed, *No.*

Panic flooded the old woman's face even as Lara's laugh filled the room, Keris's sister declaring, "Do you really think that I'm such a fool as to come alone?"

The sisters cowering in the shadows moved as one, slitting the guards' throats with shocking proficiency, gurgles filling the air even as bodies thudded to the ground. Then they dropped their veils, saying in unison, "Hello, Father."

In that moment, Zarrah could have closed the distance between her and Silas and put that nail in his skull. Could have satisfied the need that had driven her for so many long years. But she merely took a steadying breath as the room erupted into chaos.

Guests screamed and scrambled toward the door, colliding with what remained of Silas's guards as they moved to attack his daughters. But the women only picked up the swords of their victims and met the men blow for blow, cutting them down.

"Never mind *them*—get *her!*" Silas shouted at his guards.

The men all rushed Lara, and Zarrah kicked off her high-heeled shoes, not willing to let the woman stand alone. She picked up her chair and swung it at one of the guards, smashing him in the head. The wood broke, and holding tight to one of the legs, she struck him again, blood splattering her dress.

Whirling, she saw Coralyn unchaining Aren, Silas's shriek of "Kill him! Kill the Ithicanian!" filling her ears.

Follow his lead. Keris's voice rippled through her thoughts, reminding her that Coralyn wasn't the only one with a plan. Yet it wasn't her dependence on Aren for escape that had Zarrah moving, it was that she refused to stand by and watch another Ithicanian die.

Guards leapt to attack, and Zarrah swung her fist, the nail that had nearly been her damnation now Aren's salvation as the steel plunged into the guard's ear. He dropped, and Zarrah plucked up his knife, moving on to the next.

The noblemen, seeming to sense that if they didn't fight, they'd die, picked up fallen weapons and flanked Silas. With steel in their hands, they rallied around their king, now a force to be reckoned with. The ambassadors cowered in the corners, looking like they weren't certain which side they were on.

Loud hammering split the air.

Zarrah's eyes jerked toward the door. The thick wood shuddered with each blow, guards on the other side trying to break through. When they did, she and her allies would be outnumbered to the point where no amount of skill would see them through this alive.

She searched the room for a way out, but with the windows behind the curtains barred and with soldiers on the opposite sides of both doors, they were trapped.

Hands closed on her shoulders.

Zarrah twisted to attack, only to find Aren behind her. He hissed, "All this is for nothing if you get killed!"

Because Keris had made a promise on her behalf to supply Eranahl. Aren wasn't doing this to save himself but to save his people, and so she didn't struggle as he dragged her backward and pushed her behind a velvet curtain.

The windows were painted black, allowing in no light, but Zarrah grabbed hold of the bars over them, pulling as hard as she could before moving onto the next, finding every one of them secure. *What in the name of God was their plan?*

Did they even *have* a plan?

Wood cracked and splintered.

Tightening her grip on her knife, Zarrah stepped out from behind the curtain, ready to fight. A large gash had formed in the door, the soldiers on the other side almost through. But that wasn't what stole her attention: It was Coralyn.

"Did you think we'd let you get away with it, Silas? Let you get away with stealing our children?" Coralyn shouted. "With murdering our children? Did you think there wouldn't be a price to pay for your greed?"

She was taking credit. Taking the fall.

Like a mother—flawed and imperfect as she was—Coralyn was protecting her child.

"I'm going to gut you for this, you old bitch!"

"By all means, Silas, please do!" Coralyn laughed. "It will entertain me in the afterlife to watch how well you sleep knowing that every wife you have and every wife you ever take will be watching and waiting for a moment to get revenge for what you've done. The harem protects its own, and you've proven yourself our *enemy*. I think you'll not drop those trousers of yours so easily knowing that all the pretty mouths you surround yourself with have teeth. So by all means, Silas. Martyr me. All it means is that I'll have an exceptional vantage point to watch you pay for your crimes."

The split in the main door widened. They had only seconds. Zarrah lifted her weapon, ready to die fighting if that was what it came to.

But Coralyn extracted a glass jar from the folds of her dress and threw it to the ground. Thick, choking smoke filled the room, and a hand caught Zarrah's arm, Aren's voice shouting, "Get behind the table and cover your ears!"

Zarrah threw herself over the table and landed with a thump between Lara and one of the other women, all of them coughing from the smoke. But it wasn't to Keris's sister that her attention went but to Coralyn, who stood upright and in defiance between them and Silas.

Without thinking, Zarrah lunged, tackling the old woman to the ground. She'd barely managed to clamp her hands over her ears when a deafening boom split the air.

Glass and bits of stone rained down on her, so hot they burned the skin they touched, but Zarrah only gritted her teeth as she pushed herself upright.

"Go!" Coralyn wiped blood from her face. "Run, you useless bitch!"

"Silas will kill you if you stay." She could barely get the words out between coughs. Wasn't entirely certain why she was bothering, only knew that Coralyn's death would shatter Keris to the core.

"Someone has to take the blame, and I won't let it be him." The old harem wife shoved at her. "Tell Keris I love him."

Before Zarrah could say another word, Coralyn strode into the haze. Slender fingers gripped Zarrah's wrist, dragging her toward the broken window. Through the smoke, Zarrah made out blond hair, and then Lara's voice demanded, "Who is she?" before she shoved Zarrah toward Aren.

"Later." The King of Ithicana's voice was clipped. "Climb!"

Ripping the skirt of her dress so that her legs were free, Zarrah jumped up onto the window frame, climbing the side of the harem building, a knife clenched between her teeth. One of the other women pulled her over the balcony railing and pushed her inside with a whispered warning of "Stay silent."

The alarm bells rang loud enough to make her head ache, but it served well to cover their passage as they strode through the corridors. "How much did he tell you?" Aren asked her.

"Only to follow your lead." At least, to a point. Keris's voice rippled through her memory: *Some things are too valuable for me to allow others to pack. Far better for me to do it myself.* However Aren planned to get out of the palace, she wouldn't be going with him— Keris had a different plan.

As if hearing her thoughts, Aren asked, "Do you trust him?"

With my heart. "With my life."

They ran down the hall, carpets muffling their footfalls as they exited into one of the covered walkways. The interior was dark, but the smoke of the recently extinguished lamps still hung in the air. Outside, thick mist rose from the fountains, the effect eerie and strange.

Once they'd entered the tower, the group raced up the stairs, but Zarrah slowed as they reached the door to Keris's chambers. He knew the plan. Knew they'd be coming this way, so it would make sense that he was here.

Zarrah lifted a hand to reach for the handle, but before she could grasp it, the door opened and Keris stepped out.

And nearly lost his head to Lara's blade. Zarrah lunged, but Aren was faster, catching his wife's wrist, hauling her back.

"Who is he?" Lara demanded.

Keris inclined his head. "It's been a long time, little sister. I wish we could've reunited under better circumstances."

Lara's eyes widened, the queen clearly unaware that her brother had been involved in the scheme. "*Keris?*"

He smiled, but it didn't reach his eyes, and Zarrah wondered if Lara noticed. If she cared.

"You're helping us?" Lara asked.

"I'm helping myself," Keris answered. "But tonight, our interests are aligned."

His gaze moved past his sister to Zarrah, and she instinctively stepped toward him, closing her eyes as his hand curved around her face, thumb brushing her cheek. "Are you all right?"

Her skin stung from a dozen little burns inflicted by the explosion, and her eye was nearly swollen shut from Silas's punch, but Zarrah barely felt the pain through the adrenaline coursing through her veins. "It's nothing."

He gave a slight nod, then said to Aren, "This is where you part ways with the general."

"I don't think so," Aren snapped. "Zarrah's coming with us. I intend to make sure she delivers on her end of the deal."

Make her? Zarrah ground her teeth at the insult, but Keris had already stepped between them. "There's too much chance of you being caught or killed. And her life is more important than yours. While everyone is pursuing you, I'll get her out."

There was merit to them splitting up, for it meant more chance of one of them getting out alive. Which meant more of a chance that someone would escape to help the Ithicanians starving in Eranahl.

Which Aren had to know, yet he showed no signs of conceding. "I'm just your goddamned decoy?" he snarled.

Keris tensed, radiating irritation, though nothing showed on his face as he said, "Precisely. But given my plan is more likely to achieve that which you desire, perhaps you'll refrain from whining. Time is short." Keris pushed Zarrah toward the open door, but before she could move, Aren caught her arm, his fingers digging into her flesh.

Zarrah's temper flared, then softened as she saw the desperation in the Ithicanian king's eyes. His need to know for certain that this wouldn't be for nothing.

"On my word, if I get out alive, I'll have supplies delivered to drop points in Ithicana, where your people can reach them." Zarrah touched her hand to her heart. "Good luck, Your Grace."

And then, knowing this might be the last time she ever saw Aren Kertell alive, Zarrah stepped into the room.

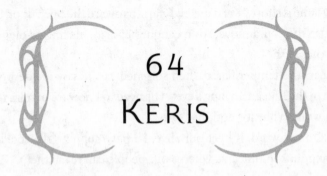

64
KERIS

AREN TOOK A STEP AS THOUGH HE INTENDED TO FOLLOW VAL-
cotta into the room and drag her back out again, and Keris's temper flared. He blocked the man's path. "Time for you to carry on.
But before you go, I need you to make it look like I at least *tried* to
stop you."

Not his favorite part of the plan, but if he were to get Valcotta
out of the palace safely, it was necessary that his innocence in
what happened tonight be unquestioned.

Aren opened his mouth as though to argue, then sighed.
"Gladly." Then he swung.

Instinct demanded that he dodge, but instead, Keris held his
ground, taking the blow.

Pain lanced through his face, and Keris stumbled backward,
catching himself on the doorframe. He touched his swelling cheek,
a black eye inevitable. "You have ten minutes until I start down to
alert the guards. Make them count."

He didn't watch them continue up the stairs, instead stepping
inside and shutting the door, which he bolted. He turned to ensure

Valcotta was truly all right, but before he could say a word, her arms were around his neck, her mouth on his.

Zarrah claimed his lips as though she intended to claim his very soul, though in truth, she possessed it already. Even if she were the devil herself, he was too bespelled by her, too lost in the feel of her, too captivated by the sound of her ragged breathing to care. She pulled on his lower lip with her teeth, driving his lips apart. Logically, Keris knew this wasn't the time, but he yielded to her anyway. The kiss deepened, her tongue slipping into his mouth, sliding over his. He groaned, wanting to pull the clothes from her body, wanting to taste her, to lose himself in the scent of her, because her presence had turned his blood scalding with the need to have her. To push her against the wall and claim her as thoroughly as she had claimed him.

The clock on the wall chimed, and his eyes flicked to it. Everything was on schedule. Everything was going according to plan. They had a few moments before he needed to head downstairs, and there was a great deal he could do in a few moments.

Then Valcotta pulled her mouth from his and said, "Your father is still alive."

Keris's skin turned to ice even as his stomach dropped. "What?"

"At least, I believe he is. There is a chance that he was killed in the blast, but I don't think we'll get that lucky."

"*Lara,*" he seethed, furious at himself for having trusted she'd deliver. Furious that he'd allowed himself to rely on a woman notorious for betrayal. "That was the deal. Our help in exchange for her putting a knife in my father's heart."

Valcotta blew a breath out between her teeth. "The deal according to whom?"

He blinked. "Coralyn."

"She lied—Lara made no such promise." Valcotta took a step toward him, then hesitated, as though she wasn't certain how he'd react. "She likely deceived you because she knew the only way you'd agree to this scheme was if you believed your father wouldn't survive it."

His spine stiffened, and he gave a sharp shake of his head, eyes snapping to the clock. "No, *she's* the one who would never agree to it—the risk to the harem would be too great."

"Which is why she set me up to do it." Valcotta's throat moved as she swallowed, and she crossed her arms over her chest. "It wasn't the first time. It was Coralyn who arranged for me to try to kill him that night in the tower, although I didn't know it until after the fact. She wanted me to try again, but I refused to do it unless she found a way for me to escape, which she did. Or you did. I . . ." She trailed off. "I had a chance to kill him, but I didn't do it. If he'd died by my hand, he'd become a martyr in the Endless War."

A dull roar filled Keris's ears, and it wasn't just that his plans had crumbled to dust but that his aunt had been attempting to use Valcotta right under his nose. He should've anticipated her meddling. Should've known she was up to something, but never in his wildest dreams had he believed she'd ally with a Valcottan just for the sake of killing his father. Still couldn't believe it. "Where is Coralyn? What happened?"

"She took credit for the plan. Then refused to leave with us." Valcotta's jaw quivered, her eyes fixed on his chest. "She told me to tell you that she loves you."

If his father was alive, and Coralyn had taken the blame for Aren's escape, then . . . "I have to help her."

Valcotta caught hold of his arm, dragging him back. "You can't help her, Keris. If you try, your father will only become convinced of your involvement and will kill you, too. Which will mean her sacrifice was in vain."

He pulled out of her grip, pressing his fingers to his temples, trying to think. But it was impossible when he considered what might be happening to his aunt at this very moment. "I should have sent you with Aren. I . . . You need to go. If you hurry, you'll catch them at the top." And at least Valcotta would have a chance of getting free.

"I'm not going with Aren." Her hands closed over his wrists, pulling them to his sides. "Because if I go, you'll do something stupid and brave and get yourself killed. And I refuse to let you die, Keris Veliant."

"Then you're condemning yourself, because my plan no longer exists." He met her gaze, silently pleading with her to go. "You need to leave with Aren. He'll get you out or die trying, that much I know."

"Then why didn't you send me with him in the first place?" She locked her fingers with his, squeezing hard. "Because you didn't like their plan? Or you had a better one?"

Because he didn't trust anyone other than himself to keep her safe. "Both."

"What was it?"

He felt like he couldn't breathe, visions of what his father might be doing to his aunt filling his head. Why had she lied about Lara's intentions? Why had she tried to get Valcotta to do the deed?

"You might never know the truth behind Coralyn's motivations," she said, seeming to sense his thoughts. "And we don't have time to deliberate. You've three minutes to explain the rest of your plan to me, and then you need to go down those stairs and cover our tracks. Do *not* destroy the chance Coralyn's gifted you."

Keris scrubbed at his face, wincing as he pressed against his swollen cheek. *Focus!* he shouted at himself. *You have the rest of your life to hate yourself for tonight's mistakes.* "Everyone will be chasing after Aren. The chances of him getting out of the city are slim, but he'll die before he's captured again. I was going to hide you, then sneak you out when—" When he was king, when he had control. He swallowed. "When it was safe to do so."

"How?" she asked, and Keris turned to the chest that traveled everywhere with him. He unlocked the lid, lifting out stacks of books until the bottom was revealed.

The false bottom.

Zarrah's eyes moved to the clock. "One minute."

They were out of time, so he spoke quickly. "I came up with the idea weeks ago but dismissed it. Your absence would be discovered immediately, and I'd be the obvious culprit. But everyone thinks that you've escaped with Aren, so no one will have reason to suspect me." He pressed a tiny button on the carved exterior, which popped up the false bottom. "You'll need to hide in here."

Zarrah stared at the chest, her throat moving as she swallowed. She hated this plan; that much was obvious. She wanted to fight her way free, not hide in a box, and he almost wished such a thing were possible. "Valcotta—"

"Lock me inside in case someone searches your room. And then you need to go."

She lay on her side on the blanket he'd padded the bottom with, her knees curled up, feet bare. His heart was racing, fear and nerves prickling his skin, because he didn't want to close the lid on her. It was too much like closing a coffin. "Ready?"

"Yes." She caught hold of his hand, pulling him down and kissing him hard enough to bruise both their lips. "We're going to get through this. All you need to do is ensure that *no one* suspects you, especially your father."

Praying she was right, Keris lowered the panel over the top of her, the latch clicking into place. Then he swiftly loaded the books inside and closed the lid.

It was time.

Taking a deep breath, he strode to the door and threw it open, leaving it that way as he hurried down the stairs, shouting, "Guards! Guards! They're in the tower!"

He raced down the curved stairs. When he'd nearly reached the second floor, he rounded the corner and almost collided with the men running toward the sound of shouts.

Their eyes widened at the sight of his eye, which was nearly swollen shut thanks to Aren and his fist, and Keris snarled, "They've gone up to the top of the tower, you fucking idiots! Go!"

The men barreled past him, and Keris continued down to the ground level. "Let me out," he ordered the men guarding the door.

"It's not safe, Your Highness. The Ithicanian—"

"Is at the top of the tower, and he has my Valcottan prisoner with him! Where is my father? Where is Serin? Who is in command of this mess?"

Instead of answering, the soldier unlatched the door and flung it open, calling, "They're in the tower!"

Pushing past, Keris ignored the dozen men who ran by him and strode into the gardens before looking up.

The air was thick with the misty fog emanating from the dozen canisters the harem had placed in the fountains, but the rising wind was whisking the cover away. And as he watched, Keris picked out the flash of a shadow flying down from the top of the tower and over the heads of the guards on the inner wall.

He wasn't the only one who noticed.

Shouts of alarm filled the air but were drowned out a few seconds later by a large *boom,* a flash of light from the exterior gate illuminating the night.

All around him was chaos and confusion as the soldiers split their ranks, half mistakenly running into the tower and the other half, understanding that their quarry was outside the sanctum, heading to the gates to them.

Get to the horses, he silently willed his sisters, running toward the sanctum's gates, though he could do nothing to help them at this point. *Get into the city.*

Because if they got caught inside the walls, his father's men would *know* Valcotta was still in the palace.

The elaborate gates to the sanctum were open, and Keris raced through, carnage greeting him. All around the large courtyard, soldiers screamed and clutched their blown-out eardrums, some—those closest to the gate—lying still, likely never to move again.

A group of his father's men raced out of the stable, throwing themselves onto their horses and galloping off in pursuit of the decoys outside the wall.

Keris held his breath. Waiting. Waiting.

Then another group on horseback emerged. He clenched his fists, certain the soldiers milling around would see what he saw: figures too small and lithe to be men, and one overlarge form that bounced wildly in the saddle, reins flopping loose in his hands.

Bastard doesn't know how to ride. Keris ground his teeth, praying that this small yet critical detail wouldn't entirely ruin their escape. Then they were gone. What Lara intended to do next, he didn't know. And to be frank, as long as they didn't get caught and betray Valcotta, he didn't fucking care.

"What do you mean, they've escaped?"

Keris turned at the sound of his father's voice, watching him storm out of the sanctum gates, soot staining his face and wine splattering his clothes. But still very much in command.

And very much fucking alive.

Girding himself, Keris approached, but his father was too busy shouting orders to acknowledge him.

"They went up the tower," he interrupted. "The Ithicanian and a group of women, including Zarrah Anaphora."

His father's lip curled, eyes taking in Keris's swollen face. "And I see you did little to stop them."

Keris crossed his arms. "I wasn't expecting to come face-to-face with a group of armed women outside my goddamned bedroom door. How did this happen?"

"Coralyn."

It took all of Keris's self-control not to flinch. "What are you talking about?"

"The old bitch arranged it as retribution. Stabbed me in the back."

"Where is she?"

If his father heard the question, he didn't bother responding, only shouldered Keris out of the way to take reports from his men.

There was part of him that wanted to press his father for more information about Coralyn. But he'd accomplished what he needed to—bolstering the lie that Zarrah was with Aren and Lara. Which meant that, for now, outside the walls would be the only place they were looking for her, and he could turn toward finding answers about his aunt's fate.

Keris went first to the destroyed dining room, but the only bodies were those of soldiers, so he headed into the harem's quarters.

It was eerily silent.

He proceeded down the hall to the grand suite of rooms Coralyn occupied, his heart skipping at the sight of the open door.

Then Serin's voice reached his ears. "Who else was involved?"

"I already told you, *Magpie*, we don't know. This is Coralyn's doing."

Lestara.

Pulse hammering in his throat, Keris stepped into the room, finding six of his aunts on their knees before Serin. The wives were all red-eyed and tear-streaked, three of them actively weeping.

His temper simmering, Keris snapped, "You'd better have a good explanation for this, Magpie. And an even better explanation for why the woman *you* trained has escaped the palace with *both* of our prisoners. This is a truly spectacular fuck-up on your part. If I were you, I'd be trying to put as much distance between me and my father as possible rather than abusing his favorite wives."

The Magpie's eyes darkened. "Coralyn conspired with Lara to free the Ithicanian."

"So I've been told. Yet it isn't Coralyn you're interrogating." Even as he spoke, Keris silently whispered, *Please don't let her be dead.*

"She's indisposed," Serin replied. "And we're rather short on time, Your Highness. If we don't capture them soon, we never will."

Indisposed could mean any number of things, and none of them eased the twist of fear in his chest. "Then why are you wasting time talking to these women?" Reaching down, he took Lestara's hand and drew her to her feet. "Instead of punishing my aunts for *your* failure to predict the actions of the woman *you* trained, perhaps you might turn your attention to hunting my wayward sister down!"

Ignoring Serin's glare, he helped the rest of the women rise, motioning for them to leave. Then he rounded on the Magpie. "Where is Coralyn? What have you done to her?"

"Nothing your father didn't ask me to," Serin answered. "The old bitch is finally going to get what she deserves for her meddling."

Keris's control snapped.

Grabbing the spymaster by the front of his robes, Keris slammed him against the wall, pressing his forearm against the man's throat. "Where. Is. She?"

Serin glared at him, but as Keris pressed hard enough to cut off his air, the glare turned to panic, and he gave a tight nod. Gasping in a few breaths, he said, "You know where he puts wives that anger him."

Suddenly, it was Keris who felt like he couldn't breathe.

They'd put Coralyn in the hole.

65

ZARRAH

THE CHEST PRESSED IN ON ALL SIDES, THE AIR THICK AND UN-breathable and filled with the scent of her own sweat. Zarrah's breath came in fast little pants, every part of her wishing that she could be on her feet with a weapon in hand. Turning her head, she pressed her lips to the hole that Keris had drilled in the chest, suck-ing in mouthfuls of air as she sought some degree of calm.

She was a warrior. Her strengths were tied to the battlefield. Not to scheming and strategizing, and most certainly not to hid-ing in a box so that she might escape like a piece of contraband.

But if she had another chance to go with Aren and the others, she would still choose to remain. Because she trusted Keris with her life, and because by remaining, she'd prevent Keris from sacri-ficing himself in a desperate attempt to save his aunt.

She hoped.

Relaxing her aching fingers from around the hilt of the knife she clutched, Zarrah squeezed her eyes shut, seeing Keris's face when she'd told him about Coralyn. The grief. The guilt. She might have spared him all of that agony by just killing his father when she'd had the chance. But the ambassadors from Harendell and Amarid and all the other nations had been alive and watching from where they'd cowered in the corner. They'd have seen. And short of slaughtering everyone in the room, there'd have been no way to keep silent that the heir to the Valcottan throne had done the killing.

This is what it's like to rule.

The thought weighed on her mind, making her understand why her aunt kept the world at arm's length. How could one do anything else when one was constantly forced to put the good of the Empire over the good of the individual? That was the choice her aunt had made in refusing to negotiate with Maridrina to get Zarrah back. And while she was increasingly wary of her aunt's vision of Valcotta's future, there was no doubt in Zarrah's mind that she'd acted for what she perceived was the good of the Empire.

Would it be possible to change her aunt's view of the future? Would Zarrah still have influence with the empress after this debacle? Unease flitted through her chest as she envisioned walking into the palace in Pyrinat and explaining, as much as she dared, how her capture had transpired. Explaining how she'd forgone an opportunity to escape on the way to Vencia in favor of the chance to assassinate Silas, only to forgo both her chances to do so. First to protect Keris and then because she'd come to understand that murdering the King of Maridrina would be like dumping oil on the fires of hatred between the two nations. Explaining how she'd then escaped by making a bargain with Ithicana, another nation the empress was at odds with, all with the help of the son of her mortal enemy.

"*Fuck,*" she whispered, because the truth was damning.

The door latch clicked.

Zarrah's heart leapt as the door opened, and she steadied her breathing, listening for the familiar tread of Keris's feet.

"He's distracted. Search the room, top to bottom, but make sure you put everything back as it was."

Serin.

"What are we looking for?" a man asked. Then he muttered, "This room is a mess. Don't the servants ever come in here?"

"Search for anything that ties him to Ithicana," Serin answered. "Or to Valcotta. And be quick about it." The door shut.

Zarrah clenched her teeth, listening to boots thud and scrape over stone as the man moved through the room. Papers rustled and objects shifted as he searched through Keris's things, muttering about the disarray as he went. Then boots came closer, stopping just in front of the tiny hole she was peering through.

"Who locks up books?" the man grumbled, and Zarrah flexed her fingers, the knife hilt slick with her sweat. *Go away*, she silently willed him even as she knew a locked box would draw his interest.

Metal scraped against metal, the man cursing under his breath as he fumbled with his picks. But there was no mistaking the *click* as the tumblers released.

He is only Serin's stooge, she told herself as she listened to him pull out books, shaking them to check for loose pages. *You are a general of the Valcottan Army. You have been fighting since you were a child. You can defeat this man.*

Except then what? She was still trapped in Silas Veliant's inner sanctum, which was swarming with soldiers.

Something scraped along the false bottom above her, and she prayed he didn't notice the difference in depth. Prayed that Keris would come back. Prayed that a servant would walk in and interrupt their search.

Yet even as she prayed, Zarrah planned her attack, because

there was only one person she could count on to save her ass: herself.

"Who needs so many blasted books?" The chest shifted slightly, and the man grumbled, "My God, this thing is heavy. And he takes it with him everywhere he goes. Wait . . ."

Silence fell, and Zarrah took a measured breath. Then another. Because this was the silence of a man who'd discovered something. Of a man who suspected he might not be alone.

Practiced hands brushed along the sides of the chest, searching.

Click.

Light blossomed above her.

And Zarrah attacked.

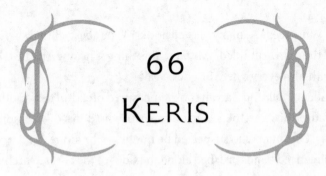

66

KERIS

Every member of the Veliant family knew about the hole, but given his propensity for pissing off his father in his youth, Keris knew it better than most.

He made his way to the staircase that led to the cellars beneath the harem's building, his stomach tightening at the sight of the guards standing by the heavy door. "Open it. Now."

One of them used a key attached to his belt to unlock the door, swinging it open, but as Keris passed, taking their lamp as he did, the man said, "The king has ordered she not be removed. Not under any circumstance."

Keris didn't bother answering, only kicked the door shut behind him, the damp scent of earth filling his nose even as darkness closed in around him. Turning up the lamp, he called out, "Coralyn? Auntie?"

No answer.

Heart in his throat, he moved down the stone corridor, bypassing the wine cellar and storerooms, heading to the door at the very end. As his hand pressed against the wood, Keris hesitated. *What if she is dead? What if those men had been told to guard her corpse?*

His breathing came in too-fast pants, his hands clammy as he prepared himself for the worst. The hinges creaked as he pushed, holding the lamp ahead of him as he swallowed hard. "Auntie?"

Silence.

"I suppose it was too much to hope that you'd leave well enough alone."

Relief shuddered through him, sending the shadows from the lamp dancing across the mildewed walls. Keeping his voice low, Keris said, "You told me that Lara swore to kill him or die trying. So which is it, Auntie? Is my sister a liar? Or are you?"

"You know the answer."

She'd lied to him.

Hurt lanced through his chest because other than Valcotta, she was the only other person living whom he trusted.

"I'd never have agreed to this plan if I'd known you intended to take the blame." Not even the opportunity to save Valcotta was worth the death of his aunt. He'd have found another way. A way that protected everyone he cared about.

"I'm aware, Keris. There's a reason I didn't tell you the truth."

Moving toward the dark opening in the earth, Keris looked down. About six feet in diameter and eight feet deep, the hole smelled of wet earth and decay, the light from the lamp only faintly illuminating his aunt's face. Her cheek was bruised and her lip split, but knowing her as he did, she was likely more aggrieved that her gown was soiled by dirt. "How badly are you hurt?"

"Your father got in a few blows, but I've weathered plenty of that over the years from him." She gave an annoyed sigh. "Since there isn't a chance of you leaving without some form of chatter, go fetch me two bottles of wine."

"Wine?"

"Yes. Be sure to pick something expensive. If I'm going to die in this hole, I might as well cost Silas money while waiting for him to do the deed."

Keris had no intention of letting her die, but he also knew arguing would be futile. So Keris hurried back down the corridor and stopped in front of the well-stocked cellar. After picking out two bottles that he knew she favored, he all but sprinted back to the hole, closing the door behind him.

Setting the lamp next to the edge of the hole, he said, "Make me enough room that I can jump down."

"Having to share my accommodations won't improve them," she said, but did as he asked.

Gripping the bottles, Keris jumped, ignoring the ache in his knees from the impact. He pulled out one of the corks, then handed her the bottle and watched as she drank from the neck. She downed half of it.

"Have they been caught?" she asked.

"Judging from the noise of the drum towers, no."

She gave a tight nod, then drank several more gulps of wine. "You need to leave. All of this will have been for nothing if your father believes you complicit."

"I'm not leaving you down here, Auntie." He fought the urge to ball his hands into fists. "Not a chance."

"You will do precisely that." Setting down the bottle, Coralyn gripped him by the shoulders. "Already you stand on precarious ground, because you were seen speaking with Aren twice, and it is no secret that you and I are close. Don't for a heartbeat believe that Serin won't suspect you were involved in my scheme and use that angle to try to turn your father against you."

"It was my scheme!"

She huffed out an amused breath that made him feel like a fool for ever believing that was the case.

"It doesn't matter whose plot it was." His mind raced for solutions. He'd smuggle Valcotta into the city. Would contact his supporters and take the crown by force, as he'd originally planned to do. "I'm not letting you die for me."

"Any good mother will willingly die to spare her child such a fate." She pulled him against her, her familiar perfume filling his nose. "More than any other child of this harem, you are my son, Keris. And I would die a thousand times over before allowing harm to come to you to spare myself pain. Besides, it's done. Nothing you say or do is going to save me from your father."

"You won't need to be saved from him if he's dead." Pushing her back, he met her gaze. "I've thousands of supporters in the city. I can take the palace by force."

"And get every member of this family killed in the process?" Her voice was filled with fury. "You will do no such thing, Keris Veliant. I will not allow you to risk this family in a futile attempt to save my life."

"What makes you think you can stop me?" He twisted away from her, bending his knees to jump and pull himself out of the pit, because he needed to prepare his lieutenants.

"Keris." She tugged on his coat, her voice tight. "You're right. I can't stop you. But perhaps the truth will make you rethink sacrificing so much to save my life."

"I doubt that." He pried at her fingers but froze as she said, "I know about you and the Valcottan woman. About Zarrah."

A chill ran down his spine. "What are you talking about?"

She exhaled a pained breath. "Don't insult me, boy. I knew from the moment you marched that woman into my rooms that there was something going on between you two. Never mind that the tension was thick enough to cut with a knife, you've spent your whole life running from your duties as a prince of Maridrina. Running from the politics and machinations and power plays. Yet the moment Otis captured her in Nerastis, you suddenly decide to play the game? Your idiot of a father believes that it's becoming the heir, and your own desire to survive, that has caused this change in you, but I know you better than that."

Denial seemed pointless, so Keris only stared at her in silence.

"If it had been only lust, I might have turned a blind eye. Except when I dressed Zarrah like a courtesan and paraded her in front of you, you didn't look at her as someone to be bedded and discarded; you looked at her like you wanted to get down on your knees and beg for her hand! As though you loved her!"

He couldn't help but flinch, especially as tears poured down her face.

"I knew she'd be your damnation. That if anyone discovered what was between you, your father would kill you, because what you two are doing is forbidden by both your peoples. If you were dirt-poor farmers, it would be forbidden, but you are the heirs to the most powerful families on the continent!"

His throat was thick as he said, "Do you think we aren't aware of that? We both know there's no future in it."

Coralyn's face crumpled as though some part of her had hoped she'd been wrong and he'd ripped that hope away from her. "You know it, but do you accept it, Keris? Or is there a part of you that believed if you took the crown, took power, you could force Maridrina to accept her as your consort? That you believed you could force peace down the throats of two nations that have hated each other for generations? Some stubborn part of you that believed you could have it all?"

Keris's lips parted to deny it, to scoff in disgust at such a suggestion, but the words wouldn't come. Because hearing it made him wonder if it was true. "I wanted peace long before I met Zarrah."

"But it wasn't until you met her that you risked anything to achieve it."

It was true, but not in the way she framed it. Meeting Valcotta, *knowing* Valcotta, had changed him. Made him believe himself capable of achieving things he had never believed possible. And made him understand that anything worth achieving required sacrifice.

"Not just your own future, your own life, but the lives of everyone in this family. For if you pursue this future, you will see the Veliant name, and all those who bear it, burned to ash. I couldn't allow that to happen, so instead, I resolved to kill Zarrah. Aided her quest for vengeance for her mother's death and got her all the way to your father's chambers in the tower, knowing his guards would slaughter her. Knowing that I'd kill two birds with one stone and you'd never be wiser to my involvement."

His breath came quickly, his anger rising. Not just anger but blistering fury. Coralyn hadn't just tried to murder Valcotta; she'd manipulated her, using the wounds her mother's murder had left behind.

"But she didn't take her chance, choosing instead to protect you from your brother, never mind that it was your affair that set him against you in the first place." Coralyn was shaking, the words coming out between sobs. "Not even your brother's death was enough to turn you from her. Instead you sought to make it worse with a coup, willing to let a hateful mob into our home for the sake of freeing your goddamned whore."

"Don't you fucking call her that," he hissed.

"Why not?" Coralyn spat between sobs. "The empress will call her that and worse should she ever learn what Zarrah has done."

"Then call me the same, for she's done nothing that I haven't done!"

"It's not the same."

"It is!" He didn't care if the guards heard. Twisting away from her, Keris pressed his forehead against the wall of the hole, sucking in breath after breath as he fought for composure. Fought to master the grief he felt over this betrayal by the one person he'd trusted all his life.

"You convinced Zarrah to kill him tonight in exchange for the chance to escape with Aren, didn't you? You never intended to take the fall—you intended to use her to martyr my father so that all hope of peace between our nations would be lost."

"Yes."

He rounded on her. "You were willing to escalate a war that would see thousands dead just to destroy any hope I might have of being with Zarrah?"

"To protect you." She choked out the words. "And to protect the family."

"Have you ever stopped to think that maybe this family doesn't deserve protection?"

Before she could answer, someone shouted in the distance, "Your Highness?" When Keris didn't respond, boot steps echoed down the corridor.

Panic flashed in his aunt's eyes. "Climb out! They can't see you down here!"

Keris was furious with her. But that didn't mean he wished her death. Far from it—what he wanted was the chance to prove her wrong. "I'm going to talk to my father. I'll convince him to spare you—he'll find it strange if I do otherwise."

"Fine. Do what you will. You always do."

Bending his knees, Keris jumped, then pulled himself over the edge of the hole. He rose to his feet, right as the door to the chamber opened. But the screech of hinges wasn't enough to drown out the sound of breaking glass below.

"Apologies for the interruption, my lord," the guard said from the doorway. "The king wishes to have a word with the lady."

Ignoring the man, Keris held the lantern down into the hole to better see his aunt, trepidation filling him, though he wasn't certain why. "Coralyn . . . ?"

There was blood everywhere.

The arms of her dress were soaked crimson from elbow to wrist, the broken wine bottle still gripped in her hand. "Forgive me."

"Get the physician!" he shouted at the guard, then jumped back in the hole. He closed his hands over her wrists, trying to stem the tide, panic filling him as blood flowed between his fingers. "Why? Why have you done this?"

"I can't risk Serin's questions," she answered between clenched teeth, already sagging in his grip. "You need to get out. You need to go."

"I'm not leaving you!" Tears rolled down his cheeks. It didn't need to be this way. He would have shown her. Would have shown them all.

Coralyn dropped to her knees, and Keris dropped with her, barely hearing the shouts of alarm from above. Barely feeling the blood soaking his clothes as his aunt slumped against him.

"I love you, dear one," she whispered.

And then she said nothing more.

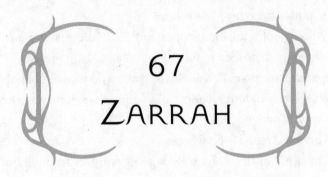

67
ZARRAH

Her hands struck the false bottom, sending it flying upward into the man's face.

He cried out, but Zarrah ignored him and the pain of her cramped body as she launched from the chest.

She dived into him, sending them both rolling across the floor into a stack of books. Grabbing one, she smashed it into the man's temple. He lay there, stunned, and she scrambled to her feet, slamming her heel down on his spine. The crack of his neck seemed to echo, and Zarrah glanced toward the door, waiting for it to open. Waiting for someone to investigate the noise. But the door remained closed.

She crossed the room and locked the door, then turned to survey the corpse sprawled across the carpet. A corpse she was going to need to find a way to hide. She'd avoided using her knife to minimize the mess, but the bastard had loosed his bowels, and the room already smelled of shit and piss.

"Where the fuck are you, Keris?" She clung to her anger because the alternative was terror. What if something had happened to him? What if Silas had accused him of being involved?

What if Keris had done something stupid to try to save his aunt?

The thoughts spun through her head, compounded by her sense of helplessness at being stuck in here while he was out there facing their foes. But if she went out, and Keris did have the situation in hand, she'd destroy his hard-laid plans. Instead, she stripped the man of his soiled trousers and mopped up the mess with toweling, all of which she dumped down the privy, wishing it were large enough to dump the man himself. Then she wrapped the man in a blanket and shoved him under the bed.

Not a permanent solution, but the best she could do. She went back to the book chest and climbed into it, debating how to close the false bottom over her again.

Click.

The door bolt turned. She whirled, pulling the knife from her belt as Keris stepped through the door.

Covered in blood.

Panic turned the room bright as she leapt out of the box and crossed the floor to him. He leaned back to close the door, closing his eyes as he rested against it. "What happened? Where are you hurt?"

"It's not my blood. It's Coralyn's."

She saw then that his eyes were red and swollen, his dirty cheeks streaked where tears had fallen. "She's . . . ?"

"Yes."

An ache filled Zarrah's chest, because she knew this pain. Could have spared him this pain, if only she'd done what Coralyn had asked. "I'm so sorry. This is my fault. If—"

Keris's eyes snapped open. "This is *not* your fault." He closed the distance between them, gripping her face gently. She could smell the blood on his hands as he said, "She told me what she did. Told me why. Coralyn dug her own goddamned grave tonight for no better reason than that she couldn't see a future different from the present."

There was a quiver to his voice, the grief in his eyes so vast it carved out her heart. Though part of her wanted to ask what Coralyn had said, what had happened, Zarrah sensed that talking about it would undo him. And they were far from out of danger. So instead, Zarrah wrapped her arms around his neck, pulling Keris against her.

She felt the rapid pounding of his heart against her breasts, her cheek pressed against his, rough with stubble.

"You shouldn't be out of the chest," he said. "It's not safe."

Zarrah swallowed hard. "Someone came in. His body is under the bed."

"Pardon?" He blinked at her, eyes hazed with grief and exhaustion, though they sharpened swiftly enough when he realized her words were no jest.

"Serin sent him in here to search for proof you're involved with this escape," she said as he crossed the room, bent to lift up the bed skirt, and swiftly recoiled. "The man was thorough and discovered where I was hidden. I had no choice but to kill him."

"Shit." Keris scrubbed his hands back through his hair, and she noticed his face was pale. "Why can't one goddamned thing go as planned?"

Battles rarely went as planned—the secret was being able to adapt your strategy. To look for solutions to problems as they occurred. They needed to get rid of the corpse somewhere it would never be found, which was impossible within the palace. Anywhere they put it, the body would eventually be found, and the blame would fall back on Keris.

"What the fuck do we do with him?"

Zarrah heard the edge of panic in his voice. Knew that he'd been pushed too hard, too far, to think clearly. But she'd been raised on the battlefield, trained to fight and to think even when bodies were falling around her. Even when her life was on the line. Which meant her mind was now at its sharpest. "We take him with us."

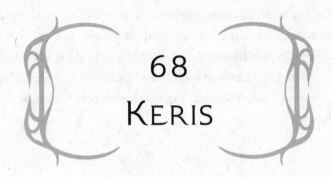

68
KERIS

HEART IN HIS THROAT, KERIS FOLLOWED THE PAIR OF SWEATING men he'd tasked with carrying his trunk of books down from the tower, keeping his arms crossed and a scowl on his face as they passed through the gardens and out the gates into the main palace.

Only for the drum towers, which had been a constant barrage of noise for hours, to plunge into silence.

Keris froze, his stomach twisting. Had Aren been caught or killed? Was that why the towers had ceased their noise? All it would take was one of Aren's party being caught alive, one of them caving to Serin's torture, for the information of Zarrah's whereabouts to be revealed.

As well as Keris's complicity in the escape.

Hooves clattered, and his father appeared before him, mounted on the back of his stallion. "They've made it up the cliffs outside the western gate," he shouted at the soldiers massing around them. "We can't let them reach the water! Go!"

His eyes latched onto Keris. "Where the fuck are you going?"

"Nerastis." He met his father's glare, not bothering to curb the venom in his voice. "As you ordered. Your Grace."

"Now?"

"You told me to be gone by dawn. And as it stands, I find there is little reason for me to remain in Vencia."

The horse sidled sideways, betraying his father's tension, and he hauled on the reins. "Coralyn deserved her fate. She's a traitor to the Veliant name."

There was no one more loyal to this family than her! Keris wanted to scream, but he bit down on the words. Because drawing his father's ire would be foolish. And because Coralyn's loyalty to her family had been what had gotten her killed. "My ship sets sail at dawn. Do you have any orders for me?"

His father stared him down, then gave a tight nod. "War will be coming to Nerastis. Make sure we are ready." Then he dug in his heels and galloped out the gates.

THE STREETS OF VENCIA WERE empty except for the soldiers patrolling them, everyone under orders to remain in their homes while the city was searched. It was quiet, but the stink of smoke from the fire at the east gate was nearly as thick as the tension that hung in the air as his carriage slowly made its way down to the harbor.

The wind had risen, the waters rippling with whitecaps despite the thick storm walls that protected it from the worst the seas had to offer, which meant it would be rough once they passed out into open water. But being out on violent seas was more appealing than remaining in Vencia a moment longer, because drowning would be a far more merciful death than would be granted them if they were caught.

Soldiers flanked the gangplank as Keris and the servants carrying his trunks approached, the men with his book trunk staggering beneath its weight. Aboard, more men searched the contents of the vessel, his father taking no chances of anyone escaping. The sight had sweat rolling in rivulets down Keris's spine.

"Your Highness." The soldier in command bowed low. "I regret the inconvenience, but your belongings must be searched before the ship can set sail."

Keris let out an annoyed sigh but gestured to his trunks. "Be quick about it. I've had a long night."

They riffled through the one full of clothing, then turned to the trunk with its precious—and damning—cargo. Turning to him, the soldier said, "I need the key, my lord."

Digging the small bit of metal from his pocket, Keris unlocked the trunk, lifted the lid, and stepped back. His stomach was in ropes as the man picked up a book, setting it on the ground before plucking up two more. The layer of books over the false bottom was only six deep. If the soldier reached it, there was no way in hell that he wouldn't guess there was something hidden beneath.

Surrounded by soldiers as they were, there'd be no escape.

Feeling ready to vomit, Keris snatched the book the man was holding out of his hands. "That's the only copy in existence. Have a care with it."

The man frowned. "It's just a book."

"It cost two hundred pieces of gold." Which was total bullshit. He'd picked up the volume from a bookseller for a handful of silver. But it had an ornate cover, so it looked expensive. "One good gust of wind and I'll lose the lot to the harbor, and it will be you I hold accountable."

The soldier hastily set the book back in its place, then stared at it, clearly warring between the cost of disobeying orders and the cost of damaging Keris's belongings. The latter prevailed, and the man reloaded the chest, gesturing at the servants to carry it aboard the vessel. "Safe travels, Your Highness. The seas are fierce."

It was a struggle not to let the breath he was holding out with a loud whoosh, and Keris pretended to pluck at lint on his sleeve as he followed the trunks up the gangplank.

The captain met him at the top, but Keris only half heard the man's pleasantries as he was led to a large stateroom, where his trunks were placed neatly against one wall, the men who'd carried the book trunk grumbling about the weight as they exited. "No interruptions," he told the man. "I prefer to study at night and sleep during the day, and if I wish for food or libation, I will call for it. Understood?"

"Yes, my lord."

"When do we set sail?"

"As soon as the soldiers finish searching my ship." The captain scuffed his boot against the ground, his eyes bright with curiosity. "Is it true the King of Ithicana has escaped?"

"Unless he's aboard this ship, Aren Kertell's whereabouts are not your concern."

The captain's eyes widened. "Certainly not, my lord! I am loyal to king and Crown."

"Wonderful. I look forward to journeying south with you." Keris stepped inside, bolted the door behind him, then searched the room for any spyholes drilled into the wall, but there were none.

He stopped next to the trunk holding Zarrah. "I'll get you out as soon as we pass the breakwater." They'd still be at risk, but not from his father's soldiers deciding they needed to do another inspection of the ship. "Are you all right?"

"Yes," came a soft whisper.

Keris went to the window at the back of the cabin, which held a stained-glass panel depicting flowers and greenery, and stared out the clear pane in the center. The ship bobbed, the faint sound of sailors shouting filtering through the walls, and then the vessel drifted away from the dock. He gripped the edge of the window frame, watching the rough buildings of the harbor, faintly lit by the dawn sun, grow smaller and smaller as they picked up speed. Then the breakwater, the opening flanked by two towers, appeared. A few minutes later, the deck tilted as the sails caught the heavy wind that tore around the point, the ship bucking and plunging on the rough surf. The vessel headed farther out to sea, then shifted direction, heading south along Maridrina's coast.

Keris exhaled, finally allowing his shoulders to slump, adrenaline fading and leaving exhaustion in its wake. Valcotta was free.

69
ZARRAH

THERE WASN'T ENOUGH AIR TO BREATHE, AND WHAT THERE WAS of it reeked of corpse.

Zarrah pressed her face to the tiny air hole, sucking in breath after breath, but it felt as though a band of steel was tightening around her chest, slowly suffocating her. The body shoved in next to her grew stiffer by the second, though at least it had finally stopped its twitching.

Let me out, she silently pleaded. *Please let me out.*

Only her pride kept her from screaming the words aloud.

Then the scent of Keris's cologne filled her nose, spicy and familiar and comforting. "We're at sea. I'm going to get you out now."

Relief tempered her rising panic, but Zarrah's heart didn't ease its gallop until he'd pulled out the layer of books, the volumes thumping against the floor like he was throwing them. Until he'd pulled up the false bottom, letting in a rush of air. Until he was hauling her out of the trunk and wrapping her in his arms.

Zarrah's muscles screamed as her body unfolded, her legs shuddering as she forced them to straighten, but she didn't care.

She was free.

"Look," he whispered in her ear, half carrying her to the window. "That's Vencia in our wake."

The hill holding the city rose above the wall of the breakwater, the palace that had been her prison sitting atop, the bronze dome of Silas's tower glinting in the dawn light. To be free of it seemed impossible, and part of her feared she'd awake to find herself back in her tiny room in the harem's quarters, her escape only a dream.

"Are you all right?"

She tore her gaze from the city to look at Keris and found herself once again short of breath. Lifting her hand, she tucked a lock of his hair behind his ear, wondering how his eyes had ever inspired her hate. Wondering how she'd ever compared them to his father's, for beyond the color, they were *nothing* alike. "Yes. Other than the fact I stink like corpse and have needed to piss for hours."

He winced. "I'm sorry. I wish there'd been another way."

"It was my idea, Keris," she reminded him; then they both turned to stare at the body stuffed into the trunk, limbs bent at awkward angles from Keris forcing the man to fit. "Let's dump him while it's still dark."

Working together, they hauled the man out of the trunk and over to the window. Zarrah opened it, air that smelled of brine and storm rushing over her, lightning crackling to the north over Ithicana. The ship rose over a large wave, then plummeted down, spray rising to mist her hair. More than enough noise to cover the sound of a body splashing into the water.

"Ready?" she whispered as the ship climbed another wave. "Now!"

They heaved the man out the window, watching him strike the

water right as the ship hit the dip between waves. The corpse disappeared beneath the foam.

"Serin will suspect." Keris leaned on the windowsill, the muscles in his forearms bunching. "There's no way around that."

"He's suspected for a long time but not had the proof he needed to convince your father." She hesitated, then added, "I overheard them that night in the tower. Your father . . . he's protecting you."

"I don't believe that. My father hates me."

Was it better that he continue to believe that? Better for her to stop this conversation in its tracks than to open old wounds? It was tempting, but Keris had kept hard truths from her out of the desire to protect her. Truths that had subsequently been delivered to her by others with hate in their hearts. Truths that she'd rather have heard from him. "I don't think he does. I think you frustrate him and piss him off, but . . . but you're the only person who isn't afraid to stand up to him, and he respects that."

"That's bullshit." He scowled at the water. "I'm fucking terrified of him. Always have been."

"But you still don't bend to him." She bit her bottom lip. "He believes you're suppressing your true nature, but that there will come a point you'll embrace it. That you'll live up to your name and be the heir he wants you to be. That's why he's protecting you."

Keris rounded on her, eyes full of anger as he snarled, "I will *never* be like him. I'll put a knife in my own goddamned heart before I'll *ever* live up to his expectations."

A flicker of unease ran through Zarrah. Not because she believed Keris to be anything like his father but because she sensed a thread of darkness ran through him. An inky stream that, if ever allowed to swell, might turn him into something far worse than Silas. Keris pressed his fingers to his temples, voice exhausted as he said, "I'm sorry. I can't . . . I don't want to talk about my family right now. For a moment, I just need to feel far away from them."

Her chest tightened. This wasn't how she imagined her first breaths of freedom would be while trapped in that cursed trunk with a corpse. In her mind's eye, she'd seen herself in his arms. Felt his mouth pressed against hers, his hands on her body. Wanted to lose herself in him in a way that had been so long denied.

A tear rolled down her cheek, and Zarrah brushed it away angrily. She used the facilities before retrieving a pitcher of water to scrub away smeared cosmetics, blood, and sweat from her body, the mirror revealing a bruised and swollen cheek where Silas had struck her. Her body also bore scrapes and bruises from the battle. From her fight with Serin's lackey. All evidence of what she'd endured to get here, yet the pain of them was nothing compared to that in her heart.

After donning one of Keris's shirts that she'd taken from a trunk, she picked up her ruined gown and went to the window where he stood, then tossed the garment into the surf. The jewels she wore swiftly followed, a hint of relief filling her. Not because she'd disliked the garments Coralyn had chosen but because being forced to wear them had been as much a form of control as the bars and shackles.

Keris abruptly turned, one arm wrapping around her body and hauling her against him, the other braced against the wall as the ship rose and plunged. She wrapped her arms around his neck, resting her cheek against his, feeling the dampness of sea spray.

"Coralyn was right." His breath brushed her ear, sending a tickle of sensation through her that made her shiver. Made her ache. "I do want to remake the world so that I can be with you. So that I can get down on my knees and ask you to be my wife. So that I can put a crown on your head and make you my queen. So I can build a shrine and worship you as my goddess. I want all of these things, yet I face a future with *none* of them, and I don't know whether I want to fall on my own blade or burn everything to ash because I do not want to let you go."

An impossible future, and yet his words made her blood sing even as the visions he painted flitted across her mind, twin to the forbidden dreams she'd had in the darkest hours of the nights. Dreams that had driven her fingers between her legs in search of release, but when the waves of pleasure had faded, had left her with only grief, because they could not be. Not unless both of them abandoned everything. "You have me now." She tangled her fingers in his hair.

"It's not enough." His hand slid down her back, curving over her ass and jerking her closer. "A lifetime wouldn't be enough. Eternity wouldn't be enough. Not when I want to map every star in the sky with you in my arms."

For a heartbeat, Zarrah felt like she couldn't breathe as the weight of what it would be like to lose him hit her with full force, driving the air from her chest. Making her eyes sting. To live a life-time without his voice in her ears, to never again feel his touch or taste his lips . . .

Tears threatened. And not just tears but great, heaving sobs that would tear her chest apart. Except she didn't want to spend any of this precious moment grieving. "This is the time we have. And I forbid you to squander it, Keris Veliant."

He didn't speak, the only sounds the grumble of distant thun-der and the crash of the ship breaking through the rough surf. His head turned, their lips so close they shared the same breath. "There is nothing I wouldn't give you," he said softly. "Nothing I wouldn't do for you."

Her skin was ablaze, every brush of the mist-soaked breeze sending shivers across her body, her thighs already slick. "There is only one thing I want from you right now. Only one thing I need."

Keris's lips met hers, and rational thought departed.

Whether it was weeks of being denied his touch or his touch itself, Zarrah wasn't certain, but the taste of him on her tongue unleashed a wildness she hadn't known herself capable of. Like a feral creature, she tilted her face, consuming him as surely as he consumed her.

The time for words and sentiment was over, and all that was left was blazing, blinding need.

Her mouth opened for him without hesitation, and she groaned as his tongue stroked hers, savage and demanding, every inhale filled with spice, making her hungrier for more of him. For *all* of him, though she knew it would never be enough.

His fingers trailed from her ass up her spine, then back down again, the sensation causing her body to buck. Causing her to tangle her fingers in the silk strands of his hair and kiss him harder, but Keris broke away from her mouth. His lips brushed her throat, nipped at the sensitive skin beneath her ears, and Zarrah panted, the sensation almost more than she could bear.

And then he moved lower.

He kissed fire down her throat, then over her collarbone, pausing only to catch hold of the hem of the shirt she wore, pulling it slowly upward, the feel of the linen brushing over her peaked nipples nearly sending her over the edge.

The ship plunged over a wave, and she almost lost her balance. Keris caught her around the waist to steady her, the shirt slipping from his fingers to the floor.

He held her at arm's length, drinking her in. "You're the most beautiful woman I've ever set eyes on. The most beautiful thing I've seen in all my life." His blue eyes were dark with a mix of lust and sorrow and something she knew they both felt but hadn't put words to. Might never put words to, for to do so might be their undoing.

And she'd had enough with words. Enough of being seen and not touched. She wanted *more*.

Her fingers fumbled with the buttons of his coat in her haste, and she tore the garment from him and cast it aside. His dark laugh filled her ears as she moved on to his shirt, nearly tearing it in her desperation to have him free of it.

The ship tacked west, and the dawn light spilled into the room, illuminating him with its glow. It turned his hair, damp from the sea spray, to gold, every muscle in his arms and torso appearing carved from alabaster. Her eyes tracked down his abdomen to the V of muscle that disappeared into his trousers, then to the hard length of his cock straining against the fabric. He was perfect. Everything she wanted, mind, body, and soul, but her desire was still tempered by an edge of fear, for outside this stateroom were dozens upon dozens of Maridrinians who'd see her dead just because she was Valcottan. Would see Keris dead for daring not to care about that damning fact. "What if someone comes in?"

"It's locked." His fingers flexed where they gripped her, sending a flood of heat through her core. "And there's a trunk in front of the door."

"They might still hear."

"I suppose that depends on how loud you scream my name, Valcotta." He let go of her with one hand, trailing a finger between her breasts and over her navel, slipping it between her thighs. She watched his eyes darken further as he found her sex hot and slick with desire. "With what I intend to do to you, everyone hearing you is a *very* real risk."

Her heart skittered, some strange, mad part of her soul relishing the risk, the adrenaline it sent coursing through her veins making her body throb, already on the rise toward climax. "Show me," she breathed.

Keris gave her a feral smirk, then pulled her down with him

onto the seat before the open window, her knees to either side of him. His mouth captured hers, biting at her bottom lip and making her whimper, her aching sex rubbing against the exquisite hardness of his cock, still constrained by his trousers.

"*Fuck*, Valcotta," he groaned into her mouth as she ground against him, then he caught her wrists in one hand, pulling until her spine arched, her head falling back.

When his mouth closed over her nipple, sucking and teasing, she nearly did scream. She drove her hips against his, hunting the rising release, her breath coming rapidly as he switched to her other breast, his teeth catching at her nipple, biting until pleasure bordered on pain. "Don't stop," she sobbed. "Please don't stop!"

His laugh vibrated against her skin, and then he let go of her wrists, his hands gripping her waist as he lifted her. Zarrah gasped, her eyes snapping wide and her hands catching at the window frame, dangerously close to falling to the violent waters that surged below.

"Trust me," he murmured, and the feel of his breath, hot against the apex of her thighs, drove away her fear. "I won't let you fall."

She did trust him. With her life and with her heart, so Zarrah closed her eyes, allowing her body to sway with the bucking motion of the ship. Her knees, which he'd rested on the back of the bench, slid wider, and Zarrah shuddered as she felt his tongue stroke the length of her sex, parting her, then delving into her.

Undoing her.

She screamed his name, but the sound was consumed by the rising wind, the thunder to the north, and the crash of the ship's hull against the surf. She let go of the window frame.

If he let go of her, she'd fall. If he let go of her, she'd die, but Zarrah felt no fear as she rode the sensation of his tongue inside of her, the sea spray icy against her overheated flesh. His mouth captured the center of her pleasure, his tongue circling her. Teasing her. Then claiming her.

Zarrah climaxed, the force of the pleasure rocking her harder than the storm-tossed ship. Wave after wave surged through her, sending stars across her vision and dragging his name from her lips. She collapsed backward, her arms dangling as she half imagined she might touch the waves; then he was pulling her back down onto his lap and into his arms.

Her forehead pressed against his, Zarrah sighed as he stroked her naked back, shivers still coursing through her as her pleasure faded. Only to be replaced by the need for more. "I want you in me." She kissed him, tasting herself on his lips. "I *need* you in me."

"As always, Valcotta"—he circled her nipple with his thumb—"we are like-minded."

Behind the ship, the storm was capturing more of the sky, the sea growing more violent by the second, but Zarrah didn't care. Barely saw the lightning dancing across the sky or the rising whitecaps as she dropped to her knees. Keeping her eyes locked on his, she unfastened his belt, then drew his trousers over his hips, her core tightening at the sight of his considerable length.

She bent her head, wanting to taste him. Wanting to give him the same pleasure as he'd given her, but Keris's hand curved around her cheek, lifting her face. "Goddesses don't kneel before men." He drew her up so that her knees were on either side of his hips, his cock pressing against her entrance, the sensation making her moan even as the sight of him made her body moisten, for it was he who appeared like a god. Too beautiful for words.

And he was hers.

So she claimed him, lowering herself inch by delicious inch, watching his eyes roll back, a groan tearing from his lips as they came together.

Zarrah thought it would be wild. Thought it would be a frantic, desperate union of two lovers long denied and soon to be parted. Instead, it was a slow and achingly sweet rebuilding of their hearts, her breasts pressed against his chest, only flesh separating their thundering hearts. His lips against hers, so his breath was her own. His body buried so deep inside hers that for this precious moment, they were one.

The ship rocked them, wind gusting over their bodies as tension rose in Zarrah's core, gathering and building until she crested with an intensity that blinded with its brightness. It rippled through her even as she felt Keris climax, heard him cry out, his cock pulsing and filling her.

All she could see was stars, the map of their story in the sky of her mind, and her heart wept because without him, she feared there would be only darkness.

He picked her up. Carried her to the bed and eased her under the blankets, though it was the heat of him that warded away the chill. She did not want to give him up. God help her, she did not want to give him up.

A tear rolled down her cheek, and she felt him brush it away. Tasted him as he kissed her. Heard him as he whispered, "I love you, Valcotta. I will have you or I will have no one, because where you go, my heart goes with you."

For a long moment, she could barely breathe, much less speak, then she said, "I want you to call me Zarrah now. Because there will be no more walls between us. No bars. And no borders."

"Zarrah." His voice caught, and he repeated, "Zarrah."

And it was with her name on his lips that she allowed exhaustion to claim her, falling asleep in his arms.

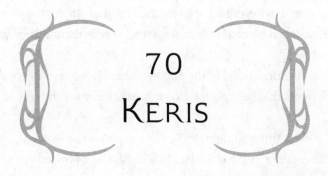

70

KERIS

AFTER SHE'D DRIFTED OFF, HE'D RISEN TO CLOSE THE WINDOW against the driving wind and rain, drawing the sodden drapes and plunging the room into relative darkness before checking that the door lock was secure. Only then did Keris climb back into the bed, his chest aching as she curled into his arms, her feet cold against his shins.

And then he slept.

And slept.

For how long, Keris didn't know, only that when he woke, it was dark, the storm rattling the windows, the seas rougher than they were before. The motion of the ship rocked Zarrah's still-sleeping form against him, her breath warm and steady against his throat.

He loved her. God help him, but he *loved* this woman more than life. This fierce, beautiful creature who'd been thrown into a pit of hateful snakes and had not only survived but had emerged stronger. No longer someone whose pain could be manipulated and used but as the commander of her own future, seeing clearly where once her eyes had been clouded by grief and hate.

He wished he could claim the same. Maybe then he'd be worthy of her.

Zarrah stirred, and in the dim light, he watched her eyes open, dark pools that he'd gladly drown in every day for the rest of his life.

"Is everything all right?"

"Everything is perfect." He stroked back her tangled curls, his cock stiffening as the blanket pulled back to reveal the pert curve of her breast, her nipple hardening under his gaze.

"The seas are rough." Her voice was breathy, and he smiled, lowering his mouth to flick his tongue over the dark peak before asking, "Does it bother you? The waves?"

She sighed, eyes fluttering shut. "No."

He closed his mouth over her breast, sucking and biting, relying half on his memory of what she liked and half on his instinct of what he thought might undo her.

He traced a finger over the hard muscles of her abdomen, circling her navel before sliding his finger between her legs. She was hot and wet, thighs parting to allow him to stroke her sex while he continued to kiss and suck at her breasts. He circled the tight bundle of nerves with a featherlight touch, knowing it would drive her wild but wouldn't make her climax.

"You're a tease." She caught his face and pulled his mouth to hers, biting his bottom lip nearly hard enough to draw blood, the sweet pain making him want to forget foreplay and drive himself into her like some wild beast. Which was very likely why she'd done it. Zarrah *knew* him like no other woman ever had. Ever could.

Instead of taking her bait, Keris slid a finger into her slick core and slowly began stroking her. Zarrah bucked her hips, trying to increase the rhythm, but he only smiled against her lips and moved his weight, holding her hips down.

"You're not a tease; you're a fucking devil," she moaned, and he laughed, adding a second finger and kissing her throat, nipping at the lobe of her ear, his teeth clicking against the ruby earring she still wore. Her nails raked down his shoulders as he added a third finger, barely keeping his lust in check as Zarrah sobbed his name, her breath coming fast, her eyes squeezed shut.

"Please," she gasped. "I need you. All of you."

And he needed her. More than air in his lungs and blood in his veins, he *needed* this woman. Twisting onto his knees, he spread her smooth thighs wide and thrust himself deep inside.

Zarrah's back arched and she pressed a hand to her mouth, biting at her own skin as she smothered a scream. Then her legs were wrapped around him, one heel digging into his back and the other his ass, adding such force to his thrusts that Keris had to brace a hand against the wall to keep from collapsing against her.

He wanted to *see* her. Needed to watch her writhe beneath him, her exquisite face tight with building pleasure, one hand on her breast and the other . . . He groaned, nearly coming at the sight of her fingers stroking and circling her sensitive flesh as he pounded into her, the faint flickers of light coming through the drapes reflecting off the lacquer on her nails.

He'd seen her do this before, the first night they'd been together, and it had broken his will.

Just as it broke him now.

He slammed into her and came, barely containing a shout of her name as waves of pleasure overtook him, his cock spilling into Zarrah even as her back arched, her tight sex contracting around him as she climaxed. He collapsed against her, burying his face in her throat and inhaling the soft scent of her hair.

Her legs eased their grip around his body, slipping down to

tangle in his, her arms wrapped around his neck. He sighed as she stroked his hair with one hand, pushing it back and unraveling tangles as his heart eased its rapid pounding.

"I can't keep doing this." He kissed her throat, aware of his hypocrisy as his cock began to stiffen again inside of her. "I'll get you pregnant."

"I know." She didn't let go of him, didn't stop stroking his hair, fingers gentle where moments ago they'd been fierce.

It was another knife to his heart, because it was another thing stolen from them. He liked children—always had—and the thought of *his* child at Zarrah's breast made his eyes burn. He'd seen the way she was with the harem's children, the sweetness she'd shown Sara, encouraging his sister to dream where others always cautioned her back. She'd be a good mother, as kind to her children as she'd be viciously defensive of any who sought to harm them.

And if they were his children, many would seek to harm them.

Zarrah murmured, "How many days until we reach Nerastis?"

He wondered if she was thinking the same thing about children. Or if her thoughts were something else entirely.

"Hard to say." He shifted off her, out of her, resting on one elbow so that he could see her face. "The wind is against us."

"Is it?" She smiled, her hand sliding down his stomach. "I rather think it's for us."

If only this voyage could last forever. If only the wind would blow so fiercely that it held the ship in place, extending this moment into perpetuity, because he'd never have it again. "Don't go back."

Her hand stilled in its descent. "What do you mean?"

"Don't go back to Valcotta." Before she could say anything that would silence him, he added, "We could leave all this behind us. Buy passage on a Harendellian merchant vessel and risk the Tempest Seas. Sail all the way north until there is no one who knows or cares who we are and then live under different stars."

Zarrah was silent, her expression unreadable. "You would leave for the sake of us being together?"

"You make it sound like a greater sacrifice than it is." He smiled, but it was forced. "Abandoning politics and scheming and war and murder to be with the woman I'm in love with is an easy decision."

Now that he'd said the word once, it was as though it needed to be said over and over, despite her not saying it in return. Because he knew why she hadn't.

"What of your family? Are they so easy to abandon? To leave to suffer under your father or whichever of your brothers eventually inherits?"

Keris closed his eyes, thinking of his aunts. Of his siblings, many barely past infancy. Of Sara, forced to toil for her meals in the church. "It wouldn't be easy. It would be a burden I'd carry for the rest of my life." He opened his eyes. "But I'll still do it if it means being with you."

"Why?" Her voice shook, but she rolled him onto his back, straddling him as she demanded, "Why are you willing to do all of this for me?"

"Because I never lived until I met you, not really." He lifted a hand to her face, thumb stroking her cheek. "And because you've not been given what you deserve. Not been treated how you deserve to be treated. I would give you everything. We'd be happy."

The storm outside was fading, the sunlight growing brighter, and it illuminated her face. Revealed the dusting of freckles on her cheeks, the highlights of red in her dark-brown hair. But it was her dark eyes he fixed on, wide and framed with endless black lashes. Doe-like, despite the mind behind them being that of a tigress.

"I need to think on it." Her voice was tight. Strangled. "I need . . . I need time to think."

It wasn't a no. But it wasn't a yes. A twist of anger rolled through his chest, because what did she have to go back to? Whom did she have to go back to besides the aunt who'd left her for dead? It wouldn't be a happy life she returned to, and he wanted more for her than that. But instead of saying any of that, he gave her a tight nod.

"It's not an easy decision." She bit her bottom lip. "For my heart, the answer is easy, and it would be yes. A thousand times, yes. But . . ."

"Honor." He couldn't keep the bitterness from his voice. "You honor the people who'd spit on you if they knew the truth."

She flinched, and guilt flooded him. "I'm sorry. I'm an asshole to have said that."

Zarrah only shook her head. "You're not wrong. They would. But this decision . . . it's not about honoring them—it's about honoring myself. I . . ." She looked away, seeming to hunt for the words she needed. "I need to do things that I believe are *right*. So I can be proud of who I am and what I've done, because there is much I've done that I feel ashamed of." Her eyes jerked back to his. "I don't mean you. I could never regret you."

Keris found himself wondering if that were entirely true. Or if it was, whether it would remain true.

"I need to consider the costs of my actions before I make a choice that I cannot undo." She curved her small hand around his cheek, her thumb brushing his skin. "If you truly love me, then you'll give me the opportunity to think."

His chest hollowed, because he *knew* her. Knew the woman she had been and the woman she'd become. Knew what the choice would be. "Whatever you decide, I'll still love you. And wherever you go, if you decide to turn back, I'll be there."

Her eyes gleamed bright, then two tears dripped down her

cheeks to splatter against his chest. "Just give me time to think, Keris."

Then she was kissing him, her tongue in his mouth as she caught hold of his cock, his body caring little for his fractured heart as she stroked him. He turned his face away from hers, feeling strangled, though he managed to say, "This isn't allowing you to think, Zarrah."

"No." She lowered herself onto him, her back arching, breasts illuminated by the rays of the sun. "But it is allowing me to dream."

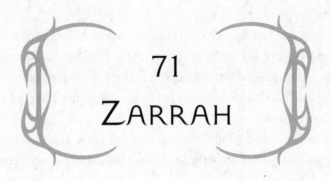

71

ZARRAH

THE MERCHANT VESSEL STOPPED IN NEARLY EVERY PORT BETWEEN Vencia and Nerastis to drop off and pick up passengers, more than tripling the time the journey typically would take. Yet Zarrah would have dragged it out longer if such a thing were possible, for the weeks were the most pleasurable of her life.

Zarrah, by necessity, remained closeted in the stateroom, but Keris rarely left her side unless it was absolutely necessary. He ordered food and wine brought to the room, and she was delighted to discover that absent Silas's taste for excessive salt, Maridrinian food was very good. And their wine even better, Keris sparing no expense, much to the ship captain's obvious delight. He read to her from the books he'd brought to disguise her escape, tomes on every different topic, even the driest subject made fascinating by his velvet voice, and she'd rest her head in his lap, listening for hours. He obliged her with stories of his past, though he steered clear of his father. Of Otis. And of Coralyn. Though she was desperate to know what the old woman had said to him prior to her death, Zarrah knew better than to press when the pain was so fresh. So instead she reciprocated, telling him of her childhood in Pyrinat. Of her mother and cousins and what it was like to grow up in the lap of Valcottan privilege. She told him of her training after her mother's murder, of the endless, *endless* hours of sparring and lessons. How she'd relished growing strong and capable even as she lost parts of her character that her mother had nurtured so carefully. And when he asked whether she'd done *anything* fun, she told him of the mischiefs Yrina had gotten her into, especially when they'd come of age. He held her when the pain of her friend's loss welled afresh, allowing her to sob against his chest until the waves lulled her to sleep.

And they made love.

Endless, endless pleasure that went beyond what she'd dreamed possible. Sometimes sweet and tender, his caresses coaxing climaxes from her body that rolled through her and made her see stars. Sometimes desperate and savage, his cock hammering into her while she clawed at him, needing more, needing him deeper, the explosion of her climax leaving her breathless and exhausted. He was endlessly creative, and as her inhibitions vanished, she unleashed her own wicked desires, little delighting her more than watching him lose control of himself, her name always what was on his lips.

Both of them knew what they were doing. Trying to force a lifetime into one ship voyage, because it was all they could ever have.

It had been a lie when she'd said she'd needed time to think. She'd only needed time to find the courage to voice the truth. The truth that would shatter her heart in a way she'd never recover from, but the truth nonetheless.

Zarrah had to go back to Pyrinat.

Her time in Vencia had cleared the smoke in her mind surrounding her aunt and caused her to see clearly. The empress didn't want the Endless War between Maridrina and Valcotta to ever cease, perhaps even wanted to escalate it in pursuit of retaking Nerastis. Whether it was fanaticism or anger or pride, Zarrah wasn't certain, only that her aunt was not acting for the good of Valcotta.

Zarrah was the *only* person in a position to tell her so. The only person capable of tempering her aunt's desire for war. And, if fates aligned, the only person in line for the throne who would ascend it with the desire to pursue peace.

To walk away now, no matter how much her heart wanted to, would be condemning her people to fight and suffer and *die* in a war that did nothing but appease the empress's pride. Zarrah knew she couldn't live with herself, knowing that she'd had a chance to make a difference for tens of thousands of Valcottans and instead had chosen herself.

Not that she believed it would come effortlessly.

The empress would not be easily swayed, and with Silas on the throne, peace couldn't be had. But if Keris remained in Maridrina, if he ascended either by inheriting or by some scheme, then it would be possible. Which meant tens of thousands of Maridrinian lives improved if only the pair of them stayed the course.

If only they sacrificed each other.

ZARRAH SAT WITH HER LEGS crossed on the bed, watching Keris, who sat at the open window, her pulse racing and her palms slick.

Their time together was over.

Though the window only revealed a night sky filled with countless stars, Zarrah knew they passed familiar landscape. Knew that, if she stood on the deck of the ship, she'd see the lights of Nerastis glowing in the distance.

Tell him, she silently ordered herself. *What are you waiting for?*

But it felt like her throat had closed up, her breath coming too fast and beads of sweat rolling down her back, though the night air was cool. Zarrah opened her mouth to speak, but her tongue was thick, and all she did was swallow his name, unable to give it voice. She knew why she was hesitating—it was because the longer she waited, the more opportunity he'd have to convince her to change her mind. To run away with him.

To be happy.

You're a fucking coward, Zarrah, she snarled at herself. *Just do it.*

Then Keris turned away from the dark sky to face her, silently meeting her gaze. He'd dressed as the prince, freshly shaven, hair loose to his shoulders, the coat he wore royal blue and embroidered with gold, boots polished until they gleamed. With the starlight glowing behind him, he was impossibly handsome—like the prince out of a fable, but that wasn't what she saw. It was the question in his eyes.

"I have to go back." The words tore from her lips, and she immediately wanted to take them back as he tensed, suddenly looking anywhere but at her. Why hadn't she phrased it differently? Why hadn't she started with an explanation? Why—

"I know you do."

There was understanding in his voice, not anger, but she still found herself rushing to explain. "I promised Aren to help Ithicana. And I need to attempt to soften my aunt's stance on the war. Need to convince her of the merits of peace. Need to keep my position as her heir so that when you take the crown, we can end this."

His jaw flexed on the last, and her chest tightened. "I wish there was a way, Keris. A way I could be with you and still do what my conscience demands, but there isn't. And I hate it. I want to scream and rage and cry because it isn't fair." She drew in a shaky breath. "I don't want to lose you."

Silence.

Vaguely, Zarrah was aware of the sounds of the sailors moving about the decks, muffled shouts of preparation, the rattle of the anchor as it lowered into the depths. But still, Keris didn't answer. Didn't move from where he stood, didn't lift his eyes from the floor.

"Please say you understand." The words croaked from her lips, fear rising in her chest to the point she felt sick. "Please say you don't hate me for doing this."

His face snapped up, and in two strides, Keris closed the distance between them, wrapping her in his arms. "I wish I could hate you," he said into her hair. "Because then I could watch you walk away and not feel like . . . like . . ." She felt him shake his head. "If there are words for how I feel about you, I've never heard them. Never seen them written in any of the thousands of books I've read."

With her head pressed against his chest, the sound of his hammering heart filled her ears, mirroring her own, and Zarrah's grip on his coat tightened even as her resolve faltered. *I can't lose you I can't lose you I can't lose you!* her aching heart screamed into her thoughts, and she clenched her teeth to keep from sobbing them aloud.

"I knew you'd never say yes. Knew that you'd never agree to running away when so much rode on your return. That your conscience would never allow it. And as much as I hate that, it's also one of the reasons I love you. If you'd said yes, it would have made you like me. And I could never love someone like me."

Her heart shattered, and Zarrah lifted her face, the words that had long been in her heart rising. But Keris pressed a finger to her lips, whispering, "Don't. It's already hard enough not to fight for you, and if you say it, my selfishness will win."

The last thing he was, was selfish. "Keris—"

"If you're going to go, it needs to be now." He twisted her in his grip, walking her to the open window. "Dawn will come soon, and you need to get into Valcottan waters before then."

"How—"

He picked up the stoppered ale cask she'd had him request days ago, though most of the contents had been poured out the window. "I knew you had no intention of getting back inside that trunk, Zarrah." He wrapped a belt around the cask, fastening it tight before pushing it into her hands.

The ship bobbed up and down, the sailors loud in their preparations, and in the distance, she could hear the sound of a Maridrinian naval vessel approaching to watch over the process of unloading the royal cargo.

This was it. The moment she'd dreaded for the entire voyage, but nothing could have prepared her for how horrible it would feel. Like the breath was being squeezed from her chest, every part of her in pain, most especially her heart.

And yet she wanted to draw it out. Wanted to cling to him for as long as possible to delay that final slice of pain.

"Zarrah . . ."

Sucking in a gasping mouthful of air, she kissed him fiercely, then climbed onto the windowsill, the water splashing loudly against the hull below. Keris caught hold of her hand, then braced himself against the frame. "Be careful." She knew it wasn't the water he feared.

She gave him a tight nod, then allowed him to lower her down until his face was lost to the dim light, their locked hands their only connection. The memory of that first night on the dam filled her mind's eye, Keris's grip on her the only thing keeping her from plunging to certain death. Then, he'd been her enemy, but now . . . "I love you," she said. "I will always love you."

Then she let go.

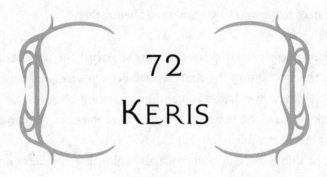

72
KERIS

I LOVE YOU.

Keris clenched his teeth, his hands screaming with the force with which he gripped the window frame, it taking every bit of his self-control not to jump in the water and follow her to shore.

You have to let her go, he told himself, the pain in his chest excruciating. *You have to respect her choice.*

And he did. But that didn't mean he had to like it. Zarrah deserved better, deserved to be treated like a queen, not to sacrifice herself for the sake of those who'd never thank her for it. Who'd never know what she'd given up for them.

A loud knock sounded on the door. Keris jumped, turning away from the window. "Yes?"

"Your Highness, the soldiers comprising your escort have arrived. When you are ready, you may disembark."

"Thank you," he forced himself to say. "I'll be along presently."

Yet he didn't move from the window, instead turning to listen for any sound that she'd come back. Any sign that she'd changed her mind. Hating himself for wishing that she would.

But as dawn warmed the sky, he saw nothing but empty waves. Heard nothing but the shouts and curses of sailors and soldiers.

She was gone.

Sucking in a deep breath, he turned from the window and started toward the door. But then he caught sight of himself in the mirror on the wall. He stared at his reflection for a heartbeat, then twisted toward his packed trunk, casting off his coat as he did. Digging into the depths, he extracted his uniform jacket, which was festooned with markers of rank that he hadn't earned. He donned it anyway before digging to the bottom and pulling out the sword.

He stared at the weapon, jewels glittering on the pommel and the edge gleaming sharp. A gift from his father, and he hated it. Wanted nothing more than to go to the window and toss it into the waves.

Instead, he belted it around his waist. Zarrah had sacrificed everything in a bid for peace, and that could only be achieved if Maridrina were willing.

Which meant that he needed to bring war upon his father.

And this time, it wouldn't be fought with words.

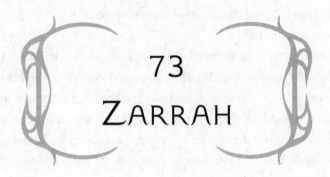

73
ZARRAH

For a long time after she reached the beach, Zarrah lay in the sand, just breathing.

Beyond the edge of the harbor, she could just make out the ship she'd abandoned Keris on, flanked by a naval vessel watchfully monitoring the unloading of passengers and cargo via longboat. *Has he already reached shore?* she wondered. *Is he on his way to the palace?*

Part of her wanted to remain where she was, watching. Yet she knew that Valcottan patrols would soon cross over this stretch of beach, and she could not be connected to the ship or to Keris. So Zarrah staggered to her feet and made her way into the city.

Nerastis was always the quietest at this hour, but she still crossed paths with dozens of her countrymen and -women going about their business, her ears filling with the familiar lilt of Valcottan voices, her nose with the scent of grilled meat and savory spice, her mouth watering despite it not being long since she last ate.

It occurred to her that this was the first time since her capture on the north side of the Anriot that she'd walked alone. That she'd walked *free*. Stopping in the center of the lane, Zarrah breathed, tasting the sweetness of the flavors, relishing the moment. Yet like iron to a lodestone, her eyes drew north, catching sight of the glint of sun off the domed towers of the Maridrinian palace.

Was he already inside? What was he doing? How were the soldiers, many of whom had been loyal to Otis, reacting to his return?

Unease flitted through her stomach, but Zarrah tamped it down. They both had their own paths to follow to reach their mutual goal, and neither could do anything to help the other. But God help her, she *hated* that he was alone among vipers. Hated that she'd abandoned him. Hated that she wasn't there to watch his back.

"You made your choice," she whispered to herself. "Don't let it be for nothing."

So she started walking, eventually finding a vendor who sold clothing and purchasing trousers, a blouse, and a pair of rope sandals. She swiftly changed into the dry clothes, then carried the bundle of Keris's garments toward a burning pile of trash. She stroked the fine linen, wanting to lift the fabric to her nose to see if it retained any vestiges of his scent, but she refrained, instead waiting until the street was clear before tossing the clothes on the fire. They smoldered, steam rising, but eventually the fabric blackened and charred, the last physical vestiges she had of Keris turning to ash.

Telling herself the stinging of her eyes was from the smoke, Zarrah squared her shoulders and turned toward the palace garrison she'd once ruled, wishing she knew for certain whether what she'd find there would be welcome.

EVERYONE STOPPED IN THEIR TRACKS as she walked through the gates, eyes widening and whispers of astonishment filling her wake, her name on everyone's lips.

But no one stopped her. No one contested her right to walk into the palace itself, her sandals making soft pats against the tiles as she made her way to the commander's offices, the two soldiers outside gaping at her as she approached. One managed a salute, but the other hesitated, then pressed a hand to his heart.

A symbol of respect, yes, but one granted only to nobility.

And to the dead.

"Who is in command?" she asked, though she already knew. Could smell the hot scent of fried batter that her cousin adored emanating from under the door, and in her mind's eye, she could picture him eating it, greasy fingers leaving marks on the reports.

"His Highness, General Bermin," the soldier who'd saluted answered. "We . . . He . . . After you were taken prisoner . . . We wanted to go after you, my lady, but—"

"I understand the decisions made." She gave him a half smile. "And I think it best to leave the explanations to the general. Would you ask if he has time to see me?"

Once, she'd have barged in. Demanded answers. Allowed her anger out in full force. But Zarrah had learned more than just patience during her time in Vencia.

The soldier knocked, then stepped inside. Whatever he said caused an eruption of motion from within, boots thumping on the tile; then the door flung open, and her cousin filled the doorway. "Little Zarrah!" he shouted. "You're alive!"

Then his arms were around her, squeezing her so hard, Zarrah could barely breathe, her face unfortunately pressed into his sweaty armpit. He pounded her twice on the back before lifting her into the air, twisting her this way and that, examining her. "We received word many days ago that you'd escaped with the Ithicanian, but it's been crickets since, so we feared the worst. Are you well? Did they harm you?"

Before Zarrah could answer, he set her on her feet with a thud and rounded on the soldiers. "Have food and drink brought, and lots of it. Look how skinny she is." Bermin laughed, loud and booming. "Apparently, Vencia is so starved even the Rat King's palace is going without. Look at her!"

Hiding her annoyance, Zarrah shrugged. "Silas's favorite spice is salt, and lots of it. If I never taste the cursed stuff again, it will be too soon."

"I think it less preference and more necessity." Bermin grinned. "We have the Maridrinians boxed in, and they are starved indeed. Though blockading them is barely necessary, as the bastards don't have coin to pay for food even if it's offered. Even the Amaridian queen has cut them off, for Silas is in arrears on payment for the use of her navy, never mind the compensation he owes her for the vessels lost to storms. It won't be long until Vencia stinks like corpse with so many starved dead in the streets, and all because Silas can't bear to give up his precious bridge."

Her cousin laughed, the delight in it making Zarrah's stomach twist in revulsion. Those who starved first would be the ones with the least control over circumstances, while the king who ruled would feast until his last breath. "I think it not half so dire as you've been led to believe, cousin."

"But soon enough. Especially once we retake Nerastis." He slung an arm around Zarrah's shoulders, tugging her into the office that once had been hers, though all vestiges of her presence were gone, down to the paint on the walls. Erased, which made her even more certain that Bermin's enthusiastic greeting was feigned.

As she sat in a chair, he circled the desk. "We'll take the city, then push north, taking land mile by mile and slaughtering any of the rats that don't scuttle ahead of us swiftly enough, and it will only be a matter of time until Maridrina is crushed onto the tip of the northern point with naught but desert to sustain them." He leaned over the desk, his grin feral. "We'll have vengeance for them taking you, Zarrah. I'll see to it myself."

Was this truly what she'd once been like? How she'd seen the world? Loathing filled her, but Zarrah mastered her expression and inclined her head. "You intend to act soon? The garrison seems undermanned for such a venture."

Something flickered across Bermin's eyes, something dark and hateful, but it was gone in a heartbeat and replaced by a smile. "You know my mother, little Zarrah. Always biding her time, waiting for the moment to be right. If it were me, I'd seek vengeance for your capture this very hour, but I bend to her will."

"The Harendellian ambassador told me that she locked herself in her room for a day and a night and wept, but I didn't believe him."

"It's true." Leaning back in his chair, Bermin crossed a leg, boot resting on his knee. "Locked herself in with orders that she not be disturbed for *any* reason, though whether she wept or raged, I could not say. Only that she emerged and gave the orders you were not to be pursued for any reason. But . . ." He hesitated. "Yrina disappeared shortly after and hasn't been heard from since."

"Serin caught her." Zarrah's chest tightened at the reminder that her friend had been the only one who'd tried to help her. "She's dead." By her own hand, to protect Zarrah's secret.

Bermin pressed a hand to his heart, lowering his head in grief she didn't think was feigned. "How did you come to be captured? What were you doing on the north side of the Anriot alone?"

Zarrah had spent a great deal of time considering how she might answer this question. "You asked how I knew the Maridrinians would attack that night by sea, and I told you that I had informants. But that was a lie. I was spying myself, going in disguise and gaining information from the Maridrinians themselves."

He frowned. "Why take such a risk? We have spies aplenty."

"Spies whose caution was reflected in the quality of information they were providing." She shrugged. "I was ambitious, and it caught up with me. I tarried too long and was caught by Prince Otis's patrol."

"Who brought you to the palace, where his elder brother decided you were worth more alive than dead." Bermin rubbed his chin. "A prince we barely knew existed until he took the position of heir but whose name is now on the lips of everyone, north and south. Is it true he pushed his own brother to his death and Silas applauded him for it?"

"So I heard." Keris's face flashed through her vision, the horror etched across it as he looked down at his dying brother. The brother he'd killed to protect her. "He's a different sort of Veliant than we are used to. He's . . . clever."

"But not a fighter?"

"I saw no evidence of such skills in the time I spent around him." She disliked the scrutiny, though it was inevitable. Bermin was a killer, and she didn't like the idea of his attention focusing on Keris. "He was disparaged often for being bookish, which I'd say is an accurate judgment of his character."

Bermin's face scrunched in disdain, but before their conversation could continue, a knock sounded at the door. "Come," her cousin rumbled, and the door opened to admit one of the guards, who passed him a folded piece of paper.

"This just came. Keris Veliant has arrived by ship."

Zarrah's heart skittered, but she only scowled as Bermin opened the paper, his eyebrows lifting as he read. Then he tossed the paper across the desk so that she could read it. "Might be time to reconsider that judgment of his character, little Zarrah. It appears the bookish fop has decided he's a military man after all."

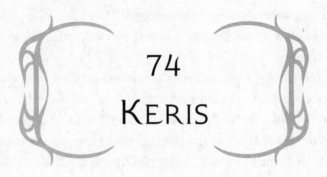

74
KERIS

NERASTIS WAS A PLACE THAT HAD BEEN FORCED UPON HIM. A tool for shaping him into a proper prince. A place where there was no desire for people like him. A punishment. Yet as he walked through the familiar streets, the stink of rot and sewage filling his nose, and shouts of madams tossing drunks out of brothels, Keris was struck with the realization that of all the places he'd lived, Nerastis was where he felt most at ease.

Where he felt most at home.

Why that was, he couldn't have said. It was a debauched shithole teeming with violence, the buildings more rubble than not, and the poverty worse than anywhere in Maridrina. But as he watched the people of the border city go about their business, faces and clothing a blend of Maridrina and Valcotta, Keris realized what he found so compelling. Nerastis was a place where a seed could take root. Where an idea could grow into reality, because for all this city was the heart of the conflict between the two nations, it was also populated by people who set aside politics every night and lived as one.

It was fitting that this was where he and Zarrah had met. It wouldn't have been possible anywhere else.

The thought had him turning south, eyes latching onto the Valcottan palace on the far side of the Anriot. Was she already there? If so, how had she been received?

Was she all right?

Anxiety rose in his stomach as his mind provided him with endless scenarios where things had gone horribly wrong, each worse than the last.

You shouldn't have let her go.

Even as the thought rolled through his mind, he grimaced. Zarrah was not one to be controlled. And neither was he interested in controlling her, for all it would make aspects of his life easier. Being controlled was as much a prison as any cage.

As it was, he now had to look to his own survival, which was precarious. This garrison was full to the brim with men who'd respected Otis, and there wasn't a chance in hell they didn't believe Keris had killed him.

Because you did, his conscience whispered, but he shoved the thought away, burying it deep, where he kept his grief for all the others he'd lost.

Then he stepped through the gates into the palace.

"Your Highness." A captain named Philo waited for him, the man bowing low. He was in his later years, hair more gray than brown, skin tanned dark from a life spent on duty in the sun. Keris had had only minimal contact with him, given his penchant for avoiding all things military, but he recalled Otis describing him as a good leader and popular with the men.

So he inclined his head and said, "I'm pleased to see you well, Captain. It's Philo, isn't it?"

Surprise flickered through the man's eyes, though whether it was for the courtesy or the fact Keris had remembered his name,

Keris didn't know. That either was a shock was a reminder that he had a great deal of damage to undo as far as his past behavior toward the men of this garrison.

Philo recovered from his surprise swiftly, gesturing to the palace. "Your rooms are ready, Your Highness. I'll have your things brought up if you care to recover from your journey."

Resting his hand on the man's shoulder, Keris pushed him in the direction of the entrance. "What I'd like, Captain, is a report on the state of Nerastis. With recent happenings in Vencia, the situation is more volatile than in recent history."

"Yes, Highness." Philo cast him a sideways glance. "Serin was here in advance of your arrival, though he has since departed. He apprised us of all the developments."

Of course he did. It was a struggle not to scowl, though the information was not entirely shocking. The merchant vessel he and Zarrah had traveled on had made port in several harbors on its journey south, which meant another ship or even a fast rider would have arrived in Nerastis far in advance of them. For all he didn't regret a moment he spent with her on that ship, it didn't mean those moments came without cost. "A long journey for the Magpie to only supply an update."

"He was in pursuit of Aren Kertell and his . . . *wife.*"

Shock rippled through Keris. "In Nerastis?"

"The Red Desert, as the case may be." Philo led Keris to the war room, then closed the door behind them. "They were pursued south and cut off by a force from our garrison, dispatched on Serin's orders. They fled into the Red Desert and are now presumed dead."

Given Lara had been raised in the Red Desert, Keris would presume no such thing, but the larger question was why the pair hadn't gone back to Ithicana. Had they been prevented from reaching the sea, and this was their only avenue of escape?

Or had they gone south with a purpose?

"Keep me apprised of any developments." Keris's eyes went to the map of the continent, tracking from Vencia to Nerastis down to Pyrinat. "What of Zarrah Anaphora? Was she with them?" What he really wanted to know was whether the spies had seen her in Nerastis. What he really wanted was news that she was safe.

Philo shook his head. "It was only the pair of them."

Which meant no news had come of Zarrah's return.

What if she hadn't made it to shore? What if she'd drowned? Or been attacked by something in the water? What if she were injured somewhere and in need of help? What if Bermin had taken one look at her and killed her?

Focus.

He turned from the map to face Philo. "I want a total cessation on raids across the border, with all efforts turned to defense. More patrols along the Anriot within the city and as far east as the Red Desert." The rest of the instructions poured from his lips, ideas he'd had long ago but had never implemented because that would have meant involving himself. Would have meant conceding to his father.

But he needed these men to respect him so that when the time came, they'd follow him against his father.

Philo stared at Keris like he'd never seen him before, but to his credit, he only nodded. "It will be done, Your Highness."

Then a knock sounded at the door. A moment later, a soldier stepped in and passed Philo a piece of paper. The captain read it and frowned, then handed it to Keris. "Likely nothing to be concerned about, Your Highness."

Keris read it and felt his stomach plummet, because Philo couldn't have been more wrong.

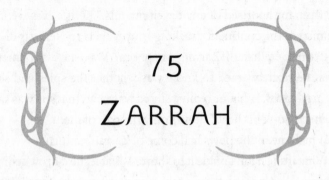

75
ZARRAH

ZARRAH READ THE SPY'S REPORT AGAIN, THEN SET IT DOWN. "IT would seem that the princeling shows no interest in lowering his defenses at the border, so perhaps the empress's watch-and-wait stance is for the best." She couldn't help but wonder how long Keris would be able to maintain this level of militance. How long it would be until Silas was forced to strip the Nerastis garrison in order to continue his fight against the Ithicanians.

A conflict that she was about to extend by delivering on her promise to Aren.

Bermin's jaw was tight, his eyes again dark. "You aren't in command anymore, little Zarrah—that is the price of your overambition, and you'd do well not to overstep."

Ah, Zarrah thought, his unease about her intentions a subtle clue that Zarrah had not entirely fallen from the empress's grace. "I've no desire to resume command of this garrison. My intent is to return to Pyrinat and, by the empress's will, to remain there permanently."

Silence.

Often, she'd called her cousin stupid, but that wasn't entirely the case, for he possessed a certain sort of selfish cunning. That cunning was now hard at work, judging the truth of her words. And they were true—Zarrah's eyes weren't on the title of general. They were on the empress's throne in Pyrinat.

"You've changed," Bermin finally said, and she gave the slightest of nods.

"I had a great deal of time alone to reflect on my choices of the past." She cleared her throat. "I do need a favor from you, though. I incurred debts in my escape that would be more easily paid while I am in Nerastis, but I will have difficulty accessing my credit, given I've little proof of my identity. Would you write something guaranteeing me?"

Bermin huffed out a breath. "You need coin."

The color that heated her cheeks was no act, and if there'd been a way to avoid this, she would have. But waiting until she could visit the bankers in Pyrinat was not a delay that she could afford, and the scheme she'd planned needed her to be here to enact it. "Yes. And as soon as I've paid my debts, I'll be on a ship south."

"It's the least I can do." He reached for a paper but paused before dipping his pen into the pot of ink. "If it had been my choice, we'd have gone after you, cousin. For all that our relationship has been strained in recent years, you are my blood. And abandoning you cost me honor."

Zarrah drew in a breath, the sentiment hitting her harder than she expected. "Thank you," she said, watching as he swiftly wrote a note guaranteeing her, sealing the purple wax with his heavy signet ring before handing the document over. As she was tucking it into a pocket, the food arrived, the servants filling Bermin's desk with plate after plate. Zarrah dug in, the familiar tastes exquisite on her tongue, her cousin also eating with relish, both of them sipping at sweet wine.

"We heard some details about your escape," Bermin said between mouthfuls. "Is it true the traitor queen orchestrated it all?"

Zarrah nodded. "She's a force to be reckoned with, as are her sisters. If Silas allowed women into his armies, I daresay we might be the losers in the encounter." When her cousin gave an amused snort, she added, "I'm not joking, Bermin. The six of them infiltrated the palace in nothing but dancing costumes, with no weapons, and took down at least two dozen of Silas's men."

Bermin blinked, then gave an appreciative nod. "When did you part ways with them?"

"In Vencia." She sipped her wine. "I expect they're already back in Ithicana." A reminder that she needed to honor her debt, not sit around drinking with her cousin.

But Bermin shook his head. "They're not in Ithicana. And they also haven't been killed by Silas's men, despite rumors to the contrary. Last word we received, the Maridrinians were pursuing Aren Kertell and his queen, who were alone, into the Red Desert."

The wine soured in her mouth. "Pardon?"

"They're probably dead by now. Or if not now, then soon." Bermin drained his glass. "No supplies, no camels, no *water*. They've not got a goddamned chance."

Zarrah's stomach hollowed, grief making her body ache, and she set her glass down with a heavy clink. What had gone so horribly wrong that they'd been pushed into the Red Desert? What had happened to Keris's other sisters? To the Ithicanians who'd been part of the rescue?

"You grieve for them?"

"Yes." She pressed her hand to her heart to honor them. "Aren is a good man. An honorable one, for all he's made mistakes. He helped me when he didn't have to." And not to save himself but to save his people. Her eyes stung, and she squeezed them shut. "I wish I could have done more."

Across from her, Bermin shifted in his chair, and she felt his discomfort. Knew it was because he hated displays of emotion that he didn't share. So it was no shock when he said, "You should rest, cousin. I'll have your things brought to you."

"Thank you." She rose. "I'll make arrangements to depart for Pyrinat as soon as I can find a ship sailing south."

"Let me know if I can assist."

He led her to the door, giving the order to a waiting servant to see her to a room and for her things to be brought to her. Zarrah silently followed the servant to the quarters, her packed clothing and personal belongings arriving while she was in the bath.

Dressing in her uniform, Zarrah strapped her weapons on and ensured her cousin's letter was safely stowed in her pocket before leaving word she was going to speak with ship captains about passage.

Valcotta had control of the Nerastis port, and the docks were currently full of merchant vessels loading and unloading cargo, with well-armed naval vessels anchored in the harbor, watchful for any sign of a Maridrinian attack. But Zarrah ignored the military ships, instead eyeing merchant vessels being loaded with grains harvested from the fertile fields south of the city. Not just any ship would do. She needed one capable of weathering the Tempest Seas—and one with a captain with the balls to do so. Spotting a familiar vessel, she approached, the sailors stopping what they were doing when one of them recognized her.

"I'd like to speak to your captain," she said, and was swiftly escorted to his quarters.

"General!" The captain clambered to his feet, eyes wide as he pressed his hand to his heart. "We'd heard of your escape with Ithicana's king, but not that you'd returned to Nerastis. It is a relief to see you alive."

Zarrah didn't correct the use of what was now Bermin's title, only inclined her head. "It feels good to be back on Valcottan soil." When he motioned to the chair across the desk, she sat. "You're loading a cargo of grain, yes? Destined for Pyrinat, I assume?"

He nodded. "We'd be happy to provide passage south, if that is your desire. I'll provide you my own cabins for the honor."

She gave him a smile. "Thank you for your generosity, but while it is my intent to travel south, any ship might provide me passage. The favor I require is for a captain who is experienced in more . . . *dangerous* waters. And one who can ensure the discretion of his crew."

Which, given this man used to be a smuggler, he most definitely could do.

The captain's eyebrows rose, and he rubbed his grizzled chin. "I might be interested."

Drawing a map on his desk in front of her, Zarrah tapped Eranahl Island. "I want you to drop your cargo here."

He snorted. "Eranahl is blockaded by the Amaridians, and anyone who approaches will be welcomed by the Ithicanians' shipbreakers. With respect, no amount of compensation is worth my life, General."

"Not at Eranahl itself," she said. "But on neighboring islands in close proximity to it. The only requirement is that you not be seen by the Amaridians and that the cargo be stored safely enough to weather any storms."

The captain leaned back in his chair, brown eyes shrewd. "This is a return of favor to Aren Kertell for your liberty, yes?"

She gave a slight nod.

He made a humming noise. "It is good you wish to honor your agreement, my lady, but this runs counter to the empress's proclamations. Aren Kertell spit on her friendship, and Ithicana is paying the price of that choice. To do this, however much I might wish otherwise, runs counter to that."

My lady. It was a struggle not to grind her teeth, for she'd gone only by military titles for all her adult life. He knew she had no power to seize a cargo.

Fortunately, Bermin did. And it seemed some of Keris's ways of getting things done had worn off on her.

Extracting her cousin's guarantee, she slid it across the desk, watching as the captain eyed the signature and seal. "Shall we get to the matter of compensation?"

They haggled for the next hour, then landed on an amount that made Zarrah wince, for the accounts she listed the funds to be drawn from were her own. While she was an heiress in her own right, possessing many estates that provided her a rich income, a cargo full of grain was still expensive. They toasted the agreement with wine, then clasped hands, and Zarrah departed in search of passage to Pyrinat.

Walking down the gangplank, her eyes went again to Keris's palace, gleaming in the distance. *He knows what he's doing,* she told herself, but it did nothing to temper the unease in her stomach. For his entire life, he'd resisted learning to fight or having any part in the Maridrinian military, and much of the reason for that choice was his fear of becoming like his father. Yet now he was embracing the role, and though she knew it was an act born of necessity, she also knew that if you played a character for long enough, you risked becoming them.

You could go to the dam tonight, she told herself. There was no guarantee he'd be there, but on the chance he might . . . She could caution him not to take things too far, lest he do something he regret. And . . .

Her stomach tightened at what else they might do other than talk, the memory of his hands on her body making her skin flush, his voice echoing in her ears . . . *I love you.*

Would being in his arms one last time be such a crime? Tomorrow she'd set sail, and all chance to see him would be lost, and there might never be another again.

A booming voice calling her name caught her attention, and Zarrah looked up to see Bermin coming down the docks toward her. "Before you depart," he said, "I've news you might be interested in hearing."

"Oh?"

"We just received a report of eighteen casualties in Jerin Oasis, most of them Maridrinian. The messenger said it started with some Maridrinian tart getting caught thieving, so they threw her in the stocks to crisp in the sun," her cousin said. "Then a man— a big Harendellian merchant who went by the name of James— poisoned all the patrons at a bar as a distraction while he rescued her before slaughtering a caravan of men to take their camels and supplies before escaping south. Only survivor was a boy, who said the man called the Maridrinian woman his wife."

An icy chill ran down her spine. *Not possible.*

They'd entered the Red Desert with no supplies. No camels. No goddamned *water.* Yet somehow, Lara and Aren had made it to an oasis at the midpoint of the desert and were headed south.

South.

Zarrah's mouth turned sour, understanding rippling through her. They weren't just running from Silas—they had a destination in mind. Aren, whom she'd made a deal with in exchange for escape. Aren, who knew it was actually Keris who'd gotten her free. Aren, who fucking *knew* about her and Keris's relationship, was headed to Pyrinat.

And Zarrah had no doubt in her mind whom he intended to meet with once he got there.

"What do you suppose the chances are"—Bermin rocked on his heels—"that this pair of violent lovers are the king and queen of Ithicana?"

She'd bet money on it.

"I need to speak with the empress." Spotting a vessel starting to push back from the dock, she sprinted toward it, shouting, "Pyrinat?"

One of the sailors nodded, so she jumped the gap, landing on the deck of the ship. The sailors stared at her as she smoothed her clothing. "I need passage. And I'll pay triple if you make haste."

Because if Aren made it there ahead of her, *everything* she'd sacrificed would have been in vain.

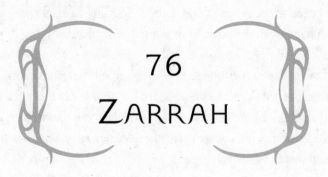

76

ZARRAH

She had a residence in the city, a towering sandstone home with large windows filled with stained glass that she hadn't stayed in for more than a night for longer than she could remember, but Zarrah didn't bother stopping there to clean up.

Instead, she headed straight to the palace.

The headwind had fought the ship all the way to Pyrinat, leaving Zarrah to pace the deck as her mind ran through every possible scenario. From Lara and Aren succumbing to the desert to them beating her to Pyrinat and using the damning information against her in an attempt to negotiate for the empress's aid in retaking Ithicana.

For there was no doubt in her mind that assistance was what they'd ask for, though what her aunt's response would be, Zarrah was not so certain.

But she was about to find out.

Her boots thudded against the bridge as she crossed the moat surrounding the empress's palace, the guards at the entrance recognizing her uniform before they latched onto her face. Hands pressed to their hearts, they opened the doors ahead of her.

The heavy doors swung inward, revealing an expansive court-yard with a large fountain at the center of it. Dispatching a young boy to deliver word of her arrival, the guard led her across the open space, through a pair of bronze gates on the far side, and into the palace.

Instinctively, her eyes went up to the twisted iron of the ceiling, which was wrought into delicate, curving shapes containing the finest colored glass, the light passing through it casting rainbows across the pathways of translucent glass tiles that wove through gardens filled with blooming flowers.

Her aunt's steward approached, flanked by a girl carrying a bowl of water and lavender toweling, the man remaining silent as Zarrah cleansed her hands. Then he said, "The empress has been made aware of your arrival, my lady." Smiling, he added, "We are most pleased to have you returned. We feared the worst with so much time having passed since you escaped Vencia with no sign of you."

A flicker of guilt ran through Zarrah, because she could have been here weeks ago if not for Keris's choice of vessel. And not once had she considered that anyone would be concerned for her well-being. "The journey took longer than anticipated, I'm afraid. And I couldn't risk sending word."

"All that matters is that you are here, my lady. Her Imperial Majesty will be overjoyed."

Zarrah could only pray that was true as she followed the steward.

If Lara and Aren had already arrived, someone would have mentioned it, which gave Zarrah some degree of relief as she followed the steward out into the open air of the empress's gardens.

They walked down the pathways in silence, Zarrah deep in thought. This had once been her home, and as a child, she'd raced through these gardens. Streams crisscrossed the space in mimicry of Pyrinat's canals, tiny bridges built to look identical to those in the city allowing one to cross, though she'd always favored leaping onto the stepping-stones or swimming where the water pooled. Even now, some of her second and third cousins swam under the watchful eyes of servants, who knew it would mean their lives if harm came to the royal children.

As they passed toward the rear of the palace, Zarrah made out the familiar clacking of practice weapons colliding. Sure enough, her aunt was sparring with her bodyguard, a massive man who'd served in the position as long as Zarrah had been alive. Welran was twice the empress's size, and tremendously skilled, but as Zarrah watched, her aunt got under his guard, staff catching him behind his knees and sending him spilling to the ground.

The empress snapped, "You grow lax in your old age. There was a time I would not have been capable of doing that, and my skill has not grown in recent years."

"Apologies, Majesty." Welran rose to his feet, and Zarrah flinched at the shame in his eyes. The man bore dozens of scars earned in defense of his empress and did not deserve chastisement. Then her aunt pulled the staff from his hands and twisted, throwing it at Zarrah. "Let's see how soft you've gotten in Maridrinian care."

Zarrah caught it easily, stepping onto the sand, saying nothing as they circled each other. Her aunt's jaw was tight and her gaze cool, but if she'd intended to send Zarrah walking back out the doors of the palace, she wouldn't have bothered with the sparring.

This time, Zarrah wasn't exhausted. Wasn't hungover. But more than that, she could tell her aunt expected her to be weak from months of captivity.

Zarrah wasn't weak.

She immediately attacked, and she saw the surprise in the empress's eyes at the force of it.

"Angry at me for not rescuing you, are you, child?"

"I'm not a child, Auntie." Zarrah knocked the staff from her aunt's hands. "I had no expectations of rescue."

She waited for her to retrieve the weapon, then went on the attack again, but this time, her aunt was ready. They drove each other back and forth across the training yard, Zarrah's pulse roaring as she hunted for an opening. But the empress didn't give her one.

Sweat rolled down her cheeks, kicked-up sand sticking to her face, but Zarrah barely felt the discomfort. Barely noticed other members of her large extended family coming to watch, the children laughing and cheering.

There.

Seeing an opening, Zarrah rolled, catching her aunt behind the knees with her weapon and sending her sprawling into the sand.

Everyone fell silent, waiting to see what the empress would do, but the older woman only rolled onto her back, spitting out sand.

Reaching down, Zarrah held out a hand. The empress stared at it for a long moment, expression unreadable, then she smiled and took it. "That's my girl."

Zarrah pulled her upright, her aunt slipping her arm in hers and leading her toward the tallest tower. Though the structures were nothing alike in appearance, she found herself struck by the similarities to Silas's tower in Vencia. The thought sent a prickle of unease across her skin, but she ignored it.

"Bermin tells me that you were on the north side of the Anriot spying, and that was how the Maridrinians caught you. Is this true?"

Bermin must have sent a courier the moment she'd left his office, and whoever it was must have ridden day and night, switching horses, to have beat her ship to Pyrinat. Not unexpected, but still irritating. "Yes. I was caught by a dawn patrol."

"So you weren't seeing a man as Yrina suggested?"

Shit. "No. I told her that only so she wouldn't follow me."

Her aunt snorted in disgust. "It was her duty to protect you. Perhaps if you'd allowed her to do so, you'd not have suffered the shame of capture, and Yrina would be alive." The look she gave Zarrah was pointed. "She is dead, isn't she?"

"Yes." Her tongue felt thick. "Or so I was told."

"The Veliants might have killed her, but Yrina's death is on your hands." Her aunt spit on the grass. "A waste of a good soldier, but at least she died with honor, fulfilling her oath."

The pain of Yrina's death welled hot and fresh, but Zarrah only nodded.

"The Harendellians say you were treated well. Is that true?" Her aunt stopped in her tracks, twisting to grip Zarrah's shoulders. "Did they *touch* you?"

She blinked, it taking a heartbeat for her to understand the meaning. "No. I was kept within the harem, surrounded by women. No one . . . *touched* me."

The empress's dark eyes searched hers, her grip tight enough that it would leave bruises, spikes of pain running down Zarrah's arms. "Better to die than to live having been befouled by one of those vermin, do you understand me?"

It was a struggle not to jerk out of her aunt's grip as revulsion coursed through Zarrah's body. Not at the suggestion of being forced against her will, as awful as that was, but at the suggestion that it would be better to die than to survive it. "The only time Silas Veliant touched me was to punch me in the face the night I escaped."

"It's not Silas who concerns me. He's loyal to the harem, so if he wants a woman, he marries her first." She laughed. "And the Maridrinians would rip him apart if he married a Valcottan. But what of the others? What about his sons?"

Too close to home. Far too close for comfort, and a bead of sweat ran down Zarrah's temple. She prayed her aunt would attribute it to the pain she was causing as she said, "Beyond being beaten when I was captured and nearly dying from the poison on one of the princelings' blades, no harm was done to me, Auntie."

"A mercy." Her aunt eased her grip, then smiled, though her gaze remained flat. Then she pulled Zarrah against her. "It was the worst form of torture knowing he had you, dear one. Every instinct in my heart demanded that I lead my armies north and take you back by force, but I had to think of the good of Valcotta."

You could have freed me by agreeing to drop the blockade, Zarrah thought, but said, "I understood your choice—knew you were acting in what you believed was the best interest of Valcotta."

Her aunt stiffened, pushing back from her. "What I *knew* was in the best interest of Valcotta. Our blockades are starving Maridrina of both coin and food, which renders them weak. To drop them would concede that advantage."

"Bermin tells me you intend to take back the other half of Nerastis and then press north."

"Does he, now? And what say you of such a venture?"

Zarrah had walked away from the chance of a life with Keris so that she might stop such a war. So that she might use what influence she had with the empress to pursue peace, in some form. Wise strategy would suggest that she ingratiate herself once more with her aunt before pursuing her goals, but Zarrah was afraid that if she didn't take a step now, she never would. "The Harendellian ambassador shared with me the losses that Valcotta has taken from the Tempest Seas for the sake of bypassing the bridge, and I think those will not be regained by taking Nerastis and a few extra miles of coast. It's not a big enough prize for the sacrifice you are making, Auntie."

This time the smile reached her aunt's eyes. "I agree, Zarrah. It isn't."

Armed guards swung open the doors to the empress's tower, which were made of twisted metal inset with glass of a thousand different colors to create the image of a woman with her hands held up to a blue sky. But before they could enter, the steward rushed toward them, breathless. "Your Imperial Majesty," he said. "King Aren Kertell is here. And the Maridrinian woman is with him."

They were here.

Her aunt let out a soft hiss, then said, "You're sure it's them?"

The steward lowered his head. "A—"

"I know their faces," Zarrah interjected. "Allow me to go to ensure they are who they say they are."

The empress waved a hand at the steward. "Keep them entertained for the time being. Food. Drink. Tell him I'll see him when I've concluded my business."

When the man had departed, her aunt rounded on her. "What did you promise him in exchange for your freedom? Because if it is Valcotta's assistance in his war—"

"I committed you to nothing," Zarrah interrupted, earning herself a cold glare. "And my debt to Aren Kertell is my own. If he's come here to ask something of you, it has nothing to do with me. I believed his intent was to return to Ithicana."

The empress's lip curled. "He knows he can't win back his kingdom alone. Yet he brings *that woman* with him to negotiate. Delia must be turning in her grave to see what ruin her son has brought to her kingdom—the fool thinks with his cock, not his brains."

"What bigger blow can you strike against Silas than to help Ithicana take back the bridge he fought so hard to possess?" Not that she wished Valcotta to go to war, but if it was between liberating Ithicana and invading Maridrina, Zarrah would push the former.

Her aunt only smiled and then flicked her fingers. "Go, darling. Retrieve them, and let us see how he who once spit upon our friendship now begs for favor."

Zarrah chewed on the insides of her cheeks as she walked away, her mind racing as she considered, firstly, how to warn Aren to keep his goddamned mouth shut about Keris, and secondly, what her aunt was planning. She had no intention of assisting Aren; that much was obvious. And while Bermin believed her intent was to retake Nerastis and much of the land north of the city, that goal seemed too shallow on ambition to account for the gleam in the empress's eyes.

Was it the bridge? Did her aunt want it for herself? Did she want Ithicana and Maridrina to exhaust themselves in a drawn-out war, which would allow Valcotta to swoop in and take it in the empress's name?

That would certainly be a bitter pill for Silas to swallow, but also made no strategic sense, for it would only put Valcotta in the same position Maridrina was in now—in possession of an asset that cost more than it earned. While the empress was motivated by pride, she was no fool—Zarrah could not see her making that choice.

So what did she intend?

Exiting the gardens and moving into the palace, Zarrah steadied her breath as she approached the gazebo where the royal pair had been left to wait. Her eyes latched onto Aren first, the Ithicanian king pacing back and forth, his nerves clearly on display, whereas Lara sat calmly, sipping on a glass of wine. Both had shadows under their eyes, faces lean from hard living, but neither showed any serious injury. A feat, given what she suspected they'd endured since parting ways with Zarrah on the stairwell in Silas's tower.

At the sound of her steps, Aren stopped pacing, his dark eyes finding her. Zarrah gave him a wide smile of welcome. "Good to see you alive, Your Majesty." She touched her hand to her chest, knowing that the empress would be appraised of her every word by the servants and guards surrounding the gazebo. "I heard you ran into some trouble after we parted ways outside the gates of Vencia."

That was the lie she'd told, and she *needed* him to hold to the same story.

Aren's eyes narrowed, noting how her words were a departure from the truth, and it was a struggle not to hold her breath as he hesitated in his response. Then he said, "Likewise—I'm pleased to see you are well."

"I didn't have the opportunity to thank you, so allow me to do so now," she said. "Perhaps there will come a time when I might repay you."

"I think we're even," he said, though there was no chance he knew she'd fulfilled her promise to him. The ship she'd sent likely hadn't even arrived in Ithicana yet, much less word of it come back to Pyrinat.

Either way, the last thing she needed was her aunt learning of her little trick, so Zarrah gave a slight shake of her head and a warning gaze, hoping it would silence him on the subject. Praying that he was enough of a politician to realize that her actions were not sanctioned by the empress. Then she gestured at the guards. "Stand down. His Grace is who he says he is." She moved her eyes to Lara's, the woman's azure eyes so remarkably like Keris's, not just in color but in their scrutiny, that it made Zarrah's chest tighten. "As is she."

The trek across the Red Desert had darkened the Queen of Ithicana's complexion to a golden brown, which made the many scars marking the woman's skin more pronounced. A woman of rare and dangerous beauty, and Zarrah thought it little wonder that Aren had fallen for her. "I enjoyed your dance very much, Your Majesty. Though not as much as I enjoyed watching you kick wine into your father's face."

Lara inclined her head, her voice soft but strong as she said, "I enjoyed that as well."

She needed to bring them to the empress, but Zarrah found herself hesitating. They'd endured so much to reach Pyrinat, and it would be for nothing. It made her sick with guilt. Not only because of what they'd done for her but because Ithicana didn't deserve the hand it had been dealt—nothing more than a pawn falling victim in a conflict between rival nations. But that was something they'd need to learn themselves.

"Come, come." She kept her voice light. "My aunt wishes to know the face behind the name. I expect she's also looking forward to a chance to berate you for every choice you've made in your reign."

With Aren towering at her elbow, Zarrah led them down the garden paths, feeling Lara's stare between her shoulder blades as she told him, "Silas has been spreading rumors of your death, Aren. Up and down the coast, though the story of how you died changes with every telling. We, of course, questioned the veracity of the claims. Silas is a braggart, and no Ithicanian heads adorn Vencia's gates."

Turning, she said to Lara, "No women fitting the descriptions of those who assisted you, either. Were they truly all your sisters?"

Lara met her eye, unblinking. "Yes."

Zarrah felt the woman dissecting her expression, looking for clues and tells of what she and Aren would face with the empress. Once, it would have unnerved her, but Zarrah only smiled and said, "Fascinating. I wonder if it's ever dawned on your father that Maridrina might win the war between our two nations if he set aside his foolish notions about a woman's role."

"That would require him admitting he was wrong in the first place," Lara replied. "Which seems unlikely."

"I'm inclined to agree." Zarrah lifted her shoulder in a shrug that belied the nerves coursing through her guts. "Your homeland's misfortune has long been to Valcotta's benefit, so I cannot honestly admit that I'm sorry."

Lara didn't answer, and the conversation died, both the King and Queen of Ithicana eyeing the interior of the palace with curiosity, although their attention focused as she brought them into the empress's tower.

Her aunt had changed out of her fighting leathers and wore loose trousers and a blouse, both of gold silk, her arms encircled with dozens of bangles and her graying hair woven with golden wire strung with amethysts. Gold bracelets climbed both arms to her elbows, her ears were cuffed with gold and gems, and her throat was encased with an intricately carved gold necklace. In her hands was a half-finished doll, her fingers lovingly toying with the threads as though she were making it for a beloved child.

Except the Empress of Valcotta did *not* have time for macrame. This was a scene staged for Aren and Lara's benefit, her aunt presenting herself in a way that was wholly unfamiliar to Zarrah. And *that*, more than the lie itself, put her on edge.

But she hid her unease, saying, "Aunt, might I present His Royal Majesty, King Aren of Ithicana, Master of the Bridge—"

"Ah, but you're not its master anymore, are you, boy?" Her aunt's gaze did not move from the doll in her hands. "That honor belongs to the Maridrinian rat. I imagine that's why you're here, isn't it?"

Before Aren could answer, she continued. "And you, girl. I assume you're the rat's get? You'll be accorded no titles in this house. Be glad I don't have you dragged outside and your throat slit."

Lara was of identical blood to Keris, and it was not lost on Zarrah that if he stood before the empress, the words might be the same. Might well be worse.

Aren tensed, but Lara only tilted her head, gaze full of challenge as she said, "Why don't you?"

"Because as much as we might wish it otherwise, your life doesn't belong to Valcotta. Nor your death."

There wasn't so much as a hint of fear on Lara's face as she said, "Your honor is my salvation." Indeed, Zarrah's skin prickled with the sense of threat, for though every individual present was a warrior of renown, this small blond woman was more dangerous than all of them combined.

Her aunt let out an annoyed huff, suggesting she also saw the threat and didn't like it. "Don't speak to me of honor."

Setting aside the doll, she rose to her feet, and Aren inclined his head. "Your Imperial Majesty. It is a privilege to meet you in person."

"A privilege or a necessity?" Her aunt circled the pair, ignoring Zarrah entirely. Lara's brow furrowed, but Aren's face was completely composed as he said, "Can't it be both?"

The empress pursed her lips, making a noncommittal noise in response. "For the sake of your mother, who was our dearest of friends, we are pleased to see you alive. But for ourselves?" Her voice hardened. "We do not forget how you spit upon our friendship."

Zarrah saw what she was doing—turning a political conflict into a personal one, which meant she intended to use personal justifications to weasel her way out of offering Ithicana assistance.

Aren only rubbed his chin and said, "You speak of my mother as your dearest friend, and yet it was she who proposed the Fifteen-

Year Treaty between Ithicana, Harendell, and Maridrina, including the marriage clause. My mother formed the alliance with your greatest enemy, and for it you held her no ill will. And yet when I followed through on her wishes, I lost favor in your eyes."

Her aunt stopped in front of Aren, her dark-brown eyes unreadable. "Your mother had little choice. Ithicana was starving. And the treaty as she wrote it cost Valcotta nothing. It was the terms you agreed to fifteen years later that were the slight." She leveled a finger at him. "My soldiers dying on steel supplied by Ithicana's bridge."

Aren shook his head. "Steel supplied by *Harendell,* which Maridrina was already importing by ship. It cost them less, yes, but to say they were at any greater advantage against your soldiers is a fallacy. It also gave Valcotta the unique opportunity to prevent Silas from retrieving his precious import for the better part of a year, so one might argue that the terms worked in your favor."

"What benefit we saw faded swiftly when you turned your shipbreakers on my fleet," her aunt countered. "You chose your alliance with Maridrina over your friendship with Valcotta, and now you come weeping because you discovered your ally was a rat."

"You put Ithicana in a position where all paths led to war, and when I gave you a path to peace, you refused it."

"It was no choice." Her aunt threw up her hands, but Zarrah suspected her frustration was feigned. "If we'd dropped the blockade, Maridrina would've gotten what it wanted without a fight. More steel to use against Valcotta. Besides, it was clear that the last thing Silas wanted was peace. Especially peace with Ithicana."

"If you foresaw what was to come and said nothing, what friend are you?"

No truer words had ever been spoken, and Zarrah saw the slight tightening in her aunt's jaw, suggesting that they'd struck home. But not in the way Aren had intended.

"Just because I see the clouds in the sky doesn't mean I can predict where the lightning will strike."

The silence that came after was tense, and Zarrah sensed her aunt revising her measure of Ithicana's king. "We have more to discuss, but I believe it a discussion best done in private." The look she turned on Lara was not friendly. "You will wait here."

Ithicana's queen's eyes turned equally frosty. "No."

Zarrah winced, knowing well what was to come, and sure enough, her aunt said, "Welran, subdue her."

Her aunt's enormous bodyguard tackled Lara to the ground and twisted her arm behind her back. Except Zarrah had seen the woman fight and *knew* the woman had allowed the takedown. She opened her mouth to warn the man, then shut it, abruptly uncertain whose side she was on in this engagement.

Aren, however, pressed his hand to Welran's shoulder, giving him an amused smile. "I can't in good conscience go without warning you. She saw you coming from a mile away. Palmed your knife when you took her down. And all that wriggling she's doing? I'd bet my last coin that the blade is only about an inch from your balls."

Smiling, Zarrah followed Aren and her aunt, Welran's laugh echoing after them.

They climbed to the top, the staircase opening into a large room with stained-glass windows featuring prior rulers of Valcotta, all with their hands reaching up to the sky. Zarrah took her place next to the door, her aunt motioning for Aren to sit on one of the many pillows.

"Let us start first with a discussion of why you are here, Aren. I have my own theories, of course, but I'd like to hear it from your lips."

"I think you know that having the bridge under the control of Silas Veliant benefits no one, not even his own people." When her aunt made a noncommittal noise, he added, "I've received word that my sister, Princess Ahnna, has secured Harendell's support for retaking Northwatch. It is my hope that you'll see the merit in assisting me in securing Southwatch from Maridrina and reinstating Ithicana as a sovereign nation."

Picking up a glass, the empress eyed the contents, though Zarrah knew she was stalling. Her aunt did not drink wine during negotiations. "Southwatch isn't assailable. Or at least, not without an unpalatable loss of vessels and life."

"It is if you know how. Which I do."

"Giving up such a secret would make Northwatch and Southwatch forever vulnerable—would make *Ithicana* forever vulnerable."

The look in Aren's eyes suggested he was well aware of that fact, yet he said, "Not if Harendell and Valcotta are true friends and allies."

Her aunt gave an amused laugh. "The friendships between nations and rulers are inconstant, Aren. You yourself have proven that."

"True. But not so the friendship between peoples."

"You're an idealist."

Zarrah started at the word, remembering when Keris had called her so. Had he been right? She still wasn't sure.

"A realist," Aren answered. "Ithicana cannot continue as it has. To endure, we must change our ways."

Ithicana wasn't the only nation that needed to change. For while Valcotta certainly *could* continue to endure as it had, Zarrah no longer believed it should.

"You look like your mother," her aunt finally said, and Zarrah frowned at the shift in subject, knowing her aunt would only go in this direction if she believed it suited her purposes. "Though your father was equally easy on the eyes."

Aren's brow furrowed. "How could you possibly know that?"

Amusement flickered across her aunt's face—and pleasure—for she enjoyed knowing that which others did not. And equally enjoyed dropping it on them to good effect. "Surely you don't believe that I'd bestow friendship upon someone who only spoke to me from behind a mask?"

"She visited Valcotta?"

"Oh yes, many, *many* times. Delia was not one to be confined, and your father chased her up and down both continents trying to keep her safe. I was bested only once in Pyrinat's games, and imagine my shock to learn that the victor was an Ithicanian princess." Her aunt smirked and rubbed a faded scar across the bridge of her nose—one of many she possessed. "She was fierce."

Aren's voice was strangled as he said, "Yes."

"Is it true your father died trying to save her life?"

He nodded.

Her aunt's face fell, and she pressed her hand to her heart, but Zarrah's instincts jangled, warning her the sentiment was feigned. "I will grieve her loss, and his, until the end of my days."

Aren seemed to believe her genuine, for he said, "If you knew my mother so well, then you had to have known her dream for Ithicana and its people."

"Freedom? Yes, she told me." Her aunt shook her head. "But I agreed with your father in that it wasn't possible. Ithicana's survival was always dependent on it being impenetrable, or at least, nearly so. To unleash thousands of people who knew all of Ithicana's secrets would see them secret no longer." Her gaze hardened. "And worse still to allow others a view from the inside. But then, you learned that lesson, didn't you?"

Aren gave the slightest nod of acknowledgment, likely thinking of the wife he'd left downstairs.

"And yet not only do you allow Silas Veliant's weapon to live, you keep her close. Why is that?"

"She's not his weapon. Not anymore." Aren was on the defense. Which was exactly how the empress wanted him. "She broke me free of Vencia, and after that, I needed her to survive the trek across the Red Desert."

"It could be another ruse, you know. Ithicana has not yet fallen—a fact that sorely grieves Silas. How better to take Eranahl than to deliver into it the woman who cracked the defenses of the bridge?"

She was seeding doubt in his mind, but to what end, Zarrah wasn't certain. Then her aunt added, "It would be nothing for us to rid you of that particular problem. She could disappear," and Zarrah saw to the heart of her strategy. She was going to predicate her assistance on terms she knew Aren would never agree to.

And as predicted, the king went still. "No."

"Your people will never accept her as queen. She's the traitor who cost them their homes and the lives of their loved ones."

"I am aware. The answer is still no."

Silence.

"And if I say that Valcotta's support is contingent on her death?"

"No."

The empress shoved away her glass, rising to her feet in a flurry of motion, feigning anger even though she was getting her way. "Even now you put Maridrina first."

Aren rose as well. "I put the chance of peace before old grievances. Which is something you might consider."

The empress whirled back around, eyes flashing with true anger. "Peace with Maridrina? Son of my friend or not, in this you go too far. On my life, I'll not lay down my staff until Silas Veliant lays down his sword, and we both know that will never happen."

"It won't," Aren agreed. "But Silas won't rule forever. And neither will you."

A flicker of fury rose in her aunt's eyes, but she smiled as Aren pressed a hand to his heart, saying, "It was an honor to meet the friend of my mother, but now I must take my leave. Tonight, I sail to Ithicana."

He departed, but Zarrah remained, waiting for her aunt to speak.

"He's wrong, you know," the empress finally said. "My will and rule will continue after I'm gone—through you, my dearest. The Valcottan Empire will grow and expand in its power, and united in mind and desire, you and I will destroy our enemies."

Except we are not united, Zarrah thought. *You will sacrifice honor and decency to have your way. Will allow a nation to be crushed, families torn from their homes and children orphaned—like I was—by violence, all for the sake of achieving power and revenge.*

But she bit her tongue, because in order to stop her aunt, Zarrah needed her to believe she was complicit. So Zarrah inclined her head. "I understand your will, Imperial Majesty." *But I will have no part in seeing it done.*

"They need to be on a ship north now." Her aunt stared into the space between them, too caught up in her own thoughts and schemes to notice what Zarrah had *not* said. "The Magpie's spies will know they are here, and it won't be long until an attempt is made on their lives. Posting guards around their accommodations will imply I'm protecting them, which won't do, whereas if they are escorted onto a ship and dumped across the border, my stance on Ithicana is clear." She snapped her fingers, and a guard stepped into view. "Arrange an escort for the rulers of Ithicana. I want them at the harbor within the hour."

When he departed, the empress turned back to Zarrah. "The sooner Aren stirs the conflict with Maridrina over the bridge, the sooner we can attack. Which is why you need to return to Nerastis. We've three Maridrinian vessels that we've captured, and I want you to fill them with soldiers and sail north on the heels of

Aren and his *woman*. Mark my words, the moment his people have him back, Ithicana will rise up, and Silas will be forced to commit his reserves."

"And when he does?"

The empress's eyes gleamed. "Then you will enact our revenge, dear one. You will sail your ships into Vencia's harbor and attack. Will burn the city, tear down the palace, and make sure every last man, woman, and child bearing the Veliant name is put to sword."

Sickening horror filled Zarrah's stomach, but she nodded, watching as her aunt moved to her desk, writing on a sheet of paper. "Give this to Bermin. Silas will pull soldiers from Nerastis soon, if he has not done so already. Once they are gone, Bermin is to take the northern half of the city. His orders are the same: Ensure every Veliant in the city is put to death, with special care given to the *crown prince*." She lifted her head to meet Zarrah's gaze. "Keris Veliant will suffer for what he did to you, dear one. My son will make sure of that."

Ice ran through Zarrah's veins, and it felt as though she was seeing her aunt for the first time. Finally seeing her for the villain that she was. Yet what made Zarrah want to vomit was that she also still saw the woman who'd rescued her. Who'd cared for her. Who'd brought her back from the edge and made her strong. And seeing her flaws, Zarrah still *loved* her. "I understand."

"You are to share our intentions for Vencia with *no one*, General," her aunt said. "Your excuse for sailing north is reconnaissance and the protection of Valcottan merchant vessels, and you'll reveal the true plans to your soldiers and crew only at the final hour. The Magpie has spies everywhere, and we *cannot* risk word of our intentions reaching Silas in Vencia."

Zarrah nodded. "I'll keep your confidence, as always."

Her aunt sealed the letter and handed it to her. "Get Aren safely to the north side of Nerastis. His ability to rally Ithicana is critical to my plans—nothing can happen to him. Or to *that woman*." A flicker of a smile crossed her face. "Ithicana suffered under Veliant hands. Let them have their own revenge."

So much hate.

There was no tempering it. No argument that would cause the empress to see reason. No speech that would make her understand that her actions benefited nothing but her own pride. There was nothing Zarrah could do, especially in the short time that she had, to convince her aunt to change her plans for war with Maridrina.

Which meant the time for words was over.

"I'll take my leave." Zarrah pressed a hand to her heart. "I love you, Auntie. I hope you know that."

"Of course, dearest." Her aunt had returned to her desk and was staring at a map, eyes distant. "And I, you."

Hopefully enough to one day forgive me, Zarrah thought, and left the palace. In pursuit of an alliance with Ithicana.

And treason to Valcotta.

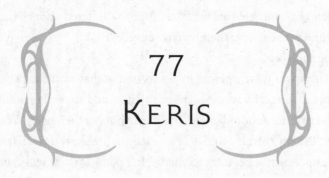

77
KERIS

KERIS READ THE PAGE CONTAINING HIS FATHER'S ORDERS, frowned, then tossed it across the table to Philo. He waited for the gray-haired man to read the contents, then asked, "How many men will that leave us with to defend the border?"

"A little more than a hundred." Philo set down the page. "And only two ships."

Not nearly enough to defend Nerastis if Bermin made a move, which was a large concern. But what worried Keris more was that by emptying the barracks here, his father would have the ships and men he needed to end the war with Ithicana and kill every last Ithicanian he found alive. His father would be victorious, the master of the bridge, and Keris's plans to use the dissent of the Maridrinian people to overthrow him would be in shambles, which meant peace with Valcotta would be a distant dream. And knowing how much Zarrah had given up in pursuit of that dream, Keris refused to allow that to come to pass.

Ithicana, even with its rulers lost to the Red Desert, needed to endure.

"That is problematic." Keris rubbed at his temples, his head foggy. His dreams had been plagued with nightmares about Zarrah, and exhaustion weighed upon him. "We risk losing Nerastis."

Faces darkened, and he dropped his hands, fixing the men with a cool stare. "Am I wrong? Is one of you actually going to sit there and argue that we are capable of repelling the Valcottans should they choose to cross the Anriot?"

They shifted uncomfortably, and Philo finally said, "You aren't wrong, Your Highness. With such low numbers, if the Valcottans made a move, we'd be forced to retreat."

"Retreat how far?" Keris asked, despite knowing the answer.

Philo opened his mouth, hesitated, then said, "Unless we received reinforcements, as far as they wished to push us."

What madness consumed his father that he was willing to take such a loss? Keris wanted to shout, but strategy demanded otherwise. He needed the criticism of his father to come from *these* men, not from him. "You're telling me that by sending these resources to my father to use in his fight against Ithicana, we risk losing Nerastis and miles of the best farmland in Maridrina?"

Yes. He could see the answer in their eyes. Yet also that their fear of his father still kept them silent. *Capitalize upon this,* a voice whispered in his head. *Turn them against him.* "The empress is notoriously opportunistic," he said. "How long can we keep our weakness hidden from them?"

Not long at all was the answer, but he waited for them to discuss it among themselves, Philo finally sighing. "A day, perhaps."

Keris said nothing, allowing the weight of that fact to sink in.

"The Valcottans haven't raided in months, despite us being undermanned," one of the other men argued.

"Because we had the empress's niece as our prisoner." Rising to his feet, Keris paced the length of the room. "But Serin's own creation got the better of him, and we lost that asset." It made him ill to speak of Zarrah that way, but it was a necessary evil.

"What would you have us do, Highness?" Philo asked. "The order comes from the king himself. We cannot refuse."

"No, we can't." Keris stopped pacing, toying with the pommel of his sword. "And yet if *we* lose Nerastis for lack of men, it will be *we* who are held accountable."

Turning, he pretended to stare at the map on the wall, waiting. As he'd predicted, Philo said, "His Majesty puts us in a position where we are destined to face his ill will regardless of what action we take."

The other men growled their agreement, and Keris felt their anger growing. Not new anger, for this wouldn't be the first time his father had put them in such a position, but anger they were only now speaking aloud. He smiled at the map, allowing them to mutter for a moment before turning. "What choice has he? For more than sixteen years, my father schemed to take the bridge, and now he has it. Would you have him give it up for the sake of a city of rubble?"

Eyes darkened at the word *schemed*. Not at his use of it, but that their king had used lies and subterfuge and his *own daughter* to win his prize.

"It's not Nerastis that has value, Highness, but the land north of it. The best land in Maridrina," Philo answered, not seeming to realize he was parroting Keris's words back at him. "Already Vencia goes hungry. If we were to lose those farms . . ."

Keris gave a slow nod. "I expect my father anticipates making up the shortfall through imports via the bridge."

Imports that would cost a fortune only a landed nobleman could afford, which none of these men were. They were career soldiers, and every last one of them had a family in Vencia that would go hungry if all of this came to pass.

Philo was on his feet in a flash. "Imports that no one can afford! This is madness driven by an excess of pride, Keris. The bridge has been nothing but a curse. Hundreds of lives lost trying to hold it, and for what? The bridge of untold riches has been rendered profitless by the politics between nations and the squabbling of kings and empresses, but it is the common people who starve." He gave Keris a pleading look. "You understand, don't you, Highness? You were against the taking of the bridge—that is well known. And it is said you listen to the concerns of the people. Even that you espouse the virtues of peace."

A flicker of an emotion Keris couldn't name filled his chest, for these very things had once earned him these men's scorn. "What I think or don't think matters little—I am as beholden to the will of the king as any of you, and just as subject to the consequences of crossing him."

Silence filled the room, the tension rising.

Then Philo said, "That hasn't stopped you in the past."

Keris returned to his seat, resting his elbows on the table. "You're suggesting I ignore orders from my father? From the king?"

"It would save lives, Highness. Hundreds, possibly thousands, of Maridrinian lives. And the cost . . ." Philo glanced sideways at his comrades, whose eyes were full of agreement. "If your father loses the bridge, well . . . maybe that's for the best."

Elation filled Keris's stomach, his pulse hammering and his skin hot, but he kept all of it from his face. "Then let us be united in our defiance." He leaned forward, finally allowing a smile to form on his face. "But know this, my friends: This step is only the beginning."

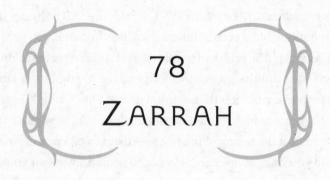

78
ZARRAH

THEY HAD A MATTER OF DAYS TO CREATE A PLAN TO TAKE BACK the bridge from Silas in one blow.

As Zarrah's ship sped them north toward Nerastis, she spent nearly every waking hour closeted in the captain's quarters with Aren Kertell and another Ithicanian, an older man by the name of Jor who had a penchant for filthy jokes and was doing a damned fine job of eating and drinking through the ship's supplies.

"You draw like a toddler," Jor snapped, jerking the pencil out of his king's hand and pulling a piece of paper in front of himself, brow furrowed as he sketched, pausing from time to time to sip at his glass of wine. But what materialized on the page was a remarkably detailed illustration of Southwatch Island, not just above the water but below.

"Here." Aren pointed at the dark circles Jor was shading at the base of the infamous pier. "And here. They are tunnels that come up through the island and let out in storage buildings. You'll need to use your best swimmers."

"What about the sharks?"

Aren shrugged as though the formidable man-eaters that haunted Ithicana's waters weren't a significant issue. "Motivation to swim fast. And it's the only way—you need to take out the ship-breakers, else you'll lose two of your three vessels before you reach shore."

Zarrah listened as he spoke, taking notes of the endless critical details of how to take what was broadly considered to be an unassailable island. An unveiling of secrets that every nation north and south would once have used against Ithicana but would now be used to save it, for Southwatch Island was Zarrah's target. Harendell, she'd learned, would be doing the same at Northwatch with the information provided by Aren's sister, Princess Ahnna Kertell, and the Ithicanians themselves would manage all the points in between. A union of three nations in a coordinated attack unlike anything she'd seen undertaken, but Aren seemed confident that it would work.

"I need to piss," Jor announced. "Don't tell him anything critical while I'm gone, General. Boy's got a brain like a sieve."

"I take back everything I said about missing you," Aren answered, though Zarrah noticed the fondness in his gaze as the older man departed. Then he turned his attention back to her. "Apologies for his language. And his jokes." He scrubbed his hair back from his face, then glanced at the door as though hoping it would open. "And for the small fortune in wine he's already consumed. He's a soldier through and through."

"Aren't we all." She sipped from her own glass, assessing Aren as he again glanced toward the door, ever hopeful Lara would walk through it, although Ithicana's queen was nearly always to be found on deck. *A distinct lack of sea legs,* Jor had told her, but Zarrah suspected Lara's motivations for staying out of discussions of strategy were more than just seasickness.

"She's not returning to Ithicana with you, is she?"

Aren's jaw tightened. "No. My people . . . they won't accept Lara after everything that's happened. Too many lives have been lost at Maridrinian hands, and for all she didn't intend for the invasion to happen, there is no denying that Lara came to us a spy. No denying that none of this would have occurred if not for the information she provided Silas. Bringing her with me would be perceived as me demanding my people bend knee to her as queen, and it would . . . *undermine* my ability to rally them behind me, which is critical. I need their support if Ithicana is to survive."

Everything Aren said was the undeniable truth, but the mix of anger and grief in his hazel eyes, and the bitterness in his voice, told Zarrah that he hated that truth. He was being forced to choose between his people and the woman he clearly loved, and though she couldn't say so, Zarrah knew how that felt. Knew what it was like to lie awake at night, searching for a way to have both. Knew what it felt like to have a wild passion take hold in the darkness and fill you with the certainty that you could *make* people accept things as you wanted them to be, only to have that certainty vanquished by the dawn light. Knew what it was like to consider turning your back on everything and everyone just for the sake of being with the person you loved.

"I'd bring her back anyway," he said, and the words sounded like a confession. "But I'm afraid . . ." He trailed off, throat convulsing as he swallowed hard, so Zarrah finished the thought.

"That they'll kill her."

Aren gave a tight nod. "If anything happened to her because I couldn't let her go, I'd . . . I couldn't live with it."

It was not her place to advise. Not even her place to voice an opinion. So Zarrah only covered his hand with hers and said, "No one can predict the future, Your Grace. Fate favors the strong. God rewards the good. And the stars never abandon those who dream of *more*."

Aren was quiet for a long moment, then he said, "Are you certain you wish to do this, Zarrah? It's not too late for you to stand down."

A question he'd asked many times since Zarrah had gone to him and Lara after their meeting with the empress. Since she'd proposed using the resources her aunt had provided her not to attack Vencia while Silas's back was turned, but to help Aren liberate Ithicana. And her answer was the same now as it was then. "Can you take back your kingdom without me?" She stared into his eyes. "I don't have a death wish, Aren. If you think Ithicana can drive Silas out without my ships and soldiers, tell me now, and I will bow out."

Aren's eyes went to Jor's sketch, and she knew he was considering what hadn't been drawn. The Maridrinian naval vessels circling the island, which he hadn't the means to combat. The sheer number of soldiers that Silas had protecting the asset. "It wouldn't be a quick battle. It would take time."

"Time is the enemy," she said. "Time means an opportunity for Silas to empty his garrisons in Vencia and Nerastis in order to fight you. And the moment he does that, the empress attacks. Vencia will be sacked and burned. Nerastis will be retaken and every Maridrinian living there put to sword before he realizes his error."

"You could get word to Keris," Aren said, rising to pace the room. "If Silas knows the empress's intent, he's not going to leave his capital undefended. The threat of her attacking might be enough for him to withdraw from Ithicana without a fight."

Zarrah snorted. "Don't tell me you honestly believe that? Silas has dedicated more than sixteen years, countless of his children, and bankrupted his kingdom in pursuit of Ithicana's bridge. And now he has it. He won't give it up without a fight; you know this. You know *him*."

"He's not going to let Vencia burn to keep it."

"Are you so sure? He's allowed Maridrina to starve and be ravaged by plague for the sake of this bridge—do you really think he wouldn't allow a city to burn?" Zarrah stared him down, willing Aren to remember the man who'd kept him prisoner for months. Yet at the same time, part of her prayed that he would see a way through this that she hadn't.

He exhaled, shoulders slumping. "You're right. Shit. *Shit*."

The fear she was fighting so hard to contain started to climb up her guts, and Zarrah clenched her teeth, forcing it down. Not allowing it any control. "If I do this, Aren, it's over before Silas has a chance to empty his garrisons. My aunt's plans to invade will be ruined, and Ithicana will be liberated."

"And you'll be executed for treason."

She would be. The empress had proven her willingness to cast Zarrah aside for the sake of her pride, and there would be no greater blow to her pride than Zarrah willfully thwarting her plans to destroy Maridrina. But she couldn't allow her aunt's pride to force Valcotta into dishonor. Couldn't stand by and watch Ithicana fall beneath Silas's heel. Couldn't stand by and watch her aunt raze Vencia to the ground. Couldn't stand by and watch the Endless War orphan another generation of children.

Her honor would not allow her to stand by any longer. Not when she had the power to take action.

Zarrah closed her eyes, seeing Keris's face even as she felt her dreams of them creating peace together slip away. "Some things are worth dying for."

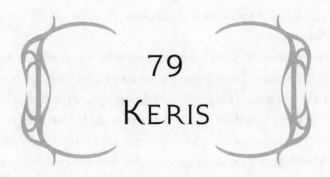

79
KERIS

NOT ALL OF HIS RESISTANCE TO GOING ON PATROLS HAD BEEN moral high ground—a good portion of it could be attributed to the task being god-awful tedious and even more uncomfortable.

Keris scowled as mud soaked through the knees of his trousers when he knelt, his eyes, and those of all the men around him, on the beach below. One of their vessels on the water had signaled that a Valcottan ship had been spotted heading inland, and Keris was using Zarrah's tactic of meeting them head-on. A good, clean battle that would show the Valcottans that Maridrina's hold on the border was as strong as ever.

Unfortunately, it meant he was going to have to fight.

You can do this, he silently told himself, trying to ignore the beads of sweat running down his back. *It isn't as though you're entirely incompetent with a weapon.*

A fact of little comfort, given the only real battle he'd ever been in was the taking of the bridge, and he'd been next to useless. It made him wonder if things would've gone differently for Raina and the rest of the Ithicanians if he'd been more skilled. Whether he'd have had the power to turn the tide.

Probably not.

From the water, Keris faintly made out the sound of a longboat being lowered. Of oars being placed into locks. Then there was only the soft roar of the gentle surf rolling against the shore.

"Only one longboat," Philo muttered from his left. "Might be scouts checking that it's safe to land before the rest come to shore. We should maintain cover and wait for them to give the signal, then attack when more hit the beach but their forces are still split. They'll take heavier losses."

Keris's jaw tightened, because a better option would be to scare off the scouts and reduce the body count to nil. These were Zarrah's people, and even if she was far away in Pyrinat, he still didn't want to be responsible for their deaths. "They might just be smugglers. Let's see what they're up to."

Ignoring Philo's protests, Keris moved closer to the beach, several of the men following at his heels. They reached the edge of the tree line as the longboat hit the beach and four people got out. It was too dark to see anything more than their shadowy outlines, their voices muffled as they exchanged a few words; then one headed in his direction.

Keris motioned to his men to keep down, then went still himself. The Valcottan who approached made not a whisper of noise until she paused, almost within arm's reach of Keris. She rested her shoulders against a tree before bending double.

"Just do it, you coward," she whispered. "Just get it over with and go—goodbyes will only make things worse."

Her accent wasn't Valcottan; it was Maridrinian. And there was something else . . . something familiar that he couldn't place . . .

Out of the corner of his eye, Keris saw one of the woman's

companions climbing back into the longboat, another pushing it out onto the surf before returning to join the fourth.

But it was hard to focus on them with the woman standing so close he could hear her breathing, so ragged he thought she might be on the verge of tears.

She abruptly whirled and headed back down to the beach, where the trio conversed briefly before one of them headed north along the waterline.

Something brushed against his arm, and Keris jerked, turning to find Philo at his elbow. "Not raiders," the man whispered softly. "Spies. We need to capture them to see what we might learn of Valcotta's intentions."

Something felt off, not the least of it that the woman had been Maridrinian. Yet the vessel on the water was without a doubt a Valcottan ship. Keris needed to get closer, needed to hear what the remaining two were saying.

Moving silently, he edged down to where those remaining two—the Maridrinian woman and an exceptionally tall man— were now arguing.

"Let Keris earn that crown he wants so badly—it's about time he got his hands dirty."

All the blood rushed from Keris's skin, his hands turning to ice. Not at the mention of his name or his plans but because he *knew* that fucking voice. That was Aren Kertell on the beach, which meant the woman had to be Lara. And they'd come off a Valcottan ship, which meant . . .

His skin prickled, and he glanced over his shoulder to see Philo and several of the others with bows in their hands, the weapons drawn.

Panic tore through his body, because that was his goddamned sister they were going to shoot in the back. That Lara might deserve it barely registered in his mind as he jerked his knife free of its sheath. Stabbing Philo wasn't a viable option, so Keris angled it into the faint moonlight, trusting that Aren would see.

Trusting that he'd save her.

The Ithicanian king reacted in an instant. Diving, he knocked Lara over, the pair of them rolling behind a boulder as arrows flew.

"Attack," Philo snarled, and more arrows arced through the air even as men slid down the slope to the beach. Keris held his ground, his mind racing as he thought of ways to get Aren and Lara out of this, the loud crunch of underbrush telling him that his men were pursuing the pair north.

He needed to improve their odds.

"Call for reinforcements!" Keris shouted. "Tell them we've got Valcottan raiders coming in from behind!"

Half the men stopped their pursuit, eyes on the water where the Valcottan ship was faintly visible, searching for approaching long-boats. Better odds, but not good enough. So Keris sprinted up the slope to where his horse was tethered.

Leaping onto its back, he heeled it down the narrow track at a gallop, heading to the fishing village the next inlet over.

His horse exploded onto the beach at the same time as Lara and Aren stumbled from the brush. Leaning over his horse's neck, he urged the animal for more speed, dragging on the horse's reins when he reached them. "What the hell are you doing in Nerastis?" he hollered. They gaped at him. "Never mind. You need to run. They're coming, and I'm not in any position to help you."

As soon as the words exited his lips, his soldiers exploded out of the brush and onto the beach, racing in their direction. And because to do anything else would render him complicit in their escape, Keris shouted, "Catch the Valcottans! They're getting away!"

Lara shot him a glower before Aren dragged her toward the waterline, where another man pulled loose the moorings on a fishing boat.

But they were running out of time.

Keris's soldiers were in hot pursuit, too great in number for them to fight. Yet his sister abandoned the boat, striding up the beach to meet her countrymen with blade in hand.

Lara fought as one born to it, relying on speed rather than brute strength, her jaw clenched in determination as she cut down man after man, leaving only corpses in her wake.

But there were too many of them.

They were going to kill his sister unless—

"Don't kill her!" he shouted. "Take her prisoner!"

If his men heard the orders, Keris couldn't tell. And it didn't matter, because Aren had abandoned the boat and was now fighting back-to-back with his wife, the two of them a match for Keris's men.

Or would have been.

The sound of galloping hooves filled the air, and a second later, reinforcements burst onto the beach.

If he didn't do something, they'd both be killed.

Coralyn's voice filled his ears: *She doesn't seek forgiveness, but perhaps you might give her yours.* His stubbornness didn't want to bend, didn't want to give that concession, but neither did he want to stand back and watch his sister slaughtered. Her death would accomplish nothing, whereas if she lived, maybe . . . maybe Lara might do some good.

Then motion on the water caught his eye. Longboats filled with armed Valcottans, and while the two forces were evenly matched, Keris seized upon the opportunity. "Retreat!" No one listened, so he stood in the saddle and bellowed, "Retreat!"

Philo's eyes tracked the direction Keris pointed, and then he shouted, "Fall back!"

Attentions snapped from Lara and Aren to the water, where dozens of Valcottans spilled out of longboats.

The sight of who led them caused Keris's heart to stutter, all the rest of the world falling away.

Zarrah sprinted up the beach, weapon in hand, the moonlight slipping out from behind the clouds to illuminate her face. "For Valcotta!" she screamed.

He should focus on his sister. On Aren. But Keris's eyes were all for Zarrah as she and her soldiers pursued his men, killing those they overtook. Heading straight toward him.

"Your Highness, run!" Philo shouted, but Zarrah's eyes had latched onto his, and it would have taken an act of God to make him turn his back on her.

She skidded to a stop and held up an arm. As her soldiers formed up around her, she looked over her shoulder. Keris blinked, seeing that Lara and Aren had the boat on the water, were kicking it out to sea, soon obscured by darkness.

"Fall back to the boats!" Zarrah shouted. As her soldiers moved to comply, her eyes locked on his. *Meet me tomorrow night,* she mouthed, then spun on her heel and joined her comrades racing back to their longboats, the battle over.

For now.

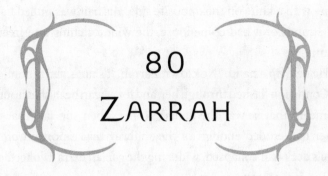

80

ZARRAH

It felt like Zarrah was walking through a dream as she made her way across Nerastis and then out of the city proper, the dim light of her lantern illuminating her path through the long grass. Overhead, there was only a slice of moon, and a million stars twinkled above like diamonds on velvet cloth. Though she'd only walked this path a handful of times to meet Keris, it felt etched on her soul, as if she'd walked it every day of her life. Her pathway to him, and this would be the last time she'd walk it.

The roar of the water rushing through the spillway reached her first, then the mist that smelled of life and earth and leafy things, her fingers trailing over the damp tips of the grass as she ascended the slope, her eyes fixed on the faint glow of light waiting for her.

He was here.

Her silent steps turned to soft thuds as she stepped onto the dam, following the arc of rock out into the open until she reached the gap, her eyes never wavering from the familiar shadow on the far side of the spillway. The lantern was bright enough to reveal he wore a Maridrinian uniform bedecked with the braids and medals and markers of a high-ranking officer, a sword belted at his waist, along with a knife on the opposite side. His hair was pulled back, but strands of it had come loose, the wind catching and freeing them.

He held up a hand. "No closer, Zarrah. It's not safe."

Confusion flashed through her, and for a heartbeat, she thought he meant that *he* was the danger to her. Then she saw that the water had eroded enough of the spillway that a portion of the dam's deck had collapsed, widening the gap an extra two feet.

Too far to jump.

A sharp, stabbing pain struck her heart, because she'd thought that she'd do this in his arms. Thought she'd say goodbye with the taste of him on her lips and the feel of his hands on her skin, but apparently fate, God, and the stars had given her enough for one night and would give her no more. Her eyes burned, and she blinked away the tears before they could fall.

Silence.

Zarrah knew she should speak. That she should start her explanation now, because time was short. But her throat was tight, strangling every word that tried to rise to her tongue. To her lips.

"Lara and Aren made it through the Red Desert." His voice carried over the roar of the water, risky names to be shouting on the outskirts of Nerastis. "Bastard has nine lives."

The corner of her mouth turned up. "I think it's your sister that's the hard one to kill."

"Recent events suggest otherwise." There was a hint of anger in his voice. "She nearly took an arrow in the back last night, she was so distracted coming up with suitable words for goodbye."

Zarrah flinched, though she wasn't certain why.

"What is going on, Zarrah? Why were they on your ship? Why did you dump them on a beach, only to sail in to save their asses?"

She swallowed hard, her hands like ice. "They came to Pyrinat to ask the empress to aid Ithicana in driving Maridrina out and retaking the bridge."

"And?"

"She declined. Gave me orders to drop them north of Nerastis so that they might make their own way back to Ithicana to rally Aren's people."

"Thank fucking God." His shoulders slumped, and though the noise of the falls drowned it out, Zarrah *felt* his sigh of relief. It made her stomach twist into knots. As if sensing something in her silence, Keris lifted his head and met her stare. "Tell me that's the end of it, Zarrah."

"I can't." She dragged in a steadying breath. "Because it's not. Not for me."

"What have you done?" He took a step toward the edge of the spillway, as though he might jump, then gave a sharp shake of his head and held his ground. "Zarrah?"

"I'm going to take ships north to help Aren liberate Ithicana. I'm going to help him end this war. And then I'm going to return to Pyrinat and accept the consequences of treason."

"No, you are not! You will do no such thing! You—"

"Did you know it's been a year?" Her heart beat against the inside of her ribs like a fist trying to hammer its way out. "A year since I stood on the deck of a ship and watched your father's fleet sail past me to Ithicana. A year since I did nothing and thousands suffered for my inaction. It feels like I've come full circle and am once again standing on that deck, watching disaster approach. But this time, I won't do nothing."

"Zarrah, no. Don't." His voice was drenched in panic, and again he stepped to the edge of the spillway. "Ithicana is Aren's problem, not yours. It was his blind love for my sister that invited invasion.

And Lara's shame that drove her to keep secrets when the full truth would have stopped my father in his tracks. What happened in Ithicana is *their* fault, not yours. Let them pay the price."

Her chin trembled, and Zarrah clenched her teeth, trying to contain her emotions because she needed to get this out. Needed to make him understand. "It's not just Ithicana that disaster approaches, Keris. It's Maridrina." She sucked in a breath. "The empress is coming for you. She knows that your father needs to end this war before Amarid withdraws its support. She knows he intends to pull every last one of his soldiers from across the kingdom to strike Ithicana a fatal blow. And when he does, when Maridrina sits entirely unprotected, she intends to strike her own fatal blow."

"Let her come!" he shouted. "I have control in Nerastis, *not* my father. I'm not sending him the soldiers or ships, so if Bermin thinks to waltz across the border and take this city, he's in for a shock. I have it in hand, Zarrah!"

"No, you don't!" Her emotions boiled over the walls she'd built to contain them. "You don't have it in hand, because it isn't *just* Nerastis she's coming for—it's Vencia. I know because it's me who is supposed to sail into its harbor to sack and burn and murder. Me who is supposed to go to Silas's palace and put every last Veliant to sword."

Silence.

"But instead, I'm going to *lie*." Tears dripped down her cheeks. "I'll tell my soldiers that her orders are to retake Southwatch for Ithicana. We'll drive your father out and send him back to lick his wounds in Vencia, and things will go back to the way they've always been."

"No, they won't, because you'll be executed." He stood right at the edge, and she cringed as rocks crumbled to fall into the water below. "This is madness, Zarrah. There are other ways. I'll warn my father. Tell him that the empress intends to attack while his back is turned. He won't risk Vencia."

"Won't he?"

Keris's mouth opened, but he hesitated, and Zarrah knew he was thinking of the depths of Silas's obsession with the bridge. Knew he was seeing how this would unfold and the calamity it would bring. "There has to be another way to stop this. Just . . . just don't attack. Delay until he's done with Ithicana, and then the opportunity will be lost."

"That's still treason, Keris." She wiped the tears from her face. "And if I'm to be executed, it won't be for inaction. If I'm to die, it's going to be righting my wrongs."

"No! I won't let you!" Lamplight glittered off the tears on his face. "I won't let you die!"

"It's not your choice." She took a step back. Then another.

"What about Valcotta?" he shouted. "What about all the good you would do as its empress? What about the lives that would be saved if it was you who ruled?"

"A dream." She bit her lip, grief rolling over her in violent waves. "Whereas this is reality. I love you, Keris, but you can't stop me from doing this." She took another step back. "My ships will set sail in a matter of hours, so don't think there is a way to stop me, because there isn't. I told you I need to do things that I believe are *right*, because that's the only way I can honor myself."

"Zarrah, please." He dropped to his knees. "I'm begging you, don't do this. Please don't do this. I can't lose you."

Her heart fractured into a million pieces, but her resolve remained whole. "Goodbye, Keris. May we meet again in the Great Beyond."

And with him screaming her name, Zarrah walked away.

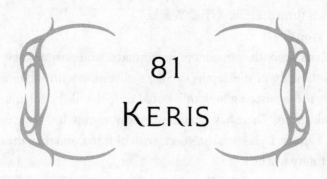

81
KERIS

"ZARRAH!"

He didn't care if anyone heard, if all of fucking Nerastis heard, because he needed to stop her. Needed to keep her from making this decision. Needed to save her.

Even if that meant saving her from herself. Because he goddamn refused to let her die.

But she didn't stop. Didn't turn around. Just kept walking and walking until the glow of her lantern was out of sight and his voice was hoarse.

Go after her.

Keris backed down the dam, eyeing the gap of the spillway, the far side cast in shadows.

It's too far.

"It's not too far," he snarled to himself. "You've jumped farther."

And there was no other way to reach her. The river was being watched by *his men,* and without his horse, he'd never make it around the lake in time to stop her from boarding that ship. This was the only way. Because he wouldn't let her die.

He broke into a sprint, gaze fixed on the far side, his lantern marking the place he needed to jump.

Thud.

The sickening sound of his brother hitting the ground filled his ears, and Keris flung his weight backward, skidding on his heels, then falling on his ass right at the edge.

He pressed his fingers to his temples, trying to force himself back to his feet. Trying to force himself to try again. But the same sound repeated over and over in his head, and he couldn't move.

All his life he'd spent climbing, and never once had he been afraid. But now terror consumed him.

Breathe, he ordered himself, lifting his head to stare at the spillway. Breathing and breathing until logic and reason and *control* returned.

Think.

It was too far to jump. All he'd accomplish was plunging into the waterfall to be dashed against the rocks below. He couldn't stop her from boarding that ship and setting sail.

But maybe there was another path.

Keris rose to his feet and turned north. The only way to prevent Zarrah from committing treason was to eliminate the opportunity. Which meant ensuring Vencia was well defended enough to ruin the empress's plans to sack it, as well as withdrawing Maridrinian forces from Ithicana, which would remove Zarrah's need to fight on Aren's behalf.

Except Zarrah was right: His father *would* risk Vencia before willingly relinquishing the bridge. It was the obsession that had dominated his life, and he finally had it in his grasp. What were the lives of everyone in Vencia compared to *that*?

Which left only one option.

Keris's skin crawled, his stomach twisting with nausea, because it was honorless. And unfamiliar.

But if it worked, it would save Vencia. Would stop the escalation of the Endless War in its tracks. And it would save Zarrah's life.

"Fuck honor."

He broke into a run toward Nerastis.

KERIS GALLOPED THROUGH THE BALANCE of the night and through the morning before trading a farmer for a fresh horse.

He'd left instructions with Philo to retain all the ships and men, warning him to be ever vigilant, as Valcotta intended to attack. He could only pray that it would be enough, if not to stop Bermin from making a move then at least to stop him from pressing north into Maridrina. There was nothing more he could do for them now.

For days he rode, stopping only to switch horses or for a few hours of fitful sleep in the brush before pressing on. By the time Vencia's walls came into view, Keris was so exhausted he could barely think, his clothes stained to the point of ruin and his stomach as empty as his pockets. The two men manning the gates didn't recognize him, allowing him to pass through with all the rest of the merchant traffic heading into the city.

The harbor was dominated by naval vessels flying the Maridrinian flag, and on the docks, hundreds of soldiers waited to be loaded. Though Keris had known this was his father's intent, he was still struck by the sight. Ithicana could not survive this without Zarrah's help, and even with it, it would be a battle for the ages.

At the palace, new gates had been installed to replace those destroyed by Ithicanian explosives during the escape—sturdier ones that were shut despite it being midday, the walls crawling with soldiers.

"Halt!" one of them shouted at him, and Keris pulled up his shaggy mount in deference to the arrows currently leveled at his chest. "There is no entrance to the palace. Be on your way!"

Pulling back his hood, Keris looked up at the soldiers. "Open the fucking gate! And ensure someone has a drink waiting for me in the courtyard. All I can taste is dust, and my ass is never going to recover from riding this creature." He switched his glower to the horse, which was the most mean-spirited creature he'd ever encountered. It seemed to sense his ire, turning to try to bite his foot. "I'm going to feed you to the dogs."

He looked back up at the soldier.

The man stared at him for a heartbeat, then finally seemed to see past the filth and shaggy horse, recognition dawning in his eyes. "Your Highness?"

Patience shot, Keris only glared until the gate slowly swung open, allowing him to trot inside. Sliding off the horse, he tossed the reins to a stable boy. "Give the bastard a good rubdown and an extra helping of oats." He swiftly rinsed his hands in the waiting basin of water. "Where's my father?"

"In his war room, Highness." The servant carrying the bowl hurried along next to him, water splashing. "But perhaps you'd care to bathe and change before attending him?"

"Later." Keris cut left and then entered the building, ignoring his aching body and taking the steps two at a time to the second level. Unlike the inner sanctum, which was lavished with creature comforts, the outer palace was austere and cold, the walls devoid of art and the floors naked stone. A reminder that this building was a fortress that had repelled more than one attack during Maridrina's tumultuous history. He made his way to the war room where his father met with his generals, his bootheels thudding from the speed of his stride.

"I need to see him," he said to one of the guards outside the door. The man ducked inside, then reemerged and gave Keris a nod.

Taking a fortifying breath and praying his nerves wouldn't betray him, Keris stepped into the war room.

Though he'd only been in there a handful of times in his life, the room remained almost identical to how it had been in his childhood. One wall contained a series of narrow windows set with frosted glass, the opposite wall holding a framed map of Maridrina. A heavy circular table sat in the middle of the room, surrounded by what Keris knew to be extremely uncomfortable chairs, and along the side wall was a cabinet containing bottles of liquor, each expensive enough to feed a family for a year.

His father sat at the table in the company of several officers in the Maridrinian Army, judging from their uniforms, but at the sight of Keris, he waved a hand at them. "We will continue later. I would speak with my son."

The men rose without argument, bowing to his father before abandoning their glasses of expensive drink on the table as though they expected to return to them shortly. Keris waited until they'd left and was about to speak when the skin on the back of his neck prickled. He turned in time to see Serin step out of the shadows, his robes trailing along the floor as he made his way to the table.

"You really need to cease crawling out of the corners," he said to the spymaster. "It's quite an off-putting behavior."

"Only to those with something to hide."

Keris leveled him with a long stare. "The dramatic statements are no better."

"Enough, Keris," his father snapped. "Instead of filling the air with useless chatter, explain where my ships and soldiers are."

"Nerastis."

His father was on his feet in a flash, his right hand balled in a fist. "You go too far, boy. I'll tolerate your complaints over my plans to hold the bridge but not you actively sabotaging them." He swore loudly, then slammed his fist down on the table, making all the glasses bounce. "Aren Kertell and your witch of a sister are rumored to be back in Ithicana and rallying forces. The Amaridian queen is withdrawing her support, and her goddamned navy once storm season begins. Which means I have a matter of weeks to destroy what remains of the Ithicanian resistance, and your peddling a fool's ideals"—his volume increased to a shout—"may have ruined it!"

"This has nothing to do with ideals." Keris watched his father warily. "The empress has guessed your intent and plans to attack while your back is turned."

His father's jaw tightened, and he glanced to Serin, revealing that he'd known the risk and had demanded the soldiers anyway. "What of it? We've lost Nerastis before, only to take it back a year later. The bridge is worth a hundred times that pile of rubble, and now we might lose it." He leveled a finger at Keris. "If I lose the bridge because of you, I'm going to cut out your fucking tongue."

It wasn't the first time he'd been threatened with the punishment, but it was the first time Keris didn't feel afraid. "Not just Nerastis, Your Grace. Vencia is the empress's target."

"I've heard nothing of this," Serin snapped, even as his father snarled, "She wouldn't dare."

"She dares." Keris's pulse was a steady thud, his palms clammy. "Zarrah Anaphora returned to Nerastis and loaded three vessels with soldiers before sailing north, her intent to wait until you abandoned Vencia to attack Ithicana, then to launch an attack of her own."

"How did you learn this?" Serin demanded.

Keris shrugged. "Spies. I'm sure your own eyes will bring the same information eventually, although if we'd relied on them, it would be too late."

Serin's eyes narrowed, but it was Silas who spoke. "And why did you feel it necessary to deliver this information yourself?"

He had to at least try to convince him, even if doing so was a fool's hope. "The bridge has been nothing but a curse. Is seeing Vencia destroyed and thousands of Maridrinian lives lost worth it, Father?"

Yes, was the answer in his father's eyes, though he said, "We'll raise the harbor chains and arm the civilians. They can defend the walls until I return."

"Old men, women, and children against three ships full of hardened Valcottan soldiers is not a fair fight."

His father crossed his arms. "Then we evacuate. Let *Zarrah* content herself with burning an empty city. We will rebuild and then have revenge against her when the time is right."

God help him, but Keris *hated* that word. Would strike it from every language in the world if he could, for those motivated by it brought only ruin. "Give up the bridge, Father."

"You want me to concede?" His father stalked around the table. "I sacrificed nearly two decades of my reign and nearly two dozen daughters to win this prize, and you just want me to give it up?"

Keris tensed, knowing what was coming. But he couldn't stop now. "Yes. For the sake of Maridrina, you must."

"I must do nothing! I am king!"

"Your pride will be the death of this kingdom." Keris's control of his temper frayed with every passing heartbeat, because his words accomplished no more than spitting into the wind. His father would never concede. "And it will be for nothing, because you aren't capable of winning this."

Face darkening with fury, his father struck, fist flying toward Keris's face.

But whereas once he'd have allowed the blow to land, this time, Keris blocked it. And struck one of his own.

His father staggered, tripping over a chair and falling on his ass, his cheek a livid red. But rather than fury, his expression was filled with a delight that made Keris sick.

"Guards!" Serin shrieked, but the king held up one hand. "No. No guards, Serin." He spit blood onto the carpet, and said, "You are always particular in your phrasing, Keris. You say that *I* cannot win. Not that it cannot be won."

It felt like a noose was around Keris's throat, choking back his words, because innocents were going to die. People who'd had no say in any of this and yet would lose their lives because they were pawns in the games played by kings and queens and empresses.

And princes.

So he said, "The key to victory is not attacking the limbs of our enemy but striking at its heart."

"Attack Eranahl?" His father shook his head. "Its defenses are formidable—it would require us taking nearly every man and ship at our disposal to assail it, which would mean leaving our strongholds on the bridge undefended and ripe for the picking."

Keris picked up a drink from the table and took a mouthful. The liquor burned down his throat to sit like a lead weight in his stomach. The weight of his father's approval—something he'd never wanted to earn, because doing so would mean becoming something he loathed. Yet here he was. "Aren fights in the belief he is going to war against you."

"He is going to war against me."

"No, he is going to war against *me*." Keris drained his glass. "And by the time he realizes it, it will be too late."

His father's eyes narrowed. "What do you propose?"

"I propose we use the bridge to withdraw all our men from Ithicana in secret, leaving only enough behind to maintain the illusion that we intend to fight to the death to keep our hold on the bridge. Once Aren commits his forces, and those of the Valcottans, to attacks on our outposts holding the bridge, we sail against Eranahl and take the city."

His father made a face. "What good is that? Aren will hold the bridge and its defenses, and given he'll suffer almost no losses to his army in the taking, we'll never dig him out again."

Even now, after all this time, his father still didn't understand that not all rulers were like him. That not all rulers were willing to sacrifice their people for the sake of political, strategic, and financial gain. Except what made Aren Kertell a better man than Silas Veliant would ultimately be his downfall. And the end of Ithicana.

So Keris detailed the rest of the plan, a part of himself withering and dying as his father's smile grew, pride radiating from his gaze. "You are my son after all. A true Veliant. I knew it. I've always known it. And I think so have you, no matter how hard you tried to fight it."

As much as Keris wanted to deny it, he knew his father was right.

Keris gave a slight nod, and he sent out a silent plea to wherever Zarrah was on the high seas.

Forgive me.

82
ZARRAH

"THE HARBOR CHAIN IS STILL UP."

Zarrah glanced left at the captain of the ship, who was lowering his spyglass from his assessment of Vencia. "That's two days it's remained up, with all merchant vessels turned away to seek berth in other harbors. And the seas are growing rougher, the winds higher. Storm season is nearly upon us."

"Agreed." The captain rested his elbows on the rail. "I'm afraid we may not be able to pursue the empress's desired course of action, General. Not with the updates we received last night."

Zarrah had sent a longboat to shore under the cover of darkness to meet with Valcottan spies, who'd told them with no uncertainty that not only had Silas *not* emptied the city's defenses to bolster his forces engaged in subduing Ithicana, he'd doubled them. Which meant attacking would be a death wish.

"Our plans must have leaked somehow," one of her lieutenants muttered. "They're prepared for an attack. I wouldn't be surprised if they keep the chain up until storm season strikes."

Zarrah knew exactly how Silas had come to know the empress's intent: Keris. How he'd managed to convince Silas not to risk the attack for the sake of his plans in Ithicana, she didn't know. But regardless, the empress's plans to sack Vencia were now in shambles, the chance of success far too low to risk so many Valcottan soldiers.

Zarrah knew exactly what Keris wanted her to do in response: to sail back to Nerastis with no fear of the empress's wrath for not completing her mission to burn Vencia.

"What are your orders, General?" the captain asked. "Do you wish to raid down the coast instead?"

"No." Zarrah straightened. "Head back to open water to rejoin our other ships. Once we're clear from view, I want every soldier on deck."

They sailed northwest, the swells beneath the ship growing as they moved deeper into the Tempest Seas, but once the lookout had called all clear, soldiers flowed onto the deck, their expressions inquisitive.

This was the moment. The moment she needed to take this final step in betraying her aunt's commands. While Zarrah had no intention of turning back, she still had a choice to make.

The soldiers watched her silently, waiting, and Zarrah bit the insides of her cheeks as she debated what to do. The easiest and surest path would be to lie to them. To say that the empress had given her alternative plans to pursue if the attack on Vencia failed. To do so would mean all these soldiers would follow her unquestioningly to Southwatch, entirely ignorant of their treason.

Would mean using them.

Except she knew what it was like to be used. Knew the sour, sick feeling that would fill their guts when they discovered that she, their trusted general, had deceived them. Knew that for all her motivations were pure, taking that step would make her little better than her aunt, who weighed strategy over honor.

Zarrah had sworn to honor herself, which left her with only one choice: the truth.

To be honest in her motivations and pray that their consciences drove them to follow her. She'd chosen these men and women specifically, every last one of them having been with her when the Maridrinian fleet had sailed past them to Ithicana. Every last one of them bearing the guilt of inaction. Zarrah prayed it weighed upon them as much as it did her, because if she was wrong, Ithicana would be the one to suffer.

"A year ago," she shouted, "we watched as Silas Veliant's fleet sailed past ours on its way to Ithicana! On its way to stab an ally in the back for the sake of one man's quest for more power and wealth. It was the honorless move of a king more rat than man. A creature who'd win wars with guile and deception rather than face his opponent with bravery and skill!"

Her soldiers murmured in agreement, nodding, several shouting, "The Maridrinians are cowards! They have no honor!"

"Perhaps that is so!" she shouted. "But what of us? What of our honor?"

Silence.

"We stood by and *watched* as they sailed past! We offered no resistance, no warning, despite knowing better than any nation on earth the horror Ithicana faced!" Zarrah walked forward, the ranks parting for her. "How many times have we witnessed the massacre of a raid? Seen homes destroyed, men and women slaughtered, children orphaned? How many times have we been only minutes too late, cursed to spend the nights awake wondering what might have been different if we'd only ridden faster? Yet when faced with the chance to stop an entire kingdom from seeing such a fate, we did not sail faster! We turned our backs!"

Circling around to the front again, she shouted, "We were the cowards that day!"

Her soldiers stared at their feet, and Zarrah could feel their shame. And she knew that, like her, they desired to atone.

"King Aren Kertell has returned to Ithicana," she continued, trusting that the words she needed would find the way to her tongue. "He is rallying his people to fight the Maridrinians and drive them out. To liberate his kingdom and take back his people's homes. But he can't do it alone." She paused, surveying them. "He needs allies. He needs *us*."

Their faces lifted, anticipation rising in their eyes, but she knew the greatest hurdle was to come.

"Yet when Aren came to our empress to ask for our help, she turned him away."

Zarrah waited, allowing the information to sink in. "Rather than seeing this as an opportunity for Valcotta to right a wrong, she sees it as an opportunity to strike a blow against an enemy. As an opportunity to attack Maridrina while its back is turned and enact upon it the same carnage as our cowardice brought to Ithicana."

Silence.

No one on the ship deck spoke. No one stirred. No one seemed to even breathe.

"We could follow her wishes and sail down the coast, killing and burning as we go." Her voice carried over them, filling the void. "Or we can sail to Ithicana and stand by its king and fight for liberty. For decency. For honor!"

Zarrah surveyed her soldiers, praying to the stars that she'd judged them rightly as she shouted, "I give you the choice: Will you fight and kill innocents to strike a blow at Silas Veliant? Or will you fight and kill to protect the innocents that Silas Veliant seeks to destroy?"

No one said a word, and a prickle of fear wormed its way up

Zarrah's spine. Because if she'd been wrong, Aren and Ithicana would pay the price . . .

The captain of the ship stepped forward and shouted, "I will stand with Ithicana!"

Then one of her soldiers lifted his fist into the air. "I will stand with Ithicana!"

A woman drew her sword. "I will stand with Ithicana! I will fight for them!"

And then it was a roar of voices, all shouting the same thing, all wanting the same thing.

So Zarrah stepped forward, lifting her own weapon in the air. "Let us to war!"

83

ZARRAH

"NO SHIPS AT THE DOCK." A BEAD OF SWEAT RAN DOWN THE SIDE of the captain's face, betraying his nerves. "Looks quiet."

Southwatch *did* look quiet, only a handful of soldiers visible, but well Zarrah knew that appearances could be deceiving. The vessel she stood on looked like a Maridrinian merchantman, the sailors disguised, but belowdecks, two hundred armed Valcottan soldiers waited to attack.

They drifted closer, the Maridrinians standing on the pier appearing unconcerned as they waited to tie the ship off.

Sweat beaded on her spine as she discreetly gave the signal for her strongest swimmers to enter the water. They'd swim under the ship and up beneath the pier. There, they'd find the tunnels Jor had mapped, which would lead into the storehouses Aren had described. When Zarrah and her soldiers swarmed the pier, the swimmers would attack from behind to disable the shipbreakers, allowing her other two vessels to sail in and join the fight.

Her pulse throbbed in a steady beat, her staff held in one hand below the ship's railing, a hood pulled forward to protect her from the light rain sufficient to disguise her skin color.

"Slowly," she muttered to the captain. "Give the swimmers time to reach the tunnels."

The ship bumped against the dock, and her crew moved to toss down ropes. But one of the Maridrinians shouted, "We're not taking cargo! Southwatch is closed—no one allowed on the island. Turn back to Vencia."

This is strange, she thought, searching for any signs that the Maridrinians had prepared for an attack, but there was nothing.

She kicked the captain in the ankle, knowing that if she spoke, it would raise alarm, as Maridrinians didn't have female sailors. Clearing his throat, the captain said, "We've got grain purchased by His Majesty for his soldiers up from Nerastis."

"Don't care if you've got a hold full of solid gold. You're not stepping foot on this island."

Something is wrong.

Zarrah's skin crawled as she listened to the captain argue with the man, the ship rising and falling on the growing surf, rain soaking her clothes.

There is a storm coming.

Thunder rolled in the east, and a gust of wind tore across the ship's deck.

On the pier, the Maridrinian's eyes widened in horror.

Zarrah's eyes snapped left in time to see the captain dragging his hood back into place, but it was too late. They'd seen.

"Valcottans!" The Maridrinian drew his weapon. "We're under attack!"

Instinct took over, and Zarrah lifted her weapon. "Attack!"

Her soldiers flung off their cloaks and drew their weapons, those below racing on-deck. With her people behind her, Zarrah led the charge.

She leapt off the ship onto the pier. More Maridrinians raced to engage even as she met a man's sword with her staff, knocking it from his hands. She twisted, slamming the butt into his head with lethal force before moving on to the next.

Blood splattered her face as she smashed his skull, but she only blinked it away, her eyes on her next opponent. His jaw was tense, eyes grim, as though he knew there was no chance of getting out of this alive. Which made no bloody sense, because this island should be packed with soldiers.

Zarrah ducked under his sword blade, then swept his feet out from under him. He landed with a thud, and she turned on her heel, bringing her weapon down on his throat. Squaring her shoulders, she turned to take on another.

But there were none.

Perhaps two dozen Maridrinians lay dead or dying on the pier, her soldiers all looking warily toward the island, waiting for re-inforcements to come.

"Where are they?" one of her men demanded, even as another said, "Maybe they went to reinforce locations being attacked by the Ithicanians?"

Except Zarrah knew that wasn't it. Knew that this island was too damn critical to be left with only two dozen men to guard it. Something was off.

"An ambush?" someone suggested.

"Maybe." Zarrah strode down the pier, her soldiers falling in behind her. She knew the layout of the building from Aren's expla-nations and Jor's drawings, and she gave orders breaking her force into groups to search the island.

Her group moved cautiously toward one of the large ware-houses that stored grain, her heart thumping. Not because she was afraid to find Maridrinians waiting in ambush.

But because she was afraid she wouldn't.

Sweat mixed with the rain rolling down her back, and Zarrah reached for the door, easing it open, then stepped inside.

Her stomach plummeted. It was empty.

All across Southwatch, she heard shouts of the same. No soldiers. No ambushes. The island was empty.

What was going on?

"Send a message to Aren that Southwatch has been taken," she ordered. "Tell him that the island was empty. He needs to be prepared, because the Maridrinians didn't just disappear."

And Silas hadn't conceded. There wasn't a goddamned chance he'd given up the bridge without a fight.

Zarrah took a spyglass from one of her men. "Take a third of our force and press into the bridge a few miles to see if you find anything. Show caution—there are more ways in and out than you can possibly imagine. I'm going to climb to the top to see if I can get a better vantage."

"Let me arrange an escort."

She shook her head. "I'll go alone."

Zarrah strode up the road leading to the mouth of the bridge, the yawning opening into the dark tunnel that snaked its way over the islands and karsts of Ithicana. A faint moaning echoed from it, a draft of wind that carried with it a peculiar smell. Like petrichor, but different, and Zarrah shivered as she bypassed it.

The island was made up of twin peaks of rock and dense vegetation, and she was soon breathing hard from heat and exertion as she climbed a narrow track leading to the top of one peak, keeping an eye out for Ithicana's infamous snakes. The air was thick with humidity to the point she felt like she was drinking water, everything smelling of lush vegetation and rain, and in the distance, lightning danced across a black storm front that seemed closer each time she lifted her head.

Every muscle in her body was tense, denied the release battle always brought with it and looking for an outlet. She'd promised Aren and Ithicana her aid against Silas, and while she'd done exactly what they'd agreed upon, that promise didn't feel fulfilled. Two dozen soldiers where there should have been two hundred, and Zarrah had no idea where they were. Had no idea how she could aid Aren, and the helplessness of it made her want to spill her guts on the path.

She'd come here to right a wrong. To atone. To honor herself.

But thus far, it felt like she'd failed on every count.

Anger quickened her steps, and soon Zarrah was running up the trail, rising higher and higher until she spotted a stone lookout at the pinnacle. Wary of Maridrinians, she tucked her spyglass in her belt in favor of her staff, cautiously approaching the opening to the small structure. It was made of the same stone as the bridge, the wet, earthy scent filling her nose as she climbed a short staircase and came out on top.

Her pulse hammered and she pivoted, forgoing the spyglass in her belt in favor of a larger one the Ithicanians had mounted in the tower. But all she saw was oceans and islands and mist.

No ships other than her own.

No soldiers other than her own.

Then a familiar voice said, "This isn't your fight, Zarrah."

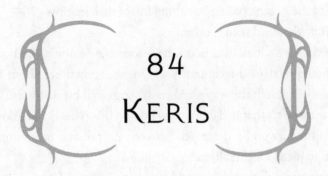

84
KERIS

IT HAD BEEN MADNESS TO REMAIN AT SOUTHWATCH, GIVEN HE'D
known what was coming. Yet as his father had sailed away in the
dark of night with a fleet of ships loaded with Maridrinian soldiers, leaving the unwitting decoys behind to die, Keris had found
himself unable to depart. Unable to get on the ship that would deliver him back to the safety of Vencia while dozens upon dozens of
his people died as part of *his* strategy. *His* plan.

His war.

So instead he'd left a letter in his stateroom with orders that
they return for him after the battle was over, knowing full well
that all that they might find was a corpse, then sneaked off the
ship. He'd spent the days since sleeping on the tops of the ware-
houses and buildings of the Southwatch market, stealing food, his
eyes always on the sea. Watching. Waiting.

Because he'd known she would come.

So when the ship bearing a Maridrinian flag had drifted toward
port, the sailors all wearing hoods pulled up against the rain, he'd

seen what the soldiers on the pier had not. That this was no vessel full of their countrymen but a ship full of their enemy.

But what he'd seen was *her*.

Even in a cloak and hood, he'd somehow known the figure standing next to the captain was Zarrah. Something about the way she'd stood, the way she'd *moved*, triggered his instincts. The same instincts that had demanded he stop this. That he race down onto the pier and put himself between Zarrah and his countrymen to plead for their lives.

Except that would have put her in the position of having to explain why she was willing to negotiate with a Veliant. With all he'd done to try to save her, Keris wasn't about to damn her for the sake of his conscience.

So instead, he'd watched as the Valcottans had swarmed the pier. Watched as the woman he loved more than life slaughtered his countrymen with brutal efficiency. Watched as she realized the situation on Southwatch was not as expected, that something was wrong. Watched her realize that *none* of this was the behavior of Silas Veliant.

And saw the moment she realized whom she'd really gone to war with.

"This isn't your fight, Zarrah."

She jerked at the sound of his voice, her eyes snapping down from the lookout tower to fix on his. "Where are they attacking?"

Not *Why are you here, Keris?* Not *What is going on, Keris?*

Because she *knew*. He could see it in her eyes. "It doesn't matter where they are. This isn't your fight. Get your people back on those ships and sail south before that storm hits." He swallowed the thickness in his throat, simultaneously struck by how beautiful she was and by the certainty that she'd hate him for what he'd done.

But it was worth it. He had to believe it was worth it.

"Where are they attacking, Keris?" She turned on her heel, and he listened to the sound of her racing down the steps, appearing at the base of the tower. "What have you done?"

"It doesn't matter where they are, because even if you board your ship right now, it's too late," he answered, bracing himself as her hands balled into fists. "It will be a fight between Maridrina and Ithicana, as it should be. Valcotta and Harendell need to stay out of it."

"What about Amarid?" she demanded. "Are they staying out of it? Or is it only Ithicana who truly stands alone?"

He lifted a shoulder because the alternative was to wince at the accuracy of her statement. "I expect they'll stay out of the thick of it."

"Where. Is. The. Attack?" Her eyes were bright with panic. "Tell me!"

The attack was already under way, and too far for her ships to make it in time. "My father and his fleet are attacking Eranahl."

Zarrah blanched, her eyes filling with horror. "Eranahl is full of innocents. How could you?"

It was a plan simple in its beauty even as it was ugly in its cruelty. Leave decoy soldiers at key points along the bridge to lure Aren and his army to attack, then move on the heart of Ithicana—the island fortress of Eranahl. Once the ruse was discovered, Aren and his army would move to defend the city and be forced to fight his father's fleet on the open water, where Ithicana was at a severe disadvantage. The war that had lasted a year would be over in a night. "People were always going to die, Zarrah. There was always going to be a battle. I just changed the ground it was fought on."

She doubled over, a ragged sob tearing from her lips, and Keris's stomach twisted with guilt. With grief. *It's worth it,* he silently chanted to himself. *It has to be worth it.*

"Load your ships and sail home, Zarrah, because no one can accuse you of wrongdoing. The empress's spies will have seen that Vencia remained too strongly defended for you to attack. As for you coming to Southwatch, given my father is about to gain uncontested control of the bridge, the empress is going to look the fool for not doing more to stop him. At least *you* tried."

The look she gave him made Keris feel sick, but he pressed forward. "Regain her favor and secure your position as heir. Become empress. Do all the good you dreamed of doing. I'll do the same and . . ." He trailed off, because the horror in her eyes had disappeared, and in its place was fury.

"Aren trusted me," she said between her teeth. "And I trusted *you*. Instead of honoring that trust, you betrayed me."

"I didn't betray you." He'd known she'd react like this. Known she'd be angry. "I—"

"Protected me? Saved my life?" Tears streamed down her face, and he took a step toward her, but she held up a hand. "Don't. I love you, Keris. God help me, I do. But right now, I also hate you because you *are* your father's son. You will have things your way no matter the cost."

It's worth it, he told himself even as her words cut deep. *She's alive and will remain alive, so it's worth this pain.*

But it *hurt* to hear the accusation from her. Like a knife to the heart, as the truth so often was. Yet he couldn't take his actions back. Refused to be sorry, because Zarrah would *live*. "Maridrina, Valcotta, Ithicana . . . someone had to lose, Zarrah. Having everyone come out of this unscathed was never an option. I tried to convince my father to walk away, but it was never going to happen, so I had to choose." His voice shook. "We could change our world, Zarrah. Create a peace between two nations who've been at war for generations. Save thousands of our people's lives. But that doesn't come without sacrifice, and that sacrifice is Ithicana."

Zarrah dropped to her knees, pressing her forehead to the dirt, but when he stepped toward her, she lifted her face. "Don't you dare come closer."

"Zarrah." He hated that he had caused her this grief. He wished that there was a way to erase her pain.

But he refused to regret what he'd done.

"You say you did it for our kingdoms, but that isn't it, is it?" she sobbed. "You did it for me. To save me. Admit it!"

"Zarrah—"

"Admit it!" The screamed words were punctuated by a sudden crack of thunder, the wind gusting over them.

He felt strangled, unable to speak. But he managed to get out, "I couldn't . . ." *Lose you,* was what Keris had intended to say, but he'd known that in doing this, he'd lose her to hate. "I couldn't let you die."

"But now I have to live knowing that my life came at the expense of hundreds. Thousands!" She sobbed the words, shoulders trembling. "And there's nothing I can do to change that."

I don't regret it, Keris silently chanted. "If there'd been another way, I'd have taken it. I don't want Ithicana to fall. I don't want people to die, but too many wanted war for a battle to be avoided."

"There was another way—my way! But you didn't like my choice, so you took it away." Zarrah scrubbed the tears from her face, then met his gaze. "I will never forgive you for that, Keris Veliant. I never want to see your face again. Never want to hear your voice. And if we cross paths, I *will* kill you."

His skin felt like ice, his stomach hollow. *I don't regret it. I . . .* The voice in his head faltered.

"I'm leaving." She straightened. "But not to go goddamned south. I'm going to try to help Ithicana."

His eyes snapped to the storm racing in from the east, the clouds dark as midnight but for the constant bursts of lightning branching through them. Not a squall, but one of the Tempest Seas' legendary typhoons. A ship killer. And it was racing west faster than any ship could sail. "No, Zarrah. You can't—the storm."

"I'm going to Aren's aid, Keris. And this time, you can't stop me." Zarrah twisted away, striding toward the path.

She was going to get herself killed. After everything that had happened, after every sacrifice that had been made, she was going to get herself killed. Which meant it had all been for *nothing*.

Keris broke into a sprint after her, desperately reaching for her arm even as he hunted for words that would change her mind.

But Zarrah whirled, staff in hand, the tip flying toward him.

And then all he saw was darkness.

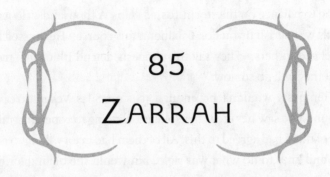

85
ZARRAH

"The storm is headed straight for Eranahl," the captain shouted over the violent winds and surf. "Even if the battle still rages, it won't for long—this storm will put every ship it catches below the sea! We must turn south and attempt to get out of its path!"

"No!" She screamed the word in defiance. Not at the captain or the storm but at Keris.

Keris, whom she'd left unconscious and bleeding and alone on Southwatch Island. Keris, who had betrayed her trust. Keris, who had condemned Ithicana to save her.

And yet for all he'd done, she still loved him.

"General," the captain pleaded, "we must turn south. Give the order. Please!"

"I can't! We have to help them!" She couldn't live with herself if Ithicana fell. If Aren and Lara and all their people died because of her. Better to go to the grave knowing she'd done everything she possibly could.

"Then you damn us all!" The captain abandoned the wheel to

his first mate, gripping Zarrah's shoulders, both of them struggling to balance on the storm-tossed ship. "A thousand Valcottan souls will perish if you don't abandon this course." He pressed his forehead to hers. "They say the tempests defend Ithicana—trust that they will do so now."

Tempests wouldn't be enough to stop Silas Veliant. Yet all around, she saw her crew, her soldiers, clinging to ropes and rails. All of them had agreed to this. All of them had been willing to risk life and limb to do what was right, but would she be in the right condemning them to death?

I need to honor myself. Her own words repeated in her head, and slowly, Zarrah bowed her shoulders. "Turn south. And may fate, God, and the stars have mercy on Ithicana."

And on her.

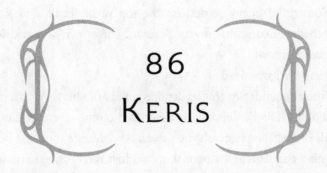

86
KERIS

FOR NEARLY AN HOUR, HE'D BEEN KNEELING ON THE DAIS WHILE A series of priests and priestesses conducted his coronation. Old men and women droning on about his divine right to rule and other such nonsense, it not lost on him that given the Veliant family's infamous lack of piety, it seemed unlikely that God had anything to do with his current position.

Keris barely heard half of what they said anyway, their voices drowned out by the endless repeat of his last conversation with Zarrah, his eyes filled with her tear-streaked face. He'd woken up on the ground, his head aching and his vision swimming, but he'd had sense enough to climb the lookout tower in time to watch her sail away. To scream her name, because he'd been certain the storm would claim her.

That despite everything, she was going to die.

I don't regret it. Those were the words he'd told himself a hundred times. That it didn't matter if Ithicana fell, didn't matter if she hated him, didn't matter if he hated *himself*, he wouldn't regret it. Yet every time he'd spoken those words, they'd been a lie.

Because he regretted everything.

Something heavy settled on the top of his head, and Keris twitched, realizing that it was a crown. The crown of Maridrina. His *father's* crown.

His father was dead.

Ithicana, under Aren's leadership and Lara's bravery, had prevailed, his father's fleet nearly destroyed by the storm and hundreds of lives lost beneath the waves. And despite it having been his plan that failed, his plan that had lost the bridge, Keris was being raised up high as king, the people singing his name in the streets and proclaiming that Maridrina would enter a new era of peace under his rule.

The last thing he deserved was songs.

His knees cracked as he rose, one of the priests handing him the jeweled scepter of his office, and as Keris turned, the man intoned, "All hail King Keris of Maridrina!"

As one, the masses of nobility filling the cathedral dropped into deep bows and curtsies, the enormous structure entirely silent as he said, "As your sovereign, I swear in the eyes of God to uphold Maridrina's laws and protect our borders from those who might do our people harm. To raise Maridrina up high so that it might shine as the brightest jewel of the known world." He cleared his throat, the next not words that had been given to him to say but those he'd given himself. "I swear to pursue lasting peace and true alliances. To listen to my people and be their voice. To protect those who need protecting and to bring the villains who would prey upon them to justice. This I swear."

The nobility all stared at him in silence, but Keris heard the whispers of his words being repeated, moving back through the building and out into the open air, where throngs of civilians waited. Heard their cheers and calls of his name.

And felt hollow.

He was supposed to walk in a stately fashion down the aisle toward the rear, but Keris found himself striding quickly, looking neither left nor right as he passed, leaving the procession behind him. At his nod, the guards flung open the doors, and he blinked away tears from the brilliant glare of the morning sun before going down the steps to the awaiting carriage.

Settling in the rear seat, he fought the urge to yank the curtains closed even as he struggled to regain control of his thundering heart, the weight of the responsibility he now wielded only just starting to take hold. The carriage rocked as it started to move, slowly making its way through the cheering throngs.

Throngs that only yesterday had been weeping for the loss of so many soldiers—husbands, sons, fathers, and brothers who'd died on the slopes of Eranahl or drowned in the Tempest Seas. Throngs that cursed his father for all that he had done, and Keris wanted to climb onto the roof of the carriage and scream, *It was my plan! It is me you should blame!*

Just like she does.

Zarrah.

Her ships had been spotted heading south, though there was no word yet from the spies on whether she was on them. But he knew. Knew in his heart that she was alive.

Keris bent forward, resting his elbows on his knees, and the crown slid from his head to land with a heavy *thud* on the carriage floor. Gold glinted in the sun filtering through the windows, the Maridrinian rubies that adorned it looking like drops of blood.

She consumed his thoughts. Ruled his dreams to the point he'd had to drown himself in wine to silence her voice. To vanquish her eyes, which always stared at him with the pain of betrayal.

I'm sorry, he silently whispered, wishing he could say it to her face. But she'd been clear: She never wanted to see him again. After all that he'd done, at least he could honor her in that. And by pursuing the future they'd dreamed of, even if it always meant standing on opposite sides of a border.

There was no doubt in his mind about the first step he needed to take as Maridrina's king.

Bring the villains to justice.

The carriage rolled through the palace gates, and he reluctantly picked the crown up off the floor and placed it on his head. The door opened, and he stepped out, not waiting for the endless carriages carrying his aunts and siblings to arrive before heading into the inner sanctum. There were things he intended to address with his family—for he refused to call them the *harem* any longer—but that could wait. This, *this,* had to come first.

Dax, beard neatly trimmed and uniform freshly pressed, met him at the base of the tower. "Your Grace." He gave a low bow, but his voice was full of amusement as he added, "Nice hat."

"It's god-awful heavy." Keris pulled it off once they were inside, then hooked it over his forearm. "Now I understand why my father never wore it."

"Hopefully you bear the weight of responsibility better than that rat bastard ever did."

Keris cast a sidelong glance at the captain of his personal guard. "Time will tell, Dax. Time will tell. Someone has been sent to fetch *him*?"

Dax nodded. "It's all been done exactly as you wanted." His mouth stretched into a feral grin. "The crowd that will gather to watch that monster's execution is going to be bigger than that for your coronation, Your Grace. You might make it a holiday."

"I'll take it under consideration." They rounded the stairs of the tower, rising up to the top level, where more of Keris's personal guards stood at the entrance, the old guard who'd been so loyal to his father dead at Eranahl or dismissed with the warning to make themselves scarce. One of them opened the door, and Keris stepped into the office, surveying what had once been his father's domain. The place where he'd ruled from high above like some false god.

"I hate this room." He set the crown on the desk, his skin crawling with the sense his father was watching. That he wasn't dead, and when Keris turned around, it would be to see him walking through the door, ready to put him in his place.

"It's your house," Dax answered, not seeming to note Keris's tension. "Redecorate."

Except Keris didn't think burning every object in this room would be enough to erase his father's presence. He poured himself a drink, then unbuckled his sword belt and leaned the weapon against the desk before sitting.

Seconds passed, then minutes, and though he should have been anticipating the sweetness of the moment to come, Keris's hands were clammy with sweat, his stomach in ropes.

A knock sounded at the door.

"Send him in." It was a small miracle that his voice was steady, because his heart felt like it was ricocheting off his ribs.

The Magpie stepped inside.

"Your Majesty." He bowed low. "My most sincere felicitations on your coronation. I was saddened to have missed it, but my flock has shared with me all the delightful details, including your speech." The spymaster smiled, revealing his rotting teeth. "So inspiring. The cheers of the masses reached me even within the depths of my workroom."

I have the power now, Keris reminded himself. *Not this creature.* But the reminder did nothing to steady his nerves, nothing to ease the growing sense that even with the crown in his grasp, he was *not* in control. "I assume you know why you're here?"

"Of course." Serin gestured to the chair. "May I?"

Keris shrugged, struggling to keep his calm in the face of Serin's composure.

Once the old man had settled into the chair across from him, having carefully arranged his brown robes, Keris said, "When you leave this room, it will be in chains, Serin. You will be taken to prison, where you will be kept under heavy guard until the time of your trial. A trial that will unveil all the many horrors you visited upon the people of Maridrina with my father's blessing. I will, of course, convict you of all of them, at which time you will be executed."

Serin's smile didn't falter. "Coralyn would be *so* pleased, Your Grace. I believe she wished for my death even more than she wished for your father's, and here, you've accomplished both."

"My father died in battle. By the Queen of Ithicana's hand, if the rumors are to be believed."

Serin huffed in amusement. "You've always been a gambler, Your Grace. All your adult life, my flock has watched you shed the veneer of the polished, bookish prince to climb into the heights and slum it with the masses, rolling dice and betting on cards, the rush you gained worthy of the risks you took." He ran his tongue over his lips. "This was no different. You gave your father a perfect plan, but you bet on his failure. Or, to be more accurate, bet on your sister's desire to atone."

It was Keris's turn to laugh, though it was entirely feigned. "You're allowing your imagination to get the better of you, Serin. How could I have predicted any of what happened? There was no way for me to know a storm would strike. No way for me to know the Ithicanian queen was alive, much less at Eranahl, to deliver that fatal blow. This was the work of higher powers than me."

"Then these higher powers must favor you, Your Grace, for *ev-*

erything has worked out as you intended." His rheumy eyes glinted. "Almost, at any rate."

Keris's skin prickled and crawled with tension. No . . . not tension, fear. Serin had something up his sleeve. Something that was going to hurt. His mind raced over what it could be, because he'd ensured his family was under guard, with the men hand-selected by Dax. That his little sister Sara had been hidden out of harm's reach. Except he knew this creature had his ways, for Keris had watched him destroy people all his life. He glanced to Dax. "Leave us."

The man hesitated, watching Serin as most people would a poisonous snake. "Your Grace . . ."

"It's fine." Even as Keris said the words, he slipped a knife from his boot, resting it across his lap. "You're not going to try to kill me, are you, Magpie?"

Serin's jaw tightened, ever hateful of that moniker. "No, Your Majesty. I have greater ambitions than your death."

Keris's blood ran cold, sweat rolling down his spine as Dax left the room. "Enough with the games, Serin. My plan is to give you a swift death via the headsman, but if you continue to test my patience, I may have to resort to my original intention, which was to nail your feet to the dirt in the garden below and then give my aunts several buckets of rocks. They dislike you even more than I do."

The Magpie only leaned back in his chair and laughed. "I neither feel nor fear pain, Your Grace. Besides, I knew in coming here that I was walking toward my death."

"Then why didn't you run? You of all people have the wherewithal to escape and stay hidden."

Serin rubbed at the gray stubble of his chin, flakes of dry skin falling like snow to join the collection dusting his robe. "True, but it is hard to give up power once one has grown used to it, and while many might wish to live out their last years in peace, I am not one of them. *Peace* has never given me any pleasure, and as such, I will always walk the opposite direction of such a fate. Which is why I walked toward you."

Keris's thoughts raced, trying to predict the man's intent. Trying to predict his plans. But his mind came up empty of anything but rising panic.

"Your father was the perfect master in that he was the perfect pawn," Serin continued. "In all but one thing: his weakness for your mother. And her spawn." He spat on the floor. "Despite all my protests that you both would be the death of him, he favored you and Lara. Saw your failings as merits, and even after your sister showed her true colors, he refused to turn on you."

"I watched my father strangle my mother." Keris couldn't keep the anger from his voice. "So I think he did not care for her any more than he cared for Lara. Or for me."

Serin giggled, a strange, insane sound that made Keris recoil. "There is no denying that your father was a flawed and violent man, but your mother is the only woman he ever loved. It was not her defiance in going after Lara that drove him to kill her, but the things she said when he caught up to her. The revelation of her *true* feelings for His Grace, which were not at all what he'd believed. How swiftly love turns to hate in the face of betrayal. A feeling I suspect Zarrah Anaphora is *deeply* familiar with."

Keris couldn't breathe.

"Did you really think you could keep a secret like that from me, Your Grace?" Serin rested his elbows on the desk. "I won't belabor the countless little clues, not the least of which was a willingness to play the game you'd run away from all your pathetic life. I *knew* there was something between the two of you, but without proof, your father wouldn't hear it. I thought the whore in Nerastis would yield something, but all she could tell me was that you wouldn't touch her and that you'd disappear into the night, returning hours later smelling of *lilac*. She believed you were visiting a lover, and an innkeeper swore a man of your description rented one of his rooms in the company of a Valcottan woman. Which was compelling, but still not good enough for your father."

The world around Keris pulsed in and out of focus, but the cursed monster wasn't through.

"I came to realize that nothing short of catching you in the act—which I suspect our dear Otis did—would damn you in your father's eyes. That even him catching you in Zarrah's bed might not be enough, for he relished your defiance, ever believing that it would one day turn you to the purpose he envisioned for you. I saw that I was destined to watch you ascend and lose my power to your *idealism*, and so I resolved to render you powerless in the one way that mattered most."

Kill him! Silence him! Keris's grip on his knife tightened, because he could not let this get out. Could not allow Serin to voice the truth—not because it would damn him.

But because it would damn Zarrah.

He lunged across the table, knife slicing toward the Magpie's throat, but then Serin's words caused him to freeze. "If you kill me, you kill her, too. If I die, my flock has orders to release the details of your sordid little affair."

Shit shit shit. Keris let go of the front of Serin's robes. "What do you want?"

The Magpie let out a strange giggle. "My flock whispered your speech into my ears, Keris. Told me that you swore *to protect those who need protecting and to bring the villains who would prey upon them to justice.*" Serin's laughter turned wild, absolutely devoid of sanity.

"If you wanted to protect Zarrah, you should have taken her far, far away, but instead, you sent her back into the arms of the greatest villain I've ever known."

Dearest God, what have I done?

"For all his faults, your father loved you. Protected you. And I think even if I were to reveal this truth to the people, they'd forgive you, Keris, because they want what you've promised. But Petra? Petra does not love. Petra does not *feel*. And Petra and I have a rapport that goes back all those years ago to when she delivered word to my flock that her sister, the true and rightful heir to Valcotta, was staying, virtually unprotected, at a villa near the border. I, in turn, whispered that information into the ears of your father."

His breath caught, horror turning his veins to ice. The empress had arranged the murder of her own sister. Zarrah's mother.

"To twist the knife deeper, Petra took her niece and raised her in defiance of *everything* her mother believed in. Taught her to revel in violence and vengeance and war, not the peace her mother sought." He smirked. "Just what do you think Petra will do to Zarrah when she discovers that her niece was not only the *lover* of her mortal enemy but that Zarrah ruined her one chance to destroy Maridrina? Because if I meet my end, Petra *will* find out that Zarrah betrayed her plans. I promise you that. My flock is loyal only to me."

Panic roared through Keris's veins, everything too bright, too loud. "Name your price, Serin. What do you want?"

Because there was nothing he wouldn't give to stop this. Including keeping this monster alive and by his side.

"The only thing I want"—Serin rose to his feet—"is to see the look on your face when you realize you've lost the game, Keris. When you realize you've lost to *me*."

Then he threw himself forward.

Not at Keris, but through the windows encircling the tower, glass exploding as he struck.

Keris lunged after him onto the balcony, reaching.

But he was once again too late.

Serin flipped over the railing and fell, a wild shriek filling the air. Yet as Keris stumbled against the rail and looked down, it was to see the Magpie smiling up at him. Smiling, right until the moment he struck the paving stones below.

Thud.

87
ZARRAH

"WE MADE WAR AGAINST THE WRONG ENEMY" HAD BEEN HER aunt's response when Zarrah had returned to Pyrinat. "I believed my adversary Silas, but it was his son. I will not make the same mistake next time."

Next time. The words haunted Zarrah as she listened to her aunt give orders not for Zarrah to be punished for her choice to assist Aren at Southwatch but for a celebration in her honor. "Let it be known that my niece and heir is responsible for ripping the bridge out of Maridrina's hands," she declared. "Without her actions, and her warning, the Ithicanian Army would never have made it to Eranahl in time to repel the Rat King and his fleet."

A lie, through and through. Because of Keris, her chance to atone and regain her honor had been stolen away, Ithicana's victory won by their own hands—and by the hands of their queen. Which was perhaps how it should be.

Silas was dead. Ithicana was liberated. And the Endless War between Maridrina and Valcotta was once again at a stalemate, all because of what Keris had done. She still couldn't forgive him. Couldn't give up her anger at his betrayal. But she also couldn't give up *him.*

Her dreams were haunted by his face. His voice. His touch.

She loved him every bit as much as she hated him, and the emotions warred inside her, giving Zarrah no peace.

Which was perhaps fitting, given peace between Maridrina and Valcotta was not on the horizon. Not when her aunt's obsession with her new adversary grew with every passing day. Keris had denied her victory and wounded her pride, and the result was a hate that made her lifelong animosity toward Silas seem a paltry thing.

It was terrifying, because what the empress wanted wasn't his death: She wanted Keris destroyed.

"Everyone has a weakness!" her aunt shouted as she stormed around the room, scraps of paper detailing everything the spies could learn about Keris fluttering to the ground. "We must find his!"

An Endless War between empresses and kings. A war of hubris and avarice. A war where people were nothing more than pawns on a board, used and discarded with no thought beyond whether they'd achieved the player's purpose. And though Zarrah dedicated herself to steering her aunt to different goals and higher purpose, it amounted to nothing. Because to the empress, Zarrah was as much a pawn as everyone else.

"We should send an envoy to Ithicana," Zarrah repeated. "Reaffirm our goodwill, yes?"

Her aunt didn't respond, her attention entirely on a report detailing the plans for Keris's upcoming coronation. "This tells me nothing!" She cast it aside. "Why does no one know anything about this man? I need to understand how he thinks, and you give me plans for dinner parties and décor! What does Keris Veliant want?"

"Peace." The word slipped from Zarrah's lips, and she instantly regretted it as her aunt rounded on her. "What makes you say that?"

"His actions." Zarrah picked up a fallen report. "He's made it clear that he doesn't want the bridge and intends to withdraw what remains of his soldiers from Ithicana."

"All that proves is he's more intelligent than his father—that structure is a curse!"

"Bermin says there hasn't been a single raid over the border," Zarrah persisted. "And not for lack of manpower, for their garrison there is full. Instead, they look to defense and to rebuilding their half of the city."

"Biding his time while Maridrina licks its wounds." Her aunt picked up a glass and swirled the contents as she eyed the report. "It says he will not follow the Maridrinian tradition of marrying his father's harem. Yet neither does he cast them aside. What do you make of that, girl? You lived with them for months yet offer little in the way of information."

Zarrah's chest tightened. "I believe his affection for them platonic."

The empress snorted. "An aversion to bedding them is not reason enough to risk angering his people by casting aside tradition. There's something else going on." She gestured to one of her spymasters. "Find out more about his motivations."

The man bowed and exited, but on his heels a servant came in carrying a tray. On it was an enamel tube bearing the Maridrinian royal seal. Zarrah's heart skipped at the sight, wondering what possible message Keris would have sent her aunt.

The empress clearly wondered the same thing, for she snatched up the tube and pulled out a thick sheaf of paper, her brow furrowing as she sat to read.

Pulse racing, Zarrah waited in silence.

Seconds passed. Then minutes. After what felt like an eternity, her aunt set the pages down, staring blankly off into the distance. Her voice was hoarse as she said, "You're just like your mother."

Zarrah went still, her skin prickling. "Pardon, Auntie?"

The empress's lip curled, her nose wrinkling as though she smelled something rotten. "Despite everything I gave you, everything I've done for you, you took her side." Her head swiveled, the eyes that latched onto Zarrah's filled with icy fury. "Both of you whores."

A chill ran down Zarrah's spine. "Excuse me?"

"You brought a rat into your bed." Her aunt took a step toward her, and Zarrah instinctively stepped back. "Which would be unforgivable in itself, but you told him my secrets. You betrayed your empress and your nation for your lover."

"This is madness, Auntie." She couldn't keep the shake from her voice. "Who is telling you these lies?"

"It is you who lies!"

The blow came hard and fast, her aunt's fist striking her in the cheek and knocking her back. Zarrah staggered, catching herself against a table.

"You were Keris Veliant's lover." The empress stalked toward her. "Not just while you were his *prisoner* but before. *After.*"

"I ask again"—Zarrah lifted her chin—"who has told you these lies?"

"The Magpie."

Her aunt threw the pages at her face. Zarrah caught several of them, eyes skipping over the spidery script laying out all the tiny damning details. A hundred coincidences that together whispered a truth that only a fool would deny. But for Keris's sake—and her own—she had to try. "Serin is a liar."

"Not to me." Her aunt's head cocked, her expression making Zarrah want to run. To hide. Because not only was what looked back at her unfamiliar and strange, it was barely human. "We have long been adversaries, and there is a trust that comes in that. What horror that I can put more faith in the words of a Maridrinian spymaster than that of my own flesh and blood. My chosen heir."

"Auntie—"

"Shh, dear one." The empress pressed two fingers to Zarrah's lips, nails digging in so hard that blood dribbled into her mouth. "I told no one but you my plans for Vencia. Told you to tell no one until you were on the high seas. Yet the princeling delivered my plans to his father in such a manner they could *only* have come from your lips. You betrayed me. Betrayed Valcotta."

"I did not betray Valcotta."

In a flash, a knife was in her aunt's hand, pressed against Zarrah's throat. "Lie to me again, dear one, and you will bleed out on this floor. And I'll feed your corpse to the dogs."

A traitor's death.

Denial was pointless. But perhaps the truth might do some good. "I may have betrayed your confidence, but I did not betray Valcotta, Auntie. You sought to escalate a war and pursue an attack that would have seen countless innocents killed. And for what? What had we to gain from attacking Vencia besides the perverse pleasure of slaughter?"

"Revenge." Her aunt stared at her, unblinking. "They killed your mother, Zarrah. Is the princeling so pleasing between the sheets that you've forgotten that? Forgotten how they cut off her head and hung her body up to rot and drip down upon you for days?"

Hearing it still hurt, but not in the way it once had. "I haven't forgotten. But unlike you, I remember that it was Silas who killed my mother, not Maridrina. And Silas is dead."

"Not all of him. You dishonor your mother's memory by not extinguishing his bloodline."

"Keris is—" She was about to say he was nothing like his father, but that wasn't entirely true. Silas had left his mark on his son. "He's not his father. He wants peace, Auntie. The Endless War could end. We could stop the fighting. Could have peace if only you would give up this . . . this fanatical pursuit of pride and vengeance. Valcotta will be better for it."

Silence.

Blood dripped down her lips into her mouth, but Zarrah barely felt the sting as she stared into the eyes of the woman who'd saved her life. Who'd brought her back from the edge. Who'd made her strong. For the first time, she saw that there was something *wrong* with her aunt. Something missing. And its lack ensured the empress would never understand the future Zarrah dreamed for Valcotta.

"You were supposed to be mine, dear one. Supposed to be the one who'd carry on my legacy. The one who'd ensure I lived on. But you're still hers. Or worse," she hissed, "you're *his*."

Zarrah lifted her chin. "I belong to no one but myself."

And she'd honor herself to the bitter end.

The empress laughed, and the wildness in it turned Zarrah's blood to ice.

Then her aunt attacked.

The hilt of her aunt's knife struck her in the temple, and Zarrah dropped to her knees, stunned. Only for a foot to catch her in the stomach, sending her toppling sideways. The world swam, and Zarrah tried to stand, but another blow caught her in the stomach, flipping her. Then another and another, each one driving deeper into her belly, agony racing through her body.

If you let her kill you, this will never end, a voice whispered from deep in her thoughts. *If you let her kill you, she'll make war on Keris.*

She needed to fight.

Zarrah rolled, catching hold of the empress's ankle and pulling her down. She landed with a crash, and Zarrah was on top of her in a flash. Though her aunt had experience and skill, youth and strength still counted for something as Zarrah pinned her. "This can't go on." She spat blood onto the tile. "It has to stop."

The empress laughed. "The war will never stop."

It was the truth. Under her aunt's rule, nothing would ever change. And the chance for Zarrah to sway her had been eradicated, if it had ever existed at all.

There was only one option left.

While she'd be executed for it, Zarrah had the hope that Bermin would be better, for at least her cousin still possessed his humanity.

Whereas this creature was devoid of the quality entirely.

Zarrah closed her hands over her aunt's throat and squeezed, silencing the laughter.

And leaving panic in its wake.

Her aunt's eyes bulged, and she squirmed and struggled beneath Zarrah. But the empress had taught Zarrah every trick she knew. And Zarrah capitalized on that knowledge even as she squeezed harder.

Her aunt's face purpled, her eyes wide and frantic, and Zarrah watched as she lost consciousness. Tears flooded down her cheeks, but she didn't let go.

Then a battering ram struck her in the side.

All the air drove out of Zarrah's lungs, her head slamming against the tiles, and she vaguely made out Welran's face above her. Boots pounded against floor as guards poured in, several moving to help her aunt's bodyguard restrain Zarrah.

The empress's voice, soft and strangled, said, "She tried to kill me. She's a traitor. A cursed traitor in bed with Maridrina. Arrest her! She's charged with treason."

The world swam in and out of focus, but Zarrah forced herself to center on the empress. "Yes, Auntie. Arrest me. Try me for treason and give me a *trial*." Because the law demanded it, and Zarrah was prepared to ensure that *everyone* in Pyrinat, and in Valcotta, heard what she had to say about their ruler.

The empress was quivering, Welran having moved to support her, but it was false weakness. For the eyes that stared back at Zarrah held *nothing* but fury. "No, dear one. There will be no trial for you. No execution. For what you've done, it must be Devil's Island."

Horror filled Zarrah's chest, and on its heels came terror unlike anything she'd ever known, bile burning up her throat because to be sent to that island was to be sent to hell on earth. "No, Auntie. Please, please don't send me there!"

"If you couldn't face the consequences, you shouldn't have betrayed me."

But treason meant execution, not *that* place. "Just kill me now. Please."

The empress only gave her a cold smile. "Put her in shackles. And gag her. Leave her traitorous words for those who will greet her on Devil's Island's shores."

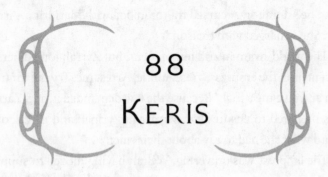

88
KERIS

THE RUMOR THAT HE'D KILLED SERIN IN COLD BLOOD SWEPT across Vencia like a tidal wave, repeated over and over until all swore it was truth. And although no one wept for the loss of Maridrina's spymaster, the knowledge that their new king had murdered him in cold blood changed things.

There were no more cheers. No more songs. And Keris felt a wariness in their eyes when he passed, his people no longer certain that he was the harbinger of change.

No longer certain that anything had changed at all.

Though in truth, he barely cared. Only went through the motions of rule, his mind consumed with waking nightmares of what the empress would do when she learned the truth. He'd wanted to shut the gates to the city. To lock everyone inside until he figured out a way to stop Serin's messengers.

Except he'd known it had been too late.

Serin had set the wheels in motion long before his plunge to his death, likely the moment he'd learned Keris's father was dead.

And neither the fastest ship nor the fleetest horse could take Keris to Pyrinat in time to save Zarrah from the truth.

So instead, he forced himself to push forward. To begin negotiations with Ithicana for the return of Maridrinian prisoners. Set things to rights in every possible way, because the moment the spies brought word of her fate, he was done. There were some hurts that no heart could endure, least of all his.

Serin's flock acted swiftly, though whether it was a blessing or a curse, Keris wasn't certain.

"News from Valcotta," Dax said, handing Keris a folded piece of paper, then leaving the room.

Keris sucked in a deep breath, then leaned back in his chair and drained his glass while he stared at the paper he'd set on his desk. Slowly, he extracted a knife, the edge glittering sharp, and set it next to the paper.

Please let it have been quick, he silently prayed. *Please don't let her have suffered.*

Then he unfolded the paper, his eyes skipping over the words. Saw that Zarrah had attacked the empress for reasons that had not been disclosed. Yet rather than a report of her execution, he saw something that turned his blood cold.

Zarrah Anaphora has been sent to Devil's Island.

"No. No no no."

Devil's Island was Valcotta's harshest prison. A small, rocky island in the cold waters of the deep south, where only the worst of the nation's criminals were sent. Men and women so vile that it was said hell itself had spat them out and refused to take them back again.

And the empress had delivered Zarrah to them.

Keris stood up, his glass falling from his hands to crash against the floor, but he barely noticed.

He had to get her out.

Except Devil's Island was impenetrable, the only route in a single dock, the rest of the island cliffs surrounded by frigid and violent seas. Valcottan vessels constantly patrolled the perimeter, with archers armed and ready to shoot anyone who made it into the water.

No one, *no one*, had ever escaped.

Think, Keris! he silently screamed at himself. *Think of a way to do this.*

His eyes landed on the letter stating the terms Aren had set for Keris retrieving his imprisoned soldiers. And next to it, a spy's report that had come via the Harendellians that Aren had declared Lara the rightful queen of Ithicana.

An impenetrable island. An impossible task.

He strode to the door, flinging it open. "Make arrangements for a ship. I want to sail on the next tide."

Dax lifted one eyebrow. "And where, Your Grace, are you planning to sail?"

Keris turned, looking out the tower window to the sea and the distant misty haze cloaking Ithicana. "We sail to Eranahl Island."

He wouldn't stop until he'd done everything in his power to free Zarrah. He didn't care if all of Maridrina turned on him if it meant liberating her from the worst place on earth.

"Eranahl, Your Grace? You think it wise to enter Ithicana?"

It definitely wasn't wise. Might even be fatal. But he couldn't rescue Zarrah without help.

Which meant it was time for a conversation with his sister.

Read on for "The Calm Before the Storm,"
a bonus short story from Lara's and Aren's
points of view that bridges the gap between
The Traitor Queen and *The Endless War* . . .

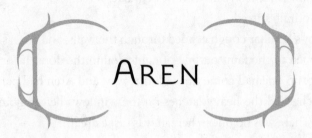

AREN

AREN KERTELL, THE THIRTY-SEVENTH RULER OF ITHICANA, jerked awake with a start. His rooms in Eranahl were shadowed, the glow from a jar of algae on the table next to the bed the only source of light. His heart thundered in his chest, his breath rapid and ragged, sweat from the already-fading dream dampening his brow.

Just a dream, he told himself. *She's alive.*

Yet his heart refused to steady, his skin crawling with unease that had his hand reaching for the dagger beneath the pillow. Outside, thunder boomed and wind lashed against the balcony doors, the scent of lightning and rain thick on the air. Aren's eyes flicked over the shadows of the room, searching for movement. For threats.

It wouldn't be the first time someone had come for his queen.

One dead by his hand. Another by Aster's. Another two languishing in the prison below the palace until the storms cleared enough for a proper Ithicanian execution.

I will gut you, he silently said to whoever might be lurking in the shadows. *I will cut your fucking throat.*

Because that was all anyone who came in the night deserved. That was all *anyone* who came for Lara deserved.

Nothing stirred.

Jor's familiar cough echoed through the walls, and Aren's eyes snapped to the faint outline of light around the door. If Jor was there, no one had come through that way, and Aren had personally checked the heavy latches on the windows before going to bed. There was no one in here. It was just a dream.

She's alive. She's alive. She's alive.

Yet his pulse continued to roar, a bead of sweat rolling down his brow as he slowly shifted his weight to look next to him on the bed.

Lara was sprawled half on her side, half on her back, the strap of her nightgown pulled down, the strip of dark silk a slash across her skin. Even in the dim light, there was no mistaking how thin she was, the infection that had taken hold of the wound in her leg having stolen away flesh and muscle. Having nearly stolen her life.

She was so still.

Aren's chest tightened, terror filling his guts. *Nana said she was over the worst of it,* he reminded himself. *Said that she'd recover completely in time.*

But God help him, he couldn't shake the memories of her lost in fevered dreams, her skin burning hot and her breathing unsteady. How he'd held her hand, all of his grandmother's potions and tonics failing, helpless to do anything as Lara had slipped closer and closer to the edge between life and death.

She's alive.

The words in his head sounded more like a plea than a statement of fact, and Aren's eyes fixed on her chest, searching for the steady rise and fall, but he couldn't make it out in the darkness.

That, or she wasn't breathing at all.

A tremor ran through him as he leaned closer to her face, waiting for the warmth of her breath to brush his cheek.

Waiting.

Waiting.

But no breath came.

Panic surged through his veins, then a whoosh of breath hit him in the face, carrying a giggle with it.

Smirking up at him in the darkness, Lara said, "I'm a touch offended that you believe I'd meet my end in such an inglorious fashion as dying in my sleep."

His heart was hammering so hard, Aren thought he was going to be sick. "You were holding your breath!"

Lara chuckled, pushing strands of hair off her face that had come loose from her braid. "Maybe."

"It's not funny."

"It *was* funny," she answered. "You've just forgotten how to laugh."

Twisting away from her, Aren slung his legs over the edge of the bed and rested his elbows on his knees. *It was just a joke. She's fine.*

The bed shifted as she crawled across it, her arms wrapping around him and her face resting against his shoulder. "Are you angry?"

He shook his head, words feeling beyond him, his heart still racing.

Lara was silent for a long moment, then said, "I . . . I'm just tired of being treated like an invalid."

He could understand that. Knew that it was against her nature to lie in bed, idle for days at a time, but . . . "I've seen you without breath in your lungs, your heart still. I don't ever want to see that again."

Lara exhaled a long breath. "There are moments I forget that.

Or it feels like it happened to someone else. A story. Not my reality. Or yours." She buried her face in his neck, her grip tightening around him. "I'm sorry."

The last thing he wanted was for her to feel guilty about more things than she already did. Reaching around, Aren caught her by the waist, ever mindful of her healing injuries as he pulled her into his lap. "Not everyone can be funny, Lara," he told her gravely. "But it's all right—I love you *despite* your comedic failings. No one is perfect."

Except to him, she was perfect. She was everything.

He sensed her considering a retort, but instead of flaying him with her wit, his wife only twisted a lock of his hair around her index finger and said, "Clearly my humor needs some exercise. I'm getting up and leaving this room today, else I'll lose my wit entirely."

Though he'd known this moment was coming, Aren still stiffened. "This joke isn't any funnier than the last. You need to get your strength back."

"Agreed. Which is why I need to start moving around."

She wasn't wrong. But in this room, he could keep her safe. Not just from those who sought her death but from the dark looks. Whispered words. The hate. "Not yet."

"Just how do you think you're going to stop me?"

She rose to her feet, and though nothing showed on her face but defiance, Aren didn't miss the way her leg quivered beneath her weight. He gave it a pointed look, then rose himself, lifting her in his arms as he did. Ignoring her protests, he put her back on the bed, pinning her wrists to the pillow and wishing he wasn't quite so keenly aware of her body beneath his.

And that his own body wasn't so quick to react.

"Well," Lara purred, the corners of her mouth turning upward. "If this is how you plan to keep me here, then here I will remain."

"Lara . . ." He dropped his face to her throat, still gripping her wrists, though he was careful to keep his weight on his elbows. "We can't. Nana said—"

"Are you really going to allow your *grandmother* to dictate what you can and cannot do with your own wife?"

The intelligent answer was *yes,* but the blood fueling his brain was rapidly abandoning it for other parts of his body. Especially as she wrapped a leg around his hips, her nightgown riding up to her waist. Leaving nothing between them. "You're still injured."

"I think you'll find the parts of me required for this particular activity are in the peak of health."

"I don't think that's how it works."

"Well, I disagree."

She rubbed her sex against his cock, and God help him, she was already wet. Clearly wanted this as much as he did, but he was supposed to be the voice of reason. Except reason was abandoning him, along with intelligence as his wife arched her back, nightgown pulling down to expose her breasts. "You're not supposed to exert yourself."

"Then you do the hard work." She dug her heel into his back, grinding against him and erasing all thought from his head.

"I'm tired of waiting," she said. "I need you in me."

His control shattered like glass, and he claimed her mouth, parting her lips with his tongue so that he could taste her, resisting the urge to plunge into her and make her his again. He knew every inch of her body, had touched it and tasted it nightly until her cursed father had invaded and everything had gone to shit, and Aren wanted her back. Wanted to kiss each curve and line of her beautiful body, to claim her with his mouth before he buried his cock in her. Wanted to hear his queen scream his name as she climaxed.

Releasing her wrists, he trailed his fingers down her arms, the whimper that exited her lips sending a jolt of desire through him. He kissed the rapid pulse in her throat, the delicate line of her collarbone, then dropped his lips to her breast, drawing her nipple into his mouth. Lara gasped, her back arching beneath him. "Don't stop."

Aren wasn't sure he was capable of stopping. From the moment he'd set eyes on her, he'd wanted her, but it was because he loved her that he couldn't deny her. Catching her other nipple between his teeth, he nipped at it, smiling as she buried her fingers in his hair. His own fingers trailed down her side, down the hard muscle of her leg, then up the inside of her thigh. She quivered beneath him, her nails digging into his scalp, her breathing rapid as she pulled his lips back to hers. "Please," she whispered as she kissed him. "I need you."

There was a tightness to her voice, an edge that made Aren pause because he'd heard that tone from her before. After he'd stitched her up following the battle for Gamire Island, then proceeded to fuck her with no regard for the fact she'd lost a quarter of her blood to the wound on her leg.

Then he'd left her.

All her life, Lara had been taught that her value was in what she could accomplish only to have those who should've cared about her, should've protected her, turn on her once she'd served her purpose. Who could blame her for allowing that to sink into her soul, especially after how he'd treated her? Who could blame her for continuing to risk her health—her *life*—just to ensure she was worth something to those she loved?

"Aren?"

There was a hint of trepidation in her voice, and he silently cursed himself because its presence was his fault. Resting his weight on one elbow, he smoothed her hair back from her face and then kissed her. Meeting her gaze, he said, "I love you, Lara.

Nothing in this world short of death will ever take me from your side, and even then, it would only be until I could find you in whatever comes after. I will never leave you." He hesitated, then added, "And I know that I said all these words before only to cast you aside. Not once, but twice."

Lara turned her face away from his, eyes squeezing shut. "You know I don't blame you for that, Aren. What I did was unforgivable. I lied to you."

"I said nothing would take me from your side but then allowed something to do so," he answered. "But I didn't stop loving you. Not once, Lara. Not once. And I never will."

She opened her eyes to meet his again, "There are moments when hearing that from you feels like a dream I might wake from."

That broke his heart. "It's the truth. You are brilliant and brave. Empathetic and kind to those who deserve it." He kissed her again, tasting the salt of a tear that had trickled down her cheek. "There is no one else I'd rather have at my back during a storm or in my arms when the clouds clear. There is nothing and no one in this life or the next that I want more than you, Lara."

"Then why are you holding back?"

"Because I don't want you to hurt yourself," he said. "I don't want to risk you."

"I'm fine, Aren."

"You always say that. You think that showing any weakness makes you worthless." Lara went still beneath him, her face abruptly unreadable, but he pressed onward anyway. "I know your worth. I see it every time I look at you, know it every time I hear your voice. You have nothing to prove, but I do. I need to prove to you that I will always be at your side, no matter what we face."

"I already know that."

"Do you?"

Her lip quivered. "Yes."

Whether she was lying to him or lying to herself, Aren wasn't certain. "No more deception between us, Lara. No more lies or half truths. No secrets. I swear to it."

She hesitated, then nodded. "I swear to it. No more secrets."

Shifting his weight, Aren kissed her. "And when the healers say that you are well enough for exertion"—he pressed against her—"I promise it will have been worth the wait."

Lara rolled her eyes and smiled, and he kissed her again, linking her fingers with his. Tasted his beautiful wife. Relished her. Prayed to fate and the stars for a moment to breathe before they were tested again.

Fate, of course, had different plans, and a knock sounded at the door.

LARA

LARA TWITCHED, THE SHARP RAP ON THE DOOR STARTLING HER, and she instinctively slipped her hand under her pillow to where her knife was concealed. Never mind that she didn't have the strength yet to fully brush her own hair, much less wield a blade.

She hated feeling weak. Hated how her heart fluttered and her legs trembled every time she stood, a visit to the water closet feeling like she'd climbed a mountain rather than crossed the room. *You did this to yourself,* Nana was fond of telling her, and it was hard to argue the old woman's point. In the days after she'd awoken from her first bout of illness after the battle for Eranahl, Lara had pushed herself to the limit, needing to prove herself worthy of the crown that had been placed back on her head. Needing to involve herself as much as she could in rebuilding the kingdom that had suffered so much as the result of her actions. One stupid misstep on the stairs had broken open the wound on her leg, and it had festered, nearly killing her.

And leaving her confined to this room ever since. Not just weak but . . . useless.

Another knock sounded, and Aren reached up to draw her hand down from the blade. "They can wait," he murmured, kissing her throat. "I'm not ready to get out of bed."

"It could be something important."

"Not as important as who is in my bed."

Aren kissed her again, tongue parting her lips as his thumbs stroked the backs of her hands. Lara's blood warmed, an aching need for him building between her legs. He was still hard, rubbing against the apex of her thighs. Though she knew he was trying to protect her, might well be right to do so, Lara still lifted her hips, his thick tip pressing inside of her.

Aren groaned, his large body shuddering as he said, "God, woman. Did you not hear a damned thing I just said? Or have you just chosen to disregard all of it?"

Instead of answering, Lara hooked her leg around him and pulled, her back arching with pleasure as he filled her. Her heart was fluttering wildly but she didn't care. She loved him more than life. Wanted him more than breath. And with everything feeling so fragile, so tenuous, Lara needed this connection to him. Knew that for all his protests, Aren needed it, too.

"Lara . . ." he gasped, the sound half protest and half desire. A third knock sounded, louder and more insistent, and he turned his head and shouted, "Piss off!"

Silence.

The door exploded inward, revealing a scowling Nana framed by the lamplight. She leveled a finger at them and snarled, "I knew it!"

"Get out!" Aren roared.

"Get off of her!" Nana roared back, storming into the room. "I didn't nurse this woman back to health only for you to break her because you couldn't keep your idiot cock in your trousers!"

"I'm not doing anything to her!"

A blatant lie, given he was still very much inside of her, but Lara said nothing. It was about time Aren stood up to his grandmother on something, even if in this, he had little ground to stand on.

"Oh? Then you won't mind if I take this?" Nana reached for the blanket and Aren cursed, snatching at the bedding, the two engaging in a vicious tug-of-war while Jor and the other guards gaped in the doorway.

Her own temper simmering to a boil, Lara jerked her nightgown back into place and then shouted, "Enough! I started it, so if you wish to cast insults, Amelie, cast them at me!"

The old woman scowled but dropped the blanket. "Idiot girl. I expect him to be blinded by lust, but you should know better."

"You don't speak to her that way." Aren dragged the blanket up to his waist, his face flushed with anger. "She's the Queen of Ithicana and you *will* treat her with respect."

Nana spat on the floor. "And you're the king. Yet instead of dealing with your kingdom's problems, you leave your sister to do the work while you play nursemaid. You do Lara no favors by ignoring your duties to Ithicana in favor of your *husbandly* needs."

"I am not ignoring my duties."

"Oh?" Nana reached down to pick up Aren's discarded clothing. "Then why is there a council meeting going on right now while you stand, naked as a jaybird, arguing with your grandmother about whether you can hump your wife?" She threw the clothing at him. "Get dressed and go rule."

Lara closed her eyes for a heartbeat, silently cursing Ahnna. The Ithicanian princess had grown used to control in Aren's absence, and this was not the first time she'd behaved as though he hadn't returned at all. "You should go."

Silence stretched, then Aren gave a stiff nod and pulled on his trousers. Bending to kiss Lara's cheek, he then said to his grandmother, "We're going to have words about this, Amelie."

"I look forward to it, Your Grace," Nana answered sourly, watching as Aren exited the room. Aster entered as soon as Aren disappeared, carrying a tray of food.

Lara bit down on a sigh of annoyance at the sight of the man. Though he'd once sought her death, since the incident with the sharks during the battle for Eranahl, the former watch commander was now her most strident supporter. "Fanatic," Aren always muttered when Aster was out of earshot, and while Lara was inclined to agree, she also knew that the old man had saved her life, and she owed him for that.

"Late to rise today, Your Grace?" he asked.

"Is it late?" She passed a weary hand over her face before glancing at the balcony doors, no light visible around them. "It's still dark."

"The storm is heavy over the island." He set the tray on the bed next to her. "I checked everything for poison myself, Your Grace."

The same conversation they'd had every day since she'd woken from her fever, yet for some reason, seeing a bite taken from every item on her plate pissed her off this morning. "It's really not necessary for you to sample my food, Aster. Jor has the cooks watched while everything is prepared." She bit her tongue to keep from adding, *Besides, you wouldn't taste the poison in something until you were dead.*

"Four people have already tried to kill you, Your Grace," he answered. "And there is a small but vocal faction within Eranahl demanding your execution, so I think it is safe to say there are assassins around every corner."

Nana snorted, but Lara barely heard her, a vision of a woman with a knife filling her mind's eye. How the woman's face had been twisted with hatred, Lara too weak to move, too weak to scream. It had been luck that Aster had come into her room, embedding his knife in the assassin's chest before the woman could strike.

She'd fallen on Lara, blood soaking the blankets, the weight of her driving the air from Lara's lungs until Aster had pulled the corpse off her.

She owed him her life.

Aster was watching her expectantly, so Lara dutifully picked up her fork and took a mouthful of fish, then another, knowing that he'd watch her eat the whole meal. Thankfully it was small, the entire island still on rations. As it would remain until the storm eased and boats could return to the water to fish and retrieve supplies from the other islands, as well as the bridge itself.

"Out," Nana said to him after Lara had finished eating, and ever unfrazzled by the woman's tone, Aster took the tray and exited the room to take up his post.

"You need to back off," Lara snapped, the moment the man had left the room. "Aren has endured enough without you berating him at every turn."

"Why? Because if I don't, you'll poison me into the shitter again?"

If you don't, I'll cut out your goddamned tongue. The words rose to Lara's lips, but she bit down on them. "You're his grandmother. You should be supporting him."

Nana stared her down. "Drowning clearly stripped you of some of your intelligence, girl. I *am* supporting Aren as a grandmother should—by protecting him from himself." She gave a sharp shake of her head. "As a king, he already suffers from people telling him what he wants to hear rather than what will help him, but I refuse to do that. He's behaving like a husband, not a ruler. If that's how he wants to live, he needs to abdicate to Ahnna and leave."

Lara's jaw tightened, and she looked away. Such was the life of a monarch, she knew that, but couldn't Aren have a goddamned moment of respite? Hadn't he earned it?

As though hearing her thoughts, Nana said, "This isn't the moment to breathe, the moment to rest, Lara. This is the moment to leverage what you and Aren accomplished. To leverage the support of fanatics like Aster who see the behavior of overgrown fish as a reason to follow you, even though we know that the creatures steered clear of you because your blood was fouled with stimulants."

That had been the reason?

Lara's stomach dropped, the world spinning around her, for not once had it occurred to her that there'd been something in her blood that had driven the sharks away.

"To that end, perhaps it is time your convalescence ends," Nana said. "Let's have a look at you."

Lara dutifully moved to sit on the edge of the bed, though her mind drifted as Nana pressed an ear to her chest, listening to her heart. *Had* it been the stimulants in her blood that kept the sharks from attacking her? She'd ingested as much of the herb as she could to push through the blood loss and pain of the injury to her leg, so it was possible her blood had tasted . . . *off-putting* to the creatures. And there had been plenty of other people to choose from in the water. She bit the insides of her cheeks, her hands cold.

Why do you even care? she snapped at herself. *It's not as though you put any stock in superstitions and myths.*

Except . . . she'd drawn some strength from that moment. From having the defenders of Ithicana allow her to pass to the gates, giving her a chance to live. From their belief in her.

Idiot. Lara squeezed her eyes shut.

"Heart and lungs are good," Nana said, then ran a prodding finger over the red line across Lara's ribs. Where her father had sliced her open with his sword before she'd stabbed him. Before she'd killed him. "This is healing very well."

Lara gave a tight nod, knowing that none of those things were the demon that haunted her.

Groaning, Nana lowered herself to the floor, knees cracking, and then began unraveling the bandage wrapped around Lara's thigh.

It was hard not to hold her breath, because her memory still drew up visions of the wound when it had turned foul. Red and rotten and seeping things she wished never to witness again. Though she knew the wound was now clear of infection, it was still a relief when the bandage pulled away to reveal the forming scar, the redness to either side faded to pink.

Nana held a lamp up to the injury, sniffed at it, then set to poking and prodding. "Any longer idle and you'll limp for the rest of your life," she finally said. "Time to get off your back and on your feet, though you'll need to take it slowly at first."

Lara lifted one eyebrow. "Seems your invasion of my bedroom was unnecessary."

A snort was the only response she got, the old woman never one to apologize for anything. Nana rose to her feet, gathering her supplies back into her bag. Then she met Lara's gaze. "There're no herbs for contraceptive tonics. Eranahl is stripped to the bones of everything, as there are women here besides you who wish to avoid pregnancy. I've requested that obtaining more be a priority, but until the storms subside enough to retrieve supplies . . ." She shrugged. "Though I suppose there is a chance that you don't need them."

Lara hesitated, for this was not something she'd put much thought to.

"That's what I thought."

Goddammit, the woman was a queen of manipulation. Not that Lara didn't believe the information was true, but—"Thank you for keeping me apprised."

Without another word, Aren's grandmother took her things and left the room, Lia stepping inside as she left. Because God for-

630 DANIELLE L. JENSEN

bid Lara have a moment alone. "I'm going to clean up," she informed the bodyguard, "and then ..."

She had no idea what she'd do.

Lia only said, "As you wish, Your Grace. We'll escort you wherever you wish to go."

The formality ground on Lara's nerves, for once upon a time, she'd drunk and laughed with this woman. Yet Lia, like Aster, had taken her swim through shark-infested waters as a sign and now treated Lara with nothing short of reverence.

Eyes on the bath, Lara slowly made her way across the room, her leg protesting each step. Her heart was pounding by the time she made it to the edge of the pool, but feeling Lia's eyes on her, Lara didn't pause before climbing into the bath. Her breath came in rapid pants, which Lara did her best to hide from the other woman by sinking low in the water, where she finally felt alone.

Her eyes burned, half from pain and half from anger at her weakness. And then all for her own stupidity because she'd forgotten her knife under her pillow on the bed, and she couldn't summon the energy to go retrieve it.

Fuck. Lara balled her hands into fists, bubbling fury rising in her chest, the emotion making her question everything. As always, one question shouted the loudest.

Is staying a mistake?

She'd planned to leave when she'd woken in the days after the battle. Had only remained because against every odd, Aren had wanted her to stay. In the time before she'd relapsed, Lara had felt hope that there was a future for her in Ithicana. That despite everything, this was the place she was meant to be.

Those hopes now felt like delusions.

She forced herself to reach for the soap. Scrubbed her hair and body, exhaustion biting at her as she eased her too-thin body out of the bath and toweled dry. Her long hair she wove into a simple braid, which she pinned around her head like a coronet, arms trembling by the time she was finished. Donning lace undergarments, she took a plain green dress from the wardrobe and pulled it over her head, the silk whispering in the silence. A belt to hold her knife, a pair of sandals, and Aren's mother's necklace completed her attire, but instead of leaving the room, Lara sat on a chair, just breathing as she stared at the door.

Get up, she ordered herself. *You need to get out of this room.*

But fear throbbed in her chest at what she'd face beyond the confines of this space. Those who wished to kill her. Those who hated her. Those who worshiped her only because they didn't know the truth.

Get up.

Lara rose, meeting Lia's watchful gaze. "Take me to the council room."

The other woman nodded. "Yes, Your Grace." Then she opened the door and leaned out, murmuring, "Aster, the queen wishes to attend the council meeting."

Lara gritted her teeth, waiting for the man to argue, but he only gave an approving nod and held out an arm. "I'm quite fine," she said, moving past him, taking in the six other armed Ithicanians standing in the corridor. All of them possessed the alertness of warriors expecting attack from every angle, and it made her wonder if there had been more attempts to reach her than she knew about. Than even Aren knew about.

Aster coughed. "They aren't in the war room, I'm afraid. The meeting took place over breakfast and is in the dining room."

Which was on the main level of the palace. Biting her tongue, Lara gave him a smile. "Good. I'm still hungry."

Half of her guard moved ahead down the corridor, the rest remaining behind while Aster and Lia strode at her side. Or rather, shuffled, for each step she took was slow and unsteady. The silk of her dress was glued to her back by the time she reached the grand staircase, her body quivering from the effort.

"Your Grace," Lia murmured, "perhaps you might allow us—"

"No," Lara interrupted from between her teeth. "I'm just stiff."

"The queen was chosen by Ithicana's guardians," Aster declared loudly. "Thrice, death has tried to claim her, and thrice was he denied. He will not test her mettle again."

The guardians didn't choose you, a dark voice whispered inside her head. *They recoiled from you.* Lara shoved the voice away, taking a tight grip on the banister, her knuckles white. *You were the little cockroach long before any of this. What are stairs compared to what you've endured?*

She took one step down, then another, painfully aware that the servants were stopping their tasks to watch. That a crowd of watchers was gathering at the base of the stairs. *Do not falter,* she silently chanted. *Do not show weakness.*

Her legs quivered as she reached the landing on the second floor, nearly buckling. But she pressed downward.

Step.

Step.

Step.

Her guards motioned for the crowd to back away from the stairs as she reached the bottom. Though her focus was entirely on keeping her grip on the banister, Lara didn't miss the flash of motion from the corner of her eye. Instinct took over, and she let go of the banister and drew her blade, whirling to face her attacker even as her guards drew their weapons. Arm back, she readied to throw, but Aster caught her wrist. "Steady, Majesty."

Lara froze, eyes focusing on the wide-eyed face of a servant woman. Then on what the woman held. Not a weapon but a cane.

"Apologies, Your Grace," the woman whispered. "Broke my

ankle last season and this served me well. I thought you might have use of it while you heal."

Bile rose in Lara's throat. *I nearly killed her.*

Would have killed her, if not for Aster's quick reflexes. "Thank you." The words came out as a croak, and she coughed to clear her throat. "I'm sorry, I . . ." *I'm afraid.* "Thank you for your kindness."

The woman handed the cane to Aster, and he examined it swiftly before giving it to Lara. She gripped the carved handle, the wood polished smooth. Using it felt like admitting how weak she truly was. Except who was she fooling? In the mirror on the wall, Lara could see what the Ithicanians saw. A too-thin form, face drained of color, and wisps of hair glued to her cheeks with sweat. Even standing still, her legs trembled, and next to her, Lia's arms were slightly outstretched as though she anticipated her queen collapsing at any second.

No one, was the answer. She was fooling no one.

Leaning her weight on the cane, Lara smiled at the woman. "This will help a great deal. I'll return it to you when I am well again. What is your name?"

"It's Emma, Your Grace."

"Thank you, Emma." Giving the woman another smile, Lara then clenched her teeth and started down the hallway to the dining room.

Click, shuffle.

Click, shuffle.

Click, shuffle.

Already she hated the sound, but there was no denying that the cane took the burden off her injured leg. The corridor seemed to stretch on forever, the guards standing outside the dining-room doors watching her progress with undisguised interest. Lara's heart pounded harder as she neared them, irrationally certain that

they'd deny her entry. That they'd not only tell her she was unwel-
come inside that room but also prohibited.

What their intentions were, she didn't get to discover, for Aster
ignored both and rapped his knuckles on the door. He paused for
barely a heartbeat before opening it and declaring loudly, "Her
Majesty, Queen Lara of Ithicana."

Lara cringed, for she was certain that Aren had entered the
room with no announcement at all. Ithicana was not a nation consumed by formalities. But there was no helping it, so she squared
her shoulders and went inside.

Aren was already on his feet. At the sight of her, he moved to
come around the dining table, but she gave the slightest shake of
her head. His jaw tightened, but he remained at his place, his voice
cool as he said, "Get off your asses and show some respect."

Eyebrows rose on the faces of the watch commanders, but all
climbed to their feet. Lara did not fail to notice that Ahnna was the
last to comply, the princess's face unreadable as she watched Lara
circle the table and take the seat Aren pulled out for her. It was a
struggle not to sigh with relief at being seated, but instead Lara
kept her shoulders square as she announced, "Amelie has announced that I am well enough for my convalescence to end."

"Most welcome news, Your Grace," Mara, the commander of
Northwatch, said, taking her seat once Aren was settled. This was
the first time Lara had seen the woman who'd once been so vehe-
mently against her presence in Ithicana, and she wondered if that
were still the case. The thought vanished from her mind as Mara
added, "We were just discussing Maridrina, and your brother."

It was impossible not to stiffen. Lara took a long mouthful of
water from the glass Aren had just finished pouring for her, then
said, "Which one? I have many."

Ahnna picked up a decanter of wine and filled a glass, then
pushed it in front of Lara. "Keris."

There was a challenge in the princess's voice, as though Ahnna were placing the blame for Keris's actions at Lara's feet for no reason more than that they shared the same blood. "Ah. Has he taken the throne? Or has someone put a knife in his back?" After what he'd done, Lara hoped it was the latter.

Aren cleared his throat, resting an elbow on the table and meeting Lara's gaze. "We don't know. The last information we received was that he was in control in Vencia, was negotiating the return of our Maridrinian prisoners via Southwatch, but the storms have prevented our spies from sending any reports. Once this storm clears, we'll know more."

"We should be prepared to act immediately," Ahnna said before Lara could answer. "Which means learning what we can about our enemy."

"He's not our enemy," Aren said right as Lara snapped, "I don't know anything about him."

Silence stretched, the commanders all watching them with interest.

"I left Vencia when I was five," Lara said. "Since that time, I've seen him twice. When we were extracting Aren from the Vencia palace and during the skirmish on the beach north of Nerastis, neither of which were opportune moments to *reconnect*. I don't know him. He means nothing to me."

"You certainly look alike," Ahnna said, pulling loose a pencil sketch from a pile of papers, then pushing it down the table toward Lara.

"Just as you and I look alike," Aren retorted. "It is nothing more than having the same parents. If you have questions about Keris, pose them to me. I'm the one who knows him."

"Do you?" Ahnna asked. "Because it seems that the information previously provided by our spies about Maridrina's heir is woefully incorrect. They claim he's a scholar and a pacifist, possessed of no military acumen but a strong proclivity for expensive wine and women."

Ahnna continued to read from a report in front of her, but Lara barely heard the description of her brother, her eyes fixed on the portrait. The spy who'd drawn it had some talent, having captured Keris almost perfectly. He was frowning, strands of shoulder-length hair spilling about his face, and his full lips were slightly parted as though he'd been about to speak. No color had been added, but the longer Lara stared at the drawing, the more her memory filled in the gaps until what she stared at was a reflection of reality. Dark-blond hair and fair skin, eyes the deepest of azures and twin to her own.

Ahnna's voice faded away, replaced by an echo of a memory. Of sitting in the sunshine picking petals from a flower while a boy sitting cross-legged next to her read aloud from a book. "You really ought to learn, Lara," he said, looking up from the pages. "Then you can read these stories yourself."

"I like when you read them to me, Keris."

Lara blinked away the memory, hearing Aren say, "I'm not sure anyone truly knows him, to be honest. The spies have only seen what Keris wishes for them to know, and it has only been recent events that have caused him to reveal other layers."

The conversation faded away again, replaced with the blurred outlines of her father's offices in his tower.

"He's coming, Lara! Hide!" the boy hissed, pushing her into a closet. "Don't let him hear you."

She peered through the slats of the door, heart racing as a man's form appeared, hands turning clammy as her father's voice demanded, "What are you doing in here, Keris?" A pause. "Did you do this? Did you make this mess?"

"Yes, Father. I was looking for ink and accidentally spilled it."

"Useless boy!"

The thud of a heavy blow landing, a cry of pain.

"You'll be whipped for this."

She waited until they were gone, then exited the closet, bending to retrieve scattered pieces of paper, all covered with the drawings she'd made.

"Obviously this information is wrong." Ahnna's voice intruded on her thoughts. "It says he knows nothing of military strategy, yet *you* say it was his plan that brought the battle to Eranahl's gates. A battle we would have lost if not for that storm."

This was a conversation she needed to be part of, but Lara couldn't tear her eyes from the portrait, memory drawing her down and down into one she remembered well.

Hands closed on her shoulders, the stink of sweat and metal filling her nose. "Mother," she shrieked as the soldier picked her up. "Mother, help me!"

A faded vision of her mother filled her eyes, a woman struggling against guards who held both her wrists even as she screamed, "Let my daughter go! I will not let you take her from me!"

The guard turned, grunting in pain as Lara's heels struck his leg. "Be still, Princess. It is your father's wish that you go with your sisters."

Her mother was screaming, loud and shrill, and this was *always* when Lara woke from this nightmare, always the last thing she heard.

But this time, she couldn't escape the horror.

"Let my sister go!" The boy was there, hammering his fists against the soldier. "Let her go!"

Her father's face came into her line of sight. "This is none of your concern, boy," he snarled, hand striking down. "Get yourself back to your mother before I have you whipped."

"Keris!" she screamed. "Keris, help me!"

"Lara?"

She jumped, realizing Aren had said her name. Perhaps more than once. "I'm sorry. What I remember of him are childhood recollections, none of which are relevant."

"But you agree that his focus is on Valcotta, not Ithicana, yes?"

Bloody hell, how much of the conversation had she missed? "Undoubtedly. We know the empress has her sights set on Maridrina, and with half his fleet sunk in the Tempest Seas, his army cut by a third, and the kingdom still plagued by famine, he has to know that he's an easy target." All of which everyone at this table knew, which meant she'd added nothing. "Given his relationship with Zarrah, I think he'll be focused on avoiding war with Valcotta at all costs."

Next to her, Aren shifted in his seat even as the watch commanders leaned forward. *Shit.*

Ahnna took a mouthful of wine. "The heir to Maridrina and the heir to Valcotta have a . . . relationship? One you know of but failed to mention?"

Lara bit the insides of her cheeks, saying nothing because Aren clearly had reasons for withholding this information. He exhaled slowly, then said, "When it comes to each other, both are tight-lipped, but I think it safe to say they were lovers."

Ahnna's eyebrows rose, but it was Mara who whistled between her teeth, then said, "There's a story here, and I, for one, would like to hear it."

Words Lara had once said herself.

Resting his elbows on the table, Aren poured himself a drink, then proceeded to tell the council what he knew of Keris and Zarrah. Lara found herself entranced, for while some of it she knew, there were seemingly endless little details Aren had observed while in the company of the two that he'd never mentioned. He finished by saying, "He'll do anything for Zarrah. Anything."

As he once had for her, all those long years ago. Yet time, as always, changed everything.

Lara's hands balled into fists. "His sentiments will fade and then he'll stab her in the back when it serves his interests. It's what he does."

AREN

THE VEHEMENCE IN LARA'S VOICE STARTLED HIM, AND HE WASN'T the only one. Every watch commander looked to his wife, who snatched up her wine and took a long mouthful, clearly having no interest in elaborating.

"It's information we can use against Keris, if he takes the throne," Ahnna said, breaking the silence. "Or before, if we wish to prevent it. The Maridrinians won't crown a man in love with a Valcottan; the blood is too bad between those nations. Sow the right seeds in the right places, and he'll have a knife in his back within the week."

"Absolutely not," Aren snapped, though in the past, that was *exactly* the sort of strategy Ithicana would have employed. "And every last one of you will hold this information in confidence. If I discover otherwise, there *will* be consequences."

Lara set her glass down with a loud *clack*. "Why? After what he did, he deserves it."

It was always *he*. *Him*. She had not once called Keris by his name, and with the way Lara had been staring at her brother's portrait, Aren was beginning to realize that she had taken Keris's actions harder than he'd realized.

"I'm protecting *Zarrah*," he answered carefully. "Any rumors we sow in Maridrina will swiftly spread south, and Zarrah will pay the price. I'll not do that to the person who risked her own neck to help Ithicana when no one else would. You were there, Lara. You and Jor know better than anyone else the lengths she was willing to go to."

Lara only refilled her glass and then emptied it. Given her health and time away from any form of drink, he had no doubt that the wine was fueling her temper. Which was likely why Ahnna had poured the first glass for her. He silently cursed his sister, who made no secret that she had not, and would not, forgive Lara's actions.

Ahnna said, "She wasn't the only one who chose to ally with us. Harendell—"

Aren interrupted her before she could finish. "King Edward himself made the choice to send a handful of ships. His life was never at risk, and Harendell is a formal ally of Ithicana. Whereas Zarrah went against the empress's specific orders. Committed treason for the sake of righting a wrong."

"Debatable," Ahnna said. "There was no battle at Southwatch. Zarrah committed no treason."

"But the intent was there." Aren rose to his feet, pacing the length of the dining room. "It isn't as though the empress won't learn that was the plan. Soldiers aren't going to keep that secret. For all we know, the empress has already taken action against Zarrah. Possibly even disinherited her."

"In which case, there is no reason not to deploy the information in Maridrina," Ahnna said, staring pointedly at Lara. "Keris has proven himself an enemy to Ithicana, and we must treat him accordingly."

Aren's temper boiled, instinct demanding that he lash out and put his sister in her place for the slight against his wife, but he forced himself to take a breath. "You think whichever of his brothers takes his place will be any better?" When Ahnna said nothing, he slowly panned the watch commanders, using the opportunity to glance at Lara's face. It was blank and unreadable. "The other princes will wish to avenge their father and will take action against us by trying to regain the bridge. Whereas we *know* that Keris hated Silas, we know he has no interest in avenging him and attempting to take back the bridge, and we know his eyes are fixed south. Call him an enemy if you wish, but he's the lesser evil and prudence demands that we stay our hand."

"Doing nothing makes Ithicana look weak," Ahnna barked. "We must take action and show that those who strike against us will face consequences."

"Do not presume to tell me what I *must* and *must not do,* Commander." His voice was frigid. "While I will never be fully able to express my gratitude for your leadership of Ithicana while I was absent, I am now returned."

"Then I'll leave it in your hands to call a vote," she answered, voice equally as cool. "Unless, of course, that's no longer how you wish to rule."

Mara coughed, then rose. "If I might interject, would it not be best to wait to decide on a course of action until we've received fresh information from the continent, else risk making decisions based on speculation?"

The other commanders nodded and murmured their agreement.

"Shall we adjourn, then?" Aren wanted to be through with this meeting. Needed to be alone again with his wife, his queen, who had no business being on her feet, much less enduring this bullshit. "Or are there other matters requiring my immediate attention?"

Ahnna said nothing, only slid two pieces of paper toward him.

Aren's stomach twisted with nausea as his eyes skipped over the documents, which were the formal orders for the execution of the individuals who'd tried to assassinate Lara, both requiring his signature. He stared fixedly at the names for a long moment, then picked up a pen, dipping it in the ink pot. But as he reached out to sign his name, slender fingers closed over his wrist.

"I grant them mercy," Lara said softly. "As queen, it is my right to do so, and I exercise it now."

"They tried to murder you." *Had nearly succeeded.* "While you were unconscious and half dead with fever, they tried to take your life. They don't deserve mercy."

Her azure eyes moved from his face to the pages. "Many see me as Ithicana's enemy, and there is no law here against killing the enemy. They did what they felt was right and just, and they don't deserve to be punished for it."

His anger boiled over. "Bullshit, Lara. They acted knowing that you are my wife, after I'd formally declared to all of Eranahl that you are my queen."

"*Your* queen." Picking up the pieces of paper, Lara ripped them in half. "But that does not make me theirs."

Aren flung the pen on the table, ink splattering everywhere. "That's *exactly* what it means." He scrutinized the watch commanders, men and women he'd known for their entire lives, before fixing his gaze on his twin. "I thought I had made myself clear, but in case I have not, allow me to reiterate. If you wish for me to remain Ithicana's king, then Lara will be my queen. If you demand she leave, then I will go with her." Jerking a knife from his belt, he drew it across his palm, then squeezed his fist, blood dripping onto the map laid across the table's center. "On my blood and honor, where Lara goes, I go. Even if it's to the fucking grave. So let's do this here and now: Vote as to whether you wish us *both* on the throne or not."

For a long moment, no one moved, and his heart sank. For Lara, to *be* with Lara, he'd walk away and never look back. Yet it still gouged at his soul that after everything she'd done, after everything that they'd both done, that his commanders wouldn't stand with him. Maybe he'd been a fool to expect they would, for his people had suffered and lost as a result of his mistakes, and Lara's. Still, he'd hoped . . .

Next to him, Lara rose to her feet, and Aren knew what she was going to say. That she'd leave, if that was what it would take. Ever and always, she was willing to sacrifice herself. Except this time, he wouldn't let her. Aren opened his mouth to forestall her words, but instead of speaking, Lara took his hand and gripped it tightly, shoulders squared in defiance.

Claiming him and daring anyone to question her right to do so.

To his shock, Mara gave an approving nod. The older woman had once despised Lara, but it seemed that she, like Aster, had changed her tune. Mara climbed to her feet. "I was beginning to fear that you'd lost your balls, girl. Good to see you still have them." Bowing low, the commander of Northwatch said, "I swear allegiance to Aren and Lara Kertell. Long may they rule Ithicana."

Nearly as one, the other commanders rose, swearing allegiance to him and to Lara, until only one remained sitting.

Slowly, his sister rose, hazel eyes unreadable. Aren struggled not to hold his breath, because if Ahnna refused to swear, he wasn't sure what he'd do.

Ahnna took the decision from him as she said, "Given that I will not be remaining in Ithicana for much longer, I formally resign from the role of Commander of Southwatch Island. This matter, and Southwatch's vote, should be handled by someone who will be here to bear the consequences."

His stomach hollowed. "You'd rather give up your position

than bend the knee to Lara as queen? Are you that fucking unforgiving?"

Lara's grip tightened on his hand. "That isn't what she said."

His sister's eyes moved to his wife, jaw tight as they stared each other down, then Ahnna said, "I've heard Lara's explanation, as well as yours, Your Grace. I understand that Lara was manipulated and lied to all her life, and that Silas was the villain. I understand that she did not intend for her father's plans to come to fruition. I saw firsthand what she did to undo the damage her actions caused. But . . ." Ahnna looked away, shaking her head. "*Knowing* does not change what happened. It does not rebuild homes, or bring back the dead, or make those who were injured whole again. There are many who, in hearing the truth, will forgive her. Yet there are many for whom the truth is not enough to earn their forgiveness, and I am one of them."

How can it not be enough? Aren opened his mouth to say as much, but in a flurry of motion, Ahnna slammed her palms down on the table, sending liquid sloshing over the rim of her cup. "You weren't here, Aren. You don't know."

"You act as though I was captured the day of the invasion," he retorted. "For weeks, I fought day in and day out. Saw men and women I've known my whole life fall beneath Maridrinian blades. Lost my whole goddamned household on Midwatch to one fucking woman."

At the reference to her sister, Lara twitched, her grip tightening on his hand, but she said nothing.

"You saw battles, Aren. Quick deaths. Soldiers' deaths." The knuckles on Ahnna's scarred hands turned white from pressure as she leaned toward him. "The rest of us saw *war*. They hunted our people. Men, women, children, it didn't matter, and when they caught them, it was no swift death. Since I was sixteen, I've fought in vicious, bloody battles, but it all pales in comparison to what I witnessed the Maridrinians do to our people. Every time I close my eyes, I see their faces, which means I cannot forget. And unless I find a way to forget, I will never forgive." She straightened. "As soon as I am able, I will leave for Harendell to fulfill my commitments. I will do what duties are necessary until you select my replacement in the command of Southwatch, but I will *not* vote. Which means I shall excuse myself for this conversation."

Not giving him a chance to argue, his twin sister strode from the room, the door shutting heavily behind her.

Silence stretched, and Aren found himself at a loss for words.

Not only was losing his sister's support a personal blow, with the way some of the commanders were shifting restlessly, it would cost him politically. Mara must have seen the same, for she said, "Ahnna blames herself for much of what has occurred over this past year and subjected herself to the worst of it in a way few other Ithicanians can claim, which has warped her perspective. It is well that she has chosen to remove herself from command in favor of someone with less . . . personal bias. Especially given that her concerns will soon be for Harendellian matters."

The unease on the faces of the other commanders eased, several of them nodding in agreement.

"Even without Southwatch's vote, we have a majority," Mara continued. "Which means that the council stands behind both of you as rulers of Ithicana. That said, you may wish to reconsider granting your mercy to the individuals who attempted to take your life, Your Grace. What goodwill you gain from granting the perpetrators mercy will not protect you half as well as fear of the consequences of attempting to harm you, and I think more attempts will occur."

As much as Aren favored mercy, he agreed with Mara. Being faced with Ithicana's worst form of execution would go a long way in dissuading anyone who might dare harm his queen, though to be honest, he'd do worse than any shark if it happened on his watch.

"Those who have lost everything fear nothing," Lara answered. "But if they are to fear anything, let it be my blade. Now that my strength is returning, those who seek my life going forward will find no mercy."

"More Ithicanian blood on your hands is perhaps *not* the best solution," Mara said, and Aren found himself snapping, "Then what is the solution, Commander? Because asking Lara to stand passive while men and women try to cut her throat is only going to mean that their blood is on *my* hands, and I will not kill them slowly."

"An heir."

Aren straightened in surprise, and he heard Lara suck in a breath. "Pardon?"

Settling in her seat and waiting for the other commanders to take theirs, Mara leaned backward. "A solution to the problem would be for the queen to produce an heir. Many who might lift arms against her will stay their hands if she is carrying the future king or queen."

"You want me to use a baby as a shield to protect myself?" Lara's voice was hoarse, and as Aren glanced down at her, it was to find her whole body rigid.

Mara eyed her, but rather than answering the question, said, "An heir creates a sense of goodwill and stability within any kingdom. It would also demonstrate your commitment to a life in Ithicana."

A shudder ran through Lara with such violence he thought she might collapse, and Aren shifted to grab her arms only for her to abruptly sit in her chair. "No. No, that is not an option. There will be no baby."

Aren lowered himself into his own seat, uncertain how he felt about her answer as emotions swirled in his core. That Lara wouldn't wish to use a child to protect her own life was her nature, and in truth, he felt the same way. Except he found himself wondering if her vehemence was against current circumstances or children in general. He realized that it wasn't a subject that they'd ever really discussed, and that perhaps he'd made assumptions he should not have.

"You're the queen, Your Grace," Mara said. "If you don't have a child, the Kertell line ends with no certainty of who will hold the crown after your time comes to an end."

"Why can't it be as it is in Valcotta?" Lara demanded. "The empress chose Zarrah over her own son."

Aren's stomach twisted, for that felt like an answer to his unasked question. *Don't leap to conclusions,* he told himself. *Talk to her first.*

"The empress must choose a blood relation as her successor," Mara answered, seemingly unmoved, though several of the other commanders were frowning. "Ahnna is to be queen of Harendell, so she cannot be named heir, and His Grace's only other living relation is Taryn."

Lara tensed at his cousin's name, and for that, he couldn't blame her. Taryn had taken Lara's culpability in the invasion as a personal betrayal of friendship, her feelings made worse by the fact she'd been held prisoner by the Maridrinians for close to a year. He had not learned the particulars of how she'd been treated, but he didn't need to know the details to understand it had left a dark mark on his cousin's soul.

Tension within the room was rising, and in truth, he'd had enough. "Your suggestion is heard, Commander," he said. "But as it stands, the queen is still recovering from her injuries and that must be her focus. I will ensure Aster has the resources he requires to protect her at all times, which will keep those ruled by their emotions from taking regrettable actions." He paused, then added, "This meeting is adjourned."

Mara inclined her head, then led the commanders from the room.

Aren rose to his feet and circled the table to the door, then set the latch into place. "Just in case my grandmother realizes you're up and comes hunting," he said to Lara. "Though I'm not certain even a locked door will keep her out."

Lara gave him a weak smile. "I'm here with her blessing, though I'm sure she'll find another reason to meddle."

If Lara was here with Nana's blessing, it meant his grandmother was confident in his wife's health. "Nana will never change."

Coming back around the table, he took two quick steps, then reached down to scoop Lara into his arms.

She gasped out a laugh. "Aren!"

He kissed her throat, inhaling the scent of lilacs, tasting the salt of her skin. Sitting in his chair with her on his lap, he pulled up the skirt of her dress until her injured thigh was revealed, the wound no longer bandaged. "Looks good," he said, trailing a gentle finger over the thick scar. "I should probably have a look at the other, just to be sure."

He caught at the straps of her dress, but she swatted him away. "How can you be thinking about sex after that meeting?"

"Because . . ." He kissed her, his cock hardening as her lips parted. Her tongue tasted like wine. "I'm finally alone with my beautiful, brilliant, and fierce queen, and that leaves no room for any other thoughts."

Lara snorted, then caught his hand, which he was using to stroke higher and higher on her thigh. "Would you please redeploy some of the blood in your crotch back to your brain so that we might have an *intelligent* conversation?"

A half dozen quips rose to his lips, but there was an edge to his wife's voice that told him she was in no mood for games. So instead he lowered her skirts and met her gaze, waiting to see what she'd say.

"I'm sorry" were her first words, and he opened his own mouth to say that *she* had nothing to apologize for, but Lara pressed a slender index finger to his lips. "I handled every aspect of this meeting poorly. I thought I'd be prepared, but I wasn't."

"Why should you have been? Ahnna should've been civil, but instead she went for blood." Exhaling slowly, he shook his head. "Your presence might have motivated certain conversations to occur sooner than they otherwise would have, but they were inevitable. Ahnna is many things, but impulsive isn't one of them. Her words, her resignation, none of that was something she decided on in the moment."

"I hate that I've come between you two. Hate that the individual who was once your greatest ally is now . . ." Lara shook her head. "I'm not sure what she is."

Leaving, and soon to be Harendell's problem, was the answer he wanted to give, but Aren bit down on the words. For one, he didn't entirely mean them, and two, as the future queen of Harendell, his sister would continue to have influence in Ithicana. "It's for the best, Lara. She's right that Southwatch's vote should be made by someone who is to remain in Ithicana as an advocate for the island's interests. As to her feelings about you . . ." He hesitated, then said, "Ahnna knows that it was Silas who invaded Ithicana, that it was his armies who committed atrocities on his orders, but there is little satisfaction to be had in blaming the dead. Likewise with blaming those who are nothing more than names and sketches on paper. Whereas you are here and an easy target for all the anger and guilt and grief in her heart."

Tears turned Lara's eyes liquid, though she blinked them away.

"I *am* to blame. If I'd told you everything, if I'd told you about that *fucking* letter, none of this would have happened."

There'd been a time when he'd thought the same, but now . . . "Even if you had, do you really think it would have stopped Silas from attacking? The bridge was his obsession, one he sacrificed more than fifteen years of his life to achieving. Do you really think he'd have given up? Or would he just have found another way?"

"I . . ." A tear trickled down her cheek, but she didn't seem to notice. "He wouldn't have let it go. He'd have died before letting it go." She drew in a sharp breath, as though she weren't getting enough air into her lungs. "He did die rather than let it go."

Died on the end of her blade. God help him, but Aren wished he'd been able to see that moment. Clearing his throat, he said, "I love my sister, but she is intense and proud and unforgiving. Please don't paint all of Ithicana with the brush she has handed you, especially not when all the rest of the commanders swore to you as queen."

"I don't paint them all with the same brush. I know there are people who see things in different ways."

The words came out too quickly, and Aren knew that the concession was an attempt to ease his mind while hers still stewed, convinced she was reviled and hated by all, when that was most definitely not the case. As he watched, her eyes flicked to Keris's portrait where it still sat on the table. "Do *not* blame yourself for what he did."

"I don't." Her face hardened. "I blame *him*."

Aren reached over, grasped the paper. Crumpling it into a ball, he then tossed it across the room. "He'll get himself killed with that smart-ass mouth of his, of that, I have little doubt."

Lara didn't answer, only toyed with the front of his shirt, her eyes distant. Thoughtful and brooding and beautiful, and God help him, he loved her. Loved every part of her, mind, body, and soul. "Do you want us to stay, Lara? Because I meant what I said to the council: Where you go, I go. If you want us to make a life somewhere else, a place where Ithicana is naught but a name on a map, we'll leave."

Her eyes shot to his. "No! I don't want to leave." She frowned. "Do you want to leave?"

Part of him did. Part of him wanted to take her and walk away from the burden that was rule. Perhaps if he were more of a narcissist, the power that came with the crown would be enough reward to outweigh the toil, but he wasn't. And these days, it felt like being king was a constant *give, give, give,* with nothing to refill the well. "My life is with you, and if we can't be happy here together, then I want us to leave." He hesitated, then asked, "Why do you want to stay?"

She was still, barely seeming to breathe. "I . . ." She shook her head, a flush rising to her cheeks. "I just do."

It was no answer, but experience had taught him that pushing her in moments like these would only cause her to put up walls. Nor was it the time to press on Mara's proposition, though that was a conversation that needed to be had. Not because it changed anything but because he'd sworn there'd be no more secrets between them. "I love you, Lara. There is no life for me without you in it."

In a rapid motion, she moved, twisting in his lap so that her knees were to either side of him.

Her hands slipped around his neck, one tangling in his hair. "You know that I feel the same way, don't you? How much I love you?"

"I know it." He pulled her closer, the apex of her thighs pressing against his stomach and her breasts brushing his chest. Capturing her lips with his, he kissed her softly, then with more urgency. Her tongue was in his mouth, her hands in his hair, and he wanted to tear the clothes from her body. Wanted to lay her on the table and claim her. Make her scream his name, the guards standing outside the doors be damned.

"How much activity are you allowed?" he asked, kissing his way down her throat.

"Why?" Her voice was breathy. "Do you want to go for a walk? Perhaps climb to the summit and admire the view?"

He snorted out a laugh. "It's a view I'm interested in, but not of the ocean."

Catching hold of her hips, he lifted her onto the table and slowly pulled her skirts up her legs.

Lara's eyebrows rose, gaze devilish. "This is hardly appropriate."

He parted her knees, revealing lace undergarments sewn with tiny silver coins around the waist, already wet with her desire. The sight nearly undid him, but he managed to say, "If you didn't want to end up with your dress on the floor, why did you wear these?"

"They're pretty and they match my dress," she purred, gaze darkening. "I wore them because I like them."

"I like them, too," he growled, catching hold of her undergarments and slowly drawing them down her legs. Rubbing a thumb across the damp fabric, he tucked the scrap of lace into his pocket. "I think I'll keep them."

Her cheeks flushed pink, but there was nothing innocent about her as she caught hold of his shirt and jerked. "Kiss me."

Aren obliged, his need barely contained as she bit his bottom lip, her free hand palming his cock through his trousers. God help him, he wanted to fuck her. Wanted to tear off his clothes and thrust into her over and over until they were both spent, but she deserved more than that from him. Deserved to be treated like a queen. "Enough of that," he murmured, catching hold of her hand and drawing it away.

Only for her to twist her wrist, freeing herself and then unbuckling his belt.

"You should know better than to expect obedience," she said, sliding her hand into his trousers and taking hold of him. He groaned as she stroked his length, his eyes on her parted lips, memories of her mouth around his cock nearly pulling him over the edge.

"There are consequences to disobedience, Your Grace," he growled, his heart thundering as she pumped him hard.

Her eyes were full of challenge as she said, "Are there?"

Ripping his belt loose, he held it up, weapons sliding off the length to clatter to the floor. Catching hold of both her wrists, he bound them together and then pushed her down against the table, hands above her head. Lara let out a gasping moan as he kissed her throat and then her collarbone, her legs wrapping around his waist.

He could feel the heat of her naked sex through the fabric of his trousers, and she ground against him, making his cock throb with need. "Behave," he said, pulling down the bodice of her dress to reveal her full breasts, pink nipples hard, "or I'll rip this pretty dress of yours apart and use the pieces to tie you to this table."

"Is that a promise?" Her sandaled heel caught the waist of his trousers, dragging them down, and Aren groaned as the last barrier between them fell away.

She moved her hips, slick sex sliding up and down his length, and he captured one of her nipples in his mouth, drawing it deep. Lara moaned as his teeth scraped across the tip, back arching in a way that caused his tip to enter her. "Yes," she gasped. "Please."

Not yet.

Letting go of her wrists, he took a firm hold of her thighs, pushing them slowly apart. Holding her wide as he dropped to his knees, the scent of her nearly making him come as he drank in the sight of her nakedness. "You're beautiful." He kissed the inside of her thigh, hearing her whimper. "Perfect."

Then he leaned forward and parted her with his tongue. "Mine."

"Yours," she gasped, her back arching as he circled her clit with his tongue before sliding it inside her. Her thighs clenched, but he was stronger than her and pressed them wider as he tasted her. Devoured her. Made her his.

His woman.

His wife.

His queen.

"Come for me, Your Grace," he commanded, then captured her clit, sucking it hard. Lara's back arched, her body shuddering as she climaxed, sobbing his name as he stroked her with his tongue.

Aren waited until she went limp, then rose to his feet and lifted her into his arms. He sat on the floor with her in his lap, her head resting against his shoulder. Slowly her breathing steadied, and Lara looked up at him. "Are you going to untie me?"

"Are you going to behave?"

"Never." She smirked, then held up his belt, which she'd managed to free herself from without assistance. "Your turn, Your Majesty."

LARA

LARA SLEPT THE BALANCE OF THE DAY AND INTO THE EVENING, exhausted by unfamiliar exertions, only to wake after the sun had set. Rising from the bed, she bit back a groan, every part of her painfully stiff. She discarded her nightdress on the floor and, knife in one hand, cane in the other, she made her way across the room and climbed slowly into the bath, the water washing away the stickiness of sweat coating her body.

Aren had wanted to remain with her, but Nana's words still sat heavily in her mind, so she'd told him to go see to matters requiring his attention. He'd protested but eventually left, patting the pocket holding her undergarments with a smirk as he'd left the room, making her laugh.

She missed laughter between them. The endless jokes and battles of wit they'd engaged in before the invasion, in the months they'd lived and loved in Eranahl with light hearts. They'd never be able to go back to that time, but laughter made her heart swell with hope that they'd find a new version of happiness.

She climbed out of the bath, toweled herself dry, and donned a

silk wrap. The storm had ended in the way they always did in Ithicana, raging in one breath and then eerily calm the next, and she
opened one set of balcony doors to allow fresh air into the room.
The sky was clear, the moon and stars already bright overhead,
and Lara pulled a chair between the open doors and settled herself
down in it. Every inhale tasted of moisture and smelled of jungle,
the *drip, drip, drip* of water falling from the eaves like music.

Why do you want to stay?

Aren's question circled her thoughts, though she'd yet to come
up with an answer. Part of it was that she didn't want to tear Aren
from his home, didn't want Ithicana to lose its king and be cast
into the uncertainty of a succession war. Another part was that
she had a hard time imagining either of them living a simple life as
common people, the visions of what it would be like living on a
farm or working as a merchant refusing to form in her head. She
loved Ithicana, and it felt like home in a way that no other place
ever had, yet even that was not the reason that demanded she and
Aren remain.

You aren't wanted here.

Lara shivered, remembering all that Ahnna had said. She had
no expectations of forgiveness, but . . . she desperately wanted to
prove to the people that she was worthy of living here. Worthy of
being their queen, because the life she saw when she closed her
eyes was of rebuilding Ithicana, defending it, and making it strong.
That was what she wanted, but she didn't think it would be possible unless she proved every single day that she was more than her
prior actions.

Acceptance.

The word resonated with truth, and Lara bit at her bottom lip
because she had no idea how she might achieve it.

Produce an heir.

She cringed as that conversation replayed in her head, realizing now that Nana hadn't been forestalling intimacy between her and Aren to protect her body but rather to protect her choice. God . . . she could only imagine how gutted she'd have felt to have been with child only to discover that everyone thought it self-serving. A way to protect herself, ingratiate herself, to gain the acceptance she craved but not earn it.

Shit.

Lara pressed the heels of her hands to her eyes, knowing that her reaction had surprised Aren. Did it change how he felt about being with her? She . . . she didn't think so. Certainly his actions when they were alone in the council room suggested otherwise, but doubt and uncertainty refused to silence their whispers into her ears.

Behind her, the door to the room opened.

Lara's grip tightened on her knife, but only Aren appeared. "I brought you something to eat," he said.

"Something that Aster hasn't eaten half of," Jor shouted from beyond. "Clever bastard is just trying to get more than his fair share of rations."

Lara smiled, then grinned broadly as she saw the plate. "Is that . . . pork?"

"It surely is." He set the plate and a fork on the table next to her. "Turns out a ship with supplies rode out the storm on an island not an hour from here. They had a pig with them, though he met his doom almost upon passing through the gates to the city. Everyone is tired of fish."

"Especially me," she muttered, digging into the meat, which was grilled to perfection. Then a thought occurred to her, and she stilled in her chewing, swallowing hard. "What other supplies did they have?"

"No herbs," he answered. "Nana sent them immediately back to the water with precise instructions, so that should be remedied soon enough."

She sighed, returning to eating, though the meat had lost some of its appeal.

Aren went to the sideboard, poured two drinks, and brought them back. Setting them on the table, he dragged another chair next to hers and then flopped down in it, stretching his long legs in front of him. She could feel the tension of the unasked question floating between them, but she was afraid of bringing it up. Afraid that her doubts would be confirmed.

"About Mara's . . . suggestion." Aren took a long mouthful of his drink, looked at the contents, then drained the glass. "Do you want children, Lara?"

She swallowed hard, the bite of pork sticking in her throat and forcing her to take a drink herself. *Don't be a coward*, she told herself. *Ask the goddamned question.* "If I don't, does that change things between us?"

"No." He met her gaze. "It does not. The only condition on my desire to be with you for the rest of my life is honesty. So I would like to know your thoughts on this, for I know you have them."

Lara gave a tight nod, setting aside her plate. "Children were not something I was raised to consider. I was sent to Ithicana with a full set of knowledge on how to prevent pregnancy, told that I must avoid it at all costs."

"Because a child would bind you to Ithicana. And to me."

"Yes." She hated talking about this, about what she'd been trained to do to Ithicana. And to him. But silence had damned her before, and she refused to do the same again. "Though Serin told us it was because our bodies would be weakened by pregnancy and that you'd use a baby to control whichever of us became your bride. He never explained anything in a way that would make it seem that it was him or my father denying or controlling us; everything was always cast at your feet."

Aren exhaled a long breath but said nothing.

Keep going, she told herself. *You can do this. You must do it.* "Though I learned the truth when we went to Vencia and realized that I'd been raised on lies, it pains me to admit that some of those lies refused to relinquish their control. The notion that a child would be used to weaken and control me was one of them. That's why when we were here before the invasion, I kept taking the contraceptive tea."

Aren's jaw was tight, the muscles in his face standing out in the moonlight as he said, "Do you still believe that?"

"No." She gave a sharp shake of her head. "Seeing my sister Sarhina pregnant vanquished that thought from my head. She was as strong as she'd ever been while pregnant, possibly even stronger. And though she was cautious and careful, being pregnant did not limit her. Nor did her husband, Ansel, try to use the baby to control her."

Her chin quivered, her eyes burning as tears formed. "I believed at that point that you'd hate me forever and I was haunted by visions of what might have been if I had been entirely honest about the actions I'd taken. Dreams of us together and happy, and after seeing my sister with child, those dreams changed to include that blessing."

Tears were pouring down her cheeks now, entirely beyond her control, because not only was she feeling the grief of *now,* she was feeling the grief of *then.* "I do want us to have a child together, Aren. In my vision of us happy, there is a child, but that vision will never come to be if I use the baby as a tool. To protect myself and win the acceptance of our people by providing them an heir, rather than earning it with actions and deeds."

Aren was quiet for a long moment. "You will never earn the acceptance of all our people, Lara. It's just not possible, and I hate that you would deny yourself what you want because of it."

"I know *all* is impossible." She wiped the tears from her face, sucking in a ragged breath. "You asked me why I wanted to remain in Ithicana, and the reason is that my dream of a happy future is *here*. But I need the chance to earn that future."

"I think you have earned it," he said quietly. "I also understand that it's not about how *I* feel but how *you* feel, and I respect that."

Relief flooded her, but before she could say anything, Aren set a small sea sponge on the table. "When the storm broke, Jor and I went diving with a particular catch in mind. He said you would know what to do with it." Aren hesitated, then added, "Not that you have to, but this gives you the choice."

Lara stared at the sponge, emotion filling her with such intensity that she could scarcely breathe.

"I'll let you finish eating," he said, rising to his feet and taking a few steps away. "I . . ."

Lara snatched up the sponge and threw herself at him. Aren caught her, but before he could say anything, she kissed him. Hard and fierce enough that their teeth clacked together, her fingers digging into the muscles of his shoulders. "Take me to bed," she whispered between kisses. "I want you. I need you."

"Lara, are you—"

"Enough talking." She bit his bottom lip, relishing his groan, then said, "I've had enough goddamned talking."

For once, he didn't argue. A few quick steps had them at the bed, and he lowered her down, the sheets cold against her back. He caught hold of the tie on her wrap, slowly unfastened the knot, and then drew the sides of the garment wide before straightening. His eyes roved over her body, and Lara curled her toes, the naked lust in his eyes fueling her own desire.

"You are so beautiful." His voice was a growl. "The world pales in your presence."

Giving him a devilish smile, she parted her knees and put the sponge where it needed to be, Mistress Mezat's training of her and her sisters in the Red Desert once again serving her well. "I said no more talking."

He grinned, and it was all teeth. He pulled off his tunic and unbuckled his belt, weapons falling to the ground with a clank for the second time that day. He kicked off his boots and slowly drew down his trousers, and it was her turn to stare.

Lifting one leg, she pressed her naked foot to his chest, holding him in place as she took her time luxuriating in the perfection of his body. Taller than most men, and broad, every muscle was thick and hard, not a spare ounce of flesh to disguise it. His skin, tanned dark by endless hours in the sun, was marked by as many scars as her own. Badges of honor earned in the defense of his kingdom, and she caught her bottom lip in her teeth, wanting to trail her tongue over each of them.

His dark gaze fixed on her mouth, and he pressed against her foot, fingers curling and uncurling. Nearly at his breaking point.

She fully intended to push him past it.

Running her eyes down his chest and over the sharply defined muscles of his stomach, she let her gaze settle on his cock, large like the rest of him. Already hard, the tip glistened, and she kept her gaze on it as she trailed a finger down between her breasts, over her navel, and between her legs. Allowing her eyes to drift up to his, she slowly circled her clit with her index finger, a soft moan exiting her lips as she heard his breath turn ragged.

Aren cracked.

Grabbing her ankle, he pulled it out of the way, his hand slipping up her calf as he caught hold of her other leg and pulled her thighs wide. In one thrust, he was inside her, and Lara sobbed with pleasure as he plunged in and out, the headboard slamming against the wall. So many weeks since they'd been together like this, and before that, longer weeks still.

She needed this. Needed him. Needed for them to be together in every way possible, because Aren was hers. Her king, her husband, her life.

Her nails raked down his back and she wrapped her legs around his hips, pulling him deeper with each thrust.

"I love you." He kissed her hard, biting at her lip. "I love you so much."

"I love you, too."

Her eyes burned even as her pleasure ratcheted higher, each of his thrusts stroking over her exactly right, because Aren *knew* her. Every inch of her, inside and out.

The climax took her hard and fast, rolling over her in waves and pulling him with her. He shouted her name, burying his face into her neck as he thrust one last time, a flood of heat filling her. His weight came down, his chest against hers, hearts thundering in unison.

Slowly, their breathing steadied, and Aren lifted himself up on one elbow to kiss her. "You all right, love?"

Lara made a soft humming noise, feeling entirely boneless and incapable of speech.

A soft laugh exited his throat, then Aren kissed her lips, her throat, before meeting her gaze. "Good," he said. "Because I'm going to have you again." His eyes were dark, his cock already hardening inside of her. "And again."

Tilting back her head, Lara smiled.

He was hers. She was his.

Tonight, tomorrow, and for all the tomorrows they ever faced.

Aren

"Feeling sated?" Jor asked as they walked down to the harbor.

Aren snorted and cast a dark look at the older man. "That's none of your fucking business."

"You want to keep your encounters secret, you're going to need to gag that queen of yours," Jor said, kicking at a rock. "Lass has a set of lungs on her, so the whole damn palace was reminded over and over again of your name."

"Kiss my ass," Aren muttered, then added, "Thank you, though."

Jor shrugged. "When you've romanced as many women as I have, you learn a few things. I'm surprised your grandmother didn't mention it. Amelie knows all the tricks."

"Likely because she takes perverse pleasure out of making my life more difficult."

Aren abandoned the conversation as they reached the entrance to the harbor cavern, which was a scene of organized chaos. Fishing boats leaving to haul in more catch. Larger vessels loading families and their belongings, ready to abandon the city that had been their prison to return to their homes on other islands, which would do much to ease the burden of supplying Eranahl.

But he and Jor were here to deal with another matter, one that couldn't be put off.

After climbing into a small canoe, they paddled down the tunnel, following the grating echo of metal saws. Aren's eyes went to the roof of the tunnel, following the deep scrapes in the rock that the portcullis had made as Silas's ship dragged it out. During a break in a storm, they'd been able to move the massive steel structure to one side of the tunnel to allow boats to pass, but the larger task of removing it and replacing it remained.

He blinked, and a vision of Lara on the far side of it filled his mind's eye. Bleeding and half drowned. Dying before his eyes and him unable to reach her.

"Morning, Your Grace," one of the smiths said. "Once we've broken it down into pieces, we'll bring them back into the city and reforge the portcullis, though we might need to source more steel from Harendell, as we lost the chains."

"No," Aren answered, staring at the twisted metal but seeing Lara caught beneath it. The bubbles rising from her lips and the light going out of her eyes. "Drop it in the sea. I'll make arrangements to purchase steel from the Harendellians."

The man made a face. "The cost—"

Jor whistled sharply. "He said drop it in the sea, so that's what we'll do. Get to sawing, you lazy arse."

The men grumbled but complied. Having no desire to sit idle and watch, Aren took up one of the saws and set to cutting bars himself. Section by section, they cut down the twisted metal, dragging pieces out to deep water and allowing them to sink. There was some catharsis to the work, ridding the island and himself of something that held so many awful memories, though the work was exhausting.

Wiping sweat from his brow, he stared out over the sea and caught sight of an approaching vessel. A small outrigger with only three men aboard, all of whom he knew. All lifted hands in greeting as he was recognized, one shouting, "News from the mainland, Your Grace." As they drew closer, he added, "Not fresh, I'm afraid, but the storm kept me cooling my heels in the bridge. But fresh or not, you'll want to be reading the report straightaway."

Aren's stomach tightened. Nothing he needed to read right away would be good. "Hand it over, then." The boats bumped together, the man jumping into Aren's canoe and handing him a wax-wrapped packet. Aren remained standing, balancing instinctively on the rocking swells as he unwrapped the package, scanning a report compiled at Southwatch of news from the continent. "That bitch," he snarled as he reached the last item. He handed the page to Jor, but before the other man could begin reading, screams echoed out of the tunnel.

Cries for help.

LARA

"You seem refreshed, Your Grace," Lia said. "Stronger already."

Lara wasn't sure about that, but she *did* feel happier despite having not gotten a tremendous amount of sleep. Not because of the sex, though that had been . . . *intense* in a way that still gave her shivers, but because telling Aren her thoughts and fears had lifted a weight from her shoulders. There was a comfort that came from him standing at her side despite knowing the worst, a security that made her feel strong though her body was not. "I want to walk to the harbor."

Lia exhaled, her displeasure over the request apparent. "I'd advise against it. All it takes is one well-placed arrow and—"

"I'm not hiding in the palace forever," Lara interrupted. "There is a difference between caution and paranoia. I'm not allowing my life to be ruled by fear."

"As you wish." Lia inclined her head, then went to the door and informed Aster and the others of her plans.

Lara retrieved her knives and the cane, which had proven to be of great assistance. The silk skirts of her dress swished around her legs as she limped after Lia, finding Aster and the rest of her body-guards waiting in the hall. "They're removing the ruined portcullis today and I wish to see how the work progresses."

He didn't argue, only offered his arm. Today, Lara decided to take it, because the challenge she wished to face was not the stiff-ness in her leg but stepping out of the safety of the palace and into the city. To surround herself with the people whose acceptance she wished to earn, though she didn't yet know how she'd do it.

With the aid of Aster and the cane, her progress was much swifter today, and Lara soon found herself standing before the doors to the palace, which were open and flanked by a pair of heavily armed women. Taking a deep breath, Lara stepped out into the sunshine.

"Many left this morning to return to their homes on other is-lands," Aster said. "Though there is some uncertainty of what they'll find, so some will return."

Those whose homes had been burned or destroyed by her fa-ther's soldiers. Those who had nothing to come back to.

What could she possibly offer them? Gold from Ithicana's cof-fers to rebuild was hardly the answer. Nor was building with her own two hands, though she was happy to do so.

Walk, she ordered herself. *At the very least, show them that you are not afraid.*

Step, click.

Step, click.

Step, click.

The hot tropical sun seared down overhead, the air nearly un-breathable with the thick humidity, but she slowly made her way around the lake at the base of the volcano's crater. Those doing laundry at the water's edge stopped their work to watch her, as did those whose shops lined the pathway. Some expressions bore curiosity. Others animosity. But what Lara sensed the most was that she was being judged.

"Be on your guard," Aster said under his breath, his free hand resting on the hilt of the long machete he favored. "Show no mercy."

I need to do something. Something worthy of a queen.

But Lara didn't know what, and the absence of any form of solution drew more sweat to her skin than the sun burning overhead.

Laughter greeted her as they reached the entrance to the harbor cavern, children playing in the waters. Lara paused on the base of the stairs to watch them, at least two dozen splashing in the calm waters, which were empty of vessels, everyone hard at work. Once upon a time, this was where she'd learned to swim under the cajoling of many of these children, and her eyes stung at the memory. She'd been so happy, then. They'd all been so happy.

A shadow passed beneath the children.

"Aster," she gasped, but he was already shouting, "Shark! Get out of the water!"

The children reacted instantaneously, swimming to the edge and clambering out. The enormous shark rose to the surface and was swimming in circles around a young girl. She screamed, shrill and panicked, and without thought, Lara reacted.

Wrenching out of Aster's grip, she took two quick steps and jumped.

Water closed over Lara's head, bubbles obscuring her vision as she kicked to the surface. Screams of panic filled her ears, terrified children as well as Aster shouting, "Calm yourselves! It won't hurt her!"

If only that were true.

Startled by the splash, the shark broke away from circling the girl, and Lara swam in her direction. Ever and always, she had been awkward in the water, and that had not changed. But even with her skirts tangling in her legs, she made it to the child before the shark resumed its circling.

Pulling the crying girl close to her, she gasped out, "Stay calm. Don't thrash about."

As the girl calmed, Lara pulled her knife.

It was madness to believe it would do much against such an enormous creature, but if she could stab it when it attacked, it was possible that the girl would get out unscathed. The shark circled, dark dorsal fin cutting the water, and Lara tracked its path, keeping herself between it and the girl.

"Call for a boat! Call for a boat!" people shouted, but above them Aster screamed, "Do not intervene! She is the true queen of Ithicana and it will not harm her!"

Yet above it all, she heard the echo of Nana's voice. *The creatures steered clear of you because your blood was fouled with stimulants.*

The shark closed in, head rising slightly out of the water to reveal one of its black eyes. Cold and thoughtless, driven by instinct and need, and entirely incapable of the things Aster and those like him believed. It cared not for what was in her heart, only for filling its belly.

She'd fight it to the end.

"Stay behind me," she said to the girl, the child's legs bumping hers as she pressed tight to Lara's back, both of them treading water.

Closer.

Closer.

"A boat is coming," someone shouted, then Aren's voice: "Lara!"

The shark thrashed its tail, agitated, and Lara tensed, gripping her knife tight. The boat wouldn't make it in time, and she'd have only one chance.

The dark shadow darted in, then veered, the tip of its tail striking her arm. Her knife spun out of her grip. She reached, trying to catch the sinking weapon, but her fingers only brushed the hilt as it dropped out of reach.

The girl was screaming and crying, the boat knifing closer, but the shark was coming in again. It would kill them both before Aren made it.

Unless she did something.

Lifting her arm, Lara bit down until she tasted blood. Then she swam. *Come and get me,* she willed the shark. *There's nothing in my blood this time.*

She felt it coming. Felt it chasing. Knew that it would be heartbeats until jaws closed on her legs.

"They've got the girl!"

There was no chance for relief as the shark swam past her, its skin rough against hers, and the world seemed to stand still. A beam of sunlight from the cavern opening illuminated the water around her, and Lara stopped swimming, then sank beneath the surface.

The shark was larger than she'd realized, but her fear filtered away as it slowly swam past her. Watching her. Seeing her.

I see you, too, she silently said to it, reaching out a hand to touch it.

Only for bubbles to explode from above, hands latching onto her shoulders and hauling her to the surface. She landed with a thump and a gasp on the floor of the boat, Aren's face appearing above her. "Are you hurt?"

"No." She sat up, leaning over the edge of the boat to watch the shark swim back out of the tunnel. "It didn't hurt me."

Small hands caught at her arm, and Lara turned to find the girl next to her.

"It's all right." She pulled the child against her, both their hearts hammering. "It will be all right."

The boat banged against the stone dock, and all was a flurry of motion. Emma reached for her, sobbing *thank you* over and over, while Aster shouted above everyone, "All hail the true Queen of Ithicana! Chosen of the guardians! Long may she reign!"

Lara hardly heard him, her eyes on the people around her. There was no way to know why the shark hadn't attacked, whether it was some sort of mystical approval or if the creature simply hadn't been hungry. It didn't matter. What mattered was that *this* was how she'd earn her place. By defending her people. By taking the risks no one else would.

Aren lifted her into his arms, carrying her up the steps into the sunshine. Dropping to his knees, he held her tight against his chest. "God help me, Lara, you can't keep doing that. You can't keep scaring me by risking yourself."

"It's who I am, so you'll have to learn to live with it," she said softly, then extracted herself from his grip and climbed to her feet. Aster appeared, holding out her cane, which she took.

Leaning her weight on it, Lara watched as the crowd dispersed, children smiling at her and a few of the men and women inclining their heads as they passed. One of the men who'd been in the boat with Aren and Jor, a man she didn't recognize, approached and bowed to her. "Your Grace."

Then he handed an open waxed packet of paper to Aren. "When you've decided how to proceed, I'll bring the message back to Southwatch."

Something about his tone sent a prickle of unease down her spine, and she asked, "Is there news? What has happened?"

Aren's face was grim as he extracted the pages from the packet and handed them to her. Ink bled from the dampness of her hands as she skimmed the report from the continent, her eyes snagging on Keris's name. On Zarrah's. "Oh no." She met Aren's gaze. "What does this mean?"

He exhaled, squaring his shoulders. "It means war."

DANIELLE L. JENSEN is the *New York Times* bestselling author of *A Fate Inked in Blood,* as well as the *USA Today* bestselling author of the Bridge Kingdom, Dark Shores, and Malediction series. Her novels are published internationally in nineteen languages. She lives in Calgary, Alberta, with her family and guinea pigs.

danielleljensen.com
TikTok: @daniellelynnjensen
Facebook: facebook.com/authordanielleljensen
Instagram: @danielleljensen